HIGHEST BIDDER

LAUREN LANDISH

WILLOW WINTERS

BOUGHT BOOK 1

PROLOGUE

LUCIAN

I slowly pace the room, letting the sound of my shoes clacking against the floor startle her. My eyes are on Dahlia, watching her every movement. Her breathing picks up as she realizes I've come back for her. With her blindfold on and her wrists and ankles tied to the bed while she lies on her belly, she's at my complete mercy, and she knows it.

The sight of her bound and waiting for me is so tempting. I force my groan back.

Her pale, milky skin is on full display as she waits for me. I've left her like this deliberately, in this specific position. She knows now not to move, not to struggle. She knows to wait for me obediently, and what's more, *she enjoys it.*

The wooden paddle gently grazes along her skin, leaving goosebumps down her thigh in its wake. They trail up the curve of her ass, and her shoulders rise as she sucks in a breath. Her body tenses and her lips part, spilling a soft moan. She knows what's coming.

She's *earned* this.

She lied to me.

And she's going to be punished.

She doesn't know this is for her own good. She should, but she hasn't realized it yet.

I'm only doing this for her. She *needs* this.

She needs to heal, and I know just how to help her. The paddle whips through the air and smacks her lush ass, leaving a bright red mark as she gasps, her hands gripping the binds at her wrists. I watch as her pussy clenches around nothing, making my dick that much harder.

Soon.

I barely maintain my control and gently knead her ass, soothing the pulsing pain I know she's feeling. "Tell me why you lied to me, treasure," I whisper at the shell of her ear, my lips barely touching her sensitive skin.

"I'm sorry," she whimpers with lust. I don't want her apology. I want her to realize what she's done. I want to know why she hid it from me all this time. She'll learn she can't lie to me. There's no reason she should.

Smack! I bring the paddle down on the other cheek and her body jolts as a strangled cry leaves her lips, her pussy glistening with arousal.

"That's not what I asked, treasure." My tone is taunting. She needs to realize what I already know. She needs to admit it. To me, but mostly to herself.

I pull away from her, just for a moment, leaving her to writhe on the bed from the sting of the paddle.

I didn't anticipate our relationship reaching this point.

In the beginning, I thought this would be fun. Just a form of stress relief for me.

But things changed.

I bought her at auction, and now she can't leave. She's mine for an entire month. But the days have flown by, and the contract is almost over.

I need more time.

I'm going to make this right. I'm going to heal my treasure.

If it's the last thing I do, I'll give her what she needs. What we both need.

She parts those beautiful lips, and hope blooms in my chest.

Say it, tell me what you desperately need to say.

But her mouth closes, and she shifts slightly on the sheets before stilling and waiting patiently for more.

I pull my arm back and steady myself.

Soon, she'll realize it. My broken treasure. Soon she'll be *healed*, but that won't be enough for me anymore. I want more.

Smack!

CHAPTER 1

LUCIAN - A FEW WEEKS PRIOR...

I stare at my jacket, laying it over the arm of the tufted leather chair in the corner of my office. I need to leave this fucking building and get home, but I don't fucking want to. It's not like I have anything waiting for me. Nothing to do but more work.

I've spent a fortune on my home. I built it from the ground up, painstakingly choosing every piece of hardware and meticulously designing each room myself. But I couldn't give a damn if I go back there anymore.

It's cold and lifeless. Empty.

My brow furrows, and a frustrated sigh leaves my lips. I could keep working. *There's always more work waiting.*

I clench my jaw and type the password to unlock my computer, the gentle tapping of the keys soothing me. It's a comforting sound. But only for a moment.

As the screen lights up and I glance at the window of emails left on the desktop, I seethe and remember why I'm in such a horrible fucking mood. My eyes focus on the lawyer's name attached to the most recent email. This is why I'm so damn pissed and aggravated.

I'm fucking tired of leeches always suing me. Trying to take a piece of me they haven't earned. Most of the lawsuits don't bother me. It comes with the territory. But my *family,* and my *ex-wife?* It

LAUREN LANDISH & WILLOW WINTERS

fucking shreds me, and I hate that I ever felt anything for them. At some point in time I had feelings for them, emotions I've long since grown cold to.

Now there's only anger.

I steady myself, knowing they've tried this before and failed. They'll keep trying, and it's aggravating, but I refuse to give them anything. I've learned my lesson the hard way. I know better now.

My eyes widen as a new email pops up.

From Club X.

It's been a long time since I've seen an email from Madam Lynn. And an even longer time since I've set foot into the club. The pad of my thumb rubs along the tips of both my middle finger and forefinger, itching to see what's inside.

Images flash before my eyes, and I can practically hear the soft sounds of the whip smacking against flesh and a moan forced from the Submissive's lips. Never to hurt, only for pleasure. Whips aren't my tool of choice, nor what I've been known for in the past. But none-theless, the memory kicks the corners of my lips up into a grin. I tap my fingers on the desk, debating on opening the message before moving the mouse over to the email and clicking on it out of curiosity.

Check your mail, sir.

I huff a laugh at the message and immediately hit the intercom button on my desktop phone for my secretary. It's not yet five, so she better fucking be at her desk still.

"Yes, Mr. Stone?" she responds, and her voice comes through with a sweet and casual air.

"Could you bring me my mail, please?" Although it's poised as a question, it isn't one. There's only one correct response, and she knows that.

There's no hesitation as Linda says, "Of course." Her voice is slightly raspy. Linda's old, to put it bluntly; she should retire.

If I was her I would, rather than putting up with my arrogant ass.

I'm happy she hasn't though. Every year I pay her more money to stay. A hefty raise, a gift here and there. It keeps her happy. Finding a good secretary is more work than it's worth. It was a pain in my ass when I started. Linda's the first I've been able to keep for more than two months and now that she knows what she's doing, with more than four years of working for me, I have no intention of finding a new secretary. So when I make a request, I say *please*.

I go through the emails remaining in my inbox, waiting impatiently for her soft knock on the door to my office. Usually I don't bother with the paper mail. Just like most of these fucking emails, they're junk. She knows what to do with them. So I leave it to her to organize and sift through it daily. She hands over the personal mail at her discretion, usually waiting until the end of the week to bring it all by, but this particular one I want right now. I'm not interested in waiting.

The light knocking at the door echoes in the small room, and I look at the clock. It's only three minutes later. *Not bad, Linda.*

"Come in," I call out and she does so quickly, closing the door behind her. She walks straight to my desk, not wasting any time. Her pink tweed skirt suit looks rather expensive. It's a Chanel, if I'm correct. I see she's putting that last bonus to good use.

"This is from today," she says, placing a compact stack in front of me, "and this-"

I stop her, waving my hand and pulling out the small, square, deep red envelope. "No need."

She collects the remaining mail, tapping it lightly on the desk to line everything up together and asks, "Anything else, sir?"

The use of sir catches me off guard, and for a moment I wonder if she knows who the sender of this particular piece of mail is, but her face is passive. And it isn't the first time she's called me sir. Most of my employees do. Linda just happens to use it less often than most.

I shake my head and say, "That's all." The lines around her eyes are soft, and her lips hold the faintest form of a smile. Linda's always smiling despite having to deal with me. She takes my hot temper in stride. That's one of the reasons I'm eager for her to stay.

She nods her head before turning on her heels. I wait until she's gone to open the envelope.

I watch her leave and listen to the door click shut, leaving me in my spacious office alone and in solitude. Just the way I prefer it.

I finally open the envelope with the letter opener on my desk, avoiding the black wax seal embossed with a bold X entirely.

The thick cream parchment slips out easily from the elegant envelope, and the handwritten message is in Madam Lynn's beautiful penmanship. If nothing else, I admire her flair.

I can practically hear her sultry voice whispering in my ear as I read the sophisticated script.

Dear Sir,

An auction is to be held and I personally wanted to invite you, Lucian. It's been far too long, and I know you're in need. Renew your membership first.

I'll see you soon,

L

An asymmetric smile plays on my lips as I take in her message. I may be a Sir, but she is certainly a Madam. I sit back in my leather desk chair and tap the parchment against the desk as I debate on whether or not I should attend.

It's been nearly a year since I've been to Club X. Even longer since I've had a Submissive, and only one of those was purchased at one of the monthly auctions. She lasted the longest, but only because she was required to.

It would be a nice distraction from the mundane. I muse, staring absently at the back wall lined with black and white sketches from an up-and-coming artist.

Before I can decide, my desk phone rings, bringing me back to the present. I lean forward with annoyance and answer it.

"Stone," I answer.

"Lucian," my sister's voice comes through the line. It's bright and cheery, everything my younger sister embodies. Bubbly is what she likes to be called.

But her happiness doesn't rub off on me. Not after reading the fucking emails from our parents' lawyer. I doubt she knows, and it's not her fault.

She reminds me of them, though. I wish it wasn't like this. I wish I could separate the two, but I can't. They manipulate her, and it's only a matter of time before they'll come up in conversation. Shit, our parents could be why she's calling now.

"Anna, how are you?" I ask her casually. I trace my finger along the wax seal of the envelope as I listen.

"I've been good, but I've been missing you..." she trails off as her voice goes distant. I don't respond. I don't care to admit my feelings either way. Yes, there's a bit of pain from losing contact with my sister, but she chooses to keep in touch with them. She made that decision. And I refuse to have any contact with them.

"It's been too long," she says in a sad voice and then her tone picks up. "We should do lunch sometime soon."

I take in a long breath, not wanting to commit to anything. Lunches are quick unless it's a business meeting. Then they aren't really lunches. But beyond that, I don't have much to tell her. I'm certainly not going to be telling her what she wants to hear.

"Maybe soon," I finally reply.

She huffs over the phone, "You say that when you really mean no." Her voice is playful and forces a rough chuckle up my chest. She may only be nineteen, but Anna's a smart girl. I can't deny her. No matter how much I wish I could, I have a soft spot for her.

I lean forward and pull up my calendar. "I can do Thursday."

"Deal," she quickly agrees, and I can practically feel her smile through the phone. It warms my chest that I can make her happy. Unlike the rest of them, she doesn't take, take, take from me. She truly just wants to see me.

"I've missed you, too, Anna."

"Well you won't have to, since I'll text you and see you on Thursday," she says confidently.

"I will. I'll talk to you then." I'm quick to end the call before she can drag me into a longwinded conversation. She can do that on Thursday for all I care.

"Talk to you then. I love you," she says brightly.

"Talk to you then," I answer and hang up the phone.

As I do, my eyes catch sight of the card and I pick it up and rise from my desk, slinging my jacket over my arm and thinking about the last time I was there.

It's been a long time since I've set foot in Club X.

And a visit is long overdue.

CHAPTER 2

DAHLIA

God, I wish I could wear this color, I think to myself as I slowly slide my fingertips over the rich, velvety purple fabric that lays across my desk. A fabric that will hopefully be turned into an award-winning gown. I suck in a breath, holding it and hoping that I'll be able to contribute to the design.

It's the new in vogue color this season, and it's only a matter of time before models will be flaunting it down the runway. I just hope that I can eventually be one of those fashion designers that proudly walks the runway at the end of a successful show. One day.

I like purple; it's probably up there with red and black as one of my favorite colors. I just don't look good wearing it. I gently lay the fabric down on the desk, thinking. Black suits me better, and it's probably why nearly all of my closet consists of black and greys. Even now, sporting dark silk slacks, a blouse the color of midnight and a cropped black leather jacket with my dark brown hair pulled up into a sleek ponytail, I look like I'm modeling for the grim reaper.

I think I need to stop wearing so much black, I tell myself, *maybe then I'll stop being so damn depressed.*

I take a deep breath and shake off the thought, taking the advice from my therapist to focus on the positives in my life. Black may be slimming, but it doesn't do the spirits any good. I just read a study on colors and the effects they have on the psyche and mood. I huff a small laugh. It was an odd thing to be tested on in my History of Fashion Development class, but it was eye opening.

Today has been wonderful, though. Actually, the past two weeks have been a dream come true. Growing up, I was heavily intrigued by fashion. Christian Dior, Gucci, Prada, Michael Kors, you name it. If it had a name, I wanted to wear it. I dreamed of cutting fabrics and sewing them into gorgeous gowns. One of my favorite gifts my mother ever got me was a drawing pad and a huge set of colored pencils for sketches. I filled the entire book up in only a month.

Over time, my obsession morphed into a lifelong dream of wanting to work in the fashion world, and up until several weeks ago, it looked like that fantasy would never come to fruition. But I finally got my foot in the door, and I'm not going to let this opportunity slip through my fingers.

Now I'm sitting here with my own office on the top floor of Explicit Designs, working one of the most coveted internships in town, living out my wish. It's unbelievable. Seriously, I absolutely love this job. I get to see all the latest designs and in-style fashions, meet quirky, interesting people and be involved in the entire creative process that goes into making these magnificent creations. It's funny how things turn out.

Especially considering how I'd almost given up.

A surge of anxiety twists my stomach, and I frown. It chills me to know how close I'd been to abandoning everything, how close I'd been to letting the darkness overwhelm me. Thinking about it makes me shudder, and I try my best to push the unwelcome thoughts away. It's a constant battle. Dark thoughts always seem to be waiting in the shadows of my mind--stalking me, haunting me, and then pouncing right when I think things are going good.

But things are better now, I try to convince myself. *And I need to focus on being happy.*

A clinking sound pulls me out of my reverie and causes me to look up. I see my boss, established fashion designer Debra Ferguson, through the glass window of my office, gathering her things and getting ready to pack up for the night.

This is the one thing I don't like about the floor I work on. The whole area is a large open space with floor-to-ceiling windows surrounding the offices, and there's virtually no privacy. Everybody can see everyone else. I suppose it isn't so bad, but I do miss my privacy.

I watch as Debra, who's clad in a fashionable red dress that hugs her matronly frame, slings her oversized Prada purse over her right shoulder and slides on her Gucci shades. For a woman in her late forties, she exudes the kind of sex appeal you would find in someone half her age, and it's one of the reasons why she's so popular. To me, she embodies everything I want to be when I'm her age: intelligent, confident, sexy and in complete control of her destiny.

As she makes her way out of her office, she doesn't bother looking my way. For a moment, I wonder if I should step out and tell her goodbye before she leaves. It would be the polite thing to do, yet I stay rooted in my seat.

I shouldn't, I tell myself, feeling a sense of self-consciousness wash over me. *I'll probably just annoy her.*

I don't know why I think that way. Debra has been mostly gracious to me. I suppose I'm intimidated by her. At least that's what I think it is. I'm new, and still trying to learn my place. There are only a dozen or so people working here, and everyone has their own routines. I need to learn mine.

Feeling conflicted, I watch as she walks out of the large room and disappears from view. I let out a slight sigh when she's gone. I don't know why I get like this, why I let my own self-doubts cause me to miss out. It's infuriating. And it's a wonder I've even landed this job with all the insecurities weighing me down.

After gently folding and putting away the purple cloth before making sure everything is in order, I grab my vintage Chanel purse and sling it over my shoulder. The purse is a hand-me-down from my good friend and coworker Carla. We shared a class two semesters ago, and I know it's only because of her that Debra even considered me for this position. I owe her so much already. *But wow, this purse.* I run my hand along the plush quilted leather, still in disbelief that it's mine.

I nearly died when she gave it to me, as I'd never owned anything so expensive before. Let alone *vintage Chanel*. For the longest time, I refused to use it, scared I would somehow lose it or someone would steal it... or worse, I'd get wine or lipstick on it. Instead, I let it collect dust in my closet. I only started using it after Carla scolded me and said to stop being so worried about it. In her mind, it was just a purse, and what was the point of having it if I was never going to use it?

I'm about to walk off when my phone dings. Quick to see who it is, I whip it out. *It's Mom,* I think anxiously. *She finally responded to my text.* Instead, I'm greeted by a message from my roommate Callie.

Calgurl182: *Gonna be studying hard for my exams. Please be quiet when you come in from work. Thx*

I grin at the message. When I need to get a paper done, I study hard, but Callie takes studying to a whole new level. And with exams coming up, I know Callie's level of anxiety must be through the roof. I can totally relate to her not wanting to be disturbed.

After making a mental note to be quiet as a mouse when I enter our tiny apartment near campus, I flip over to my last text with my mom and my grin slowly fades.

Hey Mom, I know I told you about landing my dream job recently, but things are really tough right now financially. I've had to pay for so many things, a used car, clothing, rent, tuition... all these things have left me a little strapped and I'm not sure how I'm going to afford to pay for my next semester. I hate to ask, but can you help me out? I'll pay you back as soon as I get the chance.

Love you,

Dah

Staring at the blank space where her response should be, I feel dejected. I wasn't expecting much from her, but she could have at least responded and let me know that she cared, even if she can't help me out financially. I've had to pay for college myself. Which was fine when I had a job, but this internship doesn't pay anything, and I couldn't keep my retail job and also work here. I'm fucked. I was hoping my mother would be able to help me out. But this is the third text I've sent about money, and she hasn't responded to any of them. She sure as hell reminded me that she was going on vacation with her new boyfriend though.

It makes me feel like I'm low on her priorities. But maybe she just can't handle dealing with added stress right now.

She's been distant lately, and I know even before she started dating this current boyfriend she was having a really rough time. The last few years while I've been at school, my mother has grown apart from me. I can't help but wonder if it's because I remind her too much of my father. I hope not, because it'll only make me feel worse, maybe make me resent my father more, if that's even possible.

Just thinking about him sends a shiver of apprehension down my spine. I don't know if I'll ever forgive him for ripping our family apart. For letting what *happened* to me, happen. Even now, I still can't fathom it. My father was supposed to be my protector, my guardian. *He let him hurt me.* That fact shakes me to my very core, and occasionally, I suffer nightmares over it.

It's been better lately though. I swallow thickly and grab my coat.

Stop bringing this up. I've had a relatively good day, and I don't need to screw it up by living in the past. I'm never going to get over it if I keep wishing things had turned out differently. What I need to do is quit worrying and figure out a way to pay for my tuition next semester. I square my shoulders and nod my head at the thought, feeling my confidence come back. I'm going to make this work and have a life I'm proud of.

Just thinking about my money woes stresses me out. I can't help but think I'm going to be worn thin by having to work in order to pay the bills on top of doing this internship. That's not even factoring in the time I'll need to study for school.

I need to figure something out by next month. After finals, there's the holiday break and I can do something then. I'll find a way to keep this internship *and* pay for my classes.

Steeling my shoulders with resolve, I walk out of the office as I think to myself, *One way or another, I'm going to find a way to make some money on the side. Even if it kills me.*

CHAPTER 3

LUCIAN

*M*y sister loves this part of the city, the hustle and bustle of Main Street with the crowds always walking by. I don't understand it. We could go anywhere, but she always asks to come to this particular cafe.

I take off my jacket and sit at a bistro table hidden in the shade, back in the corner. With my back to the stonewalled building, I can at least face the crowd.

We're still outside so she'll be happy, the crisp fall air rustling the newspaper in my hand. I place my forearm on the edge of the page and look out past the crowd while I watch the cars pass.

I grew up in the city. Only a few blocks from here actually. It doesn't make me like the city any more though. I huff a humorless laugh. Maybe that's why I don't care for this environment.

Too many reminders.

"Can I get you anything?" a waitress asks. Her sweet smile stays in place as she waits patiently with her hands clasped in front of her.

"Coffee black, with one sugar," I reply, and as I order I hear my sister's squeal and the loud clicks of her heels on the pavement.

She looks like she belongs here. Happy and dressed in the latest fashion, she fits right in with the people you'd expect to see in this part of town. She runs up to me and wraps her arms around my shoulders, making the waitress take a step back. She's the only person I let touch me. I just don't fucking like to be touched. But Anna can. She never hesitates to do what she feels like doing. I admire her for that.

She pulls back and takes me in; her cherry red lips make her brilliant smile look even whiter.

"Lucian," she says sweetly before turning to her left and finally taking notice of the waitress.

"Oh! Sorry!" she apologizes, her shoulders scrunching as she backs up and practically falls into her seat.

"No problem," the waitress says and laughs it off. "Can I get you anything else, sir?"

My eyes lift to the waitress. Ever since I got that invitation, it's been more and more apparent how many people call me sir.

I shake my head and give her a tight smile. She's a petite blonde, with a cute button nose and angelic face, but she's not my type. Not that it was on the table... but I'm sure it could be, if I wanted.

The waitress turns to Anna and before she can even ask, Anna orders while taking off her cream leather jacket, "Can I have a salted caramel latte with cream and four Splenda and an extra shot of espresso?"

She does not need that extra shot, but I keep my lips closed. I've learned not to give my sister advice, since she's going to do what she wants to do anyway. And me keeping my mouth shut makes her happy.

She sighs comfortably as the waitress leaves with a nod.

"How are you?" I ask her easily. She smiles brightly, pushing her hair over her shoulders and leaning forward.

"Everything is going so well." Her eyes soften as she says, "Thank you for paying my tuition." Her voice is subdued, but sweet. "It really means so much to me, Lucian. I know-"

I stop her. I know she's grateful, but she doesn't have to keep telling me. "Of course, I'm glad you're enjoying your classes."

I was honestly worried. My sister is naive, and I wasn't sure she'd enjoy college at all. She's never been much of a book person, or the studying type. But if she wants to go, I'm happy to help her so long as she takes it seriously.

She leans back, silencing her thanks and looks at the paper. "Are you in it today?" she asks. Her eyes are wide with curiosity.

I shake my head as I say, "No."

"Bummer," she says as she slumps back into her seat and I chuckle at her expression. I'm never happy to be in the paper. I didn't start this business to be a public figure.

And up until the last few years, whenever I was in the paper, it wasn't good public relations. They say any publicity is good publicity, but they're dead fucking wrong.

The tabloids were not a fan of my playboy lifestyle. And neither were the stockholders. It didn't take long for me to change the business over to a privately owned company, but still, my company suffered because of my childish antics. I had to tone it down. No more fucking every pretty little thing who begged for my cock. I thought getting married would solve that problem--fuck, I thought I was in love.

I was a fucking fool, and I have the alimony checks to prove it.

If my name is never mentioned in the papers again, I'll die a happy man.

I started this company when I was Anna's age, back when I was only nineteen years old. It's odd to think that, considering how I still see my sister as young.

That was the year I split from my family. Realistically, I'd already been on bad terms with my brother. He's a jealous prick, and I have no intention of ever allowing him to be in my life again. Even back then, things were tense between us at best. At the time, I wasn't even speaking to him. But at least I still had my parents. Or at least I thought I did. Before I knew what it was like to be stabbed in the back.

I had to drop out of college. I huff a humorless laugh at the thought. My parents didn't try to help, and I simply couldn't afford it anymore, so I left.

A friend from one of my classes reached out and said he'd front the money for the business I was always talking about, and all he wanted in return was to be a silent partner. It was almost too good to be true. Zander's been at my side more times than not, even when my family decided to rip me apart and steal every penny from me that they could.

With Zander's startup capital, I built the company of my dreams from the ground up. He had the money, and I had the vision. It was perfect. And success came easily and exponentially.

My expression hardens, remembering how proud I was to give my parents a car. A brand new car. I forget what model, and it doesn't matter at this point. It wasn't good enough for them, and they wanted more. I couldn't though. I needed the cash flow for the business, it was growing so rapidly, and I could hardly maintain the expenses.

The day my bank account was drained and checks were bouncing was the day I cut those money-hungry assholes out of my life.

They stole thousands from me. I wasn't even going to sue them until they tried to do it again and then tried to sue *me*. I couldn't believe it. My own parents. We'd never been close, but they were still family. I don't understand it, even to this day. Had they given me time and believed in me, I would have been able to give them everything they ever wanted.

And I would have.

But that's not how it happened, because that's not how the world works.

Years have passed and time after time, I've learned it's better simply not to trust a damn soul. I have Zander and a few friends, and of course my sister. But no one else. It's better that way.

The waitress brings us our coffee and Anna's quick to bring hers to her lips, not caring that it's probably kissed-the-sun-scalding-fucking-hot.

She winces, putting the coffee down and bringing her fingers to her lips. I shake my head slightly, a grin slipping into place. I hide it by blowing on my coffee, my eyes on hers, but my amusement goes over her head and she takes another sip.

She'll never learn.

"So," my sister says as she starts trying to look me in the eye, "I'm going to have a holiday party." My spine stiffens, and the answer is on the tip of my tongue. She's been trying to include me in family events and work me back into our family. It's not happening. I was never close with any of them. I don't have a need for family. I don't need relationships in general. I'll do anything for my sister, but I'm not going anywhere near my parents.

She holds up her hands defensively and says, "They won't be there."

I'm taken aback and shocked; my brows draw in, and I consider what she's saying. "Did something happen?" I ask.

A sadness crosses her eyes quickly. But I see it there, and her lack of a response tells me that something did happen.

My voice is cold and hard, but not toward her, and she knows that. "What'd they do?"

"Nothing," she says softly, her shoulders folding inward. She looks down at the lattice table.

Usually I'd snap at whoever was sitting in front of me lying, saying nothing's wrong when there's obviously an issue, but I wait patiently for Anna to continue. She's hurt, and it's showing. I know she'll tell me what the deal is, but she just needs a moment. She traces the metal openwork design of the table absently. "They were just upset that I accepted your offer to pay for my classes," she tells me slowly, her eyes finally reaching mine as she visibly swallows.

My fists clench at my side, and my jaw tenses. Those fucking bastards. Why hurt her? All they care about are themselves.

"They just don't understand," she continues, picking up her coffee cup with both hands. She takes a hesitant sip and then says, "They just need a little time. You know how they..." she shrugs, "lash out."

My heart thuds in my chest as I calm my rage. *Hothead.* I used to be a hothead. But I'm wiser now, and she doesn't need my anger.

"Are you alright?" I finally ask.

She gives me a sad smile and says, "I am." Her hand reaches for mine on the table and I take it. "I promise I'm okay. But they won't be coming to the party."

She clears her throat, and I give her hand a quick squeeze before letting go. I knew they'd make her choose between me and them. Cowards.

"So..." she draws out the word, "are you coming?" I can hear the vulnerability in her voice, and it shreds me. I can't leave her with no family at her event. But a fucking holiday party?

"Please say you'll come," she implores.

I suck in a breath and concede. "I'll go." Five fucking minutes is all she'll need. Knowing her, she'll be busy socializing and won't even notice once I'm gone. I'll just make an appearance to make her happy.

She jumps in her seat and reaches across the small circular table, giving me a tight hug. It forces a smile to my lips, and I pat her back in return.

She finally sits and all seems right with her world again.

"You need a date," she says confidently. No doubt she already has some friend from school lined up who she thinks is perfect for me.

I don't trust a soul.

I don't put myself out there to be stabbed in the back and taken for granted.

Besides, the auction is coming up.

"I don't, Anna." I click the side button on my phone, knowing it's about time to leave. And I'm right. "I do need to get back to work though."

She pouts and says, "But I just got here."

"You were late, Anna." I stand and slip my jacket back on, buttoning it while she leans over and kisses my cheek.

"Fine," she says, smiling. Her voice lowers as she says, "I'm really happy you're going, Lucian."

I give her a smile, feeling a slight pain in my chest. I'll go, but I'm leaving as soon as I fucking can.

"I'll talk to you soon."

I'm still tense as I walk away. My family, the memories... the fucking lawsuits. It's just another reason that I prefer to stick to my routines and stay away from all this shit. I don't need anyone in my life, and they sure as fuck don't need me in their lives.

CHAPTER 4

DAHLIA

"*I*s something bothering you?" Carla asks me intuitively before taking a bite out of her celery stick that's slathered with a generous smear of peanut butter.

We're having lunch on the third floor of the building in Explicit Designs' famed Divanista cafeteria. Although we share the building with other companies, this room is exclusively for our use, and it's one large open space with glass tables with shiny steel legs set up sporadically around the room. The floor-to-ceiling windows on the back wall provide a breathtaking view of the skyline downtown. Naturally, I've opted to sit right next to one of the windows. I love the landscape. It's one of the reasons I chose to come to the city here for school.

For my meal, I've decided on a diet soda and an apple. It's not much, but considering my mood, I don't have much of an appetite. The stress of not having enough money is really getting to me. I wish I could look past it, but I can't. I don't see a way out of this mess while still keeping this internship. And backing out could ruin my career before it even gets started. It's a no-win situation, and every day it's becoming harder and harder to deny that I'm fucked.

I pause in mid-sip of my diet cherry cola, taken aback by the question. While I'm not in the best of moods, I think I've been doing a good job at appearing happy. I guess I've failed. But I'm trying to stay positive. I think if I hang in there, I'll figure something out. It's just easier said than done. "I just woke up feeling a little bit under the weather," I say. "Other than that, no worries." I give Carla my most reassuring smile and take another sip.

Carla's not fooled by my fraud, and she sets down her celery stick and gestures at me. "C'mon Dah, I know you better than that."

Crap. I want to tell her my problems, but at the same time I'm reluctant. I don't want her to think I'm hitting her up for money, especially after she gifted me that vintage purse. It would be embarrassing. I like Carla, and don't want to jeopardize our friendship by appearing desperate. "No," I say firmly. "Really. I'm fine."

Carla looks unconvinced. "You sure?"

I nod. "Mmmhmm."

Carla scowls, and then a second later growls, "Liar." She holds her glare, but when it appears that I won't be spilling the beans, she lets out a resigned sigh. "Alright, I'm not going to keep prying... for now. I'll let you get away with staying mum, but you're going to have to tell me what's bothering you sooner or later." Her celery stick whirls in the air before she takes a bite. The snapping sound makes me smile. If Carla's good for something, it's making me laugh.

After a moment her expression turns serious and she says, "Dah." There's a shift in tone in her voice, and I know this must be something important.

I swallow down my bite and answer guardedly, "Yes?"

Carla's fingers play with the edges of her celery stick. "I have a question."

By now she has my undivided attention, and worry laces through my chest. *I hope this isn't bad news. Or some sort of nasty gossip about me. I don't think I can handle any more stress.*

"Yeah?" I dare ask.

Carla hesitates a moment, as if unsure how she wants to proceed, and then she leans forward and says beneath her breath, "Are you into BDSM?"

I sit back in my seat, stunned. *Whoa. What the hell?* After a moment, I let out a nervous chuckle. "Where'd that come from?" My cheeks are flaming hot with a bright blush although Carla seems unaffected. She cocks a brow with a small smile, but doesn't answer right away.

"Carla?"

Hesitating, Carla licks her lips and studies me as if she's weighing whether she should tell me anything further. "I'm in a club," she says finally.

"What kind of club?" I ask cautiously.

"Promise you won't tell anyone," Carla demands. The lightheartedness I'm used to with her vanishes from the conversation entirely. "Or I can't tell you the rest." Her eyes flash with an intensity that is unnerving.

I don't know what Carla's getting at, but she has me on the edge of my seat. "I swear," I say. At this point, I'm dying to know what the hell this is all about.

Carla stares at me long and hard as if assessing my honesty before leaning forward slightly and whispering, "I'm in a BDSM club."

I stare, not comprehending. I know what BDSM is, but I'm just not clicking with what she's saying. "Do you mean some kind of cult?"

Carla freezes, and then lets out a small laugh. "Heavens no. Nothing like that." After a moment, the amusement fades from her face. "But it's not really something we talk about, though. No one is allowed in if they don't sign a non-disclosure agreement. Absolutely no one." Her last words are uttered in harsh tones, conveying the need for complete secrecy this mysterious club demands.

Wow. "Why in the world would anyone agree to that?" I ask. My body heats some with the implications of what that could mean.

"Because of the clientele," Carla explains. "They're all powerful, rich and sometimes highly visible men. Men from all walks of life. Doctors, lawyers, businessmen, CEOs, celebrities... even congressmen and senators."

"You're kidding," I say, intensely fascinated, my breathing picking up.

Carla shakes her head and replies, "Nope." She sits back in her seat, taking a drink of her smoothie. "That's why NDAs are signed."

"So these men are married?" I ask after a moment of digesting this information. What she's saying is un-fucking-real, but I believe her.

She's too serious to be lying, and now I'm just hungry for all the details.

Carla purses her lips thoughtfully. "I suspect some might be, but there is no way of knowing for sure." She puts the cap back on her smoothie and leans forward. "The club thrives on a secretive atmosphere, and though some of the Subs know the Doms' identities, they're forbidden," her hands fly outward, increasing the intensity of her words, "to reveal or share any knowledge of them outside the club." Her brows pinch together slightly as she continues, "I think a lot of men are just young, eligible bachelors that are looking for a place to sate their sexual appetites, so most Subs get to play with a free conscience."

Subs and Doms are all familiar terms to me... I mean, everyone's read Fifty Shades, haven't they?

This is all so intriguing, and I find myself leaning in and lowering my voice. "So what happens if a Sub exposes a Dom outside of the club, or vice versa?" I have to ask.

Anger flashes in Carla's eyes. "Not only are they subject to legal action, but they get kicked out and banned for life." She emphasizes the next words, "But these are people you don't want to cross." Her face is deadly serious as she warns, "This club is fun and exciting and intoxicating, but you don't want to be enemies with these people. I mean it, Dah." The mood lightens up some as she readjusts in her seat and says, "So just keep it between us."

I let her words settle as I look out of the window. It's a bit frightening, but thrilling at the same time. I can see why such a rule is in place. The club thrives on secrecy, so divulging identities would be a big no-no if it wanted to stay in business. Also, keeping things confidential is probably a huge draw for the members. I'm sure it's a lot more fun and thrilling for both sides to know they're engaging in something so depraved that they have to hide it. The risk of getting caught only increases the thrill. The very thought sends a shiver of want down my spine.

My eyes are drawn to Carla as she takes another sip of her smoothie, her eyes fixed on me. "So why are you telling me this again?"

Carla's next words nearly knock me off my seat. "Because I want you to come and check it out."

I laugh with astonishment. "What?"

"My boyfriend, you know, Bruce? We're both members. It's how we met, actually."

My jaw literally drops. That is a total bombshell I wasn't expecting. "No way!" A blush grows on Carla's face. So she's a Submissive! I never would have thought that about her. Well, I would guess she's the Sub in their relationship... I have to stop my line of thinking right now before I get too carried away.

Carla nods. "He bought me in an auction."

What in the world? "An auction?" I breathe in wonder. Carla's boyfriend *bought* her? My eyes widen, and I'm not sure how to respond. *What in the actual fuck?*

"It's nothing like that," Carla says defensively. "Auctions are something by which Subs and Doms can take their experience to the next level, and these men pay dearly for the privilege to do so. As dark as it sounds, it's benign really if you look at it from the Sub's perspective." Her voice is much softer now, and I can tell she's practically pleading with me to understand. And I'm trying. I really am. "The Dom pays high dollar for a sex slave for a month, and the Sub gets to live out her fantasy of being dominated. Sometimes, they might even forge a relationship outside of the club's perimeters if they decide they like each other enough, like what happened with me and Bruce." She smiles sweetly and bites her lip for a moment before shrugging. "So you see, no harm, no foul. Everything is clean, consensual, and terms and conditions are outlined in the contracts. No one has to agree to accept any terms that they don't like. Rules *must* be followed, or else."

"That sounds scary as fuck," I blurt out. "To just get sold to someone."

Carla's shaking her head before I've even finished my thought. "There's so much paperwork, and all of your desires and fetishes are clearly marked. Everything is consensual, and the club is all about making sure everyone is safe. Seriously. It's all about living out your fantasies."

I squirm in my seat. My heart's racing at the very thought of being bought. I won't lie to myself. If I knew it was safe...

"That's why I'm telling you this," Carla says, though I'm barely listening, lost in my thoughts. "Because you can get paid... if you're into that sort of thing, that is. I think you'd enjoy it. I'm pretty sure you need a good hard fuck. Or two. And I know you need the money right now."

My ears perk up, and my heart stills in shock. Is it really that obvious? "How did you know-"

She shakes her head, dismissing my worries. "You're new here, and these clothes are expensive. You don't drive your car to work, though I know you have one. And when I gave you that purse, you acted as if I'd given you a five million dollar engagement ring with how scared you were of losing it." Carla shakes her head again. "I might look like an airhead, but I'm not." She reaches across the table and gently places her hand atop of mine. "I want to help you."

I want to help you strikes something in me. My eyes focus on the table, and I'm absorbed by my thoughts.

All of what she's said sounds exciting and erotic, and being dominated is something I crave more than anything else. But the reason for it is dark and twisted. Just thinking about it causes a horrific scene that used to be a constant in my night terrors to flash in front of my eyes. It's been years, and I thought I was over this. But I'm not.

I can never get over what he did to me.

"Please stop," I beg, *my voice choked with pain as I struggle in vain.* I hear my own voice pleading over and over in my head and it sends shivers down my spine. I close my eyes and try to ignore the memory. His heavy body on top of me. The smell of his foul breath as he told me to be quiet.

"I told you to be quiet, you little bitch!"

I clear my throat and breathe out deeply. I focus on remembering where I am today, and how it's in the past. But the sound of his voice won't go away. The memory flashes before my eyes. My body tenses remembering how I looked around for my father. How I screamed out for him to help me.

I tried to fight back, but it was useless. My heart beats rapidly at the memory, pumping cold blood through my veins. I wish I could forget.

"Dah?" Carla asks.

I jerk my hands out of hers, startled. My breathing is ragged, and anger tightens my chest.

"Is something wrong?" Carla is peering at me with concern, and I'm freaked out at how I so easily spaced in an instant.

I clear my throat and unclench my fists that I hadn't realized were balled up. That fucking bastard. He'd taken so much from me, and hadn't had to pay for it. When I told my father about what Uncle Tommy did, he just laughed, not believing his brother capable of such a horrible thing. He chose him over me, and he refused to take me to the hospital. "Yeah, sorry. I was just thinking about what you've told me and how interesting it all sounds," I lie. I've never told anyone other than my parents. I'm ashamed. I know I have no reason to be, but I am.

Carla looks unconvinced. "You sure?"

"Yeah." I wave away her concern and swallow the bitterness that forms in my throat. I've never forgiven my father for not believing me about what Uncle Tommy did to me. The incident caused so much friction in the family that my mom ended up divorcing him. *That* had been awful with all the screaming, arguing and accusations flying about. I liked to believe that my mom cared the most about what happened to me. After I saw how she focused on what assets she would get in the divorce instead of making sure Uncle Tommy paid for what he did, I began to feel like she'd just used me as an excuse to leave my father because she wasn't happy in her marriage. "Please continue."

Carla hesitates for a moment, studying me closely. She doesn't buy it, but I can't let her know what happened to me. I don't want her to get spooked. I give her a nod, and then she finally continues. "So anyway, if someone does buy you, half of the final bid goes to the club. But when the minimum bid is five hundred thousand dollars, you won't find much to complain about as far as the fees go."

I gape with shock. Five hundred thousand dollars? It takes a long moment for that to even register. It's a good distraction from where my mind was going. I don't want to dwell on the past. I can't.

"That much money?" I ask with disbelief in my voice. "You've got to be kidding!" I can't believe they'd pay that much money.

Carla shakes her head. "I told you, these men are powerful and wealthy beyond your wildest dreams. For some of them, a million is like a dollar bill. But that's not even half of it. They pay a hundred grand a month already for their membership; these men are absolutely fucking loaded."

I'm too stunned to speak. Everything that I could ever want is right at my fingertips... if I could debase myself enough to become someone's sex slave for a month. It's an idea I should find shameful, an idea you'd think would repulse me to my very core even, but I find myself... craving it.

I need this.

Years after my traumatic experience, I'd grown up with the desire to be dominated. Which is ironic, because my uncle was never harsh or rough. He held me down, but then I gave up. The things I need to get off are highly specific.

At first these feelings brought me shame, but I couldn't help myself. I needed to be controlled by a powerful man to get off. There was simply no other way. This caused friction with some of my partners. My first boyfriend couldn't understand why I wanted him to force himself on me, why I wanted to be choked and slapped around while being fucked mercilessly. He could never know how I'd been violated, and how the very act had perverted me in ways I didn't dare say to anyone. I didn't understand either. I felt sick after every sexual encounter with anyone. With the help of a therapist, I started to cope with everything, past and present. I need to be dominated, but I need to know it's for pleasure and know that I have control. That I can stop it at any time.

"Some Subs and Doms wear masks to protect their identities," Carla explains, cutting into my thoughts, "so you can even opt for a mask if it makes you feel more comfortable." She grins deviously. "It adds enormously to the spice and sizzle of a sexual encounter."

Unconsciously, I think about being dominated by a masked man, held down and fucked until my insides are raw. The uneasiness from my memories starts slipping away. This could be good for me. This could help me in a way I'd never considered. I'm broken. I know I am. No matter how many times my therapist says otherwise, I know I'm broken. I don't want to live like this, but I don't have a choice. And maybe this is just what I need. A Dominant who knows what he's doing, someone who can give me exactly what I need. I can picture it, and all the dark things that make my pussy clench and nipples harden play before my eyes.

"Dah?" Carla asks.

I snatch my hand away from my neck, which I hadn't realized I'd been clutching while I was engaged in my fantasy, and shake my head. "This club sounds so crazy."

Carla flashes a wide smile. "'Cause it is! Trust me, you're going to love it."

CHAPTER 5

LUCIAN

a small grin slips into place as I take in another look, making sure I'm prepared. When I built this house, I made sure to have this playroom made. Its sole purpose is pleasure. *My pleasure.* Whatever kink I want access to, it's here. The walls are painted a deep silver, and the wood furniture is all black. It's masculine with clean lines, but it's the details that matter.

Hooks line the ceiling; for the sex swing, for chains. For whatever the fuck I want. And they're scattered in various places. If I want my Submissive dangling from the ceiling with no support, I can make that happen. I can have her arms secured above her head while I'm fucking her from behind, and there's nowhere she can go, no place to hide, nothing to lean onto except for me.

My eyes linger on the Saint Andrew's Cross in the far corner. It's one of my favorite tools for punishment. My dick hardens in my pants just imagining a sweet Submissive secured to it, pleading for her forgiveness. *Yes.* I fucking need that. I need that right now. The sling stand and spanking bench are next to it, but I hardly ever use those. Although I know some Subs prefer them, and I'm always willing to compromise.

I run my hand down the leather-lined paddle and look at the other tools in the drawer. All of them are new. Never used, not even once. I got rid of the ones from my last Sub and bought new ones for this auction. Nipple clamps, plugs, paddles, whips, ropes, canes, cuffs, blindfolds, the works. Everything my Sub could possibly need.

I gently set the paddle back where it belongs and shut the drawer, feeling as though I'm prepared.

At first I wasn't sure I'd be ready to have another. I wasn't sure I even wanted one. But the more I pictured how the evening were to go, the more I decided I need to buy one at the auction.

If I'm going to do this, I'm going to do it right. And for me, that means absolute control. I want a contract in place, and I want the privacy of my own home. I know some of the other Doms, my close friends included, prefer the company of the club. They have their private rooms there, and they leave and go about their lives as though it's just a hobby. But for me this is so much more.

It becomes a borderline obsession once I've met the right woman. One who wants her needs filled, needs that complete my own.

I take a seat on the bed in the center of the room and pull out the mask from my pocket. I've worn a mask every time I've entered the club, like most of the high-powered men do. I learned the hard way that there are consequences to being open about this lifestyle. More than that, when I started my company, I realized very quickly how much my personal choices could impact the company.

Back then, when I was just getting started, I was a fool. I should have known better, but I was careless. I was angry about my family, and overwhelmed with women wanting to please me. It was more than flattering, and I was eager to enjoy their company. I was young and stupid. I shouldn't have been so reckless. It wasn't worth it, and if I could take it back, I would.

I quickly made a name for myself as a playboy in the tabloids. It was then that Zander introduced me to the club. It was a way to sate my desires, but still remain anonymous. My company no longer had to take a hit for my personal preferences, and it got the stockholders off my back. Not that they matter anymore. They can't do shit to me now.

Either way, it's best to be as private as possible. I have to avoid scandals and negative press at all costs. My livelihood is at stake, and women simply aren't worth it. The image of my wedding picture that used to hang in my living room flashes before my eyes. One failed marriage is all I need. She blindsided me and fooled me into thinking she felt something more for me. I should've taken a note from the Club X playbook and had her sign an NDA.

At least she took a paycheck to sign one after our hideous divorce. I don't know why I'm surprised. She just wanted a paycheck all along. Just like everyone else. They all just want a fucking paycheck.

I rise from the bed, feeling the need to take the paddle out again, but not having my Submissive at hand. I crack my neck and forget about the past. It's where it belongs. Tonight is about right now and needs that must be filled. I've put this off long enough. I *deserve* this.

I huff a laugh and smirk as I think about Zander's reaction to my text. He's the one who introduced me to this lifestyle. I learned to enjoy the release and the control gained as a Dominant. But it's more than that. It's the fulfillment of providing for a Submissive. Of training her and watching her become truly sated with pleasure. Earning her trust and devotion. It's a thrill, and a deeply satisfying one at that.

I've been craving it, but putting it off. It's difficult to put that faith in another person. The faith that they'll listen, and learn to trust you. It's even more difficult building trust that is real. But you can't hide your body language, or your primitive needs. My last Submissive tried to hide hers. I think she just wanted to play. But I don't do pretend and make-believe. I require perfection. I give this my all, and I expect every bit of the passion and energy that I put into this in return. But my last Sub didn't give me that. She was defiant and just wanted to be punished. Always. And each time she wanted it harder and more painful. I don't have a fetish for pain. That doesn't interest me. And she knew that. I took my collar off of her and never set foot in Club X again.

It's been almost a year since I've been to the club, a year since I've had a Submissive and given in to these baser needs. I'm more than ready to delve into my desires and put this room to good use.

I pocket the mask with a grin on my face. It's show time.

CHAPTER 6

DAHLIA

Club X.

I suck in a sharp breath as I step through the club's doorway past the lobby and into a darkened ballroom that I can only describe as pure luxury. The floor is covered with plush, royal red carpet that is intertwined with breathtaking intricate designs, and the clicks of my heels are muted against the softness. The walls are painted a soft purple and are lined with gold trim, while golden sconces give off a red glow, suffusing the room with a sultry ambience.

High ceilings give the place depth as well as an airiness that makes my skin prickle with excitement. I touch the bracelet at my wrist. This one is temporary, but everyone is wearing them. It's just cream-colored rubber, but it'll look like Carla's when I join. *If* I join. The rubber is joined by three interlocking metal rings, with the center ring being black. She said it shows the other members that I'm a Submissive and that I prefer carte blanche, so the Dom has free range with me. The very thought makes my core heat with desire. Right now my bracelet is color is limited to cream because I'm learning. It will be apparent to everyone who sees it that I'm a BDSM virgin. There are other colors, but they aren't for my tastes. The knowledge makes my breath still in my lungs as men pass, glancing at my wrist with interest, but I'm still taking in the splendor of the club.

There are scores of finely set tables throughout the large room, as well as booths with velvet seating lining the walls. At the end of the room sits a stage, the large red curtains closed, hiding the secret of what lies beyond it. On the far left side, there's a high-end bar illuminated by neon blue light and outfitted with what looks like every drink known to man. Soft, elegant music plays over surround speakers that are artfully hidden, only adding to the luxurious vibe.

But the most exciting thing about Club X isn't the extravagant finery. It's the people. I walk behind Carla and Bruce, in awe of it all. My eyes dart this way and that, trying to take in everything, and I try, unsuccessfully, to calm my nerves. I settle my eyes on Carla's backside and my cheeks grow rosy as I admire the view. She looks fucking hot tonight. She's wearing a short dress that barely covers her butt cheeks and hugs her body, showcasing every delicious curve. In fact, every woman here has on a dress that barely covers her ass.

They're everywhere.

Beautiful young women and masked young men that are dressed in slick high dollar suits fill the room. Even though their faces are hidden behind masks, I can almost feel the ambition, drive and authority radiating from these men, and it makes me weak in the knees.

Power. Wealth. Sex. It's all here, under one roof.

Looking around, I don't see a single man without a mask. Some are black and simple. Others are silver and themed with animals. The men sit at tables or booths alone, watching the room with an almost predatory gaze, while other men sit in groups talking amongst each other quietly. Other Dominants are accompanied by a beautiful girl or two, but it's clear who's in charge. Nearly all the women are in Submissive poses or in the act of being led around.

I watch as a tall man in a dark suit, his face hidden behind a metallic mask, walks past me holding a chain that clinks as he walks. It's attached to a dark-haired girl clothed in a silver shift dress. As she moves I can see the gown is nothing more than thin slits of fabric stitched together, her skin exposed in between the gaps. My eyes widen as the Dom tugs slightly, and the leash pulls at the collar around her throat. The Submissive tumbles forward slightly and the man catches her, pulling her into his hard chest and whispering into her ear. She smiles against his suit jacket as he chuckles and she nods her head slightly, looking up at him and responding with a soft, "Yes, sir," to whatever he's said.

He releases her and walks easily to a table where another man is already sitting.

The seated man, a tall blond, is eyeing the Dom's Sub with intense interest, his legs planted out wide. He mutters something to the Sub, and she blushes at whatever it is.

"Answer him," I hear the Dom command, looking at his Submissive with a heated gaze.

The Sub looks hesitant, although lust is easily read on her face before uttering something too low for me to hear and nodding slightly. At this, the Dom takes a seat at the table next to the blond man, and pulls his Sub into his lap, spreading her legs out wide and placing the balls of her bare feet on the leather-covered bench on either side of his thighs. The blond man moves in close and lowers the top of the Sub's dress, taking out her right breast. My lips part in disbelief. I watch as he takes her nipple into his mouth and as he slides his hand up between her legs. Her head falls back against her Dom's shoulder, and she moans softly with pleasure.

My breath hitches, and my eyes widen.

I glance around the room and then focus back on them. No one around seems to notice or think this out of the ordinary, and I feel my core heat at the erotic sight. Seeing as how this is a BDSM club, I expected to walk in on a wild orgy, where Doms would be fucking their Subs into submission, but the vibe is much more high class than that, giving off an almost secretive and seductive feel. But I'm still shocked to see something like that. My blood heats with desire, and my body feels aflame.

As I continue to watch the blond man suck on her tit, my nipples pebble and my breathing becomes ragged. I tear my eyes away, my cheeks burning with shame, when Carla whispers in my ear, "Sexy, isn't it?"

Carla is gazing at me, her breasts heaving as her eyes dart past me to the couple and then back to me. I can't get over Carla's dress; it looks expensive, and it's covered with glittering sequins. Both sides have long slits that show off her long legs, and nearly expose her pussy. Her hair is styled into a sultry deep side part, and her makeup is flawless. A Sub collar adorns her neck, and serves only to enhance her sexiness. It's a thin leather strap with a polished gold tag.

She leans in and whispers, her eyes still on the scene to our left, "Bruce doesn't share me. That's not our thing."

Her boyfriend and Dom, Bruce, looms behind her, his metallic mask glinting in the red ambient lighting, his dark, vested suit fitting right in with all the other wealthy men in attendance. He doesn't have a leash on Carla, and a lot of couples don't seem to have them either. Tonight, he let Carla be free of her chain, which she's told me she customarily wears, but has forbidden her to walk more than a few feet from him. I was there when he told her the rules, and I couldn't believe how eagerly she accepted them. She wants to please him. She craves his authority and his conditions. It's a dynamic that's foreign to me. I'd only met Bruce once before this. They seem like an average enough couple. But this is different. Much different. Here in Club X, he's the master of Carla's world.

Even though I know the basics of the dynamics behind a Dom and his Sub, it's going to take me awhile to get used to seeing Carla so subservient since she's such a hands-on, career-driven woman. I didn't expect this. It's one thing to fantasize about the lifestyle. It's quite another to be immersed in it.

But that's what being a Sub is all about, I tell myself, *surrendering all your control and power to another person and letting them take the reins.*

In that light, Carla is the perfect Sub.

I'm doing my best to fit in and copy Carla's behavior. I'm wearing a backless black dress that rises up to mid-thigh and the front side is cut low, showing off my ample cleavage. Salon-perfect hair, sultry makeup, spandex pantyhose and glossy nude pumps complete my look. I feel sexy, but at the same time I'm extremely nervous since this is my first time here. All the women present seem to be playing their roles flawlessly, and I'm unsure I'll be able to fit in. The thought brings my anxiety back to the forefront. I wish I could calm down, but I'm struggling to relax. Especially knowing the auction is tonight.

I can't believe I could be bought by someone. *Five hundred thousand dollars... or more.* The thought is surreal. I'm literally shaking in my heels.

"It's crazy," I breathe, making sure to keep my voice as low as possible and my eyes in a safe place. Carla warned me that even if I'm not claimed, I have to play the part of a Submissive. I can't do anything that would disrupt the fantasy the club provides. I don't want to offend anyone, and I don't want to get kicked out. Looking out among the sea of masked men, my heart pounds. These are men of power, men that could dominate me just like I want. An image of being held down by one of them flashes in front of my eyes. Before I realize it, I'm trembling with a mix of arousal and fear. "You were right about this place."

"Told you," Carla whispers so low that I can barely hear. She turns toward Bruce, looking for permission, and he gives her an imperceptible nod. "Come," she says quietly, gesturing at me to follow. "Let Bruce show you around before we grab a seat."

Without waiting for an answer, she begins following Bruce, leading me down a walkway on the right side. There's security detail as we leave the dining hall and go to the hallway where the rest of the club awaits. They check our bracelets and nod as we go through. Their presence only adds to the tension in the pit of my stomach. Bruce splays his hand on the small of Carla's back, and she looks up at him with obvious appreciation. My gait is awkward as several masked men turn their heads my way, their eyes boring into me. I feel self-conscious under their gaze, unsure about my place here. These are powerful men--doctors, CEOs, lawyers, senators, and I'm just some silly girl whose problems have led her here. But they don't need to know that. No one needs to know the reason I'm here.

I'm searching for a man of power to take control of me. To help me take control of my past. That's exactly what I need.

A dark feeling presses down on my chest as horrible images flash in front of my eyes. I do my best to push them away. I don't want to think about it. I came here to heal this darkness. This is going to help me. I know it will. I *need* this.

"How many of these men did you say work in government?" I whisper to Carla as Bruce leads us along, tearing my eyes away from those dangerous masked gazes and thinking of anything I can to ignore the stir of anxiety in my belly. Of all the men that Carla claims are members of the club, none seem more taboo than the ones holding public office. The risk of scandal is more substantial with these men, and I'm sure it makes the thrill of being with them all the greater.

"I'm not sure," Carla replies out of the side of her mouth, and I have to strain my ears to hear. "Just remember, the person that becomes your Dom could be anyone. A CEO, doctor, lawyer, governor, congressman, senator-"

"Even the president?" I interrupt. It's partly a joke, but the humor isn't evident in my voice. Mostly because of my nerves.

Carla pauses as if shocked, then shakes her head and chuckles softly. "No... at least..." a look of uncertainty comes over her face and she concludes, "I don't think so."

If the President of the United States is a member of Club X, I think to myself, *then this entire country is going straight to hell.*

I have no idea who's going to buy me. Every fucking time I signed a piece of paper to be included in the auction tonight, it nearly made me sick. I'm so anxious and worried. Anyone can buy me. At the same time, it's exhilarating. The only thing that keeps me from freaking the fuck out is knowing that all of my preferences, my hard and soft limits —meaning things I will not do and things I might try—are all in the contract. The contract itself was sixty pages long. Every possible detail and interaction between the buyer and submissive was included. And it must all be followed to the letter as to what my *preferences* are. The club is strict about filling out all the paperwork Madam Lynn emailed me. Plus, talking to her and Carla gives me faith that this is going to be the fantasy that I want and not some fucked up horror flick.

"Here's the Sex and Submission store," Carla says, gesturing as Bruce stops us in front of an opening into a large room along the wall. Inside, there are rows of shelves filled with all sorts of sex toys and BDSM devices. There are dildos, whips, chains, ropes, nipple clamps, elegant butt plugs and every kind of sexual toy you could imagine. I watch as several Doms walk around with their chained Subs, picking out their toys of choice to be used on them later. "Obviously, you'll be making stops here in the future. Just don't get too carried away."

There's humor in her voice and I appreciate it, although I still feel muted in my excitement. My inexperience in this new environment is making me tense, and I feel overly self-conscious.

We continue on the tour and Bruce leads us upstairs through a long hallway filled with rooms on either side. Like the floor below, the hall is filled with opulence, with the same lush carpeting, beautiful painted walls, luxury furniture and upscale art pieces.

As we pass each room, I can faintly hear the sounds of smacking flesh and pleasured cries through the thick, fancy doors.

"Here are the private apartments," Bruce says as Carla stops, indicating a door off to the right. "This is where... well, you can pretty much guess what goes on. These are safe places for the Dom and his Sub and where they can get to know each other's limits in private."

There are men in dark suits lining the hallway, and they look like they mean business with their dark glasses and buzz cuts. It's obvious they're here to make sure no one violates the rules.

As we move through the hallway, I hear more sounds of debauchery that make my pussy clench on air; the crack of a whip followed by a soft cry, and then more noises of smacking flesh as if a man's low-hanging balls are smacking up against a wet pussy.

I want to be in there, I think to myself, my mind racing with base thoughts. *Being dominated.* My body tingles with anxiety and heated anticipation. I take in a staggered breath. Soon. I swallow thickly as my palms start to grow damp with perspiration. It's overwhelming.

We reach the end of the hallway and then Bruce leads us down the steps into another corridor that lets out into a large room filled with Doms and Subs who are in the act of role-playing and even having all-out sex.

"This is the playroom," Bruce says, nodding at the scene in front of us.

I hardly hear him. My eyes are on a Sub who's on her knees, being face fucked by a muscled, ripped, naked stud in a mask. He thrusts forward, forcing her to take all of his big cock to the ball sack, then he throws his head back, groaning with absolute pleasure.

Fuck, I say to myself as my pussy clenches repeatedly and my nipples stiffen like stone, *that's so fucking hot.*

That dark act of being forced is what turns me on. It's what I crave above all else. It used to shame me to my core, but now it's the only way I can get off.

My breathing comes out in pants as I watch, imagining being taken by force by someone like this masked man.

"We should go back now," Bruce informs me quietly, turning to me. He watches me with a keen eye, taking in my flushed cheeks and heavy breathing, and an amused smile touches the corner of his lips. "I'm ready to eat."

I take deep, full breaths to calm my racing pulse and say nothing as Bruce leads us back to the dining room and to an empty table near the giant stage. As I take my seat, I notice several masked men's eyes on me, staring me down as if they know I'll be up for auction soon. My cheeks burn at their gazes, almost wishing one of them would come take me and relieve my throbbing pussy, but I ignore them. I know I'm not supposed to look at them unless they tell me to. Yet I feel that some of them sense the desire that burns in me, the need to be dominated. I wonder if it's attracting them, like a moth to a flame.

A wave of anxiety washes over me. What if it's one of these very men looking at me who buys me tonight? Will I be good enough for them? I'm sure that most of them are used to trained Submissives, but I'm new. I'll need to be taught, and I'll have to learn how to properly behave.

Total surrender is all I need, I tell myself. *The wants and needs of my Dom will be my wants and needs. His wishes are my command.*

I'm pulled out of my thoughts when a waitress dressed in a black uniform comes up with a gold-plated menu and sets it down in front of me and then looks at us expectantly. Bruce speaks first. "A dirty harry for my Carla," he says smoothly, "and a shot of whiskey for me." She nods, and turns to look at me.

"Just a water please," I say, swallowing thickly. My nerves are getting the best of me. My hands are shaking. Soon I'll be up for auction, and then I'll be owned by someone. A stranger. I should drink to calm down, but I need my wits.

Carla waves away my concern. "You're fine. You're going to love this."

That should soothe me, but it doesn't. She has no idea why I'm on edge. Well maybe she has an inkling about part of it, but she doesn't know the real reason that I want this. I can't shake my negative feelings. Even when we order our food and start eating, premium steak on a bed of wild rice pilaf, I feel anxious. I'm timid about how I'm going to go through with tonight. And actually, I'm fucking terrified. I'm new to all this, and as exciting and alluring as Club X seems, I'm not sure if I'm totally cut out to be a Sub, let alone being one for an entire month. I mean, what would happen, God forbid, if halfway through my contract, I decide that I can't take it anymore and want out?

But I can't, I tell myself. *More than the money, I need a Dom who's going to force me to face my fears. A Dom who's going to heal me, so I can move on with my life.* My blood cools, and I close my eyes. With everything in me, I know that I need this.

CHAPTER 7

LUCIAN

*T*he door to my Audi R8 closes with a gentle click. It's rare that I drive myself anywhere anymore. I need the time to work, and with the heavy city traffic, having a driver frees up a good hour for work. It's even more rare that I have to self-park. Club X has a valet option, but no one uses it. The clientele here is well known, and members have our own gated parking on the side of the club. The lot is littered with expensive cars all rivaling the collection I have in my garage. Aston Martins and Porsches catch my eye in particular.

It's practically a treasure chest for men like myself.

I hit the lock, which echoes a small *beep* in the chill of the night, and stroll toward the entrance. My mask is already in place. It's simple, and made of smooth, black thin leather that wraps over my eyes and covers the bridge of my nose. Silk ties keep it in place. I actually purchased this one here. The club sells a wide variety of masks. They sell everything you could ever possibly dream of or need for this lifestyle.

As I step closer to the nine foot high carved maple doors, I smile wickedly in anticipation. Inside of this club is another world entirely.

It's a world of sin and darkness. A world of high-end luxury, an adult playground.

The darkness this time of night only makes the exterior of the club more alluring. The deep red up-lighting along the columns is barely a hint at what's waiting within. From the outside, you'd have no idea what you were walking into if you weren't already familiar with the club.

Even when the large doors open and reveal the interior, at first you may be deceived.

Before I can knock, the doors swing open silently. The staff is timed so well I don't even have to slow my pace. My shoes click on the stone entryway before being silenced by the plush carpeted floors. I walk in easily, feeling the warmth of the club in the foyer. The faint seductive music hums through my body, and a grin threatens to slip into place.

The air itself is provocative and mysterious. Nothing in this world exists like Club X.

"May I check your coat, sir?" the young woman asks at the long black front desk of the lobby on my right. Her voice is soft and even, and she holds my gaze steadily. Very little of her skin is shown other than the deep V cut in the blouse of her black pant jumpsuit. Her professional look is complete with natural makeup, and her blonde hair pulled back into a sleek ponytail.

She's wearing the same uniform that I recognize from all the years I've come here. It's easy to distinguish the employees in Club X. There's never a doubt that they're off limits and not interested in play. The professional touch that Madam Lynn requires is admirable.

Some things never change.

The air of familiarity makes my blood heat with the recognition of what's to come.

"No thank you," I state easily and walk through the lobby, the music increasing in intensity. The view of the restaurant calls to me.

Most guests are in awe of the dining area with its high ceilings and dim lighting. The stage takes precedence this late at night. The silhouettes of the go-go dancers are barely visible as the lights flutter around them in beat with the music.

There may be a doubt as to what Club X is if I'd come earlier and stayed for dinner, but when true night comes and the lights dim, the curtains open and the club comes alive. Sin around every corner, and a fantasy come to life.

I take a quick glance at the guests, and see a few familiar faces. I smirk, standing behind a round, tufted booth in the back of the room, the hallway behind me. Familiar faces aren't quite the right words, considering the men are all masked. But I recognize them, regardless. Senators, professors, CEOs... all men of power. My peers.

There may be secrecy in this building, but secrets are only as good as those who can keep them. Trust is something that doesn't come easily to me. But the contracts we all sign for our memberships are held sacred among us.

Judging by the simple clothing the women are wearing, there's no theme tonight. I suppose I should have known that. Madam Lynn likes to keep things simple on the night of the auction. One a month. No wonder the restaurant is only half full.

A couple passes behind me, and I turn to watch them walk through the hallway. His crisp, dark navy suit is at odds with the chiffon shift dress she's wearing that's practically see-through. Her pale pink nipples show through the fabric, as well as a hint of her pubic hair. She has a thin gold leash wrapped around her neck and held in his hand. It's a loose hold, and the chain is so thin I imagine it would easily break if she were to pull away from him. Without a collar on her neck, and judging by how quickly she's moving, it must be a punishment. She's to obey, or she'll no longer belong to him.

There are two men for security at the entrance to the hall. The restaurant is for anyone, but past this doorway is only for members. I already have the silver bracelet granting me entrance around my wrist, and I easily lift my sleeve to reveal it as I walk by. They nod their heads and remain still, their hands behind their backs.

Madam Lynn has stepped up her game in that department, they look like the fucking Secret Service.

The man picks up his pace and pulls a bit tighter on the petite woman's leash as they get closer to their destination. She lets out a small gasp and takes a few quick steps to catch up.

The Submissives in the club who are single and not claimed are able to roam, but there are rules. They must always display their submission so they don't break the fantasy the club provides; any action that disrupts scenes can lead to being banned or potentially punished if a Dom sees fit to take over the Sub and she agrees.

The Submissive's bare feet pad on the carpet as he leads her past the stairway to the dungeon and down a hall to the left where some the private rooms are.

They can be purchased for a decent price, all things considered. A few hundred grand a month is a reasonable rate. Each is numbered or named, depending on the owner's discretion; all are expansive, and fully furnished. They're tempting for the ease at which they can be used.

I've never had one. I do have a strong desire for privacy, but not here. I prefer the confines of my own home. It makes things difficult though, seeing as how the Submissive must agree to leave and to play where I'd rather be.

It's one thing to be consumed by the aura of the club, but it's another thing entirely to unleash your desires in another person's care. And without the protection the club provides.

My steps pick up as I pass the divine pleasures of the club and make my way to the stairs so I can do what I came here for. The auction is starting soon.

Upstairs the atmosphere continues, but it's subdued. It's far more serious, and the music has vanished. In place of the dark red furniture and luxurious trimmings are simple round tables scattered with only two or three chairs around each. On the back wall is a stage, smaller than the one downstairs, with a podium off to the right. The deep red curtains are closed, leaving the room dark with little to occupy your-self with, but there's only one thing on every man's mind in this room at the moment.

"For you, sir," a man on my left says as I take in the room, my eyes adjusting to the darkness. I give the man a tight smile and accept the pamphlet he offers. My dick starts hardening, knowing my new Submissive's details are waiting for me inside. My body hums with desire, and my blood rushes in my ears.

"Lucian," I hear a deep voice call out in front of me. My eyes are drawn to a table near the back of the room and a small hand waving me to come to them.

A smirk slips into place as I pass Senator Williams. Although he's masked, I recognize the sharp features of his jaw, and the pale blue eyes peeking from the silver mask. I give him a nod, but he doesn't see. He's tapping the pamphlet on the table and staring at a man across the room. I don't recognize him, but I imagine it's someone on the senator's shit list judging by the look on his face. The knowledge makes my smirk widen into a grin.

"Interesting to find you here, Lucian," Isaac says in a smooth, lowered voice as I approach. The tables are separated enough for a bit of privacy. I unbutton my jacket and sit easily on the opposite side of Zander and Isaac. Two men I know well. Two men I trust.

"It's been a while," I say easily, taking in the sight of them. My eyes travel along Isaac's suit. It's light grey, and he's even wearing a striped silver tie. I'm not used to the look on him. The men in here are expected to be dressed in black tie attire, but it's been nearly a year since I've been back, and seeing Isaac in a suit is something that's more or less a rarity. Even though it's custom tailored, he looks like he doesn't belong in it. His rugged demeanor and casual stance offset the clean lines and hard edges the suit is meant to enhance.

He's simply not a man to wear a suit. If it were up to him, I imagine he'd be in jeans. Although I'm sure he's found ways to use the tie around his neck to his advantage. He's a contractor for private security, and you'd think he'd be used to dressing up. But he looks like he's itching to get out of his suit. Although I know the silver watch on his wrist costs a fortune. I suppose we all desire a bit of luxury, it's just a matter of personal taste in choosing how to go about it.

I glance around the room, the memories of the club coming back to me, but I stop when I see a man I recognize. It's not because I've seen him here before. Joe Levi. He has a mask on, but his sharp features are distinct, and his mannerisms are the same. He's a crook; a mobster, a villain. This room and club are filled with men of power and wealth, but a membership isn't something that can simply be purchased. There's a background check and a training course that must be completed first. Madam Lynn is out to protect the women here just as much as she aims to profit, but seeing Joe makes me question that.

I gesture slightly toward him, catching Isaac's eye.

"He's been here about three months now," he answers, and his voice is low.

"Are his tastes what I've heard them to be?" I ask soft enough that our conversation can't be heard by anyone else. Zander can hear, but he lets Isaac answer.

"He only comes to the auctions."

I nod in response and look back over to him.

"He's yet to buy anyone." Isaac's words settle in me as I take in the other buyers. Some I know, some I don't. The only one I'd rather not have in this room is Joe. But that's not my call.

"Are you suddenly in the buying mood?" Zander asks me. He's a man who fucking belongs in that suit. He was practically raised in it. Zander's from wealth; he oozes high class, and his neat black bow tie is the cherry on top. As a wall street mogul and heir to a sizable fortune, the designer look and gold cufflinks fit him well. With sharp cheekbones and piercing green eyes, his classically handsome look makes him fit in with this exclusive crowd. Isaac belongs here as well, but his suit is caging in a beast who wants out. That's the difference between them.

"I need a distraction," I finally answer.

"It's good to see you back on the horse," Isaac says with a smirk.

I huff a small grunt of a laugh. "I've just been busy."

Zander smiles at my response and looks as though he's contemplating opening his smart mouth for a response, but he doesn't. Instead he rests his elbows on the table and looks to the stage.

"Have you two already picked out who you'll be bidding on?" I ask. Although I've seen them at events and at a poker night here and there, no one's spoken about Club X or any Submissives or partners recently.

Isaac shrugs, moving his eyes from the stage to me as he answers, "I'm here more for the company. Just biding my time until the show tonight."

"Anything interesting?" I ask.

He raises his eyebrow and his blue eyes sparkle with mischief as he says, "Fire play."

"Ah," I answer and choose not to expand on my thoughts. I have no interest in fire play or anything that could cause serious scarring. No whips, no fire, no spikes or knives. My brow furrows, and I sit a little more comfortably in my seat.

49

"Don't get your panties in a twist there, Lucian," Isaac says with a grin that shows off his white teeth.

"Fuck off," I say easily.

The guys laugh, and I feel a little more at ease.

"Seriously," Zander says, "it's good to see you here."

I give him a simple nod. It is nice to be back. I can feel the adrenaline scorching my blood, and it's intoxicating.

I haven't been back since before Tricia. My ex-wife. I took her here a few times for some shows to see how things were performed. I let her pick out her favorites. The memory turns the corners of my lips down, and the excitement dims. But I shake it off, clearing my throat and ridding my mind of all thoughts of her.

I flip through the pamphlet, leaning back in my chair and scanning the verbiage I've read a time or two before.

There are strict guidelines that must be adhered to by both buyer/seller to gain entry and to continue membership.

Membership is one hundred thousand per month and allows members to attend auctions and enjoy all the privileges of membership.

All parties are clean and agreeing to sexual activities and must provide proof of birth control.

The women are displayed and purchased in an auction setting with a starting bid of five hundred thousand. Subsequent bids will be in increments of one hundred thousand dollars.

NDAs are required, and paperwork will be signed after the purchase.

Any hard limits are noted at auction and will be written in the individual contracts.

The rose color of the Submissive indicates her preferences, so please take note.

Pink - Virgin
   Cream - Finding limits/BDSM virgin
   Yellow - Simple bondage D/s
   Black - Carte blanche
   Red - Pain is preferred S/M
   No flower - 24/7 power exchange

The buyers must adhere to all rules of the club, or they will be banned and prosecuted. Submissives must also obey all rules, or buyers can take legal action and no money will be paid.

With the accepted terms and conditions, the willing participants of this auction are as follows:

As I turn the page to read about the women and their desires, the lights darken and a loud click prefaces the thick red velvet curtains opening slightly and the auctioneer walking onto the stage.

The auction is starting.

CHAPTER 8

DAHLIA

Just relax and everything will be fine, I tell myself as I step into a room backstage to prepare for the auction.

There's a group of scantily-clad girls already getting ready, and some of them are naked, looking through a rack of skimpy outfits to find which one suits them best. None of them appear to be nervous like I am, or at least they're very good at hiding it.

If they can be cool and collected under pressure, so can I.

I suck in a deep breath, my palms moist with perspiration, my heart racing, and try to calm my nerves. I have to get a hold of myself. I don't want to walk out on stage and wind up fainting because I've worked myself up into a tizzy. I can do this. I just have to keep telling myself how much I need this experience.

Trying to ignore my anxiety, I make my way over to an unattended clothing rack near the rear of the room. I begin sifting through outfits, looking for one that best matches my personality. After a moment of searching, I let out a huff of frustration. I don't see anything that I think looks better than what I already have on. But I have to find something. And quick. The auction is only minutes away.

Just try on something. Anything. I'm sure it will look okay.

I'm about to snatch a red dress off the rack when the sound of clicking heels causes me to turn around. She walks toward me with confidence; a woman in charge of her destiny. Her blonde hair is styled elegantly, her makeup flawlessly dramatic. She struts toward me as if she owns the place, her scarlet red dress clinging to her impressive curves with each step.

Madam Lynn. It has to be.

She stops in front of me, her face brightening into a friendly smile, and extends her hand. "Miss Days, what a pleasure it is to meet you." She shakes her head as if in wonder. "The picture in the email you sent doesn't do you justice. You are far, far more beautiful in person." She speaks with a polish that sounds very professional, something you wouldn't expect from a woman who profits from sex and submission for a living.

My cheeks become rosy at her compliment. "Thank you, Madam Lynn," I say, taking her hand and shaking it. Her hands are soft and warm like her personality. I'm surprised that this woman seems so down-to-earth, considering the awesome wealth that makes up her club. I originally pictured a snobby woman with her nose stuck so far up in the air that she wouldn't know what down was, even if she fell flat on her face.

Madam Lynn flashes me another warm smile filled with straight, sparkling white teeth. "You are very much welcome."

I finger my newbie Sub bracelet nervously, wondering why she's here to greet me personally. Had I done something wrong, like unknowingly violated a rule while on my tour with Bruce and Carla? It would be just my luck.

Seeing my worried expression, Madam Lynn waves away my concern. "You're fine, dear. This is simply protocol. I check on all my girls before every auction to make sure everything's running smoothly, and no one is having second thoughts." She pauses and peers at me with concern. "You aren't having those… are you?"

Of course I am. But I'm not telling you that. "No, I'm good," I blurt out almost immediately. I cringe at how fraudulent I sound and wait for a response.

Madam Lynn simply smiles, placing a gentle hand on my shoulder. "Good to hear. I think you're going to make a fabulous Submissive, and will make a very lucky Dom super happy."

Her words fill me with a confidence that I haven't felt all night, and I'm grateful for her encouragement. "Thank you, Madam Lynn," I say respectfully.

Madam Lynn nods. "Mmmhmm." She begins to turn away, but then stops. "Miss Days?"

"Yes?"

She points to a skimpy gold sheer number on the tail end of the rack. "Might I suggest that one for you? I think it will look good on you, and serve to enhance your beauty. It fits your personality perfectly. I'd stick around to see you try it on, but I need to go check on the other ladies before time runs out." She winks at me in parting. "Good luck at the auction."

I watch as she glides off and begins talking to other women in the room before my eyes fall on the dress she picked for me. It looks okay enough, but I won't see what it really is like until I try it on. I take it off the rack and examine it. Gold and sparkly. There are large gaps in the material, and it's more revealing than what I have on. Blushing, I undress behind the rack, hiding from the other women, and then slip into it, enjoying the feel of the soft material against my skin. I walk over to a large mirror and then suck in a sharp breath when I see myself. The gold material sparkles against the light, enhancing my figure and tanned skin in ways I didn't think possible, making me look utterly gorgeous.

Madam Lynn was right. This looks perfect on me. It's flattering in all the right ways. It's sheer, but the metallic color hides my body well, compared to the other women in the room. I look around at them all crowding around the vanities and chatting away. It's almost like what I'd imagine a strip club could be. Or a burlesque show. My heart pounds harder in my chest, and I pace my breathing as I calm myself down.

I'll have to remember to thank her after the auction. And also ask if I can keep this dress.

"Please check over the pamphlet one more time and make sure everything is accurate," a heavyset woman with greying hair pulled into a bun says behind me, startling me.

I've read this pamphlet over and over. The sheer amount of paper-work I've had to fill out and read is exhausting. My stomach churns as I remember the psychological section. There was a box for me to write in. I was supposed to disclose my problem. I didn't. I suck in a sharp breath as a lump grows in my throat.

I reach out and take the pamphlet, trying to catch my breath. I need to get a hold of myself. I open it up and read through the small description of me, and the list of kinks and fetishes I'm willing to try.

As I look through the rest of the pamphlet, I begin to feel like a prostitute. I try to push the thought from my mind as I take a seat at one of the chairs lining the wall, but I can't shake the feeling that I'm selling out. Cheapening myself. Just because there's a written contract involved, how is this any different than selling myself for sex?

I can end up being a rich guy's perverted fuck toy and nothing more and hating myself after the contract is over.

The thought makes me sick. It's because of my money troubles that I'm thinking like this. And I have to be honest with myself--the money is tempting, and would solve so many problems in my life so easily. I want to cry for thinking about myself that way. But that's not what this is for me. This is much more than just some easy money. And if this turns out to be anything less than what I want for myself, I'll walk away from it all. The money doesn't matter. I need more from this. I need the fantasy. My body heats, and my pussy pulses with need.

I can't back out now. I have to go through with this. Carla's gone through this same process, and look how happy she is with Bruce. She's a successful career woman by day, and a perfect Submissive by night. Looking at her, you would never guess she's leading a double life. Using her as an example, I really should have nothing to worry about. I have to believe that this will help heal me, even if the man who buys me doesn't know about my problems. He gets off on his sexual fantasies, I get the money and continue with the therapy that will help me. It's mutually beneficial for the both of us. A win-win.

Feeling slightly better, I close the pamphlet. And not a moment too soon. The large woman who handed me the pamphlet is suddenly herding all the women in the room together.

"It's time, ladies," she announces. "Good luck with the auction tonight."

As I line up with the other women, it's obvious that the rest of them have done this before and they all know each other well. I pull at the hem of my dress as the women in charge call out names. I'm the second name called, and I force my legs to move as I walk to the front of the line. I peek out as she opens the door, but the curtains are closed. The floor of the stage is a shiny dark wood, and the walls are covered with a thick wallpaper with a subtle cream paisley pattern. Other than the gorgeous wallpaper, the stage is empty. There's no detail whatsoever. It lacks the details and luxury that the rest of the club has in every other room.

I suppose the only detail on the stage will be each woman as she takes her turn in the auction.

"You seem very nervous," a woman behind me says. The blonde woman in front of me turns around, and the two women look at me, waiting for me to respond.

"A little," I breathe. No shit I am. Who wouldn't be?

"Relax, you'll make good money, and it's so much fucking fun."

The woman in front of me lets out a small laugh and then smooths her red dress. The dress itself is provocative. The deep V in front dips so low that it nearly shows her belly button, and there's no back at all to the halter dress. It's so revealing, but it suits her well. "It's always a good time, and all the times I've been in the auction, I've never seen a woman not have a man bid on her."

The woman behind me nods her head and leans forward to peek at the empty stage. "I already know who's going to be bidding on me this time."

"Your boyfriend?" I ask. The women laugh, and my insecurity is almost unbearable.

"I don't have a boyfriend, and I'm not interested in one," she answers with confidence.

The woman in front of me looks at me as though she's wondering why I'd even mention a relationship. I feel fucking sick to my stomach, but I close my eyes and remember this is just sex. Good sex. Sex that's going to give me what I need. When I open my eyes again, I see the woman in front of me smiling.

"That's what you should be focusing on," she says with a knowing look. "Just enjoy yourself," she concludes as her eyes roam my body and she looks out beyond the door to the stage once more.

Madam Lynn opens the entrance door behind us with a clipboard in her hand, and a petite brunette in bright pink high heels in tow. She looks like she's struggling to keep up with Madam Lynn's confident stride toward the front.

"Alright, ladies," Madam Lynn doesn't look up from the board as she walks toward the stage with everyone turning to face her. "We'll have Madeline first," she announces, then looks up and lets a playful smile grace her lips. "I wonder who you'll be going home to tonight?" she asks beneath her breath with a raised eyebrow. I didn't even think about leaving the club. I look around the room again and notice all the duffel bags. There are only a few. But it looks like some women have packed an overnight bag. Shit. For the first time since I've seen her, the beautiful woman in front of me actually blushes. "Dahlia, you'll be next," she says as she turns to me, and I can feel everyone's eyes on me.

Madam Lynn's eyes travel down my body and then back up to meet mine as she brushes the hair out of my face. "Let's keep your hair behind you and not cover up your breasts. Take your bra off as well." She moves on, continuing to list the ladies and doing a thorough check of each as my heart sputters in my chest. Another assistant is carrying a handful of roses, ten total, in a variety of colors. She passes each girl a rose in turn. I carefully take the cream-colored rose as she hands it to me. Although the thorns are gone, I still feel as though simply holding the rose in my hand is going to hurt me.

I step out of line and reach behind my back to unclip the bra and let it fall. My breasts are perky, but they sag slightly from their weight. I look in the mirror, feeling even more self-conscious.

"You're beautiful, Dahlia." I turn to face the woman behind me. "These men know what real women look like."

I clear my throat, taking my spot back in line and trying not to hide myself, fiddling with the soft petals of the rose. "Thank you," I say as confidently as I can.

The urge to cross my arms is strong, but I fight it.

"Madeline," Madam Lynn calls out her name as she opens the door wide. "Let's go, my dear."

Madeline walks confidently out onto the stage and I walk quickly to take her place behind the door. Madam Lynn's hand is firm on Madeline's shoulder as they walk, their heels clicking and Madam

Lynn whispering in Madeline's ear. She finally releases her, lining her up in the center of the stage.

It's so bright. Spotlights are shining on her body, and their intensity makes the dress pointless. You can see everything. Fuck. The breath is stolen from my lungs as I look down at my own dress and hear a microphone being turned on.

"Welcome, gentlemen, it's time for the auction." At Madam Lynn's words, the curtains slowly open and Madeline straightens her shoulders, standing tall for all the men to see.

Sucking in a deep breath, I prepare for the auction to start.

CHAPTER 9

LUCIAN

"*How* about her?" Zander asks with a raised brow. Neither he nor Isaac have their bidding paddles in hand. Judging from their conversation, they aren't interested in the women tonight. There are at least fifty men in this room, and the pamphlet lists only ten women tonight. So I'm perfectly fine with them sitting this one out. I'd like to find someone who'd suit me well, and there's one I'm eager to see.

I shake my head as a man I don't recognize starts the bidding off at five hundred thousand, raising his white paddle that's barely visible.

The woman is beautiful, and the pamphlet indicates she's experienced as does the black rose in her hands. But the next woman is the one I'm impatient to see.

"Six hundred thousand," the auctioneer says loudly, searching through the crowd and then nodding his head. "Seven to the gentleman on the right." I turn and see Zander's raised his paddle.

He smiles broadly as the original man yells out, "Eight hundred thousand!"

"Stop fucking with him, Zander." Zander's grin doesn't fade as he sets the paddle down and shrugs at Isaac.

"You better not do that shit to me," I tell him. Cocky bastard.

"Is that what you do here?" I ask beneath my breath.

Isaac shakes his head and watches the stage as the woman is sold for nine hundred thousand dollars. "He just started doing it out of sheer boredom. One day you're going to win one of them," he turns to face Zander, "and then what?" he asks.

"Then I'll have myself a Submissive," Zander says flippantly. Isaac answers with something, but I don't catch it.

The woman I've been waiting for walks out on stage. Her nude heels click on the ground, and it's all I can hear as she walks in what seems like slow motion. Everything else turns to white noise, and the only sound in my ears is the steady *click, click, click* of her nervous steps.

She's utterly gorgeous, but there's an obvious innocence about her. I thought I'd be interested when I looked at her information initially, but now I'm certain that I have to have her.

Treasure. She's the one. Her gold dress clings to her figure and sparkles beautifully, as though she truly belongs in it. The gold tones only make her sun-kissed skin that much more beautiful. My dick is already hard at the thought of my hand leaving a bright red flush across her lush ass.

She centers herself on the stage, looking nervously at the auctioneer and then behind her, at Madam Lynn.

The dusting of sparkles on her dress barely hides her soft curves. I want to see all of her. I want to feel her soft skin. I grip the paddle tighter and rise it up high. "Five hundred thousand," I call out, starting the bid before the auctioneer can ramble like he did with the first woman.

A man in the far corner, features behind a grey mask that covers three-quarters of his face raises his paddle. "Six."

Another man in the far back who I recognize as Stephen White, heir and owner of a few local car dealerships, raises his paddle. "Seven hundred thousand."

Although the thin wood of the paddle pierces deeper into the sweaty palm of my hand as anger washes through me, I maintain my calm demeanor and raise my paddle again. "Eight hundred thousand."

I watch Dahlia, my treasure, as her skin colors a beautiful red on her chest and up her cheeks with a blush. My dick twitches at the thought of seeing that color on her ass. I can imagine how she'd squirm in my lap as I smacked my hand down with a blistering beating. Gripping her tempting ass before spanking her over and over.

"Nine. One million," the auctioneer points at each man as they raise their paddles, upping the cost. I don't care how much I have to pay. She's going to be mine. "One million one hundred thousand. One point one."

There's a pause, and he looks around the room through his spectacles. "One point two," he says as I raise the paddle.

"One point three," he calls out as the last bidder, White, raises his paddle again. I turn to face him, and although he must be able to feel my eyes boring into the side of his face, he ignores me.

I raise my paddle once more and keep it in the air this time. "One million four hundred thousand," the auctioneer says. I watch as White raises his and then takes a peek at me as the auctioneer rattles off, "One point five," my paddle still in the air.

"One point six," the auctioneer says, pointing to me and then looking back to White.

"Shit's getting real," I hear Zander say out of the side of his mouth. His humor doesn't do anything to ease the anger flowing through me. She's mine.

White finally breaks my gaze and sets his paddle on the table. I stare him down as the auctioneer says, "One point six million, going once... going twice," he takes a final look around the room and I swear to God if anyone were to speak I'd lose my shit, "Sold! For one point six million."

I watch as the woman, Dahlia, gasps. My treasure is ushered off the stage with unsteady steps in her patent leather heels as she tries to collect herself. A smile grows along my lips as I stand to go to the office in the back where I'll collect her after the auction is done.

"Congratulations, sir," Zander says with a smirk.

"You should have bid two mil, you pussy," Isaac says to Zander, and I finally huff out a small laugh.

"Maybe next month I'll fuck with him," Zander says before taking a sip of his whiskey.

I ignore them and watch as Dahlia disappears from my sight.

I knew the moment I saw her that I had to have her.

And now she's mine. I *own* her. A few sheets of paper stand in the way. And then tomorrow morning, I'll have my Submissive all to myself. I'm dying to get a taste tonight, but the rules must be followed. And that means one last night to herself, and then she's mine.

———————

THE DOOR TO THE OFFICE I'VE BEEN SITTING AT FOR NEARLY AN HOUR finally opens, and my hand tightens around the tumbler on the table. The ice clinks as I move the cool glass, bringing it to my lips. My eyes never leave the door as I take a sip of the aged whiskey.

It opens seamlessly, revealing Madam Lynn in her scarlet dress. She's a gorgeous woman with poise and grace, but I ignore her entirely, waiting for Dahlia to be revealed. Her shoulders are hunched inward slightly, and her head's down. Although she originally walked in with her eyes on me, they immediately fell to the floor.

It's like she's scared to look at me. Maybe she's overwhelmed. I imagine that's normal, and I'll be sure to put her at ease. The pamphlet only gave a tiny bit of information about Dahlia, my treasure.

I know she's a first-time Submissive. Her information indicated she hasn't been trained, which only makes my dick harder and me more eager to get her back home and in the playroom. So her looking down is an instinctual Submissive behavior. That's fucking perfect.

She looks even more beautiful close up as she walks to the glass table and takes a seat across from me and next to Madam Lynn. The madam slaps a stack of papers down on the table, finally gaining my attention.

She smirks when I look at her.

I only care about two sheets in that entire packet. The non-disclosure agreement, and the page where Dahlia signs and consents to be my Submissive for the next thirty days.

"Madam Lynn, Dahlia," I greet them both, although my eyes are firmly on Dahlia. At the mention of her name those beautiful wide eyes look up at me.

"Are you going to be keeping your mask on? Or is it acceptable to reveal your identity?" Madam Lynn asks.

Ah, yes. I slip off the mask and place it on the table. I'd forgotten about the damn thing. I know Dahlia has already signed an NDA for the auction, and I want her to get a good look at me and read my expression.

I don't want her to question how much I truly want her.

"Dahlia, meet your new Dominant, Lucian." Madam Lynn leans back in her chair as Dahlia extends her hand to me.

A smirk plays at my lips. She's so fucking cute. I play along, shaking her hand. When our skin touches, her soft small hand in mine, my body ignites with desire. The urge to pull her close to me takes over, a spark heating between us. I release her and move my hand to my lap before I do something stupid and take her before the contracts are signed.

I clear my throat. "Let's get this over with."

"Eager, are we?" Madam Lynn thinks she's funny.

She sets a sheet of paper in the middle of the table and points to a list with a thin silver pen. The list has several boxes checked, but some are empty.

"Do the two of you consent and agree upon the following conditions?" I look through the list carefully. The checked boxes are the ones that Dahlia desires, and the unchecked boxes are hard limits, meaning we won't be engaging in those activities.

I read through each stipulation carefully, making sure our tastes are agreeable. For the most part, it's my choice on things while she's still finding her limits. She's new to this lifestyle, so she's been assigned cream as her color for now. With over fifty specific fetishes on the list there are only a handful of hard limits, such as: scat, blood, breathing and permanent marks which remain unchecked. I agree with her on all of those, and I'm not interested in them either.

The boxes checked include the usual: anal, bondage light and bondage heavy, nipple play, deprivation, spreader bars, and other kinks and fetishes. Fisting is also included, which makes me look up at this petite little thing with mild surprise. She blushes violently as I take in her expression. We could work up to that. I imagine she checked it as a soft limit.

I sit back and nod my head, accepting the pen from Madam Lynn. "Everything looks perfect to me." I sign on the line.

"Wonderful," Madam Lynn says as she takes the sheet and pulls out another. I'm getting anxious, and I can't stop staring at my treasure. She's not looking at me, and I know she's nervous; in fact, I enjoy that she's nervous. But I'm going to need some privacy to take full advantage of that.

We sign a few more papers, including the NDA I require.

"Alright, and now to summarize the above terms and conditions. You, Mr. Lucian Stone, are agreeing to act as Dahlia Days' Dominant at the locations of your choice for the duration of the next thirty days which will end at precisely one minute past midnight on the fifteenth of the following month of December. As her Dominant, you agree to the terms and conditions in the above contract, including and accepting that at any point Miss Days can terminate the contract and end the relationship entirely."

I nod my head as Madam Lynn pauses and glances at me. "And Dahlia Days acknowledges and accepts that by leaving this arrangement, all monetary gains in the sum of half of one point six million, which is the equivalent of eight hundred thousand dollars." Dahlia looks as though she's going to faint as Madam Lynn rattles off the figure, "will be forfeit." She turns to Dahlia, who's completely lost in thought; it's obvious she's still in slight shock. After a few seconds, my treasure sits upright and nods her head.

"Yes, I understand."

"I'll need you to sign here," Madam Lynn says, and I wait for Dahlia to sign, my hands itching for the pen. "And Mr. Stone," Madam Lynn hands me the pen and I'm quick to scribble my signature.

"Your thirty days starts tomorrow," Madam Lynn says, finalizing the procedure. It's about fucking time.

"I'd like you at my address at eight in the morning," I say and scratch my address down on the pad of paper. I took tomorrow off just so I could enjoy her fully for the first day. I may be a workaholic, but my treasure is a real treat, and I'm going to need time to explore every inch of her body and test how every subtle touch affects her.

"But I-"

I stop and look up at her, not knowing why Dahlia would object.

Maybe she doesn't have transportation. "I can have a car pick you up, if you'd rather?" I offer her.

"I can drive. I just wasn't expecting it to start so early. And I thought maybe we'd be at the club?"

"You'll be in my playroom for training, and you'll be available when I want you, which will be all times of the day and night, treasure." She gasps slightly, and her eyes widen.

"I-" she starts to answer, and then looks at Madam Lynn as if she's the one she should be speaking to. *I'm her Dom, for fuck's sake.*

"You what? Tell me what's bothering you." I'm getting irritated by her hesitation, and my tone reflects that. She doesn't seem too bothered by it though, which is good. She's going to have to get used to it.

"I have an internship," she answers hesitantly. The poor girl hardly looks like she's breathing. She can't even look me in the eyes. Her shyness, nerves and even the hint of fear are all endearing.

"Why was that not included in the contract?" I ask her.

Madam Lynn opens a folder and produces a sheet, sliding it across the table. I glance at it, and her schedule is listed as flexible.

"I didn't know my schedule ahead of time," she explains meekly.

"Do you know it now?" I ask her.

"For this week," she answers me quickly. I nod and let out a heavy sigh. That'll have to work.

"I'll need your schedule," I say and hold out my hand for her to pass it to me from the pile of papers in front of her. She should have brought it.

She looks at the stack on the table and then up to me. Her eyes are gorgeous, a beautiful mix of greens and blue with a touch of golden brown. They're the most stunning hazel eyes I've ever seen. Her chest rises with a sharp breath as she says, "I-" she stops, and swallows thickly. "I didn't know to bring it."

My expression hardens, and I move my hand back to my lap. My fingers grip my thigh to keep from grabbing her ass and pulling her across my lap. She's unprepared. My dick is hard as a fucking rock knowing I should punish her. But I have to remember, she's new and still needs to learn.

"I can get it to you tonight," she says in a slightly more firm voice.

"Is that acceptable?" Madam Lynn asks me from Dahlia's right. I can feel her eyes on me, but I don't take mine off my treasure. I can't punish her just yet. But I'm going to give her a taste of it tomorrow. Whenever I'm able to get my hands on her.

"How many hours a week is your internship?" I'm already pissed that I can't have her whenever I damn well feel like it.

"It's forty hours," she says softly. Her quick reply with an answer I was expecting makes me relax somewhat. I can handle forty hours of her away. It will be good for her to maintain a social life. I swallow down my selfish desire to have her on call at all times. For now, this will have to do.

"What time are you done?" I ask.

"Around six," she says, then holds my gaze and nods.

Around six. I give myself a moment to calm down. She isn't trained. She doesn't know me. But she will, and she has so much to learn. "Precision and timeliness are important to me."

She opens and closes her mouth, clearly at a loss for words and then nods her head. That's a very good start. I'm enjoying this already.

"I'll need to know when and where to pick you up." I could have my driver wait there, or I could wait outside of wherever it is that she works as well, but I don't have any desire to wait around. I have a list of shit that needs to get done, and I want to know a specific time. More importantly, I want to hold her to this time.

"No later than six fifteen," she says confidently. *Good girl.* It's irritating as fuck that I'll have to wait, but I'll have her to myself tomorrow night. I'll bury myself in work until then.

"I'll need the address and your schedule sent to this number." I jot my number down and slide it across the glass-topped table to her. She reaches for it, but I keep my fingers on the paper and wait for her to look at me. "I expect that message tonight."

"Yes..." I can practically hear the "s" on the tip of her tongue. She looks up at me and then back to Madam Lynn.

"Ask me, Dahlia," I tell her. "If you have a question, I'm the one you need to ask. No one else."

"Sir?" she asks with those sweet hazel eyes peering up at me, filled with vulnerability. "Do I call you sir?"

My dick is harder than it's ever been in my entire fucking life. "Yes, treasure. You will call me sir."

She starts to ask another question, but then pauses for a moment and licks her lips. "Always?" she asks.

I shake my head gently. "In this club and when we're playing, but if I take you out, then no, I don't want you to call me sir." She nods her head, accepting what I've told her as I let my own words settle. *Take her out.* When would I fucking do that?

"Any last questions for either party?" Madam Lynn asks. She looks between the two of us, but her eyes linger on Dahlia. She's seen many of these auctions; I'm sure she's made up in her mind what type of match this will be already.

Dahlia shakes her head as she says, "No." Her breathing is coming in shorter and heavier, and I know the reality is setting in.

"No, I'm more than ready for tomorrow to begin. And make sure you pack a bag with your essentials and a change of clothes. You'll be staying the night."

Dahlia nods her head as she says, "I understand, sir." Her voice is small and her words barely more than a whisper.

"I'll see you tomorrow at six fifteen," I tell her as I stand and fasten the middle button of my jacket and then slip my mask into place.

"Yes, sir." Those sweet words stay with me for the rest of the night. The soft sounds of her submission from those plump lips are all I can think about. Tomorrow. Six fifteen can't get here fast enough.

CHAPTER 10

DAHLIA

"Lucian," I announce to Carla. "Lucian Stone. That's who bought me."

I'm leaning against a clothes rack, standing in the fashion workroom on the third floor early the next morning, organizing Debra's designs for an upcoming fashion show. I really want my coffee, but I'm so anxious I'm scared to drink any more caffeine in fear it will make me a jittery mess. I'm still in disbelief over the amount of money Lucian paid for me. *1.6 million.* Jesus. It doesn't seem real.

But it won't be 1.6 million after Club X takes its cut, and after taxes. In the end, I'll probably end up with less than five hundred thousand. Still a fuckton though. And it'll go a long way in getting a head start in life. I'm definitely not complaining.

I turn to look at Carla, wanting to read her facial expression for any kind of reaction, but she has her back turned to me.

She's putting the edgy outfits in their respective categories with ease, but I can hardly stay on my feet. I'm so exhausted. I was up all night, tossing and turning, consumed with thoughts of Lucian and reliving the events of the auction in my head. All I could think about was how gorgeous he was, with his dirty blond hair, chiseled jawline and that brooding, yet intense expression that made me feel like I was burning up inside while on stage and back in Madam Lynn's office.

Being up close to him had been even more intense. He radiated such power and a sort of mystery that made me hungry to know more about him. Even the way he spoke, with a deep growling voice throbbing with authority, filled me with sexual desire and made me want to fall to my knees and please him right then and there.

I remember the title he made me call him.

Sir.

A shiver goes down my spine as I think about the way he looked at me. Like he owned me. Like I was his property. I want him. Now. More than that, I crave his lips on mine, his touch on my body. I crave his... domination. I can picture him now, thrusting his chiseled hips against my ass, pushing every inch of his big fat cock inside of me as he wraps his powerful hands around my neck and makes me beg for more. The raw image flashing in front of my eyes makes my nipples harden, my core heat with desire, and my body tremble with anticipation.

I can't wait for our first meeting.

Six fifteen, I tell myself, sucking in a deep breath and pushing away the naughty images. *I just have to make it until then. Then I'll be all his.*

Carla slips a glittery red halter top on a rack, the clinking of the hanger snapping me back to the present, and then turns to face me, her face twisting into a puzzled expression. "Lucian Stone," she murmurs, tapping her index finger against her lips thoughtfully. It's weird to see her dressed conservatively today, in a black pantsuit and hair pulled into a ponytail, a far cry from the slutty outfit she had on last night. I'm struck once again by her ability to live this double life. Looking at her, you would never guess that she was into being someone's Submissive for pleasure. "Hmm," she says, closing her eyes, and repeating his name over and over to jog her memory.

Her eyes pop open a moment later and she frowns at me, causing my throat to drop into my stomach. "I'm sorry, Dah," she admits, shaking her head regretfully. "But I've never heard of this guy."

My mouth falls open in shock, my heart pounding in my chest. I don't know why it matters that Carla doesn't know Lucian, but I'm really fucking nervous. Going into the contract, I knew I'd be handing myself over to a total stranger, but I would've been more comforted by the fact if it were someone Carla knew and could vouch for.

"What?" I ask incredulously. "I thought you knew a lot of these men's identities." Maybe I feel anxious because I don't know what to expect from Lucian. He has an air of mystery about him that seems... intoxicating, but dangerous at the same time. Carla knowing something about him, *anything*, would help me feel more at ease.

She shakes her head. "I never said that, Dah. I just said that I know who *some* of them are. But I'm sorry if you got the wrong idea. I wish I could tell you more about this guy, but I can't." She pauses, lost in thought, and then shakes her head. "I wouldn't worry too much. This guy sounds like he *really* wanted you. It's been awhile since a chick commanded that kind of price." She scowls. "I'm jealous."

Before I can reply, Debra struts into the room holding a stack of papers in her hand. Once again, I'm reminded of how Debra resembles Madam Lynn--not in looks, but personality. She looks gorgeous today in black spiked stilettos, tight white pants and a silk black top that showcases her impressive chest. Her hair is done up into an effortless updo with wisps of hair framing her mature face and her makeup is vibrant, taking a few years off. But the most alluring thing she's wearing, as always, is her confidence.

"Good morning, ladies," she greets us with a smile, walking over to a table on the side of the room and placing the papers on it.

"Good morning," we both reply in near unison.

Debra turns to face us and chuckles, shaking her head. "Ah. You girls are so cute! It makes me sad that I've brought more work to put on your plate."

Cute? If you only knew the depravity we're involved in.

I hold in a groan and hope it's not something too involved. I can barely keep my eyes open.

"What's that?" Carla asks curiously.

Debra points at the pile of papers. "I need you two to match the models in those folders with their respective gowns for my upcoming show."

"That should be easy," Carla says easily, and I hear the relief in her voice. "We'll get that done for you no problem, boss."

"Speak for yourself," I mutter under my breath, low enough that Debra doesn't hear. Carla grins at me. She knows I've barely gotten any sleep, but she's cheery anyway. Probably from the hard fuck she got from Bruce last night. My cheeks heat at the memory of Club X once again. I can't stop thinking about last night.

Debra shoots her a thumbs up. "That's the spirit. I knew I could count on you two." She starts to leave the room, but pauses in the doorway to add, "Oh, and by the way, I also need you two to come up with theme ideas for the after party. Usually Kevin comes through for me, but he's down with a nasty cold and I don't know if I can depend on him." She pauses to look between us both. "Can I count on you two girls?"

Carla nods and says, "Yes," but at the same time, I say respectfully, "Yes, Madam Lynn."

Debra must not have heard me, because with a flash of a grin, she's gone.

Carla turns to me, her expression shocked. "You did not just call her Madam Lynn!"

Placing a hand over my mouth, I let out a deep yawn that I can't control. "Sorry. I'm really tired." The cups of coffee I've drunk this morning have done little to wake me up, but something tells me that when six fifteen gets here I'll be wide fucking awake.

"Their mannerisms do favor each other though," Carla says thoughtfully, walking over and grabbing a stack of Debra's papers. "But you need to be careful that you don't slip up like that in the future. Madam Lynn's name is an open secret and who knows what clientele she has... even in this building."

It takes a moment for the implications of what Carla is saying to hit me. "Debra?" I ask incredulously, my jaw dropping open, "a Submissive?" Never in a million years would I think Debra would have a submissive bone in her entire body. She's just... too powerful for that.

Carla makes a face. "I'm not saying that she is. I'm just saying, would you have thought I was a Submissive without me revealing it to you?"

I shake my head.

"Okay then. Just remember the NDA you signed." She motions me over to an empty table to the side of the clothing rack. "Come help me sort through this mess right quick and then let's get lunch."

We spend the next half hour categorizing fashion designs and matching model profiles to the outfits they'll be wearing for Debra's upcoming fashion show. Carla is making quick work of the task, but I'm finding it hard to do even the simplest thing, tired and my mind filled with anxiety. When I screw up and pin a model's profile on the wrong outfit, Carla places a hand atop mine, her expression concerned.

"What's on your mind, Dah?" she asks.

Do you even have to ask?

"I just wish there was a way that we could find out more about..." I say, my voice trailing off. I don't know why I'm bothering. Carla has already said she doesn't know anything about Lucian. She can't conjure information about him out of thin air just because I want her to. I'm probably just worrying myself to death over nothing.

Carla shakes her head, her eyes filled with sympathy. She must think my worry is getting tiresome, but I can't help it. This is my first time doing something like this, and no matter how hard I try to relax, I remain on edge. "I don't think so, the club's rules..." her voice trails off as her face crinkles into a thoughtful expression. "I know!" she says suddenly, her face brightening, snapping her fingers. "We can look him up on the net!"

Oh my God, I'm so stupid. That's actually a genius idea. Why the hell didn't I think of that? I've spent all this time worrying when a simple Google search could have turned up dirt... if there is any.

Probably because all I've been thinking about is being fucked by him, I think to myself.

"Let's cyberstalk him," Carla says, slinging a black slinky dress over the rack and throwing the model profile she's holding down on a table.

Uneasiness touches my chest.

"You're not going to be able to work unless you find out more about Lucian to put your mind at ease. So let's get it over with. You only have a few hours before you meet up with him, and you don't want to go into your first encounter terrified, trust me." She begins making her way over to the nearest desk, and I hastily slip the white dress I'm holding onto a hanger and place it on the rack. "What about all this?" I gesture.

"It'll still be here when we're done. C'mon. It'll only take a few minutes."

"You think Debra will care that we're doing this on a company computer?"

Carla practically rolls her eyes as she says, "Girl, you don't even wanna know what I've searched on company time."

Fuck it. My need to find out more about Lucian overrides my caution of breaking the rules. "Let's do it."

She grabs a chair and slides it across the floor to sit next to me as I tap on the space bar to bring the screen to life. I take control of the mouse, and within a few clicks, pull up the Chrome browser.

The blank Google search bar sits in front of me, the cursor blinking.

"You ready?" Carla whispers, placing a comforting hand on my thigh and gently rubbing it.

I'm ready for anything that says this man isn't a sociopath, I think to myself.

Gulping, I nod, and my fingers fly across the keys. *Lucian Stone.* I stare at his name in the search bar, anxiety filling me. *What will this search reveal?* I wonder. Hopefully nothing. Back in front of Madam Lynn, he definitely didn't look like a bad man with his dashing good looks, but my opinion on that will change quickly if I find something I don't like.

"Dah?" Carla presses.

Screw it. Taking a deep breath, I tap the left mouse button.

The first few results that pop up on the screen are pictures of him, all of them incredibly handsome, and him with other young businessmen in suits. Some are even shirtless pictures of him on the beach, his incredible eight-pack abs proudly on display. Desire stirs in my stomach as I look at them. He's so gorgeous and built like a Greek god. Seriously, he looks like such a tall glass of champagne. It doesn't seem possible that I'm now going to be his property for an entire month.

All that is going to be mine later, I tell myself. *Holy fucking shit.*

"Jesus," Carla breathes, her eyes widening at all the eye candy of Lucian. "He's fucking hot!"

"You're telling me," I whisper, clicking through several sexy pictures of him on the beach, my pussy clenching at the thought of having this man all to myself.

After admiring a score of pictures of Lucian, I scroll down the page and my eyes settle on a bold headline.

Man becomes youngest CEO to make eight figures.

I click on the article and begin reading. Carla is as well, and I can hear the faint wispy sounds of her lips moving as she follows along. It's one of her quirks, but it's slightly distracting as I read about how he dropped out of college and started his own company. It wasn't long before he rose to the top of the corporate world and made a name for himself.

The article continues listing Lucian's accomplishments, which I find quite impressive. There's nothing in the list that gives me cause for concern. My anxiety ebbing a little, I move on from the article and skim through the next few search results. All of them are about the same thing, talking about how impressive Lucian's rise to power is and how he's the next big thing in the corporate world.

Holy fuck, he's accomplished so much.

Insecurity stirs in the pit of my stomach, replacing the dread. Next to him, I feel like a complete underachiever. It's going to be hard not to focus on his status when I'm with him. I can only hope that he makes me forget who he is when we have our sessions, otherwise they won't be pleasant.

I scroll through a few more of the same types of articles spanning the last few years and take deep breaths, my anxiety ebbing slowly.

Satisfied there's nothing else to see, I'm about to close out the search page, when I notice another eye-catching headline that makes my heart jump in my chest.

Young CEO headed for tumultuous divorce.

Married for less than a year, CEO and sole proprietor of Stone Enterprises, Lucian Stone is headed for a vicious split with Tricia Stone, formerly Morgan. The couple has filed for divorce, citing irreconcilable differences although there are several rumors of an affair. And not what you'd expect. It appears Mrs. Stone has fled their home and is staying with an unknown "former friend." Tricia has been quoted as saying, "The last few months of our marriage have been difficult, and I simply can't continue in this manner. This marriage and divorce have certainly harmed my image, and I have no doubt that it will affect me for the rest of my life. This isn't what I thought we were committed to when we exchanged vows, and I am deeply heartbroken by the turn of events." Mr. Stone has failed to comment.

I close out the page, feeling slightly uncomfortable and wincing with a twinge of guilt. I shouldn't have dug past his company's history, let alone gotten into his personal history. Shit.

"Feel better now?" Carla is looking at me with relief in her eyes. I wish I felt the same. It seems she's just as happy as I am that nothing dastardly has shown up on Lucian. I probably would've driven her crazy had I not done this. "You found out that he wasn't a serial killer... and I found out that I missed out by getting stuck with Bruce."

"Carla!" I protest.

Carla gives me a playful smirk. "Just joking. But seriously, you okay now?"

No, I'm not. But I'm going to suck it up and deal with this until tonight. I nod my head. "You're right. I didn't find out anything that makes me want to back out of my contract, thank God."

Carla smiles with relief. "Good."

THE REST OF MY DAY IS MUCH MORE PRODUCTIVE, AND I'M EVEN ABLE to come up with a kick ass costume theme for Debra's after party; Subs and Doms. Carla thinks it's an absolute hoot. She's just worried about how Debra is going to take it.

By the time six rolls around, the exhaustion I was experiencing earlier is gone. Like I predicted earlier, I'm wide awake and I can't stop trembling with excitement.

"I'm going to go freshen up and then wait downstairs for my ride," I announce to Carla, my hands trembling with nervousness and excitement as I stick the last profile on an outfit. There's still one last pile of clothes that needs to be organized, and there are sticker papers all over the floor. I'm supposed to help Carla clean it up, but if I do, I'll be late and I'm afraid of angering Lucian before our first meeting.

I can almost picture the anger in his eyes, and it sends a shiver down my spine.

Carla finishes hanging up a white ball gown, and then turns to grin at me. "Just remember to relax and enjoy yourself," she advises. "A good Dom will make you feel safe in surrendering to him." She pauses and bites her lower lip, as if unsure if she should say something else. "And let me know all the dirty details tomorrow!" she blurts out.

"Seriously?" I give her a pointed look. "But you just scolded me earlier about the NDA."

Carla scowls at me with consternation. "Fuck the NDA! Lucian is hot as fuck. I want to know what happens, or else!" She gestures at the leftover work. "Besides, you owe me for leaving me to deal with all this alone. Hopefully Lucian leaves a red print on that ass for me in revenge." She gives me a devious grin, and I imagine her mind is filled with dirty, depraved thoughts.

I blush furiously and let out a laugh. "My, my, that attitude isn't very submissive, is it? But okay. I'll be sure to take notes."

Carla mimics the thumbs up Debra loves to give when someone is doing a good job. "Good girl."

I laugh again and leave Carla to clean up our mess and make my way downstairs, my heels clicking against the floor. I walk into one of the work restrooms and make sure it's empty before I walk over to the mirror. I need to freshen up before I meet with Lucian's driver. I feel like I can barely breathe as I lean against the granite counter. I would've preferred to go home to take a shower after spending all day on my feet, but Lucian had been adamant. He wanted me right at six fifteen, and not a moment after. I shouldn't be surprised. This is a man who is used to getting what he wants. *And he wants me.* Again, I can hardly believe this is real. One point six million, with a super handsome and ultra-wealthy Dom willing to fulfill my fantasies. And eight hundred thousand of that money goes to me. It's just too much to take in.

Anxiety and desire roll through me thinking about the way Lucian demanded that I be available for him. Sitting there in that chair, he looked like a man that was dying of thirst. Like he would've done anything in that moment to get a drink of me. And I want to satisfy that thirst. My blood chills at the thought of him looking at me like my last ex did. Like somehow he'll know I'm not enjoying it. That I'll be disappointing him if I can't get off *when* he wants, *how* he wants. I take in a steadying breath. *No*, I think and shake my head. Neither of my exes would've even known about my problems if I hadn't told them. And this is about me pleasing Lucian. I can do this, and Lucian doesn't need to know about how broken I am.

After several deep breaths, I feel a bit calmer. I finish washing up, and focus on fixing my hair and makeup. When I'm satisfied with my appearance, I leave the bathroom and make my way out into the vast lobby and toward the front exit, marked by two glass double doors.

My heart seems to pound harder with each step, and by the time I reach the doors, I'm out of breath. I can't stop trembling. I'm filled with anxiety over what's to be my first sexual encounter in years. It's been a long time since I've been with a man, and the last few encounters only left me feeling disappointed and let down. A part of me is afraid this will end up being no different.

Outside, a Rolls Royce with tinted windows is waiting for me by the sidewalk. The driver is leaning against the car and immediately pushes off and straightens his shoulders when he sees me. I don't even have to guess whose car it is.

I place my hand on the cool silver handles of the glass double doors, steadying myself, my legs feeling like they're going to buckle. Another few minutes and I'll be running late. I need to get out there, but I have the sudden urge to run away.

I can do this. Everything is going to be okay.

Taking a deep, calming breath, I swing open the doors and walk outside.

CHAPTER 11

LUCIAN

I loosen my tie as I finally get to my penthouse. She should be here any minute. I wanted to be in the car with Joseph when he picked her up, but work took priority. Besides, we can discuss matters in the playroom. Quickly.

I'm ready to feel that tight pussy milking my cock. I couldn't even sleep last night I was so fucking hard for her. The last hours of work nearly killed me. I sigh heavily and toss my tie onto the large circular table in the front hall. Now that I'm home, she'll be able to relieve my stress.

Just knowing that simple fact makes every muscle in my body relax. As if on cue, I hear Joseph's footsteps and her heels walking down the hall.

I don't wait for him to enter. I shrug off my jacket, leaving it on the front table with my tie and open the door myself. Joseph's walking behind Miss Days as he looks up and answers, "Ah, here he is now. Mr. Stone," he greets me.

Dahlia's stopped and looks back at me with widened eyes, staring at me with a mix of fear and lust. *Perfect.*

Joseph brings in the duffel bag he's carrying and sets it down in the foyer. He's a quiet man. He doesn't ask unnecessary questions, and that's why I like him.

"Thank you Mr. Brennan, that's all for today."

"Good day," he says then nods his head and turns to leave. I'm not usually so short with him. But right now I have one thing on my mind.

"Mr.... sir," Dahlia corrects herself and blinks several times, still not sure what to say or what name to use. An asymmetric smirk forms on my face. She looks gorgeous. Her hair is styled into loose waves and resting over her shoulders, covering her breasts. Her blouse is baggy, and hides her figure. It's fashionable, but it needs to come off. It would look far better on the floor than on my treasure.

"Come in, Dahlia," I say barely above a murmur, stepping back and opening the door wider.

She nods, and noticeably swallows. I wait patiently as she walks in slowly. I know she's timid, but that's going to change quickly. I'm going to enjoy the transition.

I stop her, with my hand on her waist and lean out slightly to show her the keypad on the outside of the door. "You'll come here every day, and Mr. Brennan will get you up the stairs," she turns and stares down the hallway to the elevator, "and here you'll enter in a code specifically for you so you can wait for me." I've already set in her code. "It'll only be active from six thirty to seven, so don't be late."

She nods her head and says, "Yes sir."

Good girl. I place my hand on the small of her back, shutting the door and leading her out of the front room and straight to the stairs. She's glancing around and taking it all in, but I have no intention of showing her anything other than the playroom today. Well, and the guest room later tonight since I know I'll be needing her in the morning.

I'm rushing her and I know that I am, but I need to get this first part out of the way and over with. We've wasted nearly an entire day, and I'm eager to start her training.

As I lead her up the stairs she walks with her head down, and her breathing comes in heavier.

"I want you to wait for me in this room," I say as I get to the second door on the left. She stands patiently as I open the door.

I wait for her to enter, letting her curiosity lead her in. Her steps are slow and hesitant, but she walks into the room and takes everything in. Her own desire leads her to the bed in the center of the room, her fingers running along the comforter.

I close the door as quietly as possible and watch as she walks over to the row of whips and punishment tools.

"Pick one." My command startles her as she gasps and turns around. Her slightly frightened look only makes me want her more.

"I want to know what you most enjoy, and what would be the best punishments as well." I walk over to her slowly as she nods her head and looks back at the wall of toys to choose from.

Her fingers gently brush the tails of a whip and I think she's going to choose it, but instead she moves to a simple paddle. I like both equally, and so I'm fine with that.

I take it from her trembling hands and set it on the bed. The cuffs are already attached to the frame, and the spreader is ready for her, too. I set up everything last night.

"I want to jump into our first session, Dahlia." Her stance is tense, and her breathing is coming in pants. When I finally get a chance to sink my fingers into her pussy I know she's going to be soaking wet for me. I can't fucking wait.

I start unbuckling my belt. And I give her a simple command. "Strip."

She starts to slowly and sensually remove her clothes, but I haven't the time for that. I want her too badly to enjoy a tease.

"Faster. I want you naked and ready for me when I come in here. You should be naked and kneeling next to the end of the bed. Go there now."

Her eyes widen, and she looks away as though she's embarrassed. As if she's done something wrong, and I don't like it. She didn't know my preferences, so she has no reason to feel self-conscious. Maybe it's the way I'm being short with her, I'm not certain, but if it is then she'll learn not to let it bother her. Or else she'll be miserable for the next few weeks.

She leaves her clothes in a pile on the floor, kicking out of her heels and walking quickly to the end of the bed to kneel.

Her chest rises and falls with each nervous breath. She sits on her heels, moving her knees slightly apart, her hands resting on her thighs. Her head is angled down. She has gorgeous posture for a Submissive.

I step out of my clothes, keeping her waiting. The belt buckle falls noisily onto the floor and she jumps slightly, but doesn't look up. My eyes never leave her, waiting for her reaction.

"Have you used a safe word before?" I ask as I walk over in front of her, stroking my cock as I move. I'm already leaking precum with the need to be inside her hot mouth.

She gulps as she stares at my throbbing cock, forgetting to answer. I light up with the desire to correct her behavior, but she shakes her head and quickly adds, "No, sir." Although the fire to train her is dimmed by her obedience, I'm still on edge with need.

"Simply put, I'll test you. I'll push your boundaries and when I ask you where you are, you'll answer red for stop, yellow if you're getting close, or green if we're in safe territory."

She finally looks up at me with wide eyes and her lips parted with a question, but she quickly looks back down.

"Ask me," I tell her, stroking my dick again.

"What if-" she starts, but I interrupt her.

"Look at me when you speak," I snap out my words and it makes her jolt slightly as she looks up to meet my gaze. Her skin is bright red, and I love it. I love how on edge she is.

"What if you don't ask?"

I stare at her in wonder for a moment. "I should. But if I don't, you can speak up at any point." I crouch down in front of her, taking her chin in my hand and angling her lips closer to mine. "I'll be looking for your limits. I don't want to push you over the edge." Her eyes dart past me and shine with uncertainty, and I'm not quite sure why. I know she's never had a Dom, so that must be why. She just simply isn't prepared.

I stand up straight and tell her, "I'm going to show you what I mean." Her eyes glance at my cock as I stroke it again. Those beautiful hazel eyes are heated with lust. Her fingers dig into her thighs to keep from lifting her hands. She already knows a good bit of what's expected. I like that. I fucking love that she's trying to obey. But she's going to fail at some point, and I can't wait to discipline her.

"Open," I give her the simple command and she obeys, opening her mouth and breathing huskily as I put the head of my dick up to her mouth.

Fuck, she looks gorgeous. She bends her head forward, but I shake my head no and she quickly moves back to her previous position.

"Open wider," I tell her and she does her best, widening her jaw for me as I ease my dick in past her lips. I spear my fingers through her hair and push myself in deeper. Her tongue massages the underside of my dick as I push in even farther. Her cheeks hollow as I fist her hair and move her up and down my length. She moans, and the vibrations makes my dick stir with need and my toes dig into the carpet.

I shove my dick into the back of her throat, feeling it close tightly around the head as she tries to swallow it. I don't pull back, instead I push in even deeper, watching as her eyes water and she struggles to take my short shallow pumps. She feels too good and the sight of her makes me want to cum this very second, but I'm not going to let that happen. Not yet.

Her fingers dig into her thighs and her throat tries to swallow me again, feeling like fucking heaven, but I know she's at her limit and I pull back. My hand is still fisted in her hair as she takes in a breath. As she inhales, I reach down and push my fingers between her thighs. She's fucking drenched.

"Go lie on the bed," I say and stroke my dick as she scrambles to do as she's told, still taking in deep breaths and wiping the spit away from her mouth.

She lies in the center of the bed with her hands at her sides. I crawl on top of her and straddle her waist, picking up one wrist and strapping her to one of the leather cuffs attached to the bed, and then securing the other wrist.

"Safe word," I say and watch her expression as I latch the buckle and test out the restriction on her wrists.

"Green," she answers quickly and confidently.

I crawl down her body and pull her down with me, sliding her along the sheets until her arms are stretched. She looks beautiful like this. Her pale rose nipples are pebbled and I lean down, sucking one into my mouth out of pure temptation. My fingers trail along the dip in her waist, testing her. Simply playing with her body for my enjoyment, and to test how reactive she is. She's quite responsive, which I enjoy, although I know many Doms don't. I'm grateful they haven't had a chance to taint her with their preferences.

I reach to the far end of the bed and attach the spreader to her right ankle. I look up her body and to her face to gauge her reaction as I attach her left ankle and snap the steel spreader open, widening her legs so she's completely exposed to me.

She sucks in a breath, and her glistening pussy clenches around nothing. She's completely helpless as I flip the spreader bar over, making her squeal as her arms cross and she lies on her belly. She breathes heavily into the pillow as I crawl up her body, leaving small open-mouth kisses up her sensitive skin and continuing playing with her. I finally reach her neck, and I graze my teeth along her skin and then nip her bottom lip.

She moans in the hot air between us.

"You're mine, treasure. To do whatever the fuck I want to do to you." I bite down on her earlobe and my dick presses into her side as she moans. "Is that what you want?" I ask her.

"Yes," she breathes the answer with lust and I bring my hand down hard on her ass. "Sir!" she's quick to yell out.

I chuckle as I sit up and flip her back over onto her ass with the flick of my wrist as I hold the spreader bar. I bring it closer to the headboard, folding her in on herself and attaching the locks to her ankles, so she's completely bared to me and unable to move.

Fuck, she looks so goddamn beautiful. Her breathing is the only thing I can hear as I shove two thick fingers into her tight cunt.

"Safe word," I ask her as I curl my fingers and roughly finger fuck her over and over.

"Green," she yells out desperately. She likes it rough; the harder and more forceful I am, the more her skin flushes and the sweeter the sounds are spilling from her lips.

I pull my fingers out and hold them up to my lips, taking a taste of her. I close my eyes and groan at the sweet flavor. I suck them clean as she watches me closely. I had intended to make her do it, but the heated look in her eyes as she watches my primal needs is addicting.

I grab her ass and move her slightly before lining my dick up with her pussy. I don't ask, and I don't give her any more warning than that before I slam my dick deep inside of her, the cuff buckles clanging against the frame of the bed and her scream of pleasure filling the room.

I don't give her time to adjust. Instead I fuck her savagely, taking everything I want from her. My blunt fingernails dig into the flesh of her ass as I groan out in an even voice I don't recognize, "Safe word."

"Green," she moans, arching her back. I move my hands to the small of her back and fuck her harder and deeper. She never shows any sign that it's too much as I hammer my hips against hers.

I lean forward and growl into the crook of her neck, "I wanna feel your tight pussy pop on my dick." I piston my hips over and over as she screams my name. She shouldn't be using my name in this room. But I don't have it in me to correct her. I'm too lost in pleasure and focused on finding her limits. "Now," I say and then bite down on her shoulder.

Fuck!

Her hot cunt spasms around my dick, practically choking it as I ride through her orgasm. I feel my balls draw up, and I have to pull out before I cum.

I gently rub her clit in circular motions, drawing out her release as I catch my breath.

Her chest and cheeks are a bright red, and her legs are shaking uncontrollably with pleasure. She fucking loves this.

I pull away and watch her calm, still bound to the bed. So far everything's going just as I wanted. She hasn't disappointed me in the least.

"When's the last time you've been fucked in your ass?" I ask her as I reach for the bottle of lube behind me. Her pussy is soaked, and there's a good bit of her arousal and cum on my dick that's leaked down to her ass, but I need to make sure I don't hurt her.

"A while," she whispers, her breath still coming in ragged pants. She gasps as I gently prod her ass, spreading the lube over her tight ring.

I gently push my middle finger in, and she pushes back. I fucking love that I won't have to work her ass up for me. I want her now. I want to cum in her ass right now.

Fuck, yes. My dick is aching with the need to be buried inside her again. I pump another finger into her ass and watch as she writhes on the bed.

That's all I need, I can't take any more.

"Yes," I hiss with pleasure as I sink deep into her ass and she claws at the cuffs around her wrists. I don't stop my slow thrust until I feel her ass completely surround my dick.

"Safe word?" I ask her from deep in my chest.

She's quiet with her head thrashing as she tries to stretch and get accustomed to my girth.

I pull out slowly, with a hint of a smile on my face, although I can't let her know. I'm hitting everything I wanted to with ease. And now I get to punish her.

She breathes heavily as I pull out of her and grab the spreader bar with my left hand, angling her so I have a better view of her ass cheek and pick up the paddle with my right.

Whack!

Her body bucks at the blow, but I have the spreader firm in my grasp and I'm not letting her move an inch.

"You need to answer me the second I ask you a question, Dahlia."

"Green," she says with nothing but lust in her voice, but it's too late. She needs to be punished.

I spank her ass with the paddle again, watching her jump slightly and pull against the binds, but it's useless. *Whack! Whack! Whack!* I smack the paddle against her reddened flesh over and over. "Safe word?" I ask her loudly so she can hear me over her gasps.

"Green!" she screams out, exposing her throat as she arches her neck. *Whack!* I smack the paddle flat across her ass harder than before, and she draws in a sharp breath. *Whack! Whack!* Her mouth opens in a silent "O" and I know the endorphins are finally running through her, making everything hotter and more pleasurable and intense.

"Safe word?" I ask her as I gently press my palm to her hot skin.

"Green," she moans softly with her brow scrunched. Good girl.

"You'll answer me the first time I ask you now, won't you?" I say as I debate on giving her another round to get more endorphins flowing.

"Yes, sir," she says breathlessly. Her nipples are pebbled and her words coated in lust.

I toss the paddle behind me, she doesn't need any more, and line my dick up. I'm not gentle as I slam into her tight asshole.

"Ah!" she screams out as I hammer into her. My hands grip her thighs as I pump my hips, watching her face for cues. She feels so fucking good. I knew it. I knew she'd feel like this.

I almost get lost in pleasure, but I can't just cum yet.

I fuck her ass harder and harder, the buckles of the cuffs clinking, the feet of the bed slamming on the ground and her strangled cries of pleasure fueling me to continue. It's a near violent and relentless pace, and I watch her face, waiting for the limit. I know she's going to need to say it. I need to hear her. I need to know I can trust her to tell me when it's too much.

I angle my hips and shove my thick cock all the way into her ass, my fingers digging into her ankles as I push into her to the hilt, filling her ass and making her scream. She pants out her breaths and tries to struggle against me, but it's useless. I hammer into her, pistoning my hips, pushing further on the side of pain.

I start to worry as she doesn't say it. She doesn't give me any indication that she's close to her limit. She wants this, she's enjoying the pleasure and pain blending into one, but I'm nearing my own limits. She isn't a red girl. There was no indication that she preferred pain in the meeting or the pamphlet.

My own breath comes in ragged as her face scrunches and I continue thrusting my hips into her tight hole.

"Yell-" she starts to say, craning her neck with her body tensing. I still inside of her and bend down, moving under the spreader bar and kissing her lips sweetly.

"Good girl," I whisper against her lips as her face relaxes and I move easily in and out of her with slow deliberate thrusts only meant for pleasure. She opens her eyes slowly, and for a fraction of a second a spark ignites between us, something forceful I've never felt before. I'm quick to move away, regaining my position and roughly rubbing her throbbing clit with the rough pad of my thumb.

"Cum for me, treasure," I give her the command as my own orgasm slowly approaches, making my spine tingle and my toes curl.

She closes her eyes and thrashes her head as I give her a quicker pace, fucking her ass and rubbing her clit to get her off.

But she's struggling to get there. My own is approaching, and I want her to cum again. I need that. I have to have her sated and finding her release with mine.

I pull my hand away from her pussy and her eyes pop open, looking back at me as I smack the back of my hand down hard across her clit. That does it. Her pussy spasms around nothing, and I thrust into her tight asshole over and over as the waves of my release finally crash through my body.

Yes!

My balls draw up, and I hold my breath as pleasure wracks through my body.

Fuck, she feels too fucking good.

I pump short, shallow thrusts into her ass as her body trembles beneath me and she screams out my name. Thick streams of hot cum leave me in waves as I bury myself as deep in her as I can and groan in utter pleasure.

I tighten my grip on her thigh as she trembles under me and I fill her with my cum.

When I finally pull away, breathless and sated, I do so gently, pulling out slowly and watching her body as she lies limp and still helplessly bound by the spreader and cuffs. Her head is laying to the side with her eyes closed, and goosebumps linger along her sensitized skin.

A part of me wants to take more from her, but she's exhausted and we need to cover more of my expectations. Soon I'll be able to torture the pleasure from her until it's nearly unbearable for her.

I climb off the bed and head to the en-suite for a warm cloth, leaving her just as she is while she calms her breathing.

When I get back with the warm, wet cloth, I'm gentle as I clean up every inch of her. Her body tenses and trembles. Her clit is still primed for more, and her ass is bright red from where the paddle hit her.

The bed groans under my weight as I unlock the spreader from the cuffs and ease her legs down onto the bed and unlock the shackles around her ankles. I massage a bit of life into her sore muscles before unlocking her wrists and doing the same with her arms.

Her breathing is steady as she curls slightly inward, still consumed in the intensity of her orgasm.

I pick her body up gently and place her on all fours at the end of the bed. Her bright red ass is high in the air.

Her eyes widen, and her breath hitches as she looks over her slender shoulder at me.

A rough chuckle vibrates up my chest as I walk over to get the cream mixed with a little aloe for her burning skin. I use a light touch as I apply it.

"You safe worded me," I say softly. "Good girl."

Her lips part and I know she has a question for me, but she's holding back.

"Speak. You need to be able to communicate with me, Dahlia."

"I'm happy you weren't angry with me." I pause in my motions and consider her.

"You think it would make me angry for you to tell me you were reaching your limits?" I shake my head with my lips turned down. "No, I'm happy I have a good understanding of your needs."

I put the cap back on the lotion, satisfied with her aftercare and add, "We suit each other well. I'm very pleased."

She hums softly at my praise. She's perfect and so obedient. I'm going to have to push her to disobey though since I know we both enjoyed the paddle.

"Just like this, treasure," I say, planting a kiss on the small of her back and running my hands down her thighs.

"Every day when I get home, you'll be waiting for me just like this."

"Not kneeling?" she asks weakly and then adds, "sir?"

I huff a small laugh and then stroke my dick, feeling it hardening for her again already.

I lower her hips and tease her cunt with the head of my dick. "No, I want you like this instead," I say and barely get the words out before I shove myself deep inside her again.

CHAPTER 12

DAHLIA

I wince as I take a seat on the back of the city bus on my way to my internship. My breath hisses between my teeth as the decadent pain heats my ass. I welcome it though. It's a reminder of last night. I stare out of the window, the images flashing before my eyes as the bus noisily roars to life and takes me away from campus. It's been a week of enduring Lucian as my Dom, and every day I love it more and more.

I'm running late because of finals, but I'm happy they're over with. One less thing to worry about.

My only problem now is that my ass is fucking sore as hell. Every time I do anything involving any kind of movement, I'm filled with slight discomfort. It's the good type of pain though - a reminder of how Lucian utterly and thoroughly dominated my body.

Call me a glutton for punishment, but I want more. Right fucking now.

I've spent all morning thinking about our filthy encounter, with aching desire. I'm already primed to go off and if my day was planned down to the minute, I'd probably need relief. I can't believe how many times Lucian got me off last night and how many times he came. I'm sure he was shooting blanks by the fourth time, but I was too wrapped up in ecstasy to notice.

Every time he took me harder, faster, taking from me with a ruthless need, I came violently. He was everything I wanted. It was perfect. But everything I've been running from smacked me hard in the face early this morning. I swallow thickly, the lust disappearing and the shame creeping in. He rolled over and pulled my back into his chest. He fucked me from behind, but he was tender. He was gentle. He kissed my neck, and I had to close my eyes and pretend. The pleasure stopped. No matter how much I wanted to, I couldn't get off. I feel shitty, having been so aroused moments before, and enjoyed being used for his pleasure. But then numb to him.

The truth is, I want more of his roughness. I've always needed that. My heart clenches and I pull away from the window, pulling my hobo bag into my lap and holding it against my chest. I feel hollow inside. How disturbed am I that he couldn't make me cum? I had to fake it when he told me to cum with him. For fuck's sake, I'm living a fantasy. But even this morning when he threw me on the bed and fucked me like I wanted, the only thing my body craved, I couldn't get the fact that I'm broken out of my head. Fuck, it hurts.

I feel sick about it. I just don't understand it. It makes me fear that I'll never be normal and that this experience will only serve to show how depraved and fucked up I am in the head. I bite the inside of my cheek and pull out my phone. I should call Dr. Andrews. I cringe at the thought. I know there's doctor-patient confidentiality, but what's she going to think about this *arrangement*? Whore. I lean my head back against the seat as the bus goes over a bump and jostles me slightly. She's going to think I'm whoring myself out. I run my hand down my face and try to ignore those thoughts that keep me weighed down with guilt and shame. All I need to do is concentrate on the way I felt alive under him.

I'm pulled out of my musing as the bus comes to a stop in front of the Explicit Designs building. Wincing, I get up from my seat and head inside, swallowing the lump that's growing in my throat. In the lobby, I try to pick up speed, but I'm forced to take it slow. I don't want to draw attention to my awkward gait.

Damn you, Lucian.

A small smile accompanies me as I walk slowly, reveling in the slight sting that's directly connected to my throbbing clit. It takes me a while, but I make it up to my office without incident. Once inside the not-nearly-as-private-as-I-need-it-to-be office, I take off my coat, and set it down on my glass-top desk, letting out a shiver. It's brutal outside.

Which reminds me; it's winter break, and my tuition is due. At first the reminder sends a jolt of worry through me, but then I remember the money. I have enough coming to me at the end of the month to eliminate my debt and pay off my final semester's tuition. The thought should fill me with shame and trigger the whore comments I've been hearing in my head, but it doesn't. I know what I'm doing some people might consider degrading, but I don't really care. I would want this regardless of the money. That has to count for something.

I set my purse down on the desk and bring my cup of coffee to my lips. I blow on it out of habit, but it's cold by now. I don't mind though; I just need the caffeine to get me through the day. I check my email and then get started working on Debra's scheduling for her upcoming fashion show. I spend most of the day doing clerical work, getting up several times to go to the bathroom to apply aloe vera to my sore ass cheeks. Lucian told me to, and each time there's less and less of a sting that accompanies it.

Around closing time, I get a surprise when Carla, who I haven't seen all day, pops her head in the doorway, causing me to jump in my seat. I put my hand to my chest and breathe out a slight sigh of relief.

"Hey chica, how's your day going?" She's gorgeous today in tight red jeans that hug her curves and a white button-up shirt, complete with glossy red heels. I absolutely love the outfit. It makes her look like she's ready for a red-hot, sexy Christmas. All she's missing is a red Santa cap.

Carla grins at the slight pain on my face from moving in my seat. She knows exactly where it's coming from, too. The bitch. "Just fabulous," I reply, with a blush heating my cheeks. I want to tell her everything, but I'm nervous about the NDA. I should ask Lucian. Or maybe I shouldn't. …shit. I don't know what to do.

"If not for the sore ass?" Carla jokes. It's honestly not that bad. It's certainly acted as a reminder of who I belong to though.

I scowl at her, but I can only hold it for a second before I laugh.

"Shut up! Please." I have to resist rolling my eyes. "You wouldn't be talking if you were in my shoes."

Carla chuckles, shaking her head and then walks in, her heels clicking with each step, and sits down across from me. "Bet you I would. You forget honey, I'm a pro at being a Sub and have had many rough sessions." She smirks deviously. "Let's just say my ass can take a heavy pounding."

I huff out a short chuckle. It's weird hearing Carla talk like this, even after all this time. I would've never guessed she was such a sexual fiend before she revealed her secret to me. I suspect it's going to take some time before I ever get used to it. *If* I ever get used to it.

She's so different here at work in front of others. It's like two split personalities. But then again, people would probably say the same about me if they knew I was a member of Club X.

"Well?" Carla asks, pulling me out of my thoughts.

I frown with confusion. "Well what?"

She smacks her hand on the desk. "Details! You said you'd give me details." She leans forward and places her chin in her palm, greedy for the juicy gossip.

I hesitate. I'm not sure I want to tell her everything, especially the part about me not being able to get off. Part of me is screaming to confide in her. She's obviously a woman who would understand, right? But no one has ever understood. No one. Not my ex, not my mother. They knew, but they didn't understand. It's a problem. It's the only thing on the tip of my tongue. I want advice. I want help. I take in a short breath, but I can't say the words.

I try to school my expression and not show the pain that's squeezing my chest. Everything was perfect yesterday. I should be happy. I should be thrilled to tell her about Lucian. Instead all I can think about is the one moment this morning that was anything but alright.

"Dah?" Carla sounds concerned and my eyes snap to her, shutting down the negative thoughts. "Did he hurt you?" she barely breathes the words, fear evident in her eyes.

"No!" I'm quick to get that thought out of her head. I shake my head as I say, "No, no, it was… unbelievable." She looks at me for a moment, taking in my expression and posture.

Taking a deep breath, I tell her everything about this past week, except that one moment early this morning.

Carla grins, her chest heaving, her breathing ragged. She doesn't appear to notice my anxiety and seems to have gotten worked up over my tale. "I'm so glad you liked it. Sounds like Lucian really knows his stuff." She shakes her head with wonder. "And you safe worded him and everything."

"Is that bad?" I ask her in a hushed voice. I didn't want to. I wanted to be perfect for him, but it was just too much. He said it was good though. I really believed him when he told me he wanted me to tell him if I was at my limit.

Carla shakes her head, her eyes shining with a hint of awe and says, "No, it's good to know each other's boundaries."

Her words summon the image of Lucian spanking me, leaving red marks on my ass and my breathing quickens. *That.* That power. That control. It's that which I crave above all else.

"My only problem is..." I snap my mouth shut, shocked at how close I came to thinking out loud. Holy fuck. How did I almost tell her? Is that even a boundary? I pick at my nails and look past her and out the window of my little office.

Carla eyes me curiously. "Your only problem is what?"

Her eyes on me force me to look back at her, my mind racing with excuses, unsure what to say. I shouldn't tell her. But it's right on the tip of my tongue. Maybe I should give her a chance and just tell her. She might understand.

But if she doesn't? What then?

That thought alone scares me above all else, and it hardens my position. I'm not telling Carla shit.

"Nothing," I say, shaking my head and flashing her a nervous smile. "It's nothing really."

Carla isn't buying it. "C'mon," she gestures with a manicured finger at me. "You can't just leave me hanging like that. You have to tell me."

"No," I say firmly. "Really, it's nothing." Her ensuing scowl causes me to sigh and I say, "Fine. I was just going to say I wish it didn't have to end in a month." I'm surprised by how easily that lie came out.

Carla chuckles, and I'm filled with relief. She bought my lie. "Girl, with a man as good looking as Lucian, I don't blame you." She snaps her fingers. "Oh, which reminds me!" She watches her finger as she taps on the glass desktop. "Do you think Lucian will be bringing you to the club?" I don't know how to respond. "I just think it would be good for you if you had time in the club, with other Subs and such."

I freeze, caught off guard.

"Bruce did it for me," she adds. She seems really nervous and I honestly feel the same way. He *owns* me. I don't know what the rules are outside of the playroom.

"I don't know," I say slowly.

"Just ask him," she says finally. "It's just that, sometimes it's easy to get sucked into a fantasy," she says as her eyes flash with a sadness I've never seen. "And I don't want you getting hurt."

I stare back at her with a knot growing in the pit of my stomach and reply, "Trust me, I don't want to get hurt either."

CHAPTER 13

LUCIAN

I need to rein in my anger before I get home, but all I'm thinking about is taking this tension out on my sweet Dahlia. I know she must be sore from the past two weeks, but I'm not going to be able to hold back.

I *need* her.

Just the thought of sinking deep inside her makes me relax.

I've been dealing with one problem after another all day. I clench my teeth as I relive every tiresome phone call from public relations and my lawyer. My ex-wife. She had the nerve to laugh at me during our call. I know she just wanted to get under my skin. I tried to hide my irritation, but she knows she got to me. I let her in, and all she did was find my weaknesses. She wants to exploit them now. I imagine she's run out of the small fortune she was awarded right around this time last year. It took over two years for our divorce to be finalized. She wouldn't settle on a perfectly reasonable sum; she wouldn't settle for anything other than everything.

And I bent over backward and gave it to her.

That was my mistake. Not the first, though. Marrying her was my first mistake. But giving her what she wanted only proved to her that she could get more.

But I won't allow it.

The phone rings in my pocket, and I grit my teeth at the sound. My temples pound with each of the incessant rings.

I don't want to answer it; I want to get home. To my treasure.

I breathe out deep and think, *soon*. Soon I'll be lost inside of her. Where I belong.

I hit the small center button on my dashboard and lean back in my leather seat, twisting my hands around the steering wheel.

"Stone," I answer smoothly. Never show emotion. I've learned better than to let them see they can affect me. Tricia is the perfect example of why I can never let them know how I feel. They call me ruthless, heartless. Well, they made me that way.

"Mr. Stone, it's Jackson." Jackson Harris, my lawyer. "We have a situation." I cringe at the ease in his voice. He doesn't have a situation. He gets paid regardless. If my ex could afford him, he'd be on her team right now. He's not loyal to me. Neither is my PR team, but I'll pay them whatever they need to get this shit dealt with.

"And that is?" I ask as though I don't already know. Tricia's been harassing the office, calling me nonstop. I've gotten her message, but apparently she hasn't received mine.

"Tricia's refuting the legitimacy of the NDA."

I let his words sink in. During our divorce, she agreed to sign the NDA and legally cannot discuss any matters pertaining to our relationship during any period of time, married or otherwise. "I fail to see how that's an issue. She's contractually-"

He cuts me off, "She can refute it, although she has no footing."

"Then how is this a problem?"

"I've received several calls from Andrea, and it is apparent that Tricia has reached out to several editorials and is taking bids for her story." My blood runs cold as I drive down the highway. My heart pumps harder in my chest and I try to focus and not be consumed with the anger that's barely contained.

Her story. As though she's anything other than a gold digger. I gave her everything, and the moment she found someone else, she left me. She thought she had it made with me. But I worked too much. Always bitching that I needed to make more, but be home more. She was impossible to please.

I tried. I fucking tried. I slam my fist down on the wheel. At least karma bit her in the ass and the asshole she cheated on me with left her. It would've been better if I could have proved that she was cheating. Then she would have walked away with far less.

I take in a deep breath, pulling off of the interstate and getting closer to my penthouse.

"She has nothing to lose, Lucian. We can sue her afterward, but the damage will be done." I swallow thickly, hating that one mistake so many years ago can continue to cause me damage.

"And what do you suggest?" I ask him.

"We can pay her, or the magazines, but I imagine she'd be cheaper." I scoff and look out of the window as I drive into the private garage and key in my personal PIN. I check the time, it's six forty. My little treasure should be waiting for me.

"She's not getting anything. I refuse to pay her one cent."

Just as I say the words, the sound of an incoming call comes through the background.

"It will be expensive not to pay her, Mr. Stone. We can always pay now and sue later." His tone holds a hint of a warning, letting me know he doesn't approve, but I don't give a fuck. He works for me, and I don't care how much money I have to spend to make sure she doesn't profit off a damn thing from me anymore.

"No. She gets nothing." I end the call and answer the next, pulling my black R8 in next to the Aston Martin. I'm on the fourth floor of the garage. It's private and all mine. I glance around the space as I answer, "Stone."

"Mr. Stone, this is Andrea from the agency, do you have a moment to speak with me?"

I pinch the bridge of my nose and wish I could ignore these problems. Public relations is a pain in my ass.

A long inhale calms me slightly as I say, "I'm listening."

"Given the current climate, I've been working with Alena and we feel it may be best if we were to combat the possibility of your ex's story being released with a different form of press."

I open my mouth to remind her that in my opinion, no press is good press. I don't want to be seen anywhere. I can't even stand the business articles from Forbes and Business Insider. I'm not interested.

"I understand that you prefer to stay out of the limelight, so to speak, but in my professional opinion..." she pauses on the phone and I find myself watching the digital dash, waiting for her to continue. "May I be frank with you, Mr. Stone?"

"Yes." I prefer if everyone were frank so I didn't have to deal with fake bullshit.

"Your wife has held this over your head for years, and her story is going to come out whether she profits from it or not, doesn't matter. She's going to go through with this. I think it's best that we create an appearance now that will refute the picture she intends to paint."

I swallow thickly, staring straight ahead through the windshield at the grey cylinder blocks of the garage. I'm numb to this. There's nothing that she can really do to hurt me. I glance at the elevator. I just want to get upstairs to my penthouse and go straight to the playroom.

A small smile kicks my lips up. She'll be waiting for me like a good girl. Just like yesterday and every day these past two weeks. It's time to give her some real training. My fingers itch to touch the thick coarse fibers of the rope that's already laying on the bed. She's going to get a lesson in saying please and thank you today, and I can hardly wait.

"I think it would be best to create the impression that you're in a committed and loving relationship. We all love couples. So much more so than a nasty divorce. Weddings are the best sellers."

My eyebrows raise at her comment. She's delusional if she thinks that shit's going to happen. "I'm not interested in a PR stunt, Andrea."

"I'm only saying, what if you were to be seen in a romantic setting and paparazzi happened to take your picture? And let's say that the picture happened to be leaked, along with a story that you confirmed to be true. Well if that situation were to occur, it would go a long way in making your ex look like a villain and you as a prince charming that the public is rooting for."

It's quiet for a moment as I consider her request.

"It will make you look relatable. In fact, it may be better than the story she's selling," she adds with a bright and cheery tone. "Just a thought."

"Fine," I finally say with my fingers on the key in the ignition.

"Wonderful," Andrea's tone remains upbeat. I have a feeling she must have real assholes for clients since she's never bothered by my tone. "Shall we send someone out for you?"

"No," I'm quick to cut her off. I have my treasure, and I think she'd enjoy it. I pause as I realize I hadn't thought twice about whether or not it should be Dahlia. I can imagine how I'd tease her under the table. Yes. I have to remember cameras will be watching, but I'm going to enjoy myself.

"Thank you, Andrea. I'll have my reservations for this evening sent to you."

"No need, Mr. Stone. You're all set at the Ritz; a table's been reserved for you at any time you choose."

I huff a humorless laugh. "You pay us well, Mr. Stone," Andrea says. "I have faith in this plan."

I don't, but at least I have my treasure waiting for me.

CHAPTER 14

DAHLIA

a shiver snakes down my limbs as my thighs tremble from exertion, my ass stuck high into the air. I've been waiting in this position for what feels like forever. It's a bit uncomfortable, but it's how he wants me. *My sir.* He's coming for me. And he expects me to be ready to take him. *All of him.*

My breathing becomes heavy, labored, as I keep my hands firmly planted against the lush mattress. I want to be perfect for him. I need to please him and make sure I obey. The only thing he's asked of me is to wait for him just like this. And I can do that. I did it yesterday.

My body trembles again, my ass trembling with a chill, my pussy clenching with insatiable need. *Fuck.* I can hardly wait.

Keeping myself balanced, I glance around the room. My clothes are in a neat pile on a chair in the corner, but Lucian isn't here yet. *Where is he?* I want him here now. Ravaging me. Dominating me for everything I'm worth.

I turn my head back toward the wall, concentrating on keeping my ass suspended in the air. I'll wait however long it takes for him to get here. I need him to see me like this the moment he walks in. My nipples pebble as I imagine him walking down the hall toward this master suite, dressed in one of his expensive business suits, his shirt unbuttoned, his tie loosened, looking sexy as fuck. *Ready* to fuck.

I let out a groan, my pussy clenching repeatedly on thin air, wishing his cock was there. Another groan escapes my lips as I imagine him behind me, fucking me mercilessly, his blunt nails digging into my hips as he thrusts harder and deeper.

I'm so horny, I have the overpowering urge to reach down and rub my pussy. But I know I'm not supposed to. I scissor my thighs, craving some friction. Just the tiniest bit. It's a battle, and I'm almost about to give in to the desire to touch myself, when I hear the sound of the door creaking open.

Relief flows through my abdomen as excitement causes my limbs to shudder. *Yes.*

I go perfectly still at the sound of Lucian's voice, keeping my ass right where he told me to.

"Treasure," I hear him growl behind me, his deep baritone filling the room and making my clit throb even more.

I tremble slightly, feeling my breath quickening. "Yes sir?" I ask breathlessly. Just being in his presence is such a huge turn-on, knowing what's to come. What he's going to do to me. My whole body has come alive with desire.

I hear the sound of his muted footsteps against the plush carpeting and I fight the urge to turn around to catch a glimpse of him. He hasn't given me permission.

The bed creaks as he gets on it and goosebumps rise along my skin, traveling from the base of my spine toward my shoulders and down my front. A second later I feel his hot breath on my ass cheeks and I know he's level with my ass, eyeing my glistening pussy. My heart begins to pound like a war drum, beating so hard that Lucian probably hears it.

I close my eyes in anticipation, my breathing ragged and shallow as I wait for him to bury his face in my pussy and then make me beg for more.

"I asked you to wait for me here and to be still, treasure," Lucian growls from behind me, his hot breath grazing my pussy and causing it to clench even harder. He puts a hand on either side of my ass and spreads me farther apart. My eyes widen, and my fingers dig into the mattress.

I buck forward slightly, the feel of his breath on me making me shiver uncontrollably. Oh my God. He's driving me crazy, and he knows it. Why won't he just put that mouth on my pussy and take me by force?

"I did, sir," I weakly protest. I'm practically trembling with exhaustion from holding this position for so long. For him.

"No, treasure," I hear him say as I feel his fingers lightly touch my mound, gliding along the slick, swollen flesh. I groan softly as I let his fingers dip inside and explore my sore walls. I feel a little discomfort that makes me wince, but it mixes in with the pleasure and I want more. Much more. My neck arches, and I bite down on my lip to keep from moaning. "You didn't."

He doesn't give me more, though. I gasp as he pulls his fingers away and I instantly miss his touch.

The bed creaks as Lucian crawls off of it and walks over to the nightstand. I sneak a peek to the side. I can see him now, and he looks just like I imagined him; his shirt unbuttoned at the chest, his tie loosened. And he has a huge fucking bulge pressing against his expensive slacks, dying to be let out. My mouth waters at the sight.

I watch as Lucian walks over to the side of the room, messing with something in a drawer before standing in front of the whips and canes. *Uh-oh.* My heart begins pounding like a sledgehammer as I read Lucian's body language. He means business.

"You were supposed to be still, treasure," he growls ominously, "and for the last five minutes you have been anything but still." Moving slowly, deliberately, he picks up a riding crop. He walks back over to the bed, dragging out each step, his face an impenetrable mask. My heart flutters, knowing what's coming next as he moves out of view behind me.

The bed creaks again and then everything goes still. *Silence.* I strain my ears, listening for Lucian's breathing, but all I can make out is my heart pounding between my ears.

Smack!

I buck forward as pain stings my right ass cheek and a soft cry escapes my lips. Immediately, I feel Lucian probing my pussy, his finger lathered with a cooling gel. My eyes close from the soothing relief. But it's temporary.

Smack! Smack! Smack!

I buck forward again, my head almost slamming into the head-board, crying out with pain and pleasure. Lucian continues to probe my pussy, my ass on fire from his brutal slaps. It hurts, but it feels *so good* at the same time. My body's alive with pleasure, wanting more but also wanting to get away. It takes everything in me to be good for him and obey. I have to stay still, but it's so fucking hard when my instincts are screaming at me to move.

"Are you going to listen, my treasure?"

"Yes," I say weakly, my limbs trembling with need, resisting the urge to angle my pussy as his fingers barely touch my throbbing clit. I'm so close.

Lucian strokes several fingers against my G-spot, nearly fisting me and causing me to gasp and white lights to dance in my vision. "Yes what?"

"Yes, sir!" I yell as my body threatens to fall over the high cliff of pleasure.

Smack! Smack!! The relentless smacks continue, and the pain turns to something else. Instead of moving away, I find my body eager for the next. *Smack! Smack!*

He slaps the riding crop against my ass again and I cry out once more. I feel pressure building inside of my core. I'm going to cum all over his fucking fingers if he keeps this up. My cheeks burn with embarrassment at how much I want his punishment. How much I crave and need it.

Suddenly, Lucian's hands are gone from my pussy and disappoint-ment flows through my body. I was so close. I'm breathless, and my body weak with need and exhaustion.

"Your punishment is over," Lucian declares, making me even more upset. My heart tightens, and I find myself feeling unstable and weak. My ass hurts as he shifts his position.

I have the urge to protest, my lips parting, but nothing coming out. This was my punishment. I knew I should have been still. I should have controlled it. I close my eyes and try to ignore how upset I am.

"Thank you," I say, trying to keep my voice neutral and hide my disappointment.

"Thank you what?" he asks menacingly.

"Sir!" I say quickly. "Thank you, sir."

He's suddenly pressed against me, his breath hot on my neck. Behind me, I can feel his hard cock pressing up against my sore ass through his silk slacks. My pussy pulses in tandem with the blood that's pumping through his huge dick. "Good girl," he whispers in my ear, his hand snaking around my waist and up my chest to clamp down on a hard nipple. "Now when I tell you to be still, will you be still?"

I hold in a moan as he gently pinches my nipple to the point that a gasp is forced from me. The sensation is directly linked to my throbbing clit. And again I feel on edge. "Yes, sir," I whisper, immediately turned on again, and nodding my head.

He gently kisses my shoulder and strokes my back. "You will, treasure." He releases me and gets up off the bed and frustration laces through me. I feel cheated somewhat. I want him back.

Keeping my expression neutral, I watch as he walks over to the corner and grabs my clothes out of the chair.

"Is this all you have?" he asks, looking down at the black skirt and cream blouse I'd worn on the way over and examining it.

Anxiety courses through me. I know they're not the most expensive clothes, but it's the best outfit I have.

Not knowing what to say, I give him a slight nod.

"When I ask a question," he growls, narrowing his eyes slightly at me, "I expect a verbal response."

I force it from my lips. "Yes, sir."

He looks down at the pile again and I can tell he's not pleased. A feeling of worthlessness touches my chest. I don't know why, but his disdain for my clothes makes me feel like shit. Like I'm not good enough. I hate it.

"It will have to do," Lucian says. "For tonight only. But after today, I'll need the sizes you wear so you'll be prepared for next time."

My face crinkles in confusion. He told me to be naked.

"We're going out, treasure," Lucian announces, tossing my outfit down the chair and moving his hands to the belt wrapped around his waist. He begins walking over to the bed while undoing his belt, his eyes on me, burning with an intensity that causes my skin to prickle. He gets his belt off and tosses it to the side, and then he pulls his slacks down around his ass, gripping his massive, swollen, throbbing cock in his hand and stroking it as he moves forward.

"But first things first," he growls, as he climbs onto the bed behind me, lines his huge dick up with my pussy... And plunges it deep inside with enough force to make me cry out.

CHAPTER 15

LUCIAN

*D*ahlia's blouse is loose on her and the wind blows it easily, pressing the thin fabric against her skin. The night is bitter cold, but all she has is a thin cardigan and a cream chiffon blouse. Her skirt covers her legs to her knees, but I imagine she's going to be cold.

I don't have a single item for a woman in this house. I should've been more prepared, but I had no intention of taking her out. Next time I'll be ready. I've already sent a text to Linda with Dahlia's sizes and everything I want for her. The thought takes me off guard that there will even be a next time. But I can't deny that I'm already thinking about taking her out again. Just the mention of dinner made her obviously happy.

I love the look on her face, and I want to keep her satisfied.

I know Madam Lynn has extended contracts in the past, so perhaps my Dahlia will be happy enough with the same arrangements.

I slip my jacket off my shoulders and place it around hers even though we aren't outside yet. She turns in the foyer, her heels clicking on the marble floors to look at me.

"I'll be alright," she says sweetly.

"That's not the correct response, my treasure," I leave a small note of admonishment to linger and she recognizes it although it's mostly meant to be playful.

"Thank you, sir." The soft blush to her cheeks makes her look innocent.

My fingers itch to reach out to her, but I resist. I know it's harder on Submissives to see the lines between a traditional relationship and what we have.

Dahlia's doing so well though. Especially for someone who's never participated in this lifestyle. "How are you enjoying this so far?" I ask as I slip my wallet into my back pocket and grab the keys off of the table.

"This?" she asks me, gesturing between the two of us.

A smile is forced onto my lips at her confusion. "Yes, Dahlia," I open the door and splay my hand on her lower back to lead her out, "how are you enjoying our arrangement?" I lock the door behind us and pull out my phone to send a text to Andrea letting her know we're leaving.

"I'm liking it so far," she says softly, the color intensifying in her cheeks. The sight of her shy beauty captivates me. I've loved every minute of pushing her boundaries and exploring the curves of her body.

"Good." I smile down at her and she rewards me with a sweet soft hum as she rocks back and forth on her heels, waiting for me to lead her away.

"You're excited for dinner?"

"I am," she replies and her smile widens. My chest swells with pride that I can put that beautiful look on her face.

My hand rests gently on her lower back and I lead her along.

She's quiet as we walk down the hallway and get into the elevator. The lighthearted feelings wane as I think about where we're going. It's late, but the paparazzi will be there, Andrea assures me in her text back. We won't even know they're there. A late-night candlelit dinner for two in a private room. It should be enough to satisfy the PR firm.

I clear my throat and consider what Dahlia will think of this. She needs to know this is a stunt and nothing more, but the thought of telling her the truth sends a prickle of unease down my skin. I don't want her to know any more than she has to. I also don't want her to be disappointed. She's genuinely happy, and I don't want to take that away.

"We'll be dining alone tonight." I have to set the ground rules for her. This isn't a date. I'm not an eligible bachelor. This is simply a dinner that she's attending with me as a Submissive, although, things will obviously be different.

"The rules are different outside the playroom, Dahlia," I tell her as I key in the code in the elevator chambers to take us to my floor of the garage.

She huffs a small laugh and her eyes slowly rise to meet mine. "I'm not even sure I know the rules in the playroom," she says softly.

Something about the look in her eyes makes me weak for her.

"Of course you do. You're perfect in the playroom, treasure," I say and cup her chin in my hand and run my thumb along her lower lip. They beg me to kiss her, but there are lines I'm not yet ready to cross. I don't want to lead her on, and this is already pushing it.

"You submit, and do your best to obey. You accept your punishment and best of all, you enjoy it." I release her as the elevator stops and lead the way out.

"That's all I ask of you, but when we're outside of the playroom, it's going to be far more difficult." She walks quickly to stay beside me as I stride toward the grey metal key box on the wall. The key to the penthouse opens it, and I pick out the Porsche 911. It's sleek and I want something different for tonight. Something hotter.

I eye my treasure. She looks beautiful, but she's dressed as if she could be my secretary or my assistant. I don't want anyone mistaking her for anything other than what she is. She's mine.

Tomorrow I'll have the clothes sent to her place. Enough for a few dates at least. The idea of changing the rules and bringing our play out into the public is thrilling. It's new and different, and a challenge.

"Do you think you can play by a new set of rules, Dahlia?" I ask her.

She meets my gaze and nods, "Yes, sir."

"That's the first change." She pulls the jacket a little tighter around her shoulders. The wind is harsh as it blows into the cement garage.

She stares at me with those gorgeous hazel eyes flashing with a hint of uncertainty. "You'll call me Lucian when we're in public. And you're to act as though we're a couple."

"I can do that," she says thoughtfully.

My skin chills as I lead her to the red sports car and open the door. She walks quietly by my side, absorbing my words. I'm not interested in blurring these lines, and it may be difficult for her to remember what this is between us.

"Thank you," she says as she slips into the passenger seat. I wait until she's fully inside to gently shut the door.

My gut twists in my stomach knowing I'm leading myself to paparazzi. They're leeches and I hate the thought that I'm relying on them for this PR stunt, but if it works in my favor, I'll suffer through it.

I close my door and press the start button, the car purring to life. I glance at Dahlia and her legs have goosebumps, she's nearly shivering, huddled inside of my jacket. I click on the heated seats, but the heat itself will have to wait until the car heats.

"The rules are simple, Dahlia." I glance at her and then back onto the road. "You act as though we're a couple, just be mindful that people will be watching, even when you think no one is." I readjust in my seat and consider my next words, "Be respectful to me as your Dom. I know this is new to you, but you understand what that means, don't you?" I watch her from the corner of my eye.

"I think so," she answers hesitantly.

"Go on then."

"A Submissive is supposed to treat her Dominant with respect."

"As should a Dominant to his Submissive," I respond easily. I'm surprised by the flash of shock on her face and how her sweet lips part. "You don't agree?"

"I-" she starts to answer, but she doesn't finish her statement.

"Tell me about why you enjoy this, Dahlia." I keep my eyes on the road, but I'm fully focused on my treasure. It's important to me that we're on the same page here. I keep forgetting she's never done this before. That everything is new and different.

"I enjoy…" her voice trails off and she looks out of the window, tucking her hair back as she clears her throat. "I enjoy it when you're rough with me." She whispers her words, and the soft sounds makes my dick harden in my pants.

"I enjoy that, too," I tease her. "But this is more than just rough sex," I add.

"Yes," she answers diligently, nodding her head. "It's about me submitting all things and giving you control of the situation."

I wait for her to say more, but she doesn't. "And for you to trust that I know what you need, and that I'll provide it for you." I hold her gaze as we stop at a red light. Waiting for her to acknowledge that.

"Right," she says softly although there's no conviction in her voice.

"You've never had a relationship like ours before? But you've had boyfriends I assume?" It sounds odd to say the term boyfriend. I never much liked the word.

"I have."

"And would you call them dominant?" I ask her.

Her forehead pinches and she shakes her head slightly. "No. I wouldn't." She puts a finger to her lip and seems to truly consider what I'm asking.

"Tell me what you're thinking."

"My last... my ex." I drive easily, listening to her tell me about her experience. "He didn't really know how to help me in ways that I needed him to." It's a rather cryptic response, but I respect her privacy if she's not willing to divulge any more information.

"And you communicated your needs, but they weren't fulfilled. You couldn't trust him to take care of you in that way?"

"Right," she nods her head, "so yeah, I wouldn't say he was my Dominant. He didn't know how to be," her voice is soft and coated with the sound of realization. "He couldn't be my Dom."

"Is that why it didn't last?" I ask her. I'm curious. The conversation itself has made me want to know more.

"He just didn't understand." She answers with a sadness I wasn't expecting.

"What's that?"

"Hmm?" she hums.

"What didn't he understand?"

"I'd rather not talk about it, if that's alright?" The shyness and sadness mix in her eyes. Also apprehension.

"That's fine, treasure. You can keep a few secrets."

"My point was I respect your needs and your submission, and you do the same for me and my dominance. It's about trust, respect and communication."

I pull through the valet at the Ritz-Carlton and put the car in park so I can look at her. "Do you think I don't respect you, Dahlia?"

I ask her in all seriousness. I respect her and her submission. I know her needs, and what she enjoys. We share the same desires, so it's been extremely easy for me to fall into the dominant role in our relationship and fulfill her needs, but maybe I've missed something.

I lean forward and take her chin in my hand, tilting her lips to mine and planting a small chaste kiss against them. "Don't forget for even one second, that every time I smack my hand across your ass, it's because I know you need it." I nip her bottom lip and then whisper, "Every time I fuck you until you can't breathe, it's because I know you want it." Her eyes close, and her lips part with lust. I reach my hand down and let my fingers play along the thin fabric of her underwear. "I give you what you want, I respect your needs, I cherish them."

"And you'll do the same for me, won't you, treasure?"

"Yes, sir," she whispers with lust.

"Ah, ah," I say as I pull away, turning the car off and grabbing the key. "Right now, it's 'yes, Lucian.'"

CHAPTER 16

DAHLIA

Every time I fuck you until you can't breathe, it's because I know you need it.

Lucian's words repeat in my mind as I climb out of his sports car, my breath catching in my throat as I take in the gorgeous view. Holding the door for me, Lucian gives me a boyish grin as a young valet dressed in a black suit and gold vest jogs up to us and hastily greets Lucian with a slight nod, asking him for the keys to the car.

"This is beautiful," I breathe, turning to Lucian and shaking my head. The valet grabs the keys from Lucian, grinning at the sports car like a kid at Christmas, before running around to the driver's side and jumping in. "I've never been taken to a place like this. Ever." I turn back and take in the restaurant with awe, admiring the scenic view. The building, which is cut of exquisite grey stone and has gleaming tall glass windows adorning the front, sits back on a terrace overlooking a beautiful lake. Floodlighting brightens the entire area, showcasing every inch of the grandmaster masonry. Intricately designed stamped concrete steps lead up to the entrance, a sparkling water fountain with ambient lighting rests at the center of the plaza, and a fancy balustrade runs up along each side. The full moon looms in the starry night sky, milky white light reflected against the water, making the scene even more romantic.

I watch in wonder as men in expensive suits and ties walk up the steps with women dressed in absolute finery on their arms. The gowns these ladies are wearing look like they cost a fortune, dazzling jewels and all, and it makes me feel more than a little self-conscious.

No wonder Lucian wasn't pleased by my outfit, I think to myself, glancing down at my outfit that seems drab compared to the others. *He's accustomed to seeing women wearing all this.*

Lucian is enjoying my shock, watching me with obvious amusement. "I thought you might like it," he says, splaying a hand across the small of my back. "But come, I think you'll enjoy the inside even more."

Breathless, I allow him to lead me up the steps to the restaurant, and I try to appear confident like all the other women around me. Like I belong on Lucian's arm. But it's hard. I can't stop worrying about people looking at me and thinking that I look out of place. Glancing around, no one seems to be paying us any mind, and the pleasant sounds of the waterfall take the edge off my anxiety.

Unconsciously I reach for Lucian's hand, wanting to feel security and comfort, and then snatch it back, fearful that I might be crossing the line. *Shit.* I didn't mean to do that. But isn't that what Lucian wants me to do? Pretend I'm his girlfriend? It's confusing, and my emotions and anxiety are getting the best of me.

I bite my lower lip nervously, glancing over at Lucian. He doesn't seem to have noticed my misstep and even places his hand on my right hip, guiding me up the last of the steps leading to the terrace.

Inside I'm completely blown away by the ritzy, upscale setting. The high-ceilinged room is a splash of gold and white, filled with luxury seating and high-class booths. There are several crowded bars on either side of the room, manned by attractive bartenders in deluxe suits. Delicate music seems to float to my ears from nowhere and a delightful scented fragrance tickles my nose. The walls are adorned with gold lights made up of gorgeous patterns that blend in with everything else, and on the back wall, the floor-to-ceiling windows provide a breathtaking view of the moonlit lake. The room is filled with the ultra-wealthy, the din of their chatter almost making me dizzy. I take it all in with a sharp breath. The seating, the lighting, the ambience--all of it is done to perfection.

"This is incredible," I say just above a murmur, unable to find a better word, my nervousness returning. I've never been somewhere like this in my entire life, and I feel totally out of my element. I step closer to Lucian and cling to his arm, wishing I could shrink and hide behind him as we move through a crowd of finely dressed couples toward the waiting area.

"I'm happy you like it." Lucian seems unconcerned with my anxiety and even wraps his arm around my waist as a waiter immediately approaches us. My cheeks redden at how Lucian is acting like I'm his property, and I have to take a moment to remember that he's doing this for show. I can't enjoy this too much. I can't get used to this either.

The waiter nods his head at Lucian, his eyes taking me in for a moment and then going back to Lucian. "Right this way, Mr. Stone. Your reservation is ready."

The waiter leads us over to a luxurious booth in a secluded corner and I try to walk with confidence on the way over, but I almost trip. A small gasp slips through my lips, and my heart stutters in my chest. Luckily, Lucian hooks me with his arm and keeps me from falling, smoothly guiding me to the table like nothing happened. My heart's in my throat as I walk the remaining few steps, my cheeks burning with embarrassment. I don't look around to see if anyone saw.

The waiter produces two menus but Lucian politely waves him away as he says, "I already know what we'd like to order."

"Of course, sir." Another young man dressed in a crisp black suit quietly fills the crystal globe glasses on our table with water from a pitcher as Lucian orders.

"A bottle of chardonnay to drink, black cod brûlée," Lucian nods in my direction while passing the menus back, "and ribeye with goat cheese dipped in Meyer lemon honey mustard."

The waiter slips the menus back into a pouch at his waist, and takes out a pen and pad in one smooth flourish.

I part my lips to say something about Lucian ordering for me, but then close them. He's still my Dom. The rules have changed slightly, but not really.

"You'll love it," Lucian assures me with a small smile, seeing the question in my eyes.

"Of course, sir." The waiter nods as he scribbles notes on his pad. "Any appetizers?"

Lucian shakes his head. "No, thank you."

"I'll be back as soon as I can with your drinks. Please let me know if there's anything else I can do for you."

I watch as he walks away, past a few tables of romantic couples dining in luxury and try to relax in my seat. But my nerves have a grip on me. Blowing out a breath, I take a peek around and my stomach tightens even more. I can't get over the fact that I'm dining with the upper crust of society. Club X had filthy rich diners, but that's different. There, it's horny rich men looking to pay money to hook up with women from all socioeconomic backgrounds. Here, everyone's come to spend a boatload of money on food just because they can.

And I'm probably the only woman in the room who's here as almost a paid prostitute. The thought is unsettling and makes my stomach turn. I reach for my water, the crystal glass cold in my hand and take a sip.

I nervously finger my silverware, not sure how to act. I feel so anxious, I almost want to get up and leave. Why did Lucian bring me here again? Our contract said nothing about wining and dining with rich people. I thought it was all supposed to be about sex, whips and chains. Maybe this is some sort of test.

Noticing my nervousness, Lucian hooks his finger under my chin, drawing my eyes to him.

"You need to relax, treasure," he says softly. His eyes are filled with empathy and his concern goes a long way in calming my anxiety. "These people aren't any better than you are. Trust me on that." He says his words with such conviction that I actually believe him for a short moment.

Looking at him, I'm reminded again of his words in the car. *I respect your needs and your submission, and you do the same for me and my dominance. It's about trust, respect and communication.*

Before I can say anything in return, the waiter comes back, gently setting our wine glasses down in front of us one by one and pouring a small amount of the wine in Lucian's glass.

Lucian motions for him to continue pouring without taking a sip.

"Is there anything else I can do for you?" the waiter asks as he finishes pouring the wine and then gently sets the bottle on the table.

"No," Lucian replies. "Thank you."

A moment passes in silence. Lucian grabs his glass of wine and relaxes in his seat. I envy him. He seems so at ease in this setting, so used to being surrounded by such awesome wealth.

"So how did you find out about Club X?" Lucian asks suddenly, looking at me with an intensity that makes me forget about all my worries for a moment and causes a shiver to run down my spine. Although I'm still slightly on edge, I love the way he's looking at me; like I'm the only one in the room. And seeing as how we're surrounded by beautiful, wealthy-looking women that make me feel insecure, I feel pretty fucking special right about now.

I pause for a moment, lowering my gaze, my skin pricking at the soft emotions swelling my breasts. I'm unsure if I should tell him how Carla approached me and swore me to secrecy, but I decide there's little harm. He's a member of Club X, not an outsider. I won't be revealing anything about the club he doesn't already know. "My friend, Carla, told me about it one day out of the blue," I say softly.

Lucian arches a brow, his fingers running along the stem of his glass. "Any particular reason?"

I blush slightly at the memory, but I'm glad that we're talking. The conversation is helping me relax, and focusing on Lucian is making it easy to tune out the people around me. "She invited me because she said she could tell I'd like it. She said I was an obvious Submissive and that I'd enjoy it."

Lucian takes a sip of his chardonnay, still looking at me in a way that makes my skin prickle. "So, you said your friend's name is Carla?"

"Yes," I reply. "Her Dom is named Bruce, and he's actually her boyfriend." Including that small bit of information makes my blood heat with insecurity. *She's more to him than I am to Lucian.* I have to look away from Lucian and clear my throat before continuing. "I don't know if you know him or not."

A thoughtful expression graces Lucian's handsome face. "Hmm. Can't say that I've heard of those two before, and I usually know who the couples are within the club." Lucian's eyes grow distant and I know he's thinking about some event in the past, something that troubles him because his demeanor has shifted. "But then again, I've been away from the club for a while."

I clear my throat and ask, "Will we be going back to the club anytime soon?"

"If you'd like, we can." He straightens in his seat and clears his throat, the hard lines on his face softening. "In fact, I've been meaning to talk to you about that."

"About what?" I ask curiously.

"I think it might be beneficial for you to be around other couples, get used to how they interact. It'll help you with training."

I nervously half smile. I'm anxious about trying something outside my safe zone, and I prefer the privacy of Lucian's playroom, but I'm anxious to see more of the club. "I think so, too," I agree, a small thrill running through me.

Lucian seems pleased at my response and he once again gives me that look that makes my skin prick. "You're so beautiful, do you know that?"

I blush furiously, my heart doing backflips at his unabashed praise. That compliment was totally unexpected. Lucian's really making me feel like that we actually are a couple, even though this is supposed to be pretend. I have to shake my head and remind myself that this isn't real. It's all make-believe. "Thank you," I say in a soft voice, a shy smile on my lips.

Lucian shakes his head. "No thanks needed here. So why is it that you decided to enter the auction?"

I freeze as his question triggers those dark memories that are always waiting for the right moment to pounce. The very reasons that drove me to Club X. Several painful images flash in front of my face and I have to grip the edges of the table to keep my composure. I lower my gaze, breathing deeply, slowly, fighting to push those horrible images away. Not here. Not now. *Go the fuck away.*

When I look up, Lucian is staring at me with concern in his eyes and my heart is suddenly aching for him. Maybe I should just be open with him. Doesn't he have the right to know? A powerful urge presses down on my chest, bidding me to tell him everything.

I respect your needs and your submission, and you do the same for me and my dominance. It's about trust, respect and communication.

His words bear heavy on my conscience. If I truly want our relationship and contract to be successful, shouldn't I be truthful with him and let him know who he's really dealing with? Isn't that what trust is all about?

"Treasure?" Lucian's deep voice snaps me to attention.

I open my mouth, ready to tell him everything, but no words come out. I can't bring myself to say it, can't bring myself to reveal my dark secret. A secret that could possibly push Lucian away. Fuck. I feel ashamed. I wish this wasn't so fucking awkward, too.

I give Lucian a light, fraudulent smile and shrug. "I don't know... I just... wanted to try it." I feel shitty for lying, and it's so fucking obvious that I am, but what else can I do? I'm not telling Lucian about my past. At least not right now. I don't want to mess up our arrangement in any way. It's just sex. And it's over in less than a month. I don't owe him anything more.

Lucian peers at me, his eyes piercing me with their skepticism. "Are you sure there isn't something else you aren't telling me?"

I almost fold beneath his questioning gaze, my heart hammering in my chest. It's funny how the tables turn. A minute ago I was prying into his past, but now he's prying into mine. *And he didn't open up to me.* The reminder hardens my resolve. I duck my head, tearing my eyes from his and look down into my glass of water. "I'm sure," I repeat firmly, injecting as much strength into my voice as possible to get him off my back.

It's about trust, respect and communication, his words scream in my head, making me feel even more like shit.

Lucian stares at me intently, looking like he wants to press the issue, but then he straightens, a smile curling the corner of his lips as he takes a sip of his chardonnay. I relax slightly, realizing he's letting me off the hook. *Thank God.* He's definitely not buying my lie, though, and for some reason he seems content on letting me get away with it. For now.

A feeling of relief flows through me when the waiter returns with our food balanced in each hand. My stomach quietly rumbles as the rich aroma fills my nostrils and he sets the plates down in front of us.

"Anything else, sir?" the waiter asks.

"No, thank you," Lucian's quick to reply.

"Enjoy," he says. And with a flash of a smile, the waiter's gone.

Grabbing my heavy fork, I take a bite of the tender meat dipped in sauce, and my eyes widen as the sweet tangy flavor fills my mouth. Damn. Lucian is right.

"This is delicious," I remark, waiting for Lucian's gaze to meet mine. "Thank you." I hope he knows how serious I am.

Lucian grins. "I knew you would like it," he says confidently.

"So how did you become the CEO of your company?" I ask after a few more delicious bites. Having read the article about his rise to success, I pretty much know what Lucian is going to say, but I'd like to hear him tell it. I figure now is a good time as ever to hopefully turn this date around and focus on something that will lighten the mood.

Lucian eyes me. "How did you know I was CEO? Much less own my own company?" There's a bit of humor in his voice. I'm sure he knows I cyberstalked him.

I freeze mid-bite, my mind racing with an explanation other than the obvious. *Fuck.* Lucian never told me what he did, and I never asked. Nor was there any mention of his occupation in the contract. I open my mouth to say, "I just assumed that," but then snap my lips shut, feeling a bite of shame. It's one thing to tell a lie because you're hiding something too personal to share, it's another to tell one to cover something harmless.

A blush reddening my cheeks, I sheepishly admit, "I looked you up on the net."

I brace myself, half expecting Lucian to go into a rage for my intrusion on his privacy, but he just chuckles. "I was sure you had, my sweet treasure," he says. "I'd do the same thing if I were in your shoes. Hell, it's the smart thing to do. I would never advise anyone to enter into a contract with a stranger without knowing something about them, especially someone you'd be entrusting with your safety."

I'm relieved that Lucian hasn't taken offense to my prying. For some reason, I keep waiting for him to punish me for any blunders. It's like the line is blurring between Dom Lucian and real Lucian. I don't know which one I'm talking to. "One thing the articles I read kept going on about was how young you were to head a successful startup," I add. "That's impressive."

Lucian nods. "I had some help from a friend. He's a silent partner now."

"What about your family?" I ask. "Did you come from," I wave my hand in the direction of the other guests, "this?" I don't know how to word it.

"No," Lucian says simply. "I'm from a blue collar family." The ease in his voice is gone, and I can tell I've struck a nerve. "They're dead to me now," he says quietly.

I sit there awkwardly, frustrated that we somehow keep making each other upset, but not quite knowing what to do. The anger in Lucian's voice... it's raw. There's pain there. And pain is an emotion I'm well accustomed to.

Moved by emotion and instinct, I swallow back a lump in my throat, and reach over and place my hand atop of his. His gaze drops to where our hands are joined, and my heartbeat slows. For an instant, I fear I've crossed the line. But he surprises me by giving me a glimpse of a smile and running his thumb gently over the back of my hand.

I tell him softly, my voice filled with empathy, my eyes finding his, "Sometimes family can do you worse than a person on the street would."

Trust me, I should know, I think to myself as those dark images threaten to come back. Nausea twists my stomach, and I'm angry at myself for even thinking about them right now.

My words seem to have a profound effect on Lucian because he visibly relaxes in his chair. "Thank you," he says warmly to me. He pauses and takes a deep breath, then lets out an explosive sigh. "And there's something else, too."

My heart jumps in my chest. Maybe he's about to reveal something. "What's that?"

"I was going through a divorce at the same time," he forces out.

I raise my eyebrows, surprised he would bring this up, but I'm hopeful that I'll find out what caused it and maybe find out what kind of man Lucian is.

Lucian nods, his eyes burning with anger and a hint of sadness. "It wasn't pleasant."

I lean forward slightly. "Did it have anything to do with…" I trail off, but I know he gets my meaning, though I feel like I'm once again walking on the edge by prying where I shouldn't. Yet, I can't help myself.

Lucian is quiet for a moment, digesting my question. Finally, he shakes his head. "No. My ex was into the same lifestyle, actually. We both enjoyed it." He huffs out a dry, humorless chuckle. "She craved the money more."

Damn. Why do I keep bringing these things up? "I don't know what to say," I say slowly.

"There's nothing for you to say," Lucian says dismissively. "I'm the one who's sorry."

"Well, I feel awful for even having brought it up. Sorry I asked."

Lucian waves my apology away again. "What's done is done." He looks at me, his eyes assessing me in a way that makes me feel fuzzy inside. "I'd rather focus on the here and now."

Unable to take his gaze, a blush comes to my cheeks and I lower my head.

"Look at me," Lucian commands.

I raise my eyes, my cheeks burning all the hotter. "Sir?" Crap. Why do I keep doing that?

"Lucian," he says firmly.

"Lucian," I repeat.

Fingering his wine glass, Lucian studies me, a slight smile on his lips and my skin pricks at the emotion that grips my chest. I recognize the feeling and it makes me nervous. Lucian said this was all for show, but why do I keep feeling like it's something more?

I need to just focus on the sex, I repeat to myself, *because that's all this is. For thirty days.*

"Would you like to go for a walk after dinner?" Lucian asks, his beautiful eyes still focused on me. "There's a cobblestone trail that leads to a bridge overlooking the water. On a night like this, I'm sure you'll love it." He pauses a moment, glancing at my blouse before adding, "I'll have a coat brought for you."

I pause, thinking, *No, what I want you to do is take me back to your place and make me beg for that big fat cock,* but I only feel more confused. I'm not sure what's to gain from taking a walk as a couple, if it's not supposed to be real. I thought he just wanted to show me off in public and then whisk me back away into privacy.

I part my lips, feeling an urge to decline. I'm already having trouble separating my sexual energy from my emotions and Lucian is sending me mixed signals, making it worse. But at the same time, I'm scared of angering him. He's a man that won't be denied, and I still feel like I'm his Sub, even out in public. "Yes," I reply dutifully, flashing a weak smile, my cheeks turning red yet again. "I would love that."

I don't miss the satisfaction that flashes in Lucian's eyes. "Good."

We continue eating our meal, our conversation turning to lighter things, and despite my nervousness, I find myself relaxing. Lucian's charm makes me feel at ease and he's showing a tender side of himself that I didn't think he possessed. Several times throughout the meal, I have to go back to reminding myself that he's just doing this for show and that he doesn't care one way or another about me, except for being his paid sex toy.

Still, I'm so charmed by his behavior, I find myself wondering if it would be better to just tell him the truth. Outside of the playroom, he seems like such a nice guy, and I feel guilty about lying even more now after hearing the story about his ex. Maybe disclosing the truth would improve my experience as his Sub instead of negatively impacting it.

If only I had the courage to find out.

Seeing my distressed expression, Lucian asks, "Something you want to tell me?"

Anxiety crushes my stomach as I look into Lucian's eyes. He's been so gracious to me tonight, even if it wasn't real, revealing things that he didn't have to share with me. But as much as I want to, I don't think I can bring myself to tell him. I feel like he wouldn't understand. How could he? Being a Dom is just a lifestyle to him, but being a Sub is a *need* for me.

Feeling sick to my stomach, I shake my head, plaster a fake smile on my face, and answer, "No... I was just thinking I didn't save room for dessert."

CHAPTER 17

LUCIAN

I lean back in my chair, facing the large window at the back of my office. From here, the skyline is quiet, moving slowly underneath me. Nothing at all like the reality of being on the busy streets of the city. From up here, it's calming. The steel and glass shine with a sleek beauty that radiates a sense of power.

I tap my thumb along the armrest of the chair, thinking about the other night. The phone on my desk rings and it draws my attention, but I hit the button to silence it. I don't need any interruptions right now. I rise from my seat and walk to the window. Last night was more enjoyable than I thought it would be. It was a success as well. Andrea and the agency are pleased with the article that'll be going live at some point today online and hitting the magazines tomorrow.

Most Eligible Bachelor is on the Dating Scene. ...how inaccurate. I sigh deeply and ignore the ill feelings stirring in the pit of my stomach. I'd rather stay away from the press altogether, but I've chosen this course of action. I'll see it through.

One thing I hadn't quite prepared was my reaction to taking my sweet treasure out. Her lack of understanding is drawing me in more than I ever thought it would. I'm actually excited to take her to the club tonight. I never thought I'd get the same thrill from Club X that I once had. But it's ringing in my blood.

There's something bothering her though. It was obvious with the way she was hesitating last night. I don't like it. I don't like her keeping secrets from me.

I've arranged for a private room tonight so I can get to the bottom of it. I'm sure a little orgasm denial will get her talking. Especially considering how disappointed she was last night before I took her out. An asymmetric grin kicks my lips up. She didn't fuss with her punishment though. She didn't argue with me. She's so fucking perfect, and she has absolutely no idea.

It's hard to believe she had no experience as a Sub before this. I remember our conversation about her ex, and the curiosity rises in me once again.

I walk back to my desk and click on the emails. Isaac should have a good bit of detail for me on Dahlia's last relationships. She's had social media profiles for years, so her background check and history will be sent to me shortly. Maybe I should feel ashamed for digging into her past and violating her privacy... but I don't. Not in the least. She's my Submissive, and therefore my responsibility.

Isaac's a professional. He's worked in security for years, and I can trust him. It's not the first time I've asked him to look into someone and he's done it with no questions asked.

My phone rings again, and I stare at it with irritation before finally lifting it off the hook and begrudgingly answering it.

"Stone."

"Mr. Stone, it's Andrea." I recognize her voice instantly. Andrea sounds less than her usual chipper self. She sounds nervous, and the realization makes me stand tall.

"Yes," I say in an even tone.

The sounds of her clearing her throat fill the phone as I wait with tense shoulders. Whatever it is, she can just spit it out. It better not have a damn thing to do with the article or my comment though. "My comment about Miss Days-"

"Mr. Stone, it's about your wife."

"*Ex*-wife." I'm quick to correct her. Unconsciously my ring finger twitches as I think about how a ring will never lay there again.

"I'm so sorry, sir. Your ex-wife. She's taking this to a different level now."

I huff a humorless laugh. "We took care of that problem, didn't we?" With the photo and an agreement to several articles over the course of a month or so, the magazines are going for the hotter news and bigger paycheck.

I walk closer to the large window and look down at the tiny cars as they move slowly under me. Seemingly so slow. "She's decided that she's going to do a tell-all book now."

I grit my teeth, hating that she just won't let it go. What is it that she thinks is worth telling, exactly? A failed marriage because I worked too fucking much? I put a ring on the finger of a woman who was more interested in a paycheck than our relationship. I don't know how I let her fool me.

And as far as my perversions that she's willing to throw in my face, her tastes were far more extreme than my own. I take in a deep breath, trying to calm myself.

"What exactly is in this book?" I dare to ask.

"Mr. Stone," she says, then hesitates on the line. "According to the publisher who we've been in contact with," she hesitates again for a moment, "the book will have pictures of the aftermath of your sexual encounters."

My heart stills as she continues. *Pictures*? "There's no way for her to be able to verify that they were taken at the time of your marriage and I'm sure your lawyer will be able to prevent their use, but if this were to be leaked it would certainly be detrimental to your image."

"Pictures?"

"They make it appear as though there were bruises and several abrasions." Her voice remains strong as she says, "The way it's written leaves a lot of implications. The editor and publisher have been in contact because of potential lawsuits."

Anger slowly rises in me as I close my eyes.

Never. I never leave marks, never leave cuts. Even when I picked up my first whip, I learned then the importance of only bringing the blood to the surface. Just enough force to redden the skin and create a wave of endorphins. I've never bruised anyone. Never. It's simply not my kink. She wants to paint herself as a victim. Probably even more so, she wants to paint me as a villain.

Andrea speaks before I'm able to respond.

"I'm certain these pictures are fabricated, Mr. Stone. Especially considering the toxicity of your divorce."

"You are correct," I answer her in a tight voice.

"They would have come up before, had there been any truth at all to what she's implying. The problem is that there's no way for us to prove this. The best possible line of defense would be for you to continue this relationship with your..." The rustling of paper in the background fills the silence.

"Dahlia." I say her name as I pinch the bridge of my nose.

"Yes, Miss Days."

"Is she saying I beat her?" I have to ask. "She's claiming abuse?" Even after everything we went through, I never thought she'd stoop so low. I *loved* her. I loved the woman I thought she was.

I'd never do anything to hurt her. Not like that. She loved the paddle, but it was only for play, only to intensify her pleasure. There was never a bruise on her body.

"She is." The truth slams against my chest as I lean against the window, the cool glass on my palms. "The wording is ambiguous, so you'll have to speak with Mr. Harris on that matter." Her voice is soft and laced with sympathy.

I clear my throat and reply, "I understand. Thank you, Andrea."

"I'm sorry, Mr. Stone." The words hang stale in the air as I tell her goodbye and listen to the soft click on the other end.

I hold the phone in my hand, long after the line has gone dead. I can't believe I was ever fooled by that woman. I loved her. I know I did, and I was so fucking wrong about her and everything.

I push away from the window at the sound of a knock on my door.

"Come in," I call out, setting the phone back down where it belongs.

"Mr. Stone," Linda enters with a mug of coffee in one hand and a stack of papers in the other. She walks briskly to my desk, setting them each down before smoothing her skirt while looking up at me with a smile.

It instantly vanishes when she sees my expression. "Is everything alright?" she asks.

I give her a tight smile and ignore the concern in her voice.

"Fine." I sift through the stack and recognize the contracts that are due today. "I'll sign these after lunch." It's nothing that can't wait.

Linda stands there for a moment and I can see she wants to pry, but she presses her lips into a thin line and nods her head. "You'll let me know if you need anything?" she asks.

"Of course." She leaves silently and the phone rings again. There are emails and meetings, contracts and press conferences. I don't feel like doing any of them.

I know exactly what I do want though. I silence the phone and grab my cell phone from the desk.

Dahlia's number is right there from when she called last night.

She didn't stay over last night. I had a four a.m. meeting with a company in Singapore. But she called when she got back to her place. Just like I told her to.

She's not perfect, but she's the perfect Submissive for me. She gives it her best effort. The training is the best part, and of course I always give her what she needs after she's thanked me for her punishment. I got very lucky with her.

I press send and listen to the phone ring... and ring.

She doesn't have work or classes today. I almost brought her into the office, but decided against it so that I could focus. But I need her now.

Of course she's not fucking answering the phone.

I call again rather than leaving a message, and again it goes to voicemail.

Today has been a very trying day and I don't want to take it out on my sweet Submissive. I take in a deep breath, running my hands through my hair.

She's just busy for the moment. My desk phone rings as I breathe out and I glare at it. Hating the constant reminder that I'm stuck here instead of being with her. I'm tense and on edge. Close to ripping this fucking office apart.

I could do what I've done for the past three years. I could go to my gym and take my aggression out there. But I want to fuck. I want the exertion. I *need* the release.

I want to unwind and get lost in the feel of her tempting body.

You need to answer when I call you.

I press send on the text and sit in my seat, ignoring yet another phone call. I have actual work to do and I pay my lawyer and the agency enough money to take care of these problems for me. I should just let it roll off my shoulders and get this contract completed, but now I'm fixated on my treasure.

I go through at least a dozen emails, all with only partial focus. I keep thinking about Dahlia. Wondering what she's doing. I should know. I own her right now. My eyes dart from the screen to my phone.

Ten minutes later, and still nothing.

I expect you to be available for me at all times. I send the text, feeling the anger rise higher.

She knows this. Dahlia's a smart woman. She's intelligent and knows the rules of this relationship. She's never been a Submissive, but she knows enough.

And I fucking paid for her. If I wanted I could have her at my feet right now, sucking me off. My dick instantly hardens with need at the thought. That's exactly what *should* be happening right now.

I understand she's busy, and that she wasn't expecting me. I hold on to the last thought. I can be reasonable. My expectations weren't made clear, and I assumed too much. She should know to wait for my call. But I haven't explicitly told her.

Anger simmers on the surface; I paid for her. Her time is mine, and I've been generous. Maybe too generous.

This is my fault, but when I get my hands on her, I'll make sure this never happens again.

CHAPTER 18

DAHLIA

You need to answer when I call you.

I pull at the hem of my blouse with worry as I sit in the back seat of Lucian's Rolls Royce, reading his last text to me. I've texted him back several times, but he hasn't responded since he told me to wait for the car. I bite my lower lip, upset that I missed his calls and disappointed him. Worry stirs in the pit of my stomach as I meet Joseph's eyes in the rearview mirror.

I was at the mall shopping when he sent the texts and calls, busying myself with a gift for him, and my phone was at the bottom of my purse. I simply didn't hear it.

Everything is going to be okay, I tell myself, trying not to worry. *Lucian will understand.*

I glance down at the small bag at my side, my gift to Lucian. I got him a coffee mug from a gift shop. He drinks it non stop. It's the first thing he gets in the morning. The words emblazoned on the side say, "Please, sir." When I bought it, I thought it was funny. Now I think it's stupid as hell. It's been fifteen days but it feels like so much longer.

I just wanted to get him something to say thank you. Lucian has been positively spoiling me over the last two weeks, sending boxes and boxes of expensive clothes, high heels, designer purses and seductive fragrances to my apartment door.

LAUREN LANDISH & WILLOW WINTERS

I'm still in shock over how much he's splurging on me, especially after buying my contract for so much. The cost of these gifts has to number in the thousands, and they're the nicest things anyone has ever bought me. It's hard not to think that Lucian cares about me since he's going to all this trouble. I just wanted to do something nice for him in return. I feel like there's something between us. Or there was. Now I'm just filled with worry.

I could be fooling myself though. Lucian's a billionaire. Money probably means nothing to him. A few thousand bucks to spend on his fuck toy that he'll discard within a few days probably doesn't make him bat a single eyelash.

My lips part into a soft sigh and my heart does a flip as I look out of the window and see Lucian. He looks hot as fuck, casually leaned back against the club's back wall, wearing black silk slacks and a white shirt that's unbuttoned at the collar, showcasing his tanned skin beneath, his hands stuffed in his pockets. He's wearing the same black mask he had on when I first met him, his eyes gazing at me through it with that intensity that makes me shiver.

As the car comes to a stop, he pushes off the wall and opens the door before Joseph can get out. "You've kept me waiting." There's a slight edge in his voice that causes my skin to prickle.

I grip my gift bag, intent on offering it to Lucian as a peace offering, and begin to open my mouth to say sorry, when Lucian gestures sharply and says, "Leave it. You won't be needing that."

"But it's a gift for you-" I begin to protest.

"Put it away," Lucian growls dangerously, stepping away from the wall and moving toward me. "Let Joseph take it away with him. You can retrieve it later."

I lower my head with shame at how close I'd come to arguing with my Dom. My heart beats faster, and anxiety swirls in my lower belly. Shit. "Yes, sir." Joseph appears at my side to take the gift bag from me as I get out of the car and stand by Lucian. Shivering with apprehension, I watch as he starts the engine and rolls off, leaving us alone.

I turn when I hear a step at my side and I look up into Lucian's mask, seeing only his piercing eyes. I let out a gasp and jump a little when he grabs me by the hips firmly, his touch sending sparks of electricity along my skin, pulling me into him. My breathing turns into soft pants as my core heats from being so close to his hard body. Below, I can feel his huge cock pressing against my stomach, pulsing with powerful need.

"I-I-I'm sorry," I stutter, unable to think clearly under his penetrating gaze, "about not seeing your text. I was shopping and my phone was at the bottom of my bag on vibrate." I cringe at how pathetic I sound, waiting for some type of punishment from Lucian, but he doesn't say anything and the corner of his lips curl up into a hint of a smile.

"Come," is all he says, pulling me along to a door in the private side entrance where two men in black suits and sunglasses stand guard. He makes a gesture at the two men, some sign that I can't quite make out, and they nod and open the door for us.

I follow Lucian as he drags me inside to a dark hallway with dim lighting. The lighting is so low that I can't really see, and I have to hold onto Lucian to make sure I don't bump into anything. We round a corner and the low lighting changes to a dark red. I look around, trying to get my bearings, but all I see are multiple doors up and down the hall. I don't know where Lucian's taking me; I've never been in this part of the club before.

At the end of the hallway are two large double doors. Lucian stops us in front of them and quickly punches in a code on a metal box mounted on the side panel. I hear a clicking sound and the doors swing open. My breath catches in my throat as I step into a room awash with grey and white.

In the center of the room sits an elegant bed with a canopy, its lush comforter matching the colors of the room, and at the foot of the bed is a plush grey couch. The walls seem to be lined with a grey velvet fabric, and the curtains are a creamy white. Several elegant desks are placed on either side of the room and there is a large china cabinet filled with sexual toys and devices.

This must be one of the private rooms, I think to myself as I hear the doors slam shut behind me. *Elegant and high class, but still equipped with the right stuff.*

Before I can take in everything, I'm roughly jerked into Lucian's arms from behind. I tremble against his hard body, my mind racing with anticipation of what's to come, feeling his huge hard dick pressing up against my ass and his breath hot on my neck.

"Sorry isn't good enough, treasure," he growls in my ear, causing my pussy to clench with insatiable need.

"Sir," I whimper softly not knowing what to say, aching to have his cock thrusting inside of my swollen pussy. I want him to punish me for my crime, ravaging my pussy with his big hard dick while spanking my ass like I've stolen something. God. I fucking crave it.

I cry out as he grips my blouse and lets out a bestial grunt, practically tearing it apart with his bare hands and then moving on to my bra, skirt and panties until I stand before him completely naked, trembling with need. My nipples pebble as the cool air hits them, and goosebumps rise on my flesh.

Without giving me time to react, Lucian drags me toward the bed and throws me on top of it. I land on the plush mattress with a bounce, my head slamming into the pillows. Before I can move, Lucian's on top of me, turning me onto my stomach, his hard dick throbbing against my ass, tying my hands and feet with grey cloth that he's pulled off the canopy. I tremble with my breath caught in my throat as he works, bucking slightly against him, but he's too strong. When he's done, I struggle against my binds, but they're tied so tight. He has me securely locked down.

I lie there helplessly, my breathing coming in short pants and look to the side and see him grab a blindfold that's sitting on the nightstand next to the bed. He stands over me with it, almost as if he's taunting me with what's to come. I strain my neck to look up at him, and the only thing I can see are those beautiful eyes of his flashing with something dark, and I plead, "Please, sir."

Lucian responds by placing the blindfold over my eyes, eliminating my sight.

"I had to wait for you," I hear him growl somewhere nearby, "now you will fucking wait for me." I listen as I hear him walk away, his footsteps receding until all I hear is... silence.

I lie still for him for what feels like forever, and the only sound I hear is my own breathing. I accept my punishment. It's not the first time he's punished me. But this is different. This is more intense. I shiver repeatedly as a cool draft touches my skin, again and again, and I know my entire body is covered in goosebumps.

Thump! I jump at the sound of what sounded like a very deliberate footstep, my heart bucking in my throat, and then I hear another heavy footstep followed by another and another. My breathing quickens in relief and part anxiety. Lucian's back.

I go completely still, knowing that's what he wants, knowing it's the only thing that will get me what I so badly crave.

I nearly buck as I feel something hard graze my skin, leaving goosebumps down my thigh, before it's pulled back. A soft moan escapes my lips as my core heats with desire. This is it. This is what I've been waiting for. It's what I fucking deserve.

"Not only have you kept me waiting, but you lied to me, treasure," I hear Lucian say quietly from behind me. The quiet before the storm.

Smack!

I gasp with pain and pleasure, grabbing my binds to bear it, my pussy clenching violently around nothing. Immediately after, I feel Lucian kneading my ass, calming the pain pulsing through my ass cheeks.

"Tell me why you lied to me, treasure," I hear him whisper near my ear, his breath hot on my neck.

Shock goes through me, mixed with desire. Lied? What did I lie about?

"I know you've been hiding something. And you need to tell me what it is." Lucian's voice is hard. "You should have already told me."

Lucian knows? My heart races with anxiety. He knows what I'm hiding from him? I almost shake my head. That doesn't make sense. He can't know. I haven't told him anything.

But that doesn't mean he can't guess, a voice inside my head says, *he's not stupid.*

I part my lips to deny his words, and claim I don't have any idea what he's talking about, but guilt presses down upon my chest, keeping me from saying it. I don't know why I keep fighting to hold my secret. I'm tired of holding it in. I should just let it out and let the chips fall where they may.

"I'm sorry," I whimper, a soft admission.

Smack!

133

My body jolts violently and a strangled cry rips from my lips, my pussy moist with arousal.

"That's not what I asked for, treasure," I hear Lucian say somewhere through my mire of pain. His voice sounds like he's daring me to try to lie to him. And I wonder again why I'm fighting. It feels like he's already won.

I writhe on the bed from the sting of the savage blow he dealt against my ass, my mind a mix of pain, pleasure and confusion. I wait for another blow, but it isn't forthcoming. He's allowing me a moment of recovery, a moment to reflect on his words.

Tell him, my mind screams. *Tell him and let this all be over with!*
Smack! Smack!

Fuck! Tears leak from the corners of my eyes. This is different from the other punishments. There's no pleasure. Red is on the tip of my tongue. But a part of me knows I deserve this. That I *need* this.

Smack!

I suck in a sharp, painful breath, parting my lips to tell him what he wants to hear. *That I'm broken.*

Smack!

The strangled scream that escapes my lips is raw and filled with pain, but I manage to get three words out.

"I'll tell you!"

CHAPTER 19

LUCIAN

*T*he last few hours have been difficult. When the emails came through and Isaac called, I couldn't believe what he'd told me. I saw the records, the charges against her father's brother. Isaac had a timeline of how her life fell apart, the court dates and her parents' divorce. Moving from one house to the next.

I knew she was hiding something. I never expected that though. Never.

How could she not tell me?

I'm crushed by the feeling of insignificance. I feel useless. Or at least to her I was. She didn't tell me because she didn't think I'd make a difference. Isaac's still looking into her ex, but I have no clue if she told him, or anyone else before him. Maybe she wants to keep it a secret. Maybe it wasn't mine to know.

But she's mine. My body heats with guilt for taking her the way I did. I assumed. No, I trusted she was forthcoming. She's my Submissive, and I had no idea about something so crucial to her needs. I still don't know everything. I don't know how this affects what she needs.

I'm going to find out though.

"It's alright, treasure," I whisper softly, cupping her face in my hand and kissing her tears away as I release the cuff from around her wrist. "It took a lot for you to tell me; I'm proud of you."

My voice is soft and comforting as I massage her arm and then release the other wrist. Her eyes are glassed over with tears and shining with insecurity.

"I'm sorry," her voice cracks as she wipes under her eyes.

She has nothing to be sorry about though, this is my fault. It was my responsibility, but I was too eager and too presumptuous.

I grip her hip and pull her closer to me. "Relax, Dahlia," I whisper into her hair as she leans against my chest. "I need you to talk to me, Dahlia."

I hold her close, running my hand down her back in soothing strokes. I knew she was hiding something from me. I could see that she so badly wanted to confide in me, but she didn't.

What I don't know is why. Why hide it? Did she think it was truly unnecessary, and that her past has no bearing on our current relationship? That's possible, and I was hopeful. But her current state begs to differ.

"Tell me, treasure," I say and gently press my lips to her forehead. My words fall into the space between us, "Tell me why you kept this from me."

She stills in my arms. I don't want to push her. Trust takes time, but I want this from her. I need this, or I won't be able to continue the way we were.

I need to know what I'm doing isn't hurting her.

"It doesn't matter."

Her words are hollow and soft. Her voice is chilled with the sadness that's echoed in her body language as she tries to push me away.

I let her. She's not going anywhere. She's stuck in this room with me and she can turn away from me and hide for the moment like she's been doing, but she's not leaving.

She doesn't have to tell me just yet. But I'm not going to let her lie. Not to me, and not to herself.

"It does matter," I say and brace my arm around her body, caging her in slightly and refusing to let her move away any farther. "You don't have to tell me any more than you want, but whatever comes out of your mouth needs to be the truth."

Dahlia hides her face from me, burying herself into the mattress. I'll allow it for a moment. I forced her to open up to me, but I can only push her so much. If she keeps running, it'll force me to break her. She can't hide from me. I won't allow it. Not when it comes to this.

"You aren't broken."

Her eyes whip to mine. Red-rimmed and her cheeks tearstained, even in such distress she looks beautiful. Maybe even more so because of it. "I am," she says and her voice is hard. "I can't..." her voice croaks, and she trails off. "I can't get off..."

Bullshit. I know she's cum for me. I hold in a breath and wait for more.

Her head hangs low and she picks at the comforter, her voice soft as she admits, "I have to feel like I'm being forced."

I keep my expression neutral, but internally I'm breaking, going over every encounter we've had. I can't remember one time where I wasn't rough with her. I knew she enjoyed it, but I didn't consider why. It's a simple preference for me. And I made the assumption that it was for her as well.

I set my hand down on her hip and scoot her a bit closer to me. As I think of what to say, I remember being gentle with her, early in the morning at the end of our first week. She was sore, and I didn't want to hurt her.

I suck in a breath, hating that I have to ask, but already knowing the answer.

"You've only cum for me when I was harsh with you?" She tenses under my embrace, but I continue to hold her.

"Yes," she softly whispers.

I feel sick knowing, hearing her confession. I took pleasure and failed her as a Dom.

"I'm sorry, treasure, I didn't know."

I fell asleep holding her, after causing *that*. Leaving her unsatisfied, but even worse, with a trigger of what happened to her. Completely unaware. I know I'm a selfish man, but I've never felt it quite like I do in this moment.

"It's fine," she says, once again refuting the truth.

"It's not fine," I whisper, shaking my head gently. She doesn't hold my gaze, and her shoulders hunch forward. That never should have happened.

I consider my next words carefully. "Are you happy with not being able to find your release any other way?" I ask her. However she chooses to cope is just that, her choice. But this wouldn't be upsetting her so much if she was happy. I just need to hear her say it.

She shakes her head and looks up at me with pure vulnerability in her eyes. Tears fall down her cheeks. "No, no, I don't want this." I pull her soft body into my chest and hold her while she cries harder than before.

"Have you talked to anyone about this?"

"I have a therapist," she says, wiping under her eyes. I lean across the bed and grab a few tissues for her. She takes them graciously, whispering, "Thank you."

I nod my head. I think a therapist is far better equipped than I am. I'm out of my realm of expertise. I know I can help her. I can train her to find her release. I know I can give her that. I can show her she's capable.

"I'm sorry," she apologizes again, and I don't like it. I don't need her to tell me she's sorry. I need her to tell me she wants me to help. That she believes I can help her.

"Don't be. I'm here for you."

"I can give you what you need," I say quietly.

She nods her head, but she's not really understanding.

"I'm going to show you how deserving you are." Her sad expression stares back at me, she's exhausted and emotional.

And I'm sure she's hungry. One need at a time. I'll take care of her.

"Come, treasure. I need you to clean yourself up for dinner." She sniffles and nods her head, but before she can move off the bed, I wrap my arm around her waist and bring her closer to me.

"First, tell me something."

"What?" she asks warily.

"Anything," I tell her. I just want her to talk to me.

"Anything?"

I nod my head and repeat, "Anything," and kiss the tip of her nose.

She smiles and curls up slightly, leaning next to me and looking across the room.

"I like lemon flavored Italian water ice the best."

A small laugh leaves my lips in a huff. "Lemon?" I say with a smile.

She looks up at me, expectantly. It takes me a moment to realize what she's waiting for. "Cherry. I think I prefer cherry."

"YOU NEED TO HAVE YOUR BRACELET ON," I TELL HER, GRABBING HER wrist and slipping the triple-ringed bracelet on before we can leave. Security knew she was coming while I waited for her. But I don't want to piss them off parading her around without the required membership bracelet. I hold her waist as we walk to the door. She's much better now that I've given her time to get ready. She needs touch though. She's still hurting. I can see it in her eyes.

I lead her out of the room, my hand along her back and it's only then that I realize she's not collared. I can't allow that. I want everyone to know she's mine.

"To the right, treasure," I say and pull her slightly, my fingers slipping around her waist, my thumb brushing easily along her hip and bringing her closer to me as we enter the Club X store, Sex and Submission.

"You need a collar." She smiles slightly and looks up at me as the words hit her. That touch of shyness comes over her as she brushes her hair behind her ear. I love that about her. That sweet bashfulness that she has.

I should have already bought her a collar. From the moment she set foot through those doors, she should have been labeled as mine. I'll have to get her a necklace, too. I always want a symbol of my possession around her neck.

The shop's walls are made of glass and arranged in a way that makes it look as though it's all purposefully arranged decoration. Just like the rest of the club, it shines with luxury.

Dahlia's eyes lock onto the collars on black velvet display stands the moment we enter. There are a variety, but none of them are good enough. She should be draped in gold. Just as she was when I first saw her. I'll get her something temporary for now, but as soon as we're home, I'm buying her one that's deserving of her beauty.

Dahlia walks toward the collars of her own accord and then freezes, looking back at me with frightened eyes. I merely nod and stay by the register.

She gently touches a few collars, but doesn't pick any of them up although she goes back to one three times before she finally settles on it.

It's a simple flat silver band with a single loop at the front, and a lock and key closure.

Knowing she won't be able to take it off once I put it on her sends a thrill I can only partially understand shooting through me.

I'm more than happy she chose one with this type of closure, and I make a mental note to make sure her next collar has the same. I glance at the price tag on the underside before making my way to the register. $15,000. Dahlia seems somewhat uncomfortable behind me, a question on the tip of her tongue, but she doesn't ask it.

"Member ID?" the woman behind the counter asks softly as I pass her the collar.

"Mister 646D," I answer. I could use my name, but I still prefer the anonymity.

"And would you like it now, or shall I box it for you?"

"I'll have it now." I quickly take it, along with the lock and turn to my treasure. She lifts her thick locks up and shivers as I slip the metal collar around her neck. I'm tempted to put the lock in the front, so everyone can see, but I place it on her as it's meant to go and run my hands down her shoulders and kiss her hair before slipping the lock into my pocket.

"All set?" I ask the attendant. They charge my tab rather than requiring cards to be used. It's more convenient this way.

"Yes, sir. I hope you two have a delightful evening."

I can't help but glance at the collar around my treasure's neck as we leave. Her fingers gently touch the silver band.

"Do you like it?" she asks me as we walk through the hallway and to the restaurant for dinner.

"I love it, because it shows them all that you belong to me." Her lips part with a lust-filled gasp, and she reaches for my hand. Before she can pull it away, like she's done so many times before, I snatch it and give her a gentle squeeze before bringing her hand to my lips and kissing the underside of her wrist.

The hallway is empty, and the faint sounds from the playroom diminish the closer we get to the dining hall. Dahlia looks back twice at the sounds of a whip and then again at the sounds of a loud moan.

Her innocence pulls a smirk to my lips.

I nod at Isaac, the first person I see as we walk through the grand entrance and make my way over to him, proudly leading Dahlia toward him. I watch as he takes her in. She's not dressed as she should be. But she wasn't prepared, and I have no intention of taking her to the playroom now. Just dinner, and then home. We'll come back for a show and she can get a taste of what the club has to offer. But only once I know how to help her better. I need to make sure every action aids in her recovery.

Isaac tips his beer at me as we take a seat in his booth. It's in the back of the hall and facing the stage with a good view of everyone else. Working security, he's always chosen seats with ample viewing and easy access to an exit. Some things never change.

Dahlia's quiet as we take our seats and she's so tense, it seems she's not even breathing. "Relax, treasure," I whisper into her ear and gently kiss her cheek.

"How are you enjoying Lucian's company, Dahlia?" Isaac asks, and her eyes widen for a split second, wondering how he knew her name. I have no intention of telling her, so she can continue to wonder.

"I'm..." she pauses, considering her words. "It's better than I ever hoped it would be." There's clear sincerity in her voice, and it fills my chest with a warmth I haven't felt in quite some time. Pride runs through me.

"She's a natural," I say as I gently brush her hair, watching a soft blush rise to her cheeks.

"You got lucky," Isaac says, tipping his beer at me.

"Where's-" Dahlia starts to ask, but then closes her mouth and stares down at the table.

"Where's?" he asks her with a raised brow. She's slow to reach his gaze, and I place my hand on her back.

"You were engaged in conversation, treasure. You can speak your mind."

Isaac's brow furrows as he says, "He's been keeping you sheltered." He takes another swig and then leans across the table, closer to Dahlia. "He's been selfish not to bring you around." A small huff of a laugh leaves Dahlia's lips, and she smiles slightly.

My shoulders tense slightly at the accusation, not because I'm jealous of Isaac, not because the humor is lost on me, but because it's true.

I don't want to be here. I don't want to have to wear a mask. I don't want to hide, and at the same time, I don't want to be watched. I don't trust people. I haven't in years. Most notably because of Tricia.

We came here weekly when we were married. We were known to be a pair. And when our marriage crumbled, I'm ashamed to admit, I was embarrassed to come back.

It took time, and I finally gave it another chance. But it's not the same. I don't feel... welcomed. It's as though they're watching and sizing me up. Wondering why my Submissive left me. Wondering how I failed.

My own insecurities have kept me from bringing my sweet treasure here. But I'm willing to offer her this. I think it will help her. Not only to learn how a true Submissive and Dominant interact, but also to watch various erotic encounters. She needs the experience. I know it will help her.

"Where's your Submissive?" Dahlia asks Isaac as a waitress brings the menus and sets them in front of each of us. The easiness from the other night is finally starting to creep back into Dahlia's demeanor. Dahlia doesn't move to take hers. Good girl. I want to pick for her. I want something divine for her tonight.

"Could I get you anything to drink, sirs?" the waitress asks.

"A whiskey on the rocks for me," I answer easily. The waitress nods her head and then looks back to Isaac.

"I think just a water for now," he says. Club X has a three-drink maximum. Any more and you aren't able to enter the club. Only the dining hall.

"What's your favorite drink?" I lean down and ask Dahlia. The waitress is waiting, and I know she won't write anything down until I agree to whatever it is that Dahlia says.

"My favorite?" she asks, and then hums as she thinks of her answer. "A margarita, but I don't-"

Isaac laughs in his seat, interrupting her and I take the opportunity to tell the waitress, "A margarita, please."

"Frozen, or on ice?" she asks.

I look to my Submissive and she answers the waitress, "Frozen, with salt, please."

"Salt?" Isaac asks, "Is there any other way?"

"Some of my friends like sugar." Isaac makes a face that mirrors my distaste.

"So?" Dahlia looks at Isaac, "your Submissive?"

"I haven't got one," Isaac says with a smile that's plastered on. It's not meant to be there. Isaac has been soft lately. Ever since his last Submissive. He's been unwilling to take another.

"Oh, are you going to..." Dahlia stops talking as we both watch her, waiting for what's next. In my time with her, she's seemed so confident and poised. But she's not in this atmosphere. I need to fix that. Yet one more instance in which I've failed her.

"Buy one?" he asks.

Dahlia nods her head. "Yes, at auction?"

Isaac frowns and shakes his head. "I doubt it. I'm just enjoying the company and helping where I can."

I grunt a laugh. He doesn't want the responsibility anymore. He's missing out, and he knows it. But I can't blame him when I did the same thing.

At least I didn't come here though.

"Oh, how do you help?" Dahlia asks with genuine curiosity.

"Shows and demonstrations."

"Isaac is an expert with the whip." Dahlia shifts slightly at my mention of the whip. And it forces a smirk to my lips.

As the waitress comes and gently sets our drinks down one at a time from a large silver tray, Dahlia's phone rings. Her eyes dart to mine, and I nod slightly.

"I'm sorry."

"Nothing to be sorry for. If I didn't want your phone on, I would have made that clear." I lean closer to her, cupping her chin in my hand. "I think you should be in the habit of listening for your phone though, my sweet treasure." Her face brightens with a beautiful pink as I quickly kiss her lips and release her.

The uneasiness of the day settles against my chest as I lift my whiskey to my lips, the scent filling my lungs. I throw it back, knowing she's not alright. *We* aren't alright. This isn't an easy fix, and I'm going to have to be slow and patient. Two things I've never been very good at.

I lock eyes with Isaac as Dahlia busies herself looking in her purse. Isaac's worked in security for so long and dealt with a number of victims. I'm sure he has an opinion of my sweet treasure. He's a good man, and he hated to tell me what happened to her. I haven't talked to him since earlier, and I can see the questions in his eyes.

I give him an imperceptible nod. I know she's going to be alright. I'll make damn sure of it.

His shoulders relax slightly, and his relief is evident. I wrap my arm around Dahlia's shoulders, consumed by the need to touch her and protect her, my desire just to have her close.

A soft noise from behind us gains Isaac's attention.

"I'll be right back," he says with his eyes on the sweet little thing who just walked into the room, her hand gently settling on the bannister, bracing herself. Her eyes are large and full of shock and wonder. There's no collar around her neck and she's walking aimlessly in the room, searching for where she belongs. Her short jumper looks out of place, further making her stand apart from the crowd. But what captures my attention are the thin silver scars on her back. So thin, they wouldn't be visible if not for the exact placement of the sconces in the dining hall.

I watch as Isaac approaches her and she falls slowly to the floor, never looking him in the eyes. It's obvious she's been trained before. But not by anyone here.

"It's all so overwhelming," Dahlia's soft voice brings me back to her. My sweet treasure. She doesn't belong here, but not because she doesn't fit in. She does, so well. She doesn't belong here because she should be home with me. Healing and working on feeling whole. I hate that I ever acted in a way that contributed to her pain.

No matter what she says, I did.

I took her in a way that resulted in her being in pain. It's unacceptable. I need to make this right. But there are only weeks left.

I need more time.

"You're coming back with me, and I want you to stay with me." I say the words as a command although it toes the line of the freedom I've given her thus far into the contract. I can see her protests in her eyes, although she remains quiet. She's thinking that I think less of her. That I think she's broken. *That I pity her.* But I don't. She's strong and capable, just like she was yesterday. But I can offer her solace. And I want to. I desperately crave to fill those needs that she's ignored.

"I'm your Dom. I need to fix this so you can better serve me." It's easy to make it sound selfish. I am a selfish man. And I'm pushing her. But that's what I'm supposed to do. My role is to push her to her limits. She can handle this. She's strong enough.

She hesitates and looks around the dining hall, as if only now realizing where we are. Her beautiful eyes raise to meet mine and she softly agrees, "Yes, sir."

CHAPTER 20

DAHLIA

I'm your Dom. I need to fix this so you can better serve me.

Sitting at my desk at work, I mindlessly finger the necklace, a gift from Lucian, at my throat. I have emails piling up that I need to respond to, but I can't get my mind off my current dilemma; I think I'm falling for Lucian. I know I shouldn't be, given our complicated pasts, but I feel like he's the first person to ever truly understand me. I'm still in shock that he didn't call off our contract after learning my secret. Or that he didn't shy away from my claims of being broken. It seemed to only make him *more* determined to help me.

I can't believe that he's willing to take on my emotional baggage when he can just walk away and find himself another Sub who doesn't have the same hang-ups. He doesn't have to waste his time with me, he can have any woman he wants. But it shows that he cares. And I want his help. I *need* his help. Even if it makes me seem weak. I don't care.

Still, I'm worried that I'm setting myself up for disappointment. I can feel myself being weak for him. I'm relying on him, and that's something I don't do. I feel there's a good chance Lucian won't be able to help me and I'll end up with an aching heart. To add to my insecurities, last night definitely gave me doubts about our future.

I suck in a heavy breath at the memory.

I'd tried to give Lucian a blowjob when it was time for bed, but he claimed he was tired and needed to sleep. He gently brushed my hair away from my face and told me to lie down. I did as I was told, but I hated it. I wanted to accept him at his word, but I couldn't stop thinking he just didn't want me because of my problem. Because *I'm broken*. It took a lot for me to hold myself together and my self-esteem took a blow. I started to think I wasn't good enough. That *he* thought I wasn't good enough for him. And that he's only trying to help me because he pities me.

I can only hope that it's all in my head.

Breaking out of my dark thoughts, I let out a soft sigh of frustration as I look at the tons of emails on my computer screen. *I'm never gonna get any work done.*

Trying to push my situation from my mind, I begin to go about answering emails, starting with the most important ones first. By midday I'm halfway through my workload and I've taken a break to type a message to my therapist when Carla nearly breaks her neck bursting into my office. She's holding a newspaper clutched to her chest, her expression animated and excited. As usual, she's dressed stylishly today in a black pantsuit and cream camisole peeking out from underneath, her hair pulled back into a single braid, bangs covering her forehead, rosy rouge coloring her cheeks and purple shadow frosting her eyelids.

She shakes the paper at me, her chest heaving violently, making me think she's sprinted all the way up to my office without pausing to take a breath. "You will not believe what's on the front page of the Daily Observer!" she gasps.

My curiosity piqued, I quickly close out the email that I was typing to my therapist about making an appointment so that Carla doesn't see. I don't need her thinking I'm broken, too.

"What's that?" I ask, standing up to take the paper from Carla. I'm trying to be my normal self, but I just don't have the peppy outlook I usually do. I'm tired, and my spirits are dampened.

"Just look at it!" wheezes Carla.

I snatch the paper from her hands and flip it around to the first page. A jolt of shock runs through me as my gaze settles on the page

LAUREN LANDISH & WILLOW WINTERS

and I let out a soft gasp, my eyes going wide. The headline in bold takes my breath away.

Hot, Eligible CEO Bachelor's new fling!

It's a picture of me and Lucian on the night we had dinner at the restaurant, embracing and engaged in a heated kiss. Lucian's hand is on my ass, and my arms are wrapped around his neck. My heart pounds. I know right when it was taken. I remember that moment like it happened only a minute ago.

"Crazy, huh?" Carla breathes next to my ear as she looks at the picture with me, causing me to jump. I was so engrossed with the picture that I forgot that she was even there. "Where the hell were you two at?"

I'm unable to respond, my eyes glued to the picture. A surge of powerful emotion runs through me. I can't get over how much we look like a couple. Even though it was all supposed to be for show it almost looks... real. Like we really are in love.

My heart does a flip at the thought and I go weak in the knees, confirming what I felt earlier; I'm falling for Lucian. It scares the hell out of me. This, what we have, is fragile. It all hinges upon the fact he wants to *fix* me. But what happens when he decides I'm not worth the trouble? Or when my contract is up in nine days? My lips draw down into a frown as emotion threatens to overwhelm me.

And what will Lucian think about this? My blood spikes with anxiety. I can't even begin to think of his reaction. I try to swallow, but it feels like my heart is shoved up my throat and trying to get away from me.

Carla stares at me, noticing my conflicted expression. "What's wrong?" she asks me, placing her hand on my arm with concern. "Why aren't you happy?"

I set the paper down on my desk and turn to her, parting my lips to say something, but then feel a lump the size of a golf ball fill my throat, staying my words. I don't know what's wrong with me. I just want this to be as real as this picture looks. I want that more than anything.

"Dah?" Carla says, coming in closer. "Is something wrong? Did Lucian do something to you?"

"No," I say, my voice thick with emotion. "Not at all." It would be far easier to just tell her my dilemma and not have her guessing at what's wrong, but I can't bring myself to do it. I don't want to risk telling her and being crushed that she doesn't understand.

Carla places both her hands on my shoulders and gazes into my eyes. "What is it then, huh? You can tell me."

No I can't.

The lump is growing bigger. And I don't know why. Everything is happening so fast, and I don't know what to do. Just days ago, I was happy to have finally found someone who could get me off, but now he knows my secret and I think I'm falling for him. Fuck.

Tears well up into my eyes, and I feel like any moment I'm gonna start choking on them.

Seeing the anguish on my face, Carla pulls me into a tight embrace. "C'mere, girl." She begins patting on my back, not knowing she's making things worse. "Whatever's the matter, it's going to be okay. I'm here for you."

My throat constricted with emotion, I'm unable to say a word, and can only manage to think my response.

Oh Carla, if only you knew.

CHAPTER 21

LUCIAN

*T*he minute I get into the door, I make a beeline for the playroom. I can't wait to see her. I'm ready for training to really begin. I drop the keys on the foyer table, making a loud clinking sound, and start undressing, leaving the jacket on the floor as I make my way to the stairs. I loosen my tie and pull it off as I push open the door, revealing my treasure.

She's still, and in the exact position she should be in. The sight of her gorgeous curves and bared pussy makes my dick that much harder. She stirs slightly when she hears me walk in. I close the door gently, but I'm not nearly as quiet as I have been.

She rights herself instantly and goes motionless.

I know exactly what to do with my treasure. I strip down to my slacks as I make my way to the dresser. It's filled with a variety of gear and toys. I have to open three drawers before I get to the one I need. I look over my shoulder and Dahlia is perfectly still, exactly how she should be. There are a few vibrators in this drawer, in all sorts of sizes. A large wand with a round head making it resemble a microphone in its build, bullet vibrators, butt plug vibrators, an egg with a remote. There's something for every mood and whim. A rough hum comes up my throat as I take each one in.

"Good girl, treasure," I say as I place my hands on the edge of the drawer. "How was your day?"

She answers as I keep my back to her while I debate on which one I should choose. "It went well, sir." Her voice is so soft I can barely hear her. "And yours?"

"Speak up."

"And yours?" she repeats herself. I settle on the wand.

"Draining and unfulfilling up until now," I say as I shut the drawer with the wand in my right hand.

"On your back," I give the command as I shove my pants down and kick them off beside the bed. Dahlia's quick to turn on her back. Her breathing is coming in a little quicker now. Her eyes stare at the ceiling, and her arms lay at her side.

"Look at me," I tell her. "I want to see you when I talk to you."

"Yes, sir." A trail of goosebumps runs down her front as she answers me, pebbling her pale rose nipples. It takes a lot of restraint not to suck them into my mouth. But I refrain. She needs this first.

"We're going to work on what excites you, Dahlia. I'm going to train you and your body, condition you really. I'm going to make you desire me in any way you can have me."

I crawl closer to her and tap on her inner thigh for her to spread her legs, which she obeys immediately.

"I want you to tell me about your fantasies, Dahlia." Her eyes widen, and her body stiffens as I run the tips of my fingers from her clit down to her opening. She's soaking wet. Fuck, the very sight of her makes me want to take her. I'm dying to be inside of her hot pussy, but I have to wait.

Her breathing gets heavy, and she licks her lips. "I can do that."

I run the tip of the wand through her folds. She sucks in a breath of air from the chill of the steel. "You're going to tell me all your fantasies, Dahlia." I turn on the vibrator as it hits her opening. Dahlia's eyes close, and her lips part slightly. She doesn't move though, she knows better than to move. I slowly work it up to her clit, watching her face and her body for her reactions. I want to know exactly where that sweet spot is. Her thighs twitch, and her back arches slightly as I reach the underside of her throbbing clit. *Bingo*.

"But none of the ones you're thinking." I continue my path over and around her clit and then back down. I can see how much she's resisting the need to writhe with pleasure. If I have to, I'll restrain her, but I don't think I'll need to.

"So tell me your fantasies," I say easily, getting comfortable in my position and knowing this may take a while.

"Any?" she asks me.

I shrug and say, "You can. You'll see what they reward you."

She takes in a sharp inhale as I round the sensitive spot and then she starts, "I dream about being alone at night." Her voice is soft and husky. A blush brings color to her chest and face.

"There's a man behind me. I can hear him, but I'm too afraid to turn around so I walk faster, but he catches me." Her breathing comes in quicker, and her body tenses as the vibrator comes closer to where it needs to please.

"He pins me to the brick wall of an alley," her voice goes tight with need, and her thighs tremble as I hold the wand in place.

"Who is this man?" I ask her, my dick hard with need.

"No one, a stranger, I don't know," she answers quickly.

She whimpers when I pull the wand away and leave her on edge. The hum fills the room as her eyes snap open and she stares at me with hurt in her eyes.

"Let's try a different one," I tell her. Her mouth falls open, and she swallows thickly as she realizes what I'm doing. She closes her eyes and nods.

Her throat is hoarse as she slowly says, "I... I dream about being on a date." Her forehead is pinched, and I know she's lying.

I pull the vibrator away and she doesn't even look at me. "Don't lie to me, treasure. Next time I'll punish you."

"I'm sorry," she says weakly.

"Maybe I should tell you a story?" I offer, "and you can finish it?"

"Yes please, sir."

"I dream about taking a beautiful girl and locking her in my office at work." Dahlia's eyes snap open, and she looks back at me with a questioning gaze. "She stays under the desk as I sit at my chair."

"Do you think this could be your fantasy?" I ask her.

She nods her head, shifting slightly on the bed. I quicken the pace of the vibrator as she starts her story.

"I wait for you on my knees." She bites down on her lip and then looks back at me. "You take your cock out as you sit down and stroke it. A bead of precum starts to drip," her voice goes a little higher as I put the vibrator to the underside of her clit and hold it there. She struggles to stay still as she continues her story. "I lick it. You moan," her head thrashes to the side. "So sexy when you moan like that." I ease off the pressure and massage circles around her clit. "You love it when I take you in deep. Your hands fist in my hair." Her breathing picks up as I put the vibrator onto her most sensitive spot. Her face scrunches, and her mouth opens wide.

"Keep going, or I'll stop."

Her fingers dig into the mattress as she continues. "You shove your cock down my throat. You push me up and down your dick. I can feel you all the way at the back of my throat!" Her upper body lifts off the bed as she screams out, close to her release.

My dick twitches with the need to give her what she needs, but I can't. Not yet.

"And then I pull out of your mouth." I continue with the story, letting her concentrate on controlling her body. Her breathing comes in harsh pants. "I pull you up, grabbing the hair at the base of your skull."

Her mouth makes a perfect "O" and her body tenses, her neck arches. "And I kiss you. I take your lips with my own," her body trembles and I capture her screams of pleasure as her orgasm crashes through her body. My tongue tangles with hers and I eagerly climb between her legs, shoving my dick into her hot cunt.

Her back bows, and she breaks our heated kiss to scream out into the hot air between us. I buck my hips, slamming ruthlessly into her and riding through her orgasm.

I stare into her eyes, knowing I want that with her. That fantasy. I need it in my life.

I pick up my pace, already feeling my orgasm approaching and watch as the realization of what's just happened crosses her eyes.

I almost say words I don't mean. I'm just caught in the moment. But as she cups the back of my head and crushes her lips against mine, I lose control of everything. I kiss her back with a passion I thought I once knew and I bury myself to the hilt, spilling my cum deep inside of her tight walls.

As the waves of pleasure wrack through me, I ignore the thoughts creeping in. I see her beautiful eyes shining with devotion, and I close my own, wanting to deny what's clearly between us. Our ragged breath mingles as I stare at the nightstand and try to pull myself together.

I purchased her as a distraction. That's all this is. Even as I brace my body on top of hers and catch my breath while she softly kisses my neck, I ignore the feelings creeping into the crevices of my mind.

CHAPTER 22

DAHLIA

"*I* came for the first time ever without having to think about being forced," I confess to Carla while chewing on a salty french fry, and gazing out into the beautiful skyline through the floor-to-ceiling windows. We're sitting in Explicit Designs' famed cafeteria, enjoying lunch together. Ravenous for once, I'm enjoying a big fat cheeseburger, fries and a vanilla shake, while Carla is having the same thing, except her shake is milk chocolate.

I've finally told Carla about Lucian's habits in bed, though I don't think I've had much choice in the matter.

For the past few days, Carla has hounded me about the details of my relationship with Lucian and I've finally given in to her incessant prying. Mainly because I so badly want to share my dilemma with someone who understands where I'm coming from. I've kept the details to the bare minimum, keeping it casual and not divulging how my world has been completely shaken up. I still feel like I can lean on her though. Like I can trust her and share this little piece of myself with her. Even if she doesn't realize just how much it means to me.

Taking a sip of her shake, Carla chuckles, her eyes alight with mischief. She looks absolutely lovely today sporting a ruby red dress, the hem coming just above her knees and showing off her nice calves, her hair pulled back into a ponytail with a curl on the end, and her nails painted the same color as her dress. Red pumps adorn her feet, and I think she'd give even the most seasoned fashion model a run for her money with how much she's working that outfit. She sure is a vision in red, let me tell you. "So what's so bad about that?"

I shake my head, biting into another fry and doing a little shrug. "I don't know. Don't you think it's weird that I couldn't get off without fantasizing about that before?"

Carla waves a fry at my face as she swallows down a huge gulp of her shake. "Hell no. That's why we're Subs. We like it kinky... and rough. I can see how someone can find it hard to get off without that fantasy." She makes a face. "It's not something that's a problem for me, but I definitely can relate."

The way she's acting makes me want to tell her about the rape, but I fight down the urge.

I've gone this long without telling her, I think to myself, *there's no reason to tell her now. Besides, she just accepts that's it's a fantasy, and that's all she needs to know.*

Carla lets out a little evil chuckle, pulling me out of my thoughts. "Although... Lucian must be a real grandmaster in the bedroom to make you cum without that fantasy."

Lucian.

The very thought of him fills me with hope. And despair.

For the first time ever, I'd cum without the fantasy of being raped. I'm still in shock. It's amazing when I think about it. No one had ever been able to do it. Not even when I've touched myself.

And yet, I still don't know what's going to happen between us. I still don't know if I'll be able to get there continuously without that fantasy. I'm nervous and apprehensive and hopeful, all at once. I'm just a mess.

Carla is smiling at me, mistaking my quietness for something else. "Look at you!" She lets out a little chirp. "I think you're in love."

My mind snaps back to the present, and I focus on Carla's face, wanting to deny it. But I can't; she's right. I'm falling in love with Lucian. But I'm doubting our relationship will ever be anything more than what it is--a contract for sex. And it hurts. "No I'm not," I lie.

Carla laughs at me. "Don't lie to me, Dah. I totally see it in you.

The way you look when you talk about him, how you've been acting this past month. Your feelings definitely go beyond the boundaries of a Sub and her Dom. I should know, since the same thing happened to me." She waves her hand at my face as if she's fanning me 'cause I'm burning up. "Face it, Dah, you're done for."

"And you're totally dumb," I growl, causing her to laugh. "Seriously though, I don't know what's going on with us. You know when my contract is up, he can just find a new Sub, right?" A heavy weight presses down on my chest. That's exactly what I keep thinking is going to happen. That he's going to get tired of trying to heal me. Get tired of me being *broken.*

Carla frowns, put off by my pessimistic attitude. She finishes her chocolate milkshake and tosses the cup in the trash. It's ten past one. Our lunch break is over. "Don't say that, Dah. You have to have hope that things will turn out right."

That's the thing, I tell myself, as I finish off my burger and then get up to toss the rest of my meal in the trash, *I don't want to give myself a sense of false hope.*

I SPEND THE REST OF THE DAY GOING OVER EMAILS AND FASHION designs in my office, ignoring everything and just focusing on work. I'm just about to close up and head down to the first floor to await my drive over to Lucian's when I receive an unexpected call.

"Hello?" I answered in a guarded voice.

"Dah!" my mother's raspy voice greets me with more pep than I remember. With how scratchy her voice is, I can tell she's been hitting the cigs pretty hard lately, probably up to several packs a day. "Hey honey, how have you been?"

This is the first time in recent memory that I've been ecstatic that my mother's called me. I haven't heard from her in so long, her voice is like music to my ears. It should piss me off that I'm just now hearing from her, but I'm so happy to have someone to talk to. Maybe I can even get the courage to talk to her. She doesn't know about my issues, but I could tell her about Lucian, even if it's not real. I could tell her about the paper and that I'm in a relationship. I want to. I'm dying to talk about it. I don't know why, but I just need to talk to her. "Hey Mom!" I greet her cheerfully, "I've been alright, how have you been?"

"Good, good. I'm glad you're doing okay, honey. I've been worried about you."

I smile. Mom seems like she's called me with genuine concern. I open my mouth to start telling her about my situation, when she cuts me off with, "I got your text." Her voice has dropped several octaves, signaling that her mood has shifted. "I can't really help out in the money department right now," she finishes.

If it weren't so sad, I'd laugh. Figures she'd call when I most likely won't need the help. I part my lips to tell her I should be set for a pretty good while, but then close them, realizing it's probably not wise. I shouldn't tell her about the money, which I haven't received yet. Knowing my luck, she'd try to ask me for some, claiming I owed her a cut for birthing me into this world. And that money is just enough to pay off all my debt. Every cent of it. After taxes I'll have a little left over while I'm waiting to start a real job, something that'll actually pay me. "That's alright, Mom. I worked things out with the school and everything will be fine."

"Oh honey, I'm so happy for you," Mom says, zero happiness in her voice. "I'm so glad you were able to fix things, I really hated having to turn you down."

I want to say something nice in return, but I can't find the words. She really doesn't give me much to work with.

The call goes silent except for the atmospheric static.

"I'm going to see Todd for Christmas," Mom announces when the silence stretches past fifteen seconds.

I perk up at the news. Even though I'm upset with her, I would love to see her. So much has gone on in my life since we last talked, it would be nice to enjoy each other's company. And I still haven't met Todd. I'd like to though. It seems like this must be serious between them.

"Do you want me to come, too?" I ask. In the back of my mind, I'm thinking about Lucian. Our thirty days will be over soon. My heart hurts thinking we could be over, too. Even if we aren't, I don't know if he'd want me around. After all, I'm his Sub. I have to keep reminding myself that.

And he has his own family, I tell myself, remembering the sister he's mentioned to me that he cares so much about, even though he hates his parents. It's something else we have in common. He feels like his parents have done him wrong and I feel likewise, and we both have such screwed-up pasts, though I'd argue mine is a bit more screwed-up than his. Well maybe not more, but different. I almost huff at a humorless chuckle at the thought. Still, Lucian's past gives him special insight on my problem, helps him understand me. He knows what it feels like to be hurt by someone who claims to love you, to be betrayed by the very people you trust.

I hear my mother suck in a breath, bringing me back to the present moment, followed by a long pause. "I don't think Todd wants anyone else coming," she finally admits.

I sit there numbly, letting her words sink in. Why am I not surprised? I should've known better than to ask a question like that. At least she told me ahead of time. For Thanksgiving she told me she was spending it with Todd only a few weeks in advance, too. But that's Thanksgiving, not Christmas. There's a big difference. At least to me there is.

"Oh, that's okay," I say evenly. *I'm not going to break down over this. I'm not going to break down over this.* I have to repeat it over and over in my head.

"I'm really sorry, honey." Surprisingly, I detect faint emotion in her voice. I ignore it, along with my own emotions threatening to consume me.

"It's okay, really. I understand." My voice is even, practically robotic.

"I'll talk to you soon, okay? I have a plane to catch."

"Yeah." Before I can get in another word I hear the line go dead. *Click.*

I sit there for a moment, staring at my desk, feeling empty inside. If I could've gotten over leaving Lucian for a while, this would've been the perfect time for Mom and I to bond, for her to listen to me and give me advice on my problems. But that was a fool's fantasy.

She hasn't been here for me for so long, and she's not about to start now. I need to get over it and let her come to me when she's ready.

For now, I'll just stay at my apartment for Christmas.

Alone.

Gathering my things, I walk out of my office and head down to the first floor, feeling the unhappiest that I've felt in a while.

CHAPTER 23

LUCIAN

She's late. I came in, and somehow I already knew. When I opened the door and saw the empty bed, my breathing slowed, my blood cooled. Anger wasn't there, but fear was.

She's left me. I'm still standing in the doorway, trying to convince myself that I'm wrong. I know I am. I *paid* for her. She can't leave me. My heart thuds once. She doesn't care about the money. She never has. Not once has she mentioned it. But still. She's not leaving me. My own insecurities are creeping in, and I shove them away.

She's mine. I can take care of her. I am taking care of her. I nod my head and turn from the room.

I let it resonate through me. She's coming. She'll be here. I calm my racing heart and slowly close the door with a gentle click. My palm presses against my pocket, but it's empty. I clear my throat and make my way toward the stairs with a hard expression, devoid of all emotion. I left my phone on the foyer table, but I don't need it. As I hit the last step, I hear the keypad rejecting an entry.

My treasure. I imagine she's panicking in this moment. As I walk to the door, my phone goes off. I stare at it, my hand hovering on the doorknob, but it doesn't matter what her excuse is. She's late.

I open the door, my expression stern and her body jolts some. Her breathing is coming in quick as she takes a half step back.

"Lucian, I-"

"Sir," I correct her with a hard voice. My grip on the door tightens as she stares back at me with her mouth slightly opened. The lines are blurred, and that's obvious. But I'm still her Dom, and she's late and she's hesitating.

I open the door wider and she walks in quickly with her head down. "Thank you, sir," she says uneasily.

I should take her upstairs, but I can't wait. I need her now.

My fingers deftly unbuckle my belt as I walk to the living room. I stand by the sofa and wait for her eyes to reach mine as I pull the belt from the loops. "Strip and bend over," I give her the command and lust covers her expression. She's quick to do exactly what I tell her.

Every second that passes my blood gets hotter, my cock harder. Her heels slip off her feet as she shoves her dress down. She doesn't hesitate to bare herself to me and bend over the arm of the mahogany leather sofa. She has to balance herself on her toes as her upper body lays flat on the cushion. Her hair fans around her and she looks back at me, the perfect picture of obedience.

My dick pushes against my zipper as I fold the belt in my hand. I run it along her spine and trail it slowly down to her ass. Her eyes close, and she lets out a mix of a whimper and a moan.

"Why are you being punished?" I ask her.

"For being late, for addressing you incorrectly, and for disappointing you and forgetting my place, sir." I close my eyes behind her and let my head fall back.

Perfection.

She's so fucking perfect. I pull back my arm and quickly lash the belt across her ass. It hits her with a loud *smack!* and she lets out a small scream as her hands ball into fists in an attempt not to cum.

"Count them, treasure," I say calmly.

"One, sir," she says loudly.

Smack! I aim just below the soft curve of her ass on her upper thighs. I pull back the blow slightly, knowing it'll be more tender.

"Two!" she yells with her face scrunched up, but her pussy clenches and her mouth opens with desire.

Smack!

"Three," she whimpers.

This one is higher, in a fresh spot and she pushes her ass up to meet the blow. I steady my hand on her lower back to remind her. She needs to be still. The belt whips through the air. *Smack!*

"Four, sir." Four is good. Four is more than enough. She writhes slightly and bites down on her lip.

I drop my belt to the floor, the buckle making a loud clank, and gentle my hands over the marks on her ass. The red lines are slightly raised, and Dahlia seethes in a breath as I press my hand against the hot marks. She presses her ass into my touch and struggles to keep her body from squirming with pleasure. I've administered the perfect amount of pain to give her the endorphin rush she needs.

I eye them carefully, making sure they won't bruise and there are no cuts. Just four parallel red lines.

I lean forward, my hard dick nestled in her pussy, the fabric of my pants separating our hot skin. I graze my teeth along her naked shoulder and nip her earlobe. My hand travels along her waist, her stomach, up to her lush breasts and I squeeze gently and then pinch her nipple as I kiss her lips. Her mouth opens as I pull slightly, my other hand traveling to her soaking wet pussy.

"Thank me for your punishment, treasure," I say with a calmness I don't feel.

"Thank you, sir," she whimpers, struggling to stay still as I rub her swollen clit and pull on her nipple until it slips from my grip.

The need to punish her pussy and command her body is riding me hard, my thick cock pushing against my zipper as I watch her glistening sex clench around nothing.

I don't know what to do. We both want this, I know that much. But I don't know if it's detrimental to what we're working toward.

She can see my hesitation and her soft eyes flicker with self-doubt. I hate it. I won't allow it. My shortcomings won't cause her pain.

"Is this what you want, treasure?" I ask her in a hard voice, shoving my pants down and stroking my dick. I push her back down and she gasps. Her breathing is coming in ragged pants as she hesitantly looks back at me.

I line my dick up with her hot opening and slam into her. Her tight walls force a rough grunt from my lips as I pound into her mercilessly over and over again.

I push her face down into the cushions and fuck her at an angle that goes deeper than I ever have before. The sofa muffles her screams as I drill into her tight cunt, throwing my head back and groaning at how fucking good she feels.

My toes curl into the carpet as I thrust my hips harder and harder. The sofa shudders each time, and I have to lean forward to keep the heavy furniture from moving too much. Her hips dig into the sofa and her toes come off the floor as I lose control, slamming recklessly into her, loving how her nails scratch against the leather sofa.

Her body tenses and I know she's close, and that's when I lose focus. Thinking about her. About her pleasure. About her pain. I try to shake the thoughts away, rutting between her legs with a primal need, but I can't shut them out.

Her pussy spasms on my dick and she feels so fucking good, but my mind is racing with the knowledge of why she's just gotten off. Her past and her struggles corrupt every bit of pleasure in my being as she screams out my name.

I can't. I can't get off on this.

I pull away from her, still hard and slipping out, letting her fall limp and sated on the couch, her orgasm still running through her body and making her thighs tremble. She pulls her knees into her chest and tries to calm her breathing as I walk away.

I breathe in deep, running my hand over my face and trying to think. My head is fucked up, and I feel lost. I question taking her like that.

I pace the floor, not knowing how to handle what I've just done. I don't know what's best for her.

The moment she realizes I'm still hard and that I'm not able to cum this way, not knowing why she needs this, her face crumples and she covers her mouth as she's wracked with sobs.

"Treasure," I whisper her name, my heart sinking into my hollow chest. She shakes her head and tries to push me away.

"You don't want me," she says.

I grip her chin firmly and wait for her to look me in the eyes. "I want you. Don't you ever think or say anything differently."

She swallows the lump in her throat. "You couldn't cum," she says just above a murmur.

I don't know how to answer her. "You don't want me like that anymore."

"I fucking love you like that. I love fucking you raw and hard and forcing your pleasure." Her bright eyes finally meet mine again. "Don't think that I don't. I want you every way I can have you. I just... couldn't, knowing."

Her eyes fall, and I hate that I did this to her. I wish I was a stronger man. I wish I had all the answers.

I hook her chin with my finger and bring her lips to mine for a sweet, chaste kiss. But she doesn't return it. Her lips are hard, and her heart's not in it.

"I want you, treasure. I still want you." She needs to believe me. I had a single moment of weakness and doubt. I shouldn't have. But I did.

I brush her tears away with the rough pad of my thumb, hating that I hurt her this way. I can see the regret in her eyes as she takes in a staggering breath and pushes the hair away from her hot face. Her cheeks are red and her eyes are glassed over, and she won't look at me.

I fucking hate it.

I grab her chin in my hand and I force her to kiss me. I crush my lips to hers, my tongue diving into her mouth and massaging against hers. Her small hands grab my shoulders and she kisses me back with just as much force and just as much passion.

I lie on the sofa, pulling her on top of me and gently sliding inside of her hot pussy, still slick with her arousal and cum. I grip her hips tightly and thrust my hips to fuck her with a slow pace. Each thrust is hard and deep, forcing small gasps from her. She places her hands on my chest as I slowly lie flat and continue to fuck her, while she meets me thrust for thrust.

Her tight walls stroke my dick causing a numbing pleasure to grow in the tips of my fingers and toes. I hold my breath as I pick up my pace and pull her down closer to me. Kissing her quickly with a bruising force as I fuck her harder and faster. All the while holding her close to me, where she belongs.

As I close my eyes, letting the pleasure wrack through me, I roughly rub her clit over and over, trying to force her over the edge with me. Hot thick streams of cum fill her and leak between us. Her body is tense and on edge, but when I open my eyes, I can see why she hadn't cum.

She's crying. Her face is buried in the crook of my neck.

My heart shatters as I pull her away enough to see her face and kiss her sweetly.

"Treasure?" I can barely breathe, "Did I hurt you?" My heart thumps slowly as I wait for her to answer. She shakes her head, but she won't look at me. Her inhale is long and shaky.

"I couldn't. I started to think-" a sob is ripped from her throat and she falls into my chest. "I'm sorry, Lucian."

"Shh," I kiss her hair and hold her close.

"I don't want to have to think like that anymore." Her tears fall into my shoulder as I rub her back.

"It's alright, treasure. It's going to be alright."

I hold her as she calms herself, rocking her back and forth and kissing her over and over. My heart clenches with each small sob, but I'm here for her.

I kiss her forehead, breathless and consumed with conflicting emotions. The overriding thought being whether or not I deserve her, whether I'm even worthy of being her Dom. But I want to be. I want to heal her. I *will* heal her. I'll find a way. I lift her small body in my arms, cradling her to my chest. She lays her cheek on my shoulder, neither of us saying anything as I carry her to bed.

CHAPTER 24

DAHLIA

*P*lacing a hand over my eyes, I wince as I lower myself down on the pure white sofa, a throbbing pain pulsing my ass. It hurts like hell. But I still love it. It always reminds me of Lucian, of his dominance. It gives me something to cling to, allows me to momentarily ignore my confused emotions. Yet that lost feeling returns as I sink into the couch.

Which is why I've come to see my therapist. Doctor Sandra Andrews.

She's seated cross-legged across from me, in an oversized tufted leather chair, dressed in a white blouse and blue silk slacks, the outfit complementing the room's pale blue carpet and cream-colored walls, a notepad and pen in her hand. For a therapist, she seems young, but that's one of the reasons I like her so much. She possesses a wisdom that's beyond her years, and through the year she's given me sound advice that I've found to always be on point.

Sandra's gazing at me with concern. Her gentle eyes regard me from behind eyeglasses with thin metal frames. "It's been quite some time since you've checked in, Dahlia," Sandra remarks softly, her smooth voice soothing my ears and calming my anxiety.

"I know," I reply in a soft sigh, my voice sounding small. I clear my throat, feeling slightly nervous, pulling my knees into my chest, wincing slightly as pain pulses my ass. My bare feet sit on the sofa, brushing against the chenille fabric. No shoes is a rule Dr. Andrews has. I guess it keeps the area cleaner, but even more than that, it's supposed to make you more relaxed. I pick at the bit of nail polish on my toenails as a sigh leaves me.

"Are you alright?" she asks, seeing my distress.

I huff a small laugh, resting my chin on my knees and looking up at her. "My Dom punished me with a belt last night." I'm shocked at how easy the words come out. As if it's normal. As if *I'm* normal.

Shifting in her seat, Sandra takes off her glasses. Her brows are pinched as she taps them against her lip. "And how did that make you feel?"

I almost chuckle at how much like a stereotypical therapist she sounds. But I don't have any humor in me. I push my hair out of my face and consider her question. It made me feel alive. And wanted. But that ended far too quickly. Too good to last.

It takes Sandra a moment to realize what caused my reaction, the faint huff of a laugh at her question, and when she does, she sets her glasses down on the end table and shakes her head. "I'm sorry, Dahlia, you've simply caught me a little off guard. Would you mind expanding for me please? I'm not sure what you mean by 'your Dom.'"

It's time to just let it all out. *Let it flow.*

I suck in a deep breath, feeling that oppressive weight on my chest. Slowly, I exhale and begin to tell her everything about Lucian, except I leave out the part about the auction. I know there's doctor-patient confidentiality, but I don't feel comfortable telling her. I don't want to. Sandra listens to me intently while I weave my tale, almost frozen like a statue, her soft eyes compassionate.

"Okay," I say, letting out a soft sigh. I debate on how much information to give her. Our names are in the paper, but I still feel uncomfortable saying his last name. "As you know, I've never been able to get off without fantasizing about being… raped." I swallow thickly as a surge of shame, guilt and worthlessness threatens to overwhelm me, but I squeeze myself tight, warding it off. "But I finally met someone who I felt could help me. Lucian."

"And this man is your Dom?" she asks.

I nod my head, and continue as she jots down notes. "All I had to do was be his Sub and let him take control, and the rest would come naturally." I look over at Sandra, wondering if she knows enough about BDSM to be familiar with what I'm talking about.

Sandra's very still, but she doesn't look confused, her eyes assessing me inquisitively. "By 'his Sub,' you mean his Submissive?"

So she does know a little something.

I nod my head.

"I see," she says softly, doing a little gesture and then scribbling something on her notepad, "Go on."

I gulp down the lump forming with my throat. "When I became his Sub," I shake my head, my chest feeling increasingly tight, "I finally felt like I was in control, knowing I could stop my fantasy any time I wanted. I could safe word him and it would all stop. I had that power." I sniff, tears burning my eyes. "But at the same time, Lucian had no idea how messed up I was, and he was unknowingly giving me what I thought I needed. Until..." The tears threaten to spill down my face and Sandra reaches for a Kleenex on the decorative stand beside her chair, but I gesture for her to stop. I'm trying to be strong.

"Until?"

"Until he forced my secret out of me," I sigh, my voice a whisper thick with emotion. "I'd been trying to hide it from him from the start, but he knew something wasn't right with me." *Even he could tell I was broken.*

"And what happened next?" Sandra asks.

"He said he could help me." I breathe the words, closing my eyes and remembering. "I was really shocked." I look back at Sandra, and she's nodding. "Up until that point, no one's really understood. My exes sure as hell didn't."

"So, that must've been really encouraging for you then," Sandra remarks. "Knowing that you found someone that not only understood you, but was willing to help you."

God. This lump is growing so big I'm going to choke on it. "Yes," I say and nod my head. "But I didn't really believe it, like, I didn't believe that it would end up working... but then Lucian made me cum for the first time ever without the need of that fantasy." I swallow thickly, feeling like I can't breathe, hoping like hell I can hold it together.

Sandra places the notepad on her lap, her expression brightening, not realizing how I'm about to fall apart. "Why, that's wonderful news, Dahlia." She shakes her head. "That must have been really gratifying, and reassuring. Did that finally give you hope for yourself?'

I close my eyes, feeling a sharp pain pierce my chest, and nod. "It did... for a very short time. And even then, I doubted it. I thought it was a fluke. But then..." I suck in a breath that feels like it's filled with little daggers.

Sandra peers at me intently. "But then?"

I exhale sharply. "Lucian wasn't able to climax when he was being rough with me, which is how I want him to be with me and it totally," I gulp, "killed what little confidence I had in our relationship. In that moment, I felt like he was disgusted by me."

Sandra's face morphs into a frown. "I'm so sorry, Dahlia." She puts her glasses back on and scribbles in her notepad as she asks, "Did he say why he wasn't able?"

I shake my head no as I answer, "We had sex again, right after that... when he could see I was upset."

"And how did that go?" she asks.

I lean my head back against the sofa and stare at the ceiling. He made love to me, he came and I didn't. Because I'm fucked up and broken. "Not good. He came, but he wasn't rough and so I didn't." My head falls forward and I wait for the doctor's judgment. I just want a solution. I want to be normal.

I'm trying my best not to cry, because I know if I do, this session is over. I won't be able to recover.

"I'm broken," I say just beneath my breath. I could feel something so strong between us, something I've never felt before. But I couldn't give it back to him. I couldn't make love to him. It's so fucked up. It just hurts.

Sandra shakes her head. "No you're not. The progress you made shows that you can recover from this. You *will* recover from this." She gestures at me, her words firm and commanding. "You are a beautiful, talented young woman who's had horrible things happen to her... but that doesn't mean you can't recover, that you can't go on to live a fulfilling normal life." Slightly leaning forward, Sandra's words gain passion as she speaks, so much so that I momentarily forget my pain and focus on her face. After letting her words sink in, she relaxes back into her seat and picks up her notepad. "Now tell me, what's good about your relationship outside of the Submissive and Dom roles?"

"Oh," I say, crossing my arms around my torso and clutching myself. I feel so chilly even though it must be seventy-five degrees in this office. "It's... it's really good at times, although it's new and I feel like it's going so fast. He's quiet a lot and it takes some time for him to open up." Sandra nods her head, jotting down notes as I talk.

"He treats me... like... like I mean a lot to him." I finally look her in the eyes. "I know he wants to make me happy."

"And does he?" she asks me.

"Yeah," I say and nod my head. He makes me so happy. "It's so much more than..." my voice trails off. The pain is back again.

"Is it not a relationship beyond the Dominant and Submissive roles?" Sandra presses gently.

"I don't know what to think of it all. I'm confused about where we stand in our relationship. This was supposed to be an..." I fumble for words, not wanting to tell her about the auction. "A temporary arrangement, not something that would turn into anything longlasting. And after that last session..." I shake my head as a surge of emotion chokes my speech. "I don't think we'll ever be able to get past my issues, so all the other aspects don't even matter."

"I disagree with you saying those things don't matter," Sandra says tenderly. "They do matter. If Lucian treats you as good as you say outside the bedroom, and the only problem you're having is the hang-up on your past, I think there's hope here and something you can definitely work with. The question is--is Lucian the man that can do it... and is he willing to commit and stick by you to see you through these issues?"

Numb, I sit there, hugging myself, fighting back those ugly tears. Sandra's right of course, but I don't know what to say. I feel like I'm falling for Lucian, but in doing so, have set myself up for a broken heart. Lucian is a very rich man, with very many options. He could easily one day decide I'm not worth the effort and find himself a new

Submissive. Or I may only ever be a Submissive to him. I want more. But I want it from him.

"I don't know." I whisper the answer.

"What I would suggest," Sandra says softly, pulling me out of my thoughts, "is having an honest talk with Lucian about what your wants and needs are. If you want him to commit to you, tell him that. And expect him to give you an answer on it. Otherwise, despite the progress you've made, this relationship could be harmful and cost you a lot of emotional and mental distress." She sets the notebook down and says, "This is just my opinion, but it seems as though there's more than a Dom/sub relationship and that's what's driving these changes for you. Make sure that's the case, and work together to continue your progress."

I don't know what to say. I feel so tense and on edge. I'd be asking him for more. I don't think it's an option. He's going to leave me or just fuck me until the contract is over. I cover my heated face with my hands and try to just focus on me. I want this. I'm scared to death to ask him for this, but I want to. I have to. But he's already given me so much. He's showed me it's possible. I'm so conflicted.

"Go talk to him, Dahlia." Sandra's words make my eyes snap to hers. "Let him know what you need. I hope he can continue to help you and that you're able to work on this foundation you've built."

I hope so, too, I think to myself feeling growing resolve as I leave her office and knowing that there's only one thing left to do.

CHAPTER 25

LUCIAN

J'm no good for her. I've already come to terms with it. I don't know how to help her. I know some of my own desires and needs could harm her. Emotionally, psychologically. I want to be strong enough for her. I want to have the experience to know how to heal her.

But I don't have all the answers. My heart clenches, knowing I should let her go. Cut ties from the contract and make sure she gets the help she needs from someone else. I keep hurting her. I don't mean to, but I know that I am.

I clench my jaw and pull out my cell phone, waiting on my sister to get here. I'm in the same spot that I was before. The same cafe we always come to. Today it's darker. The grey clouds block the sun and rain threatens to start falling at any second, but I don't care. I'm staying outside. At least for now.

A glance at my phone shows a text from Isaac.

It's done.

My body stiffens slightly, and adrenaline spikes through my blood.

Her uncle is dead.

That bastard took my treasure's innocence. Even worse, she wasn't the first and she wasn't the last.

The law gave him five years in prison, that's all. And he never even went to trial for what he did to my treasure. That's not justice. And the last girl, the second one he was prosecuted over after hurting Dahlia, was his neighbor; there wasn't enough evidence for the judge to proceed, but I know the truth. I saw what they had on him. I read the testimonies. He needed to die.

I should feel guilty, and maybe I should even be disgusted with myself. But I don't feel a damn thing other than satisfied. He hurt my treasure in a way I know I can never fully understand.

"Your coffee, sir." The waitress flashes me a sweet smile, her cheeks a bright red from either the chill or more blush than necessary. "Can I get you anything else?" she asks, leaning in slightly. Too close for my comfort.

"No, thank you." I'm short with my words, and the look on her face falls. Again, I should care. But I don't.

"Lucian!" My sister appears from behind the waitress, sparing me whatever looks the young woman was giving me.

She wraps her arms around my shoulders, not even giving me a moment to stand.

I always look forward to seeing Anna. But as I look down to click my phone off and ignore the text message, I feel... broken. Everything is off-center and an emptiness fills my chest.

She squeezes me one more time and looks for the waitress, but she's gone.

I huff a humorless laugh as Anna pouts and almost shrugs off her coat, but decides against it, falling into her seat and looking past me, into the cafe.

When her eyes reach me once again, that bright smile lights up her face. "You have a girlfriend," she says, and her voice etched with awe.

I pick up my coffee and blow on it, not knowing how to handle this. I don't give a fuck what anyone thinks really. Zander and Isaac know the truth. My sister's the only other person in my life who matters. But I'm sure as fuck not going to tell her the truth.

She leans across the small table and playfully smacks my arm as I set the cup down.

"Come on," she urges me, "spill it!"

Her excitement brings a small smile to my face, although it doesn't reflect what I'm feeling at the moment. "She's a sweet girl, but I'm not sure how serious it is." *Lies.* I tell my sister lies. I've never been more serious about anything in my life. But I know I'm not good for her. I don't know if I can keep her.

"She's so pretty!" Anna's eyes go wide and she lets out a soft sigh. "I can see it in your face," she says, and her voice is teasing.

I grunt out a laugh. "Leave it be, Anna."

"You'll bring her to the Christmas party?" she asks me. The hopeful look on her face is too much. Christmas is less than three weeks away. I already turned her down for Thanksgiving. I'd only just gotten my hands on my treasure, and with neither of us committed to spending the holiday with family, I made sure she spent it on her knees. It was the most successful holiday I've had in years.

"I have no idea if we'll still be seeing each other by then." As I say the words, I realize how much pain they cause me. The very thought that my treasure may be gone in less than a month physically hurts. Doubt and uncertainty are two emotions I don't handle well.

"Tell me, how are your classes going?" I ask quickly to change the subject.

"Are you high?" she asks incredulously. "It's Christmas break." I take a sip of the bitter black coffee, wishing this meeting were over. I have three conferences left today and only then can I go home and take care of her.

"So, Mom called me." Anna's words bring me back to the present.

I can feel my facial expression harden as I wait for more.

"She said she's sorry."

It takes a lot for me not to roll my eyes at my sister's naiveté. She's a sweet girl and I love her, but she's a fool.

"What else did she say?" I ask, although I can't keep my voice even.

She looks hurt by my harsh tone and I instantly regret it.

She softens her voice and says, "She's really sorry." Her eyes plead with me, but I can't. I won't.

"'I'm sorry, Anna," I shake my head and look away, "I can't-"

She quickly reaches across the table, taking my hand in both of hers as she continues, "I'm not asking you to do anything. I promise you." My heart clenches looking at the tears in my sister's eyes.

"I know what they did, and it was wrong. I just wanted you to know…" her voice cracks, and she sucks in a breath. "But I know you don't trust them," she says as her face falls.

I stand up and hug my sister close, rubbing her arm as she holds me back.

I hate that she's so emotional and pulled in different directions. "It's alright, Anna." She's put herself in the middle of this feud. She's suffered from both sides. I went a long time without seeing her. I regret it, but at the time I didn't want to be reminded of what I'd lost. I wish I could take it back. I wish I could protect her from what happened.

"I love you, Lucian." She looks up at me, brushing away the one stray tear rolling down my cheek. "I hope you know that."

I nod my head once, holding her gaze.

"I have to go, Anna."

She gives me a quick squeeze and regains her composure.

I hate that I have to leave her like this. But I have no solutions for her.

She sniffles and looks past me for the waitress as I put two twenties on the table and lean in to kiss her forehead.

"Take care, Anna," I tell her as I turn away from her.

"You too," she whispers.

THIS FUCKING MEETING IS NEVER GOING TO END. AND IT'S ONLY THE first of the three I need to take care of before the day is over. I'd run my hand over my face, but it's a video conference. So instead I stare straight ahead, listening to the pros and cons of moving the manufacturing of casings for the new prototype to South Korea while leaving the remainder in the US.

I need the numbers and I need the statistics, but what I don't need is the two heads of the two opposing divisions to get into a fucking argument and take up my time.

I finally speak up, putting an end to this nonsense. "Mr. Crenshaw, I fail to see the point of this debate."

"It's about timing, Mr. Stone. This is going to destroy my timeline."

"The bottom line is what matters," Mr. Jenkins answers in a stern voice.

THERE'S A KNOCK AT THE DOOR, INTERRUPTING THE CONFERENCE. I ignore it.

Knock knock, it comes harder this time.

Crenshaw and Jenkins continue to debate on whether or not their shipping methods are reliable and I look up to the door as I say, "Come in." Linda knows my schedule and she should know better than to interrupt me, especially when the head of my development department is telling me my timeline may be fucked because of this change.

I glance at the door when it opens, and I have to do a double take.

"Dahlia?" I look up past the monitor and ignore the conference. Their voices pour from the speakers, but it's white noise. Dahlia's in my doorway, with Linda right behind her.

"Mr. Stone," Linda says with an uneasiness as she looks between the two of us. "I wasn't-" she starts to explain herself, but I wave her away.

"Leave us."

Dahlia looks unsteady. She seems lost with what to do with herself. I wait for her to tell me what's going on. Or to come over to me, but she just stands in the middle of my office, twisting her hands around the strap of her purse. With doubt in her eyes and uncertainty clear on her face.

My forehead pinches with confusion. What the hell is she doing here? *It looks like she's been crying.* The realization snaps something inside of me.

I stand abruptly from my desk, and it's only then that I hear the voices coming through. It was all white noise before.

"Mr. Stone," several men call out. Fuck. I look back at the monitor gritting my teeth, but the moment I do, Dahlia turns to leave.

177

"I'm sorry, I shouldn't have-"

"Stay." I give her the command, and she freezes. Her breathing is coming in harsher than before.

I walk past her to the office door, ignoring the questions coming through the speakers, and lock it before moving to the blinds and closing them all. I can feel Dahlia's eyes on me, but I don't turn to face her gaze until we have privacy.

"When Mr. Stone..." a voice rings through the speakers and I quickly walk over to the other side of the desk and lean forward, hitting mute and exiting out of the conference without a word. I don't owe them an explanation, and they still need to have this sorted by tomorrow at the latest. I pay them well, and I expect no less from them.

"Lucian, I-" Dahlia finally says as I walk toward her. I take her small hands in mine and bring her closer to me.

"What's wrong?" I ask her.

"I shouldn't have-" she looks down at the grey carpet and shakes her head, the doubt and regret spreading through her.

I hook my finger under her chin and tilt her up so her soft hazel eyes are forced to look back at me. "What's wrong?"

"I..." She's so hesitant. Last night was hard on us, and I failed her. Again. This is my fault. "I feel like," she chokes on her words, looking past me and out of the window. "I need more."

"I'm sorry about last night," I apologize to her. Her eyes widen slightly as I lead her to the sofa on the side of the office. "Please forgive me for not being as strong as I should be. I've never..." my voice trails off slightly as I debate on how to word this.

"I need to find a balance between giving you what you need, and fulfilling your desires." I pull her into my lap and rub soothing circles along her back. "I also need to curb some of my desires, treasure. And last night that's where I failed you." I cup her chin in my hand and place a soft kiss on her lips.

"I can be a better Dom for you. I will." The look in her eyes is filled with uncertainty. My heart beats frantically at the realization. "Tell me what you're thinking," I command her.

"I want that," she says softly. But there's still hesitation clearly present in her expression.

"What else do you want?" I ask her.

She's quiet and obviously worried, and I don't know why. Maybe she's lost faith in me. I won't let her think that. I won't let her slip through my fingers.

"Get on your knees," I tell her. I'll make her see how good this is. I won't let her question it. I know I failed her, but I can make this right.

Her lips part with a small gasp and she crawls off of me, keeping her eyes on mine until her knees are on the carpet and her hands rest on her thighs.

"Good girl," I say and her expression lifts with my praise. I slowly unbuckle my belt and pull out my cock. I stroke it once and her eyes dart to it and then back to mine.

I keep stroking my dick, making her wait for it. The heated look in her eyes and the quickening of her breathing only makes me harder. It feels like velvet over a thick steel rod in my hand. I groan as a bit of precum leaks from the tip.

"Lick," I utter, and the second the command comes out, her hot tongue laps at my head and she cleans it off with a deep moan. Her beautiful eyes look up at me while she continues to obey me, and it's all I can take.

She wants it hard and rough, and so do I. I can give her that and keep her from taking this to a dark place that she doesn't want to go.

I will.

I pull her up by her hips and throw her down on the sofa, pulling her skirt up over her waist and ripping her panties down her thighs. I can't get them off fast enough, and the thin lace tears. Her neck arches at the sound, and her glistening pussy clenches.

I spread her thighs wider, and slam into her tight pussy without warning. Her back bows at the intensity, and she screams out.

"You'll be quiet, treasure." Her wide eyes look back at me as she bites down on her lip, and I quickly lean forward, fucking my treasure on the leather sofa with short fast strokes. My fingers dig into her hips with a bruising force as my lips crash against hers.

Soft moans mingle with our hot breath and she struggles now to writhe under me as I pound harder into her. My pants fall down around my ass as I pick up my pace, thrusting into her with a savage force, all the while kissing her with devotion and holding her close.

I can give her both. I can, and I will.

"Lucian," she moans my name as her head falls back. Fuck, the sound of her voice full of pleasure, and the feel of her tight walls, hot and wet with her arousal makes me groan into the crook of her neck. I want to rut between her thighs with the primal desire I feel for her. I want to let loose and take from her. But I don't. I can't. I force myself to stay in control and grip the back of her neck as I whisper against her lips.

"Cum for me, treasure." Her eyes stare into mine as I slide in and out of her slick pussy easily, with a force that makes her gasp slightly. Her body jolts with each hard thrust. Every time she closes her eyes, I kiss her gently, passionately, with everything I have.

I'm on edge and ready to cum. It's hard not to with how good she feels. My toes curl, and I hold it back. Her first. I need this from her. She needs this.

"Cum for me," I command her again, slipping my hand between our bodies and rubbing her swollen clit.

Dahlia's eyes go half-lidded and her lips part as her head falls back. I can see she's close, so close. I lean forward, spearing my fingers through her hair, maintaining my steady pace and bringing her forehead close to mine.

I fist her hair and pump my hips faster, gazing into her eyes. There's a spark there, staring back at me, keeping me focused on her. Soft moans pour from her lips and I'm quick to muffle them with my kisses. Our tongues tangle in a heated need to be as close to one another as we can. Her arms wrap around my shoulders, her hands in my hair as I thrust deeper, jolting her body slightly.

I tighten my grip on her hips as she pulls away, moaning my name. Her neck arches, and her mouth opens as her pussy spasms around my dick. I groan into the crook of her neck, loving the feeling and needing more. I kiss along her neck and up her jaw to her lips.

She greedily kisses me back with a passion I've never felt, her hot breath filling my lungs. Her fingers dig into my back, pulling me closer to her. And I lose my composure. "Treasure," I murmur reverently, kissing every available surface of her soft skin as I thrust into her again and again, until I reach my own climax.

The tingling pleasure rolls through my body, building with a tension in the pit of my stomach and then explodes outward. My eyes close and I pull away from her as a rough moan is torn from my throat, but Dahlia takes my head in her hands and forces me to kiss her. She presses her soft lips to mine, and I give her everything I have.

She takes every bit of me in that moment. It's all for her.

CHAPTER 26

DAHLIA

I walk through the hallway of Lucian's penthouse, my chest heaving with excitement, my heart pounding with anticipation. I'm feeling nauseated, and I don't know what from.

Things are different. Yesterday was different. The rules have changed. At least for me they have. I was too chickenshit to tell him that I want him as a partner, a boyfriend, whatever he wants to call it. I need more than a Dom. But I think he knows that. Maybe I'm just pretending. Playing house so that I don't have to believe that I'm just his pet. Just a Submissive he bought at the auction. It feels like so much more though, at least to me.

I'm too afraid to put a label on us. I'm afraid of what he'll say.

I key in the code and open the door. Just like I've done every day for almost a month, it feels natural. Setting my purse on a stand in the foyer, I stop for a moment to touch the necklace at my throat. Lucian gave it to me this morning. It's beautiful, made of gold and diamonds and has a bold, but elegant thickness to it. He wants me to be collared at all times. And he's obtained a variety of them for me. I'm spoiled. I'm very well aware that he's spoiling me in the jewelry department.

Reaching up behind my neck, I delicately take off the chain and slip it into my purse, grabbing out my new Sub collar in its place and locking it around my neck. This one is even more beautiful, with spiked diamonds and gorgeous gold accents dotting the sumptuous, cream-colored leather. It's very flashy, and I would never wear it unless I was alone with Lucian.

I continue down the hallway on my way to the playroom, when I see him standing at the foot of the double-sided staircase. My breath catches in my throat at the sight of him. He's never home when I get here. I'm supposed to wait for him. For a moment fear grips my chest, and I think I must be late. But he smiles at me as he walks toward me. No hint of a punishment in sight. He's looking fucking hot as hell this afternoon, which shouldn't be surprising since I saw him earlier this morning and he looked fucking hot as hell then, too.

It's obvious he's been waiting for me, and I've shown up exactly when he wants me to. My pulse begins to pound between my ears, and my legs tremble slightly as his gaze falls on me.

I quickly kneel, falling easily to the floor and submitting to him. I place my hands on my thighs and wait for him obediently. It's the position he first made me get in on our first day. The memory puts a small smile on my face.

"Come here, treasure," he commands in a voice I can't deny.

I drop onto all fours and slowly begin crawling my way over to my Dom. It feels awkward. I've never crawled to him before, but I'm his Sub right now and I think this is what I'm supposed to do. I don't want to mess up. I jolt slightly when he commands me to stop, his voice harsh.

"Don't crawl," he says, a hint of irritation in his voice. "I don't want to play right now. Get up and walk over to me."

Ashamed, I climb to my feet, my cheeks burning. I hesitate, feeling insecure now, my anxiety returning.

"Now, treasure," he demands with even more authority.

My stomach twisting with apprehension, I walk over to stand in front of him. Up close, I can see something's off about him. His whole body seems tense and he looks like... just worn down, like he's had a rough day. At least, I hope that's what it is.

My contract is almost over. Maybe he's about to tell me he doesn't want to renew it. That he's ready to move on.

I'm filled with nausea over these thoughts, and it's hard to keep my composure. Before I can ask him what's wrong, he pulls me into him, kissing me on the lips passionately. Sighing softly, I melt into his arms, letting him hold me, surrendering my entire body to him.

When Lucian pulls back, my chest is heaving as I release breathless pants. That kiss was intense, and it goes a long way in calming me. Lucian obviously isn't calling things off. Yet.

"What was that all about?" I ask breathlessly.

"You asked for more. That was me giving you more."

I try to respond, but I'm not sure how. I didn't expect this. This can't really be happening.

I part my lips to say something, anything, but Lucian places his fingers against them, quieting me. "Shhh. This is about me and you right now. Let me give you what you asked for. We're not going to the playroom tonight. Tonight, it's just *us*."

Just us? I stare at him in shock, hardly trusting what he's offering. Lucian appears to be dangling everything I could ever want, right in front of me. I should be jumping for joy, yet I'm still worried that this is all some sort of cruel joke.

"Will that make you happy, treasure?" he asks, looking me straight in the eyes and making me weak in the knees. I can't believe it. I want to clarify what more means to him. But I can't. I'm afraid of the answer, and the deadline approaching us.

"Yes… Lucian," I respond softly.

"YOU'RE DOING WELL," LUCIAN WHISPERS IN MY EAR, HIS BREATH hot on my neck as he places his large hands atop mine and gently guides them in kneading the big ball of dough on the cutting board in front of us.

For dinner, Lucian wanted to pass on takeout and bond over making homemade pizza. I was apprehensive about it as I've only made it a few times before, and it's never turned out well. But Lucian assured me it would be fine, that I had all I needed, chiefly him to guide me. Turns out he was right, the dough is almost perfect. And the experience has been one of the most pleasant things I've done in a while.

I could learn to love this, I think dreamily, enjoying the sensation of Lucian's closeness.

A soft sigh escapes my lips as I'm pulled out of my thoughts and feel the heat of his body behind me, his hands guiding mine in a very sensual and deliberate manner, and his big hard dick pressing up against my ass.

"Do you like that, treasure?" Lucian says in my ear, nibbling on my neck, gyrating his cock gently up against my ass cheek, while pressing my hands into the soft dough, molding it into a flat surface.

"Yes," I moan, my pussy clenching repeatedly with need. "Please give it to me, sir."

Lucian kisses me several more times on the neck before saying, "Uh-uh, treasure. Not until we finish this pizza." He huffs out a small chuckle in my ear. "Or at least get it in the oven."

I feel like this is cruel and unusual punishment, pressing his big cock up against me, and then telling me I can't have it until we finish. But I know better than to argue. I just need to get this pizza crust done pronto, throw on the sauce and toppings: pepperoni, sausage, bell peppers, onions, four cheeses, and then throw it in the oven. So I can get all of that big fucking cock.

I continue to let Lucian guide me with molding the dough, and by the time we finish the crust I'm completely covered in flour. But worse than that, my panties are soaked.

"See, treasure?" Lucian asks, stepping out from behind me and filling me with disappointment. Unlike me, Lucian only has flour on his hands and a little bit on his blue apron. He nods at the crust we made and places it on the pizza pan next to the cutting board. "That wasn't so bad, was it?"

I shake my head, blushing, wishing he were still behind me. "No, I enjoyed it. A lot."

Lucian gives me a hooded look filled with desire, and a promise of what is to come and my breath quickens. "As did I."

I blush harder and I'm about to reply when my cell, which is lying on the end of the counter, goes off with rapid dings. Lucian glances at it and then gives me a look.

I shrug, wiping my hands off with the towel and wondering if it's my mom. Maybe she changed her mind about Christmas.

Before I can take two steps, my phone goes off several more times and I pause. It's unusual I get that many texts in such rapid fashion. Maybe I should check to see who it is. Wiping my hands on a dishrag, I walk over and pick up the phone, but I almost drop it a second later when I see the series of texts, a cold chill striking my spine.

"Oh my God," I gasp, my heart pounding wildly in my chest, dropping my phone to the counter.

Lucian tears his eyes away from the stove and settles them on me. "What's wrong?" he asks with concern.

I place a hand over my chest to calm my rapidly beating heart. "Those texts I just got... they were from my mom."

Lucian goes rigid and he clenches his jaw, but I'm too freaked out to really respond to his strange reaction. "And?" he asks.

I take a deep breath, trying to calm my pulse. "She said my uncle was found dead..." my voice trails off as my mind races in disbelief. My blood heats, and my breath is coming in short pants. The person who'd caused me so much grief is now dead. It doesn't even sound real. *He's gone.*

Lucian doesn't immediately respond, but I take his silence as shock.

"I can't believe it." The words fall from my lips as I read the texts over and over.

I glance at Lucian, noticing that his entire demeanor has changed. The playfulness I enjoyed while we made the crust is gone.

His face is emotionless. I've seen the look before. It's his mask. He's hiding what he truly thinks. A wave of a chill runs through my body, turning my blood to ice. I almost ask him if he knew. He doesn't look surprised. He seems to be waiting for something. Or hiding something.

My heart thuds hard in my chest as I tear my eyes away from him. The thoughts in my head are just paranoia; horrible suspicion pressing down on my chest, a suspicion I desperately don't want to believe.

"Lucian?" I say his name as a question although I can't ask what I really want to know. Something deep down in the pit of my stomach is telling me he did this. Maybe he's not the one who pulled the trigger. But Lucian murdered him.

I swallow thickly as his heavy footsteps approach me.

I have to hold on to the counter to keep myself upright, suddenly feeling like I'm going to faint.

"Are you alright, treasure?" Lucian asks, concern returning to his voice as he walks over and wraps his arms around me, holding me close. I feel awful for leaning into him. For even thinking he did this. *The club is full of powerful men. You don't want to be their enemy.* Carla's words echo in my head as he rubs soothing circles on my arm.

Swallowing back a wave of uncertainty, I reply, "I'm fine."

CHAPTER 27

LUCIAN

I haven't taken a day away from the office in a very long time. But there was no way I was going to leave Dahlia today. We only have today and tomorrow left.

I still have work to do, and so does she, but as soon as I'm finished, she's all mine.

My treasure is waiting for me in the living room. The last I saw her she was sprawled out on the rug with several textbooks and sketchpads, preparing for her final semester and an event for work.

My body relaxes as I remember how she asked me to go with her. She's still coming around to being open with me and telling me what her needs are, but she's doing much better now. It was so obvious that she thought I'd say no, but she's my priority.

I open the desk drawer and take out the contract. I need to extend it, and I've been typing up the language for my half of the contract for the last hour. I've been distracted by the incessant phone calls from PR and my lawyer. I couldn't care less at this point. If my ex is going to publish her tell-all, I'll sue her. I'm not giving her another penny. They don't seem to agree with my tactic, but I don't care anymore.

I'm done with her. Tricia is my past, and that's where she'll stay. If she wants to publish lies, then she can make herself a liar and wind up in court.

I sigh heavily and hate that I've given any more energy to her at all. My head is pounding with a relentless headache. My temples throb with pain that just isn't leaving. I take another two Advil from the bottle on my desk and wash it down with my coffee.

It's almost room temperature now, but I only need the caffeine. A smile graces my lip when my fingers run over the engraving on the outside of the steel mug. *Please, sir.*

She thinks she's cute, my treasure. And she is.

My heart swells for a moment, but then my computer pings with yet another email. This one is from the executives that head up development.

I put my mug down on the desk, intent on getting to work and tying up these loose ends. Once I'm done for today, I'm going on vacation. I want time for just the two of us. She'll be busy once school starts, but until then, her time is mine. And I want it all. Linda's processing applications for another two executive assistants. I need to start delegating more work. It's a slow going process, but I'm working on it.

I focus on the tasks at hand and make the final decisions on several contracts with ease. Knowing that once this is done with, I'll be able to enjoy my treasure makes the time go by quickly.

A timid knock at the office door makes my fingers pause on the keyboard.

"Come in."

Dahlia peeks her head in, only partially opening the door. "Are you busy?"

I have a moment." I really do need to get this shit done. But I can put it on pause for her.

She walks easily to the desk and I turn my chair so she can sit on my lap. I love the feel of her body against mine. Her warmth and gentle touches soothe me.

I lay a hand on her thigh and plant a small kiss on her neck.

"Will you be done soon?" she asks me. Tricia used to ask me that all the time. At first, anyway. She stopped a few months into the marriage, when she gave up.

I close my eyes and pinch the bridge of my nose. The headache is coming on full force now. I hate that the thought of Tricia ever came to my mind because of something my treasure said. They're nothing alike.

"I have another two hours at least," I tell her, knowing that it'll possibly be more, but I'll come back and finish once she's gone to bed. I'll make time for her. I'm committed to that.

"I was going to make dinner," she wraps her arms around my shoulders, "or maybe order something?"

"What do you want?" I ask her. A sweet smile slips into place on her lips.

"That's what I came in to ask you." I hug her waist closer to me, her ass slipping against my cock and stirring desire. I nip her neck and debate on taking her now. Sating her so she can relax while I finish this.

"What's this?" she asks, her forehead pinched.

I glance down at the contract on the desk. "It's not ready yet. It's the new contract."

She picks up the papers and skims through them.

My body tenses as the crease in her forehead becomes deeper and the look of unhappiness is evident in her eyes.

"I don't want to sign this," she says finally. Her voice is full of apprehension and soft with doubt. But she looks back at me, setting the papers down with strength and finality. She shakes her head. "I don't want to sign it."

I didn't expect that. My body chills at how resolute her decision is. "Do you want more money?" I ask her, not knowing what other problems she could have with it. I've put in her needs. I know I'll meet them. These past few days have been nothing but perfection.

Dahlia pushes away from me and climbs off of my lap, her warmth leaving me wanting her. I grip her hips to keep her from leaving me but she slaps me away, catching me by surprise.

I quickly rise from my desk, the chair falling backward onto the floor. A touch of fear flashes in her eyes as she walks backward.

I raise my hands, although my voice is strong and my eyes are narrowed. "Dahlia," I say and her eyes fly to mine. She looks angry, but more than that, upset.

"What's wrong?" I ask her, although I'm not a fucking idiot. I shouldn't have implied that it was about money. It's a habit of mine.

It's hard breaking them, but I know my treasure better than that. It's not about the money for her. I should have known that.

"I don't want your money," her voice cracks slightly as she crosses her arms and looks away. "I'm not-"

"I'm sorry." I walk toward her, slowly moving my hands around her hips. I can tell she wants to push me away, she wants to leave, but she's my Submissive.

She should have known better than to leave me like she did. She knows better than that. But then again, I knew better than to bring up money.

"Look at me," I say and as the words leave my lips, she obeys. A small frown mars her beautiful face. "Whatever you want to change in the contract, just let me know."

She shakes her head, and her face crumples. "I don't want a contract."

My grip on her tightens, and my heart races in my chest.

"I don't know why you want this if we're... if we're more than this." Her voice is shaky, and she's obviously extremely upset. I don't understand why though.

I hate that she's questioning me. I need contracts. Whatever she wants to change, I can alter. I don't mind that.

"I want this, treasure. I need this." I understand it's fucked up. But I do. I need to know that when I make her angry, or when I fail her, she can't leave me. I need to know she'll still be here and I'll be able to make it right.

"This is what I want from you... equality," she stresses the last word and I still don't understand. I don't get what this has to do with the contract or anything for that matter.

"You are my equal. How can you not see that?"

"I'm your Submissive. I can't be both!"

"You are my Submissive, my other half and my equal. They're all one and the same." It pisses me off that she would think less of herself.

She looks lost again. I'll show her what it means to be mine. My everything. She's best when she submits. She's more comfortable in that role. This questioning everything isn't what she needs.

"I'll change whatever you want, and you'll sign the contract." I'm forceful with her. It's what she needs, I know it is.

"Now get on your knees." She just needs a hard fuck. I've been too busy for her. I won't make the same mistake I made with Tricia, not with her. I can't let her get away from me. I won't let my treasure slip through my fingers.

She looks back at me with uncertainty. "Did you kill him?" she asks me.

My heart stops in my chest, my blood running cold. She hasn't asked. She hasn't brought it up since she got the text messages from her mother. I could tell she knew. It has to be obvious.

"Where's this coming from?" I ask her.

"That's not an answer." Her voice is low, and wavers.

"I'm your Dom, you'll do well to remember that right now."

"I thought you said I was your equal?" she asks as she cocks a brow at me, her voice broken and raw. My heart twists in my chest.

"Yes, you are, and yes, I had him killed." The words slip from my lips before I can stop them, my heart beating so hard it slams with pain on each beat.

She gasps and steps back slightly. My breathing comes in ragged as I wait for her response. I never intended on telling her. I didn't want her to have to carry the weight of knowing. But I won't lie to her.

"He deserved to die, Dahlia. Not only for what he did to you, but what he continued to do after." My words are full of conviction, but she doesn't respond.

She looks toward the door, but I don't want her to leave me. She's scared, and I can comfort her. I can make this right.

I breathe out deeply. "I need you to understand that you're safe. I'll always make sure you're safe."

Her breathing comes in quicker, and she looks so lost. She's forever lost and insecure. If only she'd listen to me. "Come here."

"No," she's quick to respond, and it pisses me off.

I narrow my eyes at her. "Treasure," I say and my voice holds a note of admonishment. She's going to be punished for deliberately disobeying me.

"You're not leaving, Dahlia." I won't let her go. I can't. I can't lose her.

"I have to." I close my eyes at her words, hating them. My hands ball into fists at my side.

"You don't have to do a damn thing but do as I say. Come here."

"Don't make me stay. Please, don't make me stay." My body heats with anxiety at the fear in her voice. She's afraid of me. Tears leak from the corners of her eyes. No. I shake my head, denying that this is even a reality. This wasn't meant to hurt her. I only meant to give her justice.

"It's me, Dahlia. I'm still the same man I was."

"You killed him?" There's a mix of disbelief, fear, and something else in her voice.

I nod my head once. "I hired the hit." Regret starts to creep in, but I refuse to allow it. I had to do the right thing. I only wish she'd understand.

"Come here." I soften my voice, waiting for her Submissive side to come through. I take two steps toward her and she backs away.

"Red." My lungs stop working as she whispers the word, shaking her head. She walks to the door, her soft footsteps echoing in the room and I let her go, standing still and just trying to breathe.

She just needs time. The door closes behind her and I try to move, but I can't. She safe worded me. She left me.

She just needs time. I take in a ragged breath.

I knew that her uncle's death would affect her. I want to be there for her. I know what she needs.

But she doesn't trust me yet. She hasn't given herself fully to me.

I sink into my chair, hating that I had to let her leave, but knowing I'll have her back. She can't leave me. I know she loves me. I fucking love her, too. I'll give her whatever she wants. I just need her back.

CHAPTER 28

DAHLIA

I can't believe he did it.

I suck in a deep breath of guilt as I drive to Sandra's office in my beat-up, piece of shit Mazda. I should be incredibly upset about what Lucian did. I'm still trembling. It's one thing to have suspicions, it's another thing entirely to have them confirmed. I wish I'd just lived in denial.

He murdered someone on my behalf. But ever since getting over the initial shock, I feel relieved that the person who caused me so much pain is gone from the world. I'm a horrible fucking person for being happy with his death. I'm torn and conflicted. I need help. I'm not okay.

I suck in another deep breath as I turn off the highway, taking the road that will take me straight to Sandra's office.

I'm free. Tears prick at my eyes. I hadn't realized how much pain I was in just knowing that man was still breathing. I feel... relief. And guilt.

And what about Lucian? I don't know how to feel. *But nothing matters without him.*

The thought causes a large lump to form in my throat and tears to sting my eyes.

When I step into Sandra's office, she's waiting for me in her leather tufted chair, her legs crossed in front of her, her notepad and pen in hand. It's after hours, but when I called she said she'd be here. She'll never know how much that means to me. Her hair is loose in her bun and her cream-colored blouse is a bit wrinkled from being worn all day, but she's here for me.

"Dahlia," she greets me warmly with a gentle smile. She gestures at the couch across from her. "Please, have a seat."

"Thank you," I say softly, feeling nervousness start to set in, and trembling slightly. Barefoot, I walk over and sink onto the couch, pulling my legs up under me, sucking in a deep breath and exhaling slowly.

"Now, would you like to tell me what's bothering you?" Sandra asks me when I'm fully seated, her soft voice soothing the turmoil that's roiling beneath the surface. Her pale blue eyes focus on me behind her glasses.

I open my mouth to speak, but then close it when I realize something critical I missed on the way over. *I can't tell her anything that will incriminate Lucian, so I'm going to have to be very careful talking about my uncle's death.* I sit there for a moment, my mind racing on what I could safely disclose. I run my hand over my face, hating this and hating everything.

"Dahlia?" Sandra prods gently.

"My uncle is dead," I announce, suddenly deciding that I will just go with a variation of the truth. Hopefully Sandra won't read too much into it.

Sandra lowers her pen to pad, scribbling, and frowns. "Oh, dear, Dahlia. I'm sorry to hear that."

I nod. I should be crying right now, but I can't summon a single fucking tear. Or maybe I shouldn't. I know it must look odd, but I can't help it. "Shot in the back of his head twice." I hate how flat my words sound, I could be talking about a piece of trash off the street.

And that's what he was, I tell myself. *A piece of trash.* But that doesn't make his murder right. And I know it. I just can't bring myself to care. I bite my thumbnail, just trying to think straight.

Sandra shakes her head, anguish flashing in her eyes. "That's horrible. I'm truly sorry, Dahlia." She sets her pen down on the pad and leans forward. "Was this the uncle who hurt you?" her voice is soft and full of understanding.

I nod my head, brushing the bastard tears away. "Yes, and he's dead now."

"I see. How do you feel about that?"

"I…" I pause, feeling a weight on my chest, "I feel like I'm somewhat responsible for his death."

Sandra writes something down on her notepad and then looks up at me, her face twisted with curiosity. "Why is that?"

I shrug while shaking my head. Of course I can't tell her everything, but I feel like admitting a partial truth will help me deal with my guilt. "I just do."

Sandra scribbles several lines and then focuses her kind eyes on me, compassion flashing in them. "You can't blame yourself for your uncle's death, Dahlia. It's not healthy."

I shake my head. "Yes, I can. It's because of me he's dead."

Sandra frowns at the conviction in my voice. "Why do you say that?"

"I don't know, I just feel responsible for it in some way." I choke on my words. "But I don't feel bad about it," I admit. "Except for the guilt I feel about not caring, I feel kind of relieved actually. Like, I'm totally happy he's dead." The silence that follows presses down upon me, and I cringe. I hate how that makes me sound, but I can't help it. It's the truth. I look over at Sandra and she's watching me, sitting very still. I wonder what's going on in her head. "Does that make me a bad person?"

Sandra scribbles more notes down on her notepad before looking back up at me. "Considering what he did to you, no. Not at all." She pauses as if thinking about how to formulate a question. "But now that he's dead, do you think his death will help you?" She pauses again, but I know exactly what she means. "It's important I document the impact that it has on you."

Hugging my knees to myself, I shake my head. "No. I can't believe I'm saying this, but I think I finally was able to let that all go."

That same guilt comes back over me, but I push it away. I hate the fact that I'm happy about my uncle being dead, but I can't help myself.

"I see."

I cover my face with my hands as I lean forward crying. *It's because of Lucian. It's all because of him.*

"Dahlia," Sandra's soft voice prods me as she rises from her seat, the sounds accompanying my sobs.

He killed him for me. My heart clenches. I'm a horrible person for loving him for that. That's truly what I feel. It's so fucked up.

Her small hands rub soothing circles on my back. "Have you been able to talk to your partner about this?" she asks me in a small voice. "Lucian?"

I nod my head, wiping under my eyes and reaching for the Kleenex in her hand.

"Do you think you'll be able to confide in him?" she asks. I don't know. My heart squeezes with pain. This is so real. It's so much to take in. I love him. I know I love him, and I can't bear the thought of him leaving me. The contract is over, but I'm not signing another. I want him. I want a commitment. I need it. I need *him*.

CHAPTER 29

LUCIAN

I gave her a chance to come back to me on her own, and she didn't. I'm not going to wait. I refuse to.

The thirty days are over, we have no contract. This is just me and her.

I check my phone one last time before grabbing my keys and opening the door. I swing it open and my heart stops as I stare back at Dahlia. Her eyes are red-rimmed and her hair is a mess.

She came back to me. I'm still in the doorway as she looks up at me with uncertainty. I can't believe she's here. My heart thuds in my chest as she brushes her hair behind her ears and parts her lips.

"Lucian," she says and her voice is soft.

"You came back."

She visibly swallows and takes in a sharp breath. I open the door wider and step to the side. I still can't believe she's here. I thought I'd have to drag her back here. I'm hesitant to think anything positive though. She's obviously not well. And we need to set ground rules. We need to make sure we're on the same page.

She walks in slowly, her hands gripping the strap of her purse. This is either going to go one of two ways. Either she's here to end it, or she's here to stay. And if she's staying, I'm never letting her go.

Her heels click, the sound reverberating off the walls of the foyer as I close the door.

"I'm struggling, Lucian." She turns to face me, still tightly gripping the strap.

I know she is, but everything is going to be alright. "Talk to me, treasure; I want to help you."

She takes in a shaky breath, finally putting her purse down on the table and walking toward me. I open my arms and she walks into my embrace freely. I breathe easy, feeling her pressed against me. Knowing she wants to be held by me. I kiss her hair as she nuzzles her cheek against my chest.

"I'm sorry I made you feel like you had to leave," I apologize. "What I did was something that needed to be done. It wasn't meant to hurt you or to make you afraid of me."

She nods her head in my chest, but she's quiet. I just need her to open up. I need to know what she's thinking.

"I don't want you to leave again. I need you to stay, treasure."

"I don't want to leave, I want you," she whispers into my chest.

"Forgive me." My voice is pained. If I had to do it all over again, I still would've killed him. I know I would have.

"It's not about forgiveness. I think... I love you, Lucian. And that scares the hell out of me." Her confession breaks the wall of insecurity between us. I breathe easily, holding her closer to me and rewarding her honesty with a sweet kiss. My lips mold to hers and I pour my passion into the kiss, needing her to feel it. My hands travel along her body, wanting to claim every inch, but she pulls away slightly, breathing heavily with her eyes closed.

I can feel a but coming. I blink the lust-filled haze away and wait for more. *Just tell me what you need, treasure. I'll give you anything.*

"I'm not okay right now, and all I want is you, but it's not the same for you..."

I pull away from her with my brows pinched. "What do you mean it's not the same for me? You don't think I want you? I've given you everything I can. I don't want to lose you."

"It's just. The contract-" The fucking contract. Just hearing her bring it up makes me snap. I don't care about it. I don't want anything in between us. My blood heats, and all I want to do is show her how much she means to me.

"Fuck the contract! Just don't leave me!" I stare deep into her eyes, feeling the emotions consuming me. I'm just as raw and vulnerable as she is. "I love you, Dahlia. I want you, and I'll do whatever it takes to keep you."

She takes in a sharp breath, her eyes searching my face. They're filled with hope and doubt.

I need to erase that doubt. I can handle anything but that. I want her passion; I want her heart. I want her everything.

"I love you and I can't let you go," I whisper as I pull her close to me, crushing her small body against mine and molding my lips to hers.

She pulls away from me, and I don't want to let her go. I don't want to break the kiss and lose her.

My eyes are closed as the warmth from our breath comes between our lips, but her body stays pressed against mine. My hands slip up the back of her shirt, feeling her soft skin against mine, keeping her close to me.

"Let me love you forever," I say softly. That's all I want. It's all I need. "Don't leave me again."

"Never. I'll never leave." A weight lifts off my chest as I crash my lips against hers again, needing to feel her. Needing to show her what she means to me.

"I love you, Lucian." Her words make my eyes slowly open and I stare into those beautiful hazel eyes.

"I love you, treasure."

EPILOGUE

LUCIAN

I love that collar around her neck. *My collar.* The gold and diamonds belong there, letting everyone know she's a treasure. *My treasure.*

What's better is how much she loves wearing it. She loves being mine. That's all she wants, and that's something I can always give her. Every day that passes I want her more.

"Are you ready for the show?" I ask my treasure as the waitress collects our empty dinner plates. We've been coming here more often. Club X. It's definitely helping her to learn how Dominants and Submissives are equals in their partnership. The show tonight will really bring that to light.

Her eyes still light up with awe at everything the club has to offer. She's certainly not a voyeur, but when the lights dim and the curtains open, she always asks to climb in my lap. She knows my fingers will travel right where she needs them as we watch. My lips are at her neck. My dick is already hardening. *Soon.*

Isaac invited us to see the show tonight.

He'll be on the stage tonight, but it's not with his Submissive. He's yet to collar her, or rather, she hasn't been willing to let him collar her. It's been nearly a month of them finding each other's limits within the club's boundaries. No Dom has gone near her since they've started their play. But there's still no collar around her neck. She submits for the shows and in the playrooms. She lets him take her to the private rooms. But it ends once she leaves the club, and she's yet to accept any commitment.

I don't understand the dynamic, but it's not my place to question it.

Dahlia breathes in deep, setting her spoon down on the dessert plate. "I'm really excited." She's hardly eaten. It must be her nerves.

"Stop worrying."

She's been letting the stress of going to my sister's party get to her. Christmas is only a week away and I know she's anxious. They hit it off last week when we went to dinner. We even got Italian water ice afterward, despite the cold temps. Both of them got lemon, of course. My treasure has nothing to worry about. Anna loves her already, for showing me I can love again. I'll always have my sister, and now with treasure it feels more like a complete family. I'll never be able to let the rest of my family in, but I'm finally at peace with that.

I take her small hand in mine and turn it over, kissing her wrist. I close my eyes and hum at her soft touch.

"I love you, treasure," I say and kiss her wrist again. It's her left hand and I know I'm going to be putting my ring there soon. I want everyone to know she belongs to me.

"I love you, too," she says sweetly, leaning in and kissing me on the lips. I can feel the eyes of other couples on us.

"Settle down, treasure," I warn her, nipping her bottom lip. She smiles sweetly and obeys. She's still the perfect Submissive. Even when she doesn't think we're playing. I'm still not sure she quite understands, but she trusts me and that's what matters. The trust between us is the only thing that matters.

Continue on for Book 2, Sold.

SOLD BOOK 2

PROLOGUE

ISAAC

I'm silent as I step into her room, taking in the sight of her tempting curves. She's spread for me as she lies on her back, her knees bent and heels digging into the mattress. My dick hardens in my pants as I see her pussy bared to me and glistening with need.

It's been so long since I've wanted something so intensely; she's devouring my every waking moment. Katia, my little kitten. Even when I close my eyes, she's there. I'm practically obsessed.

And now I have her.

My heart pounds with anticipation as I walk slowly toward her, the plush carpet muting the sounds of my movements.

In this moment, she's lost in her thoughts. Her expression is smooth, and her chest rises and falls with easy pressure. She belongs to no one. Not to me, not to her past.

The thick comforter beneath her small frame appears completely white, but upon closer inspection I can see the thin silver threads woven throughout create a faint damask pattern. The strands match the color of the thin scars that mar her soft skin, trailing from her shoulders down her back.

They only partially display her pain, but they also show her strength; they're proof of what she's overcome.

She has more healing to do. I'm going to help her. I know what she needs, and I can be the person who soothes her pain by showing her the intense pleasure this kind of relationship can bring. A dark part of me craves it.

She refused my collar for weeks. I knew she wanted it, but the last one she wore wasn't by choice.

It's only several steps until I'm standing over her, admiring her gorgeous features. Her plump lips that beg me to kiss her, and her long blonde hair fanned out beneath her sun-kissed shoulders.

My gaze drifts to my collar, firmly fitted around her neck. She could take it off if she wanted. But she won't. She craves the trust and the bond between a Dominant and Submissive. But she needs the relationship of a Master and Slave.

And now she has that. I'm proud that I gave that to her.

At my seemingly sudden touch, her whimpers fill the silent room. Fuck. She's soaking wet waiting for me. My fingers trail over her soft, wet folds and I marvel at how ready for me she is, my dick straining against the zipper of my pants. Her head falls back slightly while soft moans escape her lips, but with the blindfold over her eyes, she can't see me. She didn't even know I was next to her until the tips of my fingers were hot and slick with her arousal.

I can prove to her that she can trust again, and she can sate my desire for complete control.

The moment she agreed and stepped onto that stage to be sold, *she was mine.*

"I've missed you, kitten," I murmur in a deep voice and even cadence that make her lips part with desire.

"I've missed you, Master," she breathes into the hot air, her breath coming in ragged and need lacing her voice. Her soft voice mirrors her skillful obedience. Obedience she learned from someone else, but it's mine now.

It's only been a few hours, but knowing what I had to do, the pressing matters that kept me away, made the hours seem like days and I truly missed her touch.

Her tight walls squeeze my fingers as I shove two in. I have to close my eyes as the divine feel of her begs me to take her in this moment. Instead, I pump my fingers in and out, listening to the wet noises mixed with the sounds of her soft moans. She deserves to be rewarded for waiting like the good girl she is.

Katia bites down on her lip, muffling her cries of pleasure. Her sticky wetness drips down my wrists. She's obviously missed my touch just as much.

I watch her gorgeous body as she resists the natural instinct to writhe on the large bed as I stroke against her front wall, feeling the fires of desire stoking ever higher.

Sometimes she prefers to be bound, the thick coarse rope holding her to the bed. Sometimes she even enjoys having it tied around herself. The sight of her waiting for me bound and helpless... I won't lie; I fucking love it.

Never her ankle though. I'll never wrap anything around her ankle.

The dim light in the room barely reflects the jewels shimmering from her studded ankle bracelet. It hides scars that have yet to fully heal for her. It's heavy, mimicking the weight of the chain that once pierced into her skin at the bone. It's her choice to wear it. One day, when I've truly given her freedom from her past, she'll throw it away forever.

She may be a Slave to me, but I'm her Master, and I know what she desperately needs.

Her thighs tremble as her orgasm approaches, but I don't let up. She knows not to cum yet. Not until I give her permission. I own her pleasure. We both know that.

I slide my fingers in and out of her and watch as the lust on her face changes. The thrusts of my wrist make her body jolt slightly and her legs are shaking with need for her release, but other than that, she's still.

I could do whatever I want to her right now. Not because I'm stronger, not because of a contract. But because she wants me to. No. Because she *needs* me to do whatever it is I want to do to her in this very moment.

"Why do you need me?" I ask her. I know she's meant for me. I knew the second I saw her that she needed me just as much as I needed her.

"Master," she whimpers, her head slightly turning to the side with the need to thrash as I continue the ruthless motions.

Even with the heavy, jeweled metal covering the scars over her ankle, she hasn't realized. She has no idea why she needs me.

I grab her throat with my left hand, halting my movements. I put heavy pressure on her rough, sensitive G-spot with both fingers inside her. She's close and she needs this release, but I need to hear her say it.

"Why call me a Master, Katia?" My voice is harsh as I withdraw my hand from her welcoming heat and rip the blindfold off of her. I'm careful to make sure I don't catch her hair, but she doesn't know that. She has no idea how careful I am around her.

She doesn't answer, fear flashing in her pale blue eyes. Her breath hitches.

She wants to please me, but she can't answer me. *Because she doesn't know the answer.*

"Because you are my Master,." she says with faux confidence.

I lean forward, tightening my grip on her throat and whispering into her ear, "Why?" My breath tickles the sensitive skin of her neck, creating a shiver down her shoulders.

Her shoulders rise and fall with deep breaths as her eyes stay focused on mine. "Because you bought me," she answers in a soft voice, and even as she speaks the words she knows it's not what I was looking for. I can see the disappointment in her eyes.

My lips press against her forehead, reflecting the pain I feel from her answer. "No, kitten," I reply. That has nothing to do with it. Her safety is guaranteed with me. Her worries are nonexistent because I take the burden. She doesn't understand that, because to her, the word Master meant something much different. It was about control. And I have that, yes. But this is so much more than that.

I step back, leaving the cool air to replace my warmth as I unbuckle my belt.

I'LL SHOW HER WHY I DESERVE THE TITLE. THE THICK LEATHER SINGS in the air as I pull it through the belt loops.

She'll learn. And then she'll truly be mine.

"Get on your knees, kitten."

CHAPTER 1

ISAAC

The rough pad of my thumb brushes against my bottom lip, my elbow resting on the desk as I stare at the monitor in front of me. There are twenty on this side of the room, and another twenty behind me. The screens flip between cameras, and I take it all in effortlessly. I'm not usually in this room though. I actually prefer being on the floor, but I'm the boss and right now this is where I'm needed.

Shifting in the large desk chair, I let out an easy sigh from the tiresome day.

Club X needs extensive security and constant monitoring.

The members, both male and female Dominants, go through extensive training before being allowed to engage in any activity, but accidents are bound to happen. And sometimes they aren't accidents, no matter how strict our acceptance policies are. It's been quite a while since we've had any issues that required serious attention. But a lot of these members are new to the scene, and with inexperience comes errors.

Errors like Submissives who forget to safe word, and Dominants who don't recognize the signs that their partner isn't alright. They get caught up in the moment, and trust that their Submissive will safe word.

Ninety percent of the time when we intervene it's for those reasons--miscommunication and misguided trust.

I fucking hate safe words for that very reason. A good Dominant should know when enough is enough. But a lot of the people here are new; they're still learning, pushing each other's limits. More than half of the relationships are new or knowingly temporary.

Mistakes are inevitable. Still, it's my job to make sure they happen as infrequently as possible.

Security lines each doorway in the club, and I personally trained all of them. Protecting the members is number one on our priority list and for that reason, privacy is an illusion at Club X.

By that I mean there's a reason these men and women *play* here. The atmosphere that's created is intoxicating and alluring, but it's more than that, they're *safe* here. Whether or not a Sub or Slave trusts their Dom or Master, we're here to ensure they'll be okay. We provide a sense of safety that's needed for many of these women to let their guard down and completely immerse themselves in the lifestyle.

When a couple exits the club, there must truly be trust between them... except for the auctions. Those are a different beast entirely.

A chill washes through me in a slow wave at the thought of the auction. It's rare that the buyer and buyee don't know one another intimately already. But on occasion, it happens. Just like it happened last week with Lucian and his new Submissive. The reminder heats my blood.

Yet another D/s. I clench my jaw absently, my eyes moving from one screen to the next. I've been to the last six auctions. Although I work here, and workers aren't normally allowed to partake in the scene, I've dabbled in play. Madam Lynn turns a blind eye so long as I'm discreet. One of the perks of helping to mold the club and shape it into what it is today.

I sit up straighter in my seat, repositioning myself and keeping my mind from wandering to the dark corners of my mind where my depraved fantasies lie. I'm working, and now is no time for me to unleash my desires. There's no one here to fulfill them anyway. I've gotten used to it over the past year.

I watch a monitor on my far left as Dominic's attention strays from the large carved maple doors of the front entrance out to the dining hall. He's one of the bouncers at the club, and looks like he was built to work in security. He can't see much of what's going on in the dining hall, but the thick red curtains are pulled back and several girls are on the stage. This isn't any typical club. And it sure as hell isn't a strip club, although some of the men and women do enjoy exotic dancing during theme nights. The reason the women are lined up on the stage is so they can be trained. Regardless, the sight of beautiful women displayed and chatting captures Dominic's attention.

Some of the Submissives are collared, their Dominants giving them permission to learn while they sit patiently in the audience or accompany them onto the stage to do the training themselves. The uncollared Submissives are mostly unattended. One has a suitor, but he's merely watching from the audience.

Being collared is a serious commitment. Only a minority of the couples within the club are collared. Several have paired off and continue their play exclusively, but without a collar the commitment has yet to be made and the Submissive is not off-limits. It's not an offense to not be given a collar, it's simply something that isn't rushed into. There's a sense of respect and commitment surrounding the process, and every Dominant or Master has their own way of going about it.

I've never had the honor of giving out a collar. None of the handful of women I've kept as slaves have wanted to stay. They may have said one thing, but I knew better. I have yet to meet the woman who is my match.

The women on stage I've seen before. The club has regulars, and the exclusive invites rarely allows for new members. It creates an environment of familiarity, which aids in allowing the members to feel at ease.

There are several trainers with them as well. The trainers are experienced in BDSM, another pivotal feature of this club that I played a part in. We needed a safe way for the Submissives and the Dominants to learn. This club isn't a free-for-all. Although each Dominant has their own way of doing things, their own preferences and kinks, and we encourage the variety.

Dressed in leathers, the trainers are lined up and waiting for the women to choose instruments from the extensive collection. Their sole purpose is to provide a means for the women to explore their limits. One woman, I believe her name is Lisa, is concerned about her positioning. Although she's dressed in a simple cream chiffon romper, she's on the waxed floor of the stage, practicing with a trainer offering advice. She's not very graceful. Poor girl. She's going to really have to work on her balance.

A quick vision flashes in front of my eyes of how I'd train her. I'd use a flogger, certainly not a cane or paddle. Every unstable waver of her body would earn her a lashing. At first I'd have her balance on one foot, but ultimately I'd have her end up in the position she's in now. On her back, on the floor, her legs spread and opened for me. And as she worked on balancing herself, the heavy braided tails would whip against her glistening pussy. I can visualize how the skin on her thighs and ass would be flushed red from the punishing strokes. But the ones at the end of her training would already have her on edge. What was a punishment, would turn into a reward.

I glance back at the Submissive, Lisa. I can see it happening, but not with her. She's not for me.

Most of these women want a Dominant. They want to be able to rely on safe words. I don't provide that. It's something I'm not interested in. I want a woman's complete trust. Or at least her utter reliance on me, and total obedience.

I recognize Lilly on the stage as well. She's fairly new to the club, and she's yet to find a Dominant. She's eager to learn and excitable, but her energy is excessively positive. I've heard many men talk about how she seems more vulnerable and breakable than even the more experienced Subs in the club. *Bubbly* is a good description of her.

Oddly enough, she's the only one walking to the whips on the right side of the stage. Her bracelet is cream-colored, indicating that she's finding her limits.

I glance at the other screens before coming back to hers. Her fingers trail down the knotted ends of a cat o' nine tails, and several men in the audience perk up at the sight. I wouldn't have guessed she'd be a red woman. The women with the red in their bracelets are ones who enjoy pain. Masochists. She may be interested in the whip, but her reaction will be enlightening, I'm sure. Many underestimate the intensity of the pain. It takes time and several punishing hits before the resulting adrenaline rush and flood of endorphins work their magic and turn pain into pleasure. It takes the right partner as well.

My eyes flash to the next screen, and a rough chuckle makes my shoulders shake as Madam Lynn catches Dominic lingering in the large opening between the front lobby and the dining hall.

One look from her, and he's quick to go back to his place at the front. He may be nearly six and a half feet tall with broad shoulders to match his intimidating height, but Madam Lynn doesn't compromise. Everyone knows that. Dominic returns to his post while he adjusts his dick in his pants. I snort a laugh. I'm not hard in the least.

Nothing has excited me for years, but Dominic never fails to be aroused. I imagine it would be different if the employees were permitted to play in the club. But there's a zero-tolerance policy against it. Professionalism is the most valued attribute to Madam Lynn. I'm fortunate she makes an exception for me.

I glance around the monitors, but my sight is once again drawn to the stage. The cat o' nine tails is whipping across the screen and landing with a loud hiss against a dummy. Lilly walks closer to the dummy and runs her fingers along the marks left by the whip while the trainer talks to her, wrapping the whip around his hand and walking toward her.

I can't hear what he's saying, but she's listening intently. She's showing him her full attention and taking the lesson seriously. The Dominants may not realize it yet, but in the years I've been here, I know an excellent Submissive in the making, and Lilly will certainly be one.

Although she won't be mine. She's not my type. None of these women are. I'd rather be picky and choose one who is meant to fit my desires, just as I'm meant to fit her needs. I'm not interested in a quick fuck; most of the men here aren't. It's better to find a match that you can grow to trust. Someone who can help you delve deeper into your darkest desires.

"Poker on Saturday?" Joshua's deep voice distracts me from my thoughts. I turn in the swivel chair to face him. The room is a mirror image, and he's been in charge of monitor display of the second floor, while I've taken the first. The screens behind him flip among the other rooms as he looks over his shoulder at me.

Joshua is a co-owner of the club with Madam Lynn. We went into business together with security, and his relationship with Madam Lynn created all of this. They're good friends and nothing more. The ring on his finger and the collar on his wife make that more than apparent.

"Yeah, Saturday," I answer. I've been hosting the card games the last few weeks now. My cabin's on the outskirts of the city with no neighbors or wives, or in Joshua's case, children.

It's empty, which I used to enjoy. I'm fond of privacy. The only time I hear a voice at home besides my own is poker night. It hasn't bothered me much before, but now that most of the men seem taken with their partners, the halls seem quieter in a way I find slightly disconcerting. Especially this last week, with Lucian being quieter than usual and preoccupied with his Submissive.

I crack my neck, feeling the stiffness of my muscles. I'll hit the gym in my basement and take a shower before bed. I need to do something to get out this tension.

"How much you planning on losing this week?" I say and smirk at him.

Joshua's face scrunches as he focuses on a screen. He visibly winces as he watches one of the red rooms in the dungeon. I'm surprised anything gets to him anymore.

Finally recognizing my words, he answers, "I'm taking every chip you got, Rocci." I snort a laugh and hold back my yawn.

I stand up and stretch, picking up my worn brown leather coat off the back of my chair. It's time to go home anyway. I'm going on a fourteen-hour shift here. Derek called out unexpectedly, and I covered for him on his short notice.

I think about what's waiting for me back at home.

The mess is still on the table in the game room from last week's poker game. A few bottles and cigar wrappers. Nothing worth bitching about; the maid will clean it up tomorrow anyway.

I watch the monitors in front of Joshua, consumed by the image that's holding his attention. A Master and a Slave. They're a rarity here. The red rooms in the dungeon require the most attention, for obvious reasons.

I've seen Masters come and go in the club. Many are Sadists and that creates serious problems, so we don't allow many. I'm one, although my desire to use pain is only to enhance pleasure. And that's not the situation that's occurring on the screen at the moment. Joshua looks tense and concerned, but there's no reason to be. Becca loves the pain. She doesn't need a safe word because her limits are much higher than her Master's. She arches her back toward the cane, accepting the blow and greeting it with a look of ecstasy etched on her face. She's the only Slave here, and she's collared. I don't even know why they come here anymore.

It's been a long time since a Slave has arrived. Someone who's capable of trusting so wholeheartedly that they're willing to give herself completely over to a Master. Who's willing to give over to a 24/7 power exchange.

Maybe that's why nothing has interested me. My tastes are specific. *A Slave.* I crave the power being a Master allows me, and the desire to control and provide her every need.

Across the hall from the game room in my home is the door to a room I created for one sole purpose. A room fit for my match.

I shrug the leather jacket on my shoulders, trying to remember when the last time I even opened it was.

Too long. It's been far too long.

CHAPTER 2

KATIA

I can practically hear the clock ticking as I go about my daily routine. *Tick. Tick. Tick.* It's a quarter past five and I'm running behind schedule. I'm usually on time, but I had difficult time sleeping last night, tossing and turning for most of the night. I frown at the memory as I pull on my faded wash jeans over my hips, and tug down my cozy red sweater.

I haven't had a night that bad in a while. I cover my mouth with a yawn and try to ignore the unsettling feelings as I make my way to the bathroom sink. But I'm hoping it's just a fluke. It *is* just a fluke. I won't let things get back to the way they were.

Pushing the unpleasant memory away, I swipe on my favorite lipstick in a shade reminiscent of crushed rose petals, and smoosh my lips together. Then I peer critically at myself in the mirror. The quick ponytail I coax my hair into is going a long way to hide my disheveled blonde hair, but when you're the owner of Paws Apartments, a doggy day care and shelter, your hair doesn't need to be pretty. You just need to show up and be there.

I've found dogs only care about two things. Well, three. Food, exploration and companionship. I love it actually. Working and caring for these dogs fills me with purpose and gives my life meaning. It's the one thing I look forward to every day. Just thinking about the excitement on their fuzzy little faces when I walk in to greet them warms my chest and brings a small smile to my lips as I reach for the small tube of thick concealer.

Another part of my routine.

My smile slowly vanishes as I run my fingertips along the scars littering my neck. No matter how much time passes, they barely seem to fade. It's been four long years, but they're still there, reminding me of a darker time in my life. As I stare at my neck in the mirror, a weight presses down on my chest, but after a moment I push it away in defiance.

I survived all that, I think to myself, dotting the concealer on my neck and right shoulder and then reaching for my foundation. *And I'm stronger now.*

He didn't ruin me. I won't let him hold any power over me anymore.

Straightening my back, I swallow thickly and square my shoulders as I delicately press the foundation onto my skin and smooth the concealer on the scars on my neck until they're all gone. After I'm done with my face, I toss the foundation into the decorative velvet-lined box where I keep my makeup, the memories already fading. Coffee is the next thing on my agenda.

Tick, tick, tick. The small ticks echo in my head, reminding me how far I'm behind already. I grit my teeth. *Crap.*

I almost call out, "I'm coming, Roxy!" as I make my way to the kitchen, but then I catch myself, a feeling of sadness coursing through me. I take a deep breath and rub under my tired eyes. It's a habit I have yet to break. I'm so used to Roxy being there every time I turn around that I still haven't gotten over the fact that she's gone.

Tears prick my eyes as my bare feet pad on the linoleum and I start the coffee maker. Two clicks, and it's brewing. I should grab something to eat, but instead I find myself lost in thought as the sounds of the water heating fill the empty space. The quiet space. Quiet because she's not here anymore.

Roxy, my Golden Retriever, was such a lovable dog. She was always there for me whenever I needed her. She was so happy. I swear dogs can smile, and she was always smiling. We were practically inseparable. And she didn't give a rat's ass that I had scars all over my back or that I was scared of things I couldn't see, of dark memories that I desperately wanted to leave in the past.

She just loved me unconditionally and only wanted to comfort me. I clung to that love, fostering it. She was my therapy, and I came to depend on her for so much. I can't count how many times I woke up out of a night terror, frightened out of my mind, only to find Roxy sitting right there, nuzzling against me and whining with true pain from worrying over me. Her calming presence would almost always soothe my anxiety. It's times like last night, when I'd been plagued by a particularly dark terror, where I miss her the most.

It hurts so badly to think that she's never going to lay with me in bed again. To think I can no longer hold her close and pet her with long strokes as I whisper, *thank you* into her thick fur. She'd done so much for me, more than anyone else has: loving me, healing me, that even if she were here now, I'd never be able to repay her for it.

I try to lean against the counter and my elbow knocks the plastic travel mug off the counter. I try to grab it but miss, the plastic hitting the tips of my fingers before falling onto the floor with a loud clatter. I wince from the loud noise and wait for it to settle before picking it up.

"I guess it's just going to be one of those days," I mutter out loud to myself, wiping at the tears in the corner of my eyes with the back of my hand. At least it's not broken. I bend down, scooping the mug up and finally resting against the counter as the smell of coffee fills the room. Since Roxy's death, some days have been harder than others, with me nearly overcome with emotion. Unfortunately, this was shaping up to be one of *those* days. I suppose that's just how grief works.

It's even worse considering Roxy was the first pet I've ever had, and that she was the only companionship I had when I first came back home. I pause as I pour cream and sugar into my coffee cup. Maybe it's not right to call this place home. I'm still hours away from what used to be home. The small suburbs of New York will never be home again. I just can't face the constant reminders. I feel guilty about distancing myself from my family and the life I used to have, but it's for the better. It's the only way I'll find happiness after everything that happened.

I take a deep breath, setting the mug on the counter and inhaling the smell of fresh hot French vanilla coffee, doing everything I can to let go of the painful reminder. Losing Roxy was very difficult, but I can't keep going on like this. I'll always love her, but she wouldn't want me living with this constant negativity. I just know in my heart she wouldn't.

Closing my eyes, I take a small sip of the coffee and let the warmth fill me, comfort me. When I open them a moment later, they focus like a laser onto the clock on the microwave.

5:45

Shit, now I'm really running late. Sighing, I take another sip of my coffee, trying to relax. I'm only behind by fifteen minutes, but the dogs are there and waiting. I don't want to disrupt our routine. They need it just as much as I do.

A low ding from my phone draws my eyes over to the kitchen table where my laptop is sitting open from the previous night, and I see my cell screen lit up on the edge of the lap top with a text. I let out a sigh and quickly grab it off the side of the table, hitting the keypad and waking the laptop to life. I don't really have time for this, but I can't not answer it. Before I can check my message, I see a notification pop up in the lower right corner on my laptop screen.

Darlinggirl86 has come online.

My phone dings again, but I ignore it as my last DM with Kiersten lights up with a message. I smile as I read what she's typed.

Darlinggirl86: *<3 you girl. You were right! I should've gone shopping. It made me feel so much better. I finally got that red dress that I've been eyeing for like a month now. And you wanna know the best thing? I look damn good in it too!*

Smiling, I type a response while huffing out a small chuckle.

Katty93: *<3 you too! I bet you look damn good in it too!*

It always makes me feel good to talk to Kiersten. I consider her to be one of my best friends, even though we've never met. I've never even seen her face. We've spent the last four years bonding over this support group message board, engaging in conversations about how messed up our lives were, sharing our dreams, hopes and aspirations. And most importantly, moving forward.

I wait for a response, but after almost a minute passes, I type in that I have to go. I really hate being late. I don't like making the pups wait for me. I finally take a look at my phone and let out a heavy sigh when I see who it is. *Mom.*

Katia, I miss you honey! When are you going to come home?

Seeing the message gives me mixed emotions. I'm lucky to have my mother, to have a loving family. But they're a part of my past I just can't come to terms with. In this new city, with a new life, the past doesn't matter. I can be anyone. But with them, I'll always be Katia, their daughter who was taken for four years. And worse, when I look at them, I see how the years changed them.

Maybe it's wrong of me, but when I think of her, I want to see the mother I knew. Seeing her reminds me of the time I was away. All the times I missed. When I last saw her, before they took me, she was happy, young and vibrant. That was over eight years ago.

I want to see her blonde hair that looks just like mine, not the silver shade that's taken its place. Her gorgeous smile that I always envied, and blue eyes that sparkled with laughter. She tries, but the pain is still there. And it hurts me too much to see it.

When I was gone she never stopped looking for me, never once gave up on finding her precious daughter. I hate that I caused her so much stress, so much pain. Even if it wasn't intentional, I still feel responsible. I still feel fucking guilty. I hate that she had to worry about me night after night, hoping, praying that she would one day find me alive.

But she couldn't save me. No one could. I had to save myself.

And looking at her only reminds me of that.

I REALLY CAN'T DEAL WITH THIS TODAY, I THINK TO MYSELF, TEARING my glassed-over eyes away from the screen and not bothering to look at the five other messages she's sent.

I love my mother dearly. But it's better this way. I don't want her tainted any more by what happened to me. That's not to say that I'm not better now. I'm a survivor.

I suck in a deep, trembling breath. I don't want to tell her that I'm not coming home. I'm trying to get over everything. And despite my trepidation about dealing with my mother, I do want to see my family again. But I can't right now. I'm just not ready. It's been four years of recovery, only nine months out here on my own, and I know I'm a stronger, better person for it. Yet, deep down I still feel like I'm... not whole. I'm still healing. And that's okay. But being away from home makes everything easier. It hurts me to admit it, but I just want to be alone.

Well not alone, alone.

My fingers find the dip of my throat as my heart pounds in my chest as I think back to my previous conversation with Kiersten before she abruptly logged off. I'd finally confessed what I'd been thinking for some time. Something that I knew I deeply wanted, but was afraid to admit; my need for a Master.

I shake my head at the memory, still not believing I admitted this, to me or to her. After everything I went through, how more fucked up in the head could I get?

Tick, tick, tick. Fuck, I need to get my shit together and get going.

My eyes stray back to my cell's screen and I read my mother's first text again, my heart feeling like it's being tugged down by an anchor. I want to answer her and soothe her worry. I want to reassure her that I'll be there soon. But deep down, I know that's not enough.

Taking a deep breath, I let my fingers fly across the touch screen keys.

I love you mom. I promise I'll come home soon.

I stare at the text for a moment, debating on whether I should delete it. I don't want to make a promise I know I can't keep. Yet at the same time, I don't want to cause her any more pain or guilt. I want her to feel better, just like I want to feel better.

After what seems like an eternity, I close my eyes and hit send, hoping desperately that I don't regret it.

CHAPTER 3

ISAAC

*M*y bare feet tread the cold porcelain tiles of my state of the art kitchen floor. The steel gleams with the bright morning light streaming through the large floor-to-ceiling windows on the far wall of the breakfast nook. My house may be quiet and empty, but it's luxurious and fitted with every upscale feature I could find.

Modern, and sophisticated. It's exactly what I wanted.

The coffee maker is already going and the sounds of steaming water get louder as the addicting scent of fresh ground coffee fills my lungs.

I cover my yawn and then stretch my arms above my head, feeling the stiff muscles ease. My flannel pajamas hang low on my hips as I crack my neck. Same shit, different day, but I'm ready for the excitement of the club. I'm determined to look into recruitment and go through candidates. I've been talking to Madam Lynn, hinting at the fact that I'm interested in finding a potential Slave.

She hears me, but I have no idea if she's really listening.

The door to the fridge opens with a small hum and I crouch down to grab a pepper and a few eggs for my morning omelet.

I love cooking. It's the one thing my mother used to do for me. Before things changed, she always cooked me breakfast. Even after things changed... for a little while.

I shake off the memories threatening to suffocate me and crack the eggs on the side of a bowl, whisking them as I try to ignore the memory of her laugh. She had a beautiful laugh, my mother. The sounds changed as she did. They were once light and airy, but they changed to a rough voice that cracked when she spoke. In the end, I didn't even recognize her.

I turn on the gas burner and let the pan heat as I grab my cell.

I work at Club X and its safety is my priority, but my security business is still private and taking inquiries.

I put the phone on speaker and listen to the voicemails from yesterday. I rarely get a call for RP Security. That's what we were called before transferring to the club. R and P, for Rocci and Knight. Zander and I still own the firm 50/50, but we hardly ever take clients. It's simply not worth it. Well Zander never took clients. He's a silent partner. Still, it's not worth it.

I listen to a message from a man wanting a security detail at an exclusive getaway trip for him and his mistress as I dice up the pepper and half of an onion. I shake my head, deleting it and not even thinking twice about calling him back as I toss the knife into the stainless steel sink.

That's not what my business is for. I started it myself around the same time Lucian quit college and created his company. It wasn't long before I followed suit. The three of us were inseparable, and in many ways we still are. Zander footed the bill for both Lucian and me. He's good for fronting money in exchange for stocks, and not doing any of the work. Hiring Joshua as my right hand man took the business to the next level and turned it high-end.

But I'm not interested in being a lookout while a cheater gets his dick wet.

I created this business for one reason. My mother's laugh echoes in my head again as I watch my breakfast cook in the pan. I'm losing my appetite more with every second that passes.

Murder. Vengeance. I needed the man who killed her dead.

She may not have been a real mother to me in the last two years of her life. The alcohol she used to numb the pain of losing my father overseas eventually turned to coke. Holding me close and crying on my shoulder because she missed my father turned to beating me because I reminded her of him.

She was responsible for her actions. I know that. But he didn't help. He made them worse.

Jake Shapero. Her boyfriend who got her addicted to harder drugs and led her down the path that ultimately destroyed the mother I once knew.

Also, the asshole who broke my jaw because I dared to talk back. I flex my jaw at the memory as I use the spatula to lift the perfect omelet off the pan and onto a plate. I have no desire to eat it at this point, but I still add salt and pepper and sit at the table. Routine is important.

I close my eyes, and he's there. It wasn't just one punch, but I didn't see him. As I covered my face with my forearms, I saw her in the background. Sitting at the table, bent over and wiping the coke from under her nose, not even bothering to show emotion.

That's not what made me want to kill him. That's not why I got into this business.

When I was fourteen, I watched him kill her. It was the culmination of two long years of abuse and neglect, night after night. I watched him hit her; I watched him strangle her. He didn't see me there, and I'd longed stopped defending her. A broken jaw, busted ribs, and beatings from both of them for interfering taught me to stay away.

I hadn't realized he was actually killing her. I couldn't believe she was really dead, even after she fell to the floor and his anger changed to fear as he shook her.

I watched him, and did nothing. The guilt weighs heavy on my chest as I take a bite of the tasteless eggs. Hating the memory.

I was tortured for years while I lived with my distant Aunt Maureen. She's much older than my mother, almost like a grandmother. She gave me a good life; she took care of me as though I wasn't troubled. But I never forgave myself.

How could I?

I never wanted to go to college, but Aunt Maureen made me. I was happy to keep her preoccupied with me being in college while I learned more useful skills. Meeting Joshua and Zander was the best thing that happened to me in college. I learned how to track down targets, how to hack into databases and effectively get someone's records and backgrounds.

That someone being Jacob Shapero.

I wasn't surprised to learn he was in prison for assault and battery, as well as possession. I had to wait over a year. A year of growing my security business with Joshua and making it legit. Thanks to Zander, a silent partner, we had the funds and clientele to make it exclusive. But every day was just one step closer to my goal. The night he was released, I waited for a sign of activity. I had ten close contacts' phones monitored. And he made the call not fifteen minutes after leaving the station. The second night, I crept into his deceased grand-mother's house and shot him in the back of the head. Waiting that long fucking killed me, but I had to do it right. I spent years preparing, and it only took two days to see it through once I had the opportunity.

I have a lot of connections now, six years later. Many powerful and also corrupt people, due to this clientele and because of the deals I've taken. It's not about the money. It's about making things right. The business is legit, although some of my methods toe the line. Occasionally I break the law to obtain information. That's the busi-ness I run. We call it security, but we've been known to do things a little less legal.

I haven't taken a private client in a long fucking time. It's been years. The club takes a lot of my time and if there's a client in need, I hand them off to someone who's qualified. The money's good, and the business is streamlined.

Sometimes I wonder if my focus on routine and careful practices, my seclusion and most notably my past, are why I am the way I am. Why I thrive on privacy and control. Not in everything. Just things that matter.

In relationships, especially.

I need complete control. I need trust so deep that she'll give herself to me completely.

I'm not interested in normal. I've had a few relationships, but none that meant anything to me. None that lasted very long.

The two M/s relationships I've had in the club didn't last long either. Neither of them gave me what I needed. And they sure as fuck didn't need me. They wanted the relationship as a way to give up control, but not because they needed to; they just didn't want responsibility. They didn't want the other aspects of being a Slave. Neither lasted more than a few weeks. I want someone who needs me. I'm desperate for it.

I know what I want from my partner is fucked up. I want her devotion, and her only desire to be to please me. I want more than I deserve, but I'll provide every want, every wish, every need. In exchange for her worshiping obedience, I'll give her the same in return.

I don't want a safe word, I don't want negotiation and compromise. I demand complete submission, and nothing less.

It's fucked up, but I want it. And I'm tired of waiting.

It's Lucian's fault. Him wanting a Submissive and buying one on the spot is what's fueling this need. I know it is. I'm pissed. I'm jealous. It was so fucking easy for him.

I'll never have that.

What I crave is too rare. Too depraved to be so easily found and taken.

I don't know why, and I don't give a fuck. But I'm ready and tired of waiting.

CHAPTER 4

KATIA

I hum a Katy Perry song playing through my radio speakers as I pull into my designated parking spot of Pine Brook Apartments, my spirits high. Today was an awesome day, and it was something I desperately needed after a week of night terrors.

An older couple who were leaving for vacation boarded their Miniature Schnoodle, Mr. Higgins, for the week. He has to be the most adorable dog I've ever seen with his tiny, bearded face. He looks like an old man and my heart just melted whenever I laid eyes on him. The day got even better when three eager high school kids, bless their hearts, dropped in to volunteer. I had a blast working with the kids, and they absolutely fell in love with Mr. Higgins and his puppy dog antics. It was so cute to watch. It's not uncommon for kids to volunteer. I have a program set up with a local school, but it makes it that much better when the kids obviously enjoy themselves.

Since the kids had so much fun I'm hoping they'll go tell all their friends about the dog shelter so more of them will come play with the pups. That's all I ask them to do. Just give the dogs some attention.

I love each and every one of the dogs, but there's not enough time in the day for me to give all of them the attention they deserve. That's not to say I and my other four employees don't do enough for them, but these dogs deserve more than what we can give.

Stretching as I go, I climb out of the car and make my way to my apartment. I wince as I make it to the paved walkway that leads to the stairs, a sharp pain spiking up my back. I'm totally sore from hauling bags of dog food.

I take the stairs slowly, feeling the strain of the day on my muscles. I don't mind it, though. It feels good to just *feel*; even if it is because I'm sore. It lets me know I've had a productive day. Even if all I did was lift dog food all day, it makes me happy. Helping the dogs gives my life special meaning.

I take in a deep breath, still clinging to that happy feeling, but at the same time I feel a sadness trying to creep in. A sadness that is trying to remind me of what my life could be. I hate it.

I reach the door of my apartment and try to push that unwelcome feeling away, taking out my keys. I'm about to unlock the door when I look up to see the mailman coming my way with a small box in his hand, along with an electronic signature pad in the other.

I furrow my brow as he approaches, wondering what's in the box. I'm absolutely certain that I haven't ordered anything in the past few days.

"Miss Herrington?" he asks me, stopping right in front of me and giving me a friendly smile. He's an energetic young man, with blond hair and bushy eyebrows.

"Yes?" I say, flashing a friendly smile back.

He hands me the electronic device, along with a stylus. "If you could just sign for me here, please?"

I take both and quickly scribble my name and hand it back over to him.

He smiles at me again as he hands me the box. "Thank you Miss Herrington, have a wonderful day."

"Thank you," I reply absently, my eyes still on the box in my hands. "You, too."

With the box tucked under my arm, I open the door and kick it shut behind me. I turn it in my hands, the keys jingling as I toss them onto the kitchen table and look for the address label. There's no return address listed, but I recognize the sender's name. Kiersten. A smile graces my lips as I plop down into my seat. She's such a freaking sweetheart. She knows this past week has been rough, and it's not unusual that we give each other a little gift here and there when we're going through something hard.

I instinctively look past my kitchen and into the cozy living room at the wooden owl on the bottom of my end table. It was a gift from Kiersten. She knows I love owls. I think it's a door stopper, but it looks just right where I put it.

My place is a nice, one-bedroom apartment with a spacious, open floor plan. It's not cheap, but it's not too expensive either, considering it's in the city. The kitchen and living room join seamlessly with one another. There's a large sliding glass door at the end of the living room that leads to a small patio. There are two windows with sheer curtains on either side of the couch. I always keep the curtains open because I like the sunlight. It helps keep the darkness away. I went a long time without sunshine, and I'll never take such a simple thing for granted again.

There's not much to the rest of my apartment, just a small hallway and then my bedroom and an adjoining bathroom. But I love it. It has a cozy vibe, and I've surrounded myself with little things that help keep my mood upbeat, like the stone bunny bookends on the shelf next to the couch, owl pillows, and beautiful glazed ceramic planters by the large windows filled with succulents. I forget to water the plants often, so they have to be succulents. And I filled this place with warm yellows that seem to pop out at you. I use yellow because I've always heard that it helps with depression. Just seeing the color stimulates endorphins that make you happy. And I want to be happy. More than anything; it's all I want.

My eyes stray back to the box and I wonder again what it is. Deep down, I know this is something different. Something... special.

There's only one way to find out.

I walk over to the cabinet and retrieve a letter opener and then come back to the box. My heart racing in my chest, I pry it open.

My breath catches in my throat when I see what's inside. A fancy golden envelope sits on a bed of purple plush velvet fabric. Holy shit, this is fancy. I pick it up, marveling at the soft feel of the parchment. It's unlike any paper I've ever felt before. It's thick and luxurious. After a moment of staring at it, I carefully open it to reveal a golden card with tassels on the side. There's a simple message inscribed inside.

You've been invited to Club X.
Madam Lynn

CLUB X. THE WORDS RUN OVER AND OVER IN MY MIND. I CAN'T FOR the life of me figure out what it is. It sounds like some sort of secret underground club, yet I can't make any sense of it. Why send me an invitation without any information about what I would be joining? And who the hell is Madam Lynn? It's just strange. I check the box again, and there's Kiersten's name. I can't get the scrunched expression off my face.

I turn the invitation over in my hand, examining it several times, looking for any clues of what this club is about. There aren't any.

Shrugging off my coat, I walk over to my desk in the corner of my living room, thrumming with excitement, sit down and open my laptop. When the screen lights up, I quickly type in my password and bring up the web browser. I type in Club X in the search bar and then hit enter. Kiersten won't be on till tonight. And I'm too impatient to wait to ask her.

My heart drops in my chest at the results that pop up. Nothing with "Club X" per se. But a bunch of porn websites and pornographic pictures are the first things listed. Some information about ecstasy. Certainly not what I expected. I click through a couple of them, but the sites are all set up to get you to put in your credit card. Screw that. I click through a bunch more websites, trying to find any information that links to the invitation, but I come up short. There's absolutely nothing here. After clicking through a couple more, I shut down the browser, a feeling of disappointment running through me.

I'm about to close down my laptop when an email notification pops up in the lower right corner of my screen. The title of the subject makes my heart jump in my chest, and I almost click on it immediately.

Your invitation awaits

I sit there for a moment before clicking, my heart pounding in my chest as my skin pricks from a sudden chill. How eerie.

From: Madam Lynn

To: Katia Herrington

Katia, I've been notified that you've received my invitation, and I'm attaching information for your consideration before we move forward. I feel it's in your best interest as well as Club X's for you to consider enrollment. I personally invite you to check us out. I know you'll enjoy it. A bracelet is included in the package. Please bring it with you. I'll see you soon.

Yours truly,

Madam Lynn

My heart is nearly beating out of my chest as I quickly download the forms, open them and begin reading. My eyes go wide as I skim through pages and pages of what essentially amounts to a non-disclosure agreement. If I want to be a part of the club, I have to sign it and adhere to the rules listed. There are four other downloads, one with a list of themed nights. Another with rules for the club. And there are *a lot* of them.

Another download with testimonies.

And the last one, pictures of a gorgeous building. It looks almost like a mansion. But the inside is what steals my breath away.

I sit there for I don't know how long, greedily devouring every word that scrolls across the page. It takes a while, but when I finally reach the end, my mind is reeling from the wealth of information. A lot of what I read was legal jargon, but there are three words that stick out in my mind.

Auction.

Submissive.

Master.

Club X is an exclusive BDSM club.

I suck in a heavy breath as I stare at the screen, excitement coursing through my limbs, but at the same time feeling slightly sick to my stomach. Am I really going to do this? It could be a way to confront that part of me that isn't fully healed, the part of me that's still dark and twisted.

I mentioned it to Kiersten, but I didn't expect this.

I have fantasies. I have cravings. I don't want normal. I tried to have a sexual relationship with someone who doesn't want complete control. But I want to give someone my everything. I want the fantasy that I found sanctuary in. I survived because of it. It's so deeply ingrained in me, and I don't want it to leave.

I don't know if I was always like this. But there's a power in submitting wholly to someone. To giving them everything and trusting them. I want to do it again.

It feels wrong. But I know deep down that it's what I want. It's what I'm missing.

I know people live with the illusion I created for myself. It's their life. I want that. I want to trust someone to take me as their Slave, and cherish me like I made myself believe my Master did.

I try to push this feeling and dark thoughts away, but they remain.

I pick up the letter again, letting the tips of my fingers trail over the engraved "X." I want it, but I'm terrified to let go. In a place like this though... Maybe this is exactly what I need.

CHAPTER 5

ISAAC

I'm two whiskeys in, and I can't help myself.

I've read her files over and over. My poor Katia. Kidnapped at sixteen years old while walking home from school. It was a nice neighborhood, low crime. No reason to worry. But one day she just vanished. Marcio Matias kidnapped her and three other women that day. He was well known in the sex slave traffic industry, and is currently incarcerated and on death row. Which only makes me angrier that I can't get my hands on him myself.

Katia is only one of hundreds of women who Marcio kidnapped over a decade.

She was a virgin, and traded to a drug lord and head of a cartel in Colombia, Carver Dario. He went by Master C, and had many slaves and shared them freely. From what I can tell, Katia was no exception and her police reports go into detail about what a man named Javier Pinzan, second-in-command of the cartel did to her. Her life was hell. She was surrounded by abusive men who took pleasure from her pain. Her arm and jaw were both broken while she was held prisoner.

Her arm more than once.

In her psych transcripts I read about how she murdered him. How she broke a liquor bottle and stabbed Dario repeatedly, running away in the middle of the night wearing nothing but a large man's dress shirt. She was filthy when they found her in a village on the outskirts of the tourist areas. She was bruised and scarred, and almost died of malnutrition and infections.

A group of tourists just happened to be in the area. Without them, I'm not certain what would have happened to her. My heart clenches in my chest, and I take another swig of the whiskey.

She saved herself.

It's been four years since she's been home. She spent a good amount of time in protective custody, adjusting to life again. She was in and out of therapy for the first few months until she started seeing a young woman named Meredith Beck. She stayed with her for two years, attending regular sessions that eventually dwindled. She hasn't been to her in over eight months and the last time she went, Dr. Beck prescribed Katia sleeping aids, a prescription that Katia never filled.

I've hacked into the support group that I know Katia is an active member in. Extremely active. She comes on daily, and is one of only a handful of users in here. This seems to be the only social interaction she has.

At first it was just to find out more about how she's healing. Just to read her messages and figure out if she still has problems sleeping. I've learned a lot about my Katia since logging in. She's a kind girl with a beautiful heart. She wants to be happy.

I take another sip of whiskey, ignoring the papers on the desk detailing her dark past, and focus on how she is now, in the present. How much better she is. How healthy and happy she is. Although there's still pain. Still a void in her life... for now.

I've created my own account and made a false identity. I didn't provide any major details, but most of the profiles here are lacking.

I know it's wrong, but I want to get to know her.

Madam Lynn would be pissed if she found out, but I'm curious. I have to know more about *her*. Katia Herrington. Her information was easily accessible, and I've been through all of it. All her background, multiple times.

Curious doesn't even begin to describe it. I know what she's been through, what she's survived. Even more, I know what she's looking for. I know what she *needs*. At first, when I read her transcripts from the protective unit, I was horrified. She endured abuse in every possible way for years, along with malnutrition, and constant violence. The poor girl has survived too much.

She's strong. She's fierce. But she's in need.

And I desperately want to fulfill that void for her.

I already know my ways are twisted, so something like this is just a drop in the bucket.

I check the blank screen again. She should be on soon. She's a creature of habit. Her login info has her on here almost every night. It's something I'll have to give her if I decide she's a good match. And if she agrees to be mine.

Her paperwork sits in front me on the kitchen table, just to the right of the laptop. I know everything that happened to her after she was taken. Everything she's done for the last four years. She's such a strong, brave woman. And lucky. So fucking lucky that it was a group of tourists who found her on the outskirts of the city. If it'd been anyone else, who knows where my kitten would have wound up.

She spent four years locked in a cell and treated like shit. Constant abuse and neglect until she caved to what Carver Dario wanted. She did what she had to do to survive. He wasn't a master. He was an abuser who deserved to die a painful death.

GROUPCHAT

Katty93 has logged in.

My heart races as I watch the blip appear on the screen. I've been waiting for her. It's wrong. I know it is. I'm not disillusioned into thinking this isn't fucked up. I just don't care.

Catlvr89: Hello Kat!

Katty93: Oh hi there!

Are you new here? Welcome!

A smile slips across my face at her willingness to please. Her happiness that's apparent on the screen.

Catlvr89: I am. Today is my first day.

Katty93: It's a nice place here. I think you'll find it really supportive.

Catlvr89: So far I have!

Katty93: …

The dots signifying Katia is typing a response appear on the screen, but then vanish. I consider typing something, but then I wait a few more seconds.

Katty93: How are you doing today?

Catlvr89: Today is good. It's been a long time since I've had a rough day.

I type in the answer before I have a moment to think. I'm not blind to the fact that this is a support group and there are more people here than just Katia. I'm not interested in taking advantage of Katia or anyone else. I just need answers to make sure she's the one I've been waiting for. I know she's usually on late, and I'm only here for her. But I'll do my best to blend in and be discreet.

I may not have gone through what some of the people on here have. But others here are coping with death. I can relate to that.

Katty93: Oh! That's really good! What brings you here?

Catlvr89: Could we message in private?

GROUPCHAT

Darlinggirl86 has logged in.

Katty93: Of course Cat! And hi Darling!

Darlinggirl86: Hi all! Welcome Cat!

I don't respond to Darling. I don't want to create an illusion that I'll be staying here. I just wanted a taste of Katia. I wanted to see what she was like. To see if she's the woman I think she is. Strong and vibrant, but tainted by a sinful darkness that makes her perfect for me.

PRIVATE MESSAGE

Katty93: I'm happy to chat. But I do promise you the group is really supportive and judgment free.

Catlvr89: I'm trying to decide what I want in a partner. It's difficult with my needs

I stare at the blunt answer I've given her, and I know it's truthful at least.

Katty93: Oh! I see. Have you recently left a relationship?

Catlvr89: No, I haven't had one for years.

Katty93: I haven't either.

My heart thuds in my chest, and my brow furrows at her response. I was under the impression that she hadn't had a relationship since she'd been freed.

Catlvr89: How did your last relationship end?

Katty93: Horribly. I left... he was my abuser.

It's odd to me that she would call what they had a relationship. Her mental records don't show that she had Stockholm syndrome or any type of psychological problems other than the occasional night terror. Which seems reasonable.

Catlvr89: Did you love him?

Katty93: No. I hated him. But I was safe with him at least.

Catlvr89: Safe?

Katty93: I knew I wouldn't die. I'm sorry if this is …dark. I didn't mean to bring it up.

Catlvr89: I like talking. You can talk about whatever you'd like.

Katty93: Thank you. Let's talk about you! Lol

Catlvr89: Lol I think I'm more comfortable talking about you if you don't mind. …Unless you have questions for me.

Katty93: Oh! Well if that makes you more comfortable. We can talk about anything.

Catlvr89: Why do you call it a relationship? What you had with your abuser?

Katty93: Idk. I'm sorry I shouldn't have.

Catlvr89: Don't be sorry. It's okay. I was just curious.

Katty93: I guess cause he's the only …idk how to say it.

Catlvr89: Has he been your only sexual partner?

Katty93: No, he shared me.

Catlvr89: Outside of who he shared you with?

Katty93: Yes. I tried to have other relationships. It just doesn't seem …idk. Like I don't feel like …idk how to say it.

Catlvr89: Like they can handle you?

Katty93: I guess something like that.

Catlvr89: What can they not handle?

Katty93: I want to be submissive. I want to feel protected and cherished.

I stare at her answer and I'm filled with confusion, revulsion. Anger. He didn't protect her. He didn't cherish her. My fingers tap angrily on the keys, the loud clicks filling the room.

Catlvr89: You felt that way with your abuser?

Katty93: I pretended I did. It made it easier to live. I created this fantasy and it made it easier to survive I guess.

My heart hurts so badly for her upon hearing her confession.

Catlvr89: I'm so sorry.

Katty93: It's fine.

Catlvr89: It's not fine. I didn't mean to bring up what happened.

I wait nervously for her response. I want to gauge just how affected she still is. What she went through is something that stays with a person for life. But what she makes of that life is her decision to make. I'm shocked she considers that a relationship. Or even thought of calling it that.

Catlvr89: So now you aren't interested in a relationship?

Katty93: I want one, it's just ...I tried other things. Normal relationships. It just didn't work.

My lungs still. We're so alike, yet so different.

Catlvr89: I'm the same way. I don't want normal.

Katty93: What do you want?

I debate on answering her. But I don't want to prime her responses.

Catlvr89: You first?

Katty93: LOL

Katty93: I'm weird I think.

Catlvr89: It's okay. I'm weird too. We can be weird together.

My blood heats, and my dick stirs at her answer and the playfulness of the conversation. I feel as though I'm luring the kitten, my kitten, out to play.

Katty93: I think I like to be dominated.

Catlvr89: What's weird about that?

Katty93: Like really dominated.

Catlvr89: Does it have something to do with what you went through?

I know it does, but I want to ask. The paperwork and her history, the fucking shrink report I looked up--all of that were other people's opinions. I want to know what she thinks.

Katty93: It does kind of. In that he was my master.

Katty93: And now I want another.

I suck in a sharp breath and force my dick to calm the fuck down. Seeing her confess only solidifies what I want from her. I need to see her. I need to evaluate our chemistry.

Catlvr89: So you want a master? What do you want from him?

Katty93: It's fucked up.

Catlvr89: I like fucked up. I want fucked up too.

Katty93: I want him to own me. I want to be a true slave to him, but I need my life too. I've been reading these stories. They seem too good to be true. A normal life, but with a M/s relationship. Maybe that's why I want it. Idk. But there's a club I've been looking into and I'm thinking about going. Just to check it out.

Catlvr89: Why not just do D/s?

Katty93: I don't want a Dom. I want a Master. There's a difference and I know what I want. I want him to rule over me. But to do it justly. The way it's fantasized about. Where I'm cherished and safe and protected and his everything and he's mine too. I want it to be real.

I close my eyes and force my groan back. It's like she's teasing me. Taunting me by saying all the right words. I start to type a response, something about measuring her desires, asking her what she specifically wants. But all of this will be for nothing if the chemistry between us isn't there, or if she's simply not ready. I delete the words and the "…" signifying that I'm typing disappears.

Katty93: I realize that I don't know your history and I really hope you aren't offended. It wasn't my intention.

A huff of a laugh leaves me as I sip the whiskey, feeling the warmth flowing through me. She hasn't offended me in the least, merely given me every indication I was looking for to pursue her. I could push. I could chase. But I need to handle her delicately. She's like a kitten in a sense. My kitten. Sharp claws, and born into this world ready to claw her way to where she needs to go. But curious. I can rely on that curiosity.

If she wants me, if she truly wants this, she'll make the initiative.

I'm not a patient man, but good things come to those who wait.

Or so they say.

I down the last bit of whiskey in my glass, the ice clinking and the harsh burn down my throat spreading through my chest. Finally, I respond. Just one little push.

CATLVR89: YOU WON'T KNOW IF YOU DON'T GO, KATTY93

CHAPTER 6

KATIA

*T*he sound of soft, elegant music envelops me as I step into Club X, my heels softly thudding against the plush, rich carpet. It takes a moment for my eyes to adjust to the dim, ambient lighting as the bouncer that ushered me in gestures to the center of the foyer before leaving to walk back to his post. My eyes are drawn over to where he pointed and I inhale a shocked breath at the sight before me.

The club is absolutely luxurious with a huge ballroom that sports high vaulted ceilings and gorgeous, yet erotic Victorian paintings plastered along all the walls. My feet walk of their own accord closer to where the hum of chatter is coming from. In the middle of the enormous room, finely decorated circular tables dot the area, while a large stage lies in the background, its vast red curtains pulled shut. From what Madam Lynn's told me, the stage is used for BDSM shows, though there must not be one scheduled for tonight. On one side of the room is an upscale bar with blue ambient lighting that contrasts with the red lighting on the walls from the sconces. It's all very elegant and alluring. Every detail exudes sex appeal.

My body chills as I realize how far I've walked in. I cross my arms over my chest and the bracelet that I found in the box bumps against my breast. I stare down at it. It's simple but elegant, just two thin silver bands with an empty space in between. It means I wish to be a Slave. It's my membership here, but also a sign to those who are looking for partners. Madam Lynn asked me at least half a dozen times if I was sure. She told me if I changed my mind, I could always have a band put in the middle. A color that would signify my limits. But I'm certain.

I glance up at the large room, and again I'm in awe.

But all of this pales in comparison to the guests milling about the room.

Handsome men wearing party masks, some with animal prints, some adorned with angel wings, and others with full joker masks, fill the large space. Their expensive-looking suits radiate wealth and power, as do their posture and the tone of their voices. Some are sitting at tables, talking with each other, while others are coming in and out of the room, flowing in from a large hallway off to the side that I'm sure leads to other, darker parts of the club. But most of the men have one thing in common--a chained, collared and barely dressed woman at their bidding.

These women follow their Dom or Master with absolute submission, that much is obvious. They're all so beautiful too, dressed in sparkly and elegant, yet racy dresses that show off their gorgeous curves. They look... healthy. And happy. It's what surprises me most. My body heats with the realization and I lean slightly against the wall, needing support. This isn't like my past. This is the fantasy.

I take in a shuddering breath, calming myself. I'm safe here. I open my eyes and watch as a woman seated in a kneeling position on a pillow next to her Master laughs at something he's said. Or maybe he's her Dom. I'm not sure. I can't see her bracelet or his. But what I can see is her obvious devotion and his.

My heart races and as I take in each of the couples, again taken aback by the beautiful clothes they're wearing, although many of them seem to be no more than scraps of cloth.

Fingering my newbie bracelet, I feel self-conscious with my short black dress that comes up above my knees. It's not anywhere close to as sexy as the outfits these stunning women have on, but I know I'm just here to check the club out. I'll have time to dress like them later... if I decide to join. I nod at my inner thoughts. I'm only here to get a taste. A dark voice deep inside of me stirs, whispering that I belong here. I ignore it.

My breath quickens as I watch a Master stop in his tracks to pet his Slave who is obediently following him on her hands and knees. The room spins around me as I watch him gently stroke her hair, and I clutch a hand to my throat, my lips parted in awe.

EVERYTHING ABOUT THIS PLACE, THE LUXURIOUS INTERIOR, THE moody lighting, the powerful men and breathtaking women, is intoxicating! I take in a deep breath as a euphoric feeling runs through me. It's like I'm getting high off my surroundings, drunk off the interaction between the Subs, Doms, Slaves and Masters. My pulse races, and my core heats. Seeing these women following around these powerful men obediently, reminds me of how much I crave a Master. How much I *need* a Master.

I want to feel the safety they're feeling. The pleasure of being rewarded and cherished. My heart twists in my chest.

Madam Lynn, in a discussion we'd had online after I responded to her email, told me everything I wanted to know about the club and policies, but I would've never expected this. This is just... I shake my head. I have no words. It looks nothing like what I went through, but at the same time it carries a familiar feeling. For the first time since being back home, I have hope that I'll be able to find sexual pleasure. The thought thrills me to my core and terrifies me all at once.

My heart races and my palms sweat as I slowly begin to move through the club, picking up confidence as I walk past the couples. My hands are clasped and my head bowed slightly, but I'm taking in every detail. Keeping my eyes low, I begin the descent into the ballroom, my hand gripping the railing for dear life. My emotions are a stormy mix, but the overriding feeling is lust.

I ignore the stares of the men I pass, knowing not to look them in the eyes and waiting for them to address me. None of them do, and I'm grateful for that. My heart is racing so fast; it feels like it's going to shoot up my throat. I'm here of my free will, but I don't want to give offense to anyone. As I step down into the ballroom, a few of the men at surrounding tables stop to stare at me. Two even approach me and I stand perfectly still, my gaze on the floor, waiting for them to command me, but when they spot my bracelet they look away. One gently fingers the bracelet and tells me in a hushed voice, "Welcome."

I respond quickly, "Thank you, sir," and wait for further instruction, but he simply leaves me and goes back to his table. I dare to look up, and the men seem to be enjoying whatever conversation they were having before.

Before I can ponder their actions, I watch as an untethered young woman, who's talking to a group of men at a table, rises from her seat and approaches me. As she gets close, I'm struck by how beautiful and sexy she is. Moving with an elegance I usually only see in a woman twice her age, she's dressed in a red babydoll dress with a black belt at its center, fishnet stockings and glossy black heels. Her dirty blonde hair is done up into a messy bun with wispy bangs that frame her eyes, and she wears a smile that is so warm and welcoming.

She holds out a manicured hand as she reaches me. "Hello, Katia," she greets me, her voice low and sultry. "It's so nice to finally meet you. Welcome to Club X. I'm Madam Lynn."

Her grip is soft and welcoming, and I feel completely at ease in front of her. "Madam Lynn?" I ask, unable to keep the disbelief out of my voice.

Madam Lynn flashes me a friendly grin filled with perfectly white, straight teeth. "In the flesh."

I know it must seem rude, but I stare at her, eyes wide, unable to respond. I just can't believe it. How in the world is someone so young in charge of all of this? Talking to her online, she seemed wise beyond her years. I assumed that she'd be much older than the youthful woman standing before me. It was so easy to confide into her online, I felt like I was talking to a maternal figure. It's a shock to see that she's only a few years older than me at most

"Is something the matter?" Madam Lynn asks when I'm silent for longer than a few seconds.

I shake my head. "No, I'm sorry," I add quickly.

She chuckles at me, waving a dismissive hand. "No need to apologize."

I get the feeling there's more than meets the eye to Madam Lynn, but I'm not about to question her. It's none of my business.

She turns and gestures at the grand ballroom. "So what do you think?" she asks. "Does it suit your tastes?"

I turn my eyes back on the room, seeing all those powerful men dressed in suits with their Subs and Slaves, my breathing becoming ragged again. "It's wonderful," I say breathlessly, and mean it. I shake my head as I continue, "I never thought it would be so…" and my voice trails off as I struggle to find the words.

"Intoxicating?" Madam Lynn supplies.

That's exactly what I was thinking. I nod my head and shoot her a grateful grin. "Yes."

She gives me a kind smile. "It truly is; you won't find a place like this anywhere else. And like I told you, all of the members here have had background checks. In addition, they're safe and clean, and the club is secured. I promise you." Her eyes shine with sincerity. Before the emotions overwhelm me, she adds, "But there's so much more to it than what you're seeing here. Would you like a tour?" She gestures to a hallway up on the walkway overlooking the ballroom.

I shake my head gently; it took me nearly a year to feel comfortable saying no again. And even now, I can feel the tightness in my throat as I deny her. "Could I look on my own?" I ask softly.

"Of course," she replies and nods her head slightly before turning her attention to someone calling for her a few tables away.

It's rude, but I walk off without saying a word, leaving Madam Lynn standing with an amused expression behind me.

I make my way to the hallway, the hum of the sultry music dimming, trying to keep my eyes to myself as Subs and Doms pass me by. They're enjoying the power play of their relationships, and I don't want to interfere by staring. Despite my nervousness, I'm excited as I step into the hallway. This place is a living, breathing fantasy.

I reach the end of the hallway and come to a room with several sliding glass doors. Through them, I can see naked masked men and woman engaged in all sorts of foreplay. My breathing catches in my throat as I watch a woman on her knees, sucking the massive cock of the man standing in front of her. My pussy pulses with need as I watch her head bob back and forth, the man watching her and gripping the back of her head to lead her movements.

I'm so engaged in the display of absolute depravity in front of me, I almost don't hear the approaching footsteps.

"I'm not sure what you're into, Katia," I hear Madam Lynn's voice behind me, and my heart leaps in my chest. I jump, startled and moving my hand to my frantically beating heart. My cheeks burn with embarrassment as I try to catch my breath.

"Sorry dear, I just wanted to let you know that the dungeons are downstairs."

As I turn to face her, her words make my blood run cold. *Dungeon.* I told her about some of my fantasies. And I do want to have a true Master who disciplines and punishes me. But the thought of seeing that right now... I just can't. I'm on edge and trying to take all this in.

"Katia?" Madam Lynn asks with concern. seeing the distress cross my face for a brief instant.

I straighten and flash her a brief, nervous smile. "Sorry."

Madam Lynn waves away my worry, shaking her head. I'm impressed by how forgiving and down-to-earth she is. "It's no problem at all. I can see you're a bit... overwhelmed."

"I think seeing the playrooms is fine for now," I answer, changing the subject from her earlier suggestion. A part of me wants to go to the dungeon, but I want to see it in a way that fills me with desire, not trigger me. I know I do want to see it. Just not yet. I'm not sure why, exactly. I don't know if it's because I'm destined to crave this wickedness, or whether it's something that's burned into my soul because of my past. But I want to feel the sting of the whip. I learned to worship it, and crave the pleasure it led me to. I desperately want it. But not yet. Not right now.

So far, Club X is like a den for sexual pleasure, exactly the fantasy I've dreamed of. Desire fills my blood as my eyes fall back onto the Subs and Doms fucking each other's brains out. I even notice whips on the back wall of the playroom, and my skin burns even hotter as I remember how good my Master was with them. He was so good with whips; I learned to love their bite. In fact, it brought more pleasure to me than anything else he ever did.

"If you're interested in finding someone..." Madam Lynn says, startling me out of my trance, "you could wait here." My heart races, thinking about feeling it again. Would it bring me the same pleasure?

"Who would...?" I start to ask, my words trailing off. *Whip me.* But Madam Lynn knows exactly what I mean.

She gestures at men walking in and out of the hallway, and others who are watching what's going on inside the playrooms. "Whoever you choose, Katia. You have no collar on your neck. Everything here is a choice." She lets that sink in for a moment before she adds, "Don't be offended if not many approach you."

My eyes dart to hers, feeling self-conscious once again. "You're wearing the bracelet of a Slave. And that's a lot of responsibility. Most men here aren't interested in being Masters." Her eyebrows are raised, and she's looking at me as though she's wondering if I follow.

I swallow thickly and nod. "I understand."

"Good." She takes my hand in hers and pats it. "If you show your submission, men will come and offer you their partnership. You can always deny them." I nod again and whisper, "Thank you." My heart clenches.

And then she turns and walks off, her heels clicking across the floor. I'm left alone, trembling with excitement and desire, my mind racing with possibilities.

Fingering my bracelet, I look back inside of the playrooms, my mouth watering with hunger. I want that. I crave that. I want someone to dominate me. *Own me.*

Every inch of my skin is humming with desire. Madam Lynn's words come back to me, *Everything here is a choice.*

Sucking in a deep breath, I close my eyes and make a decision.

There's no time like the present, and I didn't come here to let my fear rule me. I need to see if this is what I want.

I kneel on the floor at the front of the room, bowing my head, placing myself into a submissive posture. The sounds of the sex coming through the playrooms reaches my ears, and my breathing becomes heavy as my pussy clenches with need.

It doesn't take long before masked men coming in and out of the playroom approach me. A few stop to speak with me, but once they see my bracelet, they're gone like the wind. I feel disappointed, but eventually others that are bolder stop to interact. One man even stops to tell me how beautiful I am, and what a good girl I'm being. Yet his words are hollow, because after a few more compliments, he leaves just like all the rest.

It shocks me how their denial affects me. It shouldn't, but I desperately want to be kept.

I keep my position, though I start to worry that none of these men want what I want.

It also shocks me how they prefer Submissives. Being a Slave means you're more vulnerable than a Submissive, and for men who crave power, this should make me a very attractive partner. But in a way, the fact that a lot of these men respect the differences between a Sub and a Slave, and aren't taking advantage of my vulnerability, the fact that they're respecting my desires, makes me feel even more comfortable with the club. It makes me hopeful that if I do find a Master, he will be someone that I can give myself to entirely and entrust with my safety.

I stay kneeling, my forehead lowered to the floor for what seems like an eternity, watching masked men stop to glance at my bracelet and then continue on as if I wasn't even there before I hear the heavy thud of footsteps approaching me from behind.

I resist the urge to raise my head as the footsteps come to a stop at my side. If this is finally someone who wants to be my Master, I want to show that I can be the most obedient Slave. At least for a taste. Just for a moment. I can always walk away. My heart pounds as I wait for them to say something, anything, my breathing slow and ragged. I jump slightly as a warm finger hooks my chin and I'm forced to look up into the masked face of a man with sharp, patrician features.

"Are you truly looking for a Master?" he asks me, his voice low and deep, his gaze penetrating. He speaks with authority and power. He has an air of dominance about him. But my desire is replaced by fear.

As I slowly nod my head, I feel a slight tremor go through my body. I breathe heavily, trying to calm myself as I see his bracelet is like mine. He's a Master. I try to imagine him whipping me, but the sexual tension is absent.

This was a mistake.

The moment the thought hits me, I catch movement out of the

corner of my eye. A masked man walks up behind the man who's still gripping my chin, but this one radiates something far more than power, his walk filled with confidence, his piercing green eyes staring deep into mine. There's an air of anger, possession even, that's rolling off of him in waves and lighting my desire aflame. My nipples pebble and my pussy clenches as his heavy footsteps beat on the ground with his threatening presence. Just looking at him causes my heart to race and my pussy to clench with desperate need.

I can't even see all of his features because of his mask, but what I can see tells me that he's handsome as fuck, with his chiseled jawline that sports a six o'clock shadow, and his intense green eyes that cause my skin to prickle from his gaze alone. He's tall, broad-shouldered, and his dirty blonde hair is slicked to the side almost like an old school gangster, increasing his sex appeal.

Good God, he's so fucking sexy. My breathing refuses to regulate itself. *He* is a Master.

As he approaches, I forget that the man holding my chin is even there. This walking deity becomes the only thing that exists in the room for me, and his eyes seem to silently say to me, *You're fucking mine.*

CHAPTER 7

ISAAC

The moment Katia walked in, I was drawn to her. Her gorgeous blonde hair flows almost down to her hips. Her eyes are a paler blue than I thought they were. They're wide and full of curiosity.

My kitten is finally here.

It's killed me to stay away and let her make this decision for herself, but I knew she'd come when she was ready. She wants this. She *needs* this.

I watched her as she took in the club, walking slowly as she nervously picked at the hem of her dress. Her chest rose with heavy breaths as she peeked into the playrooms. I wanted her to grow accustomed to the club. I wanted her to feel safe here and make herself comfortable with the atmosphere.

But I'm sure as fuck not going to let some prick steal her out from under me before I have a chance.

Joe Levi has his hands on her. Just a firm grip on her chin. But it's a display of ownership and interest. He's debating on whether or not she's worthy to take on as a Slave. Some men like to break them, some like them already trained. In a way, Katia is both.

But not for him.

She's mine. And he needs to get his hands off of her.

"Kitten," I call out to her past Joe in a voice that makes him turn. My heavy steps echo in the room as I approach. I can feel several eyes on us, but I don't care if I'm making a spectacle. I won't allow it.

Joseph Levi is known to have dark preferences. Like me in some ways, but darker. He enjoys degradation and humiliation. Or so I've heard. It's his reputation, but he's only been at the club for a few months and he rarely interacts. He's been to every auction though, but he's yet to place a bid. Like me.

I should have known he was waiting for the same thing I was. *For Katia.* But he can back the fuck off. He has no idea what she's been through. He can't give her what she needs like I can.

But she doesn't know me. She has no clue what's in store for her. And ultimately it's her choice.

Katia raises her eyes to mine. A shuddering breath raising her shoulders. There's an instant spark as her breath hitches. Every inch of my skin prickles with recognition. My heart beats faster, and my blood heats with desire. She's kneeling and waiting for a Master. She was waiting for me.

"There's no collar here," Joe says, looking at me with narrowed eyes. I turn at the sound of his voice, ripping my attention from Katia and pissing me off even more. Irritated doesn't begin to cover it.

"No, there isn't." I fucking hate that he's right. And I intend on remedying that situation before she leaves. I don't want her in here with anyone thinking they can take her. She's vulnerable, impression-able. I need to make my claim on her now.

"Then you can wait," he says in a cold voice, turning his back to me and stepping to the side to block my view of her. Rage spikes through my blood

Fucking bastard. My hand balls into a fist and from the corner of my eyes I can see a crowd forming, security making their way over to us. Everyone knows I won't be taking that disrespect lightly. I have no right, but I don't give a fuck. My heart races, and my blood boils. I won't fucking allow it.

She does *not* belong to him.

I crack my neck, ignoring the approaching footsteps of Joshua and

Dominic, and step up to him, my hand pushing on his shoulder to get his attention. I'm ready to beat him to a bloody fucking pulp if I have to, and I have a good feeling it's coming to that.

I'm not a hothead; I'm not an overtly angry person. But when it comes to her, things are different.

His dark eyes dart to mine and his grip on Katia's drops as he makes a fist of his own, preparing for what's to come.

But before either of us can do anything, Katia speaks up, slicing through the thick tension. "No," she says in a strong voice that rings out clearly. She instantly hunches in slightly, regret and fear clearly evident. We both turn to look at her, her wide blue eyes focused on the ground as she struggles to compose herself. Insecurity is washing off of her in waves. She lifts her head to look at Joe, vulnerability shining brightly in her eyes.

Fuck me, my heart crumbles in my chest. It will shred me if she feels something with him. I can feel the spark between us, the pull to her. Does she not feel it in return?

"I'm sorry," she speaks barely above a murmur, her voice crack-ing. She clears her throat and then her eyes find mine. "Sir?" she addresses me, turning slightly still in her kneeling position to face me and placing her small hands on my shoe before resting her cheek on the floor. A sign of complete submission.

She chose me.

My chest fills with pride and I'll admit it, arrogance.

Joe snorts at me and glances at Katia, but doesn't say anything as he storms off. He brushes past the crowd that's gathered and it's only then that I really notice them.

Madam Lynn and Joshua are staring at me with contempt. This certainly isn't discreet, and it's not going to go unnoticed. I hadn't planned on this. But I couldn't let her slip through my fingers.

I ignore them. I ignore the whispers and the way Madam Lynn crosses her arms with obvious disapproval. I give Katia my full atten-tion, crouching low to place a hand on the back of her head.

"May I look you in the eyes?" she asks with her gaze forward, focused on the floor.

I hate that she has to ask that question, but she has no idea what the rules are. She doesn't know what it's like here, and her perception of a M/s relationship is skewed and inaccurate. But I'm going to fix that.

"You may. Always." As her eyes reach mine, I cup her chin and take a good look at her for the first time. Her skin is soft and sun-kissed. Her neck and shoulders are gorgeous; they're my favorite parts of the female body. The elegant curves drive me wild. She has a splash of freckles along her skin, and thin silver scars scattered along them as well.

She's beautiful.

"Always look me in the eyes," I say softly as I rub my thumb along her jaw, willing her to look at me. Those soft pale blue eyes seem to look through me, chilling my body. "Never hesitate to speak or to respond. Understood?"

I'm already laying down rules, but that's the way it works here. We all have preferences, and it's much easier to be upfront about them and ensure that the time spent isn't wasted. Tastes within the club are specific, so it's best to be forthcoming. And she needs to know what I expect.

"Yes," she replies, and her voice lingers, as if she's not sure what to call me.

"Master."

She sucks in a deep breath. I can see she's uncomfortable. That's to be expected. She's new to this. I need to slow down my approach and keep that in mind.

"When you're ready, you will call me Master." I debate on allowing it, but I concede, "Isaac is acceptable as well."

She looks hesitant, and I hate that. She's clenching her thighs slightly and her breathing has picked up. Which is a damn good sign since it means she's aroused at least. But she's still frightened and new.

"Yes," she says, and again she seems as though she's going to say more, but she doesn't. She hasn't budged an inch. She's on edge and tense.

What she needs is to get off.

"And what should I call you?" I ask.

"Whatever pleases you," she answers in a sultry voice, her body shuddering with pleasure.

I smirk at her response, feeling the adrenaline calming down and my dick hardening. "What's your name?" I ask her, even though I already know. I've already decided I'm not going to tell her what I know. I'll let her confide in me what she'd like to, for two reasons. The first is that I may have misinterpreted something and I don't want her to assume I know everything, especially when her perception may be different from what's written down on paper. And the second is that I want her to desire confiding in me. I want her to open up to me at her own pace. But to be a good Master, I needed to know her background, so I have no guilt or shame about looking into her past.

"Katia." She's quick to answer. Her voice is soft and soothing. It bothers me in some ways that she's well trained. Someone else has taught her obedience, and I hate that. It's even worse that she was trained with methods that are wrong and disgust me, by a fraud. An abuser is not a Master.

I whisper her name, loving the way it rolls off my tongue.

"Did you come here to get fucked, Katia?"

"No," she answers quickly. Her breathing is coming in pants now, and I can tell from the flush in her skin that it's because she's close to her release already. She's going to be easy to satisfy. I like that.

"What did you think would happen when you came here?"

"I just wanted to see what it was like." There's a soft innocence to her response I hadn't expected. I pull her off the ground and move her to a bench in the room, sitting her next to me and placing a hand on her thigh. I take a quick look over to where the small crowd had gathered and smile when I see they've gone. Good. I'm grateful for the small amount of privacy.

"Are you happy with what you found?" I ask her, angling my body toward her so she can see my focus is on her.

Her pupils dilate, and she licks her lower lip. "Yes."

"You're horny, aren't you, kitten?" I tease her, loving how close she is to me, how I finally have her here.

She blushes, and a small smile slips onto her lips. "I am."

"What turns you on?" I ask her.

"Just," she gestures between us, "just this."

"I need you to be specific."

"I like you taking control."

"Your bracelet has no middle band, so that means you'd like to be a Slave? You want a twenty-four seven power exchange?"

"I think so," she says as the smile vanishes, and the playfulness turns into uncertainty.

"What do you need to convince you?"

She looks up at me through her thick lashes. "It's been a very a long time."

I know we're compatible, that we would fit well as Master and Slave, but she doesn't. I need to show her.

I slowly unbuckle my belt. I'm going to push her limits, take control, and show her that she can trust me. And then reward her justly.

I'm vaguely aware that a few members of the club are watching from their places around the room. Although I've taken two Slaves from here, I've never participated in the playrooms. I've always brought them to a private room or taken them home. I have my mask on, but that doesn't mean that they don't know who I am. At least the ones who matter.

I'm glad they know though. I want them to know she's mine.

I pull the belt from the loops, watching as Katia visibly tenses. The leather slides across the fabric, hissing as remove my belt.

I let the belt hang from my hand.

"I need to know your preferences."

Her shoulders rise and fall quickly. "I'm not sure I know what you mean..." Her voice trails off and she visibly swallows.

"For instance, right now I want to fuck your throat." I crouch low, wrapping the belt over the back of her neck. "I want to hear the pretty noises you make when you choke on my cock." Her lips part, and the most beautiful moan spills from her lips. "Would you like that, kitten?"

"Yes," she says eagerly, lust dripping from her softly spoken reply.

I unbuckle my pants with my left hand, her eyes watching as I pull the zipper down and unleash my cock. I stroke it a few times. "You'll take what I give you."

"Yes," she answers obediently, moving to all fours on the bench.

I stroke my cock with my right hand and move her head down with my left. My fingers spear through her hair and make a fist.

"Lick it clean first," I command her. A bead of precum leaks from my slit and she quickly laps at it. Her hot tongue sends a chill down my body and forces my toes to curl. I remain stiff and in control, but the feel of her, the eagerness to please, makes me want to groan in utter rapture.

I tighten my grip on the base of her neck, knowing the slight pain I'm causing her. Her thighs clench and tremble, and a sweet sound of pleasure escapes her as I lower her hot mouth onto my cock. It's a clear sign that she enjoys the pain. I don't know how much she wants though. That's something we need to discuss before I push her limits.

"Good girl," I tell her, pushing her down farther until I can feel the back of her throat. I close my eyes and groan, letting her know how good she feels. I hold her down, loving the sensation of her throat tightening around the head of my dick. I pump my hips and push her all the way down, all of me cutting off her air supply with her nose nearly touching my pubes. I let her up, pulling her off of my massive cock. She heaves in a breath, her chest swaying and her fingers gripping onto the bench.

"Again?" I ask her. If she were my Slave, I wouldn't bother. But I'm also learning her desires.

"Please," she begs as her voice comes out with desperation and I immediately react, shoving her face down as she eagerly devours my length.

I let her move this time, and she pushes herself down, as far as I did. Widening her jaws and taking in as much of me as she can. I let my hand roam down her back to her lush ass and inch her dress up. She's wearing underwear, but that's something that's going to change. I want her pussy and ass easily available. For now, I push my fingers against the thin fabric and buck my hips up when I feel how hot and wet she is.

Fuck. She's so ready. She's fucking soaked for this. I pinch her clit lightly, and the vibrations from her moan around my dick nearly make me cum. But I hold back my own pleasure. Our first time will be together.

I push the damp fabric out of the way and tease her. Without any warning, I push three fingers into her tight pussy as I shove her head down farther onto my cock. I pump them in and out while thrusting my hips. Keeping up a rapid pace, and loving the noises from her wet cunt mixing with the sounds of her choking on my dick.

I pull her head off of me and let her suck in a breath. She's shaky and wobbles slightly, her eyes glazed over and spit on the side of her mouth. She heaves in a breath and then another before I release my hold on the base of her neck. All the while I keep steadily fucking her with my fingers. Stroking her walls and pushing her closer to climax.

"May I please cum?" she cries out with desperation.

"Cum for me, kitten," I say before shoving her head back down. She sucks me vigorously, bobbing her head and hollowing her cheeks, both in an effort to get me off and an eagerness to race toward her own orgasm.

She enjoys this. I throw my head back as my balls draw up. My spine tingles, and I know I'm close. I pull my hand out of her pussy and spank her clit, smacking my wet fingers against her pussy as she screams her pleasure around my cock.

Her throat opens, and I shove my dick down deeper. I continue thrusting my hips in short pumps while I resume fingering her over and over until her body tenses.

Yes!

Her cunt spasms around my fingers, and that's my undoing.

Wave after wave of hot cum leaves me, and she obediently swallows it all down. The feeling only adds to my pleasure. I continue pulling her orgasm from her as she cleans my dick of every last drop, her body shuddering and her soft moans of pleasure filling my ears.

The sight of her with her eyes closed, enjoying the taste of my cock so intensely, makes me rock fucking hard again. I could take her for hours.

Her thighs are still trembling from the intensity of her orgasm as I lick her cum from my fingers. She's fucking delicious. And tight. Next time I want her cumming on my dick.

It takes a moment for me to catch my breath as I pet her hair and let her lay her head on my lap.

Perfection.

I grab a blanket from the side of the room; they're here specifically for aftercare. Pulling her panties back in place first, I pull her small body into my arms and sit down on the bench, nestling her into my lap.

"Did you enjoy that?" I ask her softly, kissing her hair. Her sweet taste is still on my tongue and I want more, but not here.

"Yes," she says softly, her cheek resting on my shoulder. Her hot breath tickles my neck.

"Is it what you came here for?"

She clears her throat and shifts slightly in my lap. "I'm not sure what I came here for."

"You're looking for a Master," I answer her.

"Yes."

"You found one."

She fidgets in my lap. The lack of a response makes me nervous.

"I'm not interested in play. I want the real thing." I speak while holding her gaze.

"I do, too," she answers softly.

"I want you, Katia. And I don't want to share."

She's perfect. I can give her what she wants, and what she needs.

Everything is exactly how I imagined it would be. Up until this point. She isn't giving me the answer I require.

"I don't want anyone thinking you're not off-limits." I can feel my heart race as I talk to her. I want my collar around her neck. I want everyone to know she's taken. No one else can give her what I can. She doesn't know it yet, but I'm going to provide for her in ways she's never dreamed of.

Her pale blue eyes fly to mine, and her body tenses. For the first time since she's been in here, she's showing signs of fear. Fear of commitment.

But I'll be damned if she lets anyone else touch her. If she's having second thoughts about me being her Master, I'll convince her. "Are you unhappy with me?" I ask her.

"No, it's not that. I'm just not ready."

"In here, without a collar, others will approach you." And I'm sure as fuck not going to allow that.

"You have my word." Her voice is shaky.

"I don't want your word," I say in a gravelly voice displaying my dominance over her, and signaling the severity I feel at her denying me this request. I won't give her an ultimatum. She's not mine yet, and this demonstration of disobedience isn't a good sign. But she has a past. And I'm acutely aware of the fact that her perception is different from mine. She has real fears that need to be addressed. Still, I want her marked as mine. "It will displease me if you deny my collar."

She wraps her arms around herself and looks away, sadness apparent on her beautiful features.

She slowly raises her chin, her eyes finding mine. "That's all I can give you for now..."

Her voice trails off before she gets the title out. But I can hear it on the tip of her tongue. *Master.* Now that our play is over, she's reverting back. She's giving herself safety. I don't mind it, but she will have more than enough safety with me. She only needs to let go.

"What do you need from me?" I ask her, gently cupping her chin in my hand.

She's hesitant at first, but she leans into my touch. Her eyes are closed as she answers, "I don't know. I'm afraid."

"You already know not to be afraid." As her Master, I'm to carry the weight of her worries. "I want you as my Slave, Katia."

"I have problems." She looks away, toward the door and I can see exactly what's going through her mind. She doesn't want to be taken advantage of, and she doesn't know if she can handle her. That's fine. I can soothe her worries. I have to remember that I have a very large advantage here. And she has no idea how much I know.

She needs to be comforted, probably fed, and have a simple conversation. I can try to take this slow. I don't want to. But she obviously needs that.

"Come," I say as I take her hand and lead her out of the playroom, toward the dining hall. There's a show tonight. Fire play, which should be enjoyable to watch. It's not something I toy with, but nonetheless it's entertaining.

"I have to go." Her feet stay planted, and she looks up at me as though she's begging me for permission to leave. She's not mine yet.

259

That's painfully obvious. But I'm not going to let her get away with that shit.

"You will never lie to me again." My voice is hard. She doesn't *have* to go.

She furiously shakes her head and insists, "I'm not lying." Her voice is laced with fear. "I really do have to go. I am not well right now." Her breathing is coming in panicked breaths.

"That doesn't mean you need to go. If you're in need, all you need to do is tell me." Adrenaline courses through my blood. I'm frustrated and angry. I should have planned this out better.

"I don't want to." She answers honestly, and I rub my thumb on the back of her hand. This is too much, too soon. I fucking hate Joe Levi in this moment. I wanted her comfortable. I wanted to take things slower.

I kiss the back of her hand and nod.

"This was too much for you, wasn't it?" Her eyes widen and she starts to answer, but closes her mouth.

"You don't understand." I do. I fucking understand everything. Had I played this right, she wouldn't be feeling so insecure. I can fix this.

"You'll come back here. Tomorrow night." I give her the command. She focuses her full attention on me. Her submission is obvious. "If you'd like to continue this, of course."

"I would," she answers in a hushed voice.

"I would too, kitten. I understand you need time to process this. Take tonight and tomorrow during the day to think about things. And then you'll come back here. Wait for me in the dining hall. I don't want you coming back here without a collar on."

She nods her head obediently. "I'll do that."

"You're going to think of me tonight, kitten," I lean into her, whispering and gripping her a little tighter, "but you will not touch yourself."

I can see the desire back in her eyes as she whispers, "Yes". Part of me wants to push her further tonight. Take her to a private room and talk to her about her needs. I can reassure her that I can provide for her, just as I know she can provide for me.

But she does need to process this. I need her full commitment, and without her willing to wear my collar, I don't have that.

Tonight I will make her a list. I should have already made her a clear set of rules. She's a creature of habit and routines, and she desires a Master. Which means she needs rules.

This is my fault. But I will make it right.

CHAPTER 8

KATIA

I roll over in the bed, unable to sleep, my nipples hard, my clit pulsing with desire. A low groan of sexual frustration escapes my lips as I scissor my legs together, trying to calm the incessant clenching of my pussy. It's been plaguing me ever since I left the club, along with the memory of my mouth being used for Isaac's pleasure.

Fuck.

I loved it. I loved every second of being with him. Being used and commanded. I roll over again, my body covered with a sheen of sweat. It's so fucking hot in here. It doesn't help that I'm on fire with desire, primed and ready for another explosive orgasm. Fuck, fuck, fuck. I wish I hadn't left. I need more. I want more. I should've stayed.

There was so much left to say to Isaac, so much to explore. God, I want him. The way he walked up and challenged the other Master for my body and then took control of me was so fucking sexy. My skin pricks as I remember the determination Isaac displayed in getting his way with me, the way he made me take all of his length.

My limbs shudder, and my clit throbs as the memory of choking on Isaac's massive cock while he plunged his fingers in and out of my pussy runs through my mind. Another moan of frustration escapes my lips. It was so fucking hot. Isaac had been in complete control the whole time. It was unreal. He'd instantly known what I wanted. What I fucking needed.

And I need more of it. Now.

I have to go back, I decide, resisting the urge to reach down and smack my throbbing clit the way he did. I can't wait. The only problem is I'm afraid of committing completely. Afraid of the unknown. In the club though, I'll be safe.

I roll over again, feeling frustrated and wanting to grind my pussy against the bedding so I can get some relief. But he told me not to. I don't have permission. The very thought makes me breathe easier. I will obey him. I will not disappoint him.

I can't get over how powerful and commanding he was. The look in his eyes behind that mask... full of desire. I hear the roar of engines outside, cars passing by on the highway, adding to my frustration. The sounds aren't helping keep me from falling asleep, but even if they weren't there, I wouldn't be able to sleep. I'm too wound up and needing his touch. It's been so long since I've wanted like this. Since I felt this need.

But it isn't like not being able to sleep is anything new. There've been many nights I've been unable to sleep, but for a different reason entirely. A shiver goes down my spine, and a weight presses down on my chest. I close my eyes and shake my head, refusing to go there.

I ignore the emotions threatening to smother me, suffocating me like they have night after night as another pulse rocks my clit. I'm too excited. Since getting my life back, I've dreamed of a place like Club X, somewhere I could fulfill my fantasies and make myself whole again. I deserve happiness in every way. Including my sexual needs, but I hadn't found an outlet. Until today.

But he wants more. A collar. I grip my throat, my pulse picking up speed, remembering the metal chain around my neck and the spikes that dug painfully into my skin.

No, I think and shake my head, not wanting to go there. To the dark memories. But it's too late. I can't stop feeling the sensation of the choking collar my Master used to train me. The desire burning up my body flees as a flood of fear washes over me and I sit upright in the bed, my heart pounding like a battering ram. The burning sweat covering my skin turns cold as I try to gain control.

Isaac is not like that, I tell myself. *He won't be like that.*

There should be no comparison. The two aren't even remotely the same. A collar would be the only thing that they have in common. And the title. Master. I already feel something with Isaac that I never felt with my previous Master. Respect. It's hard to understand, though. In some ways, Isaac reminds me of Master O.

Tears prick my eyes as I remember the only Master that was nice to me. Whenever I was around him, I felt safe. He was caring, and always sensitive to my needs and wants. In a way, I hated him for making me feel safe because I wanted him to take me away and make me his. But he never did. He had the power to save me, but didn't. I felt betrayed by that, like he'd put on this show to be nice to me when he really didn't care about me. None of them ever did.

I pull my knees to my chest, instinctively wrapping my fingers around my ankle. I was so filled with desire from tonight's events, I forgot to cover my ankle with my weighted blanket. But I need it now. I sit there for what seems like hours, but it's only a few minutes. Listening to the cars pass by outside, my heart thudding in my chest, I keep trying to push away those dark memories.

It's gone. It's in the past. I've dealt with these emotions. I thought I'd come to terms with them.

Lies, the dark voice whispers inside of me. *You'd barely acknowledged their existence.*

I take in a shuddering breath, refusing to listen and counting softly in my head as I repeat the poem *Fire and Ice* over and over again. It's a trick I learned to lessen my anxiety, long ago. *Some say the world will end in fire, some say in ice.*

I close my eyes, whispering the poem I've memorized and letting the calming cadence block out all other thoughts until my heart has settled and the rush of adrenaline has waned. I just need to try to get some sleep.

Sighing, I crawl off my small bed, and it groans as I place my bare feet on the cold floor and go over to the chair in the corner where my heavy blanket lies neatly folded. It's weighted and not meant for this use, but it works. With it under my arm, I walk back over to the bed, climbing in and then laying the familiar throw across my left ankle.

I need it. I need to feel the weight as though it's the shackle. Without it there, sometimes I wake up late at night, feeling just how I felt before. Right after I stabbed him to death and took the keys from his pocket, frantically searching for the one that fit the lock on the cast iron shackle that had been on my ankle for four years. The deepest scars I have are on the thin skin covering the knobby bone of my ankle. Whenever he'd drag me, replacing the other end of the chain with a weighted ball, the metal would cut into me. He didn't care.

To tell the truth, I learned to take that pain and focus on it rather than what he'd do to me.

I didn't fear much, but that night, when he told me he was giving me to Javier and that I should be good for him, I was terrified. He warned me that I had better not be bad and make him break my arm again. He said I was getting old, and he'd have no use for a Slave with a bum arm. I couldn't take it anymore. Something inside of me finally snapped.

The fear wasn't fully realized until the lock came off and the weight was lifted from my ankle. I had the fear that I'd never get out. That they'd catch me and slowly torture me. That fear was so strong it nearly crippled me. If I failed to find my freedom, I knew I was dead.

Without the weight on my ankle at night, I tend to wake up feeling the same racing pulse through my blood and fear of death that nearly suffocates me.

I lie back and go still, waiting for the sleep to take me and the memories to fade. It's this position that I learned to sleep in years ago. Images of Master O and Master C continue to haunt me, causing me to want to toss and turn. But just like all those years ago, I don't move with the weight on my ankle, holding me in place.

Finally, I close my eyes and try to concentrate on Isaac. His calm, commanding presence. His piercing green eyes. His massive, throbbing cock. My body relaxes as the vision of my possible new Master pushes the other two from my mind. My breathing becomes more stable, and the sweats leave my body as I'm finally able to drift off into a deep sleep.

CHAPTER 9

ISAAC

The thrum of excitement is pulsing through the club as the pounding of the bass makes everything come alive with the need to sway to the beat. The lights flicker in time with the sultry music, and the women hanging from the swings in the center of the room and dancing in the cages on the stage sway their hips and flip their hair, their hands traveling along their bodies seductively.

Strips of their hair are decorated with a glow-in-the-dark paint in different neon colors. The dining hall is no longer a restaurant. The tables have been removed, and the dance floor and up lighting have created what's needed for the themed night. And this side of the club is dark.

It's meant to allow for some particular kinks tonight. Voyeurism being clearly evident.

Several couples are on the dance floor, and although at first it may seem that they're grinding in beat to the music and dancing like the others, they aren't. A woman on the outskirts of the crowd has her lips parted as her Dom thrusts from behind her. Her dress is only slightly raised in front, but I can see that it's lifted from behind. A rough laugh rises up my chest as he pumps in time with the music, holding her small frame to him. Her eyes are glazed over, and her neck is turned to the side.

This room is alive with sin.

The four women swinging from the ceiling are tempting the men below. They don't work for the club. Neither do the women in the cages. They're simply Submissives who are enjoying the clublike atmosphere. Nights like tonight provide the women a little more room to be free spirited, so long as their Dominants allow it.

I'm not on duty tonight. Nonetheless, my eyes scan the room. I'm just waiting for her. For my kitten. I have a small bag with a pure white simple silk dress, the straps made of thin gold chains. I brought a toy for her too that I'm eager to attach to her. It's a thin gold chain that matches the dress. It'll wrap around her neck, but it's more of a necklace, and very lightweight, so it's comfortable. The best feature is the long chain that will fall between her breasts and under the dress with a clip that secures around her clit. It's not tight, not painful, but a simple tug will elicit a spike of pleasure through her body. I intend to use it as a training mechanism for her tonight. I have my list of rules and requirements. One being she must wear this in place of a collar.

It's a fair compromise. I don't know what I'll do if she denies me this request. I want her, but I need her submission. Her complete submission. Both for her benefit, and for mine.

"I'm assuming you collared her?" A deep voice from my right grabs my attention. Joe Levi. It pisses me off. Not because he's out of line for asking, but because I have to answer that I didn't.

"She's not ready," I answer easily, as though I'm not in the least upset by the fact.

"Oh?" he says, and his eyebrows raise and I can tell he's genuinely surprised.

"She's mine." I don't care if she doesn't have a collar. He had better not go near her.

"Understood," he responds easily. "I have no intention of encroaching..." He takes a sip of whiskey from the short glass in his hand before adding, "so long as she shows no desire for me."

My eyes narrow, and I take the man in. His crisp suit is fitted perfectly to him. His broad shoulders mean it's custom. The man has an air of darkness around him, and it doesn't help that I know he's a crook. He's associated with bad men, with criminals. I have no fucking clue why he's even in here. Of course he's masked. We all are. But no one here is a fool, and it's obvious to one another who most of the men here are. There are only a few I'm not privy to knowing. Joshua and Madam Lynn are fully aware all the patrons though. Beyond them, some of the masked men are a mystery, even to me.

But there is no mystery to Joe Levi. His name has been headlined in the paper, and by some dumb luck he's never been convicted of any of the crimes he's been accused of.

The lights bounce around the room, glinting off his mask as he turns to walk away from me.

"No hard feelings, I hope?" he asks with his hand on my shoulder.

"None yet," I answer in a low voice. He only chuckles and walks toward the edge of the room, setting his empty glass on a silver tray held by a waitress. She gives him a tight smile and continues making her way around the edge of the room, avoiding the sea of bodies on the dance floor.

I'm not interested in staying here. I'm merely waiting for Katia. As soon as she walks into the foyer, I'll see her from this position. I watch Joe's back as he disappears into the darkness, searching for whatever he came for.

There's no way in hell we're staying here. In fact, as soon as she agrees to the rules, I have no intention of keeping her here at all. I want her in my home. In her room. Available to me at all times.

That's where she belongs.

Fuck, I need her, too. I need her to ease this tension. Lucian called and needed a loose end taken care of. It was easy to find the perp, but setting up the hit required a delicate balance with two of my contacts. I'm on edge and in need. I can't let it affect her. But I fucking need her.

But first she has to submit to me. I know she's scared of taking that jump, but all she has to do is agree and then I will make everything so much easier for her. I'll take the weight of her pain away, and give her a new purpose to replace the past that haunts her.

My fingers itch to check the rules again. My nerves are getting the best of me as I pull the paper from my pocket.

I rewrote them a few times, paying close attention to the wording of each line.

Rules are not something easily transferred from one slave to the next. Each is different, and each has their own needs and requirements. Katia is especially different and sensitive in what I must have her agree to.

The music seems louder as I unfold the paper and read each line.

RULES

1. You will wear my chain. Always. In and out of the club with pride, signifying my ownership of you.

2. You will not allow anyone to touch it, and you will also not touch the chain.

3. When we are apart, you will write my name on a body part of my choosing. Your attire and the place of my name will be decided by me and sent to you the night before.

4. You will stay with me when you're able. Conditions may be discussed.

5. You will serve, obey, and please your Master. And you will never show disrespect for your Master.

6. You will worship my body, and I will worship yours in return.

7. To receive pleasure, you must earn it.

8. You will trust me in all things.

9. You will not hesitate when responding to me, and you will be specific in your speech.

10. You will thank me for your discipline and punishments as much as your rewards.

11. You will always be in submission to your Master.

12. All of your choices will be based on whether or not they will please me.

13. Your eyes will never be cast down, and your head never bowed. You represent me, and you will demand respect.

14. You will keep your sex shaved and never wear undergarments. In my presence, your sex and ass will be available to me at all times. As well as your mouth.

15. All of your worries and fears will be the burden of your Master.

16. You will not hesitate to obey your Master.

17. You will always be ready to please your Master.

18. You are my greatest treasure, and your trust in me will not be taken for granted.

19. You will never reach an orgasm without explicit permission given. Should you do so, you will be swiftly and severely punished. I own your pleasure.

20. Through discipline and reward you will learn to behave properly and become a better slave for your Master.

21. You are allowed to suggest ways to further your training or your preferences, so long as you address your Master properly.

22. You must always respond both physically and verbally to whatever I choose to do with you. Your expressions are important to me, and you will not hide them.

23. If you choose to be marked by your Master, you will never tighten your body when you are being whipped, caned, cropped, slapped, paddled, belted, spanked, or anally or vaginally fucked. I want to see your flesh squirm and when you tighten your body, it hurts more. You will be proud to wear the marks I give you.

24. You will not be shared at any time, and you will not offer yourself sexually in any way to anyone else.

25. In my bondage, you will be made free. In submission you will find your true self.

These rules are specific to Katia's needs. I understand it's quite soon for her, but I'm not interested in having a different sort of relationship with her. The is the only relationship I'm able to give. And it's the one she desperately needs. In time, she'll come to see that.

I have a contract ready for her to sign. The rules are included in there as well, but I wanted them written down to give to her. So she could see exactly what I want from her. It's not uncommon for the Masters and Dominants of Club X to provide contracts. We're men of power and wealth. We need contracts for everything. This one though, is more for her benefit than it is for mine.

As I fold the list in my hand, readying myself to slip it back into my pocket, my eyes hone in on her walking toward me. Her hips sway gently, and I swear I can hear her heels clicking on the ground as her eyes take in the sight behind me. My breath stops short as she sees me, halting in her path. Her breath hitches, and her eyes fall to the floor as she slowly lowers herself to the ground, kneeling and waiting for me.

Submitting to me.

CHAPTER 10

KATIA

*M*y heart's racing as I press my cheek against the floor, the bass of the club music thrumming against my body. As I lie there in submission, I sense several men walk around me, causing the skin on my neck to prickle. They're watching me, almost taunting me. But I dare not move. I don't belong to them, and I'll stay like this until my Master says I can move. To do anything else would be disrespectful. He saw me coming over. I know he did. When his eyes met mine, I felt the same shock, the same awe I felt yesterday.

My heart pounds in tandem with the heavy beat of the music, my limbs trembling with anticipation. I can't wait to serve him. To please *him*.

I hope he doesn't make me wait long. I feel insecure without his collar, without his mark on me.

I'm ready to give him more. I shiver as I wait for him to come to me, my mind on the displeasure he must feel that I didn't submit to him yesterday. My heart skips a beat as I wonder, *What if he's pissed off and doesn't want me tonight?* It could be his first punishment, his first lesson for me.

But he told me to come. And so I did. And I'll obey. I'll do anything he wants me to do to please him. Even if he doesn't want me tonight, I'll do as he says. I need him. I *want* him as my Master. And I'll do anything to show him that I'm willing to obey.

My eyes pop open and my body tenses as his strong hand cups the back of my head, sending sparks down my neck and back. "Look at me, kitten," his deep voice growls over the bass of the music.

Chest heaving, I look up into those gorgeous green eyes as he brings his full lips against mine and parts the seam of my lips with his tongue. I deepen the kiss, loving his possession of me. How he didn't hesitate to take me. He pulls away before I've had enough, leaving me breathless. I instantly crave his lips back on mine, but I don't say anything. I'll take what he's willing to give me.

"Do you remember my name?" he asks after he pulls me up off the ground and steadies me.

"Isaac," I answer immediately, almost panting. My heart sinks at the flash of disappointment in his eyes. *Fuck!* He wanted me to say Master. How stupid am I? I've disappointed him already. Worry flows through my chest as doubt sets in. Maybe I was never a good slave, and this will end up being a major disappointment, leaving me with a broken heart.

Isaac splays his hand on my back and cups my chin, bringing my focus back on his masked face. "What are you thinking?" His tone is harsh, and I can sense his irritation. I'm already fucking up.

"I'm not being a good Slave for you," I say weakly, my voice nearly cracking and my body trembling. I'm afraid of failure.

I feel so hot, so vulnerable. The excitement is gone, and fear is very much present.

Isaac squeezes my chin and his words come out strong, but soft. "You are perfect for me. And I will not have you think otherwise. Do you understand?"

"Yes," I answer obediently, and the word almost slips out. *Master.* I want him, so badly. But I can't push myself to say it. So long the title belonged to someone else. Someone who didn't deserve it.

He stares at me for a moment, his magnificent green eyes searching my face before nodding and leading me down the hallway and into the ballroom.

I have to keep my jaw from dropping as we enter the large room.

The vibe of the club is so much different today than it was yesterday.

The thick curtains to the stage are open tonight, with scantily-clad dancing women and gilded cages swinging from the ceiling. There are women in each cage, dressed in those same beautiful gowns as before, some even in bondage gear gyrating, twirling and dancing within the few square feet of room on the floors of the cages.

Some of the women are even in the acts of masturbation, their cries and moan overlaying the soft beats of the rhythmic music being played as powerful men watch from the tables below. My eyes widen, and my heart beats faster at the realization. I don't get time to marvel at the incredible scene in front of me because Isaac continues on through the ballroom and down the hallway and past the playrooms.

My heart begins to race frantically as I follow him. *Is he taking me to the dungeon?* A feeling of pure panic surges through me and I almost pull away. I pause for a moment, almost hyperventilating, but scurry forward when Isaac turns a raised eyebrow onto me. I will obey him.

Placing a hand over my throat, I try to calm my rapid pulse and chaotic emotions. I don't know if I can handle the dungeon right now, but I'm willing to take whatever punishment Isaac deems necessary. If he's taking me there, it's because of a greater good. I have to believe that. Trust and submission are key to this relationship. I have to obey even when I don't want to, trust even when I have doubts.

We reach another long hallway that's dimly lit with shades of dark red. I can hardly see, and move closer to Isaac as he leads me through the darkened corridor. Up and down the hallway, there are men in suits who look like the fucking Secret Service, guarding the doors we pass.

I feel their eyes on me as we walk by and a shiver goes up and down my spine, but I keep my eyes straight ahead. We reach large double doors that are manned by a single guard at the end of the hall-way. The guard gives a nod to Isaac, and my cheeks burn as he turns his gaze on me. I don't drop my head, refusing to be ashamed. I know it would displease Isaac. I know he wants me to be proud that he's taken me as a Slave.

Isaac pushes the double doors gently and they easily swing open, revealing the room within. My breath catches in my throat as I step into pure opulence. The luxurious room is awash in vibrant neutral colors, grey and mauve. Even the ceiling is sumptuous, draped with panels of dark grey silk fabric and adorned with a gorgeous crystal bubble chandelier. Resting on plush, but shaggy grey carpet, a California king-size bed sits in the middle of the room with velvet grey throw pillows and a matching silk tufted comforter. The headboard is also covered in grey velvet and rises all the way to the ceiling, taking my breath away.

It's absolutely breathtaking. I've never seen anything like this bed. Or this room. Two glass nightstands sit on either side of the bed, and a swivel chair sits off to the left side. The wall has an abstract painting on it and there's a glass door that leads out to somewhere dark. But the most exciting thing is the gorgeous glass cabinet. Filled with whips, chains and other tools and toys meant for both punishment and reward, it makes my skin heat with desire.

Isaac pulls the double doors shut behind us and the room plunges into silence. The faint beat of the music vanishes instantly. My skin pricks as I wait for his command, my heart racing. He doesn't give me one. Instead, he grabs me by the hand and leads me over to the bed, bidding me to sit down. My heart beats faster and faster with every second that passes. Somewhere in the mix of my awe and desire is fear. But I'm safe here. I trust Madam Lynn. In this club, I am safe.

The plush bed creaks slightly as my weight settles onto it, and I almost moan at the soft caress of the lush material against my ass. I suck in a breath as Isaac remains standing, my eyes on the massive hard-on pressing against his pants. My mouth waters as I remember him forcing his massive cock down my throat and my pussy heats with need, my nipples turning hard as fucking stone. Isaac watches my eyes with amusement.

He must know how hungry I am; how much I want him. I hope he knows there's more to it than that. I want to please him. Badly. I wait for him to give me a command, but disappointment flows through me as he walks over to the side of the bed and reaches down. He walks back over with a beautiful bag with satin handles in his hands and sets it down beside me. I resist the urge to look at it. I know he wants me to only have eyes for him, and to always give him my full attention. I need permission first. Always.

"May I?" I ask, looking up at him questioningly.

His beautiful green eyes watch me closely. "Yes."

"I missed your touch," I blurt out. I don't know why the words slip out, and I hate it the moment they do. It's the same words I used to tell Master C. The thought of it causes my blood to chill, and it's an effort not to show my disgust with myself.

Isaac's strong hand cups the nape of my neck and he leans down, pressing his lips to mine. I melt into him, reeling under the force of his powerful lips. It's a passionate kiss, one that makes me forget the pain summoned by thinking about my past. Just when I think the kiss is going to lead to something more, Isaac breaks away, resting his forehead against mine.

I swallow the disappointment that follows, knowing that I must accept what he gives, even if it's not as much as I want. "You think of me and only me when I'm with you," Isaac says firmly. "I don't care what is on your mind. Only I matter. Only pleasing me matters. Fuck everyone else. Do I make myself clear?"

My heart nearly jumps from my chest. He's right. He's the only thing that matters. I know better. But I'm worried I'm going to keep disappointing him. "Yes, Master," I say. Shock runs through me as I say the words. I hadn't planned on saying the title; I don't know if I'm ready. But too late now.

Without warning, Isaac pushes his hands between my legs and up my dress roughly, shoving me back onto the bed. I fall back onto the velvet pillows, my head coming dangerously close to slamming against the headboard as Isaac exposes my glistening sex and ruthlessly shoves his fingers inside of my pussy, causing me to gasp out.

"Say it again," Isaac demands, his voice hoarse, but filled with both authority and desire.

I arch my back, my walls clenching around his fingers, wet sounds filling my ears as he thrusts his fingers in and out of my pussy like a mad man, forcing my arousal to pool down my thigh and all over his fingers. My body ignites with passion and pleasure. My limbs stiffen with an impending orgasm. "Master!" I cry, my voice filled with aching pleasure. I'm already close to climax, my core heating up like a fucking furnace, my stomach twisting into tight knots.

Isaac is obviously pleased by my obedience and he picks up the pace of his punishing fingering, and kisses along my jawline, his strong body lying against mine, forcing me to be still and take everything he gives me. I blush as I know the guard outside must be hearing the sounds of my pleasure, but I don't care.

"Good girl, cum freely." His rough voice sends a chill of desire through my body. "Cum for your Master." Isaac lowers his head and bites down on my hardened nipple with a stinging force as he continues to assault my pussy. It's more than I can bear. It's what takes me over the edge, and rewards me my release.

Throwing back my head, I cry out as thousands of shockwaves blast through my body. My limbs jolt with each spasm of my pussy around his fingers. My breathing stills, and my body feels paralyzed with the intensity. When it's all over and he finally pulls away from me, I lie still. Waiting for him to command me. I settle back onto the bed, lying limp with a shuddering sigh as Isaac walks over to get a small hand towel off one of the dressers where they're neatly stacked. He smiles down at me as he wipes gently between my thighs, the rough texture sending a residual wave of pleasure through me, though there are still fluid spots all over the bedding.

When he's done, he tosses the towel aside and sits next to me, petting my hair and comforting me.

After a moment he whispers, "I'd rather not be here, kitten."

My pulse spikes with fear. Had I done something wrong? "I don't understand."

He lifts me into a seated position in his lap, calming me. I'm exhausted and I lean against him slightly, although I pay close attention to his reaction, in case that's not what he wants.

"I want you in my home," Isaac clarifies, filling me with slight relief. "I have a room ready for you there. But I need your complete submission." Isaac reaches into his pocket and pulls out a piece of folded paper. "You need to read these now and you'll tell me if you find them acceptable to follow."

What's this?

My heart racing, I slowly take the folded piece of paper from his hand and open it, my eyes hungrily devouring every single word on the neatly creased paper.

RULES

1. You will wear my chain. Always. In and out of the club with pride, signifying my ownership of you.

2. You will not allow anyone to touch it, and you will also not touch the chain.

3. When we are apart, you will write my name on a body part of my choosing. You attire and the place of my name will be decided by me and sent to you the night before.

4. You will stay with me when you're able. Conditions may be discussed.

5. You will serve, obey, and please your Master. And you will never show disrespect for your Master.

6. You will worship my body, and I will worship yours in return.

7. To receive pleasure, you must earn it.

8. You will trust me in all things.

9. You will not hesitate when responding to me, and you will be specific in your speech.

10. You will thank me for your discipline and punishments as much as your rewards.

11. You will always be in submission to your Master.

12. All of your choices will be based on whether or not they will please me.

13. Your eyes will never be cast down, and your head never bowed. You represent me, and you will demand respect.

14. You will keep your sex shaved and never wear undergarments. In my presence, your sex and ass will be available to me at all times. As well as your mouth.

15. All of your worries and fears will be the burden of your Master.

16. You will not hesitate to obey your Master.

17. You will always be ready to please your Master.

18. You are my greatest treasure, and your trust in me will not be taken for granted.

19. You will never reach an orgasm without explicit permission

given. Should you do so, you will be swiftly and severely punished. I own your pleasure.

20. Through discipline and reward you will learn to behave properly and become a better slave for your Master.

21. You are allowed to suggest ways to further your training or your preferences, so long as you address your Master properly.

22. You must always respond both physically and verbally to whatever I choose to do with you. Your expressions are important to me, and you will not hide them.

23. If you choose to be marked by your Master, you will never tighten your body when you are being whipped, caned, cropped, slapped, paddled, belted, spanked, or anally or vaginally fucked. I want to see your flesh squirm and when you tighten your body, it hurts more. You will be proud to wear the marks I give you.

24. You will not be shared at any time, and you will not offer yourself sexually in any way to anyone else.

25. In my bondage, you will be made free. In submission you will find your true self.

The words burn into my memory as I look up from the paper at Isaac. I expected some of the rules and they're easy to agree with, but I wasn't expecting a list this long. As far as I'm concerned, there is only one rule. Obey my Master. I look back down at the paper and consider each one with careful diligence.

Isaac is staring at me, his green eyes boring into me with intensity, as if waiting for me to protest. "Understand that the only relationship I want with you is one in which these rules are followed. Some issues may be negotiable, but others are not."

Unconsciously, I bring my hand to my throat, my fingers trailing my scars. This all feels so real. I try to swallow but a lump grows in my throat, it's painful and threatening to suffocate me.

Isaac's next words causes my blood to turn to ice. "I have a contract for you to sign." I already signed so many, but I know this one will be different. One where I agree to be his Slave. It won't just be something I can do as I please. Coming into the club when I want to *play*.

My heart skips a beat as anxiety washes over me. I want this. I know I do... but I don't know if I can allow this. I part my lips to speak, but no words come out. I didn't anticipate this happening so quickly.

"You can walk away at any time without fear of losing me as your Master." Isaac rests his hand gently on my thigh as the paper crinkles in my hand.

I want to take solace in his words, but it's difficult. "I was a Slave before," I nearly whisper.

Isaac nods. "I know you were trained in some ways, but I have different tastes and preferences. I think that should be clear from some of the rules."

"It is," I say. I certainly could never look at my other Master without bowing. I couldn't look him in the eyes without permission. I learned those rules the hard way. They were never written out, nothing ever was. Nor was I able to demand respect from others. I was to act like I was nothing. Because I was nothing. It's hard to breathe as I compare the two. Isaac is not at all like my previous Master. Shame and guilt flow through me. The memories of what I went through consume me, the same chill and fear take over. "I can't," I blurt out, standing up quickly and nearly falling off the bed. I need to get out of here. I feel lightheaded and I need air. I can't breathe.

Isaac places a hand on my shoulder and another on my hip, bracing me, steadying me from falling. He can tell that I'm not alright, and he's not pressing me. I'm grateful.

"Shh, you're with me, kitten," he shushes me. Calming me, but I still can't breathe.

"Bathroom, please."

"Of course," he says and leads me out of the room, the men watching us as he takes me to a private bathroom in the hall. I grip onto his hands as he tries to leave me, not ready to let go.

"I'm here. I'll be here when you get back. I promise you, it's alright."

Slowly, I leave his side and concentrate on the click of my heels on the tiled floor and taking one breath at a time.

Inside, I slump against the sink, bowing my head, my mind racing with panic. Slowly the sound of the blood rushing in my ears is replaced by the dull hum of the music I heard when I first walked in. I'm safe here. I'm safe.

I whisper the words to *Fire and Ice* over and over again. Slowly, my pulse calms, my vision clears. I blink away the flashes of memories and look at the woman staring back at me.

I'm strong. I'm healthy. I'm healed.

Healed? I don't know. I don't know anymore. I'm unsure about everything. Sucking in a deep breath, I turn on the faucet, letting the cool water wash over my heated skin and greedily drinking some of it to soothe my dried, aching throat. The sound of the door opening causes me to jump, but I relax just as quickly as Madam Lynn walks in, her vibrant red heels clicking against the floor.

She walks directly over to me, her eyes wide with concern. "Are you alright, Katia?" she asks me gently, placing a hand on my shoulder.

I turn off the faucet, concentrating on the sound. My lower lip trembles as I answer her honestly. "I don't know… I'm trying." I let out a ragged sigh, feeling tears sting the back of my eyes, but I don't cry. "It's hard to let go and to trust that everything is going to be okay." Despite my confusion, I know I still want Isaac as my Master. All of him. But I can't submit so much power and control so quickly. I can't do it. I won't. I'm just worried that he won't be able to wait for me, that he might think I'm too broken to fix. But I won't do it. Not yet.

"This is about your Master?" she asks me. "Is he even your Master?"

"I don't know." Again I answer honestly, and it pains me as I realize he isn't. A Master needs control in all things. "No, he's not."

"Do you want him to be?" she asks in a comforting voice.

"Yes," I answer quickly. "I'm afraid I can't submit right now though." I have to close my eyes and push the emotions down. I know I can't fully submit to him, even though I want him. I want him as my Master. But I just can't.

"And you're afraid he won't wait for you?"

I nod my head, brushing the bastard tears away from my heated cheeks as I whisper in a choked voice, "Yes."

Madam Lynn is eyeing me with cool compassion as her words pull me out of my reverie. "Something tells me that he'd do anything to have you, Katia. So don't underestimate the power you have in this relationship." She rubs her hand down my back as I try to pull myself together. "Be honest with him, and what you want will come to you. I promise you." She lets her words sink in before leaving me alone with my thoughts.

God, I hope she's right.

CHAPTER 11

ISAAC

I cannot let her leave like this. I run my hands through my hair, pacing the hall outside the women's restroom. I know this is a lot for her. I do. But I need her commitment so that I can start her training and help her.

I'm all in. I'm taking this completely seriously. I need her to commit.

Maybe I'm asking too much? But I don't see how I could be. She says she wants this, and I know she needs it.

Madam Lynn walks out first, and I stop in my tracks.

"I saw what you did," she says and I know she almost says my name, but someone walks behind us, stealing her attention and reminding her where we are. "You need to be gentle."

I stare at her, my blood heating with anger. "She is not your concern."

"Correction, she is not yet *your* concern." She takes a step closer, lowering her voice. "Maybe if you tried a different approach?" Her eyebrows raise as though I'm missing something obvious.

"You know I don't do subtleties," I say beneath my breath. I know I'm fucking this up royally. But how? I have no fucking clue. I only need her to agree, and then this will all be so much easier.

"Maybe show her what it's like first. Give her a taste, ease her into it." *Ease her into it.* How the fuck am I supposed to do that?

I let her words resonate with me as the sound of the bathroom door opens and my kitten walks out with her hands clasped and her head down, a solemn look etched onto her face.

"Think about it," Madam Lynn says quietly before walking off, leaving me with the bit of advice she's cared to offer.

"Katia?" I close the space between us, waiting for her to look at me. When she does, my heart breaks for her.

"I'm sorry, Isaac -" I press my fingers to her lips. She instantly silences and her sad eyes widen, her breath hitching.

"No need to apologize. You have done nothing wrong. I am only displeased with myself." I move my hand away and plant a chaste kiss on her lips and then her neck, taking her small hand in mine.

I turn her hand over and kiss her pulse. "I need you to come back with me and talk to me. I have to know what you're thinking so I can make this right, kitten." I keep my eyes on hers and gently rub her wrist with the pad of my thumbs in strong soothing circles.

"Yes, Master." A smile threatens to slip across my lips, but I don't allow it. Not until I figure out what I'm going to do with her.

As I lead her back to the room, I'm quiet. Lost in thought. I don't want to take it slow. I don't want to let her return to her own home and be without me in the evenings. I have needs, but more importantly, she has night terrors. I'm supposed to be her Master, and what good would I be if I allowed her to suffer through them alone?

I can't. I only need her to realize that.

I unlock the door, ignoring the fact that my own men are standing outside the room. The door opens with a loud click as I realize something.

She can't know that. Because she doesn't understand what a true Master is.

She only knows what an abuser is like in the guise of a Master.

I close the door, feeling a surge of renewed strength.

"Come here, kitten," I say as I sit easily on the edge of the bed and pat the seat next to me. She obeys obediently, placing the palms of her hands on her thighs. I'll show her what a good Master is worth.

"You do some things so well, Katia." I compliment her. "Like this." I place my hand on hers. "You know how to kneel and bow, how you're expected to sit and stand while you wait for me." Her eyes stay on mine, but in the soft, pale blues stirs a wealth of sadness and self-consciousness. She's waiting for the other foot to drop.

"Are you self-taught?" I ask her.

"No," she says and her voice is weak. "I had a Master."

"Just one?"

"He shared me, so I had many Masters." Although she remains still and gives me her attention, her body tenses and the shine in her eyes dulls. We need to get through this, but I hate that it's happening now. Without my collar, and with the very real chance of her leaving without a commitment to me. I can do this gently though.

"Did you enjoy being shared?"

"No," she replies and her breathing picks up with fear. I'm quick to calm her worries.

"That pleases me. I don't share well with others." I give her a small smile and gently rub her neck.

Her eyes close for a moment as I rub strong soothing strokes with my thumbs down her neck and her shoulders. She's tense, and her muscles extremely tight.

"Was it your Master who left these marks?" I ask her casually. Some M/s prefer permanent marks. But I already know that these weren't her preference.

"Some, and the others were left by another man." The way she says the words leaves a chill to run down my body. I already have an idea of which *man* she's referring to. I've been investigating his whereabouts. And several others in case I can't find him myself.

I knead her shoulders, hating that I'm bringing up these memories.

"I don't like leaving permanent marks," I say easily. I do want to mark her. I want to give her pain to heighten her pleasure. But not like this.

"Were these punishment or pleasure?" I ask her.

"My punishment, and their pleasure." I stop my ministrations at her confession.

"Your Master enjoyed your punishment?" I pause for effect and continue rubbing her shoulders as I speak quietly. "I don't know a Master that would enjoy punishment. It should be carried out with disappointment." I plant a small kiss on her neck. "I assume this Master wasn't very good to you?"

"No, he wasn't."

"I want to be good for you."

Her eyes lift to mine with a spark of desire, breaking through the negative air surrounding the conversation.

"Were the rules he gave you like mine?" Again I hand her the piece of paper to read through them. "I can modify some if you'd like."

She opens the paper slowly, smoothing it on her lap and reading each line carefully. Her full lips part slightly as she reads silently.

"He didn't give me rules like this. I was just to obey him at all times."

"And what do you think of that? So long of course that his commands are for your benefit and safety, I think that's something that's inherent between the Master-slave relationship." I trail a finger over her scars as I continue, "But obviously some aspects disregarded your wellbeing, and that's not alright."

She nods her head slowly, clearing her throat and rustling the paper in her hands.

"It wasn't a good relationship, no."

"It doesn't sound like he was a Master to me." That gets her attention. "Violence and abuse shouldn't be tolerated under any circumstance." I move my hands to her arms, gently caressing her skin and kiss her neck. "Everything that we do, will be all be consensual. Every bit of training will be outlined for you with known consequences and rewards." She remains silent, but her eyes are wide and focused on me.

"Is this the Master-slave relationship you're looking for?" I ask her, looking deep into her pale blue eyes.

"Yes," she answers quietly.

"I want to dominate you sexually, Katia, but in other ways, too. I want to be responsible for every aspect of your wellbeing. At first, during training, it will be difficult for you. I won't lie. I want control, and I need honesty and trust in return."

"I want to make you cry, kitten. I want to whip you. I want to comfort you after. I want to give you a heightened pleasure that devours your very being." I kiss her gently on her lips and whisper into her ear. "I want to see my marks on your naked body. My intentions aren't pure; I assure you that. But I will be a just Master. I will provide for you in ways you never dreamed."

She stares at me for a moment, her breathing coming in ragged. My dick is so fucking hard just thinking about all the things I want to do to her.

I can't take it any longer. I lean in, gripping the nape of her neck and crushing her lips to mine. She moans into my mouth, parting her lips and letting me take her. I push her down onto the bed; she gasps and her hands fly to my sides, gripping onto me as she kisses me back with the hunger I know she has for me. For *this*.

My other hand moves under her dress, my fingertips tracing the lines of her underwear. My dick digs into her hip. I want to take her how she needs to be fucked. But not yet. Not until she gives me what I need.

I break the kiss, breathing heavily. My dick is hard as fuck and I want to take her right now. But I need to know she wants what I want. I need to be sated. As much as I want her for the person she is, I have needs, too. And I need to know my own desires will be met. I open my eyes, and watch as the dim light reflects off the faint silver scars.

"I want to leave my mark on you. Not permanent, but weekly." For the first time in a long time, I feel shame admitting my dark desires. She has yet to react to my needs. I need to know she truly wants this aspect of our presumed relationship. I want to whip her, to bring the blood to her skin and let the wave of endorphins give her a higher pleasure than she could attain otherwise. I need it for myself as well.

I want her senses overwhelmed. I want her consumed by what I can do to her.

"Yes, please." She answers with a soft voice, her eyes half-lidded. "Master, please mark me."

"I told you what I want, Katia. But what do you want from me? You want a Master, but what does that mean to you?"

"I want to feel complete. For me," she breathes heavily, clasping her hands tightly together, "it means I want to have someone command me." Her eyes look at me with vulnerability. "I want to satisfy your every need and desire and be good for you." She brushes the hair out of her face. "I don't know if that even makes sense," she says as she shakes her head.

"It's perfect. You're perfect." She flushes at my praise.

"I need you to agree to these rules. Or tell me which changes need to be made."

The lust slowly leaves her as she lies on the bed, her eyes searching my face.

I remember Madam Lynn's words. Give her a taste, and ease her into it. But I don't see how it's possible. The appeal for me is complete control in all things. I don't know how to meet her halfway.

I close my eyes, sighing heavily. I'm failing at providing a middle ground.

"This is what you described, this is what you want. All you need to do is agree," I tell her with complete sincerity.

"What about if we meet here?" she says, and her soft voice breaks the silence. "I agree to all of your rules, I just want our time limited to within the club for now. Until I'm ready." She swallows thickly, her eyes darting to my face and then back down to the lush comforter on the bed.

She looks guilty and uncomfortable. I touch her neck, where my collar should go. Faint marks of the collar she wore before are still there. Scars proving how it wasn't placed there with her consent. "I still want to collar you, but I'll take what you're willing to give me for now." She looks at me with surprise. I suppose she wasn't expecting that.

"I'll show you what it means to be mine while we're here. But I expect you to adhere to the rules when you're away from me as well."

"I will."

"Katia, what does being a Master mean?" I ask her to gauge her understanding.

"It means you own a Slave," she answers simply.

"Is that all it means?" I ask her.

She looks at me with curiosity.

"I want you to think about it."

"I will, Master," she answers with her forehead still pinched and

her eyes narrowed as though she's really thinking about it. I hope she is.

I grab the gift bag and pull out the pale blue box from within, setting it in her lap. "I want you to wear my chain until you're ready for my collar."

She opens the box slowly.

Her fingertips gently trace the thin gold chain. It's cut with a diamond edge so that it sparkles in even the faintest of light.

I take the box from her hands, removing the chain and holding it up so she can turn for me. She lifts her hair over her shoulders and barely breathes as I lock it into place. I brush her soft skin with my fingers as I lay it against her collar.

"It's beautiful. Thank you, Master, for such a gift." The sight of her wearing my chain excites a dark part of me that's difficult to tame.

"You'll never remove this. Only to wash, and then it will be put back into place." I have the accessory in another box in my jacket. But it will have to wait.

She answers obediently, "I promise."

CHAPTER 12

KATIA

 WO WEEKS BEFORE CHRISTMAS

THIS DOESN'T FEEL REAL. I STEP INTO THE REAR ENTRY OF CLUB X, my fingers gently trailing along the beautiful chain around my neck. Each step makes me feel the lingering ache between my legs. Isaac has been thoroughly using me. And I've been thoroughly enjoying it.

It's been over a week of seeing him every night, letting him take me and dominate my body, bringing me to sexual heights that I never dreamt possible. I enjoy our time together immensely, earning my pleasure, doing everything he commands so he rewards me. I live for it. I never stay here though. It's temporary. Every day I know I will see him, and I obey him when I'm outside of the club. My fingers gently run along the thick wallpaper lining the hall to the private rooms.

I don't want to stay here, and neither does he. But we have different reasons. He wants me all to himself 24/7. I don't. I can't commit to that.

It's gotten to the point where I can't wait until nightfall to see him, finding myself anxious all day out of my mind at work, which is unusual for me. Usually the adorable, playful dogs at the shelter can make me forget anything.

But not Isaac.

I feel guilty, knowing that I should be devoting my full attention to my dogs when I'm with them, but I can't get my mind off Isaac. He told me I'm free not to think about him at work, but I can't stop. He's in my thoughts every waking second. All I can think about is pleasing him and becoming a better Slave for him. A better pet. *His kitten.* A small smile tips the corners of my lips up and my cheeks heat with a blush. I love how he calls me *kitten.*

Isaac wants me at his house under his command at all times, and he tells me every night that it would please him. I crave it, but I can't pull the trigger. It's so close to the fantasy I've been dreaming of, but I'm terrified that once I accept, it'll turn into something terrifying. Something like my past.

The warmth leaves me, replaced with a chill that makes me hold myself, my arms crossed, my hands gripping my forearms. I can't let that happen.

I make my way to the bed, my thin, see-through robe flowing out behind me, confident in where I'm going even under the dim light. I've been through these halls enough over the past week that I won't get lost. The guards know me, and they know where I belong. Unlocking the door for me and letting me in to wait for my Master.

I suck in a deep breath as I take in my surroundings, enjoying the rich smell and all the luxurious materials in the room. I'm still not used to all this yet. It doesn't seem real. I'm happy thinking of it as a fantasy.

I walk over and sit down on the lush bed, sighing as I gently place my palms on my upper thighs and wait for him. Isaac has forbidden me to be anywhere else inside the club without him until I wear his collar. I can only walk to his private room, and that's it. I take in a shuddering breath at the thought of being collared again.

I don't know why I just don't accept his collar. He said he'll give me one with a buckle at first. One that can be easily removed, and has no lock. But even that makes me feel uneasy. The light chain that hangs at my collarbone is bearable, but anything tight around my neck elicits more fear than pride.

I swallow thickly and try not to think about it as my mind turns toward tonight.

Yes, tonight. I've been looking forward to tonight.

My heart begins to race with excitement and my stomach twists with anxiety as I think about what lies ahead. Tonight Isaac's showing me off. I'm going to be on the stage while he demonstrates subspace to the club. He'll whip me for our shared pleasure, and bring me closer and closer to the intoxicating state. I claw my fingers into the lush bedding, needing something to cling to as my legs tremble with weakness. I'm more than ready for it. In many ways I'm excited, but in others, I'm terrified. I still have faint raised marks from the cat o' nine tails he used this past weekend. They're nearly gone, but they'll be replaced with new ones tonight. It's odd how the thought of a collar causes fear, but the idea of being whipped and flogged only arouses me.

I have trust in Isaac. The pain is temporary, and quickly turns to pleasure. He doesn't break my skin. He doesn't hurt me to cause pain. It's all for pleasure.

I bring a hand up to my neck as I think back to when Isaac took me to a level of pleasure so intense that I lost control of my consciousness. After over an hour of him playing with my body, doing whatever he saw fit, I was awake and aware, but I couldn't react as I normally would. It was almost like being in a trance, my body humming with pleasure so intense that I was literally paralyzed. He commanded me not to cum anymore, but I couldn't help myself. Worse, I couldn't respond to him. I lay there limp on the spanking bench, feeling nothing but the tingling delight of the intense pleasure overwhelming me.

Isaac yelled at me and the whip ripped across my skin, but instead of the sharp spikes of pain I felt only moments before, I felt a rush of intense heat, lighting every nerve ending in my body aflame. My nipples pebbled and I moaned loudly attempting to move, but only weakly thrashing my head as my pussy spasmed and a warmth of fluid leaked from my hot core down my inner thigh.

"Kitten," I remember him asking me, his voice full of a threat. "Are you deliberately disobeying me?" He growled as he gripped the hair at the base of my neck and lifted my head up.

"No," I breathed the word, or at least that's what I think I said. Or tried to say. "Master," I barely whispered, pleading for his mercy and understanding. If I could have felt fear, I would have in that moment. But all I could feel was the heated pleasure and the desire for more of his touch. He raked his teeth along my neck before crashing his lips against mine, and then he lined his massive cock up with my dripping wet pussy and slammed into me so hard I screamed.

I came over and over and over as he tore into me, fucking me like he owned me. And in that moment he did. And every moment since then.

He's given me so much. But I've yet to give him the one thing he's asked for.

"Kitten."

I gasp, as I look up to see Isaac standing in front of me, dressed in a crisp black suit, looking sexy as fuck, his gorgeous green eyes watching me with an intensity that causes me to shiver. I was so engrossed in my fantasy, I didn't even hear him come in. "Master," I say reverently.

"You look beautiful," he compliments me, his voice low and filled with desire, his eyes roving over my body.

A blush burns my cheeks as I softly reply, "Thank you, Master." I want to be perfect for him; I want to please his every need.

So why won't you wear his collar then? Why don't you allow him to have you when he desires? a voice in the back of my head says. My inner voice needs to shut the fuck up.

He walks toward me, each step making my breath come in faster and faster. His fingers trail along my shoulder at the edge of the silk robe. He bends down, leaving an open-mouth kiss on my neck and then a sweet, chaste kiss on my lips. I have to work hard not to lean into him. I want more. So much more.

"You'll show yourself on the stage," Isaac says, holding my gaze, the look in his eyes making my skin prick. It's a statement of a fact.

"Yes, Master," I say obediently. In his proximity, I feel nothing but desire. Overwhelmed by the urge to please him and be rewarded.

"You know that it's safe for you to do so, and that I would never ask you to something that would cause you harm."

"Yes, Master," I agree. It's essential for the demonstration. And I don't mind. I'm proud to be used by my Master in front of them.

Isaac runs a long finger along my jawline, stopping to hook my chin with it. "You'll be perfect tonight," he says and his voice is overflowing with ardor, and I'm getting even more turned on by the deep cadence, my sore pussy clenching with need. "Many of the members here have no idea how to perform this act. We'll be doing them a service in teaching them how to to do it safely."

I nod my head, my heart racing in tandem with the want that's pulsing my pussy.

Isaac looks like he wants to say more as he brushes my hair behind my shoulders and kisses my neck, but then he lets out a sigh. "I missed you today," he admits.

My heart swells at his admission. I missed him as well. I want to tell him that I'm sorry as a deep hurt settles in my chest. It's my fault. I'm broken, and can't give him what he deserves. Because of my past. Because of the Master who had me before him.

Isaac hooks my chin and pulls my lips to his, seemingly reading my mind. "You will only think of me when you're with me," he whispers against my lips.

"Yes, Master."

He pets my hair, soothing me.

"Come, kitten." Attaching a thin, matching leash to my chain, he leads me from the room, to the stage.

CHAPTER 13

ISAAC

"*D*ahlia is all wound up now," Lucian says with a smirk. He's been excited since he got here. I've never seen him so happy.

"It's not as easy as it looks," I warn him. He enjoyed the show last night. Everyone did. Subspace is a particularly alluring mental side effect of BDSM. Katia was a perfect example last night. At the end of the show, I only had to blow gently on her clit to make her cum. She'll be sore tonight. I instinctively look toward the foyer as I put the cold beer glass to my lips.

"No shit. She also doesn't have a pain tolerance like your kitten does."

My body tenses as he calls Katia by my pet name for her. It's odd how I don't mind a room full of capable, powerful men watching my sweet pet cum on command and get so lost in pleasure that she's incoherent, yet the mention of her pet name by another man has me on edge. By my best friend, no less.

He raises his hands in defense. "*Your* kitten." He emphasizes "your," and my hackles lower some.

"You've been on edge lately," he says softly. Lowering his voice, he asks, "Is it because of the," he clears his throat, "the hit?"

My blood runs cold, and I shake my head. I hate even mentioning something like that once it's done. "That went off easily, just like I told you."

He nods his head, a grim look on his face as he takes a sip of his whiskey. "You'll never know how much good that did for her."

I looked into Dahlia's uncle for Lucian. Killing that bastard did the world a justice. A man who hurts little girls doesn't deserve to live.

"I'm happy to put her mind at ease." I truly am. Life and death are two things I take with serious consideration. It was easy to find that prick. With a criminal record and a current location available in the databases because of his past conviction, he was an easy target.

I look down at my hands as I think about the men I've killed. I can count them all on both hands. And each deserved their deaths. But I hate it. I hate the man I am.

With all this blood on my hands, I'd never be able to keep a woman like Katia. She doesn't deserve a murderer. But I can give her justice. I can heal her before I have to set her free.

The two men I'm searching for in Colombia for my kitten... they're harder to find. Everything indicates they're dead. But I won't believe it until I see more evidence. I have friends in many places. Low and high both. And if they're still breathing, I'll find them. I won't stop until I do.

Even if she never submits to me, I'll make sure they pay for what they did to her.

"I'm sorry I brought it up." Lucian sounds remorseful. "I can tell something's bothering you."

I sigh heavily. "You would be too if Dahlia denied you."

I'm growing tired of it. She's perfectly content living this way, but I need more.

Weeks have passed and each evening Katia comes and waits for me, with my chain around her neck. When I'm not there at the entrance to greet her, she denies everyone who gives her attention. She's respectful, but she answers that she's waiting for her Master.

It only took a few times of me fetching her and bringing her to the office for everyone to know she's mine. She sits at my feet while I work and then I take her to the private rooms.

The playrooms are entertaining when I wish to mark her, but I feel hollow.

She won't wear my collar.

She won't let me take her home.

She has night terrors still. She tells me after the fact, but it kills me that I'm not there with her.

She's denying me my role as Master... for this. I don't even know what I'd call it. It's like playtime. Yes, she's obedient and I enjoy her company. But this isn't what I wanted. It's only a taste of what she truly needs. And barely a fraction of what I want with her.

But she won't give me more.

I don't know how much more of this I can take.

Last night I punished her for denying me. I finally lost it. I have needs, and she's to meet them. She's my Slave, for fuck's sake! She can't be that if she doesn't see me outside of the walls of Club X.

I picked up the paddle and forced her onto her knees. Smacking the flat wooden paddle over and over against the flesh of her lush ass.

Right, left, center. Her pale skin turned a bright red. She screamed out the count of the hits and tears fell from the corner of her eyes.

Forty hits. Her skin was hot and blistering red. I know her ass is bruised.

She was hot and wet and ready for me when I was done. Angrily I took her, fucking her with every bit of anger I had. She wanted it. That's what throws me off so much. She wanted me to punish her. She'd rather that than to give me all her power.

I hated it. She came over and over on my dick, but I couldn't get off. Not like that.

I need something to change.

She feels guilty, and she wants this relationship, I know she does. But she can't commit. She's scared.

But I'm fucking tired of waiting.

I was restless as she lay next to me, nestling into the crook of my arm as I kissed her hair and rubbed soothing strokes over her arm. I don't just want sex. Yes, she follows the rules, but what's the point if I'm not there when she needs me?

I want *more*. But this is all she's giving me.

Madam Lynn walks past us and I quickly stand up, nearly knocking over the heavy table. Lucian pulls back his drink and steadies it. His brow furrows as he looks at me questioningly, but I don't respond. I need to go talk to her while I can.

"Madam Lynn," I call out to her.

She graciously turns on her heels. "Yes?" she asks.

"I'm in need of your advice," I say quietly.

"Is that so?"

"It is." I'm irritated by how casually she's speaking, but then again, I've been irritable for days now. "Katia is... content."

"She has no reason to further the relationship." I say to her.

"I see," Madam Lynn says, her eyes falling to the floor.

"She needs to be pushed. She's too afraid to give herself what she needs."

"You knew when you took her that she may not be ready?" She says the statement as though it's a question.

"Of course I knew, but she needs this. You know she does." Anyone looking at her know she's in need. I'm failing her as a Master because she's denying me. I can't allow it!

"That's not for me-" Madam Lynn starts to say, but I cut her off.

"She still has night terrors. Do you know that?" I ask her with a harsher voice than I should, anger and desperation flooding into my voice. Several men turn to look at me, but I ignore them. It's not okay. "Late at night she screams, and she's alone. She doesn't even message me!" I only know because I look into her messages online. She needs me. "She doesn't realize how much she needs this."

Or maybe she does. Lately I've been wondering if she's denying herself this. If she knows that I can help her, but she's choosing to avoid it in favor of the pain.

It may be unconscious.

It may be her way of punishing herself for wanting this lifestyle. It rips my heart into two. I hate it. I can't fucking stand it any longer.

"Convince her," Madam Lynn says to me. I huff a humorless laugh, pinching the bridge of my nose as a pounding headache takes over.

"How?" I ask her.

"The auction will seal her fate." Madam Lynn's words turn my blood to ice. I don't want her to go up for auction. I can't stand the fact that she would be seen as available to anyone else.

"I don't see how-" I start to say, but Madam Lynn cuts in.

"I'll see what I can do for you." She gives me a small smile and nods, holding my gaze.

The auction. My heart beats slower as I picture her on the stage upstairs in the dark room, the lights on her. I don't know how Madam Lynn could possibly convince her. Katia has no interest in money.

But in this moment I trust her. I don't know what else I can do.

CHAPTER 14

KATIA

"Go get it, Toby!" I cry, throwing the squeaky stuffed lizard across the shelter's backyard and watching Toby, a Golden Retriever, take off like a bolt of lightning to retrieve it. I let out an easy sigh as he reaches the toy and grips it in his powerful jaws, resting back on his haunches as he chews, making it squeal.

"Now bring it to me!" I command, gesturing at my feet. Toby understands my command, but he doesn't move, the squeak of the toy blending in with the noisy cacophony of playful whines and barks of the dogs behind us. "Now!" I demand. Toby continues to ignore me, and I let out a groan, shaking my head and placing my hands on my hips and making a face.

He's taunting me, wanting me to come after him. I don't mind it though, I've been needing some playful bonding time with my dogs. It's the only thing that helps my mood when I'm down. I gesture again at Toby, asserting my authority, but he's stubborn, his eyes on me as he chews the toy. "Okay, if you want to play that way…" I begin to rush forward, but before I can take more than a few steps a dull throbbing pulses my upper thighs and ass, reminding me how sore I am.

Reminding me of Isaac.

A heavy weight settles over my chest as my thoughts turn inward, and I sink to my knees in the grass, letting Toby play with the damn squeaky toy on his own. I don't want to think about my troubles today, preferring to just get lost in my work. But who am I kidding? I can never keep Isaac out of my mind, no matter how hard I try.

What's worse is that I feel practically sick about it all. He's upset with me. For the past week, there's been an edge to his whippings, an anger that causes him to be more savage when he whips me. They're true punishments. He always soothes me afterward, and the pain combines with the pleasure of his touch once he's done with me, but nonetheless, they're punishments.

The worse part about it is that I crave it. I get wet just thinking about it. How fucked is that? I don't know what's wrong with me, wanting him to whip me so hard. He never breaks skin, and it's never more than I can take. I think I only crave it so much because after he's done, he holds me, soothing my pain and then fucks me, giving me intense pleasure and showing that he forgives me.

But in the end it doesn't solve anything. We both know that I'm still going to deny his collar and refuse to be with him outside of Club X. I rub my temples as they suddenly begin to pound. Just thinking about how fucked up this all is makes my head hurt.

I feel a slight nudge against my side and look down into clear brown eyes. Toby's walked over and placed his toy at my knees as if he senses my discomfort. I feel a twinge of guilt as I look at him, as if my relationship with Isaac is a betrayal of my covenant with my dogs. Our whole relationship relies on kindness, gentleness and nurturing, while my relationship with Isaac is a dark, twisted thing, meant to sate my deepest desires.

"Come on, Toby," I say with a sigh, climbing to my feet. Other nearby dogs rush to my side, hip to the routine. "Let's go inside. It's your dinnertime."

I'm followed back inside the shelter by a pack of yelping, barking and excited dogs, my mood lifting slightly. I huff a small laugh, patting Toby's head as I open the door.

Seeing all their excited, furry faces around me makes me feel fuzzy inside. They depend on me. They need me. They don't care that I'm being whipped by a man at night. They love me unconditionally.

After penning each of them and giving them their food, I grab a bucket of soapy water and a scrub brush to go about sanitizing the toys. As I scrub, my thoughts stray back to Isaac.

My owner. My master.

He wants me to depend on him, for me to need him. I look up at the sound of one dog barking and think about how it's similar in some ways. I shake my head, sighing heavily and wanting to scream in frustration.

I am not a fucking dog, and I should not be comparing our relationship to this.

My phone beeps, distracting me and bringing me back to the moment. Thank fuck. I clear my throat, dry with emotion, and stand up from the floor where I was washing the dog toys and walk over to the counter, grabbing my phone out of my purse. I bring up the screen and my heart drops slightly in my chest. It's a text from my mom. My breath tightens in my throat as I read.

Hey honey, the family is getting together for Christmas Eve. I would really, really like to see you this time around... and so would everyone else. Can you please come home?

Love,

Mom

I drop the phone back to the counter as the sounds of dogs barking in the background assault my ears, increasing the pounding in my temples. I really don't want to go. I hate that I feel this way, but I just can't bring myself to put myself through it. They all look at me like I'm broken, and worse than that, when I look at them I *feel* broken. It fucking shreds me.

What could I actually talk about if I went, anyway? Living in filth and absolute squalor, being whipped by a sadistic man while in chains? Or about how I found a new Master and how I'm grappling with the decision of giving him a 24/7 power exchange? I shake my head, desperately wishing I had something to make this headache go away. There's no way they'll ever understand.

I look back to my cell's screen and feel a heavy weight settle on my chest. I know my mother is hurting, and I know she wants to see me. If I tell her no after I've been avoiding her all this time, who knows how she might take it. I don't want to disappoint her, but at the same time, I just don't want to see them.

Sighing, I pick up the phone and type out a response. I figure if worse comes to worst, I can always use the dogs as an excuse. They always need me. It's easy to hide behind work and pretend like it's not them. It's not the reminder of where I was, and what life was like before they took me.

I'll do my best to try to make it. But I can't make any promises.

Love you

Kat

As I hit send, the doorbell chimes at the entrance. I hear the click of heels against the concrete floor and smell a sweet floral fragrance before I see her. I blink in surprise as Madam Lynn steps up to the counter, her hair pulled up into an elegant bun, her piercing eyes framed by wispy bangs. She looks totally out of place here, dressed in a designer black and white color block dress with a glittery black belt at its center, her heels a glossy white patent leather. She's stunning.

I part my lips with surprise, my pulse racing in my chest. What in the world is she doing here? For a moment, I worry that I've done something wrong, violated some obscure rule of the club. "Madam Lynn-" I begin.

"You're going to walk onto a stage upstairs in my club," Madam Lynn tells me in a voice throbbing with authority.

Unconsciously I take a step back, my eyes wide. I've never heard or seen her act like this before, but the way she's looking at me, her eyes filled with an intensity that makes my skin prick, I know she means business. I feel relieved that she isn't here to tell me that I'm in trouble or that I'm being prosecuted for violating something I hadn't been aware of.

"I'm sorry?" I ask her, not understanding what she's talking about.

"It's time to take a leap of faith, Katia. You know you need it. Stop hurting Isaac, and stop hurting yourself. You're going up for auction."

My hand goes to my throat, gently tracing over my scars and I find myself answering, "Yes," almost as if against my will. I'm still shocked more than anything. Madam Lynn has taken time out of her busy schedule of running the club to visit me at my shelter. I never anticipated this.

"You're going to stand there and offer yourself to be owned for one month," Madam Lynn continues, and her voice is full of power.

"You will be sold. And you will go through with your end of the contract."

I tremble as her words wash over me, my limbs going weak over the realization. I need this. I know I do. And Madam Lynn knows it. I should do as she says, but I'm terrified.

The sharp edge in Madam Lynn's voice draws my attention back to her. "You are going up for auction, do you hear me, Katia?" She leans forward slightly, her elbows on the counter, her sunglasses in her hands tap, tap, tapping against the counter. "I don't do this usually. You're an exception."

The way she says it makes my eyes fall.

"There's nothing wrong with that, but I don't like to see relationships fail when they could be so successful. Some people need a push, some a swift kick in the ass, and some need to be told exactly what to do."

I take in a shuddering breath, at a loss for words. I know I should say yes; I've already been thinking about it. It will force me to commit. Kiersten was just asking me last night if I'd consider doing it, and now this.

She suggested I donate half of the money I received from the auction to an abused dog shelter, and half to the women's shelter I was at temporarily. I could finally give back. I've always wanted to.

"Katia." Madam Lynn's voice is so powerful, I'm shocked to my core to see tears in her eyes. I thought I imagined the emotion in her emails. We sent them back and forth for a week or so. And I truly felt connected to her, why, I'm not sure. I knew she cared about me on some level, but her display of emotion clutches my heart. There's no way I can bring myself to deny her request. "You cannot treat your Master like you are." She shakes her head slightly, her voice hushed and cracked. "You cannot continue to deny him. Worse, you're denying yourself."

"He'll be angry with me, won't he?" I whisper, clutching my throat. How could he not be? If I were to make myself available for another? He would be furious.

"To be given the chance to ensure your possession for one month?" She shakes her head, but keeps her eyes on mine. "No, he will be grateful. You will please him." She puts her sunglasses back on, making her look chic and confident, and hiding the fact that she was nearly in tears a moment ago. "He already knows. You will do this. By pleasing him, you help yourself, Katia."

"If I do this, I don't want anyone else to have a chance to buy me," I blurt out, my heart racing. I won't go to anyone else. I don't want to. There's no one else that I want to give my power to. "It has to be Isaac."

Madam Lynn is quiet for several moments, studying my face. "I'll make sure of it," she reassures me. She reaches across the counter and gently pats me on the hand. "Everything is going to turn out fine. You'll see."

As she bids me farewell and walks out of the shelter, her fragrance wafts through the air, leaving me wondering how I can possibly go through with this.

CHAPTER 15

ISAAC

ec. 15th.

"I WILL FUCKING MURDER YOU," I SAY IN A LOW THREATENING TONE as Zander picks up his paddle.

"I'm only holding it. What's the big deal?" he asks with a shrug.

Cocky fucker. He grew up with a silver spoon in his mouth, and everything's a game to him. He's a good man with a big heart, and I owe him more than I can ever return. But I will seriously smash his pretty boy face in with my fist if he bids on my kitten.

"I think he's just fucking with you," Lucian says quietly, although there's a trace of humor in his voice. He's a lucky fucking bastard, I think as I stare at his hard jaw and handsome smirk. Dahlia is his, only his, and he's keeping her. He bought her here a month ago, but she loves him. She'll never leave him.

And why would she? He's worked his way from the bottom to the top. He wants a family--fuck, he has one to give her, if he wanted to. His parents are dead to him, but he has a sister who already loves Dahlia. He has wealth and a normalcy I'll never have. I'm sure in only a few years, they'll be a happy family, complete with children.

He's not haunted by the fact that he watched his own mother die. While he did nothing.

He's not a murderer.

I am. I'll never be anything more than that.

What's worse? I don't want anything other than this relationship with Katia. I only want the exchange between a Master and Slave. I've never known anything else. And I never will.

I may be able to buy Katia now. She may learn to love being my kitten. I'll make sure of that. But one day she's going to want more. I know she will. I'll just need to end it before she realizes it.

"I still don't understand why you even let her participate," Lucian says.

"There's no collar on her neck. He has no say." I grit my teeth at Zander's immediate response. As the last word comes out of his mouth, he catches my glare and at least has the decency to seem apologetic.

Lucian shoots him a look, and I fucking hate it. It's the same look everyone's been giving me. I'm hung up on a woman who refuses to wear my collar. I have ideas of what they think about her going up on stage.

The first being that she wants someone else.

The second that it's a punishment given to her, to give her to someone else for a month.

Both situations have happened before between couples in the club.

A few have gone to auction monthly. The Dominant purchasing his Submissive each time, like a game. Role playing of sorts. A fucking expensive one with bidding starting at 500K.

Of course, none of that is true for my Katia.

I owe Madam Lynn for this. I don't know how I'll repay her, but I will.

I tap my foot anxiously on the ground as I wait in the darkened room upstairs where the small stage is. There's red and black everywhere with small circular tables covered in pure white linens.

It reminds me of a burlesque room, only the show is the women, allowing themselves to be auctioned.

I glance at the pamphlet I was given when I walked in.

There are strict guidelines that must be adhered to by both buyer/seller to gain entry and to continue membership.

Membership is one hundred thousand per month and allows members to attend auctions and enjoy all the privileges of membership.

All parties are clean and agreeing to sexual activities and must provide proof of birth control.

The women are displayed and purchased in an auction setting with a starting bid of five hundred thousand. Subsequent bids will be in increments of one hundred thousand dollars.

NDAs are required, and paperwork will be signed after the purchase.

Any hard limits are noted at auction and will be written in the individual contracts.

THE ROSE COLOR OF THE SUBMISSIVE INDICATES HER PREFERENCES, SO please take note.

Pink - Virgin
Cream - Finding limits/BDSM virgin
Yellow - Simple bondage D/s
Black - Carte blanche
Red - Pain is preferred S/M
No flower - 24/7 power exchange

THE BUYERS MUST ADHERE TO ALL RULES OF THE CLUB, OR THEY WILL be banned and prosecuted. The Submissives must also obey all rules, or buyers can take legal action and no money will be paid.

WITH THE ACCEPTED TERMS AND CONDITIONS, THE WILLING PARTICIPANTS of this auction are as follows.

I turn the page, and there she is. She's the first one tonight.

A large movement at the entrance to the room makes me turn. My blood runs cold. Joseph Levi. He looks me in the eyes behind his mask before taking a seat on his own at an empty table across the room.

Thick waves of smoke from the cigars a few men are smoking cloud my view of him. Out of everyone here, he's the only one I'd consider telling what's going on.

Zander and Lucian know. But the other men? I couldn't give a fuck.

But Joe wants a Slave. And I'm tempted to let him know why I've allowed her to go up for auction.

Why I'm eager and grateful that she accepted Madam Lynn's proposal.

I don't know exactly what she said. But I do know that I'll have my kitten how I rightfully should in less than an hour.

My heart's beating frantically in my chest, and my nerves are high. I just want this to be over with.

"It'll be fine," Zander says, putting his paddle down on the table. "No one wants to fuck with you." He meets my eyes but I instinctively look back to Joe, whose eyes are on the stage.

The already dim lights in the room lower, and the room darkens.

With a click, the spotlight shines on the thick red curtains. The auctioneer, dressed in a simple black suit and slim black tie speaks into the microphone, "Good evening, gentlemen. Let the auction begin."

The curtains draw back slowly, and my skin prickles with a mix of emotions.

My kitten is standing front and center. Alone on the stage with lights shining on her sun-kissed skin. It's so bright that the scars are hidden. You can't see from here how they speckle her shoulders. But I know they're there.

She stands with her hands clasped in front of her, no rose present, and her head bowed.

My lungs still in my chest, and my grip tightens on the paddle.

She's going through with it. She's really taking this leap of faith.

"We'll start the bidding at five hundred thousand dollars," the man says, and I raise my paddle silently. I'll gladly hand over my entire fortune to have her. I only need this one chance.

"Six," Joe's voice rings out in the room, and my jaw clenches. My body heats with anger as I feel the eyes of every man in the room on me.

"Six hundred thousand, do we have seven?"

I raise my paddle silently, not trusting myself to speak. "Seven to the gentleman in the right corner."

Katia's head lifts slightly, and she looks up at me. Her eyes are wide and pleading. They fall as Joe yells out, "Eight." Her fingers play along the hem of her sheer black dress.

I know she's frightened, for many reasons, and I fucking hate that she's suffering in yet another way. Fear of a different man taking her.

"She's mine. Nine hundred thousand," I spit out, standing from my seat and making my position known.

"Gentlemen, please. The rules will be followed," the auctioneer reminds me, but I refuse to sit.

"One million," Joe says, looking straight into my eyes and then back to Katia. "Kneel," he yells out and her legs waver slightly. But she resists. She looks up at him with her bottom lip trembling. She's fucking terrified.

"Kitten. You will bow for me," I say confidently. As she lowers herself to the floor, bowing for all to see, I raise my paddle again.

"One million and one-" the auctioneer starts to say, but he's interrupted by the sound of Joe's chair scraping across the floor as he storms out. He brushes past a few men and it's obvious that he's pissed off. But he's conceded. Her preference and obedience toward me have been made clear.

There's a murmur in the room as the auctioneer clears his throat and speaks into the microphone.

"One million one hundred thousand, going once," he says, but his voice lacks enthusiasm and he doesn't even bother looking around the room.

My eyes are focused on my sweet pet, obediently bowed on the shining wooden floor of the stage, her eyes straight ahead, focused on the fabric of the curtains pressed against the side of the stage.

"Going twice."

I watch as she takes in a shuddering breath and her eyes become glassy. She closes them tightly, and tears fall down her flushed face.

"Sold."

CHAPTER 16

KATIA

J can't stop shaking as I sit in a chair across from Madam Lynn and Isaac in her office. I can't *believe* I actually went through with it. I still have the rush of endorphins running through my body from standing up there on the stage in front of everyone. I was vulnerable and alone.

My mind goes back to the auction as I try to still my trembling hands. The lights were blinding and I could hardly see, but I knew they were there, watching me. Assessing me. That brought back memories. I close my eyes, hating the flash of my dark past.

My skin pricks as I force myself to think about the present. About the auction and all the emotions that ran through my body. I almost fell over, my knees screaming at me to buckle, when the masked man began the bidding war with Isaac, giving me an order to submit to him. I was scared that he'd outbid Isaac and take me as his property just for revenge. Even worse, if the man with the half mask won, I feared he would be a horrible Master to me, punishing me unjustly for denying him in the first place. Although something tells me he wouldn't be like that. The eyes behind his mask are full of sadness. It radiates from him in a way I relate to, yet something so different.

But I refused to obey him. He's not my Master. And he never will be. I wouldn't go through with the contract. I'd forfeit the money, my membership, I don't care. Isaac is my only Master.

The sound of leather creaking as Isaac shifts in his seat brings my attention on his handsome face. He's staring at me, the intensity of his eyes causing my skin to chill. He was here before I came in, waiting eagerly for my arrival. His eyes have never left my face since.

I can tell he's anxious to just get this over with and take me home like he's wanted to do for weeks. I can practically feel to the desire and excitement radiating from him. My eyes fall to the stack of papers laying in front of him. My contract. The rules are on top, written in large, black bold letters. I'm sure Isaac has memorized them all by now. I sure as fuck have.

My eyes are drawn to Madam Lynn as she says something else to Isaac. They've been talking for a while now, but I can barely breathe, let alone listen. There's also a stack of papers in front of her, a few that I have yet to sign. Papers that say I'll be consenting to a 24/7 power exchange. I suck in a deep breath, the realization of what this all means washing over me. There's no turning back now. I'm *his*.

He's a good Master. I know this. But it still does nothing to quell the fear I feel. Isaac's taking me out of Club X. I tremble at the thought of losing my safety net and having to rely solely on him.

"And about her work?" Madam Lynn asks, her voice coming into focus. She's been speaking on my behalf this entire time, and I've been too out of it to hear anything she's said. Although when they look at me, I know to nod and agree.

Isaac keeps his eyes on me as he replies, "She will attend all social gatherings and predetermined functions as usual."

Madam Lynn slowly nods her approval. "Christmas is in 10 days."

"I'll make sure she celebrates as usual," Isaac says confidently.

THEIR WORDS DRONE ON IN THE BACKGROUND AS THEY CONTINUE going over the contract and I find myself going back into a slight daze. I nod and answer yes as needed, my mind finding its way to my last Christmas. I'd gone home after New Year's, thinking the attention of the holidays would have passed, only to find that my mother still had the Christmas tree up, waiting for me. Everything was still decorated.

She'd done it for me. Saved everything and made sure to give me a proper holiday. She'll never know how much it hurt. I don't want a holiday. I don't want the life we had before. I don't know why she doesn't understand how much it hurts. Everything from before, the traditions she's so eager to celebrate with me. They're tainted and a part of my past, where I want them to stay.

They were all there, her, the rest of my family. They had gifts wrapped and everything. Waiting. Watching. *Staring.* I hated it. Being there in front of them brought back flashbacks of being taken, but I had to force a smile and pretend to be thrilled while I unwrapped the gifts while they all watched as if waiting for me to break down.

I exhale sharply, something Madam Lynn uttered bringing me to the present. *I can have rules and conditions, too.* I need to state them before the meeting ends and I end up fucked.

"I—" I begin, my voice hoarse and unsteady. I shift in my seat and stare at the table. He is my Master. He is to have control. But there's one thing I can't do.

Under the desk, I feel Madam Lynn's hand gently rub my thigh in an effort to calm me as I speak. I'm grateful and I feel my anxiety ebb just a little. It's Isaac. I can tell him.

I lick my lips and swallow and try again. "I would like sunlight. Please don't take that away," I plead to him. "I can't go back into darkness." I shake my head, feeling a cold chill touch my spine. "Even as a punishment, please."

Isaac leans across the table and places his hand palm up in front of me.

I instantly grab his hand for the comfort and to show him my obedience.

"Of course you will have sunlight," Isaac assures me, squeezing my hand. "You need it. You can rest assured that I will never take a need away from you. *Ever.*"

His words are filled with such conviction, it's hard not to believe him. I relax slightly as my breathing comes in steadier. And I try to remind myself again, that as my Master, Isaac will only be looking out for my best interests. All I need to do is trust him. He's already had me multiple times, bringing me such pleasure that I didn't think was humanly possible. He's not going to hurt me, and he's more than shown that he's a capable Master.

I INHALE A CALMING BREATH AS MADAM LYNN SETS A GOLD PEN down in front of me. She seems to approve of how this session has come along, her eyes warm and caring. I know this must be gratifying to her since she went through all the trouble to ensure Isaac got his collar around my neck, showing up at the shelter unannounced like that.

"Sign here, my darling," she urges me gently, her calming voice washing over me like a soothing, healing balm.

"If you'd like to take the night and decide-" she starts to say and Isaac's eyes whip to Madam Lynn for the first time, pissed off and not agreeing.

I shake my head, ignoring the rest of her words as I pick up the gold-plated pen and quickly signing on the dotted line. It takes a lot of effort to keep my hand steady as a mixture of powerful emotions flows through me and I sign my name. Fear and anxiety are present, but excitement outweighs them.

It's official. Isaac is my Master for the next thirty days.

Twenty-four hours a day; seven days a week. He will have control of everything. Every. Single. Aspect of my life.

I belong to him.

"I think it's best I go home with Isaac tonight," I say, trying to keep my fears from owning my voice. If I don't leave with him now, tonight I'll want to run. I know it. I don't want the chance. I lay the pen flat on the stack of papers, staring at the scroll of my signature.

I'M AFRAID OF GIVING AWAY MY POWER, AND GOING OFF THE CLUB grounds with Isaac where I'll be in his domain, completely at his mercy. I'm terrified, and yet, I know I need it. No more delays. Just do it. I've sold myself to Isaac so I would be forced to confront my fears. Now I just need to put on my big girl panties and face them.

Madam Lynn studies me for a long moment, her eyes soft and

filled with concern. I feel like she sees and senses my emotions, but she's not disturbed by them. If she were, she'd call the meeting. I realize she's doing this because she feels I need this. She feels it will help me. After a moment, her eyes flicker over to Isaac before she nods and grabs the stack of papers, including the last one I signed and rises from her seat. Without saying a word, she quietly leaves the room, leaving me alone with Isaac.

"Are you alright, kitten?" Isaac asks as soon as Madam Lynn is gone, his deep voice filled with concern.

"I'm scared, Isaac," I admit after several moments of nervously biting my lower lip. I pause, my heart skipping a beat, hoping I didn't already break a rule now that he's officially my Master. "Can I even call you that anymore?"

To my relief, Isaac doesn't look angry. "We'll talk about the rules when we get home," is all he says, looking like his mind is on other things.

I nod my head, my fingers unconsciously finding my neck, trailing my scars. "And a collar?" I dare ask, my body going tense. Just thinking about it is causing my stomach to twist with anxiety.

Isaac hesitates. "When you're ready," he says finally.

Shock causes me to suck in a surprised breath. I didn't expect him to say that. At all.

"I know this is hard for you," Isaac says, his deep voice filled with absolute confidence. "But don't be afraid. I will care for all of your needs. You need not worry. *Ever*."

God, his words sound so reassuring. So seductive, even.

I close my eyes, sucking in several calming breaths, telling myself I can do this. When I open them a moment later, I feel the faintest threads of determination thread through my chest as I breathe, "I'm ready," praying I feel the same way tomorrow.

CHAPTER 17

ISAAC

I twist my hands on the leather steering wheel of my Porsche Carrera GT. It's fucking freezing outside, but the heated seats and my nerves are making my back sweat. I look out of the window as we pull up to one of the last street lights before taking a private road to my home.

I take a glance at my kitten. She's looking out of the window, twisting her fingers in her lap nervously. Her back is stick straight, and she looks like she's not even breathing.

The first thing she's going to do when we get home is drink. A large glass of sauvignon will do her well. I think I'll make stuffed peppers to go with it. I'm going to need to occupy myself while she gets accustomed to her new role and new environment.

I didn't imagine her taking it so hard. She's completely changed before my eyes. The confidence is gone, and the sexual tension between us has vanished.

She's scared, quiet. She hasn't said a word other than yes. Her eyes are heavy with exhaustion and her face still flushed from crying.

The drive home has been silent, but I'm ready to change that. As much as I feel for her, I'm still excited. Adrenaline is pumping through my veins, filling me with an electric spark. I've waited so long for her, to have her here. I'm ready to show her what she's truly capable of. And even more so, what I'm capable of.

"Do you like to cook?" I ask her. It's been almost two weeks of seeing her every night. But I've barely learned much about her, other than her desires and a bit about her past. Of course I know much more than she's told me. But the finer details, those are important and I need her to open up to me so I can learn them.

"I do, Master," she answers softly. There's a trace of fear in her voice.

"Are you good at it?" I cock a brow, giving her a humorous look as I slow the car at a stop sign. The hum of the engine vibrates up my back and fills the car with a quiet purr.

She opens her mouth and almost hesitates, but she quickly answers, "No."

I let out an easy chuckle. "That's more than alright, kitten."

Her relief in my response is evident. "I enjoy cooking. I want you to help me though."

"Yes, Master," she says with a lighter voice than she's had all day.

"We're going to go over the rules and what's required of you in the house while I make the sauce," I say easily, pulling up to my house, the car jostling slightly as I drive up the driveway and wait for the garage to open.

I have a decent collection of cars. An expensive but carefully curated collection.

Katia sucks in a breath as she takes in my home.

It's simple. I like simplicity, and the modern clean lines.

The house itself is very much like a cabin, except instead of stacks of logs there are large sheets of glass on the front. Being so far away from anyone else affords me the luxury of having privacy while also being able to expose my home. The entire front of the house is open to the deep woods we're nestled in. I own the ten acres the house sits on, so it will always be like this. Quiet, serene and one with nature.

The soft grey sky disappears as I pull into the garage and quickly park the car.

"Come, kitten, come see your new home."

I SLIP OFF MY JACKET AS I LEAD HER INTO THE OPEN KITCHEN. I HAVE to take off the cufflinks in order to roll up the sleeves of my dress shirt. I don't enjoy wearing a suit. I'd much rather be in jeans. But Club X has a strict dress code. Thank fuck we won't be going there anymore.

Every step she takes seems deliberate. She's on edge and waiting for something. Maybe waiting for my demeanor to change? I'm not sure.

"Have a seat," I tell her easily, turning my back to her as she climbs onto the bar height chair at the granite island.

"I need to know your daily schedule and the plans you have every day for the next thirty days that I have you." I continue to talk with my back to her, letting her get comfortable without having to worry about the possibility of me scrutinizing her.

I am. I'm taking in every little move and change. The angles of her body and the way she's presenting herself. But it's not for the reason she thinks.

I'm not judging her. I'm gauging her emotions. And so far it's worse than I anticipated. It's like the last two weeks haven't happened.

I pluck three tomatoes from the basket next to the sink and set them down on a wood cutting board.

"Start with tomorrow."

"I have work. From seven in the morning until seven at night." She clears her throat slightly, and I can hear the slight squeak of the chair moving under her weight. "That's all I have planned."

"And the next day?"

"The same. Every day."

"And the holidays?" I ask as I scrape the knife across the board, pushing the first diced tomato to the side.

"Nothing. Just work."

The knife slices easily through the tomato and hits the cutting board. I'm still for a moment. I know her mother has sent her messages.

"You weren't invited to go anywhere with family?" I ask as I grab a hand towel off of the counter, wiping the juice from my fingers.

"I was."

"And?" I ask, my eyebrow raised. She's a very lucky girl she didn't lie to me.

"And I said I couldn't go."

"I see, and where was it that you were invited to go?" I ask her.

"To see my parents a few hours away." She shakes her head slightly, dismissing the invitation. "They won't be expecting-"

"We'll both be attending," I say, cutting her off. I don't know why I made the decision so quickly. I hadn't decided on whether or not I'd be going. But she sure as fuck is. She's in desperate need of contact and conversation in person. From what I can tell, all of her friendships are online. I want more for her.

And it should start with her parents.

She stiffens in her chair, but she nods her head and says, "Yes, Master."

"And for New Year's?" I ask her.

"I have no plans, nor was I invited to anything." Her voice is quiet, but clear.

"We'll spend that together then," I announce and turn my back to her again to continue dicing the tomatoes.

A moment later I pipe up and say, "Well, that's easy enough. You'll find someone else to work on the days I have off."

She's quiet until I turn to look over my shoulder. "Yes, Master."

I can't stand this tension anymore.

She needs to get off. That'll calm her ass down.

"Kitten," I say and wipe off the blade and gently set it down, putting dinner on hold. "Come here."

I take a look at the utensils and kitchen tools, my eyes scanning them to find something useful. Finally, I settle on a French rolling pin. It's a pale hard marble and cold to the touch, but it'll do nicely.

"Strip," I tell her as she stands to my left.

She's barely wearing any clothing at all. Without her coat, all she has on is a sheer black dress with skimpy straps that end mid-thigh, and a lace pair of panties. She slips the straps down her shoulders and the thin piece of fabric pools at her feet into a puddle of shiny black. Her nipples instantly harden. And so does my dick.

I lean forward, taking one of her pale rose nipples into my mouth and gripping both of her wrists in my hands as she attempts to pull her thong down her thighs.

She gasps at my quick movements and pushes her chest into my face. Like a good girl. I pull back, letting her nipple pop out of my mouth and then swirl my tongue around the other.

"Let go," I command her and in that instant she does, immediately releasing her grip on the lacy straps of her underwear.

I take a step back and look at her.

"You're gorgeous, Katia." The small intake of air and slight flush to her cheeks warms me. It touches a cold part of my soul I'm not used to feeling. I shake off the sensation and concentrate on the matter at hand.

"You will never wear those again. Or any underwear." I loop my thumb around the straps and easily rip through the lace, shredding the sides of her thong and letting them fall to the floor.

My dick stirs with desire as her lips part in shock. "Your cunt and ass will always be available to me. Easily."

I trail my middle finger along her lower lip, and she obediently opens her mouth. "And your mouth." I slip my finger into her hot mouth. I don't have to tell her to suck; she greedily suctions her lips around my finger, keeping her hands at her side and hollowing her cheeks. Her tongue massages the underside of my finger as she closes her eyes and moans.

Fuck! She's so fucking sexy. She has no idea what she does to me. "Ah ah, kitten," I admonish her, pulling my finger away and turning back toward the counter. "I have something else for you to suck."

I grab the rolling pin, and it's cold and smooth. She's really going to want to heat this up.

Fear flashes in her eyes for a moment, but I ignore it. I'll never hurt her. Not that way she's thinking. "Suck on this," I tell her, placing the pin to her lips. There are no handles, just one long smooth pin. She has to stretch her jaw a little more than my finger, but the pin itself isn't very wide.

I push the pin in a bit farther, letting her take a few inches and rock it in and out of her mouth. "Get it hot, kitten. Suck it like it's my cock." With my left hand I cup her pussy and reward her by pinching her clit and rolling it between my fingers.

Her brows pinch, and she moans the softest I've ever heard while taking a little more of the pin deeper into her mouth. "Do you remember how you took me?" I ask her.

She tries to push more of the pin in, but I stop her. The head of the pin is blunt and it'll hurt her throat. I don't want that. "No more." I stop her, pulling it back and releasing her clit to grab her throat. The lust vanishes from her eyes, realizing she's done something wrong. "You only get a few inches. Don't be greedy," I add playfully to lessen her anxiety.

She closes her eyes again, but I'm done preparing her. "Lie down on the floor." I kick her clothes to the side as she crouches down and quickly lies against the tiled floor. Goosebumps flow down her skin. I imagine she's cold, but I'll have her hot and bothered in no time.

"Get wet for me," I tell her as I crouch down and rub her clit and then trail my fingers down the length of her pussy. I feel her lips and the hot entrance to her cunt. Petting her gently as my dick starts leaking precum. My fingers move slowly and I watch her as she tries to stay still on the floor. Resisting the natural desire to move.

"I don't want you still or silent." My voice comes out sharp, but I soften it.

"Never hide from me." As her eyes meet mine and she parts her lips, her tongue licking along the lower one, to tell me "Yes, Master," I shove two of my fingers into her and curve my fingers upward, stroking the rough wall of her G-spot. Her back bows, and her mouth opens with a gasp. Her fingers are clawing at the smooth tiled floor as though she can grip it. "I want to watch you squirm under my touch."

It doesn't take long until she's soaking wet. Her pussy lips are glistening, and soft moans pouring from her lips without effort.

I stand up, breathing heavily and shoving my pants down so I can get my cock out. The fucking zipper was pressed against it. I stroke it a few times with the hand that's coated in her arousal. But I need to wait. While I'm standing I grab the French rolling pin. It's smooth and long. I don't have any intention of using more than a few inches of the smooth pin on her, but it'll be enough to overwhelm her. And hopefully throw her off.

I want her to realize her expectations are wrong.

"Grab your knees and pull them up as high up as you can."

321

She instantly obeys, showing me all of her.

I slip the pin into her pussy while spreading some of her arousal down to her ass. Her mouth opens with the sharp sound of her sucking in a breath. Her puckered hole clenches around the tip of my finger.

I pull the pin out and watch as her tight pussy closes. I tease her entrance, pushing the pin in slightly, and then pulling it out.

She whimpers, soft and sweet and desperate for more.

I take more of her arousal and rub it over her ass and then pull my hand back and quickly smack her. She jumps as my palm stings her lush flesh.

I don't wait for her to settle, instead I push the pin back in and pump it inside of her, angling it to rub against her front wall.

Her head lolls to the side as she moans. With her juices coating my middle finger, I push against her puckered hole and she instantly pushes back, granting me entry easily. I pump in and out a few times and her soft moans turn to louder groans. Her head thrashes, and a sheen of sweat forms across her gorgeous sun-kissed skin. I only wish I had another hand to pluck at her nipples.

Instead, she'll have to obey.

"Play with your tits, kitten."

She breathes heavily as she quickly lets go of her one knee and pinches her nipples, pulling them away from her and arching her back. Fuck! I pull my finger from her ass and the pin from her pussy. It's soaked with her arousal. I tease her asshole as my thumb brushes her clit.

"Cum!" I yell at her as her back bows harder and she grips her breast with a force that leaves a red mark behind. She instantly obeys my command, cum spilling from her pussy and leaking down her thigh. The second the first wave passes and her tight body relaxes, I push the pin up her ass.

Her mouth opens, forming the perfect "O" as I quickly pump it in and out, prolonging her orgasm.

With my right hand still pumping the pin in her ass, I line my dick up to her pussy with my body angled and my hand bracing me on the floor and I plunge deep inside of her. Filling her.

Fuck. She feels so good. Every time it's like this. I knew she was made for me. I knew she'd feel like this.

I don't give her time to get used to my girth; instead I thrust my hips in and out, at first in time with the pin in her ass, filling both her holes at once and then leaving her nearly empty. Then I tease her a bit by fucking her with one after the other.

Her thighs shake as she lies on the floor, taking more and more as I fuck her mercilessly.

"May I cum?" she screams. "Please-"

"Cum!"

Her body shakes and trembles as she screams out her release. Her head is thrown back on the floor and her hair a mess, fanned around her as her head thrashes. She looks utterly gorgeous.

I lean forward for more leverage as she cries out, her pleasure sounding strangled as I pump the rolling pin into her ass in time with my cock in her hot, tight cunt.

I groan in the crook of her neck then graze my teeth along her jaw, shoving my dick as far and hard as I can inside her while quickly picking up the pace with my right hand.

Her pussy is so fucking tight, dripping wet.

I lay my body on top of her, letting go of the pin and leaving a few inches in her ass. "Cum with me," I breathe, thrusting my hips faster and faster, fueled by the smacking of the rolling pin hitting the tile with each hard pump. Smack, smack, smack. Louder and louder as I lose control and rut between her legs, racing for my release.

My body heats, and Katia cries out her pleasure. Her hot body is trembling and her nails are digging into my sides.

My balls draw up, a tingling sensation at the base of my spine shooting through my body all at once. A blinding pleasure paralyzes me as I throw my head back and cum violently, harder than I've ever cum before, hot wave after wave filling Katia's tight pussy.

I pump my hips a few times, drawing out both of our orgasms.

It takes a moment for me to catch my breath. I slowly lift my body off of hers and pull out, taking the rolling pin still in her ass out with me. She still has one hand wrapped around her knee, and I tap her hand to let her know she can let go.

She lets it fall to the floor limp as she stares at me, her breathing erratic and her chest heaving.

I run my fingers along her asshole and then her pussy. Looking for any signs that she's hurt in the least.

"How do you feel, Katia?" I ask her.

"Good. So good."

"Just good?" I ask to toy with her, raising a brow.

"I feel wonderful, Master. Thank you."

A smile plays at my lips. "Good girl, kitten." I kiss her hair as her body shudders with a lingering wave of her release as my still-hard dick brushes against her clit. "Now clean yourself up while I make dinner."

CHAPTER 18

KATIA

I let out a sigh, my thighs still being rocked by occasional tremors, my limbs weak as I kneel on the dining room floor, still naked. I'm exhausted, but content. The way Isaac fucked me so thoroughly, and with that rolling pin... gave me pleasure that defied belief. My cheeks blaze with a blush and another shudder runs through my body, my nipples pebbling. Even now, I'm still being jolted by aftershocks that are rapidly fading, leaving me wanting more. Needing more.

I let out as a soft sigh as I feel wetness around my ankle where my ass is sitting. I'm not sure if it's my arousal or his cum, but I don't care.

The sounds of clinking glass break me out of my reverie, while the faint smells of the stuffed peppers and spices still fills the air.

I'm so full. But I want more. I feel like a glutton for sex and food.

Isaac is setting a dish for dessert down on the dining room table, some sort of fruit concoction.

I sat at the chair to my right for dinner. Eating as politely as I could and careful to mimic the way he gently set the fork on the side of his plate. It was odd to be sitting at the table.

I'm not anymore. For dessert he wanted me here. Beside his chair and on my knees.

How fucked is it that I prefer it this way?

He watches me, the corner of his full lips pulled up into a slight grin as he lowers himself into the carved walnut chair at the head of the table. "Are you hungry for dessert, kitten?" he asks.

Not trusting myself to speak, I nod softly.

I watch as he takes a silver fork and spears a slice of strawberry along with a raspberry, drizzled in some sort of thickened sugary cream.

"Open," he commands, bringing the fork to my lips. Immediately, I part my lips and take the fruit into my mouth. Mmm. I close my eyes with pleasure as my taste buds are assaulted by a rich, sweet flavor. It's absolutely delicious.

Isaac is watching me intently, enjoying the delight his dish has brought me. "Do you like that, kitten?"

A soft moan escapes my lips as I swallow the last of the fruit, and I nod my head. "Yes, Master."

"Good." Isaac drops the fork on the table and swipes his finger on the edge of the bowl, covering them with the cream spread. He brings his fingers to my lips. "Suck," he orders.

Eagerly, I wrap my mouth around his fingers, sucking them as if they're his cock.

"Look at me," Isaac orders.

My eyes dart to his while I continue to massage my tongue along the length of his middle finger holding his beautiful green eyes with mine, savoring the sweetness of the taste.

"Fuck," Isaac groans, and I watch as he palms his cock in his pants.

Fire burns in my core and I'm filled with anticipation, hoping he'll take me again and give me even more pleasure, if that's somehow possible. I suck every last drop of cream from his fingers, making sure to hold his gaze, and pull away when I'm done with an audible *pop*.

I wait for his next command, my chest heaving with desire, wanting badly to be used by him.

He lets me lick the servings off his fingers, and I find myself wanting it so much that I grab his hand forcefully, greedily sucking his fingers, imagining it's his dick that I'm sucking.

My heart skips a beat as Isaac lets out a chuckle at my behavior.

Fuck. I instantly freeze, the lust-filled haze vanishing as I'm snapped out of the fantasy.

I shouldn't have done that. I lower my hands to my thighs where they belong. He didn't give me permission to take control like that. I know better. I'll be better. It was a stupid mistake.

I stare into his eyes as I slowly pull away, his finger licked clean and waiting for his admonishment or a smack or some kind of punishment.

I know better.

I wait a moment, my breathing coming in shorter and shorter.

"I'm sorry, Master.*"* I clear my throat slightly, sitting back on the balls of my feet and awaiting the consequences of my action.

"I don't mind your enthusiasm, kitten. I'll allow it."

A breath I didn't know I was holding leaves me, and I can feel my body sag slightly.

"You must really enjoy strawberries, kitten," he says, his deep voice filled with amusement.

"No, it's you," I say, the words slipping past my lips without my consent. I blush after I speak, realizing it's all true. I'm so caught up in pleasing him, I'd made an error in my strict obedience. Isaac doesn't respond and just looks at me, his green eyes so intense that I'm forced to look away. I shiver slightly, never remembering him looking at me like that before.

"Let me show you to your room, kitten," he says, adjusting his cock as he stands. "Come," he commands.

I'm quick to rise and obediently follow him through the opulent house, taking in everything in a sort of detached awe. The house is large, simple with modern features, yet elegant. I like it. It looks like something out of a magazine.

We pass a large den as we go down the hallway and then take a spiral staircase up to the second floor. The wide hallway has dark hardwood floors, and simple black and white scenic paintings that line the wall. At the end of the hallway are two large double doors, which I assume lead to the master suite. Isaac leads me nearly to the double doors, but stops at a single door that's closest to it.

"This is your room," he informs me, gesturing at the door and then to the double doors. "That one is mine. Both my doors and yours shall remain open at *all times*. Understood?"

Biting my lower lip, I nod. "Yes, Master."

Isaac stares at me, his striking green eyes causing goosebumps to rise on my arms. "If you need me during the night, you're to kneel at my bedside and call my name until I wake. Though I'm sure I'll hear you the moment you walk in."

I'm shocked. My old Master would never allow me such freedom. I was never allowed to go anywhere without his consent or without him present. *Ever*. Even with him present, the chain was always there, making each step difficult and painful.

Letting his words sink in, Isaac turns and opens the door to my room, motioning me inside. The memory of the chain, the comparison of then and now completely vanishes as the door swiftly opens and reveals what lies beyond it.

My breath catches in my throat and my lips part in surprise as I step in the room, with a push from Isaac. It's not what I was anticipating. It's a normal bedroom. No chains or sex swings or glass cabinet filled with toys and tools for punishment. Just a normal room. It's quite lavish with a fancy white plush rug underneath the queen-size bed with matching comforter, grey and white paint on the walls in stripes, and gossamer silk curtains adorning the windows. Their softness reminds me of butterflies. This is just so... normal. My breathing comes in faster. I feel completely at a loss. I look over my shoulder at Isaac, feeling somewhat betrayed. Although it's my own fault. I don't know what to expect from him. I am his Slave, yet this is where he's keeping me.

"You can roam wherever you'd like in the house," Isaac says, his eyes focusing on my face as I nod. "But when I go to bed, I want you in this room."

"Yes, Master."

"Do you like your new room, kitten?" Isaac asks, still staring at me intently. He seems to be waiting for me to question all this. And I want to, but I don't want to seem disobedient. I don't want to tell him that I feel like I'm not worthy.

"I love it," I say and quickly add, "Thank you." In a way, it reminds me a lot of my living room with light colors that brighten my mood. There are even small copper birds on the ends of the curtain rods that I hadn't noticed at first glance. The whole room is just gorgeous. Quirky and cozy, yet spacious and luxurious.

"If it's missing anything, you'll let me know," Isaac says as more of a command than a statement.

"I will, Master," I answer quickly.

A slight smile plays across Isaac's full lips. "Good." He glances at the silver Rolex watch on his wrist and then looks back at me. "It's late, but it's time for your first lesson."

A chill goes down my spine at the intense look in his eyes. Excitement. Eagerness. Lust.

"I want to whip you," he says, slowly closing the door with his back to me, his voice low and filled with passion. "Every night I want you crawling into bed, your ass red and tender."

My breath quickens as my sore pussy begins to clench around nothing, and I close my eyes as images of being whipped by him fill my mind, my lips parting with desire.

Isaac steps in closer and I nearly fall to my knees, turned on by his closeness. "It's a reminder that you're mine. Your body belongs to me. Do you understand?" His voice is hoarse and coated with lust.

"Yes, Master," I sigh obediently, trembling from the heat radiating from his body.

"Whichever hole I want to use, you'll make available to me," he says, the tone of his deep voice making my clit throb. "And you'll be satisfied once I've cum."

If he means this to be a lesson by the way of torturing me with this dirty talk, then he's definitely succeeding. I can hardly breathe, my sore pussy soaking wet.

His eyes never leave my face. "If I've decided you've earned your pleasure, I'll make sure you cum as well. If not, you better not fucking touch yourself." His words come out quicker, his eyes holding a threat. As he talks, he walks the length of the room and I follow his steps. "Denial will be your punishment, and taking your own pleasure will only result in a whipping meant to cause more than just a sting. Do you understand?"

"You own my pleasure, Master," I manage to say as if in a trance, feeling weak in the knees and wanting him to end my torment. I want him to use my body for his pleasure. Right now.

A satisfied grin plays across his chiseled jawline. "Good girl."

He sits on the edge of the bed and then motions at me. "Tonight I want to use my hand."

Obediently I crawl onto the bed as he pats his lap. My breath quickening, I lower my body, lying in the end of the bed and across his lap, my hips digging into his thigh and my ass perfectly seated for the spanking. He moves his right leg over both of mine and lays his forearm across the length of my back, pushing my hair out of the way, so his heavy arm is laying across my naked back. "Put your hands behind your back and grip your wrists," he orders.

I do as I'm told, struggling to stay still as my clit throbs. My cheek lays flat against the bed and I stare straight ahead at the mirror sitting on top of a vanity across the room.

I want this so badly. After him talking to me in that dark, forceful way, I'm eager for his touch.

The sight in the mirror makes me even more turned on. Him still in his suit, the power radiating from his broad shoulders and perfect stature. But there's a heat in his eyes as the roam the length of my body that makes me feel like the powerful one.

I watch in the mirror as he runs his fingers along my spine, sending a tingle of need and want flowing through me.

"I want my hand to sting when I'm done with you." His dick hardens beneath me and I feel it pulsing against me. I whimper from the teasing torture he's putting me through.

He sets his hand flat against my ass and lowers his lips to my ear, his piercing green finding mine in the mirror. "I'll let you watch tonight. And if you're good, I'll let you ride my face and then fuck yourself on my dick. But if you make one sound, one movement, you'll get none of that, and you'll go right to bed once I've rubbed the cream on your ass so you can at least sit tomorrow."

I want so badly to breathe, to blink, to move. But his dirty words and dark promises keep my gaze straight ahead, locked into his trance.

"Yes, Master."

I count the smacks along my ass in my head, each one making me wetter and wetter, anticipating the reward for being such a good girl for him. My body jolts and after only eleven, my thighs are soaked.

At fifteen, the tears start to leak from the corner of my eyes and he starts fingering me, playing with my pussy between the blows.

At twenty-one, he picks up the pace, eager to end it, I think.

I was such a good girl for him.

He whispers it as he fucks me. *Good girl.*

I pass out in his arms, sated and exhausted, and I think… I think he whispers it again as he kisses my hair and then leaves me alone in the room.

CHAPTER 19

ISAAC

I sigh heavily, hearing the words of my mother and that abusive prick. *Worthless.*

That's the word she loved to use.

"Why are you up?" she asks, and my mother's voice is flat and hoarse. She's at the small kitchen table wearing nothing but a ripped nightshirt and a hot pink bra underneath.

Memories of what life used to be like flash before my eyes. The laughter and pancakes. Mom used to cook. Back before everything changed.

Now the fridge is always empty and the linoleum floor is always dirty from whatever she did last night with him. I'll clean it all up after school. It'll be okay. I can fix this.

Her eyes are so red as she rocks at the table. I know she's high. I'm old enough to know. I think my teacher knows. Mrs. Klintsova keeps asking me questions. But I don't tell them anything. I don't want her to get in trouble. She just needs help. I can help my mom. I love her.

She must know that.

"I never should've kept you. I knew your father was going to leave me."

I stare at my mother, not understanding. Dad died overseas. "He died at war." The words come out before I can stop myself, and I wish they hadn't. Mom lunges from the table, her ripped night shirt exposing the bright bra underneath. She smacks me hard across the face, gripping my shoulders and yelling into my ear.

"You're just like him!" She keeps shaking me, and I let her. She just needs to get it out of her system. I know she's hurting. I wish someone would help her. Tears roll down my cheeks and that only makes my mom angrier, but I can't help it.

It all hurts. I just want my mom back.

I stare at the ceiling, not moving. These memories come to me often, and they only remind me of the fucked up past that made me who I am. But I'm fine with that. I've grown to realize I can live with knowing who I really am.

I'm not worthless to Katia. I can do so much for her. She'll put her faith in me, she'll give me control, and I'll give her everything she needs.

It's important that she has privacy, a place that she feels at home. I know this, but I hate it. I want her tied to my bed so I can take her easily in the morning.

I roll onto my back, the sheets and thick comforter pulling with me. The dim light of the moon spilling through the slit in the curtains and casting shadows across my bedroom floor.

She's doing so well. She'll adjust soon. She's going to realize this isn't what she anticipated.

She thinks she knows what a Master is, what's required of a Slave... she has no fucking idea.

I can faintly hear the crickets from outside as a smile creeps up to my lips.

Just as quickly as it comes, it vanishes. A shrill cry from her room makes me leap from the bed.

My heart races as my feet slam against the hardwood floors on my way to her.

Her small frame is twisting under the sheets, fighting them as a strangled scream is torn from her throat.

"Katia!" I yell, grabbing her hip to pin her in place and her wrists with my other hand. I still both of her wrists above her head, holding her down with a good bit more strength than I thought I'd need.

"Katia, wake up!" I scream at her, so loud that I feel the wretched soreness in my throat. I imagine hers is worse. The screams haven't stopped, and she's only fighting harder.

Tears are leaking down her face, although her eyes are closed tightly.

She may think this is play, or a fantasy come to life. But for me this is real. I know she needs someone to heal her, and I so badly want to be her Master. I want to take those terrors away from her, to replace them with the pain and pleasure she needs.

My Katia. My kitten.

"Kitten," I lower my head to the crook of her neck, bringing my body closer to hers and forcing her head to stop thrashing. I keep my voice low and soothing as her screams turn to sobs. "I'm here, kitten, you're safe."

I press my body against hers, my hip on her hip and gently stroke her side.

"It's alright. You're safe. I'm here," I gently murmur into her ear.

I can't describe the rush of relief, pride, and satisfaction that washes through me as she settles her body and her breathing calms. Her struggle dies, and her fear vanishes.

A sense of ownership, and worthiness. I kiss her neck, my lips leaving open-mouth kisses along her skin, prickled with goosebumps.

"You're alright. You're safe. You're with me," I almost say, *your Master.* I almost speak words that I know are true. But she doesn't. Not yet.

My resolve strengthens as I pull away from her and gently run my thumb along her jaw, wiping away the residual tears.

My poor kitten.

Her eyes slowly open and sorrow and disappointment shine clearly in them, even with the dim light in the room.

"I-" she starts to speak, but I press my finger to her lips.

"Come, kitten. I want you in my room with me," I say easily, scooping her small body up in my arms and carefully balancing her as I climb off the bed and walk swiftly to my room.

Katia nestles her head under my chin, her arms wrapped around my neck. She buries her face in my chest, and I know she's ashamed more than anything.

"I'm sorry, Master," she whispers as I lower her into the bed.

"Why are you sorry?"

"It's my fault."

"Why's that?" I ask her, hating that she would think having a night terror is something she needs to apologize for.

"I use a blanket. I brought it with me, but I was tired. It was my laziness, Master. I'm sorry." Her voice is choked. "I won't do it again."

"A blanket?" I ask her. This sparks an interest. She's never mentioned a blanket before.

"I like the weight on my ankle when I sleep."

It takes me a moment to register what she means. "Like the shackle." My blood goes cold, and I pull her closer to me. My poor kitten.

"Yes, I'm sorry-" I cut her off before she can once again apologize when she shouldn't be.

"You're my responsibility, so it's my fault. Not yours. "

Her breath hitches and her body tenses.

"You'll sleep here tonight, and tomorrow I'll fix this." I kiss her hair gently, at odds with the strength in my voice. It's an effort to soften my tone as I say, "Sleep, kitten."

Her wide eyes look up at me with slight wonder and disbelief. So pale, so clear it once again feels like she can see through me. She licks her lower lip and lays her head down on my forearm, but she doesn't close her eyes.

After a moment she tilts her body some to look at my face.

"Why are you doing this?" she asks me softly. "Master?" she tacks on my title at the end, and we both know she shouldn't have. She should have started with it. She looks frightened for a moment, that she let the question slip without respectfully addressing me, but I haven't the energy to care.

My mind is reeling with the revelation of what she's just told me. And how I need to find a solution to this problem.

"Why do I want to be a Master?" I ask her.

"Why are you trying to help me?"

She still doesn't realize that being her Master dictates that I have to help her. Her welfare in every way is my responsibility. The room fills with the soft sounds of our breathing and the chirps of the crickets and other soft sounds of the night.

Why do I want to be a Master?

I've thought about that a lot over the years. Especially when the nights are cold and lonely and a simple, quick fuck holds no interest. I don't have an answer, but I want to give her one.

"When I was younger, I tried very hard to help someone." My heart hurts as I think back to when I was younger. When I first felt needed, and failed so miserably. "It only hurt me when I tried to help her. She hurt me. I gave up. I stopped trying, but I still wanted to love her." I think I did love her. I don't think I ever stopped. How can you stop loving your mother? I was only a child. I think it's ingrained in our DNA to forgive and continue to love them.

Katia moves her small hand from my chest, cupping it and putting it under her head. I trail my finger down her cheek as I continue my story.

"One day she needed me badly," I take in a deep breath, the vision of that night flashing before my eyes. "But I didn't."

"So now you try to help others?"

"No," I respond quickly. I don't, not really. I'm not interested in many people. But something about Katia called to me. It's still forcing me close to her. Wanting to give her more and more.

"Oh, I don't understand."

I grunt a response. I don't understand either. I was just thinking out loud. I don't even know why I said anything.

"Who was she?"

"My mother," I answer simply.

"What happened?" she asks, and I run a hand down my face. The vision of her lying cold and lifeless on the ground haunts me in that moment.

"Go to sleep, kitten." I shouldn't have said anything. I shake my head slightly; none of my past means anything. It has no relevance to Katia and her night terrors. The exhaustion from the day is clouding my judgment.

"I just..." Katia starts to say something, but her voice trails off. The worry is evident in her voice. It shouldn't be there at all.

I shouldn't have opened my fucking mouth. I regret saying anything.

"This conversation is over. I'm a Master because I take pleasure in it." My voice is strong and she should more than understand that I mean what I say. "That's the end of this conversation."

"But-" Katia starts to question me, eagerness to learn more in her voice. She doesn't use my title, and I've had it. My kitten is a playful one, curious and wanting to please me and learn more about me. But she should know better.

I grip her hip in one hand and flip her forcefully onto her back, pressing my body against hers and pinning her wrist above her head.

She gasps from the force and my rough hold on her.

"Did you question me?" I ask, my eyes narrows, my voice low and full of a threat.

"I'm sorry, Master." Her words come out quickly, full of fear. Her body is tense and still.

"Did. You. Question me?" I repeat louder, my dick hardening simply from the feel of her soft body beneath mine.

"I did and I'm so sorry, Master." Her pale blue eyes tell me everything. She's truly repentant. But she needs to be punished.

"On your knees," I hiss in the crook of her neck, my hot breath sending a chill down her body. I release her and sit on the balls of my feet, waiting for her to get into position.

She does so quickly and obediently.

I have to lean over to the nightstand and turn on the light. Her pussy and ass are sore, I'm sure of that. As I click it on and move back behind her, I gentle a hand on her ass. It's still bright red. Her upper thighs are virtually untouched, which leaves possibilities. I don't have the cream in this room for aftercare though.

Fuck. I clench my jaw. I hate being so limited. I spread her pussy lips to see how swollen and red she is.

Denial it is.

"You will not cum, do you hear me?"

"Yes, Master," she says, her voice clear, yet low and full of agony.

"This is a gentle punishment. Do not push me again."

"I won't Master."

I shove my fingers into her tight cunt, stroking along her G-spot before she's even able to finish. I'm quick and rough, watching how her body moves roughly with the force from me finger fucking her.

Her soft moans and her thighs trembling only make me want to fuck her more. But this is a punishment. Not a reward.

As soon as her pussy tightens and her upper body shifts and twists, trying to avoid the inevitable, I know she's close. Katia pleads in a whisper, "Master," as I pull away from her. I watch as she stays on all fours, letting the intensity of her impending orgasm fade. Her eyes are closed tightly, and her breathing is coming in pants.

I could do this for hours, but I don't fucking want to.

I'm hard as fuck, but I'm irritated. I ignore my own needs. We'll both suffer tonight.

"Go to sleep, kitten," I say flatly, lying on my back, but holding my arm out for her.

She cuddles beside me and I kiss her hair. Hating that I'm leaving her in need, but she needs to be punished.

Even after she's fast asleep and safe in my arms, I'm wide awake, wondering if I'm a capable enough Master for her.

CHAPTER 20

KATIA

I stifle a yawn as I lower myself into the cushioned chair in the corner nook of Isaac's large chef's kitchen, the smell of rich coffee filling the room mixing in with smell of bacon, eggs, sausage and pancakes. My heart skips a beat as I look out through the beautiful large windows at the early sunrise, marveling at the spectacular view of the immaculate landscaped grounds. Isaac's property is truly picturesque, and the golden halo from the morning sun makes it almost look worthy of a scenic postcard portrait. It's a far cry from the hell that I lived in under my last Master.

I shake my head slightly, by forehead pinched, feeling like this isn't real. Instead of a Slave, I feel more like a pampered pet. Like I'm really his actual kitten. More than that, there's been a shift between us. Last night, something changed. It's only been one day and I'm already feeling like I've seen a side of Isaac that I'm sure he hasn't shared with anyone. I just don't know what to make of it.

"You need to eat something, kitten," Isaac says, drawing my eyes over to him where he's standing at the coffee maker. He's stopped manning the multiple skillets he has going on the stove to pour sugar into a cup of fresh coffee. The long silver spoon clinks against the ceramic mug as I watch him stir it.

My heart jumps in my chest again at the sight of him. God, he's so fucking sexy. Just like this is how Isaac should always be. He has no shirt on, his rock-hard abs on display, and his black silk pajama pants hang low on his chiseled hips, showing off his perfect V. His large cock imprint is easily visible and makes my mouth water with need. He's not wearing any boxers and I'm just waiting for his cock to slip out of the slit in his pants.

Isaac finishes stirring the coffee, licking the residual drops off the spoon and walks over to the table and sets it down in front of me. "I know you normally skip breakfast, but I want you to eat when you're with me. I will not eat breakfast alone; do you understand?" It's hard to focus on his words with his cock imprint in my face and I swear he has a semi hard-on. I can practically see the vein running through his shaft. "Look at me," Isaac orders.

I swallow back the sudden dryness in my throat and look up into his stunning green eyes.

"You will eat," he says as a statement. As a fact.

I'm not hungry. I don't do breakfast, and he knows it, but I must do as he commands. "Yes, Master," I say, doing my best to keep my eyes on his. The way he's looking at me, like he wants to devour me, is making it hard to concentrate. This is nothing like what I thought it would be.

I pull the pink silk see-through robe a little tighter across my chest. It already hugs my curves. Even more, the outline of my breasts and hardened nipples are clearly evident and the outline of my mound is visible whenever I'm walking. He's told me that he wants me to wear this every morning, so I can be accessible to him whenever he pleases. I shiver as I remember his words. *I want your pussy available to me at all times.*

"Good." A twinge of happiness goes through me as he turns away and goes back over to the stove to operate the skillets he has going. I didn't imagine it'd be this easy to please him. I pick at the hem of the robe, and take a small sip of delicious hot coffee. I had no fucking idea what I was getting into.

I take solace in staring at his back, admiring each ridge of his muscles, the outline of his muscular physique, the crack of his chiseled ass. The small dimples on his lower back that my fingers itch to touch. I still can't get over the fact that he's making breakfast for me and serving me coffee. I should be serving him like the Slave I'm supposed to be. My last Master never did anything like this for me, never even cared if I ate at all. This relationship isn't like what I thought it would be at all, and I have to keep reminding myself that Isaac is my Master. In this moment it doesn't quite feel that he is. But I suppose even pampered pets have *Masters*.

I watch the muscles in his back contract with each movement as he deftly turns over bacon, scrambles eggs and flips pancakes in the skillets. I sit back against the cushioned seat, my mind turning to the previous night. What he told me. God, my heart hurts for him.

How could I not have realized? I was so concerned with fixing myself, and facing my own past that I never once stopped to think that Isaac might be hurting, too. That he might need help just as much as I do. I felt terrible when he held me so early this morning, comforting me, trying to make me forget about my night terrors, when it's clear he needs to forget, too. When he told me about his mother, it all clicked. He's had a darkness around him from the moment I met him, a sadness that I missed because I was too self-absorbed with my own issues.

Absentmindedly, I bring my cup of coffee to my lips and take a sip, enjoying the rich taste.

"Today you can go to work," Isaac says, pulling me into the present and drawing my eyes back to him, "but the rest of the week, you'll have someone cover for you. I've taken some time off for your training," he finishes, as he piles several pancakes into a neat stack on a large plate.

I part my lips to object, but then close them. My dogs are my everything, and I would hate to upset their routine they've become accustomed to. And dogs are nothing if not sensitive to routine. If I don't come in for several days in a row, I know more than a few of them will get worried; we're a pack, I'm supposed to be there. It distresses me to think that I could upset them by obeying Isaac's demands, but I signed a contract. I have to obey his rules. He *owns* me. "Yes, Master," I reply dutifully, hoping he doesn't notice my hesitation and praying that my dogs will forgive me.

If he notices, he doesn't say anything. "Good," Isaac says, half-turning to me as he continues to scramble eggs.

I have enough help to take over what I do in person.

"Master?" I ask.

"Yes?"

"May I do some of the administration work on my laptop from here?"

"Yes, when you have a moment, you may."

"Thank you, Master."

WELL AT LEAST THAT WON'T CAUSE ANY PROBLEMS WITH MY WORK. It's easy enough to handle. My laptop is still open on the counter. Isaac wanted me to go about my morning routine. Which means coffee and checking my messages. It makes me feel uneasy to be on my support group with him in the room, but at the same time I can see that he should know. Kiersten had sent me a slew of messages last night that I wasn't able to answer until early this morning. I'd told her all about my contract with Isaac and she wanted to know all the details of my relationship. I pull the laptop into my lap and click the spacebar until it's awake again.

I open to screen to find that Kiersten is already online and has replied only a few minutes ago.

DARLINGGIRL86: WHAT'S HE LIKE?

I nervously pick at my fingernails. Both loving and hating that I'll be talking about Isaac while he's in the room. He could easily walk over and see.

My hands resting above the keys, I think for a moment, wondering if I should tell her. The truth is, this relationship resembles nothing like what I think a true M/s relationship should be. While Isaac is still demanding, I have more freedom than I think I should as a Slave, and his kindness totally throws me off.

Katty93: Not what I expected.

I only have to wait half a second before I hear a ding.

Darlinggirl86: What do you mean?

I sneak a peek at Isaac; he's almost done with organizing breakfast, piling bacon on one plate and eggs on another. I bite my lower lip, wondering how to best answer her question.

Katty93: He's too nice.

Crap. I feel awful after typing that, but I had to say it. That's why this feels so wrong to me.

Darlinggirl86: Too nice? Is that good or bad?

I take a sip of coffee, staring at the screen and not knowing for sure if it'd be okay to tell her about what happened early this morning. It's one thing to be vague about being purchased at an auction and not providing any concrete names or scenarios. It's another to divulge something so personal. Plus I don't want to violate the non-disclosure agreement I signed.

Katty93: It's good in some ways, bad in others. But I'm only just learning what he truly needs.

Darlinggirl86: It's only been one day, Kat. Give it time.

KATTY93: I WILL.

FEELING GUILTY, I SHUT MY LAPTOP AND SET IT ON THE WINDOWSILL just as Isaac brings breakfast over to the table, setting down plates of everything he's prepared.

"Is everything alright, kitten?" Isaac asks me as he sits down across from me.

"Yes," I say, flashing a smile that I hope doesn't betray my nervousness. "Just was chatting with a friend who wanted to know how I'm doing."

"What's your friend's name?" Isaac asks as he grabs a butter knife.

"KIERSTEN," I ADMIT.

Isaac slathers butter on each layer of pancake. "Ah. A coworker, I assume?"

I shake my head. "She's an online friend I met on a support group message board. I've never met her before. She's good people though."

I hope he doesn't ask me about her past. I honestly don't know much about it, even if he insisted I tell him more about her.

Isaac grabs his fork after layering his pancakes with a river of syrup and cuts into the stack. "I see."

I'm surprised that Isaac doesn't inquire into Kiersten's background further. I thought he'd be very interested in the dynamics of my relationship with Kiersten and want to control my interactions with her.

I pick up my fork, and spear a small piece of eggs, but I'm unable to bring it to my lips. Instead, I watch Isaac devour his pancakes. I don't know what game he's playing here. I feel so lost and like I don't belong here.

Isaac swallows his mouthful and gestures at my untouched plate. "Eat," he commands. "Don't make me have to tell you again."

"Yes, Master," I say immediately. I pick my fork back up and can only take a few bites of eggs before I'm forced to put it back down again. My appetite is nonexistent, and I can't get my mind off how much I want to know more about Isaac. "Master, may I bathe you?" I dare ask.

ISAAC LOOKS UP FROM HIS PLATE WITH SOME SURPRISE, ARCHING A sculpted brow as he looks at me.

"In the shower I mean," I say quickly, my heart beating erratically. I want to give him more of me. Help him the same way that he's trying to help me. *Please don't deny me.*

Isaac shakes his head, filling me with disappointment. "Not this morning, no. I have to leave after breakfast."

I try to hide the hurt that flashes in my eyes, but he sees it and sets his fork down, pushing his plate away from him.

He scoots his chair back away from the table. "Come sit on my lap, kitten."

I'm quick to take him up on his offer.

"Tonight," Isaac promises as he looks down at me with his lust in his eyes. "Tonight I'll let you wash me... if you're good today."

At least that's something. "Thank you, Master."

CHAPTER 21

ISAAC

I set the small gift bag on the bathroom counter, the silk handles falling gently to one side as the steam fills the room. I'm not sure if this will work, but I'm hopeful. It's a heavy anklet, two inches thick and studded with Swarovski crystals. I would have had it studded with diamonds if I intended on her keeping it, but I don't.

I had two errands today, and both were successful in some ways. Although I feel cheated by the second. The first was to get this anklet. Easy enough. The second was to meet with my contacts deeper in the world Katia was once a part of. When she killed Carver Dario, she set off a chain reaction of events. His territory and contacts were vulnerable with him gone, leaving two rivals fighting for his territory. His cartel is completely shattered. The other men in her past—Master O, and Javier Pinzan--are dead. I fucking hate it. I had to know for sure, and the dental records confirmed it.

I wanted to kill them for her. I wanted them to truly suffer for what they did to her. Every last one of them.

They're all dead, but I don't know how to tell her. Worse, I don't know if she should know. I'm not certain how it will affect her. I need to wait for the right time.

The soft, rhythmic sounds of Katia's bare feet padding into the bathroom make me turn toward the open door. Although the room is hot with the steam from the shower already pouring out, her nipples are pebbled. As my eyes travel down her body, she's still, her arms at her side. Her fingers are fidgety though, betraying her inner anxiety.

I know if she didn't know any better, she'd want to cover herself. I'm just not sure which part of her body she could possibly feel the need to hide from me. I circle her once, making it that much more obvious that I'm assessing her. My steps are slow and deliberate.

I watch her face as I near the front of her again. Her eyes are closed for a long moment until she hears me step in front of her. Those soft, pale blue eyes, staring straight ahead and then sneaking a glance at my face. I let my eyes move slowly, waiting for a reaction.

As I focus on her slender shoulders, her body tenses. And I have my answer.

Her scars.

"You're beautiful, Katia," I say easily, unbuckling my pants with my eyes still lingering on her body. "Every inch of you."

"Thank you, Master."

My words aren't enough. But I'll prove to her I mean what I say. She'll see her beauty. And if she detests her scars, I'll take them away.

I won't let her think she's anything other than the gorgeous creature she is.

"Into the shower you go." I shove my pants down and follow her to the other side of the spacious bathroom.

The river rock on the floor of the large shower stall travels up the wall. The rainfall showerhead and three side spouts are going at full steam.

Katia's lush lips part as she steps under the warmth of the spray. Her skin turning pink and the water darkening her hair and spilling over her lips, her shoulders, her breasts.

She's so fucking gorgeous. She only affords herself a moment before she opens her eyes and turns to face me, waiting for her next command.

I let her stand under the spray as I open a bottle of lavender and vanilla body wash and pour it into the palm of my hand. I slowly lather it, thinking about which inch of her I want to wash first.

"Spread your legs," I say and barely breathe the command, but she instantly obeys.

I crouch down, the water pouring over my back as I massage her calves and work my way up her body. I keep moving in slow, soothing circles. As I rise and my fingers inch closer to the insides of her thighs, she closes her eyes, nearly falling backward and reaching out to steady herself by gripping my shoulder.

She almost pulls her hand away once she's straightened herself again, but I hold her hand down and look into her eyes as I kiss just above her wrists. "Stay."

With her breath coming in quickly, she nods her head and says, "Yes, Master."

I continue my ministration, working the lather over her body, teasing her sex slightly and grinning as her eyes heat with lust. She stays still as I massage her ass, taking great care to make sure she's healing nicely, which she is. I suck her nipples, my dick hard and pressing into her soft curves. But only for a moment. I just want to see them reddened from my touch.

"Rinse and then get on your knees," I give her the command while I pour the shampoo into my hand.

I massage the shampoo into her scalp while my dick brushes against her lips.

It's a tease. Her lips slowly open until the head of my cock is being licked as I move slightly.

I shouldn't allow her to tease me back. But I fucking love it.

"Lean back."

She does as I ask, and the water rinses her hair clean. My fingers spear through her thick blonde locks.

I do the same with the conditioner, but I allow more of my cock to enter the heat of her mouth. She closes her lips around my head and gently sucks, a tingle of need shooting through me as her soft tongue runs the length of my slit accompanied by the soft vibrations of her moan.

As I pull her hair back slightly, she releases me to rinse the conditioner from her hair, and our eyes lock.

"Your turn, kitten," I tell her reaching a hand down to help her up from her position.

She takes her time, grabbing the bar of hard milled soap and looking over my body. She's aroused, but taking her task seriously. She lathers the bar, large suds covering her hands, before gently caressing my body.

I close my eyes, enjoying the strong motions from her small hands.

She works her hands over my shoulders as she stands on her tiptoes, and then moves them down my back and over my ass. I have to smile as she hesitates to move lower.

She moves in front of me, her eyes focused on my hard cock and quickly lathers her hands back up, and runs them over my chiseled abs. The look of desire reflected in her eyes makes me want to take her against the shower wall right now, but I stay still.

She moves lower, making her circles smaller and smaller until her hands wrap around my cock.

I let her stroke me a few times, loving the feel of it.

"Enough," I say and admonish her.

Her eyes fly to mine and she stills, but nods her head and continues washing my legs.

I love both her desire and her obedience. And she'll be rewarded for it soon enough.

It doesn't take long until we're both cleaned and I can turn the water off.

I grab a towel off the heated bench and pat her dry in the stall, opening the glass door to let the cooler air in.

Satisfied with her being patted down and quickly drying myself, I take her hand and lead her to the front of the sink.

Without speaking, I put her chain on her, kissing her neck. And then I attach the leash with the clip at the end, and fasten it to her clit. It's tight enough to stimulate and stay attached, but not nearly anywhere near tight enough to cause any pain.

I tug it gently, outward from her stomach, watching the pleasure on her face as the chain round her neck pulls away from her, clinking softly and then pulls at her clit. Sending a bolt of pleasure through her body.

"You'll wear both of these and nothing else in this house."

My dick is nestled in her ass as I speak. The sight of her in my chains, even if they are thin and more like jewelry, makes me want to spill my cum deep inside of her.

But not yet. There's one more thing, one very important addition.

I stand behind her, splaying my left hand on her lower belly and pulling her closer to me. "This is for you." I hand her the gift bag with my right. "But you'll need to put it on yourself."

She turns to look at me over her shoulder, hesitantly taking the bag.

"Put it on now," I tell her.

She quickly set the bag down on the counter, pulling out the large, black velvet box. She opens it slowly and then runs her fingers along the crystals.

"It's beautiful," she whispers.

"It's for your ankle," I tell her. Her body tenses for a moment, and recognition flashes in her eyes.

"You and you alone will put it on and take it off." I swallow thickly, hoping this is going to work for her. "I'll throw it away the moment you leave it. You can only take it off when you shower."

"I don't understand."

"If you need to wear this at night, then you must wear it all day as well. If you don't wear it, I'll throw it away."

"It's a shackle?" she whispers.

"It's yours. It's whatever you want it to be."

I give her a moment to let the rules and the meaning of the anklet to register. "Put it on," I tell her.

She bends down and clasps it into place. It's a little large on her and slips down, but firmly stays in place.

Once she stands, I pull her closer to me and kiss her neck, running my fingers through her folds. She's no longer wet. But I'll make it up to her.

I pull the chain at her stomach, reminding her of the chains she's wearing that are mine. "This is how I want you while you're home, unless I tell you otherwise."

I kiss along her neck and nip her ear, looking between the soft curve of her neck and her pale blue eyes in the mirror.

I tug the chain again and I'm rewarded with a sweet moan of pleasure and arousal moistening her pussy.

LAUREN LANDISH & WILLOW WINTERS

I lead her with the chain to the large whirlpool tub in the middle of the bathroom, loving her soft whimpers. I sit on the edge and turn her so she's facing away from me. The anklet clinks as I pull her down on top of me roughly, her back to my front, my dick hard and ready to be buried in her heat.

"Do you think you were a good girl today?" I whisper against her ear. My lips gently caress her sensitive skin and cause a shudder to go through her body.

"Yes, Master," she answers with lust in her voice.

"You were," I admit as I slam my hips up, shoving my cock deep inside her. She tries to buck forward out of instinct, but I keep her close to me, fucking her roughly and tugging at the chain.

Rewarding my kitten.

And sating us both.

"Katia, what does being a Master mean?" I ask her as she crawls under the covers.

"It means you have complete control over someone."

"Is that what it means, kitten?" I ask her.

She clears her throat, looking as though she's questioning her response. "There's more to it than that," she finally says.

"It's very simple, kitten. Soon you'll know." Her eyes flash with disappointment as she takes in a heavy breath.

Sleep well, I tell her before turning off the lights and leaving her alone. Wearing my chain and contemplating what it truly means for me to be her Master.

CHAPTER 22

KATIA

I step into the steam-filled bathroom, dressed in my flimsy gown, my skin prickling from the inner fire inside the pit of my stomach, my body on edge. I'm sweaty and dirty from crawling on my hands and knees all day, obeying every wish of my Master and now he's ordered me to take a bath and to let him clean me. And if I'm good, he's going to let me bathe him.

I couldn't be happier to oblige. I hunger for his strong hands on my body, giving me the pleasure I so badly crave and he's tempted me with all day. It's hard to even think of myself as a Slave when I feel more like Isaac's pampered pet. It's definitely not what I was expecting going into this relationship, but I fucking love it. It feels like I'm living a fantasy.

I'm his fucktoy, his kitten, his everything. But what he does to me, what he commands me to do only makes me feel desired and cherished.

I catch sight of the faint scars on my shoulder and my mind drifts back to earlier today, to one of my training sessions that left me appreciating him even more.

"I want you to paint your scars," Isaac told me as I sat on a *leather training bench. He grabbed a bowl of whipped cream and strawberries off a stand nearby and held it out to me. With the bowl in*

his left hand, he held the long stem of a large, fresh strawberry and dipped it in the homemade cream.

"Open," he commanded me. "Stick your tongue out flat."

I did as I was told and he traced a line down my tongue with the point of the berry and then around my lips, teasing me. "You'll paint them with the cream for me to lick off."

He pulled it away from my mouth and I responded as I knew I should. "Yes, Master." I've learned to love those words. I love pleasing him. He makes it so easy.

Obediently, I took the strawberry from his hands, and only then did I really register what he'd told me to do. I didn't know why he wanted me to paint my scars with cream and fruit, but I knew I shouldn't question him. Everything he makes me do is for my own good.

My skin pricked with his eyes on me as I carefully dipped the strawberry into the cream in the bowl and began painting my scars, slowly and deliberately. My eyes watched my movements in the trifold mirror from the vanity he'd placed me in front of. The vanity was from my room, but the bench was in his. I started with my neck first, covering all those ugly marks I so hated, before moving to my collarbone and then my shoulders.

I remember how I got them. How my old Master would chain me to the bed and let the whip rip across my back. Occasionally it would break skin, but that's not what made the scars, it was the tips of the braided tails. In the beginning, when I wasn't perfect, he'd attach the punishment spurs. They'd stick into my skin and when he pulled back... I closed my eyes, hating the memory.

The second I shut my eyes, I felt Isaac's strong hand between my legs and his tongue licking along the faint bit of cream painted over my scars.

I gasped with pleasure at the sensation, reveling in the feel of his warm wet mouth, and had to fight the urge to wrap my arms around his neck and keep him in place. I knew I could only accept what he gave me, and nothing more.

He moved up to my neck, kissing away the cream, sucking on my neck.

Isaac continued kissing and sucking on my neck until all the cream was gone, and when he pulled back I was so fucking out of breath. I'd never experienced having food literally licked off my body, and the sensation of it had been incredible. The places where he licked me felt alive, tingling with sexual energy from his hungry lips and tongue. God, I had felt so good.

"Master," I breathed, panting, my chest heaving and my pussy clenching uncontrollably. Seriously, I almost came just from that. "More. Please."

Isaac responded by grinning at me and standing tall in front of me. "Be careful what you wish for, kitten."

I wasn't sure what he meant until he walked away and came back with a buzzing object. A huge fucking vibrator. Grinning, he placed it on the bench, making the tip of the head barely touch my pussy lips and clit. I instantly shivered at the sensation, so turned up already and wanting so badly to cum.

Smack!

I cried out from the pain and pleasure stinging my ass as Isaac drew back the riding crop he'd picked up from the side of the bench.

"You're not to move," he told me. "You're to stay perfectly still while that vibrator teases your pussy and the only thing I want to see move is your arm as you cover your scars with whipped cream again. Understand?"

I was breathless, wanting to protest. I needed to cum so bad. I was so turned on it was unreal. But I did as he commanded.

"Yes, Master," I replied.

The session went on to last another hour, and I was whipped several times for moving, but each time I didn't, Isaac rewarded me with his mouth and a bit of pleasure, licking and cleaning my scars. By the time it was over, I'd gotten better at being perfectly still and I was rewarded with one of the hardest fucks Isaac had given me.

My eyes flicker back to the mirror, to the scars on my body. Scars that now have a different memory. My heart clenches in my chest. This isn't what I thought it would be. It's so much more. Submitting to Isaac makes me feel liberated.

My past is losing its grip on me. And it's all thanks to Isaac.

. . .

As if summoned by my thoughts, a terror that constantly haunts me, one of the recurring images that has viciously torn me from my sleep and kept me a captive to my past for years, rages in my vision.

I can see my old Master's sick smile as he hits me, delighting in the perverse pleasure my pain brings him. I can see the scene unfold as if I'm having an out-of-body experience, and I see myself cowering in the corner as he beats me over and over again, the back of hand slamming against my cheek, splitting my lip open and filling my mouth with the metallic taste of blood. Unconsciously, I raise a hand to my face, touching where he struck me.

But there's no pain there. No bruises.

It's not real, I tell myself confidently, shocked at how little I'm affected by that horrible image, just a fading memory.

"You need a bath, kitten," Isaac says, breaking me out of my reverie.

I take in a sharp breath as I see him standing in front of the beautiful garden tub, cloaked in steam, his dress shirt unbuttoned and rumpled, his black dress pants doing little to hide the huge bulge in his pants. My nipples pebble, my mouth waters, and my pussy clenches with need as I think about how he will soon be cleaning me himself, his hot hands roaming every inch of my body. I want it. I want him.

"Yes, Master," I say obediently, a feeling of warmth lacing with my desire. I feel so safe in Isaac's presence. I could not have asked for a better Master. But I'm starting to feel a little lightheaded from the steam. Today has been such a long day, and I'm tired. Taking a warm, steamy bath will hopefully help me relax.

He gestures at my robe. "Take that off."

. . .

354

I DO AS HE SAYS, LETTING THE PINK ROBE SLIP OFF MY SHOULDERS AND fall to the floor. I don't miss the flash of desire in Isaac's eyes as he surveys my naked body, my hardened nipples, my flesh riddled with goosebumps, and the chain attached to my clit. Exactly how he likes me.

HIS EYES BURNING, HE WALKS OVER TO ME AND PLACES A HAND ON MY abdomen, tracing his name he's written across it before taking the chain off from around my neck and then unclipping the other end from my clit. The action makes my back bow with the sharp release on my tender throbbing clit. My head falls back and his fists my hair at the base of my neck. "Good girl, kitten," he whispers, kissing my exposed neck and releasing me. I glance down at my midsection where his name is scrawled, feeling a sense of pride. Every day he writes his name on me, reminding me that I belong to him... but I want so badly to ask if I can write my name on him. I haven't, afraid it might displease him.

HE'D PROBABLY LET ME IF I ASK, I TELL MYSELF. AS MUCH AS I WANT to please him, my happiness matters to him. It's obvious to me now.

"TAKE OFF YOUR ANKLET, KITTEN," ISAAC ORDERS NEXT, HIS VOICE heavy, his eyelids hooded with lust. He never touches the anklet. It's truly mine. And so far, it's helped at night. The weight mimics the shackle. But the way Isaac looks at it makes me uneasy.

I'M QUICK TO BEND DOWN AND REMOVE IT FOR THE SHOWER. JUST like I've done every day.

I know where the clasps are and I lean against the wall, still feeling exhausted and weak from the day and unhook the first, and then the second.

My heart stops short as the metal falls over my ankle.

So much like before.

I'll always be your Master. I hear his voice, and see his cruel, smiling visage. My heart races, and the room starts spinning around me. Oh my God. Not here. Not now. I feel like I'm going to throw up as a crushing weight settles on my chest and my whole body begins shaking. Fuck. I can't catch my breath as my heart pounds out of my chest, and my vision begins to narrow into a tiny little dot.

I can't breathe. My fingers grip the anklet, but I don't feel the studded Swarovski, instead it's the rough cast iron. I lean against the drywall of the luxurious bathroom, but that's not where I am. It's the hard, rough concrete walls of the small room he kept me in.

He's dead. My Master's dead. I can feel the key in my hand as the shackle falls to the ground with a loud clank.

Did they hear? My heart races faster. What I have I done? Fear grips me. I have to run. I need to run. They can't find me. I can't let that happen.

The metal slips from my hand as I cover my mouth and feel paralyzed, knowing if I can't escape, they'll kill me. Slowly, painfully, for nothing more than their enjoyment.

As the floor rushes up to meet me, the last thing I see is a blur rushing at me and deep voice yelling, "Kitten!"

CHAPTER 23

ISAAC

*F*uck! My fingers dig into Katia's waist as her knees buckle and she nearly topples forward. I saw it happening in slow motion. I've been waiting for something, anything to come of the anklet, but I didn't think it would be this.

"Kitten!" I hold her close to me, keeping her upright as her nails dig into my skin. Shit! I seethe through my teeth as her nails scratch down my arm. My heart twists in my chest so tightly, as if it's wrapped in barbed wire. The pain is unbearable.

I hate this. I never thought this would be the outcome.

"Katia, I'm here." I call to her, holding her close, but she's not listening. She's not here with me. She's far away and caught in a hell that was meant to be lit on fire and left in her past where it belongs.

She cries out, her eyes open, but not seeing what's in front of her. I shake her, I cup her face, forcing her to look at me. "Look at me!"

But she's not listening. She's fighting me, pulling away and scratching and trying to run.

He has her.

Her former Master. I want to spit the word.

He's not allowed. He's dead. I won't let him have this control over her.

She's mine!

I push her back against the wall and shove my forearm under her chin, keeping her from biting me. With her wrists pinned above her head and my hip pushed against hers, I have her still.

"You think of only me when you're with me," I command her, pushing my thigh between her legs and pressing her back firmly against the wall. She whimpers, and her eyes finally find mine.

"You belong to me. No one else." Her body tenses as her pupils dilate and recognition flashes in her eyes. My kitten. Stay with me. Only me.

I crash my lips to hers, slowly lowering my arm and she responds. Her lips part and she fights me again, but it's to hold me back. To grip onto me and kiss me with a passion that makes her heart beat so hard I swear I can hear it even over the sound of my own blood rushing in my ears.

"Only me."

"Only you."

"Who do you belong to?" I ask her, pushing my hand between her thighs and rubbing her clit.

"You," she says in a strangled cry.

"Why did you take it off?" I ask her.

She breathes in a sharp inhale and her eyes widen, afraid to answer for a moment. But she obeys. "Because I was told to. You told me to."

"You're such a good girl," I whisper into the crook of her neck as I rub my palm against her clit.

I kiss along her jaw and down her neck, rocking my hand and feeling her grow wetter and hotter. I need to get her off. I need her to be rewarded for facing her past like she did.

I bury my head in the crook of her neck, feeling her long blonde hair against my nose and cheek. "Such a good girl."

I slip my fingers into her heat.

"Thank you, Master," she moans. Her head turns to the left and then the right.

She runs her hand down my forearm and I can feel the blood smear along my arm from where she scratched me. Her eyes are closed. She's just enjoying my touch.

Thank fuck. She needs this. She can't be afraid to take it off. She needs this more than she could possibly know.

"Cum for me," I tell her, pulling away slightly and looking at the soft curves of her face. Her forehead's pinched and her soft lush lips are parted. Her flushed skin and quick pants of heated breathing only prove to me that she's close. I can't take the sight of her so wound up and turned on. So fucking gorgeous. This is how she should always be. Lost in the pleasure I give her. Never in pain.

"Please cum for me," I practically beg her, my heart hurting and my body feeling cold and nearly numb.

She cries out as the warmth of her arousal leaks from her and her thighs tremble. Her body stiffens as she grips me with a force equal to the intensity of her orgasm.

"Good girl," I softly say as I pull my hand away and hold her close to me.

I kiss her hair, then her cheek and her neck as she lolls her head to the side, gripping onto my shoulders and resting her cheek on my shoulder.

It takes a moment for her to calm, and all the while I just hold her to me.

"Are you alright, kitten?" I ask softly, pulling away from her for just a moment. She hides her face at first and I hate it. I hate that she's ashamed of confronting her past.

I grip her chin in my hand and force her to look at me.

She pulls away, moving her head to the side and responding softly. "I'm okay."

I think about questioning her. Making her talk about it. But we both know what happened.

I don't want her to hurt anymore. I pull her into my chest and rock her slightly. She holds me back with a force that's new to her. She's holding me as though she'll fall if I let her go. As if she'll shatter without me here to hold her up.

My poor Katia. I kiss her sweetly, my heart breaking.

I wish there was more I could do.

But this will take time.

Every time she puts that anklet on, she knows what she's doing, what she's enabling.

This was bound to happen, but I still hate it.

I lay her on the ground, breathing heavily and catching her breath while I turn the shower on. The loud sprays hit the wall, drowning out her heavy breathing. I turn to look at her, my hand under the stream, waiting for the water to warm and she's still, her eyes wide open, staring at the gorgeous anklet, laying across the bathroom floor from her, as though it's a snake waiting to strike.

I'm not surprised though, when she's showered and pampered and the time's come to either wear it or throw it away. I'm not surprised that she puts it back on to keep the night terrors at bay. But the look in her eyes is different now.

It's progress.

"KATIA, WHAT DOES BEING A MASTER MEAN?" I ASK HER AS I SIT ON her bed and gently pet her hair.

"I don't know, Master." She answers so quietly I almost don't hear her.

"What do you think it means?" I ask her.

"I feel so confused," she admits.

"What if I told you you've only had one Master, Katia? What would you say then?"

She turns in the bed, finally looking me in the eyes. "I'd say a Master is a good thing. A Master is a savior."

Her admission makes my heart hurt. I want to save her. And I will.

CHAPTER 24

KATIA

I can't believe I'm doing this.

I look over at Isaac as he drives us down the road toward my family's house in his spare Mazda CX-5, handling the car in a way that manages to turn me on, even when I'm on edge. Everything he does is just so sexy. His mannerisms, the way he talks, the way he moves. The way he *owns* me.

I shake my head. I can't believe I'm letting this man meet my family after only knowing him for a few weeks.

10 days into being his slave... A man that owns me, mind, body and soul no less. It almost makes me laugh that we're even coming with gifts, after I've avoided my family like a plague, all because he thinks meeting them will be for my own good. As much as I don't like this, I have to trust him. And deep down, I know he's right. I still love them. And I know they love me.

But that doesn't change the fact that this entire situation is fucked.

My heart jumps into my chest as we turn onto Waverly Road, the familiar houses popping up in front of me, my childhood memories coming back to haunt me. I walked down this street the day they took me. I close my eyes, trying to block the visions, not wanting to get emotional. The last thing I need to do is break down in front of my parents with Isaac standing there. Who knows what might happen? I suck in several calming breaths before opening my eyes and focusing on the present as Isaac pulls up in front of my childhood home, parking the car next to the curb.

There it is. *Home.* I sit there for a moment staring at it. It looks just like I remember. A two story rustic brick home, with partial cream-colored vinyl siding and a cozy porch with several rocking chairs sitting out in front of it.

"You okay?" Isaac's deep baritone penetrates my thoughts.

I look over at him, blinking rapidly as something pricks the back of my eyes. That better not be a fucking tear. I just need to hold it together for maybe an hour. Hopefully by then we'll be long gone. "Yes," I reply, trying to keep the dread out of my voice.

Isaac's lips draw down into a point as he frowns, but I hardly notice it. Even with dressing down, in just blue jeans, a red sweater, and a worn brother leather coat, he looks hot. His hair is parted and slicked to the side, the scent of his masculine cologne filling the car.

I was surprised when he didn't wear a suit, but when he brought out the Mazda for us to drive in, I figured he didn't want to show up looking like he was drowning in cash.

"You will not lie to me, kitten," he growls, his voice low and dangerous.

I lick my lips. I know I can't argue with him. "I'm terrified," I admit. "I really don't want to do this."

Isaac shakes his head. "I know you don't. But you will. Do you understand?" His voice is firm, indicating that he'll accept nothing less than my perfect obedience.

I hate it, but I force myself to nod, not trusting myself to speak.

Isaac stares at me, the intense look in his beautiful green eyes making me squirm. "You will engage in every conversation that's initiated, and you will answer honestly. Even questions you find make you emotional. The only exception is questions about us."

I hold in a groan. Oh God, why is he doing this to me? I can lie about the two of us, but everything else that makes the pit of my stomach churn is fair game? Does he want me to cry? 'Cause that's exactly what's going to happen. I know it. I'm tired of crying. I've never wanted to defy him more than in this moment. But I don't. "Yes, Master," I reply, barely able to keep the tremor out of my voice.

I can't take staring into his stern gaze, so I look back over to my family home.

My mother refused to leave it after I was taken. She had deluded herself into thinking I'd come home somehow. Like one day I'd just appear for her, but if she moved, I wouldn't be able to find my way back to her. Bless her heart.

Thinking about it causes tears to form in my eyes, and I fucking hate it. I hate that I feel so raw still. I've been on a roller coaster of emotions the past week, feeling as though I'm invincible and then completely raw and vulnerable. I don't know what I am, but right now I know I don't want to do this shit. It's just too much, all at once. Why can't Isaac see that?

"Text your mother," Isaac says, taking my hand and gently kissing the back of it. His tone has softened, and he seems to recognize how terrified I am. But he's still going to make me go in there when I don't want to. "You're going to be perfect for me, kitten," he reassures me in an attempt to boost my confidence, and giving my hand a slight squeeze. "Trust me, you can do this. You *will* do this."

I want to tell him no, tell him that I can't do this. I don't want to have to face my mother, to have to be reminded of the pain I caused her. But looking at Isaac, I know there's only one answer he'll accept. "Yes, Master," I whisper.

"KATIA!" AS SOON AS I WALK THROUGH THE DOOR, MY MOTHER IS pulling me into her arms, gripping me into a fierce bear hug. I'm already filled with anxiety, so I can hardly breathe as she squeezes me and kisses me, telling me she loves me and how much she's missed me over and over.

"I've missed you so much, baby!" she cries with tears in her eyes, finally pulling back and allowing me to breathe, giving me a chance to look at her. She looks really nice, dressed up in a tweed skirt suit with heavy makeup on, something that is totally unlike her. I don't remember her this way at all. She always had pajamas on for most of the day with her hair in a messy bun during the holidays. It was typically even worse on Christmas Day, when she'd have stayed up the whole night before wrapping presents and baking treats for the family.

Today, she looks beautiful.

"I missed you too, Mom," I say, my voice quavering from emotion.

Don't cry, don't cry, don't cry, I tell myself over and over in a litany meant to strengthen me, knowing that if the first tears fall that I'll turn into a blubbering mess. I don't know how I can't do anything but break down, I feel too weak.

Isaac's words come back to me in that moment. *You're going to be perfect for me, kitten.* As if he knew I was thinking about him, I feel a gentle squeeze on my left hand and I look over to see Isaac gazing at me with strength and confidence in his eyes.

My mom freezes as her eyes fall on Isaac, her jaw going slack as if she's just now noticing he was there. "Well," she says, her voice filled with wonder, her eyes wide with shock, "who is this handsome young man?"

I know seeing Isaac with me must be hitting her pretty hard, since I've never had an official boyfriend. She probably can't believe I wound up in an actual relationship. But what I have with Isaac is anything but normal, and probably never will be.

"Mom," I say, swallowing back a tide of emotion, "this is Isaac, my-"

A quick pinch on the ass from Isaac reminds me to be careful of what I say next, and my cheeks burn with fire, my heart pounding from the oh shit moment. I hesitate for a moment, not wanting to make a mistake, but Isaac steps in.

"Boyfriend." It's such a strange word, especially coming from his lips.

"Boyfriend," I agree quickly, hoping my mom doesn't notice my flub. "Isaac is my boyfriend." *Boyfriend.* I can't believe that word just came out of my mouth. It sounds alien, and it certainly doesn't fit the description of what Isaac is to me. Nor the name I call him every night. And he sure as fuck isn't a *boy*.

My mom can't keep the shock from her face as she extends her hand in greeting. It's like she thinks Isaac must be a hologram that's going to vanish at any second. "Well, it's nice to meet you, Isaac. Kat told me that she had someone new in her life, but she didn't tell me that you were so handsome." She shakes her head and gives me a look.

Isaac takes her extended hand. "It's a pleasure to meet you too, Mrs. Herrington. I see who Kat inherited her beauty from."

My mom turns a furious shade of crimson. A warm sensation flows through my chest at her expression. I haven't seen her light up like that in... well, I don't remember when. And I must say that I'm impressed by Isaac's demeanor and charm in front of my mother; he's nothing like he is when he's at the club where everything revolves around sex. It's a side of him that makes me curious. I like his charm, but it has me wondering how much of this is an act.

"Oh stop it," Mom says when she can finally find words, waving away Isaac's compliment and chuckling nervously, trying to hide her embarrassment. She turns and motions us toward the living room. "Please, come and meet the rest of the family."

Isaac looks over at me and winks before we follow her into the living room. I'm really liking this side of him. He wraps his arm around my waist, and the display of affection catches me off guard. But In a good way though. It's just something I wasn't expecting.

The minute we step into the room, I'm greeted by the sight of my family huddled together and overwhelmed by everyone talking at once as they rush forward to greet me.

"Well, long time no see, Katia!" My father's voice comes from across the room as my sister hugs me, saying softly in my ear, "It's so good to see you!"

"It's been too long." The voices seem to blend as I imagine turning right around and leaving. Of course I don't, and instead I plaster a smile on my face, hugging each person in turn.

"Why, you look like you've lost so much weight!"

And from my cousin Lyssa, "Who's the hot guy?"

I'm surrounded by relatives, each one pulling me into one hug after another, telling me how much they love me and how happy they are to see me. I have to once again start chanting to myself, trying to keep my emotions in check. I try to answer every one the best as I can, almost becoming dizzy with confusion from all the questions, and not even knowing who's talking to me. I think I count ten people in the room, several aunts, uncles and cousins who are around my age. But the last person to come to me is someone I've been avoiding just as much as my mother.

"Hello, pumpkin," Dad says, holding his arms out to me. He's dressed in grey slacks, matching tie and a white dress shirt. Like my mom, he's aged quite a bit with his almost fully grey hair and a spider web of wrinkles around his eyes. He worried himself to death over my disappearance. "God, how I've missed you."

Once again, it's an effort not to just break down and I know if I let out one sob, one sigh even, it's over for me. I have to keep reminding myself of Isaac's words. *You're going to perfect for me, kitten.* If I can get through this without turning into a complete mess, I know I'll be rewarded. It'll make him happy. It's my job to please him. I cling to that fact, letting it be my strength to pull through, letting it be my armor.

"I've missed you too, Dad," I say, my voice heavy with emotion, but not in danger of cracking as he pulls me into his arms for a fierce bear hug, kissing me multiple times on my cheek and telling me how much he loves me, much in the same way Mom did.

When he's done showering me with affection, he pulls back and eyes Isaac with slight apprehension, his body language instantly changing and on edge.

He's definitely not giving Isaac the warm welcome my mother gave, but I understand why. "Who's this young man?"

I open my mouth to tell him, but Isaac steps forward, extending a hand. "Isaac Rocci, your daughter's new boyfriend." Just hearing the word *boyfriend* come from Isaac's lips again nearly causes me to swoon. I just can't get used to thinking about him in that context. "It's a pleasure to meet you, Mr. Herrington." Isaac's words are smooth and confident as he places a hand on my lower back, sending a subtle but powerful message to my father.

My body tingles with the wave of anxiety. This is something I hadn't anticipated. I didn't give any thought to it whatsoever.

My dad seems taken aback by Isaac's boldness for a moment, his mouth opening and closing several times before he takes Isaac's hand and shakes it. "It's a pleasure." I'm not sure, but I think Dad's respect for Isaac has gone up several notches, which is surprising. I half expected him to challenge Isaac to a duel right then and there.

"Now," says Lyssa as she steps forward and playfully pokes me in the arm, "Kat, can you please tell me where you found Isaac?" She shakes her head and pretends to wipe imaginary sweat from her brow. "Because Lord Jesus, please tell me there's more where he came from."

My mother snickers, and my aunts erupt with laughter in the corner of the room and even I have to chuckle a little, my face turning red and my mood slightly lifting. Somehow I know one of my crazy aunts put Lyssa up to it.

"So, how did you two meet?" Dad asks as everyone settles in their seats. He's sitting across from us in a loveseat with Mom, leaning forward with intense interest, his elbows resting on his knees.

"At a business club," Isaac says easily.

Dad furrows his brow and asks, "A what?"

Isaac nods. "It's a business club, for young entrepreneurs. It's a place where likeminded, business-driven individuals can come together and share tips and ideas to help drive sales and success." Isaac sits back easily in the seat, and I watch him with interest. I've never seen him speak like this. It's different. "I own my own security company, and Katia runs her own business with the dogs. We didn't have much in common in terms of business needs but I gravitated toward her. She's strong, and smart. Independent." Isaac smiles at me. "The first time I laid eyes on her, I knew she was something special. But when I heard her speak, the sound of her voice..." Isaac looks at me, rubbing my back and causing warmth to spread up and down my torso. I'm just sitting here awkwardly, blushing like a fiend, and with a stupid look on my face. "...She had me sold." I almost choke on the irony of his words.

My father sits back in his seat, a look of relief crossing over his face. "Oh, Katia didn't tell us about all that."

Isaac nods, and takes my hands in his. "I'm a very lucky man. This has been the most... satisfying relationship that I can ever remember being in. I'm very happy to have found her." My cheeks burn even hotter, turning a crimson red.

Before we came, I thought I was going to break down and die from crying, but now I think I'm going to die from embarrassment. I'm so not used to being treated this way, much less being complimented in front of my entire family. I just don't know how to take it all, or how to react. It's crazy going from being Isaac's pampered pet/Slave, to pretending to be his new, doting girlfriend. Is that what this is? Pretend? I have to shake off the question as my aunts "aww," from across the room.

Act normal. Act normal. Act normal, I repeat to myself over and over.

"I'm happy, too," I add in quickly, shyly. My voice is low compared to Isaac's. I'm hoping all my blushing just makes my family think I'm nervous to be in front of them with a new boyfriend after so long.

Daddy says to Isaac, "Tell us a little bit more about yourself, Isaac."

Isaac sits back in his seat. "What would you like to know?"

"Well, where's your family from? Have you already celebrated the holidays with them?" My father asks the natural question, but I wish he hadn't.

Isaac pauses, pain flashing in his eyes as he searches for the right words. "I only had my mother, and she passed away when I was younger," Isaac admits finally, clearing his throat, his deep voice very quiet. Looking at him, a feeling of sadness presses down on my chest. I remember his confession, him telling me how his mother needed help and how he didn't help her. Tears burn my eyes, but I blink them away rapidly. I didn't know she'd passed away. I find myself scooting closer to Isaac, wanting to comfort him. Wanting to ask how it happened. My blood feels ice cold. I made it this far through the meeting, I can't start crying now. I have to be strong. I reach out and grab Isaac's hand without thinking. It's not something a

Slave should do, but an adoring girlfriend would. And I feel like he needs me.

"I'm so sorry to hear that, Isaac," my mom says, speaking for the first time since we sat down. She turns to me and gives me a sad, small smile and pats my thigh as she says, "I'm happy our Katy cat brought you home for the holidays at least. We expected her not to make it."

Katy cat. My old nickname. Tears threaten to spill from my eyes again as I remember how I used to run through the hallway of this house, and swing around the banister just a few feet away. Hearing my nickname being yelled by my mom and dad, even my aunts, uncles and cousins.

Before they took me. Before that bastard stole my innocence. Back when I was just Katy cat. Just a girl, getting yelled at for running through the halls. A lump forms in my throat, and I have to continue smothering my feelings.

"Katia, are you alright?" Mom asks, seeing the conflicted expressions cross my face.

God, if I get through this without crying, it will be a fucking miracle.

"It's just been a long time since you've called me that," I say, trying to keep my voice steady.

"It's a cute nickname, Katy cat," Isaac says, giving me a wink, all traces of his unease and pain gone. He looks so cheerful that I almost forget he was even upset a moment ago, and I'm forced to laugh as I wipe at the tears that threaten to spill from my eyes.

"You know why I called her that?" my father asks. *Oh God, here we go.* Dad proceeds to tell a story I've heard a million times before, of how I kept my cat costume on for nearly two weeks after Halloween one year, refusing to believe I wasn't a cat. As he goes into detail, I drown out the sound of his voice, a small smile stretching over my face.

It's a good memory. One that makes my father happy to tell. My mom is smiling in the corner. Happiness overwhelms me.

Isaac gives my hand a squeeze, and I wish I could just crawl into his lap and hold onto him. I rest my cheek on his shoulder and give him a quick kiss, whispering, "Thank you." I didn't realize how much

I was missing by avoiding my family. How much happiness was still here, waiting for me? How much love was here?

I look back over to Isaac as he chuckles at something my dad says and my heart does a backflip as the strongest feeling that I've ever felt surges through me. It frightens me. And it can't be what I think it is. Isaac is my *Master,* not my boyfriend. And only for less than thirty days. I need to remember that. I can't be falling for him. How could I? It's too fast.

But as I watch him laugh at my father's joke, I know I'm lying to myself.

CHAPTER 25

ISAAC

The little box is sitting on the edge of the outdoor coffee table. Taunting me. I should know better than to give her a gift and create expectations. I didn't go out of my way to gift her something for Christmas. After all, I provide her with everything she wants or needs on a daily basis. But it hasn't been sitting right with me.

I want to spoil her. I want my kitten to be nothing but happy.

The silver wrapping paper is folded perfectly; the edges of the box are sharp with a white ribbon tied neatly on top. It's picture perfect, and inside is something I think she'll love.

A bracelet, or an anklet if she'd like. It's from Pandora, and customizable with trinkets on it. The first is a yellow topaz charm surrounded by small diamonds, for the month of November. It signifies the first time I ever saw her. A little silver dog is the second one I picked, and was the easiest to decide on. She's told me a few times about Roxy, her dog, passing and I'm hoping this will give her happiness to see it dangling from the bracelet. I picked out a cat as well. I'll have to tell her it's because of her nickname, Katy cat. Not that there's a difference between a cat and a kitten on these little charms, but still. There's a difference to me.

Then there's a Merry Christmas bauble for the holiday we shared together, and a New Year's charm with champagne glasses and the year for tonight. A turquoise charm for the month of December, when she finally became mine.

The last one is a silver heart with "kitten" engraved on it. It looks like a tag that would hang from a collar. Even though she hasn't yet told me she's ready for a collar, I want her to have it.

I wouldn't give her a collar with that anklet still on her. I don't know why it bothers me so much, but it does. I won't allow her to wear my collar while she has that anklet on. Simply because of what it symbolizes. He still has a part of her, and I want all of her. We're halfway through this arrangement already. But we can always renew the contract.

A bit of insecurity weighs down on my chest, making it feel tight and uncomfortable as I light the last candle in the enclosed patio.

The glass enclosure all opens to the outside, as though they're extravagant windows, but it's far too cold to open them in December. But with the candles lining the room and the stars lighting the night, it's gorgeous out here.

I have the large flat screen TV on with the ball drop from the New Year's countdown on, although it's muted.

It's... romantic. Which isn't my normal scene.

But for her, I wanted to give her something. She'll never know what spending Christmas with her family did for me. It wasn't a selfish act. It was all for her, but in the process, something switched and I owe her this.

Being with her family only showed me how different we really are.

And how much is available to her.

The lies flowed so easily for me as I tried to blend in. They couldn't know who I really was. They'd never understand. But it was nice to fake it, at least for a little while. It was a real pleasure to feel a sense of family.

She has a collection of people who love her, and who want to be loved by her in return. They'll be there for her when I'm gone. When I send her away. I'll have to. I can never truly fit in with her family.

Lying about us only emphasizes that fact.

. . .

"YOU KNOW ALL YOU DO IS MAKE ME SICK." MY MOM SITS ON THE SOFA, staring straight ahead and for a moment, I pretend she isn't talking to me. I'd just walked through the door. I stole for the first time. Christmas is next week and I know my mom needs shoes. Hers have holes in them. Mine do too, but I could only fit one pair in my coat. I was so afraid of getting caught. I think the cashier saw me, but let me walk out. I don't know for sure. So for my shoes, I'll have to go some-where else. I'm too afraid that the cashier from before will recognize me.

I hear my mom talking about how I'm pathetic and weak, but I pretend those words aren't meant for me. Like she's talking to the wall she's been staring at since I walked in. But I know she is, and when she finally turns to look at me, I can see she's high again. "He wasn't supposed to go to war. It's your fault. It's all because of you," she sneers at me.

She tells me I drove him to leave. They fought because of me. He went to war because of me.

Sometimes she admits that she loved him. Those moments at least make me a little happy. I thought I was starting to imagine the memo-ries of us being a family.

She doesn't tell me she loves me. She doesn't admit that.

But she does. I know she does.

The sound of the front door opening makes me move faster through the living room to my bedroom. I'm not safe there, but if I stay away, I may be able to avoid him beating on me.

"Yeah, run away, Isaac. Run away, just like your father did," I hear her voice continue to taunt me as I shut the thin veneer door to my small room. "Run away, coward!"

I CLEAR MY THROAT AND STRAIGHTEN MY DARK RED TIE, IGNORING the painful past.

I fucking hate these suits. I have to wear them at the club, but I wasn't meant to wear them. But again, it's a romantic date of sorts. And I bought her a dress to wear.

It's short, but elegant. A sparkling silver shift dress that'll probably come off as soon as I get my hands on her, but I thought she'd like it. The way the fabric flows made me think of her twirling in it.

I hope that's what she's doing now, twirling in her room to make the ends of it swish around her upper thighs.

A small huff of a rough laugh leaves my lips as I sit down on the modern white sofa and take a look around.

It's simple, but it's something.

Champagne and chocolate-covered strawberries, a bracelet and candlelight. My gift to her. It's not enough. I can never give her enough.

The thought makes my skin prick with a chill that runs from my shoulders down to my toes. I crack my neck and try to ignore the thoughts that have been creeping into my head late at night.

Seeing her family... did something to me. It reminded me of her purity. The life she's working toward gaining back. The life she wants, although she doesn't realize it. Again it makes me think I'm not a capable Master for her. It's a life I don't belong in.

I enjoy having her here. But the time with her family made it very obvious that this arrangement is temporary. She may not know it yet. She isn't looking that far ahead.

Until it's time, I'll continue my role as her Master.

She does need to pick a collar. One that will suit her. It's time that she wore one. It's time to push my kitten a little. I won't make her wear it until she's ready, but she can choose which one she wants.

I picked out new anklets, too. Just to gauge her reaction.

I don't want her to get so used to it that it replaces the shackle. I hate that she's still using it. Although I'm not surprised, not really. She fears the memories more than she desires her freedom. Although the latter does seem to be taking on more of an edge since the bathroom incident.

Every time she takes it off, there's still a hint of pain there.

She's quick to put it back on after the shower.

One day she'll take it off, and it will give her strength. When I'm a worthy Master for her.

The faint sounds of clicking heels from behind me snap me from my thoughts.

My heart stutters in my chest, the world blurring behind her as she walks into view. Her head is partially bowed, but with shyness, not from submission. Her cheeks are flushed and with a touch of makeup, her natural beauty is only heightened.

My Katia is utterly gorgeous.

Her eyes widen and her lips part slowly as she takes in the room. She stands still at the entrance, not sure where to go or how to react.

I'm quick to walk to her, taking large strides until I'm by her side, planting a small kiss on her cheek. My heart seems to come to life once again, pounding rapidly and heating my blood as I wrap my arm around her back and let my thumb run up and down over her hip.

"Thank you, Master," Katia breathes, looking up at me through her thick lashes as I lead her to the lounge.

I kiss her cheek again and she does something she's never done. She leans into me, resting her head on my shoulder as we walk and wrapping her arm around my waist.

No one has ever done that.

I continue walking as though nothing's changed, but as soon as she sits I leave her.

It was one thing to engage in that display of affection for her family's sake. For her sake in front of her parents, really. But here, it means something different.

And I allowed it.

I should correct it. I should draw the line once again since it seems to have blurred, but instead I reach into the bucket and pop the cork off the champagne bottle with a flourish.

Although I'm not facing Katia, I can still see her smile. She even brings her hands up as though to clap, but she stops herself.

She has a brightness about her. Desire to be happy. It's one of the things that drew me to her, but also one of the reasons I know I should stay away.

"Master?" she asks me as I pour the chilled champagne into our glasses. The fizz of the bubbles and clinking of the glasses make a smile stretch across my face. It's been a long time since I've enjoyed this type of luxury.

"Yes, kitten?" I turn to face her, a glass in each hand. The dress has slipped up on her thighs and I was right. It looks fucking gorgeous on her, but it'll look better on the floor.

I set the glasses down and sit easily next to her. My dick is already hard from sitting so close to her. The easy touches and soft sounds of her sigh as she leans against me make me want her that much more.

I don't see how I'll ever have my fill of her.

"I'm afraid." She whispers her words, looking away from me and out into the woods.

"Don't be," I tell her easily. Her worries and fears are my burden, not hers. "Let me take your fears away."

"It's not what you think. "

Her breathing picks up as I flick the chain at her neck, kissing down her body and enjoying the soft sounds of her sighs.

"What is it?" Whatever it is, it can wait till after tonight. I plan to reward her with overwhelming pleasure until both of us have had our fill.

I slip off the lounge and onto my knees in front of her, my fingers trailing along her upper thigh, playing with the hem of her dress and inching it upward.

"This seems so real," she says, and her voice cracks. Her fingers dig into the thick, white fabric as I lean forward, my eyes roaming her body.

I leave an open-mouth kiss on the inside of her knee and work my way upward, moving closer to her clit. She's been such a good girl. She's earned this.

"This is real, kitten."

"I'm afraid… That it's going to be more for me than just … more than a Master."

My hands still on her thighs, my fingertips just barely touching her soft skin, and for a moment I don't respond.

"I'm afraid I'm falling for you," she admits. I already felt that she was, but her admitting it makes it worse.

I kiss just below her hem and then push her dress up higher, scooting her ass closer to the edge for me. Remaining calm on the outside, but my heart's beating faster.

I can't give her more. But I'm too selfish to send her away just yet. I glance down at the anklet she's still wearing. She needs me still. I can't let her go.

"Who do your worries belong to, kitten?"

"You, Master."

I pull her pussy into my face and give her a long languid lick.

"And your body?"

"You, Master."

I suck her clit, moving her hand to the back of my head. And then her other. Letting her know she can touch me, she can lead me.

I pull away slightly, her fingers spearing my hair.

"And your pleasure? Who does that belong to?" I ask.

"You, Master."

I'm a selfish prick for allowing it. But I make a promise to myself that once she's healed, I'll let her go. There are only fifteen days left.

I won't break her.

I'll only heal her and then let her walk away.

"Tonight it belongs to you, kitten." I lick her once and then look into her beautiful eyes glazed with desire. "Take it from me."

"KATIA, WHAT DOES BEING A MASTER MEAN?" I ASK HER AS I LAY HER in bed.

"It means you own someone. Mind, body and soul. They belong to you completely. And their Slaves desire it. They are complete with their Master."

"Is that all, kitten?" I ask her.

"I don't know, Master," she answers in a hushed voice, exhausted from the long night. She's so very close to understanding.

CHAPTER 26

KATIA

I lie still in bed, my eyes wide open and staring at the ceiling. Just like I have the last few nights. The terrors don't come in my dreams. Now they flash before my eyes as soon as I lie down.

The soft sounds of the night turn into something else. The chirps of the crickets morph into the drips of water from the pipe in the dungeon. It leaked every fucking day I was in there. Drip, drip, drip. In my mind it became a part of my fucking punishment. No daylight, and never any quiet.

But the sound I keep hearing over and over in my head is different. The sound that keeps me wide awake and on edge is the sound of metal. Of the chain scraping on the bare concrete floor.

The chain. Always the chain.

They'd drag me by them, either the one on my ankle or the one on my throat. Choking off my air supply, not caring whether they broke my neck or how much pain it caused me. I can still feel it now, biting into my tender flesh as I'm dragged across the concrete floor. My thighs would scrape against the floor as I was dragged, opening wounds and causing nasty abrasions that would last for days. I learned to be good because of those chains.

The ankle was worse, because even when they weren't there, I was enslaved by it. And the scratching of the chain followed me every-where; the pain in my ankle from the shackle was a constant in the four years I spent there.

I sit up with my hands clenched, anger consuming me in my dark-ened bedroom, sweat covering my forehead. There's a stream of moonlight coming through the window, making it easy to see. Every-thing seems so easy to see in this moment.

I rip the covers off to gaze at my anklet. My heart skips a beat the sight. It's gleaming in the moonlight, seeming to taunt me. Rage fills me. I hate it. I hate this. I hate what those bastards did to me. I could never take the anklet off. *Ever*. Tears fill my eyes, but I refuse to acknowledge them. Instead I stare at the blurred vision of the beautiful anklet. I'm still imprisoned, still under his control. The thought sends a chill through my body. He doesn't own me.

He *never* owned me. Never!

I CLENCH MY TEETH AS A FIERY RAGE BOILS UP FROM THE PITS OF MY stomach, spurring me to rip off the anklet. I nearly scream with frus-tration as my fingernails cut into the tender skin as I try to get this fucking thing off of me.

Get it off!

The tiny cuts are nothing; they can't scar me any worse than I already am.

Because of *him*.

Because of this! I scramble from my bed, the anklet in my hand, staring at it as though it's him. The sparking of the crystals are akin to his gleaming smile. Always smiling. I made him so happy. A sickness stirs in my stomach. I hear his laugh, smell his breath. Even the night I murdered him, just moments before I stabbed him, plunging the shard of glass deep into his throat over and over, even then he was smiling.

I rush over to the nightstand and set it down gently, ever so gently even though my hands are trembling. I quickly grab the lamp sitting next to it. It's beautiful, with a crystal base, but it's sturdy. And heavy.

Screaming with fury, I smash the base of the lamp over and over onto the beautiful piece of jewelry.

But that's not enough. I throw the lamp down and grasp the anklet, slamming it into the nightstand while it's in my fist. And then the wall. It needs to be destroyed. That's all I know. I need it gone.

"Fuck you, fuck you, fuck you!" I scream, slamming the metal into the wall over and over with all my might. I feel something wet and warm flow down the palm of my hand and my arm and then drip onto the floor. A chill goes through me as I realize it's my own blood. I've torn open my skin in my rage, but I don't care. I want to be free. Free of it. Free of *them*.

"You don't fucking own me!" I yell at the ceiling, my throat dry and aching with a pounding I know will hurt later. Slamming the now twisted and mangled anklet into the wall again, tears stream freely down my face. There's now multiples indents all over the wall, and the fancy paint is chipped in places. But I don't care.

"You were never my Master!" With another furious yell, I throw the anklet across the room where it hits the wall, making a jagged dent, before falling to the floor with a loud *clink*. I stare at the object, my breathing ragged and my shoulders heaving.

It's only an ankle, only a piece of jewelry, but it had so much power over me, power I didn't willingly give. Power that I'm taking back.

Exhaustion takes over my body as I realize I don't fucking need it. I don't want it either. Maybe the nightmares will come, maybe they won't. But I won't give that bastard any power over me.

Never again.

SNAPPING ME FROM THE REALIZATION, I HEAR THE DOOR CREAK OPEN and the flick of a light switch. The light stings my eyes, even though I can barely see through the tears. I didn't even realize I was crying. I wipe the tears from my eyes and suddenly feel like I can't breathe. I stare at my hand, seeing it shaking. I close my eyes and try to calm down, the adrenaline coursing through my veins suddenly feeling like too much.

"Katia?" Isaac's deep voice is filled with worry, but I hardly notice. It hurts so bad.

"I'm sorry," I croak, my voice so hoarse and garbled that it doesn't even sound human.

I hear the sound of heavy footsteps and suddenly I feel myself being lifted and gently placed on the bed. I look up through my tears to see Isaac's handsome face looking down at me in disapproval. His green eyes slowly trail down to my bloody hands, and anger flashes in his eyes.

"Isaac," I croak, shaking my head. I can't have him disapproving. Not of this. Please. Please don't.

He sits down on the bed next to me. It groans with his weight as he leans forward and brushes my hair away from face. "Shh, kitten," he tells me softly as I continue to sob. "I need you to calm down now so I can clean you. Then you can tell me what's wrong."

The sound of his deep voice is soothing and I relax a little, pressing my palms to my hot, stinging eyes to keep from crying any more. I don't want to cry. I don't want to feel *anything* for my past anymore. Isaac stares at me for a moment, before leaving me for a moment to gather something from the cabinet in the bathroom. I listen as the door opens and he rummages for something, all the while my heart hurting. It's worse than the throbbing pain in my hands. He goes about cleaning up my hands. It burns like fuck, and I seethe from the pain, but he has my wounds cleaned and dressed quickly. Neither of us speaking all the while.

I'm dreading telling him. I don't know if he'll quite understand. But if anyone could, it would be him.

"Now, what happened?" he asks, when he's done, placing the dirtied cloth down on the nightstand.

As I stare into his green eyes, I suddenly realize what I've done. I've let my emotions overcome me and acting in a way that could displease him. Looking at the battered walls, I feel like I've disrespected his house. Ashamed, I quickly try to climb off of the bed and fall to my knees at his feet, but he grabs my waist and stops me, pulling me back onto the bed.

"Please, Master, don't be upset me with me," I cry, trembling. My heart hurts so fucking bad. I want to hide. I don't want him to see what I've done. I don't want to admit it either.

"Shh. None of that," Isaac says softly, pulling me beside him and wrapping his arms around me, rocking me gently back and forth. I feel so safe in his arms, enveloped in his warmth. I just wish I could stay here *forever.* "I could never be upset with you over your pain." He pushes the hair out of my face again and cups my cheek, forcing me to look at him. His hand feels so cool against my hot skin. "You just need to tell me what caused this."

Isaac's peering at me, his gorgeous green eyes soft and caring. There's no judgment there. I'm grateful. I thought he'd be angry with me.

I shake my head slightly, trying to swallow the lump in my throat.

"I don't want it anymore," I say, and it hurts just saying those few words.

"I can see that," he says with a touch of humor before taking my chin between his thumb and forefinger. "Tell me what caused it."

I take in a long and shaky breath. "I don't know why. I just know that I don't want it anymore. I don't want any more reminders." I swallow thickly, closing my eyes and not knowing how to explain but not wanting to explain any more either.

SEEING MY RAVAGED VISAGE, ISAAC GENTLY SMOOTHS MY DISHEVELED hair out of my face and moves in close, kissing me on the cheek, my lips, and then kissing away my tears with his full lips.

"I NEED TO TELL YOU SOMETHING, AND I THINK YOU NEED TO KNOW now." I stare into his piercing gaze, my heart refusing to beat. He's serious, and his expression tells me it's something he doesn't want to say.

"They're dead," Isaac tells me. His words are firm and filled with finality. It's a statement of a fact. "The other men in Carver Dario's cartel. They're all dead."

Shock twists my stomach, taking my breath away. Did I really hear him right? I couldn't have. But I look into his eyes, and my skin pricks at the ruthlessness I see in them. "Dead?" I whisper.

Isaac gently strokes my cheek, his caring actions at odds with what he's telling me. "I did some digging. I needed to know." They're really dead? The words seem to slowly sink in, a warmth of satisfaction surrounding me and then moving through me, giving me a sense of strength I didn't feel before.

"If I could, I would've killed them myself." He hooks my chin and makes me look into his gorgeous eyes. "I wanted to. I wanted to make them suffer. But I can't. And I'm so sorry I can't give you that."

My heart beats faster and I feel a strong pull toward Isaac, a strong bond forming and drawing me closer to him.

"They will never harm you again. You are safe. Always. Do you understand?"

I nod my head, searching his green eyes for the same thing I feel. "Yes, Master," I whisper.

CHAPTER 27

ISAAC

"I want you to choose one, for when you're ready to wear it." There are only five days left in our contract. Even if she only wears it for a day, I'll be satisfied. I haven't decided how to tell her that we may not be able to continue this... once the contract is done. Her wounds are still fresh from what she confronted days ago. I won't leave her on her own while she's healing, but any longer than that would be unfair of me.

I know I need to tell her, but not yet. I'm not ready to say goodbye.

"I'm ready now, Master." Her soft voice and confession shock me. The ease of her tone and the way she looks at the row of collars I've purchased for her as though they're a reward and she's choosing the best one. It's not what I anticipated.

It should make me relieved. I should be happy. But I'm not.

It only means she's so much further along than I thought she was.

I know I need to send her away.

I don't want to though. And we have a contract. I at least need to see that through.

But once it's over, I have nothing more to offer her. I can't provide for her in the ways she'll need. I can direct her, but she'll only grow more attached. It's too selfish.

She purses her lips as she lifts one of the five collars. The bracelet on her wrist, the Pandora one I gave her on New Year's, jingles as she lifts the collar and holds it up to her throat.

It's the thinnest of them all. It's rose gold and two thin bands of metal that cross at the center. It would look gorgeous on her. All of them would.

In truth, I'd like her to desire all of them. I want a collar on her neck every second of the day. Even when she's out of the house and around people who aren't in the lifestyle. That's why four of them resemble jewelry.

The fifth is a traditional collar, but the leather band is a soft pink the color of rose petals.

"I really love this one," Katia says as she turns and presents the collar to me. She knows better than to put it on herself. My chains are to be placed on her by me, and taken off by only myself.

"Master?" Katia asks softly as I clasp the collar around her neck. "May I wear the chain as well?"

"Of course." I absently touch the thin chain, once again satisfied with my claim on her. "I expect you to."

As she plays with her collar in the mirror, I remember last night. She asked to sleep with me and when I asked if it was because of her missing anklet, she answered no. She hasn't asked for the weighted blanket either, and for the last three nights she's slept soundly.

She wanted to be available for my needs. And she admitted she enjoys it when I hold her when she sleeps.

I enjoy it as well.

I almost said yes, simply because I wanted to feel her soft body against mine as we slept. I wanted to be there in case she has another night terror. But there was something else in her eyes, something that made me push her away.

Things have changed for her, I know they have. The way she touches me, kisses me, even the way she talks to me.

She's at ease and trusts me. She's given me control of everything. Completely.

"Do you think I'm a good Master?" I ask Katia, my fingers teasing down her side before pulling her back into my chest and resting my chin on her shoulder. Her pale blue eyes find mine in the mirror.

385

"You are. I'm grateful to have you," she says sweetly, turning her head slightly to rub her cheek against mine.

I close my eyes, loving her warmth, her sincerity, but New Year's continues to play through my mind.

How she told me she was afraid. She has every right to be afraid. Her life and her goals aren't aligned with mine. She knows this, but she'd continue to put faith in me and the fucked up relationship we have for as long as I'll allow.

I have five days left.

I kiss her softly on the lips, hating how much I love the tenderness in her touch and the soft sounds of her sighs.

I don't want to tell her goodbye, but I must.

I'll carry out the contract for the next few days, only because I'm selfish. But I'll keep my distance. I'll make this as easy on her as I can. I don't want to hurt her, but I have to let her go.

"KATIA, WHAT DOES BEING A MASTER MEAN?"

"It means loving someone so strongly that your life revolves around them. That every action is made with their wellbeing in mind. Their happiness is yours. Their pleasure is yours. Their life is yours. And the opposite is true for them."

Love? I wish I could tell her she's wrong. But she's not. "My happiness is yours?" I ask her.

She looks me in the eyes and answers confidently, "Yes, Master."

CHAPTER 28

KATIA

I sit back on my heels at Isaac's desk, watching him work on his laptop. I can feel the warmth of his leg and I want to lean against him, but I don't. His brow furrowed, he's typing something important, not paying me any mind. Yet, he's all I can think about. I've been worried about him. About us.

He hasn't been himself lately, his words and actions distant, his eyes filled with pain as if he's losing something. I want to help him with whatever is bothering him. Like he's helped me. But when I try to get him to open up, he shuts himself off from me. A surge of emotion threatens to choke me, but I push it away. I hate it.

I STUDY HIS PROFILE, HIS CHISELED JAWLINE AND THE STUBBLE shading it, the clicking sounds of his fingers running across the keyboard in my ears. I don't know what it is, but something's off. Something has shifted. I feel like he's less attached to me.

Maybe it's his collar, I wonder to myself, unconsciously bringing my hands up to my neck to feel it. I love it and his claim on me. But ever since I put it on, it seems like a wall has sprung up between us. *I hate it. I want back what we had. I want to get past whatever is both-*

ering him. We can get through this together. All he needs to do is allow it.

I think he may be doing this on purpose, being distant from me. He knows our contract is over soon. I constantly remind myself that our days are numbered, and the contract is ending. But I don't want them to be. If he wanted to keep me, I'd happily stay. I don't care about the money. I care about everything he's done for me. I would never have this inner strength without him. I know I wouldn't. I feel whole again. I feel untouchable even.

I don't want to leave him. I may not say it out loud, I may not want to admit it. But I love him. Whether that's wrong or right, I don't care.

I need to give him a reason to keep me.

"Master?" I ask.

Isaac pauses midtype, looking down at me. My heart skips a beat as those green eyes prick my skin. But not because of the intensity that used to be there. He doesn't look at me the same anymore. His eyes are filled with sadness. "Yes?"

Disappointment flows through me that he doesn't use my pet name. Another sign that something is wrong. But maybe I'm paranoid and am reading too much into it. Something tells me I'm not though. "What can I do to please you?" I ask, swallowing the lump in my throat, hating the tightness that constricts my chest.

Isaac stares at me, and I bite the inside of my cheek, increasingly feeling as if there's something wrong. It's there. "You're already doing it," he replies, gently petting my hair. Normally, I would feel assured, but his words only make me more uneasy. They have no strength to them, no passion. Even his petting of me is weak.

I lick my lips, not wanting to outright accuse him of lying, but I know I can't let this go. "But I don't feel as if I am pleasing you right now. I feel like... I need to do more to satisfy you."

Isaac frowns, his hand falling from my head to hang lifelessly over the side of his chair. "You don't need to do more."

His words are saying one thing, but I'm feeling something entirely else from him. It almost feels like a spear of ice is slowly being pressed into my heart. "I can't take that you give me so much pleasure, yet I give you nothing in return." *I know you're in pain. I can see it every day.*

Isaac flashes a me a look that makes me tense. His eyes narrowed as if daring me to continue with my train of thought. But at least there's passion there. "How can you think that you give me nothing? You give me so much, Katia."

"I want to make you happy," I say thickly. I look him directly in the eye as I say, "And you aren't," challenging him to say otherwise. Challenging him to *lie* to me.

Isaac takes a long time responding, his emerald eyes studying my distressed face. "You're worried for me?" he asks finally.

I nod my head. "Yes." *I'm more than worried. I think you want to get rid of me as soon as this contract is over. You don't want to deal with what's hurting you.* Just thinking the words brings tears to my eyes. I'm hoping desperately that I'm wrong and I'm just imagining things. But I know I'm not.

"Then that's my fault." My breath catches at my throat at the pain reflected in his eyes. "I'm sorry I failed you in that respect, Katia."

Oh God no. My heart pounds in my chest and my breath comes in pants as I cry, "No, Master. You haven't failed me at all." I'm trying to stay calm. We can talk our way through this. I can help him. Please just give me something.

"I have." His words are emotionless, as if he doesn't see me breaking down right in front of him. God, he's fucking killing me! "Your worries are mine, not the other way around."

I tremble at his feet and try not to break down, hoping this is all just a bad dream. It isn't real.

"Go to your room," he orders coldly, not appearing to notice my distress.

I look at him, seeing the pain in his eyes, and feel defiance. He can't fucking blow me off like this. He doesn't have to do this. "No," I say rebelliously. "I'm not going anywhere."

He reaches down, gripping my chin. "Go," he growls right in front of my face, his hot breath sending chills down my neck and shoulders. "Now." His voice holds a threat. But I don't care.

I try to shake my head, but can't. He's holding my head in place.

"No," I say breathlessly, my heart beating frantically. "I don't want to leave you. I feel like you don't want me anymore." It hurts saying the words and admitting the truth.

At first, pain flashes in his beautiful eyes, but then anger twists Isaac's handsome face. He releases my chin and rises to his feet, pulling me up along with him. "Is that what you want?" he growls, grabbing me by the hips and pulling me into his hard body. He takes both my arms and pins them behind my back, his powerful grip sending sparks of want through my body. I just want this passion. Always.

"Yes," I whisper. "Take me. Use me. Do whatever you want with me." *I just want to help you.*

Isaac stares at me for a long moment, his chest heaving, and then without a word, he pulls me from the room, dragging me down the long hallway. I don't resist as he takes me all the way to my room, opens the door, and slings me into the room.

"Please stay!" I cry imploringly, scrambling to my feet and rushing for the door. "Talk to me, Isaac! What did I do wrong?" *Let me fix you.*

"Nothing, Katia. There's nothing you did wrong." His voice is hard, but at least he's talking to me.

"Just tell me, tell me what happened! I want to fix it. I want you back!"

He stares at me for a moment, his expression vulnerable, wanting and raw. He needs me. His grip tightens on the door and I swear it's so hard it's going to crack. *Isaac, please, just tell me.*

"Stay," he commands.

Before I can get there, he slams it shut with powerful force.

I stand there staring at the door, a range of powerful emotions running through me. Pain, sadness. Rage. I feel so helpless, so incredibly lost. I don't know what's going to happen from here, but something tells me this could be the end.

I bring my hands to my collar, wanting to take it off and throw it against the wall in rage. If he's going to just break up with me at the end of our contract, why draw it out? It only has a few days left. I should just get it over with now. I place my finger over the latch, my heart racing as tears stream down my face. But I can't bring myself to do it.

I don't know what he's feeling or going through right now, but I know one thing for sure.

I want to be his.

CHAPTER 29

ISAAC

She thinks I'm in pain.
    I'm the one needing help?
She's wrong.

I pace my office, hearing her words over and over. A rage building inside of me. I'm not broken. I'm not in pain. I have a scarred past, I know that. But I'm fucking fine.

I breathe in, ragged and trying to calm myself. She shouldn't be trying to *fix* me. Or heal me.

That's not her place.

And it's not mine to require that from her.

I knew I should have sent her away.

Selfish! It was selfish of me, and now I'm paying the price.

She's paying the price.

I run my hand down my face, clenching my jaw and trying to calm down, but as the anger wanes, a sadness replaces it. My body trembles as I sink into the leather chair at my desk, my breathing erratic.

I don't deserve her. Not at all.

She shouldn't have to bear my pain. It's not her burden. I can't ask her to live with a man like me.

I lean forward, rubbing my forehead with my hand and closing my eyes tightly, wanting to deny it, but I can't. I'm not worthy of her.

She needs to get out. Now.

I've already been thinking of reasons to keep her.

There are two days left, but I can't continue. My Katia is full of happiness; a purity has survived in her that I will taint. I can't do that to her.

I won't.

I rise from my desk, feeling a surge of conviction and hating it. I fucking hate who I am. I hate that I'm only capable of breaking and scarring and causing pain.

Feeling the rage coming back, I swipe at the clutter on my desk as I scream in fury, spewing it over the floor, the papers fluttering in the air as if taunting me.

She needs to leave. She needs to go now.

I can't have her here. I'll hurt her. I know I will.

"Katia!" I scream her name so loudly it makes my throat feel raw. "Katia!" I yell even louder, anger apparent in my tone. I've never called her for like this. I stare at the open door, and when she doesn't instantly appear, I stomp over the papers and folders now scattered on the floor and grip the door as I swing it open harder, slamming it against the wall and storming toward her room.

It's not like her not to come when I call. *It's my anger*, I nod my head at the thought as I approach her doorway.

For a moment, I think maybe she's already gone.

Maybe I scared her away. She knew she needed to leave a monster like me.

My heart stops and I nearly topple forward, bracing myself against the wall.

No.

I take in a breath, torn between the pain that just the thought caused me, and the necessity to save her.

I feel torn into two, and I don't know which side will win. I want to keep her forever. I don't want to deny these feelings I have for her any longer. But I want to save her beautiful light from my darkness.

I need to let her go.

I take the last few steps with my eyes closed and slowly open them as I walk into her room, half expecting to find it empty, but she's there.

Kneeling on the floor.

She's naked, in only my chains and even with a sadness surrounding her, a hint of anger even, she's perfect in her submission.

"Get dressed, Katia," I manage to say easily. I need her to leave. Now. Before I lose my resolve.

As she stands I catch a flash of anger in her eyes. A look that verges on disrespectful and it begs me to take her. I want to push her onto the bed and punish her.

But I can't. In this moment, I have the strength to send her away. And I need to do it now before I lose it. I watch her as she opens the dresser drawer, the sound of it opening is the only noise in the room. I'm on edge and holding on by a thread as she dresses with her eyes shining with tears. But she doesn't question me. She pulls on her jeans and I grip onto the door, closing my eyes. Hating that I'm doing this. Hating myself and that I'm not good enough to keep her.

"Master?" she asks me.

It breaks my fucking heart to hear her call me that. For the last time.

"Yes?" I answer as she opens a drawer and slips on the clothes she brought here. Simple jeans and a tank top.

"Why are you doing this?" she asks and the anger slips, replaced with something worse. Sadness. She pulls a sweater over her tank top, not looking me in the eyes. "I'm sorry, Master.

It hurts to see her like this. But it's for her own good.

I ignore her question. I ignore her apology.

"You can go now. I'll have your things sent to your place tomorrow."

Katia takes a step back, looking as though I'm going to hurt her.

"You can go."

"I don't want to go," she says, shaking her head with wide eyes.

"You must."

"Don't do this." Her voice is weak. She's begging me, and I so badly want to submit to her wishes.

"I am not what you need," I finally admit to her.

"You are-"

"I'm a murderer!" I scream at her, cutting her off. She cowers from the harsh tone. I finally said it; I told her.

"I've killed men before, Katia. I'm not a good man."

She looks up at me with a coldness in her eyes that I've never seen. "So have I."

"You need more than what I can give you."

"I want you! I can decide for myself." She's on edge and angry, but mostly upset. I don't think either one of us is thinking clearly, but this needs to happen now, before this goes too far.

"I'm your Master! You will listen to me!"

"You need to go home, Katia." I tell her with a straight face, refusing to acknowledge the gouging pain in my chest. I give her the keys to my car. She can have it. Fuck, she could have it all if she wants. But she needs to go now before I snap and keep her forever.

"No!" she yells at me, and I can't take it. I grab her waist and pull her body close to me, lifting her off the floor and storming to the stairwell.

"Stop it!" she screams at me. "Isaac, no!" Her body shudders with a sob, and I hate myself. More now than I ever have for hurting her. But I have to. I have to save her. I can't let her stay with me and ruin her beauty. Her strength. I need her to leave me.

"You have to go." I try to tell her flatly, but my voice breaks.

"I need you to know how much you own me," she screams at me, her voice so loud it hurts my ears, but I don't care. I drag her toward the front door. She hits me, pulling her fist back and slamming it against my chest. I feel a tug and hear a snap of something, but I'm not sure what. My eyes fly to her bracelet, but it's still intact.

"You can't throw me out," she says, pushing me away with no success as we reach the foyer.

"I won't let you." Her voice lacks conviction and strength. Tears stream down her face and onto my shoulder, breaking my heart at her pain.

Better now. Better this way. I finally put her down and she stumbles as her feet struggle to find purchase. I swing the front door open.

"Leave," I tell her, trying to rid all the emotion from my voice.

"I love you, Isaac." Her voice cracks with emotion.

Hearing those words from her lips almost makes me fall to my knees.

To beg for her forgiveness.

To beg her not to leave me.

I stand there silent, not moving, not responding.

"Please," she says and her voice shakes, "Please don't, Master."

"Go, Katia." The words are forced from my lips. I'll only be her Master. That's all I can promise her. And she needs more. This is the only way I can give her more.

Her beautiful lips part and a huff of disbelief leaves her. The pain still there, but a hint of anger is slipping in. Hold onto that anger, my kitten, it will make this easier.

It takes her a moment to gather herself. Grabbing the keys and walking out the door, but before she leaves for good, she turns to me.

"I won't stay with someone who doesn't want me." Her words are soft and full of pain. Her wide eyes are pleading with me, begging me to tell her everything I selfishly want to say. "Do you not want me?" she says with her composure breaking, tears slipping down her face.

I want so badly to take her in my arms and crash my lips to hers, to brush her tears away and keep her.

But I can't do that to her.

Not if I truly love her. And I do. I know so strongly in this moment I do.

"No," I finally say the word. It's hard to push it out, but once it leaves my lips, it's done. She turns abruptly, taking in a breath and walking straight to the car. She doesn't turn around, not once. Even when she's in the driver's seat, she refuses to look at me.

My knees threaten to give out as every inch of my skin burns with the need to go to her, to stop her.

I watch her walk away from me.

I watch her leave me.

And I stand there in the doorway, waiting to realize that I've done what's best for her. And this pain is justified.

But it hurts too much.

As I start to shut the door, I see what broke earlier, when I brought her down here while she was fighting me. The chain. *My chain.* I close the door and bend down to pick it off the floor. The thin silver with diamond cuts shimmers as I pick it up and clench it in my fist.

I broke it.

The vision of my mother's necklace, as she lay on the cold hard floor of the kitchen, flashes in my eyes as my thumb rubs along the chain.

Why is she so still? My heart beats faster and faster but my body only gets colder as I slowly come out from the hallway and walk toward her. He left, the monster left after I watched him do this to her.

I didn't know. How could I know that this time he'd kill her?

"Mom?" I call out to her in a whisper, still scared that she'll beat me for interfering like she always did.

But her eyes are open. They're red, but not like they usually are. Not from the drugs. It's blood. Her blood vessels broke and her eyes are so red.

"Mom?" I say louder as I walk closer to her.

Her chest isn't moving. She's so still. So quiet. I stare at her chest, waiting for it to rise with a breath as I kneel down next to her. My eyes are so blurry, why am I crying?

She's not dead. She can't be.

I shake her shoulders. "Mom!" I yell at her, and my heart beats faster with fear. Both that she'll hurt me for yelling, and that she's really dead.

I shake her, but the only sound is the chain around her neck. The necklace I bought her with the only money I had. She's wearing it today. She wears it on days when she wants me to know that she loves me I think. She wore it today.

I sob as I shake her shoulders harder, screaming her name.

The necklace clinks and clinks as I pull her up, and I break it. It's an accident. I just wanted her to breathe.

I didn't mean it.

I didn't mean any of it.

I wish I could take it back.

It's my fault.

I hold the broken chain to my chest, leaning against the door.

Struggling to breathe and cope with the fact that she's left me. I wanted her to though.

She can't be with a monster like me. I only wish I was able to hold her longer.

I wish I was good enough for her.

CHAPTER 30

KATIA

*M*y shoulders shake as I sob uncontrollably as I sit at my desk chair in front of my open laptop. The pain is searing and I haven't been able to sleep at all. Not that I want to. All I've been able to think about is him and how he sent me away. And how much it fucking hurts.

I desperately need someone to talk to, someone who understands me. But Kiersten isn't online. I almost want to call my mom. Just to hear her tell me it's going to be alright. But I can't. Not yet. I don't want to admit what's happened to anyone. I want it to just be a nightmare.

I glance at the screen again, waiting for Kiersten to come on. She's always here at night. I know I've been busy with Isaac, but I've kept up with her messages. I'm there for her. I made sure to tell her that. I always will be. And I need her now. I feel so selfish. But I truly need her now.

I've waited for the last two hours for her to appear, but she hasn't logged on. I've sent direct message after message, hoping she'd get a notification on her cell, but nothing. I wipe away my tears with the back of my hand, trying desperately to get a hold of my emotions. I don't know what to do.

I pull my knees to my chest, my feet sitting on the microfiber seat, biting down on the inside of my cheek with enough force to almost break the skin.

You can survive this, I tell myself. I am a strong woman. I've been through hell and back, and look at me. I survived.

"I'm a survivor," I intone, but my voice cracks and a wave of emotions threatens to send me over the top, and I cover my mouth to keep sobs from escaping. *Stop crying. I can't let him do this to me.* It's my fault for pushing him. But I knew something was wrong. I just wish he'd tell me how to fix it. I will. I'll do anything I can to fix it.

Fighting back more tears, I look around the house, trying to gain comfort from the yellow color, my animal ornaments, every little knickknack that was put here with purpose. To create a happy, soothing environment. A place that feels safe and inviting. But right now, it does nothing for me. I feel so empty.

A knock on the door causes my head to snap up so fast, I almost get whiplash. Hope spreads through my chest. Isaac?

Knock. Knock.

The sound is soft, not like Isaac. But I can't help but hope. I know he didn't mean what he said. I know he loves me, even if he won't admit it.

I quickly rise from my seat, the chain lock sliding and then clinking as I move it off the track and open the door without looking to see who's there.

STANDING IN THE DOORWAY IS MADAM LYNN, LOOKING GORGEOUS AS all hell. She's wearing a claret red dress with a white belt at the waist and matching white pumps; her hair pulled up into a gorgeous sleek ponytail , her makeup flawless. A soft earthy scent tickles my nose as she gives me a gentle compassionate smile that calms my anxiety somewhat. She's holding a thin envelope in her hand, but I'm more worried about how awful I look right now with my red-rimmed puffy eyes and disheveled hair. She has to think I look an absolute mess. I want to question why she's here, but more than that, I want to run into her arms and just be held, to confide in her and tell her how I fucked it all up.

She must see how upset I am, as if it isn't completely obvious. But

I ignore her look of sympathy and let her come in, shutting the door as she walks into my tiny apartment.

"Hello, Katia," Madam Lynn says, handing the envelope out to me. "I came to give you this."

I look at it for a moment before taking it. "What's this?"

"I got a call from Isaac, stating that the contract ended before schedule, but that you were to be paid in full."

Anger tightens my chest and I offer the check back to her. "I don't want this," I say stiffly. "He can keep it." *I just want him, or nothing at all. Fuck the money.* I cross my arms and back away. I'm pissed, but more than that, hurt.

Madam Lynn refuses to take the check back, placing her hands behind her back and peering at me closely. "I see things didn't end well between the both of you. I normally don't inquire into the business of my clients, but if someone was hurt... well, I have to know. Can you tell me what happened?"

My heart pounds as I think about a response. "I-I-I think I pushed him." My heart clenches. If I'd just stayed quiet and behaved... but I thought, he needed me to push him. I thought he needed me. "I just wanted to-" my throat hurts, and it's hard to say what I'm feeling. It's hard to form what we had into words. "He wouldn't let me in, when all I wanted to do was help him, just like he helped me."

Madam Lynn's expression is sympathetic as she looks at me. "That sounds like him." She shakes her head. "I wouldn't take it too personally. I've known Isaac for a very long time, and because of what happened to him, he doesn't let many people in."

*But this is different. I'm not just any person. He cared about me. I know he did. What we had was **real**.*

The pain gripping my sore heart is almost enough to bring me to tears in front of Madam Lynn, but I fight them back.

"You can find someone else?" Madam Lynn suggests tenderly, her expression turning hopeful. "You don't have to go to pieces over just one man, no matter how good he was to you."

I suck in a breath, anger gripping my throat. I've never had reason to be angered with Madam Lynn, and I know she's just trying to get me to see another point of view, but the very idea of finding another Master is appalling. There can be *no* other Master for me. Only Isaac.

"I have no desire for a new Master," I say with utmost confidence. "I only want Isaac."

Madam Lynn shakes her head, a small smile stretching on her lips. "And I'm sure he wouldn't want you to have another Master either." Her eyes shine with mischief. "He's going to be regretting this. Very soon."

I want him to regret it, but more than that, I want him back.

"Do you really think so?" I ask, trying to not sound too desperate.

Madam Lynn nods, a devious smile playing across her lips. "I do; I think he just needs a push to realize what he really wants and how desperate he'll be to make that happe.."

I swallow thickly, not knowing what to think. "I don't want another Master. Ever. If I can't have Isaac back... if he doesn't want me," my voice trails off and it's hard to think that he's really through with me.

"Isaac is being foolish, and he will have you back. Trust me, I know when a man is in love."

Love. My heart hurts so fucking much.

I close my eyes, praying that what she's saying is true. I don't want to hope if it's really over.

As if reading my mind, Madam Lynn says, "It's not over, Katia. Just give him this push."

I nod my head, feeling as though I at least have a plan. "I'll go."

It's not over just yet. I won't give up hope.

CHAPTER 31

ISAAC

*T*he faint hum of the car seems louder than usual as I drive through the dark night on my way to Katia.

It's only been hours, but I know I've made a horrible mistake. I've thrown away the most beautiful and pure creature to ever light up my life.

I can't believe I let her go. No, I threw her away.

Fuck!

I grip the steering wheel tighter. It hurts so fucking much. I keep seeing the look in her eyes.

She told me she loved me. I know she does. She did.

But now...

If she doesn't forgive me, I'll never recover from this. I had my perfect kitten. So gorgeous and full of life and hope and happiness. And *healed*. So strong in every way.

I take in a breath so violently it hurts my lungs. My chest feels like it's collapsing in.

My kitten. My Katia.

I lean my head forward, resting on my fists as I sit at a red light and fight with the emotions tormenting me.

I'm not worthy of her, that's the problem. I've murdered. I've watched men die. Worse, there's a darkness in me that will dim her beautiful light. That's my biggest fear. I need to remember that.

But for her, I'll try. I promise to fucking God, I will try to be better for her.

I just need a chance. I need her to forgive me.

I need her back. I'm a selfish man for it, but I need her back in my life.

It's a reckless thing for me to do. To go take her back. But if she lets me, I'll never let her go.

My phone rings in the car, and for a moment I think it's her. My kitten.

I swerve on the road, nearly losing control, but only for a moment. Fuck! I'm losing it.

Because I lost her.

I nearly throw the fucking phone out of the window when I see it's Madam Lynn. I don't know what the fuck she wants, but I don't have the time. I almost toss it onto the floor, but I can't. It's late. It's really fucking late, and if she's calling at this hour, there's a damn good reason for it.

"Fuck," I curse beneath my breath and try to answer the phone without anger as I drive closer to Katia. I'll have her back soon and then everything will be alright.

"Hello?" I answer.

"Hello, Isaac," her voice is even and calm, no hint of urgency.

"Now's not a good time," I grit out between my teeth. I instantly regret answering.

"Oh? I thought you should know as soon as possible that Katia has agreed to go up for auction tomorrow. But I suppose if you don't have the time..."

My blood chills, and my heart nearly stops beating. "Bullshit."

"No, that's what stomping on a woman's heart will do to you, Isaac."

I slow the car and drive off the road, stopping in the shoulder. My throat dries, and I can't fucking stand the pain. It's only been hours. It was one mistake.

One fucking mistake.

And she's done.

I threw her out. I deserve this. I shake my head, denying it. I didn't want to. I didn't mean to.

I was scared. Scared to let her close. Scared that I would destroy the strong woman she is.

"I'm sorry," I say into the phone, but it's not for Madam Lynn, it's for my Katia. "I fucked up."

"I know you did."

"She can't go up there. I can't let her."

"You don't have a choice," Madam Lynn huffs into the phone.

"You don't understand-" I start. I'm not going to let anyone else have her. There's no fucking way anyone in there deserves her more than me.

"Oh, don't I, though?" Madam Lynn's voice is hard. "She fell in love; you fell in love. You need to go get her, Isaac. You need to apologize and make this right."

Before she's even finished, I'm slamming my foot on the gas and making my way to her.

"She's not going up there tomorrow," I tell her.

"I hope I don't see her, but if I do, I will feel very sorry for you."

"She won't be there," I say flatly and hang up without waiting for a response.

She belongs with me.

Knock, knock, knock. I slam my fist against the door. The outside air is bitter cold and harsh on my skin. Making my knuckles pain with every hard blow to the door. I relish the pain. I'd rather feel it than the hole in my chest.

As my hand slams down against the door, it opens. The swift swoosh brings the cold air past Katia's bare shoulders and she covers herself with the shawl wrapped around her.

Her long blonde hair blows slightly and the chill causes her shoulders to shudder. Her cheeks are flushed and red, and obviously tearstained. My poor Katia. I did this to her.

But I'll make it right. I'll fix this.

"Isaac." She says my name softly.

"Katia." I want to pull her into my arms, but I can't. Not knowing what she did. Agreeing to go up for auction. "You're going up for auction?" I ask her, although it's more of a statement.

Her eyes flash with a heated anger. "It's none of your business, if that's why you're here." Her grip tightens on the door and I know she's going to slam it shut in a moment.

"I won't allow it, Katia." I say the words hard and take a step in. Katia slowly closes the door and it looks like it takes restraint not to shove it closed with an angry push, but the look on her face is anything but submissive.

She's pissed.

She shakes her head and says, "You told me you didn't want me." She's trying to be strong, but the pain in her voice is evident. It shreds me.

"I was wrong to say that," I say calmly, holding my hands up and approaching her like a wounded animal. My poor kitten. I did this. This is all my fault.

"I will have a Master," she says slowly, her voice gravely low.

"Then you will have me," I say with conviction, balling my fists at my side. There is no fucking way I'll let another have her that way.

"Will I?" she asks, crossing her arms. I tilt my head slightly, my heart beating frantically and anxiety coursing through my limbs.

Please don't deny me, kitten.

I don't show fear. I take a step closer to her, and she holds her ground. "You will," I answer her.

"You will never lie to me again, Isaac." Katia stares at me with red-rimmed eyes. Her bottom lip is trembling, but strength is the dominant feature in her expression.

I'm struck by the strength, but also the hurt in her voice.

"Lie to you?" My eyebrows raise in surprise.

"You said you didn't want me."

Fuck, my heart drops in my chest.

"I'm sorry, Katia. It wasn't true."

"I know it wasn't true. But you will never lie to me again," she says as she brushes the tears angrily away from her face.

"Never," I say just above a murmur, moving forward to take her in my arms, but she takes a step back.

"You need to tell me," she says softly. Her defenses are crumbling around her. My breath is stolen from my lungs at the raw vulnerability on her face.

Tell her what? Whatever she needs to hear, I'll tell her. Anything, just to get that hurt look off her face. I need her happiness back. "I'll tell you anything."

"Then tell me!" she yells at me, and I'm at a loss for words. I take a step toward her again, so close to touching her, but she steps back, moving from my reach. I drop to my knees in front of her. Desperate for her to stop moving away from me, to stop denying me.

"I'm sorry! I'm so fucking sorry! I'm broken. I'm hurt. I need you in my life. I need to lean on you and learn to put faith and trust in you like you do me!" I reach out for her, gripping onto her thighs and pulling her closer to me. "Is that what you want?"

Her shoulders rock forward with a sob as she shakes her head no. My heart shatters into a million shards.

"Just tell me what you want to hear!" I'll tell her whatever she needs to hear. Whatever it is, I need her. I have to have her back.

"I told you I loved you!" she yells at me before covering her mouth and breathing in deep.

That's what she wants?

"Of course I love you!"

She falls to the ground, wrapping her arms around my shoulders and finally letting me hold her again.

"I've loved you since I first laid eyes on you," I whisper in her ear, kissing her shoulder, her cheek. Finally, her lips. She kisses me with the same intensity I feel. She's equal to me in every way.

"You deserve better than me. More than what I can give you. But if you want me, I won't deny you." I give her a soft chaste kiss, pressing my lips to hers and feeling closer to her than I've ever been to anyone. "I fucking love you, Katia."

"I love you, Isaac." Her voice is soft and gentle. "My Master," she says in a whisper. "I love you."

"I LOVE YOU, KITTEN."

EPILOGUE

"*I*'m gonna bring you home to daddy," I coo, rubbing Toby's belly, the Golden Retriever I've fallen in love with, even if he is a stubborn dog sometimes. Toby grins at me, his mouth open, his teeth exposed as he paws playfully at my hands. "Yes I am, boo boo."

Looking at him makes me think of Roxy, but today I'm not filled with sadness when the image of her pops up in my mind. Roxy would be ecstatic for me right now. I've finally found someone who I can spend the rest of my life with. I only wish Roxy was here to spend it with us.

"But you're going to fix that, aren't you, Toby?" I ask, tickling his belly, eliciting a cute whine from his canine lips. Toby will never take Roxy's place in my heart, but I think he'll be a good substitute. I just know that Isaac is going to love him. He told me he's ambivalent with dogs, but I'm positive that Toby will win him over. He can win anyone over. His adorableness is infectious. "Aren't you, boo boo?" Toby continues to grin at me, pawing at me and my eyes fill with tears of happiness. God, I'm so happy. I can't remember ever feeling this complete. Things are going far better than I expected.

It's been two months since I moved in with Isaac, and everything is perfect. Not just between us, but everything. Absolutely *everything*.

I know it's early to say that I want to spend the rest of my life with Isaac, but what we have is stronger than anything I could ever imagine having with someone else. I can't even imagine being with anyone else. Isaac is my heart and soul. My Master. But he's so much more than even that. One day, hopefully soon, he'll know how much meaning he's brought to my life, how much I appreciate him for saving me.

I feel normal now. Which is a weird thing to say, since I'm anything but. But I'm making friends and feeling at ease. I feel whole.

I've even made a friend at the club named Dahlia. Isaac's been taking me to the club more and more. I love it there. Not only because of the allure, but for the company. Like Dahlia. Her Dom and Isaac are close. I don't know what all they've been through, but I know he helped heal Dahlia. They're going to therapy together, which is new for them. Lucian said they should go together. She's proud of it. She's proud of him. But she still hasn't told me why. I understand not wanting to open up to me just yet, but she tells Lucian everything. And it shows when they're together.

"So is this the one?" asks that deep familiar voice.

Speak of the devil.

I suck in a breath as I take in Isaac standing in the doorway, his hands casually stuffed inside his pant pockets. He's a fucking vision today, wearing a breezy dress shirt that's unbuttoned at the chest, showing the beautiful tanned skin beneath. I almost feel guilty at the sinful thoughts that run through my mind as I pet Toby, ashamed that I'm aroused in my place of work. But I can't help myself. Isaac *always* does this to me. I could be in the same room with the pope, and one look from Isaac would have me blushing violently.

"Why yes he is, Master," I answer playfully. I'm not supposed to call him Master in public. Only at home or at Club X. But fuck it, I can't help it. He shouldn't be so fucking hot, and then there'd be no issue.

Isaac smirks at me, looking to his left and to his right, wary of any employees as the dogs bark in the background. He needn't worry. They're all in the back. "Are you looking to be punished, kitten?" he says threateningly under his breath.

I return his smirk as I say, "Maybe I am."

Isaac

"PLEASE, MASTER," KATIA BEGS ME FROM THE BED AS I WALK TO THE dresser.

She's heaving for air and her fingers are digging into her thighs to keep herself from taking over.

She wants more. She always wants more. I'm going to have to take a fucking Viagra just to keep up with her.

Fuck, she feels so good. I'll never get enough of her. I could fuck her all day and still not be sated. All I want to do is give her unmatched pleasure.

Not today though. We're helping her cousin move into Katia's old apartment. Lyssa's excited to be moving to the big city, and Katia's happy to have her close.

In fact, she's been wanting to see her family more and more. Especially her mother. It's about time she opened up to her. She doesn't talk about the depraved aspects of our relationship. But she tells her mother everything else. She's honest and open. She's raw and vulnerable. She's not afraid to share her pain, because she knows with that there's healing. For all of them. Katia and her family.

She's finally accepted that.

I've never seen her happier and more confident. She's a beautiful woman, inside and out.

How I got suckered into helping her cousin move, I have no idea. Well, the movers I hired will be doing most of the work, but still.

I have to admit, it's nice being included. There wasn't even a question as to whether or not I'd be there. They all just assumed I would be. If it were anything else, I'd be irritated. But it's Katia's family. She says they're my family too, and I may one day feel that they are. But not yet.

Just like Katia, we need time.

I'll have more of it to dedicate to her now that I'm not taking new clients for the security firm.

I don't see the point. I don't want to be the man I saw in myself when I pushed Katia away.

I want to be the man she sees. She keeps telling me every night what a Master means to her.

And I promise I'll be that man. I'll make every effort to be the perfect Master for her.

As I open the dresser drawer to pick out what toys I'm going to use on her, I see the black velvet box in the corner of the drawer.

Her family is having a dinner to celebrate Lyssa's departure into her independence, or so Katia thinks. Her entire family already knows that I'll be proposing. I promised them she'll forever be surrounded by love. She deserves it.

Her mother cried when I told them, and even her father got teary eyed. I feel an odd sense of family with them. Something similar to what I had with my Aunt Maureen before she passed.

With time it will grow, and I'll make sure Katia is there, front and center, surrounded by love and family.

"Master, may I touch myself?" Katia begs me, her voice desperate but respectful.

I pluck the vibrat from the drawer.

"No, you may not." I'm stern with her, and she nods her head in recognition. My kitten is needy. "On your back," I command her. "And hold onto your knees. "

My kitten instantly obeys, falling backward and gripping the inside of her knees. Her pussy is glistening and clenching around nothing. She glances at me as I click the switch to turn on the vibrator and the gentle hum fills the room. Her head falls against the bed, and a lusty moan spills from her lips.

"Please hurry," she begs me, and it forces a chuckle to rise up my chest. She makes it hard sometimes to stay in this *Master mode.*

One truth I'll never deny is this:

I'm more of a Slave to her than she ever was, or will be, to me.

Continue on for Book 3, Owned.

OWNED BOOK 3

PROLOGUE

Joseph

I'm quiet as I walk into my bedroom, hoping to get a look at Lilly without her knowing. But those doe-eyed baby blues are shining back at me the second I enter.

Hating me. They pierce into me, giving me a look that could kill a lesser man.

I've been given more hateful glares. From deadly men who intended on killing me, who despise me and my very existence. I've never been affected.

But the look in her eyes guts me.

Because I know she's hiding pain behind the hate.

"Let me out," she says in a low voice as she wraps her fingers around the silver steel bars. Her voice lacks the strength and conviction she'd rather I hear. She adjusts slightly, and as she does she winces. My eyes follow her movements; the grates of the cage have left an imprint on her knees. It's only been a few hours since she's been given her punishment. And I'm already regretting it.

413

I have to remind myself that this is for her own good. She's being punished for a reason.

She *wanted* this.

She *asked* for this.

And now she wants to leave?

I won't allow it.

My hands ball into fists as I stalk forward, my bare feet sinking into the lush carpet with each heavy step. The cage is large, much taller than her own height, and she rises to meet me although she remains on her knees.

Here's a side to her I've never seen before. The fierce woman who was always there, hiding behind the facade of obedient eyes.

She liked to *play* the submissive. She thought this was a game.

She thought wrong.

Lilly looks back at me with daggers in her eyes as I crouch lower, leveling my gaze with hers. Even with the anger swirling in her blue eyes piercing into me, she gives off an air of purity, of innocence. She's so delicate, so sweet. *My flower*.

Her rage only makes me want her more.

"Are you ready to *obey*?" I ask her, tilting my head slightly. My words piss her off. And I fucking love it. The comprehension of her predicament makes her eyes narrow for a moment. I watch as her hands attempt to ball into fists, but she corrects herself, warring between what she craves to do and what she feels she's expected to do.

She clenches her teeth, but her eyes water. Tears form in her eyes as her lush lips part, but then quickly close without a sound being uttered.

I question everything in that small moment.

"Fuck you," she finally responds with a sneer, but then instantly lowers her gaze. She's strong, courageous even, but she's a true Submissive. I have yet to earn that side of her. But I will.

"You want to," I answer with a sharp smirk that curves my lips up, and that brings her glare back. We're at an impasse. If she'd give in, so would I, but she's fighting it.

She didn't realize how intense this would be when she signed that contract giving her freedom over to me. Neither did I.

She doesn't respond, but I see her thighs clench ever so slightly. The small action makes my dick instantly harden with desire. She loves what I do to her. She still wants me, even when she hates me.

"All you need to do is obey, my flower." I regain my strict composure, waiting for her answer.

My nickname for her makes her lips part just the tiniest bit with lust. It makes me lean into her that much closer. Wanting more. My fingers wrap around the bars just above hers, barely touching her, but feeling the heated tingle I always do when I'm with her.

She knew I wasn't a good man.

That's part of what drew her to me. I know it is.

"Fine," she says in a mere whisper. I cock a brow at her answer, daring her to continue with that disrespectful attitude.

Our days are numbered, and if I let her, she may leave me the moment she can and never look back.

But she craved this arrangement for a reason. The same darkness that drives my desires is also in her. Stirring low in the pit of her stomach, fueling her hatred for me, but making her want me so much more.

"You know that's not the way I'd like you to address me."

"Yes, sir," she says obediently, her voice the proper tone as she squares her shoulders. She's still eye level with me, and there's still a fierceness to her, but she's willing to play. *That's just how I want her.*

I'll show her how good this can be.

But first, she needs to be truly punished. The cage door opens slightly with a gentle creak. I need to leave a lasting impression.

She may be angry with me, but she's still mine.

I *own* her. And I'm not letting her go.

CHAPTER 1

Lilly

"*W*hat in the effin' hell?" I slam *Playback*, the romance paperback I'd been reading closed with an angry growl. My blood is boiling like an evil witch's cauldron.

"How could it end... like *that*?" I grit my teeth, shaking my head at the gall of whoever's written this. I fell in love with this storyline, and totally felt the heartache and brutal pain the hero and heroine went through. I was rooting for Liam and Tilda. Their story gripped my heart from the very first page, and I was quickly drawn into their struggles to overcome the heartbreaking obstacles keeping them apart.

I'd read each page breathlessly, flipping through the book like a hungry wolf in search of his next meal, practically dying to find out how it all ended, and then... I gulp as my throat constricts into a ball of tight anger, unable to understand how someone could be so cruel. I'd invested so much of myself into the story, hoping to be rewarded with a satisfying conclusion to such a tragic relationship.

Then it ended abruptly. Just like that, with no happily ever after, no resolution. Only a tragic heartbreak that left me feeling raw. I can't believe how completely engrossed I was in the book, feeling like I was part of the characters' lives, only to be shafted at the very end.

Burning up with anger, I turn the book over and peer at the binding, determined to commit the author's name to memory so I can make sure to stay clear of reading any more of their future work. *Lauren Winters*. "More like Slutty Winters," I mutter angrily, feeling thoroughly cheated.

I know it's fiction and it's not real, but I hate when I get emotionally invested in characters and then something like this happens. It makes me feel absolutely cheated.

I groan my frustration, tossing the book on the end table. My eyes are drawn to the roaring flames of the marble fireplace in front of me. The heat of the fire pricks my already heated cheeks, and I relax slightly as I'm enveloped by cozy warmth. Despite my sour moment, I *love* this.

It's one of my favorite pastimes during the cold winter months, sitting in front of a roaring fire with a hot mug of coffee and burying my nose into an engrossing romance novel. I just like it better when it's a book that doesn't leave me feeling like my heart's been ripped out of my chest and stomped on in front of me.

"I need something more mindless and smutty after that," I mutter, picking up my cup of coffee and taking a sip. I'm calm now, but I still have a slight urge to toss the book into the flames. I must admit the author did a good job with everything else. I just didn't like her ending.

I just wish I hadn't stepped on my Kindle. I had like fifty awesome books piled up on my to-be-read list.

Sighing, I get up from my cushioned recliner with the book in my hands and stretch out my limbs, several of my bones popping as I stand. But it feels so good, I hold the position, letting my limbs come back to life.

My eyes take in my living room, and my mood lifts again slightly. It feels so homey in my new townhouse, especially with how cold it is outside. I've decorated it with warm earth tones that make me feel right at home. The walls are lined with decorative shelves that are filled with books. I've read every single one of these books. A few of them are even autographed.

I love my new bookends, too. They're pale blue mice carved from stone stone to look like they're holding the books up. Just seeing them makes me smile.

This room is completely mine, and finally feels like a home. I still have the rest of the rented townhouse to put my stamp on, but this one room is just perfect. I walk to the large window across the room to open the curtains and let the evening light in. I can feel the cold from the winter air coming through.

Outside, I can still see confetti lining the streets from the New Year's Parade as I place my hand against the window. It's a few days past the first of January, and a few pieces are still blowing along the edges of the building.

I grin as I take it all in, the ending of the book quickly forgotten. I could write a romance that would leave me with feelings that would brighten my day. It's okay to make my heart hurt a little, but I don't want it broken. That's not why I read romance novels.

I've actually had a very good year, albeit a long one. I just finished my next-to-last semester at North University and I've passed all my classes with a B or better. I even managed to get a B+ in Advanced Calculus, something that's always been a struggle for me, all while working hard as a guidance counselor with troubled students at a local high school. I will never understand why psychology students have to know calculus. At this point, I just want to graduate and start giving back by helping make a brighter future for others as a teaching counselor in the local youth detention center. It's their last chance before their delinquency sends them beyond public schools and straight to jail. It's not a job I take lightly.

I can't handle the high school kids though. That's for damn sure. For this past paid counseling internship, the program threw me in a classroom with twenty students. I'm only twenty-four and petite, so even on my best days, I hardly look over twenty-one. To say the students didn't take me seriously doesn't even begin to cover it. I cannot handle working with older teenagers. At all. Sure as hell not twenty of them at once.

Some of those kids got under my skin so bad that I thought I was about to have a stroke. It takes a lot to get me worked up and thinking negatively. But I found it difficult to stay positive as the semester progressed. I still managed to persevere though; a few students showed so much improvement, and I know I made a positive difference in their lives. In the end, that's all that matters.

That internship is over, thank God. Next year, I'll be in a middle school and that's where I really want to work. I feel like I could do the most help there.

And now I have the entire winter break to catch up on all the romance books I've neglected as reward for my hard work.

I glare balefully at the book in my hand, thinking, *I just need to make sure I don't read any more disasters like this one.*

Huffing out another small sigh, I walk over to my bookshelf and pause before I slip the book back into its spot. I really should toss the damn thing into the fire. I'll probably never read it again. In fact, I know I won't. But I can't bring myself to do it. Books are my biggest obsession; even ones I don't love. They keep me sane and positive. They give me hope.

It's time to get dressed and move on. I love my book boyfriends and getting lost in romances, but I have other plans tonight.

My body crackling with excitement, I put the book back on the shelf and make my way to my bedroom. I'm going to Club X tonight, a place that literally embodies the BDSM fantasy elements I love reading about. It's a fantasy come to life, and I freaking love it. It's been my secret pleasure for a while now, and I'm having a blast just showing up and observing the BDSM lifestyle. From the rich, powerful men, to the beautiful and willing sex slaves, and the hot and heavy playrooms with wild, untamed sex—it's all so incredible. I suck in a breath as heat burns my cheeks, and my nipples pebble at the thought. The experience has been so much more liberating and intoxicating than I thought it would be. Even if I haven't actually participated yet.

It's exactly the place I need to be to research the themes I'm putting in my romance novel that I've been writing on my downtime while at school. The book isn't anything I'm taking too seriously, and I don't expect for it to ever be published or seen by anyone else's eyes but mine. I just love writing the stories that come to me. It's a stress-relieving outlet I enjoy indulging in, especially when I've had a particularly bad day.

I walk into my bedroom, tingling with excitement, and dig out a beautiful red nightgown out of my closet. I bought it just for tonight. There's a PJ theme tonight at Club X, and I don't want to be sent home for breaking club protocols. I set it down onto the bed, running my fingers along the soft silk fabric, thrilling at how luxurious it feels.

My skin pricks as I stare at it. I hope I'll look beautiful in this tonight. Just thinking about the looks I'll get from those powerful, handsome masked men causes my breath to quicken, and my pussy to clench. A fiery blush comes to my cheeks, a little bit ashamed at how turned on I am. I don't engage with them though. I stick to the safety of the trainers. I'm not ready for this to truly be real.

I can't imagine how people at school would react if they knew I was attending a place like Club X. A twinge of worry pricks my chest at the thought. I don't want anyone finding out, and I'm filled with anxiety every time I show up at school after a night at Club X. I worry that someone will recognize me and out me. But with how strict the rules are at the club, and the non-disclosure agreements that have to be signed just to get through the doors, I let the worry slip by.

I'm still slightly shocked about how I found out about it. Or rather, *who* told me about it. One of the teachers at the high school I work at, Mrs. Nicole Flite, mentioned the place to me after she saw me with my nose stuck in an erotic romance novel over lunch break. She was cautious at first, probably scared that I would look down on her or rat her out to the principal when she told me about the darker elements of the club. But when she saw how intrigued I was by the whole thing, she let loose, filling me in on all the exotic details.

I couldn't believe that a teacher who looked as sweet and unassuming as her could even be part of such a dark, sexual world like that. But then again... so am I. And now I'm hooked. This place embodies what I've been dreaming about after reading my romance novels.

It took a lot of work to build up the courage for me just to go. But I finally did, and I don't regret it at all.

I still haven't seen Nicole there yet in the weeks I've been going. And I'm not sure I will. From what I know, she's married with kids and she doesn't get the chance to go often anymore.

I haven't been able to go that much either, occupied with school and work. Only on the weekends during this past semester.

But now that I have all this free time over the winter break, I'm going to make the most of it.

I slip the red nightgown into my bag, feeling the adrenaline rush through my blood, and walk out of my bedroom, intent on spending a night lost in fantasy.

CHAPTER 2

Joseph

I bring the whiskey to my lips, taking a swig and then wiping my mouth with the back of my hand.

The amber liquid warms my chest with a vicious burn on the way down. I revel in the feeling. I need it just to feel at this point. My life is devoid of anything meaningful to me. I have wealth, I gave up power, and now I'm alone.

I made the right decision though. I left the *familia*, taking the fall to get the heat off their backs. But now I have nothing, and no one. I'm bored, and that's what's pissing me off the most.

It's better than taking over the familia though. Even if that does make me an outcast.

I clench and unclench my hands into fists. My knuckles are sore from boxing earlier today. I spend most of my time in the gym in my basement. It's all I do at this point, workout and survive each day. Just like the prisoner I am. Caged within a prison of my own making.

I don't fit in anywhere. Like the fucking Beast in his castle. I huff a humorless laugh, swirling the whiskey in the glass before taking another swig. I can feel the warmth flowing through every bit of me, coursing through my blood and finally giving me the buzz I was after.

I want to drown in this feeling. I need it just to sleep. The visions of what they've done and the blood still on my hands burn into me when I close my eyes.

I killed them. I helped eliminate those thieving, lying murderous bastards. Not for revenge, not for a righteous vindication. Killing the Romanos was a message. One that the community and our business partners heard loud and clear.

But someone had to take the fall for it, and I was eager to leave. I don't want to be a monster. I don't want a life of corruption and pain. It's a ruthless lifestyle. But it's the one I was born into.

I stare down at the worn leather journal in my lap. I'm writing every memory down as they come to me. Partly for documenting it, partly to relive it. It's fucked up that I'm trapped by the memory of a world I was so eager to leave, but the sins of my past refuse to let me move on. And I don't know why yet.

I close the journal and run my finger along the stamped name on the front. Passerotto. *Little sparrow.*

But that's not my name. It's what my mother called me. And this journal is all I have left from her, save a few dark memories.

Joe Levi. Murderer. Villain.

That's the only name I go by now.

I'm sure this wasn't what my mother imagined this journal would be used for, but she's buried six feet under in the cold hard dirt. I down the whiskey at the thought.

I was raised to be ruthless and cold, brought up in an environment that breeds sick fucks, like my own father.

They think I'm corrupt or maybe even a snitch 'cause the charges got dropped. The ones I was meant to take the fall for, but they don't know how or why they got dropped. Some think I have more power than I do, which is helpful at times. I'm still feared, which is better than having a target on my back, but it leaves me lonely.

The fire crackles in the large den. I stare at the logs, the fire spilling from the splits between the wood. The back of the brick firebox is black with soot.

I enjoy their fear. I need it to continue to survive. What's worse is that it breathes life into me.

I didn't have a choice.

Lies! The voices in my head sneer at me. They hiss that I could have done more.

They all should have died. My father, my brother.

I shouldn't have stopped at just the Romanos.

I set the empty glass down and lean forward, my head in my hands and my elbows on my knees.

I've done horrible things. I didn't have to. I chose to, so I could survive. So I didn't have to run my entire life with the threat of death hanging over my head. But I still didn't have to do it. And now the memories haunt me.

My phone pings on the end table, drawing my attention and breaking the repetitive thoughts that I can never escape.

I slowly reach for it. There are only three people it could be. I dread the ones from my *familia*. They can all go fuck off. But they don't seem to get the message. I read the name on the lit screen, and relief and something else flow through me. Comfort.

Kiersten. Or Madam Lynn, as she likes to be called nowadays.

She reminds me of the one good thing I ever did. The whiskey pales in comparison to the warmth that memory brings to my chest.

They left her for dead. But I helped him save her.

It wasn't enough for all my sins to be forgiven, for all my wrongs to be righted, but I'm proud that she's still here, even if he isn't.

She's a close friend and nothing more. It's only recently that I've begun to leave this house, and it's all because of her. She's always talking about how she owes me; she has no idea how wrong she is. There's no doubt in my mind that I'm the one who owes her.

She wants to help me, but she can't. I'm beyond repair, and there's nothing I want from her. It's a sweet gesture that she tries to fill my dark days with *something*.

I rub the sleep from my eyes. It feels late in the dimly lit room with the thick drapes closed, but the darkness is just setting in beyond the walls of this house. This prison I keep myself in willingly.

Are you coming tonight?

425

. . .

I READ HER TEXT MESSAGE AND DEBATE ON MY ANSWER.

I have sinful fantasies, some a product of the way I was raised, but others I've grown to desire of my own accord. I've yet to give in to the impulse driving me to keep going to Club X. It's alluring and intoxicating in its nature. The atmosphere is a heady mix of sex and power; so intense, it alone is a drug.

JUST LAST WEEK I BID ON A SLAVE AT HER AUCTION IN CLUB X. I'M not a fan of the term, I prefer pet, but neither really matters.

I've never paid for sex before. It's not about the money at the auctions, it's about the contract. About getting exactly what I want, and ensuring the lines are clearly drawn and everything is written in black and white. Everything consensual. ...even if its nature is not.

That bid wasn't a bid for pleasure. Although she made me curious, I didn't want her. Her Master called her Katia, his kitten.

I thought Isaac was humiliating her, making her go onto a stage knowing no one else would bid on her. Making her feel undesired. I know the man, and I know what he's capable of.

I was pissed. How could he treat her like that? She was trembling on the stage, her apprehension and fear apparent. I wanted to make him pay for what he was doing. And steal his kitten, set her free even.

But I was wrong.

I don't understand them, the members of the club and the elite circles who have grown comfortable there. This lifestyle is new to me.

But control isn't. Sex isn't.

Power is in my blood.

My phone pings again. I don't want to read it. She always convinces me to go. Maybe it's because I feel for her and what she's going through, but I'm not interested in playing games and trying to fit in where I don't belong.

I toss the journal and pen onto the end table and rise from my seat, feeling my muscles groan with a pain I find pleasurable. I take a peek at my phone in my hand when the reminder ding goes off.

. . .

KIERSTEN'S TEXT READS:

SHE'S GOING TO BE THERE.

I STARE AT IT, THINKING ABOUT THE ONE THING THAT'S INTERESTED ME in the last three years of living in this void. I ran into her when I left the last auction. Literally. I ran straight into her small, delicate frame and nearly knocked her over. I wasn't paying attention. It was my fault entirely.

But she took the blame.

Kneeling, improperly, and apologizing in a hushed voice.

She was perfectly imperfect. In need of a Master. But not yet accepting of one. She's still learning. Kiersten caught on to my interest when I started coming to the club more often.

I've been watching her. I needed to observe her.

She has desires I'm not sure I can fill. The way she craves pain is something that feeds a monster lurking inside of me. A depraved beast I've tried to keep chained.

I should stay far away from her. But she piques my curiosity, and she's made me truly desire her. Or at least I crave hearing those soft moans and forcing them from her lips myself.

I've watched her closely this past month. I'm not sure she's noticed. No one pays her much attention since she's still finding her limits. She's not eager for a partner either. She sticks with the trainers and stays in the shadows and corners, keeping out of sight.

I can't deny that she tempts me to possess her, to teach her proper techniques. I tap my fingers on the wooden end table rhythmically as I consider going tonight.

I picture the curve of her ass as she practices her poses, the way her lips part with lust when she touches herself discreetly. She may think no one's noticed her, but I have. And I want her.

I TEXT KIERSTEN BACK, *I'LL BE THERE.*

427

CHAPTER 3

Lilly

$\mathcal{I}$ walk up to the doors of Club X, the huge mansion-like structure looming in the background, its red ambient lighting illuminating the front of the building and casting a glow on its esteemed guests that are waiting to be admitted. A cool breeze blows through the area. My skin pricks as the air softly caresses my flesh, crackling with electricity, and the dark-suited bodyguard at the door recognizes me.

His eyes trail the skimpy outfit I'm wearing, the red silk short nightgown I changed into before getting out of my Honda. I feel almost naked under his gaze, but at the same time incredibly sexy; he makes me feel wanted. Although the attraction is firmly one-sided.

I should be used to this now, but I still get nervous with anticipation. I know that in a few moments, men far more powerful than him will be looking at me, and it makes me feel anxious. Unconsciously, I trail my finger along my bracelet. It's rubber without any metal rings, meaning I'm still just learning. I haven't yet chosen a membership bracelet that will indicate what I want in a partner, Dominant or

Master, or someone who enjoys the more painful side of BDSM. I'm afraid to admit that I'm still a virgin, although there's a bracelet for that. I would rather have a Submissive or Slave bracelet, although I'm not sure which one yet. The lines are blurred for me still. And I'm not sure how much control I'm really willing to give up. The fantasy of being completely at someone else's mercy makes me weak with desire. But the reality has an entirely different effect. I think the aspects of pleasure and pain are what intrigue me most. I haven't felt the sting of a whip yet. But I really want to. I crave it like a sweet-toothed freak fiending for their next Twinkie. I just haven't asked for it. It's as easy as letting a trainer know that I'm ready. But I haven't taken the plunge yet.

Deep down, I know that actually committing to it is going to take a lot. So right now, I'm just observing. It's all just research for my book. Or so I tell myself.

I'm admitted through the doors by the dark-gazed bodyguard, and as I step into the club I have to suck in a breath. I've been here a lot, at least half a dozen times, but I'm still floored every single time I walk in. Club X is beyond beautiful with thick lush carpet, extravagant furniture, gorgeous ambient lighting and soft, tantalizing music that makes my blood heat.

But the thing that gets me the most is the very air that surrounds the people.

The men who walk the floors of the club radiate power and wealth beyond imagine, and the women who follow them are too beautiful for words. I watch as a masked man pulls his timid partner along by a gleaming silver chain, his eyes filled with determination and swirling with lust. I keep my gaze safely away, knowing it's not my place to look a Master or Dominant directly in his eyes unless I want to draw his ire. I'm supposed to be Submissive, and acting anything otherwise will get me in trouble. Even if I'm only here to watch. I can't ruin the fantasy that Club X provides so perfectly.

I shiver as the atmosphere of the club seems to wrap around my body, my nipples pebbling. I love this place. It's even better than reading my books, and that says a lot.

My lungs fill with a deep, steadying breath, as I try to get control over my emotions. It's almost as if I've taken a hit of a powerful drug and I'm getting high. That's what this place does to you. It gets you high on lust, power... sex.

I lean against the bar just past the foyer and breathe in deeply, cooling my heated blood.

I know I want to go to the dungeon, but first, I think I need a drink. It's dark down there, and I'm not sure I can handle it without at first numbing a part of myself. I need to free my inhibitions.

As I wait for the bartender, I glance across the large hall. The stage on the back wall is dark tonight, with the curtains closed, and I don't know if that's a good thing. I look forward to the shows, since not only are they exhilarating, they're a great learning experience. I order a shot of tequila, making sure to keep my gaze in a safe place. Within seconds, the shot glass is placed in front of me by a beautiful bar vixen with long dark hair, wearing the same professional uniform the other employees have on. There's no mixing up who's working here, and who's here for play.

The liquid burns as it goes down my throat, but it's a comfortable feeling. I know it will help me deal with the experience of the dungeon. Even though I'm hungry for it, the alcohol aids me in handling the intense sexual emotions that run through my body. The alcohol is nothing in comparison to how intoxicating the sights in the dungeon can be. I bite into the lime and let it wash the taste of the liquor out of my mouth, the sourness making my eyes close tightly.

When I'm done with my drink, the fiery liquid warming my belly, I leave the bar and make my way through the halls, blending in and trying to disappear amongst the crowd.

A few men approach me as I pass the playrooms. I swallow thickly, my heartbeat racing as I pause in my steps. I don't look at them, but I make sure that my bracelet is in view. Once they see it, they move on. No one seems interested in someone who still doesn't know what they want.

With the rubber bracelet on my wrist, the only people who talk to me are Submissives waiting for their partners, or the trainers. I like it that way. It makes me want to keep the bracelet forever. It makes me feel safe. But the days are limited. The membership here is expensive. Too fucking expensive. The first month with this bracelet was on the house. Madam Lynn, the owner I think, said that I could stay to see if it suited me. But next month I have to pay up if I'm not paired up. And I'm not sure I'm ready for that. Or if I ever will be. But the month is almost up.

It's hard not to stop and stare at the sexual acts taking place in the playrooms as I pass them. The men and women going at each other with untamed depravity. Their moans and cries and grunts and groans assault my ears, the smacks of their flesh pounding against each other filling my already heated blood with sexual desire.

I ignore it as best I can, although my breathing is coming in faster, and continue on into the darkened corridors, my pulse racing with excitement.

There's nothing in this world like the place I'm about to enter. The playrooms are an intense experience, but down here it's far more... primal, possessive. Raw in every sense of the word. I make my way down a dim hallway to where two men dressed in dark suits wait on either side of a large iron cast door. They're employees, guards who make sure that everything runs smoothly. And that no laws are broken. They give me a cursory glance before opening the door, the sound of its creaking making my heart jump in my chest.

I take in a ragged breath before I walk into a dark stairwell, the only lighting being small, glowing red sconces on the wall, giving the area an almost evil feel. A few masked men pass me on my way down and their way up, their dark gazes holding secrets that chill my blood. One man even stops to look at me as if thinking that I am looking to be taken, but when he sees my bracelet, he keeps moving like the men back at the playrooms.

They respect that I'm not ready, and not a single person has tried to push me. There are rules to the club, and they're strictly followed. It makes me feel safe. It's odd to think that way, given the nature of this place. But I do feel safe.

I shudder to even think about what goes on through the heads of the Masters and Dominants when they look at me. It arouses me in a thrilling and exciting way. A way that hardens my nipples, and sends a pulsing need to my clit. I'm almost ashamed at how turned on I am by their questioning glances and piercing stares, and the sinful thoughts I know are lurking behind their eyes.

It's just like how I imagine things in my books. I only hope I can write about this in a way that does this place justice. A way that captures the sensual seductive side along with the other emotions coursing through my blood.

As I get closer to my destination, a shrill scream that's a mix of pleasure and pain rips through the stairwell. It's followed by whimpers and moans. I pause, gripping onto the banister for support, my breath stalling in my lungs. I've been here many times, but I still can't prepare myself for some of the darker things that happen in the dungeon. It's so sexually intense that I become dizzy with desire and emotion. Thank God I've taken that hit of tequila. After I calm myself, I continue on until I make it to the bottom floor. The sounds of groans and seductive pleading fill my ears. It's a place that resembles a seventeenth century English dungeon, with cages and racks on either side of the room, and lit torches along the walls. The ambiance is everything that makes this room... it's all so tempting and forbidden, mixed with danger and fright.

It's more private here, especially this early, but I've seen many things here I never imagined I would. Things that have turned me on. Scenes I've watched play out, and then later been ashamed to have gotten aroused by. I've seen a woman beaten with a whip until tears were falling down her cheeks, her ass bright red from the lashes. But she leaned into it. She begged for more. Her Master gave her what he felt she needed, and the way he took her after made me desire the same ruthless touch.

I want to feel what she felt. I want to experience it to understand why she desired it as much as she did.

I watch, stalking along the edges of the room, as a naked, dark-haired woman is bound to a bench. The rough rope is coarse and would chafe her skin, but her masked Master places a thin piece of silk under it. Her lips part in a soft mix of moan and whimper as he binds her so tightly she can barely move. I can see his huge hard cock pressing against his silk slacks. It forces an intense wave of arousal through every part of me.

The Master, or Dominant, I'm not sure, is wearing the membership bracelet. His rubber bracelet is joined by two interlocking metal bands of silver, and in the center, a red band. I shiver at what the bracelet signifies. This dude is into some dark shit. Sadism and Masochism.

I've seen this couple before, though I don't know their names. I don't know anyone's real name, actually, other than Nicole. It's funny--I've been coming here for a while, and I don't know anything about anyone. But it doesn't bother me. I'm here for the experience. And names are rarely used inside Club X.

Another couple is seated on a bench, and I've seen them before, too. The man gives me chills like no other. And not in a good way. His eyes are beady, and pure black. His hand is gripping his pet's shoulder, squeezing. He's always touching her, or pulling her collar. I've never seen them interact in any way other than what they're currently doing. She's on her knees on the ground, looking straight ahead and he's behind her, whispering into her ear.

Her hair is wispy and unkempt, which also makes them stand out. None of the others look like her. They're taken care of in ways she's not. Most of the women here are given looks of jealousy from me; I can't help it. But not her. I can't help the sympathy I feel for her.

Of all the people here, he's the only one that doesn't seem to belong. And it's all because of the way he treats her. The way she doesn't beg him for more. The way his touch seems to wilt her spirit, rather than enhance it.

I rip my eyes away from them, hating that they're here. I have to ignore them whenever they come down to the dungeon. Instead I focus on the couple in the center of the room, the reason most everyone is in this room. The ideal couple. The one that exemplifies what I consider to be the fantasy of this lifestyle. I watch as he kisses her softly on the lips and places a blindfold over her eyes. There's a guard to the right of them, watching vigilantly. There's another one stationed at the end of the room, also watching the couple and the onlookers like me. These men observe every detail. They see everything. The men in the suits are here to enforce order in case things go too far. They know the safe words ahead of time. Although everything is done discreetly. And some couples don't use safe words at all.

I was shocked the first time I saw one of these men disrupt a session. I could understand why though, because the woman was screaming for her partner to stop. The very fact that the guard felt the need to step in made me fear for the Submissive. The guard merely stepped forward and requested that the Submissive give her safe word. The Dominant stepped back immediately, lowering the paddle he was using on her, and the Submissive gave it, out of breath and still writhing in the binds that held her down. She whispered the word green and then looked to her Dominant, waiting for more. I got the feeling it wasn't the first time a guard had interrupted them.

The man in the suit stepped back, and the scene continued. The Submissive kept screaming as her Dominant fucked her ruthlessly, using her body mercilessly, fucking her with vicious need and smacking the paddle against her skin as he took her almost like a caveman from prehistoric times.

It was a rape fantasy reenacted before my very eyes. It was very difficult to watch, and my eyes kept going over to the guard that was standing nearby. But he didn't move again. As long as the Submissive didn't say the safe word, the Dominant had complete control over her. They were free to act out whatever fantasies they shared in complete safety.

For couples without safe words, they merely nod at the guards when asked if they're alright. Or so I've been told. I've only seen a guard interrupt once. I'm surprised how many couples don't have safe words. Some simply use 'stop'. I suppose it's different for every partnership.

Most of the clients in here seem paired up, like these two. It makes me envy them. Especially when they're collared. Collars are like wedding bands. My eyes fall to the floor, and my heart thuds. Maybe that's more of my romance novels slipping in. I don't know for sure that the people here regard collars so highly.

It's hard not to confuse reality and fantasy. But that's easy to do here. This place is like a fantasy come to life.

A movement out of the corner of my eye causes me to look around. The breath stills in my throat, and my heart skips a beat. There *he* is. Looking at him, I can hardly stand, my knees are so weak. He's like a dark prince, dressed all in black with his matching half mask, the edges of it looking torn. It only serves to enhance his chiseled features. My breath quickens as his eyes bore into me with an intensity that makes my skin prick. The room seems to bow to him. Everything urges me to bend to his will. *And I want to.*

My heart pounds rapidly in my chest as I stare at the floor. A chill travels down my shoulder and through my spine. He has a power over me more intense than anyone else. A pull to him so strong I nearly give in and fall to my knees as I feel his gaze on me.

I've seen this man before. In fact, I ran into him when I was new to the club. My cheeks burn at the memory, remembering his dark regard of me, the flush of my skin as I sank to my knees and apologized for being so clumsy. He watches me sometimes when I come into the club, and I'm always almost overwhelmed. At first I thought it was all in my head that he was checking me out, and then I thought I was just getting carried away by my fantasies. But he followed me down here.

He must want something from me. The thought makes my body come alive with desire.

Or maybe it really is all in my head, I think to myself. No one knows me here. I've tried my best to make myself as invisible as possible.

But as I move away and walk over to the Saint Andrew's Cross that sits next to a rack of whips and rope, I can feel him following me, stalking my every move.

My breathing quickens as I do something new. I slowly fall into a kneel, trying to remember every detail one of the trainers showed me about proper posture. I can't believe I'm about to do this. But my body feels compelled by a mysterious force.

I show him submission.

I invite him to have power over me.

CHAPTER 4

Joseph

I can't take my eyes off of her. It happens every time she comes in here. *Lilly.* I follow her, staying a safe distance away, her gorgeous curves stringing me along. I'll never admit to her how much power she has over me; I can't help but follow her through the club, watching her and gauging her reaction to the variety of kinks. I know she's seen me this time.

She's not put off by it. She doesn't seem frightened, although I obviously affect her. It's as if she's waiting for me. She's never done this before. She's never invited anyone into her personal space. Let alone kneel as though she's been waiting for me, offering me a chance at her submission.

Seeing her kneeling there, looking vulnerable and sexy as fuck in that red nightie makes my cock harden, my heart beat faster. I take a quick glance around the room, a possessive side of me rising from deep within my veins, but no one moves to go to her. A few eyes are on me, narrowing with questioning looks, but they fall when I look their way.

I ignore them all. I always do.

They don't know shit about me. And I give zero fucks about what they *think* they know.

These masks are good for hiding the identities of the men from the Submissives. But it's no secret who we are to one another. The tight social circles that run this city, both from the highest highs of skyscrapers and penthouses, to the dirtiest lows of the pulses that run the streets—are all infamous in their own way. We all know each other. We know who has business with who, and what side each of us is on. Right now, I belong to neither, but I'm well-known to both.

I can tell from the way they look at me out of the corner of their eyes without moving an inch, without even breathing. By the way they stay away and avoid me at all costs. I know for a fact that they *know* who I am. And I sure as fuck know who they are.

We're all powerful men here, and with too much to lose to engage in this kind of activity around people we don't know. Even with contracts and NDAs, we're bred not to trust. With so far to fall and so much to lose, most of these men stay in the private rooms once they've found someone to pursue and indulge in.

But me? I have nothing to lose. And I know exactly what I want. Or rather *whom* I want.

I approach her slowly, almost cautiously, as if moving too quickly will frighten her away. The very notion that she's offering this gift to me, thrills me.

She's been coming to the dungeon more often as if she's looking for something, as if she needs some kind of depravity that she can only find here. But she's yet to engage with anyone. That's what I've been waiting for. For that moment when she's ready to test how her pleasure reacts to pain, and how much freedom she'd get by giving over control.

It piqued my interest to see desire flash in her eyes when she watched the tails of the whip hit against the soft skin of a Submissive. She wasn't frightened by it. She was intrigued. She was *aroused*. She hasn't experienced the pain yet. I have no idea if she'll actually enjoy it.

But I'm excited to find out. The anticipation clouds my judgment, and makes me focus solely on her.

The guards in the room are watching over the other couple. David and Nadine. They're well-known in the club. They've been together for over a year, but they don't have any safe words. They take their sessions to the extremes. It's intoxicating to watch, just as my Lilly is drawn to them, like a moth to a flame.

I stand next to Lilly for a moment, shifting my Barker Black shoes slightly across the cement floor. Her eyes dart toward them, and her head tilts slightly. A sharp breath is pulled through my clenched teeth at the thought of my flogger smacking along her back. She should be still. Her back is curved. She has so much to learn. I pivot and face her, but I don't address her; I'm merely letting her feel my presence.

From the way her breathing picks up, I know she's filled with anticipation as well. She's practically trembling beneath me.

I already know her name, since I've heard her tell it to a few others in the club. But I feel compelled to ask anyway, as if it's the polite thing to do. I crouch down next to her, my hand resting gently on her head. Her soft blonde hair is like silk beneath the rough pads of my fingers. The strands slide easily through my fingers and whether it's unconscious or not, Lilly leans slightly into my touch. Her eyes close, and her plump lips part. She is a woman in need of approval. And desperately in need of touch.

I clear my throat as I take my hand away, testing her obedience and knowledge. She remains in place, her eyes locked on the floor, although her tongue darts out quickly, wetting the seam of her lips. I wait a moment, rising to stand, but she still doesn't move. Good girl. It's not until I give her permission to look, that her pale blue eyes lift to reach mine. As soon as her baby blues meet my gaze with a look of pure desire, tiny golden flecks swirling in the mist of blue and sparkling with lust, I feel a spark between us that sets my heart afire.

This is the closest we've ever been; the first time I've ever touched her. I almost have to reach out to brace myself, surprised by the electricity flowing through me. It's the intensity in her eyes, the vulnerability that shocks me. I hadn't anticipated how emotional she would be so quickly, how trusting. Maybe it's in her nature. I don't like to think that way though. I want it to be just for me, and only me. The sight of her eyes in this moment will stay with me once we've parted, I know that.

"What name do you go by?" I ask her easily, ignoring the attraction screaming at me to claim her right here, right now.

"Lilly," she replies, and her voice is low and gentle. *Lilly.* It suits her. I call her by her name for the first time, letting the soft sounds of her name fall from my lips.

"And you?" she asks, chancing a look up at me, her doe eyes calling to me in a way where I almost feel a need to look in another direction. To break the intense contact, but I don't. I accept the challenge. "You can call me Sir," I tell her. She licks her bottom lip, her eyes darting away as her breath leaves her, and then quickly looks back to meet my gaze. I smirk down at her and ask, "Does that turn you on?"

I already know it does, but hearing the "yes" fall from her plump lips gives me undeniable satisfaction.

Nadine moans from across the room and then hisses in a sharp breath that echoes off the walls. It distracts us both. David has a lit candle above her, a match in his hand while keeping the fire on the wick. The wax slowly drips down onto her naked body, leaving splashes of red covering her milky white skin. She's bound to the bench on her back, unable to move very much, but each time the wax hits her she wiggles slightly to get away.

I faintly hear David admonishing her. "You need to be still, my love." Immediately, she stops writhing on the bench, her head falling back, and her mouth opening in a silent scream as the next drop of wax falls between her breasts. Her hands ball into fists and her feet move outward slightly, but the rest of her body remains perfectly still as she obeys her Master.

"Do you want to watch them?" I ask Lilly softly, gently lifting her chin and drawing her attention back to me.

She starts to look up at me. But she stops herself. "I would like to. If you would allow it." She barely whispers the second sentence. My dick hardens instantly, loving the vulnerability in her voice, loving the way she gives me power. And reveling in the fact that she's uncertain about her behavior. It's the uncertainty that makes me crave her as a Submissive. She's breakable. And I fucking love that about her.

"Are you playing with me, my flower?" I ask her in a deep rough voice.

439

Her eyes look up into mine, widening as my words register. She stutters to answer, her breath coming in quicker. Fear flashes in her eyes, not understanding what I'm asking her. I give her a soft smile to put her at ease and say softly, yet in a stern voice, "Meaning that you want me to play the role of your Master?"

I can practically see the relief flooding through her veins. The tension leaves her body as she looks up and answers me confidently, "I would like to play." The strength in her voice diminishes as she adds, "I'm not sure if I need a Dominant or a Master."

Submissives have more power than they realize. They truly control the relationship. They set the boundaries, they start and stop all acts with what they allow the Dominant to get away with. The Dominant has an illusion of control. I'm not interested in an illusion. I want absolute power. I want to be her Master.

"I'm not looking for a Submissive, my flower," I state clearly. I don't want her to get the wrong impression. I'll determine her boundaries, then I'll push her much faster than she's pushing herself.

Her eyes quickly look beyond me, staring at the row of cages that line the left wall as she considers what I'm saying. "I'm willing to play with you, for now." My body heats, and adrenaline pumps through my veins with an anxiety I'm uncomfortable with, something I've not yet experienced. I don't want her denying me.

She nods her head slowly.

"So would you like to play with me then?" I ask her.

"As a Slave?" she asks me, clarifying what I've just said.

I tower over her small body. "In this setting it doesn't matter. We'll only play for a moment."

Her forehead pinches slightly as she considers what I'm saying. "You'll do as I say while we're down here. And if you don't like it, you can simply leave."

She seems dumbstruck by my words at first, and the connection between us wanes as something else settles in between us. Insecurity. She's confused and uncertain not about what she should do, but about what I can give her.

I'm quick to put her at ease as I say, "You can always leave. Regardless of whether I'm your Master or Dominant. You can always leave without fear." Her expression softens as she comprehends what

I'm telling her. In a sense, I'm twisting words to put her at ease so I can keep her. But I don't give a damn. I'll do what I must to get what I want.

Her voice comes in breathy as she responds, "I think I'd like to play."

"Good girl." My lips curve into a noticeable smile, and when she responds with a faint huff of a breath, it's slow and easy. And sexual. Everything about her right now from her posture and dilated pupils, to the way she's breathing and clenching her thighs depicts how turned on she is by my approval.

I walk over to the bench while she remains kneeling. I'm highly aware of the other men in the room, but there's no way they'd approach her. They'd be dead men if they dared to try.

I want her in my lap while we watch, grinding on my hard cock. She gets up on all fours before I tell her to, eager to come over to me. I wonder if she wants to crawl, if she wants to be degraded. I've yet to learn her limits. I'm confident that *she* doesn't even know her limits. But I'm going to find them by pushing them.

I need to see what her true fantasy is, and how much she can take. It may frighten her, but she'll thank me in the end.

"Come to me." I give her the command and wait for her reaction. She immediately crawls to me. Watching her move catlike across the floor, her bare knees against the cold, hard ground and her nightie riding up high on the back of her thighs while she obeys my command so swiftly, turns me the fuck on. It makes me harder than I've ever been before. As soon as she gets to me, I reach down and lift her up by her hips, settling her in my lap. She lets out a gasp at my powerful grip, which only makes my cock throb harder for her.

That sound. I want to hear it again and again and again.

I grip her by the nape of her neck. A powerful hold, yet I'm still gentle, barely holding her still in my grasp. Her body is so much lighter than I had anticipated. It's easy to move her, to grip her hips and direct her body which way I want it to go. Feeling the weight of her ass in my lap I can only imagine how easily I can take her. Her petite, pear-shaped body was meant to take a punishing fuck.

"You came down here for a reason, my flower." My hot breath tickles her cheek, causing her to shiver slightly.

"Yes, Sir," she says staring straight ahead, but she turns to me, looking me in the eyes as she adds, "I'm curious."

The focus of the dungeon is pain. The name is fitting, and we're gathered down here because the things that happen in the confines of these walls may be disturbing to others. I've watched Nadine and David before. I enjoy their play. I've also seen much, much worse. But what they do is nothing short of erotic to me.

"Put your hands behind your back." Lilly looks at me hesitantly, but even as she does, she obeys me, putting both of her hands behind her back and balancing herself by shifting slightly in my lap. I want to get rid of that hesitation. The more she plays with me, the more she'll learn to trust.

My dick throbs against her soft ass, and I know she has to feel it. I shift in my seat, making sure it presses deep into her flesh, allowing her to feel the pulsating thickness. I want her to know how much I want her.

There are rope ties, leather belts and all sorts of instruments of bondage in a storage bench next to me. More different varieties hang on the wall on hooks to my right. I'm quick to choose a hobble for its versatility and ease of use. It's a wide piece of leather with holes in it for a buckle, complete with D rings and O rings so that the band can be used as restraint, like handcuffs or, without the rings, a simple collar. I wrap the leather around her wrist and secure it and then do the same to the other wrist before fastening the two ends together with the buckle.

I make sure that both are tightened and fastened all the way so that her wrists are completely restrained behind her.

"I want a safe word," Lilly speaks quickly, her words laced with fear, as I tuck the leather strap into the loop. I can practically hear her heart beating faster and faster, mixing in with the sounds of Nadine's pleasure.

A scowl forms on my face and knots my forehead. I fucking hate safe words. I'll know her limits before she does. I'm good at reading people, and I know the difference between pleasure and pain all too well.

I can feel the eyes of the guards on me, no longer watching the scene unfold in the center of the room. Instead they're focused on the two of us, and my reaction to her wanting a safe word. My body heats with anger. But I need to get the fuck over it, she's only just now let me hold her. She's never done this before. She'll learn.

"And what would you like that word to be?" I ask her. I don't miss the look of surprise on some bastard's face across the room when I give in so easily. I don't know his name, and I don't give a fuck; he's seated across the room and enjoying the show. And not the one starring David and Nadine.

"Lollipop," Lilly answers quickly.

I almost huff out a laugh at her answer. *Lollipop?* Does she think this shit is funny? That it's some sort of a joke? I furrow my brow for a moment and then I nod my head, shoving the anger down. It doesn't matter if she thinks this is a game, she won't be thinking that once I'm done with her.

"Lollipop it is then." I lean forward, placing my lips just barely against the shell of her ear and whisper, "Now that I've given it to you, you need to make sure that you use it wisely." Her thighs clench in my lap as she nods her head. I quickly spread her thighs apart, gripping both her knees in my hands and placing her legs outside of my own. The shocked gasp that spills from her lips at how quickly I've made her available to me makes my lips curve up.

My hand slips between her thighs, my fingers barely caressing her skin. I make sure that my movements are slow, not so that she can see them coming, but just so I can send a chill of goosebumps down her body as I slide my fingertips along her soft skin. I want her to *feel* everything. I want her soaking wet by the time I slide my fingers inside her tight cunt.

I run my finger down the center of her lace panties. And again I whisper, "Next time you'll take these off before you come here." A soft moan escapes her lips as I brush my fingernail against her clit, back and forth. "Do you understand?"

"Yes, Sir," she breathes her answer. Her nipples are hardened and poking through the thin fabric of her nightgown. I want to take it off and suck her nipples into my mouth, swirling my tongue around them and heightening her pleasure. But not here. Not with everyone watching. I need to take her home. But I have to be patient. She needs to learn, and I need to find her limits.

Fuck, she makes me so fucking hard. I want to take her right now, thrusting my dick into that wet, tight pussy of hers.

My back hits the concrete wall as I spread my knees wider, which in turn spreads hers. She bites down on her bottom lip, but she has no protests. I push the thin lace fabric away and run my fingers over her soaking wet lips and groan in the crook of her neck. "You're so ready for me." Her eyes close as a shiver runs down her body.

I'll focus on her clit as she watches the scene. She's so fucking responsive. I'm in awe of how beautiful the subtle changes of her pleasure are expressed on her face. "You are going to watch what a Master does to his Slave," I lean a little closer, gently kissing the lobe of her ear and then adding in a softer voice, "and you're going to get off to it, but only when I say."

She nods her head and immediately answers, "Yes, Sir."

I grip the nape of her neck, not hard, just enough that she knows I have control of her positioning. With her wrists bound, her legs spread, one of my hands between her thighs and the other on the nape of her neck, I have complete control over her.

A silver gleam shines across the room as David produces a knife. He scrapes the wax from Nadine's body, the knife tickling her skin as he does it.

Nadine whimpers as he gets close to her hardened nipple, scraping her sensitive skin but careful not to cut her. She moans as the sensation becomes overwhelming. Every little touch gives her pleasure. Even those that are dangerous.

"It's a good thing that she learned to be still," I whisper in Lilly's ear, careful not to disturb the scene. A few other members of the club have gathered and are watching. Scenes like this are rare in the club. It takes a lot to trust someone so wholeheartedly. Most have their eyes on the couple in the center of the room. These two always manage to draw a crowd.

But some of the men are focused on us.

I run my fingers down her lips all the way to her entrance, teasing her and then trace back up to her clit. I'm toying with her and testing her sensitivity. "She must have so much trust in him." I kiss her neck, breathing in her scent. So sweet. She's truly a flower.

I open my eyes and see that David has traveled down Nadine's body, flicking off the wax as he goes along with the knife. The skin on her belly is red from the pressure of the blade. The sensitive stroking of the sharp edge against her skin brings the endorphins to the surface. That's the entire point. It makes every feeling that much more intense. I watch as he travels down farther, crouching between her legs. A few drops of red wax have pooled and hardened around her pubic hair. And he scrapes them off, cutting the short hair as he goes.

I slip my middle finger down the center of Lilly's hot pussy, and then back up to her hard, throbbing clit, putting more and more pressure on her as I rub in hard circles. I pinch the hardened nub slightly as David leans in between Nadine's legs and begins licking her pussy.

I wasn't anticipating her to react so strongly, so quickly, but Lilly's body trembles and her thighs tense, immediately trying to close in my lap. Her head falls back, hitting my left shoulder and she moans loudly as she cums in my lap. My dick pulses with need at the knowledge that I brought her to her edge so quickly.

I make my strokes harder, rougher, making sure to get every bit of her orgasm out of her trembling body. She shakes in my grasp, my left hand moving from the nape of her neck to wrap around her waist, steadying her as her orgasm reverberates through her.

I stare at her in wonder, amazed by how fucking beautiful she is. It only makes me want to get her off even more.

Her body wavers in my grasp, completely unsteady, unhinged from the intensity of her orgasm. I've seen her touching herself before, but it was nothing like this. I should admonish her for cumming without permission. A wicked grin slips into place on my lips. My sweet girl needs to be punished. She's really going to enjoy this.

Before I can move her back to my chest and spread her wider so I can feel the arousal dripping down her pussy and onto my lap, she calls out to me, "Lollipop."

Her eyes are wide open, seemingly just as shocked as I am. I hesitate, but only for a moment. Only because I'm pissed. I don't want a safe word; I know she doesn't need it. I feel ripped off in some ways. My grip on her tightens for a moment, hating whatever I've done to make her safe word me. I imagine it was the intensity of the situation.

I can only begin to guess that's why. Unless she knew her punishment was looming...

I'm quick to unbind the hobble around her wrists. Not because I want to, and certainly not because she can't handle this. Only because I agreed to it.

"I'm sorry," she breathes the apology, her breath coming in faster. "I just didn't-"

She doesn't finish, looking up at me with wide eyes shining with fear and shock. I press my finger to her lips. "This is new to you. You're going to be surprised by what I can do to your body, by what arouses you. Don't let it scare you."

She swallows thickly and starts to apologize again, but I won't allow it. She seems genuinely upset. But I don't want her to remember this moment with a single negative thought.

Still hard and pissed that I wasn't able to bind her to the Saint Andrew's Cross and give her a lashing, I steady her on her feet and stand behind her. "Don't apologize, my flower. You did very well." She could have done better. If only she'd given me more control. But that requires trust. And I'm willing to wait to earn it.

As I lead her out of the dungeon, I pass a few men. All of them wear masks, but their eyes follow us as I walk by them, a look flashing in their eyes that lets me know what they think of me. None of them trust me. But I don't give a fuck. I don't trust them either.

Even here in this dungeon beneath a house of sin, I can't escape my past.

CHAPTER 5

Lilly

A rush of endorphins flows through my limbs, filling me with excitement as the previous day's events run through my mind. I'm trying to remember everything as I prepare to write, sitting at my Ikea desk in the corner of my living room.

I've never felt anything like this before. I've never had someone own me so utterly and completely. So quickly taking possession of me. The feel of that masked man's hard body pressed up against mine, the way he took control of me, his hard cock pressing against me, throbbing and pulsating, making me want to beg for it...

I have no idea what came over me, submitting to him like that. But I don't regret one moment of the experience. It was so intoxicating that even now my body refuses to relax, little jolts of electricity shocking my nerves throughout the morning. I can already see myself mirroring a scene in my book, making it even hotter and heavier than what went down in that dungeon room. What I wish had taken place afterward if my fear hadn't made me safe word.

Fuck. I'm already getting wet, and the day hasn't even started yet.

Shaking my head to clear it, I open up my laptop and bring up the desktop. I need to write to get my mind off my sinful thoughts. Before I can open my Word document and begin writing the scene that won't leave me alone, I see an email notification pop up on my screen followed by the telltale *ding*.

FROM: ZACH WHITE
To: Ms. Lilly Wade
Subject: I need ur help.

HEY, I KNOW UR PROBABLY BUSY WITH UR FAMILY OVER VACATION and all, and I really hate to bother u, but can u do me a favor? I got myself into some major shit and now I have to do community service if I don't want to end up in juvey. I'm not going into details about what happened because I don't want u to be pissed off at me. I remember the talk we had before the semester ended and I'm really ashamed that I didn't listen.

I'm lucky as fuck tho. The judge said he might let me choose where I put in my hours if I show him that I'm really sorry, but it has to be something that he will approve of. Right now, they have me signed up for public bathroom cleaning. I can't do it. Public bathrooms make my skin crawl. Like seriously, I'm a total germaphobe after the shit mom put me thru with her dirty fucking needles and pipes all over the place and those cockroaches she had crawling everywhere. I know it's shitty to ask, but can you please help? Could you get me assigned somewhere else or something?

I can fucking hardly stand it when I have to use one at school and there is no goddamn way I'm doing that shit unless I have to.

ZACH

I SIT BACK IN MY CHAIR AS I READ HIS WORDS. MY FIRST REACTION IS to respond and tell him to just grow up and deal with it. Cleaning a public bathroom, while pretty gross, is a small price to pay in exchange for not winding up in a more serious place. I'm pissed off, too. We had so many talks, and I poured my heart and soul into every single one of them, about him getting his act together and putting more effort into his schooling. And figuring out where he wanted to be in a few years. He could do great things. We set up a plan together, and he promised that he'd do better.

But then I remember all the things he's gone through, and my anger subsides.

Zach was dealt some rough cards coming into this world. He had an abusive father who beat him regularly before he abandoned him, leaving him with a mother who was strung out on drugs and let her son live in absolute squalor, resulting in his germaphobia. He's just a kid in so many ways. I could see the pain in his eyes every day that he came into my office, the hurt that haunted him. Seeing that tore at my heart. No child should have to go through what he went through. I let out a soft sigh as I position my fingers over the keyboard. I can't be angry with him, that's not going to help him. Without someone in his life that shows that they care about him, he might as well give up. I can't let that happen. No matter what bad thing he's done, I have to offer what help I'm able. I refuse to give up on him, and I refuse to let him give up on himself.

But I can't enable him either.

BLOWING MY BANGS OUT OF MY EYES, MY FINGERS FLY ACROSS THE keys as I type my response.

FROM: MS. WADE
  To: Zach White

ZACH,

. . .

449

I'M SO VERY SORRY TO HEAR THAT YOU'VE GOTTEN YOURSELF INTO some trouble, but I did warn you that if you kept on your current path, that something like this might happen. I'm not going to lie and say I'm not disappointed. I'm pissed, actually. I put a lot of time and effort into trying to help you, and it doesn't look like it stuck with you. I hope that you're able to prove me wrong. I understand why you don't want to have to clean public bathrooms, given your past with your mother.

And I will try my best to figure out the options that are available to you... but only if you tell me what you did, and why. I want to help you, but I'm not going to let you walk all over me. I can't help you if I don't know what exactly you've been caught doing. I'm available to talk and work on the plan we've set for you. This is yet another obstacle that I know you'll overcome. I look forward to hearing from you.

SINCERELY,
    Ms. Wade

I SIGH AGAIN AS I PRESS SEND. MY HEART HURTS, HATING THE FACT I can't give him an easy out. I can't just pluck him from where he is now and move him somewhere better, where he's surrounded by encouragement and more opportunities. This very situation is going to close even more doors for him, and I hate that simple truth. He's just made things harder on himself.

I hate that the kid is in this predicament and I feel really bad for being tough with him, but I can't let him off easy. He can't come asking for my help and then try to gloss over the crime he committed. I hope he does the right thing and comes clean. I really like him and want to see him do something with his life, not end up a deadbeat father, or a druggie like his mom, living a life of crime.

Helping troubled students like Zach gives my life meaning, and it means a lot to me. There are times where I wish I could just wave my hand and change all of their lives for the better. Ha, if only such magic existed. The world would be a much better place. But sometimes... I just have to admit...

You can't help them all. They need to want to change. And I don't know if Zach really does or not.

Ugh. Just thinking about how helpless I feel in the moment, makes me depressed. I need to try to write, get my mind off this.

After making a mental note to check my email for his response later, I go back to my Word document. For the next five minutes I sit there looking at the blinking cursor trying to think of what to write. Nothing comes to me. It's frustrating. I have so much material from the previous day, yet I can't write a single word. Seriously, my fingers should be flying across the keys like a roadrunner, filling the screen with steamy paragraphs that would have even the most chaste woman wanting to go on a date with Mr. Rabbit.

I let out a frustrated sigh.

I guess I'm just not in the mood to write anymore.

SIGHING AGAIN, I GET UP FROM MY DESK AND GO OVER TO MY bookshelves and begin rummaging through my erotic romance sections. There's nothing like a good book to pull me out of a slump. I grab one with a shirtless hot guy with six pack abs on the cover, entitled *Deep Inside*. I already know what I'm getting with such a title, and I'm hoping it's just what I need to forget about my depressing work. Some days are hard. But it makes the good days that much better.

I settle down in my favorite recliner and begin reading. After a couple of paragraphs, I decide that I need something hotter. I skip straight to the first sex scene, but after several paragraphs of that, I find my mind wandering. The words are filled with passion, but I don't feel any of it. They seem dry. Empty. It doesn't even begin to compare to...

My mind wanders back to my masked Sir that I submitted to the day before, and the sadness I feel falls away. Images of how he handled my body and how he got me off flash before my eyes. A soft moan escapes my lips.

God, it was so hot, so incredibly intense. Just thinking about it now, leaves me breathless. The intensity of my orgasm and how he controlled me made me call out the safe word without even realizing it.

Lollipop.

I huff out a little giggle at the word. I don't know what I was thinking when I told him that I wanted it to be that. Maybe I thought it was cute. He didn't look like he thought it was, but in the end, he didn't care. He was more concerned with my body and pushing me to my limits.

I think I pissed him off by saying it. But I couldn't help myself. I was overwhelmed.

One thing that keeps bothering me though, is that he didn't show any commitment to me. He didn't ask for my number, or show any interest in following me from the club. He let me leave without mentioning anything, other than not wearing underwear next time. It's not like that's a normal occurrence. I'm sure there are rules against men following a woman from the club, but it still would have made me feel special if he'd asked me for more. I sure as fuck want more.

I'm curious to see where this goes. I've read all about BDSM, and I've researched Master and Slave relationships. I figure that I can at least try this if he pursues me, knowing the only way I'll really understand a M/s relationship is if I experience it for myself. My knowledge from reading about it makes me feel confident that I can handle it. It's a win-win relationship for me. I get to explore this dark sexual world, and further my research for my book at the same time.

Still, the forbidden and dark aspects keep me from committing fully. Thank fuck for Club X. A knock on the door pulls me out of my reverie. Clearing my throat, I get up to see what it is. The postal truck is driving off when I open the door, and down at my feet there's a large parcel sitting on my front steps, a beautiful white box with a white bow tied around it. Furrowing my brow with curiosity, I pick it up. It's rather light for its size, and I take it inside, setting it down on the kitchen table.

As I unwrap the item from the tissue paper, I can't stop the gasp that escapes from my lips, my heart skipping a beat. It's a rather revealing white lace dress that is see-through in seductive places. My cheeks flame with a blush at the thought of wearing it. As I hold it up to the light, my heart races.

It's so beautiful. Luxurious and obviously expensive. And exactly my size. As I press it up against my chest, the significance isn't lost on me. Tonight, Club X's theme is all white. I can hardly wait. I set the dress on the table, but something brushes against my arm. I look down.

THERE'S A NOTE ATTACHED TO THE DRESS. I PICK IT UP, AND MY heart only speeds up even faster as I read the simple words.

I'LL SEE YOU TONIGHT, MY FLOWER.

YOUR SIR.

453

CHAPTER 6

Joseph

*A*s I wait at the long mahogany bar at the front entrance of Club X just outside of the foyer, I take another look at the text from my brother. I don't know why I do this to myself. I have no intention of texting him back. There's no reason for me to be involved at all with my family anymore. They have nothing to offer me, and I have nothing to offer them, despite what my brother seems to think.

Roberto may be a few years younger, but he'll be the one taking over the *familia*. I don't need to listen to a damn thing that he says right now though. I sure as fuck don't have to listen to my father either.

I'm not getting sucked back into that life. I have no intention of going back to them. I'm not going to be a puppet for them. I'm not going to take over like I was supposed to. I played my part and took the fall; I'm done with them.

I don't ever expect to live a normal life. I know that's not meant for a man like me.

I wasn't brought up to be normal. There are things I've done that are unforgivable. The sins of my past will always stay with me, and they made me into the man I am. Whether I like that or not, it's true. My own mother was a whore. My father, Angelo, and the Don of the Levi *familia*, wanted sons, so he knocked several women up, one after the other, until he was given two boys. I grew up surrounded by prostitutes and drug cartels. I've sat through dinners that were ended with gunshots or stabbings. It was normal, and there was never a moment where safety was a possibility. There was a promise of loyalty, but in actuality any and everyone was waiting to stab one another in the back.

That's the kind of life I'd be living. It's the shit that I lived through. Even when I left the *familia*, my past followed me. My name still follows me.

Not responding to my brother, half-brother really, sends a strong message. I don't give a fuck though. I have no intention of sending one back. There's no reason for us to meet up. We have nothing in common. I have a conscience. It may have taken me a long time to find a way out, but I have a desire to lead a different life, even if I'm already condemned to hell. My brother doesn't share that desire. All he cares about is money, greed and selfishness. I wouldn't be surprised if he kills our father one day. Not that I'll shed any tears over it. They're both despicable for what they've done.

I have enough money I never need to work a day in my life again, one of the unforeseen bonuses of having the Romanos' funds sent to my account. It was meant to be evidence used against me, but never came to fruition. I need a new life; I need something to look forward to. Something to give me purpose.

I think back to Lilly, and my hand gently starts swirling the whiskey in the tumbler. She more than interests me. I click the button on the side of the phone before slipping it back into my pocket and take a swig. The burn does nothing to soothe the sickness stirring in the pit of my stomach at the thought of Lilly not coming back.

I know I need to be gentle with her. I can't be the ruthless man that I used to be. I need to hide the darkness that's inside me as best as I can until I have her fully and completely trusting me. I need to get the fuck out of here, too.

The couples walk around me, the Submissives completely

unknowing, nor do they care who I am. Most of their eyes are focused on the ground. Some of the men walk by me without taking a second look, but most of them hold contempt for me. The newspapers crucified me, as they should have. My name is practically a slur. I look up at the one man that dares to give me a hard look. The moment my eyes meet his, he breaks his gaze, pretending to stare past me. Fucking coward.

I look to my right, signaling the bartender for one more. There's a two-drink limit in Club X for obvious reasons, but my tolerance is high enough now that the drinks hardly have an effect on me. As the bartender catches my eye, I notice a man to my right staring at me once again.

It's Zander. Zander Payne. I'm well aware of who he is and what he's capable of. Even if most of the men in here have no idea. I snort at the thought. He's someone the men here should truly be afraid of.

There's an odd look on Zander's face. A look like he has something to say.

I hold his gaze as the bartender sets my glass of whiskey down on the counter in front of me. I wrap my fingers around the glass and bring it to my lips, not moving my eyes off Zander. He doesn't drop his gaze either.

I've never said a single word to the man. I've never said a word to any of the men here except for Isaac, the head of security, but that was brief and inconsequential. I have no fucking reason to talk to them.

I only came as a favor to Kiersten. She was worried about me. She's always worried about everything and everyone.

As the whiskey burns down my throat and fills my chest with the heat I've come to rely on for comfort, Zander finally walks toward me with purposeful steps. He has to walk around a few of the couples. One girl notices Zander walking by and obviously pushes her breasts up and out. She's sitting on a stool leaning forward, her white lingerie wrapped around her body and tied around her neck. Her head lowers until she looks up at him through her thick lashes, attempting to be submissive, although she's doing a poor job of it. But he ignores her.

Just as he ignores all the women here. No one else may see it, but I know the only reason Zander's here is for business. He likes to keep an eye on his assets. He likes to have an eye over everyone around him. That's just the man he is. And I truly admire it, although it's hard to admit that. I do the opposite, I try to stay away from anything and everything that reminds me of what I used to be. The only problem is I have no idea what that leaves me with.

"Mr. J? Is that what you go by here?" Zander asks me, standing a few feet from me as he rests his hand against the bar, in a seemingly casual stance.

"I prefer Sir." I set the whiskey down and leave it there, squaring my shoulders and waiting for him to say whatever it is that's on his mind.

"Ah," he says easily. This is the way he approaches all things in his life. With a casual air that makes him seem harmless. Charming, even. But I know what he's capable of. I've seen it firsthand. Everyone owes him but me. And I won't be making any business deals with a cunning shark like him.

"Sir?" He lets out a small laugh while shoving his hands into his pockets and looking past me. "I was wondering when you were going to begin indulging."

I don't respond to him. I'm not sure if he's referring to Lilly, or my bid on the auction last month. Either way, I don't give a fuck. What I do in here and outside of the club is none of his business. The less this man knows about me, the better. I look past him, toward the front entrance, waiting for Lilly. I know that she received my package. I'm only curious whether or not she's decided to obey me, to wear the dress I've given her and to come without any undergarments on. The latter is what I'm truly curious about. Not only did I give her the order yesterday, but from what I know about her, it's out of her element to be so brazen.

Zander shrugs as he says, "Not that it's any of my concern." He signals the bartender and orders a draft beer.

"Is there something you wanted to ask me, Zander?" I say to get to the point and end this charade.

His pretty boy face flashes a smirk, although he still staring at the back wall where the shelves of liquor bottles are lined up. "I may have heard something I thought you would be interested in knowing."

A man walks quickly in our direction. I've seen him before a time or two, although his name doesn't come to memory. He's a businessman, not someone that I would ever be involved with in the past. Although he does seem to know who I am, judging by the way he avoids my gaze at all cost. The last time I saw him was while I was in the dungeon with Lilly. I search around him for his pet, Adela, but she's absent today. My blood simmers, thinking he's hurt her again. Kiersten told me about him, about an *incident*. I glare at the man, hating that I have to share the same air he breathes. He clears his throat as he pats Zander's right shoulder, taking his attention away from me.

"Master Z," he says, and the man's voice is rougher and lower than I would've anticipated. My eyes hone in on a bruise at his throat, like fingers still wrapped around his windpipe. I look back at Zander and put two and two together. I back away slightly, turning and giving them privacy. Before I can turn from them completely, I notice Zander's annoyance with the man. He looks at the man's hand pointedly before responding in a low voice laced with a threat, "Yes?"

The man seems fidgety, leaning forward and whispering not so softly, "If you have a minute, I'd like to talk."

Zander nods at the man and then turns back to me, grabbing the beer off the bar.

"If you want to talk," Zander says to me, only looking me in the eyes for a moment as he stands. The permanent smile on his face is nowhere to be seen, "I heard something you may be interested in knowing." Without anything else he leaves, walking from the bar of Club X down the hallway with the man following him and away from the onlookers.

I have no idea what he could have heard, or why it would concern me. I'm not willing to make a deal with him, but I won't deny that I'm the least bit curious. My eyes follow the two men as they disappear from view.

I down what's left in my glass, setting it on the bar behind me as I swallow the amber liquid.

As soon as the glass tumbler hits the wooden bar, the doors open for Lilly. The bouncer gives her a small nod and she continues forward with confidence, both hands gripping her wristlet. She's in a long trench coat that goes down to her knees, although her calves are bare. Her high heels are nude with rose gold tips and matching rose gold heels.

She walks to the desk to check her coat, just as most of the other guests do. Some walk past her and make their way past me and off to the right down the hall to the private rooms. Many guests here don't even bother with the public. They just like the privacy and protection that the club offers. The black and white tweed trench coat slips off her shoulders down to her elbows, exposing her bare back from the white lace halter dress that I've given her.

She's a vision dressed all in white. The shimmering silk only makes her tanned skin look that much more kissable. As she takes off the coat, it brushes against the hem of the dress, pulling it up slightly and unbeknownst to her, showing more of her upper thigh. Several men around her take in the sight of her gorgeous curves. She doesn't notice them. She doesn't realize how tempting she is. I could wait for her to come to me. She's obedient. And the fact that she wore the dress I sent her, signifies that she wants me still.

After seeing the two of us interact in the dungeon, she'll be getting more attention than she ever did before. So long as I don't put a collar around her neck.

But I'm not going to give any of these men a chance to come between us.

I push off of the bar, walking straight toward her as she hands her coat to the man behind the counter.

I'm going to make sure they all stay away and that they know she's mine.

CHAPTER 7

Lilly

I step into Club X, my limbs trembling with excitement, my eyes taking in the themed decorations. There's white everywhere, the usual red sconces on the wall giving off a soft, pure glow, the tables decorated with silk ivory tablecloths, and even the walls have been draped with temporary white lace curtains, giving the ballroom an almost heavenly feel.

The air inside the club seems to crackle, only adding to the anxiety twisting in my stomach. Keeping in with the theme, everyone is dressed in white finery. I inhale in a sharp breath as my eyes flit about the room, in awe of the other women. They all look gorgeous, angelic even. The men still wear masks, but they're all white.

If I didn't know any better, I would think the attendees were dressed to gain entry to the gates of heaven, or a slutty version anyway, I imagine. I huff out a small laugh at the thought. It's comical when I think about it. I'm pretty sure with all the debauchery and fornication that goes on under this roof, everyone here is going straight to hell. Worry mingles in with my excitement as I peer down at my white lace dress that Sir gifted me. I think I look alright in comparison to the other Submissives and Slaves, but it's hard not to feel a sense of inadequacy. I thought I looked good in it back at home, but I'm slightly nervous that I may disappoint him. *My Sir.*

Slowly, I remove the overcoat from around my shoulders, the cool air of the club hitting my flesh and causing goosebumps to travel over every inch of my body. I shiver at the sensation, my nipples almost pebbling against the soft white fabric as it shifts against my skin. That's when I see *him* over at the bar, his intense, dark eyes boring into mine. My heart skips a beat as I gaze back into his handsome visage. He looks heavenly, dressed in an all-white suit, and I love how his white winged mask frames his chiseled features. His hard jawline and piercing eyes remind me somewhat of Thor, but I know this hero would rather wield a whip than a hammer.

My breathing quickens as I stare at him, my mind filled with the image of him wielding a whip. My skin pricks from the desire that flows up from my stomach.

His eyes seem to call to me with hypnotic power, and before I know it, I'm moving toward him without even thinking about it. My coat falls into the hands of the coat check attendee, quickly forgotten. By the time he reaches me, I feel as though I'm completely under his control. He could tell me to jump, and I wouldn't even ask how high. I'd just do it.

Up close, he's even more handsome than he was from across the room, putting my memory of him to shame. His white suit is crisp and spotless, his winged mask glinting in the soft lighting. His eyes, which are a deep brown, continue to hold my gaze, enchanting me with their intensity. My legs tremble, and it's hard not to show the anxiety coursing through my limbs as I resist the urge to reach out and run my fingertips along his chiseled jawline, wanting to feel him to make sure he's real.

I can't believe this is the same man that took control of my body the other night. The man who wanted me. The man I safe worded and walked away from.

I swallow as I take in all of him in his majestic glory, barely remembering to breathe. He's almost too sexy to be real. He radiates a kind of cold power that makes me shiver, his eyes filled with dark secrets I know should horrify me, but only serve to turn me on even more. It's an odd contrast, the darkness in his eyes, and the pure white he's wearing, but I fucking love it.

For a moment, I consider kneeling before him. I've seen other women do it, but I'm not sure if I should. I'm not even sure what we are, or what this is yet. He's not my Master, and yet...

He chuckles as he appraises me, his deep rich baritone sending electric shocks through my clit. "Do you like it?" he asks, his dark eyes sparkling with amusement. He must be able to sense my anxiety and uncertainty, and it pleases him immensely. "Like what?" I ask breathlessly, trying in vain to seem confident.

He smiles at me broadly. "Your dress."

I know he thinks I must be a fucking idiot. How could I be so clueless? What else could he have been talking about? The snow in Antarctica?

It's because he's so damn hot that I can't think around him, I tell myself. I blush furiously, my cheeks flaming. "I do, thank you," I reply.

"You mean 'thank you, Sir'," he corrects me firmly, an eyebrow arched sternly.

My skin pricks at my mistake, the heat of shame making it feel as if my cheeks might burn off. "Sorry, Sir. I thank you so much for the dress, Sir. It's beautiful." My words almost trip over themselves to get out. My heart seems to trip in my chest as well.

His eyes roll over my curves, and my skin tingles everywhere they seem to go. "Beautiful," he agrees huskily. I can only stand his hungry gaze for a moment before I'm forced to look away. All I can hear is the thumping of my heart in my chest. He isn't having it. He cups my chin, forcing me to look back at him, and pulls me in close, his hot touch burning my flesh. As he gazes into my eyes I can almost feel the possessiveness radiating from him. It should make me want to run away, but it only draws me to him like a moth to a flame. I didn't think it possible, but I desire him even more than the night before.

"Come, my flower." His words are not a request, but an order. I *must* obey. *Flower.*

He leads me through the club, walking with a confidence that's undeniable. As we walk through the hall, several men look our way, but each time they do, my Sir looks at them as if daring them to challenge him, and they look away. I thrill at the power he radiates, impressed by how some of these men, who are powerful in their own right, don't want to fuck with him.

It makes me feel secure. *Safe.*

Still, I feel eyes on me as we walk past the playrooms. This is different now. Before I was hidden in plain sight, but now that I'm with *him*, they're all watching. I pick at the hem on the dress, realizing how self-conscious I feel as we walk down the darkened hallway, past the double bodyguards, and to the stairwell of the dungeon.

There are a few more people here than the night before. I wish it were empty; I want privacy, but that's not going to happen. All eyes turn on us as we enter the room. Even the couple who obviously had the attention of the crowd before, stops to stare at us. Anxiety twists my stomach, and I look away.

"Look at me," my Sir commands.

I bring my gaze up to his eyes, trying not to shiver. In the background, the couples go back to their sessions and I hear the sing of whips flying through the air and smacking against flesh, followed by pained, but pleasured cries.

"What are you most interested in?" he asks, his deep voice punctuated by another *smack*. I want to look at the couple, the woman writhing in her rope binds as the man alternates the vibrator and the whip.

I shake my head, trying to keep my gaze focused on him as another lusty cry echoes off the walls. "I'm not sure. There's so much…" my voice trails off as I try to find the words. My heart won't stop racing in this room, especially standing here with him. I don't want to tell him that I'm partly here for research, and that I want to live out the fantasies I've read about in my favorite erotic romance novels. He might not like that. It'll only give him more evidence of my inexperience.

His eyes search my face. "Why do you keep coming down here?" he asks.

Smack. Smack. Smack. Another cry assaults my ears. "The pain," I whisper almost as if in response to the cracking of the whip and the cries that follow. "I'm curious." I swallow thickly and add, "I want to know why they beg for more."

He arches an inquisitive brow, the trace of a smile on his lips. The thought that I've pleased him with that knowledge makes my pussy heat for him. "Have you been whipped before?"

I shake my head vigorously, my breath quickening, my nipples pebbling. "No."

A grin plays across his firm lips as if my reply delights him in a way that I can't imagine. "Would you like to?" he asks, his deep voice dipping lower than I thought possible.

My heart races as I gaze into his eager expression, my pussy clenching with need. "Yes," I whisper. I've read about the pleasure it can bring. Every scene I've read turned me on with a passion that surprised me, and now I get to experience this sensation firsthand. I'm excited to see what it's like, but also apprehensive. To be completely honest, I'm terrified.

"Come." Taking my hand, he leads me over to the Saint Andrew's Cross. I watch as he loosens the leather straps on the cross, my legs slightly trembling, my pulse racing. His grip on my wrist is firm as he binds it to the cross. And then the other.

A guard I hadn't noticed before steps forward, a serious expression on his face.

"Lollipop is her safe word," Sir says before the guard can say anything, his voice laced with irritation. He doesn't even turn to face the guard as he straps my ankles to the cross, spreading my legs. The cool air flows up my white dress, and my heart stalls as the guard looks at me, searching my face for any objection. I clear my throat and nod, trying to swallow my heart as it tries to climb out of my throat, then he steps back into the shadows. Sir moves on to binding my other ankle, as if nothing had happened. As he tightens the leather strap, a realization washes over me.

This is *real*.

My heart skips a beat and I swallow thickly. This is not a fantasy I've read about in my books. If he whips me, I'm really going to feel it. I gulp again, my chest rising and falling sporadically. Based on everything I've read; I should like it. Love it, even. At least... I hope.

But it's a fucking whip.

Trembling with anxiety, I watch as Sir grabs a cat o' nine tails off the wall, and the ends of the braided tails look frayed. He holds it up for me to see before letting the tails tickle down my body, over the pure white silk and down my belly. To my surprise, they're soft to the touch, but at the same time thick and unforgiving.

My throat constricts as anxiety threatens to overwhelm me, and I find myself struggling a little against my binds as sweat beads my brow. I need to chill. I can endure this. I've read about it in my books. The pain mixes in with pleasure, and you don't feel it after a while. Or so they say.

I need to just keep telling myself that, and I'll be fine.

He runs the whip along my flesh again, and I almost laugh at the sensation. It tickles. But I know it won't for long. I suck in a breath at the pain I know is coming.

Sir gentles his hand on my waist, his touch soft and comforting. "Relax, don't tense your body." His command is soft at the shell of my ear. His low voice is seductive and washes a sense of ease over me. My breathing still comes in deep, but this time it relaxes me. He relaxes me. I loosen my hands and try to ease my muscles. *Relax.* I must obey him. *Don't tense.*

"I could use this to make you feel... so many different things," Sir says, his breathing heavy and husky, and his eyes are darker than I've ever seen them. I know he's turned on by what he's about to do, but that still doesn't make me feel at ease.

Without another word, Sir pulls back his arm and then brings it forward with an almost animalistic grunt, the whip singing through the air.

Smack!

I gasp as the air is ripped from my lungs and the thick leather lashes my flesh, my raw cry ripping through the chamber. Fuck! It hurts, the sting bringing tears to my eyes. But at the same time, my nipples harden and my pussy clenches repeatedly around nothing, my breath coming in short, panting gasps as I try to recover.

I pull at the binds as Sir runs his fingers gently over the slight marks. From the pain, I expect the marks to be a bright red, maybe even breaking my skin, but they're merely a soft pink. All on my upper thighs. The throbbing pain dims instantly.

His touch is so soft, but it feels like electricity, directly connected to my clit. That's the best way I can explain it.

It's an odd sensation, feeling pain and pleasure at the same time, but I like it. The adrenaline that's rushing through my body is downright intoxicating.

Sir gazes at me, watching my reaction intently, his eyes blazing with intensity. "Did you like that, my flower?" His deep voice is low and husky, his breathing ragged. I can tell he enjoyed the lash as much as I did, his crotch sporting a huge bulge pressing against his dark pants. My mouth waters just looking at it.

"Yes," I whisper weakly, my limbs trembling uncontrollably, my palms moist and clammy as I clench my fists and teeth at the residual stinging pain.

He cocks a brow at me as he says, "Yes?"

I realize my mistake, but it's too late.

"Sir, my flower," he says as he twirls the whip a bit, watching the tails sing in the air. "You keep forgetting."

"I'm sorry, Sir."

I close my eyes, tensing my body.

"You should be punished," he says in a husky voice while he grips the tails of the whip in his left hand. "A little more pain this time."

The sing of the whip whistles in my ears followed by a powerful lash against my thighs that forces another raw cry from my lips.

The pain is more intense this time, making my skin prick all over my body, my flesh red and heated in the areas where the leather tails have struck me. It's crazy what it does to me. It hurts like fuck, but it feels so good. I'm wrapped in almost dizzying euphoria, the room feeling as if it's spinning around me.

After a moment, I force my eyes open to see Sir gazing at me, an amused grin curling the corner of his lips.

"You will call me Sir," he says firmly with authority, his chest heaving from exertion. He put a lot of strength behind that last blow, and I can feel it, my flesh feeling like it's caught fire. The flames sending a hot sensation to my pussy.

"Yes, Sir," I gasp, barely able to fill my lungs with breath, my body teeming with pain and arousal.

The words haven't even finished leaving my lips before his fingers are tracing the marks and then his lips, and then his tongue. I hardly pay attention to it. Pain and pleasure become my existence as the room whirls around me, and my vision blurs almost to the point of darkness.

He pulls away from me while my eyes are closed. I instantly miss his soothing touch over the stinging heated marks.

Pain and pleasure, wrapped in leather. The sensation is addicting.

I want him to whip me again, harder, taking me to the next level, but a part of me knows I won't be able to take it. If he does it again, it will push me beyond the brink. I don't want to say it, but the word *lollipop* starts to form on my lips as I sense him preparing for another blow.

As if sensing what I'm about to say, Sir suddenly drops the whip to the floor, the loud clack on the floor making it obvious even with my eyes closed. He steps right in front of me, his shoes thudding against the stone floor, his breathing heavy and ragged from his exertion. Close up, I can see the sweat on his brow and the slight perspiration making his dress shirt cling to his chest. The smell of his masculinity fills my lungs and I breathe it in deeply, almost as if I'm inhaling a powerful drug.

"You've had enough, flower?" he asks me although we both know it's a statement, his deep, sexy voice low and filled with lust.

I'm unable to speak, my skin burning like it's on fire, but I manage to shake my head no. I can't be left like this. After that, I need a release. *Now.*

He grins at me, as if expecting my inability to answer, and runs his powerful fingers along my heated flesh, my skin stinging wherever he touches. A sibilant hiss of pain escapes my lips as I tremble with need at his touch, watching him trail his fingers down further until he reaches where I'm soaking wet.

He pulls his fingers away, and I instantly pull against the leather straps to bring his touch back to me. "Yes, Sir," I answer with the last bit of breath I have.

I watch him close his eyes, a satisfied groan leaving his lips at being able to touch my pussy as he feels my wet, dripping folds. I shiver at his seductive touch, moaning with pleasure.

"You're soaking wet for me, flower," he growls, slowly rubbing my clit in a circular motion, causing me to throw my head back and my eyelids to flutter. Fuck, his touch feels so good, heightened by the pain he's given me. I've read about this, but nothing could prepare me for it.

I want more of this, more of *him*. But before I can say anything, he suddenly curves his fingers into my pussy, stroking me hard and fast against my front wall. I cry out, fighting against my binds, my eyes rolling into the back of my head. I quickly forget the harsh pain stinging my skin, it feels so fucking good. Wet noises mix in with the pleasured cries of the other Submissives surrounding me as my thighs tremble around his arm, his fingers massaging the walls of my pussy. I let out several cries as I struggle against my binds, wanting to arch my back, but unable to. The intensity of the sensation is driving me wild, and I know I'm not going to be able to take it for much longer.

A thought makes my breath come to a halt, interrupting my pleasure for just a moment, although I'm not sure if he can tell. I've yet to be touched by a man. Not in any way. My anxiety courses through me, but the pleasure is too much.

Sir stares up at me as he pushes his fingers deeper inside of me, his eyes burning into my face, almost bidding me to cum for him. But all I can think is, *can he tell? Does he know my secret?* My head thrashes, and I close my eyes. I don't want to think about it. Right now, I'm someone else. It's only a fantasy.

I writhe against my binds, whipping my head this way and that way, crying out for release, a fiery crescendo building inside the pit of my stomach. *Fuck.* I can't take it. I'm about to cum.

Just as I'm about to find my release, Sir stops, leaving me gasping for breath, my forehead covered in a cold sweat. Anger surges through my breasts as I stare down at him in disbelief, my pussy clenching in fury as the orgasm it was chasing flees.

Sir rises to his feet and leans in, giving me an intensely hungry look as I breathe raggedly in his face. "You've been a good girl and you can cum, but I want to fuck you and make you cum on my dick," he explains as my lips part in protest.

His words should fill me with overwhelming excitement, but they don't.

My desire ebbs somewhat as I stare into his hungry eyes, a feeling of wariness washing over my limbs. I wasn't expecting it to go this far. Him getting me off with his fingers was fine, but I'm a virgin. And though he's sexy as sin, and turns me on like nothing I've ever felt before, I'm not going to give myself to him. Not like this. I don't even know his name.

A part of me wants it badly, though. As my breath comes in frantic pants, I can already imagine him plunging deep inside me with his thick cock, fucking me with a ferocity that would have me screaming with pleasure within seconds.

But I know it'll be a mistake.

Looking at the absolute hunger in his eyes, I feel the heavy weight of fear pressing down upon my chest, constricting my breathing.

I have to break this off before I cave to the desire he makes so hard to resist.

Lollipop, a voice urges in my head as Sir moves in closer, softly brushing his hard bulge against my leg and causing my skin to prick and my pussy to throb with insatiable need. *Say it now before it's too late!*

My skin flushing a deep scarlet shade, I suck in a deep breath, parting my lips to say the word that will bring me to safety.

Before the first syllable escapes my mouth, he surprises me by suddenly releasing me from my binds.

Immediately, I slump to the cold stone floor covered in sweat, my limbs sore, stinging and red, feeling drained and exhausted, his arm wrapped around my waist and holding me up.

"Are your ankles alright?" he asks me, bending over to massage my wrists, his voice coming out clear.

A feeling of confusion washes over me at the tone of his voice. His demeanor, which was hot and heavy moments before, is replaced by a coolness that makes my skin burn.

He knows you're hiding something, the voice at the back of my head says as my heart pounds wildly within my chest. *And that you were going to safe word him.*

I hate not being able to tell him the truth. But I'm not ready. Not ready to tell him, not ready to lose my V-card, I'm not even ready for a real M/s relationship… or whatever this is.

"Yes," I barely manage with a strained whisper as he helps me to my feet.

My skin stings as he examines me in the places where I was bound, making sure that I have good blood flow to those regions.

My lips part to tell him I'm sorry, that I'm a virgin and not sure if I'm ready, but then I close them. I'm not sure he'll even care to hear my pathetic excuse for denying him. He just seems ready to leave.

And there's no sense in making things worse.

Our session for tonight is over.

CHAPTER 8

Joseph

*L*illy's gone for the night. And yet again, I feel as though I've scared her off.

It's my own damn fault, but I'm still in shock.

I knew there was an innocence about her; I assumed it was because this lifestyle was new to her. But when my fingers slipped into her tight cunt even deeper, I felt her hymen. I couldn't believe it. How could she keep something like that from me? The look in her eyes told me everything I needed to know.

I stare at the lush carpet as a couple passes me in the halls of Club X, remembering that look on her face. Scared and vulnerable... and raw. She was completely at my mercy in every way.

No wonder she's taking this so slow.

This should ward me off of her. I should stay away for her own good. No matter how much she wants this, the mere fact that she's a virgin is going to make what would be an erotic exploration into something *emotional*. I'm not an idiot. I won't be fooled by the notion that she knows better. If I take this from her, there will be an attachment that can't be undone.

It makes me even more of an asshole that this knowledge only fuels my desire to take her. I fucking wanted her right then and there. The moment I realized... I'm damn proud of my restraint, but my reaction made her run away... again. She'll come back. I won't let her slip through my fingers. Not that easily, anyway.

"Kiersten," I call out to her as she walks through the main hall of Club X.

Her heels are muted on the carpet, and her eyes whip up to me as she purses her lips and searches the empty hall.

"Quiet!" she snaps in a hushed voice, scowling at me and gripping my arm to pull me aside to a darkened corner. It's comical that the sweet little woman thinks she can pull me around, but I let her. After all, she's been a close friend of mine for a lifetime, and at this point, she's the only person I trust.

"That's not my name here." Her voice is low and her eyes dart down the hall again, but it's empty. The theme night has nearly everyone in the dining hall.

A chill goes through my blood. I forget sometimes. "I'm sorry... Madam Lynn." I give her a small smile and she purses her lips, but I know she's not angry with me. She's too forgiving.

"What is it that you want?" she asks, crossing her arms and cocking a brow. I resist the urge to smirk at her. Here she's in control, the Madam of the house. But I know her too well to look at her the way the other members do.

"I wanted to make a Submissive an offer," I clear my throat and tear my eyes away from hers for a moment. When I look back, confusion is etched on her face, so I continue, "Outside of the auction."

"Oh!" Her posture relaxes slightly, although she remains skeptical. "And what offer is that?"

"A monthly contract outside of the club. I'm willing to split the fees of course. I'm simply not interested in the charade of the auction." I try to make my stance and voice casual, but the reality is that I don't want my flower coming back here. Not until we both know she belongs to me, and every person in this club knows to stay far away from her.

Kiersten raises her brow and I add, "No offense." I don't at all mind giving the Submissive whatever amount she desires, and the club the same. The money goes toward women's shelters. It's a good cause I already donate to, for the same reason Kiersten's chosen it.

It's not about the money. It's about ensuring I'll get exactly what I want.

I've been wanting to take her away from here. I don't have an interest in engaging in activities here, but I want her. I want to break her. That sweetness about her, I crave it. But I covet her tears of desire more. I see the way her back arched as the braided tails of the whip smacked against her skin. The way she touched the marks with a reverence after being lashed. I could show her so much more. I could give her indescribable sensations; things she's never dreamed of. And I want to.

All in time, but not here. She's taking things slowly and going under the radar. I need to take her away now.

"May I ask who?" Kiersten asks with a teasing smile on her lips. She knows exactly who. She's going to take credit for this, I know she will.

"Lilly." My flower.

"I'm sorry Joseph, but the rules are in place for a reason, and Lilly is still finding her limits." Kiersten looks as though she's ready to leave, and if it were anyone else, I'm sure she would. But it's me. So she rocks on her heels, waiting for my response.

I know Lilly is still learning, but she can handle everything I want to give her. She's perfect.

I CLENCH MY FISTS, HATING THAT I'M LIVING BY THESE SETS OF RULES.

Since when did my life revolve around the commands of others?

I've lived my life making demands and seeing that they're met. I've murdered, committed crime after crime and lived a life without consequence. I have more power than any man in this room. More wealth.

I do whatever the fuck I want, when I want it.

But in the last few years, I've simply been biding my time in this empty world I'm living in. I don't feel at all like the man I used to be.

It's time for a distraction. And Lilly is the perfect candidate.

"Don't give me that look," I hear Kiersten's soft voice, laced with sympathy. "I know you're hurting, Joseph," she says just beneath her breath.

I scoff at her. "This has nothing to do with that."

"If you want Lilly, you can approach her and ask to be her Master, although I'm not sure she's ready. If she goes up for auction, you may claim her that way as well. But there will be no deals outside of that." Her voice is strong, although her face is an expression of compassion. I hate it. I hate that she knows me better than I know myself.

A couple's footsteps echo in the hall as she speaks. I concentrate on the patter of the Submissive's bare feet and clacking of her partner's shoes. I'm sick of being here. Surrounded by other people I don't give a fuck about. I want Lilly where she belongs. In my home, in my bed, *in her cage when she forgets to call me "Sir"*.

"Joseph?"

My eyes snap to Kiersten's, her soft voice bringing me back to the moment.

"Are you sure you should be taking a Slave? Outside of the club, that is?"

My heart sputters in my chest, and my blood runs cold. I know why she's asking. But I'm tired of waiting and living in this limbo. I'm done living by *their* rules. I've never known anything other than the environment I've grown up in, but that doesn't mean I can't care for Lilly. I know I can.

"I'm certain." My words don't convince her, and I know Kiersten's unhappy, but I don't care.

I want Lilly.

And I'm going to take her.

I'm going to *own* her.

CHAPTER 9

Lilly

$\mathcal{I}$ blow my bangs out of my eyes with a sad sigh as I go through my emails and work documents. I'm trying to make sure that my lesson plans are ready for my new students. My heart breaks when I think about them. They're just middle schoolers, but they've already been through so much. I've read over each and every one of their files, and I can't believe what they've lived through at such a young age. Some of the kids already have a record, some of them coming from families so abusive that it makes me wish that I could take these kids away from their shitty parents.

MY PEN TAPS ON THE DESK AS I GO THROUGH EACH STUDY PLAN, making sure that they all draw from everything I've learned in these classes. I try to make them as perfect as possible for the kids, hoping that they'll take something from it that helps them. If it can change even one student's life, it will make me happy. I want each and every child to have a chance at a good life, no matter how hard their upbringing, no matter how terrible their circumstances. Just like I did.

A knock at the door pulls me out of my thoughts. I twist in my seat, looking at the door and wondering who it could be. I'm new in this city and I don't really have any friends other than classmates, but all of them are busy right now, most of them home for the winter break. I know it can't be one of them at my door. No one here even knows where I live. *It's probably a package or a neighbor*, I think as I scoot the chair back from the desk.

It makes me wish I was home with my family. But I only have my father, and now that he's remarried, we've lost touch. I know he still loves me, and I still love him, but I don't want to intrude on his new relationship and family. My birthday's coming up soon, and I know he'll be thinking about me. I smile at the thought. He always manages to send me something nice and sweet. Something from the heart.

I at least need to call him, to let him know I'm doing fine.

I make a mental note to give him a ring as I open the front door. There's a white box with an elegant bow on top sitting on the ground outside.

Sir? My heart does a backflip, and the small smile grows on my face. It can only be from him.

Arching a brow and sinking my teeth into my bottom lip to keep the smile from growing, I pick it up and bring it inside to the kitchen table.

I can't wait to open it. He's been all I can think about, although my thoughts have been a confusing mix with me being a bundle of nerves and insecurities. I suck in a breath when I open it and see what's inside.

Several white roses, and a smartphone with a platinum cover on it. My heart pounds in my chest as I pick it up out of the box, examining the high quality finish. A phone? *He could have just asked for my number!* I shake my head at the thought, but my heart won't stop beating erratically and my head won't stop shaking.

I place my fingers against my throat as I stare at the sparkling phone. I'm not sure why he would get me a phone. It's gorgeous, and more than what I could ever hope for or afford, but I already have one. It seems like such an awful waste of money, even for someone rich.

I'm shocked that Sir got me this and sent me flowers, especially after the way we left things yesterday, with me turning him down. I wasn't sure he'd want to see me again. I thought I'd ruined it all.

Maybe there's something really there. God, my heart. I stare down at the roses, gently petting the petals and inhaling their floral scent.

I'M ABOUT TO CLOSE THE BOX, WHEN I NOTICE A NOTE AT THE BOTTOM with a phone number and several words scribbled on it in a smooth font, a strong masculine one. It's definitely his handwriting.

IF YOU NEED ME, YOU CAN REACH ME HERE.
Sir.

MY BREATH QUICKENS AS I STARE AT THE WORDS, MY PULSE RACING inside of my chest and my knees going a little weak. I know that I should just box this and put it away, that this may have gone a little bit too far. But I want more... of whatever this is. I hate it. It feels like I'm getting ahead of myself, like I'm running straight into trouble. I've never had a relationship that lasted more than a few weeks. I'm always the one to send them away, not wanting them to get too close to me.

But this isn't like that, is it? I want him to get close. I'm practically haunted by the thought of him almost taking me against the cross. He could have. I was bound and there for him. The very thought sends shivers down my back.

Whatever this is between me and Sir, doesn't have to be anything more than what I want it to be. It can just be the fantasy I've always wanted to explore. It doesn't have to go any further than that. It doesn't have to be *real.* ...although I'm starting to think I want more than a fantasy.

The air fills with the ringtone on my real cell, going off across the room and pulling me out of my thoughts.

I set the note down and walk back to my desk, trying to calm the mix of emotions as I answer the phone absentmindedly.

"'Hello?"

"Miss Wade?" a woman asks on the other end.

"Yes?" I furrow my brow, wondering what this could be about.

"This is Sarah Parker with Parks and Recreation."

My heart drops in my chest as I realize this is about Zach. That's the only explanation. I pulled every string I could to get his public service moved. I lean slightly against the chair, my hand resting on the back as I lower myself down into the seat. "Yes?" I ask again cautiously.

"I'm calling because Zach White didn't show up for his service today. And he had you listed as his contact." I nod my head, my throat closing and my eyes shut tight.

"Oh," I finally manage to say, disappointment lacing my reply.

There's a slight pause before the woman continues. "I just wanted to let you know that I'm going to have to give a call to his parole officer."

Anger rips my chest as I force out my words. "Okay, thank you for letting me know. I'll try to get a hold of him." I'm so pissed at him. I'm upset, but more than anything, I'm angry. Why couldn't he just do this? Why?

"I'm sorry. You have a nice day."

"You, too," I say as the line goes dead.

Feeling the hurt spread through my chest, I turn in my seat and face the laptop. I need to email Zach and try to talk some sense into this boy's head. It really pisses me off that he wasn't there today. I thought he was really going to try. He told me he would. He told me he was grateful. Some gratitude.

Muttering angrily under my breath, I open my inbox, but before I can start drafting an email, I see a message pop up.

To: Ms. Wade
From: Zach White

Hey don't be mad at me

. . .

I KNOW UR GONNA BE PISSED AT ME AND THINK I'M LYING BUT I wasnt able 2 show up to my community service because I cut my hand really bad and ended up in the hospital. Then I went home and caught a fever. If you can call my parole officer and tell him what's up? My cell doesn't work and the land line is dead.

THANK U

ZACH

"OH ZACH, HOW I WANT TO MURDER YOU," I PRACTICALLY GROWL AS I finish reading his message. I'm not sure that I even believe him. I grit my teeth, trying to decide what the right move to make is. I remember the way he was in class. The way he tried. He was honest with me then. I nod my head, remembering the days where he really put forth effort. He is a good kid. I know he is. I'm going to call his parole officer and try to smooth things over.

I pick up my cell and dial the officer's number. No one answers, but I leave a message on the voicemail, stating that Zach is going through some things right now and if the officer can please bear with him and not come down too hard on him. He'll be there next time. I let out a frustrated sigh when I hang up the phone, wondering what I should do. After a moment I mutter, "fuck it," grab my coat, and walk out the door. I need to check on Zach. I slam the door shut behind me. I shouldn't go there; this is a job for his parole officer. But I need to really talk some sense into him. And I need to see if he's lying to me and playing me for a fool.

ANXIETY GRIPS MY STOMACH AS I ROLL THROUGH THE SEEDY neighborhood, the dilapidated houses making my skin crawl. I don't ever like coming to the south side of town. It's known for its gangs, drugs, violence and prostitutes. I only come this way if I have to. Or if

I care so much about a person that I'm willing to risk my personal safety, like now.

Damn it, Zach, I growl inwardly, trying to calm my frayed nerves.

After passing several rundown townhouses, I turn a corner onto the street Zach lives on, my palms clammy as hell as I grip the steering wheel, my eyes darting around like a cat, looking for any sign of danger. I relax a little after I pass several residences that have decent lawns. The houses look a little better on this street, but I still wouldn't want to be caught walking here after dark.

I drive past several more slightly beat up houses until I see a crowd of kids standing just outside a gated two-story stucco house. I spot Zach almost immediately, his tall figure and platinum blond hair standing out like a sore thumb. They're all out there laughing, some of them smoking weed, while others twist around on skateboards on the cracked concrete. Anger washes over me as I watch Zach laugh at a joke one of the kids cracks as he huffs out a large cloud of smoke from his lips. Both hands are visible. He cut his hand so fucking bad that he had to go to the hospital, but doesn't need a bandage? Yeah, okay. Tears prick my eyes, but I hold onto the anger.

I grip the steering wheel tightly, gritting my teeth as it hits me. He *lied* to me. I knew he probably wasn't telling the truth, but seeing it confirmed before my eyes makes my blood boil.

A part of me wants to jump out of the car and drag him to community service. But he has his own car, and I know he can take himself. He obviously just didn't want to.

I roll up alongside the crowd and several heads turn my way, including Zach's. I give him a look as he spots me, letting him know how much he's pissed me off. He stares back at me for a moment, but makes no move to come toward me. I tap my fingers against the steering wheel, waiting, hoping he will. I'm giving him a chance to come over, apologize and explain himself. To make things right.

But to my absolute surprise, he turns his back to me, pretending as if I'm not even there.

"Zach!" I call out to him and he pauses in his step for a moment, but keeps going.

Shocked, I watch as he walks off with the group of kids, one of them even pointing at me and making some sort of joke that causes Zach to burst out into laughter.

Anger and hurt twist my chest as I watch them walk away, being rowdy and unruly. I know he may not want to seem uncool in front of his friends, but I can't believe Zach would do this. This isn't the kid I know.

I don't know what to do. I want to help this boy, but you can't help someone that doesn't want to be helped. That's what's so hard about this job. It's not easy to turn someone's life around. You can give them the best advice in the world, but if they don't listen or take the initiative, there's nothing you can do.

It's definitely not how I thought it would be when I signed up for this. I thought I would be able to tell children my story, give them a sense of hope, let them know that I was here for them, and everything would be alright.

It's a job that's much harder than I ever thought it would be.

Maybe it will get better with the middle school kids, I tell myself. But deep down, I feel like I'm lying to myself. I shake my head as I sit at the stop sign in my car. I refuse to let Zach give up on himself. I won't stop trying. Even if he doesn't listen. I won't give up on him.

I reach the highway and get on it, flying down the road like a bat out of hell. Shaking my head and biting back tears, I turn the radio on full blast, mindlessly singing along to a pop tune. I don't even slow down when I pass the highway exit that will take me to my townhouse. Instead, I turn onto a highway that will take me to the upscale part of town.

I need a distraction.

And I know exactly where to get it.

CHAPTER 10

Joseph

*I*t's private in the dungeon today. Without the crowds of people, the air is chilled. It's perfect for Lilly's training. "Curve your back more." I swish the flogger in the air, and Lilly's eyes are drawn to it as she curves her back, raising her ass beautifully on all fours, and showing me her glistening pussy.

She loves it when I use the flogger. I think it's her favorite.

We've only had three sessions here since I've found out her secret, but each one makes me more and more anxious. I want her out of here, but she doesn't take me up on my offer to play outside of the club. She's always anxious at the end of training. She expects me to want more in return, she expects me to push her for sex. But I haven't, and I won't. Not yet, and not here.

This week, I've been showing up every night, because she has been, too.

I keep forgetting to tell her that she needs to call me before she comes, and ask for permission. Not that she needs to, with the tracker and the phone I gave her. But she needs to start using it. Or else the phone will be useless to her and forgotten. I can't have that, not until we've made different arrangements.

The tails of the flogger gently brush along her back as she crawls on all fours in large circles around me. I can just imagine training her in the study at my house. Her knees would be on lush carpet, rather than this concrete floor. I've already started gathering things for her arrival. She's yet to consent to it though. Every night she comes here, and she obeys every command that I give her. The commands are simple; the tasks at hand are her choice.

I've given her so much control, although she doesn't realize it. I never thought I'd want to give up control, to win her over, but it's becoming addictive. Like a game.

I know she wants a collar more than anything, and I've been hanging it over her head. I see the way her eyes linger on the couples whose Submissives have collars and leashes. She's jealous. I can give that to her, and I want to. I want her to be mine in every way. I have no reason to give it to her here though. No man here would come between us. No one has even tried. They're all aware that she's mine-- with, or without a strip of leather around her throat.

And the only bargaining chip I have to get her out of this club is that collar.

"Stop," I tell Lilly, my firm voice echoing off the walls of the empty room, although the command was spoken softly.

Lilly's breathing comes in quicker, and I watch as her pussy clenches. She loves being told what to do. She holds her position easily. She's learned well. Every small mistake that's corrected with the whip or paddle, she's quick to memorize. Not because she doesn't like the sting that travels through her body and the heated pleasure left behind. No, it's not that. It's because she wants to please me. Lilly desires approval.

I can give her that. I want to.

I let the tails of the flogger scratch along the concrete floor so she can hear it. I enjoy it when I tease her like this. Making her wonder what I'll do next. Heightening her anticipation.

"Are you enjoying this, Lilly?" I'm tempted to purchase us a private room upstairs. I could have it fitted with any equipment I need. But it's not the same as being home. And I'm not interested in only having this arrangement within the walls and confines of Club X. I'm holding back so much. For nearly two weeks I've been holding onto this desire for her.

I unbuckle my belt and unbutton my pants as she answers, "I am, Sir." I circle her a few times, lifting the flogger in the air before gently slapping it against her ass. She hardly feels it, although each time her body gently pushes forward; she's expecting more. It's a natural instinct.

I'm conditioning her to be still, to stop expecting my reaction during play. She'll get what I give her. Part of me doesn't want to though. I love this side of her. I love that she's not broken in. I love that I can train her to be exactly what I want her to be. She's a virgin in every way.

I bring the flogger up higher in the air behind her, whirling it to make a perfect circle and landing it directly on her right ass cheek.

Smack! She didn't see it coming. She takes the hit well even though she tenses her body, which I'd rather she didn't do. It creates more pain that's unnecessary, and the point of this isn't to hurt her. It's to elicit a higher threshold of her sense of touch that will intensify her pleasure beyond what I could give her otherwise. She knows this, and she knows better than to tense her body.

"Curve your back!" I give her the command, and she's quick to obey. I slowly crouch in front of her as she catches her breath, recovering from the sting on her backside. My hand wraps around her throat as I talk, my lips just inches from hers. "Don't you dare move." I watch her thighs tremble as she stays in position. With a flick of my wrist, the flogger rips through the air and strikes her along her upper right thigh. It's not a hard blow. I still don't know how much to push her, but more than that, from this angle it's difficult for me to see whether or not the tails of the flogger are only hitting her thigh or whether they're also hitting her pussy. And I sure as fuck don't want to hurt her there.

She gasps and nearly straightens her back, but after her instinctual reaction, she curves her back a little bit more. The tempting curve of her body is gorgeous. I kiss her shoulder as she moans into the air, swaying her hips slightly. "I told you not to move, flower," I say teasingly against her lips.

Quickly moving away from her, I release her throat and bring the flogger behind me, hiding it from her sight. I circle her again, loving the heavy pants spilling from her lips. Her panting is the only sound in the room other than the smacking of my boots against the floor. I take a look at her ass, and her right side is beautifully flushed. Tails of the flogger have left red lines in their place. They've blurred together as the adrenaline and blush of her skin spreads. I smack her again on her left cheek. *Smack!* And again on her right.

Each time she gives me a beautiful cry of pleasure, breathing raggedly between the blows. She doesn't move anymore though. She acts like the good girl I know she is. I continue cracking the whip through the air and landing it on her tender lush ass. Her left side, then her right side, hitting only her cheeks and upper thighs. With her focused on her back, her body is less tense. And the lashings are affecting her as they should.

The natural reaction to move away from the flogger greeting her flesh with a hot sting soon turns to her pushing her ass higher in the air, greeting it eagerly upon impact. Wanting more. And that's when I know she's there.

I place my hand along her heated flesh, massaging her ass and thighs before bending lower to lick the center of her pussy. I suck on her clit, but I don't get her off. She tries to stay still, I know she does, but she shifts her balance and arches her back. I've yet to take pleasure from her while she's learning. But I'm ready to change that.

Her curiosity and being my pet have evolved to a genuine desire and craving of my touch. Last night was the first time she asked me if she could please me. I knew what she meant, but I answered her with a simple fact, "You already are." She didn't press the issue, although she kept her gaze on my hardened cock.

I lick the taste of her from my lips as I stand. She groans slightly in protest, but she's quick to be quiet. She's learned that she'll get hers; I'm good to her, she knows that.

I unzip my pants, pulling out my throbbing cock and stroking it once, and again as I stand in front of her. Her chest rises and falls with heavy quick breaths. She looks up at me through her thick lashes, her baby blues begging me for my cock. She nearly crawls forward, my dick so close to her lips, and her so eager to please me.

"I'd like to be your Master," I tell her with her eyes on my dick, watching me stroke myself.

"You are, Sir," she answers me with a breathy voice full of desperation. Her hips sway again, and her thighs clench. She's so close to getting off. We both know I'm not really her Master though. I want more.

"You've been so good, my flower," I tell her sweetly. "What would you like most right now?"

Her eyes dart to my dick, focusing on it, and then quickly move back up to meet my gaze as she says, "I'd like to suck you off, Sir." She hesitates before saying "suck." She's so innocent. Fuck, it's hard to keep my eyes open and hold back the groan threatening to climb up my throat.

A blush rises to her cheeks, and she shifts slightly in her position. Out of all the things we've done, simply telling me what she wants seems to be the most difficult. She's not very good at voicing her desires. But she'll learn.

A rough chuckle rises from my chest. "Don't worry, my flower, you'll be doing that soon. Is there anything else?" I ask her.

"I want to know your name." She tells me immediately, with no hesitation, no shame, and she holds my eye contact the entire time.

"I'll tell you if you come home with me," I'm quick to answer. Her eyes widen slightly, comprehending what I'm telling her.

She's quiet for a moment, truly giving my request consideration. It's the most she's given me so far. I asked her to come home with me three days ago, and she made it clear that she wasn't ready. I'm tired of waiting. "Would I see your face?" she asks me.

"Yes." Although I've given her the answers I know she wants, she's still hesitant. My heart races, waiting for her answer. *Don't deny me.* I know she wants me, but I also know she's very aware of the fact that she's a virgin. That she's scared to commit so much.

She looks at the ground for a moment before telling me, "I'm scared."

"You should be." I hold her gaze as I tell her, "I want full control, and that's a hard thing to give someone." Her eyes close slowly as she sucks in a breath. The idea turns her on; I've known that from the start. She's smart to be so resistant though. I can't be angry about that.

Maybe I shouldn't be so forward, to tell her I want so much. But at least I'm being honest.

"Open your mouth," I tell her after a moment. She keeps her eyes on me as she does what I tell her. "Wider." My own breathing quickens as my body heats at the sight of her curving her back, her wide mouth opens eagerly, waiting to please me. I place the head of my dick just inside her mouth. Only the head. "Suck."

Her mouth closes around the head of my cock, her tongue massaging the underside of the tip. Her hands move along the cement floor as I pull back slightly, desperate to touch me and stroke my length and do everything she can to get me off.

The sight of her so desperate for me makes me crave even more.

I want this whenever the fuck I desire her. I don't want to have to come here. I'm getting sick of it.

She moans around my dick, but I pull away. Leaving her wanting, and falling forward slightly. Worry makes her beautiful eyes seem that much wider. She's concerned she did something wrong. She didn't, but I'm not ready to give her what she wants. I need more from her.

"I want you to come home with me tonight. I don't want to have to come here to see you." I'm completely honest with her.

Her wide eyes stare up at me, flashing with genuine concern. "I'm just not sure if I'm ready," she answers softly with disappointment in her voice.

I need to sweeten the deal. I need to be able to provide her with something that she won't get from coming here.

"I can pay you... two hundred and fifty grand... if you come with me." My thoughts are on the monthly auction the club hosts when I make her the offer. I know it's a bit lower than what she'd get from the auction, but it was the first number that came to mind. Even if Kiersten disagrees, I don't give a fuck anymore.

But the second the words come from my lips, I regret them. She moves from her position, still sitting in a respectful kneel, but she knows that moving from how I requested her is displeasing.

"I'm not a whore." She doesn't look me in the eyes as she answers me, barely above a murmur. Her chest seems to stutter on her inhale. Fuck.

"It's just an incentive," I say quickly. "It wasn't meant to offend you. I'm fully aware that you are not a whore. And I would never see you as that." I'm quick with my words as my heart races, and my body heats. Fuck!

I crouch in front of her, meeting her eyes and taking her hands in mine, rubbing soothing circles on her wrists. I ignore the fact that she's completely disobeyed me.

I'm that desperate, and I should have known better than to say it the way that I did. "I apologize, my flower." I lean in and kiss her. Her lips are hard at first as she holds onto the anger I've caused her, but then they soften, molding to mine. The tension ebbs from my body. Good girl. *Forgive me.*

"I know leaving here is going to be hard for you," I whisper against her lips, cupping the sides of her face and trying to explain myself. "You deserve to be compensated. Especially with what I want from you."

"It doesn't feel right," she answers calmly; at least she's looking me in the eyes now. The moment is lost between us. I nod my head, my chest feeling tight, disappointment lacing my blood.

I stand, tucking my dick back in and buttoning my pants, feeling like a fucking fool. I reach my hand out for her as I lightly say, "Let's go see the show." I haven't gotten her off yet, but I will. I always do. Especially during the shows. I offer her a tight smile, but what we had was ruined.

Her brow furrows, with concern etched on her face. Her eyes focus on my crotch as she stands and frowns. "I'm sorry," she says and her voice cracks as she realizes that I'm once again not allowing her to please me sexually. Not that she'd want to now anyway.

"You haven't done anything wrong," I answer her honestly. I lead her to the exit as the door to the stairwell opens, taking her away from here, and having no commitment from her to leave yet again.

CHAPTER 11

Lilly

*I*t *will definitely make me a whore,* I tell myself over and over again.

I've never read a book where a woman accepted money in exchange for sex and I didn't think she was a whore. So if I'm going to judge myself by that same logic, then that makes me one, too.

If I accept Sir's offer. The key word being "if".

No matter which way I look at it, no matter how it's said, I can't see the offer in a positive light.

Sir called it an incentive, but the wording doesn't matter. You can put lipstick on a pig all you want, but it's still a pig. What he wanted was a contract with me.

And isn't that what prostitution is? A contract between two consenting adults involving sex and money?

Anger burns my throat.

I feel insulted that he would offer to pay me. It cheapened the experience that I had with him. I don't even know why he felt the need to offer me money. Did he think I was that cheap and could be bought after I rebuffed his advances to take me out of the club?

I bite my thumbnail, remembering the look of want in his eyes. I fucking want him, too.

I'm tempted. The kind of money he was offering could make such a huge difference in my life. I could pay off my student loans, my car payment and stash the remainder of the money away for future investments. There's no shortage of things I could do with that money. And it means I'd get him. I'd get to live out a forbidden desire that keeps me awake late at night.

Do whatever you want with it. It will still mean you're a whore, that annoying voice at the back of my head whispers.

I grit my teeth, angry that I'm even considering his offer. But at the same time, I'm breathless just thinking about it. The very idea of being *paid for* makes my body tingle with excitement and exhilaration. It's something forbidden. And that in and of itself is tempting.

"But I am not a whore," I mutter, closing the textbook on my desk. It's not like I could focus on it anyway.

Every time I'm with him, I feel safe. Even though there's something behind his eyes that scares me, something that warns me away, it's what draws me to him. I know I love the way he turns me on and how he gets me off. I've never experienced anything this sexually intense with anyone. And I think... I bite down on my thumbnail again, staring aimlessly straight ahead, I think I want to give myself to him.

I need to shake this off. I want to just pretend like he never offered, but I know the topic of me going beyond the safety of club acts is going to come up again. Not only that, but he's going to keep withholding himself from me. At first I didn't get what he was doing, but now I know exactly what he's been up to. I should be happy, I get all the rewards of being an obedient pet to him, and I don't have to pleasure him in the least. But I want to. I feel like I *need* to. Even worse, the pit of my stomach sinks as I think I'm failing him. He gives me so much, and I give him nothing. I groan, arching my neck back and staring at the ceiling. Why is this so fucking complicated? Why can't I just be normal?

I flip open my laptop to my document for my book, brushing the hair out of my face and ready to focus on something else, *anything* else. My fingers itch to tap away at the keys and get out all of my frustration by getting lost in the world of romance. I stare at the cursor blinking on the screen of the blank Word document for several moments as I run through the images of me with Sir in my head for inspiration. My breath comes in shallow pants, and my thighs clench. After a moment I close my eyes, place my hands over the keys and begin writing the scene that plays before my eyes.

It's a quarter past eight and I can't get him out of my head. His chiseled, handsome smile, his rock hard abs, and his thick, ten-inch cock. Fuck. He's so sexy. I can't stop thinking about his slicked-back dark hair, or the way he looks at me. His incredible eyes bore into me with an intensity that makes my skin burn with desire. I've never met a man that's looked at me in this way, who's made me feel this way. His hands caress my body, running along every curve, making me feel like a possession. Like he owns me. A soft groan escapes my lips as I feel myself clenching below. I need his hands on me now, caressing me, feeling me. I want to be fucked hard, and...

My eyes pop back open and I suck in a deep breath, pulling my hands off the keys. I was getting carried away with the last passage. I swallow the tightness in my throat, and shift in my seat. I shouldn't be ashamed, it's what some books are about. I place a hand on my chest as my breathing picks up. But I don't want my heroine to come off as an oversexed horn dog the entire book. At least not hornier than the male lead.

I want this story to be...

I purse my lips, wondering how I can make something that's just about sex... something *more*. The darkness in Sir's eyes immediately come to me. They stare back at me, luring me to write about them. About what happened in his past that made him into the dominating man he is today. I place my elbow on the desk, my pointer tapping on my bottom lip as I wonder if he'll tell me. I imagine my heroine, knowing she'd have the courage to ask. If she met a man like Sir...

What would she do? Chewing my bottom lip, I sit there for a moment and try to come up with something. But all I can think about is how the heroine in my book has the courage and strength that I don't.

LAUREN LANDISH & WILLOW WINTERS

After a moment I get up from my seat, deciding to pull inspiration from one of my many romances. The second my ass leaves the seat; I hear a telltale ping. I sag back into the seat, clicking on the email notification that pops up on my screen.

I crinkle my nose at the sender. It's from the director of the counseling department. I wonder what it could be about. My heart jumps as I read the subject line. What the fuck?

FROM: JAMES CRICKET
To: Lilly Wade

SUBJECT: NOTICE OF SEVERANCE

DEAR LILLY WADE,

YOU ARE RECEIVING THIS EMAIL BECAUSE YOU ARE PART OF A counseling internship program that has been defunded by state lawmakers.

Over the last year, the Children in Need Foundation has fought tooth and nail to keep the funding for our program. We realize how important it is that children who are disadvantaged get the help they need so they can get a fair shot at life.

Unfortunately, the city council doesn't agree, and has voted to take away the funds that keep the Children in Need Foundation running.

What this means is that all members working under this program are being terminated forthwith, and you will no longer be employed by the Department of Education. It saddened us deeply to have to send out this message to all our hardworking employees, knowing how much so many of you care about these children, and how you all want to make a difference in their lives.

The world needs more people like you, and the entire Children in Need family wishes you all the best of luck in future employment.

492

Don't hesitate to use us as a reference for any future employers. You will all receive our highest and most glowing recommendations.

<small>IN THE MEANTIME, WE WILL BE DOING EVERYTHING IN OUR POWER TO</small> get funded in the future.

<small>YOURS TRULY,</small>

<small>JAMES CRICKET</small>

<small>PRESIDENT & CEO OF CHILDREN IN NEED FOUNDATION</small>

<small>MY BODY IS LIKE ICE AS I SIT THERE STARING AT THE SCREEN, NUMB</small> with shock. I can't believe what I just read. My eyes stop at every word, not wanting to comprehend what's written on the screen. I'm hoping that this is some sort of cruel joke. But when I check the sender address, I know it's real. A pulsing pain hits me out of nowhere in my temples. I wince and seethe in a breath, rubbing my suddenly throbbing temples. Great. Now I have a fucking headache.

I continue to massage my temples, hoping it will all just go away. I just can't get over how sudden this is. I really wasn't expecting it. My heart squeezes in my chest as it really hits me. I just lost my job. I lost my fucking job. And the kids... fuck. The pounding in my head intensifies as I focus on just breathing.

For a while now, I believed that I could depend on this job, that I would remain employed until I was done with school.

Boy, was I dead wrong. Now my entire living situation is in jeopardy if I don't find another job in a reasonable timeframe. I only *just* moved into this place. I lean back in my chair, trying to calm my breathing and get rid of this headache. Tears threaten to form in my eyes, but I won't let them. I won't cry over something like this. I rock back and forth in my chair, taking in soothing breaths like I learned in a yoga class. I will fix this. I will find a way. There's always a way.

I don't know what to do, but I *will* figure out something.

My cell goes off just as I feel like I'm starting to calm down, the shrill beeping making my head throb even more. For a moment I debate on not answering it, but then I think it might be my job calling with some miraculous news, and I jump to answer it.

"Hello?" I answer breathlessly, hope soaring in my chest. It has to be one of the counseling administrators. Please God, let it be.

"Miss Wade?" a deep, authoritative voice that sounds somewhat familiar asks. I narrow my eyes trying to place the voice, but nothing is coming to mind.

I hold in a groan of despair. My left hand rubs the throbbing pain from my head as I keep the phone to my ear, closing my eyes and wishing I would wake up from this nightmare. This isn't my job calling to deliver a fairytale. This is more bad fucking news. I just know it.

"Yes?" I try to keep my voice steady, though I'm inches away from breaking down.

"This is Officer Johnathan Johnson with the Department of Corrections. You left a message on my voicemail the other day for Zach White."

My mouth goes dry, and I'm unable to even put forth the effort for an answer.

"I'm calling to inform you that Zachery White is in jail for committing a third offense." If my laptop wasn't right in front of me, I'd slam my head against the desk. Today is nothing but a cruel joke.

"What was the crime?" I ask, my voice barely above a whisper. My heart sinks in my chest, and my throat closes. The state has a three strikes law. My hand runs down my face as my elbows fall to the desk, my left one hitting the keyboard. I want to shove the whole thing off my desk right now I'm so upset and angry. I'm so emotional and feeling overwhelmed.

"Vandalism. He and several other kids went onto an elderly woman's property and spray painted the side of her house." Officer Johnson snorts a derisive grunt. "They almost gave the woman a heart attack.

I close my eyes, my temples pulsing even harder as I remember the crowd of kids Zach was hanging with. Why couldn't that boy have just gotten in the car and gone with me? It would have gone a long way in helping him, and none of this would've ever happened. I shake my head as my eyes close, and I wish I could go back in time and just grab him. But you can't force people to change. I can't force him to make the right decision. No one can.

Now things are fucked.

A sharp pain lances through my skull. *God.* I definitely don't need any more shit right now.

Officer Johnson obviously hears me sigh and must sense the anger and sadness behind it, because he quickly speaks up. "Don't worry Miss Wade, I'm recommending that he be sent to The Boy's Academy, one of the best juvenile corrections program in the United States. If anything will turn your boy around, this place will. It has an impeccable record."

Officer Johnson sounds very hopeful and upbeat. I suspect it's mainly for my benefit, but I don't share his optimism. I just can't right now. The Academy is a few counties over. Strings will have to be pulled to get him there. It makes me happy though, because it really does have a good reputation. I suck in a breath and try not to cry. I couldn't help him, but maybe they can. I feel like I failed Zach.

"Okay," I say, trying to sound strong, but my voice cracks. "Thank you for calling to tell me, Officer Johnson. I'm going to try to reach out to Zach as soon as I'm able. You have a wonderful day."

"Zach's going to be all right once he's in that program, Miss Wade," Johnathan tries to assure me one last time. "Don't you worry. You'll see."

The line goes dead and my headache seems to increase tenfold, my head pounding like it's stuck in a vice.

Just when I thought things couldn't get any worse, more shit hits the fan. Now I lost my job and probably Zach, all in one day. It makes me sick to my stomach.

I open my eyes to see the email still up on the screen. The one telling me I've been dismissed, and the program doesn't even exist anymore.

I need to find a job. *Fast.* I need to find a way to raise funding for the program. My to-do list just got a lot longer. I need money for my rent, and the bills aren't going to stop coming just because I unfortunately lost my job.

My heart skips a beat as I suddenly remember Sir's offer.

No, I tell myself, shaking my head. *No fucking way. I can't- I won't stoop that low.*

Surely I can find another way to support myself. But every option I can think about requires immense time and work. Time that I may not have.

The offer from Sir is immediate. *Easy.* And more money than I could ever dream of having all at once.

I don't have to be Einstein to know which path I should take.

It doesn't make me feel any better about it though.

Fuck it. It's not like I don't enjoy being with him. Like I haven't been fantasizing about exactly what he offered me.

Sucking in a deep breath, I walk over and grab the phone that Sir gave me. My head pulses even harder, almost as if warning me away as I bring up his number and the text screen.

My heart beats along with my pounding headache as I stare at it. Everything in my mind screams at me to drop the phone, but my hands move of their own accord.

I close my eyes briefly before I tap out the message.

SIR,

HOW SOON CAN WE TALK ABOUT YOUR OFFER?

CHAPTER 12

Joseph

Kiersten is so pissed. I didn't have to tell her that I was doing exactly what she told me not to. But I did.

I don't know why I bothered, but now I'm looking at all these text messages and avoiding her phone calls. I don't have to explain myself to anyone. The only thing she can do is kick me out of her club. I'm sorry that I've hurt her and that I've broken her rules, but I'm not going to allow her to get in my way of getting what I want.

And I fucking want Lilly.

I rise from my seat at the dining room table at the back of the restaurant as I see the maître d' walk through the aisle with Lilly. I button my jacket as I walk toward them.

She's already checked her coat, at least I assume she has, because the thin lace dress she's wearing would have her freezing outside in the chilly January air. The black fabric clings to her curves and ends just about mid-thigh. What's most striking are her exposed shoulders, the lace straps hanging loosely off her shoulders. She's so tempting. She calls to me like no one else ever has.

She's absolutely breathtaking. Her lips are made up a darker shade of red than I've ever seen them before. Any other makeup she's wearing only emphasizes her natural beauty. Her long blonde hair is pulled into a loose bun, looking slightly messy with her bangs swept to one side.

Lilly sucks in a breath the moment she sees me, and takes a small step back. She's obviously nervous. I nod at the maître d', letting him know he can fuck off as I take Lilly's hand in mine, wrapping my arm around her back. She walks with me, her strides even, but she stares straight ahead. My throat tightens at her distress. I lead her to her seat across from me, pulling out her chair and helping her sit down. She desperately needs the help, she's practically shaking.

I take my seat, eyeing her curiously. The sound of my heart thudding in my chest is getting louder. This isn't starting as I imagined it would.

"Thank you," she says nervously, finally looking me in the eyes.

Her small hands grab the white cloth napkin off the table and she places it in her lap, smoothing it over and she seems to calm slightly. But then her eyes hone in on the stack of papers on the table. Instead of looking eager and excited, she looks uncertain and scared.

This isn't what I anticipated. I didn't know why she finally agreed, but I wasn't expecting her to be so... terrified.

"What's bothering you?" I ask her.

She twists the napkin in her lap nervously and takes a deep breath. Her mouth opens with her eyes still closed, but then she shakes her head, placing an elbow on the table and putting her head in her hand.

She's obviously not all right. I'm not sure what's gotten to her but whatever it is, I don't like it. I've never seen her like this.

I place my hand palm up on the table in front of her. Her eyes open at my words. "I'd like you to tell me now, my flower."

She holds my gaze with her beautiful doe eyes. "I lost my job," she says, and her voice is hoarse.

So it's about money. Maybe it's not a bad thing that I offered to pay after all.

She adds, "The entire department lost funding." Clearing her throat with her eyes on the glass of water in front of her, I watch her break down in front of me. My heart hurts for her.

She shakes her head and swallows thickly, looking past me and at the wall blankly. "So there aren't any more of-" she clears her throat again and takes a sip of water quickly before continuing. "So there aren't any more programs at the schools, and I don't know how to change that or help."

"Funding?" I ask. I can fund whatever the fuck I want. My heart pounds in my chest as my fingers slide down the cold glass of water in front of me. Maybe I can take some of the burden off of her, whatever it is.

"I work with underprivileged kids that have gotten into a little bit of trouble." She takes an unsteady breath, but it seems to calm her. "It's only an internship for now until I finish the last semester of school." She takes a deep breath before adding, "It was both my job and coursework for this past semester until the last two classes are available next semester." Her blue eyes meet mine as she answers the question on the tip of my tongue, "I'll be done in December." She readjusts in her seat and finally places her hand in mine. "I'm sorry. I know that-"

She starts to apologize, but I cut her off. "Don't be sorry," I say and rub the pad of my thumb on the back of her knuckles, giving her hand a comforting squeeze. "So that's what you do?"

She nods her head, a small confirmation coming from her lips. "Yes."

She's nothing like me. She's good and pure, so sweet and innocent. For a moment I consider backing out of this. I could give her the money and move on, continuing what we have at the club, or not.

But I fucking *want* her. And I haven't wanted anyone or anything in a long fucking time. Maybe it makes me an asshole for taking advantage of her and the situation. But I don't give a fuck. It's not like I only offered it now when I know she's in need. I never claimed to be a knight in shining armor. Everyone knows I'm the fucking villain. I push the papers in front of her, letting go of her hand and getting back to the contract. She came here for a reason. I need to strike while she's willing and vulnerable.

"Have a look and see if this is to your liking." As I say the words and look up over Lilly's right shoulder, I catch sight of the waiter holding a decanter of red wine as he returns to pour me a glass. I chose cabernet just before my flower arrived.

Just as Lilly's eyes settle on the papers, his presence startles her; she pulls the papers close to her chest, hiding them from his sight. But it also draws attention to her and to the papers. I hide my smirk behind the goblet of red wine, swirling it gently and inhaling the sweet scent before taking a sip.

I nod at the waiter, letting him know it's to my liking and setting the glass back down. I can't take my eyes off of Lilly as the waiter refills mine first and then fills hers. I can practically hear her heart beating out of her chest. This isn't her simply agreeing to something she's familiar with. She's yet to tell me she's a virgin. I'm not taking this lightly.

Although this isn't an auction at Club X, I'm still taking the same precautions. As the waiter leaves, another comes behind him, setting down a tray of hors d'oeuvres. Arranged neatly on the silver pebbled tray are two of each: mini caviar parfaits, pancetta crisps with goat cheese on thin pear slices, marinated mozzarella with chili and thyme, as well as a variety of olives, soft cheeses, and shaved meats.

I'm not sure what my flower really enjoys eating yet, but I'll be finding out shortly. Lilly's eyes glance to the tray and then back to the waiter, as he turns his back to us, leaving us alone and to our private dinner as I requested. Her eyes don't linger on any of the items on the tray. Instead she sets the contract back down on the table, focusing on each line.

"Would you like to eat first?" I ask her, popping an olive into my mouth.

She gently shakes her head and returns to reading the contract before her eyes widen, realizing what she's done. She looks up at me with slight fear in her eyes as she says, "No thank you, Sir."

I nod my head once, keeping my eyes on hers. She waits with her body stiff before I reply, "I know it's different here, in a new environment." I quickly lick the salt from my fingertips before wiping them on the cloth napkin in my lap, her eyes drawn to my mouth. "It'll be like this when you come home with me. But you'll get used to me being your Master at *all* times, and in *all* settings."

She sucks in a breath, and her eyes cloud with lust as she answers,

"Yes, Sir." She maintains my gaze, waiting for me to give her permission to continue reading. Such a good girl. I nod down at the papers in her hands, and say, "Go on."

I have the contract nearly memorized.

CONTRACT TO BE SIGNED ON THIS DAY, JANUARY 13, 2017, BY THE following participants.

Master: Joseph Levi.

Slave: Lilly Wade.

DEFINITION OF MASTER AND SLAVE NEEDS.

The Master requests the Slave to be available to him at all times for any needs he deems suitable.

The Slave requires safety at all times, as well as free periods when her Master deems appropriate. There will be no punishments during these free periods, however, the Slave must continue to respect her position and address her Master appropriately.

DEFINITION OF MASTER AND SLAVE RESPONSIBILITIES.

Lilly Wade agrees to obey Master in all respects with her mind as well as her body. She is also responsible for the use of her safe word, lollipop, when necessary and trusts that her Master will respect the use of that safe word.

She will keep her body available for whatever use her Master deems appropriate at all times.

Joseph Levi may use her body in any manner within the parameters of her safety.

Lilly is responsible for answering any questions from her Master honestly and directly, and will volunteer any information he should know about her physical and emotional condition.

She is not to interpret that as permission to whine and complain. She must always address her Master in a respectful manner.

It is the Master's responsibility to make it clear when a punishment is being given, and why it has occurred.

In public, the Slave will conduct herself in a manner that doesn't call attention to the relationship.

No part of this agreement will interfere with Lilly's career, her physical or emotional wellbeing.

Of her own free will, Lilly Wade offers herself in slavery to Master Joseph Levi for the period beginning on January 14, 2017 at noon, and ending on February 14, 2017 at noon.

Both parties must also note and acknowledge that this contract is not legally enforceable. It is a tool to help guide the relationship, and monetary gains will be provided to Lilly as compensation in the form of two hundred and fifty thousand dollars. Lilly Wade, Slave, may at any time leave without fear of losing Joseph Levi as her Master for the duration of the contract. Although in doing so, may be met with punishment if she is to return.

With my signature below, I agree to accept and obey what is detailed and outlined for the contract noted above.

Slave,   Lilly   Wade   _____

Date_____

Lilly looks up at me hesitantly. "Joseph?" She says my name softly, so sweet coming from her lips. I've always hated my name, but hearing it from her, with that look in her eyes, makes me proud of it.

I clasp my hands on the table and nod once, holding her baby blues firm with my gaze.

She smiles shyly before returning to the contract.

"The terms are negotiable," I say easily, waiting to see if she's comfortable with the amount I blurted out in the dungeon. It's the minimum of what she'd get if she were to go up for auction. I should offer more, but I'd rather keep the opportunity open for me to extend the contract into the next month if I'd like to.

"This contract ends on Valentine's Day." Although it's a statement, Lilly looks at me as though it's a question.

"Yes," I nod again and say, "It's exactly one month."

I stare deep into her pale blue eyes, willing her to tell me that she's a virgin. It's been days since my fingers have been pressed inside of her tight cunt, but I can still feel her hymen on the tips of my fingers. I know she's untouched, and I expect her to tell me before signing.

She looks like she's going to tell me something, but she doesn't. Instead she returns to the paperwork, but she's not reading it. Her eyes are focused on the line she's supposed to sign.

"If you're not comfortable with this..." I hate myself for even giving her an out. But in this moment, I fall victim to the vulnerability in her eyes.

"I want to fuck you," Lilly blurts out, covering her mouth with both hands. Her cheeks brighten with a beautiful blush of embarrassment.

Although her little outburst is adorable, I need to make sure she's ready for this. "But are you ready to be my Slave? To give yourself to me in all things for a month?"

Lilly takes a deep breath and then another, all while staring into my eyes. She nods her head and without speaking a word, she picks up the pen on the table, and signs her name on the line.

CHAPTER 13

Lilly

I blow a strand of hair out of my eyes as I pack away another tank top, one thought running through my mind.

It's only one month.

It's something I've been telling myself all morning to make myself feel better about accepting the money. That, along with, *after thirty days, I'll be free.* The words are helping some, but not totally alleviating my anxiety about the contract. I went over every single line of it several times. It was nothing like the contracts Madam Lynn showed me at the club when I first came. There weren't any specific boxes for things I was interested in or uninterested in. There weren't any hard limits or soft limits that were indicated on the last line.

I was agreeing to be his Slave. Period.

My heart skips a beat at the thought, my breath quickening. The whole contract is very much in Joseph's hands. It scares the *shit* out of me, yet at the same time, it turns me on. It's a paradox.

There's something about giving this man total control over me that drives me absolutely wild.

I should be ashamed, but I'm not. I want it.

I want *him*.

It isn't lost on me that I'll be giving him my virginity. My *V-card*. It's not that it's something sacred to me, something that I've been holding on to as long as I can remember. I've just never... been with anyone who's made me want to give it to them. I wasn't waiting until marriage. Just waiting until I found someone who turned me on and wanted me just as much. Joseph is definitely that man.

I hardly know the man, and here I am, knowingly about to give myself away. I shouldn't be doing this. I should know better. At the same time, I can't help but think there's something more between us, something I've never had with anyone else. I toss another tank top into the small pile on my bed.

Or maybe I'm just trying to justify it.

He's so much like one of the heroes in one of my romance novels; handsome, dark, brooding, mysterious and most likely hiding a damaged past that'll pull at your heartstrings. That's part of what draws me to him, how much of a living, breathing fantasy he seems to be.

But I need to remind myself this isn't a fantasy. It's real life. And I've gotten myself into some serious shit. Except it hasn't really sunken in yet. I'm not sure when it will. I'm infatuated with the romanticized version of Joseph.

Even now, my heart flutters at how concerned he seemed with making me feel comfortable with the contract.

I stare at the pile on my bed, remembering how he told me to bring only the things that make me happy. I glance down at my half-stuffed bag, looking to see what I have so far. My most favorite books and a new Kindle I bought that has loads of titles on my to-be read list already downloaded, but I'm still missing a few things.

I glance at my list, and go down the line of things I still need to grab, then go about gathering them.

I grab a small blue pillow that's on my bed that I use to prop up my knees when I'm sleeping and toss it in the duffel bag. Walking into the bathroom, I grab my aromatherapy oils and some cherry bath bombs and stuff them in my small toiletry bag. While I'm in there, I grab some nail polish and my three favorite lace nightgowns that are hanging on the rack. I rub my fingers over the lace; they're not nearly as beautiful as what Sir gifted me, but maybe he'll like them.

My body heats, imagining what he'll say. I close my eyes and stop that train of thought. I walk out of the bathroom with my personal items and I go down my list again, getting anything else I might have left out. Comfortable socks and flannel pajama pants that I wear when I'm really happy are next.

In the kitchen, I grab a box of my favorite homemade tea that I absolutely love and get from the farmers market. I start packing it away, but then pause, wondering if he'll even let me use this. I have to remember. He owns me. I have to do what he says, whether I like it or not. So if he doesn't want me to drink my favorite tea, I can't drink it.

Anxiety twists my stomach as I begin to doubt my decision to sign the contract. I'm not sure if I can make it through thirty days of being told what to do. I like to think that I can, but it might be harder than I imagine.

Even though it's a contract, you can always walk away, that voice in the back of my head whispers.

I shiver at the thought of breaking the terms of our agreement. But if I find that I can't handle the situation, I'll have to.

Pushing away the troublesome thoughts, I finish packing and go through the house, making sure I have everything that makes me happy or feel good. My laptop is the last item on my list. I'm about to pack it away when I decide that I want to check my email one more time before I leave. I've been hoping to hear some good news back from the counseling administration and from a lady that I sent the first two chapters of my novel to.

As soon as I open my inbox, two email notifications pop up. My heart jumps in my chest at the first email.

FROM: JENNA RAMEY
   To: Lilly Wade

LILLY,

. . .

I JUST GOT DONE READING THE CHAPTERS YOU SENT ME. AND I HAVE to say… I absolutely love them! I love how sensual you made the heroine seem, and how dark and dangerous you made the hero. I think you're definitely on the right path with the story, and you should really explore the hero's dark side. Trust me when I say that you have great potential as a writer. And I look forward to reading your next chapters. If they're good as the first two, you might have a bestseller on your hands!

LOVE,
  Jenna

A FEELING OF WARMTH FLOWS THROUGH MY CHEST AS I READ JENNA'S words. It feels good to get feedback on my work. I've always thought of myself as a crappy writer, and have had horrible confidence in my ability. To actually hear someone say that I have potential fills me with joy and almost brings me to tears. Even if she is just a friend who edits for a publishing company. Still, it means so much to me.

I READ JENNA'S WORDS OVER AND OVER, EACH TIME FEELING A LITTLE bit better, until my eyes fall to the next email and my joy dampens slightly.

FROM: ZACHERY WHITE
  To: Lilly Wade

LILLY.

I'M SORRY.

· · ·

ZACH

I STARE AT HIS WORDS, TRYING NOT TO FEEL ANGER AFTER GETTING such a lifting message about my writing. He's sorry? That's all he can say after everything I've tried to do for him? I take a moment, sucking in a deep calming breath, trying to look at the entire situation, rather than being consumed by my immediate feelings.

Zach is going somewhere where he'll be able to turn his life around. What he did before is in the past now. Getting mad over it won't help either of us. My eyes flicker across the one line on the screen again. I should just be relieved he's being given the opportunity at a second chance.

Rising from my seat, I shake off the uneasy feelings and close the laptop, putting it into my travel bag.

I leave the bag on the desk chair, as I go through the house and make sure that I haven't missed anything else.

A whole month away. Of giving myself to someone else. *All of me.*

Is it really worth doing this?

I heard about the auction. It would've paid me more than the amount Joseph offered. I'm fully aware of that. Maybe even three times the amount. Possibly more. I overheard a few of the girls talking about how much the virgins go for. But when I think about how anyone other than Joseph could have put in a higher bid, essentially taking me for their Slave, I don't regret it.

IT HAS TO BE HIM. I WANT IT TO BE JOSEPH WHO I GIVE MYSELF TO.

Shame burns my cheeks as I think about what I've done. I've sold myself to another human being. For money. I would have been with him in time, without this though. My heart clenches, and the nasty voice in the back of my head whispers, *does that make it any better though?*

I pick up the strap of the bag after zipping it closed, and hoist the heavy thing over my shoulder. The strap immediately digs in. I may have packed too much.

I'll never tell a soul what I've done. I'm ashamed, but this is about more than just me. This money is going to be used for a good cause.

I'm sorry.

I think of Zach's words in his email. I'm sorry, too.

I'll never tell anyone, but as I turn out the lights to my living room, I know I want Joseph. And nothing's going to stop me now.

CHAPTER 14

Joseph

*J*know that I fucked up the moment that Lilly walks through my front door. Her shoulders are hunched inward as I carry her duffel bags into the foyer, leaving them in the corner of the room.

Her vulnerability is intoxicating. I know it's taking a lot for her to do this, so I'll make today easy. The first few days I'll be gentle with her, and ease her into this lifestyle. I only have her for a month though, and I intend to take full advantage of our time together.

Although it's freezing outside, she wore a beautiful dress that ends above her knees. The hem brushes against her thighs as she walks in, taking off her tweed winter coat and hanging it over the crook of her arm. She shivers slightly as she walks in, holding onto the coat as if it's her anchor.

The chill from outside has made her cheeks a bright red, as well as the tip of her nose. The house is warm and inviting though, the sound of her heels echoing as she walks closer to the hall.

I close the door, my back to her as I imagine all the things I'm going to do to her. She's mine now.

I could bend her over the foyer table right now, I could take her with a bruising force from behind and fuck her like I've been dreaming of doing. I can practically hear her hips banging against the wooden edge of the table. I can see how the trinkets I've gathered from all the places I've traveled would rattle as I pounded her tight cunt, taking her virginity in a swift thrust.

I own her; I can do whatever the fuck I want with her.

I know it would turn her on. I know in the moment she would enjoy it. I would make sure of that. Strumming her clit while I positioned my hips against her ass, shoving my dick deep inside of her over and over again until she screamed out her orgasm.

I clear my throat and the thoughts from my head as I lock the door. The gentle click fills the room and makes her turn on her heels to face me. I ignore all the ways I could claim her as I walk to her, embracing her and planting a small kiss on her cheek.

"IT'S ALL RIGHT, MY FLOWER." I LOWER MY LIPS TO HERS, PRESSING them against her mouth gently.

She pulls away for a moment, pushing her small hand against my chest and breaking away. I don't like it. I don't like her pushing me away at all. That's not what she's here for. My heart races in my chest, and my body stiffens slightly. I'll allow it for the moment. But only until she's comfortable. Only until she fully realizes what this is between us.

"It's different here," she says, her voice small.

I stare at her for a moment, registering what she's said. Different? Looking to my left, I take in the open layout of my home. It's modern and dark. From where we're standing in the foyer, she's easily able to see the kitchen and den.

She focuses on the white marble fireplace on the back wall to the right. It's lined with large rectangles of black slate. Although the stone holds a cold feel to it, the warm coloring of the worn leather loveseat and chair, combined with the lush carpet balance out the room.

I watch her face as her eyes skim across the room, taking in the details. Her curiosity makes the corners of my lips kick up into a smile. She obviously approves.

My home is littered with two things: fireplaces, because I love the atmosphere created by the crackling of wood in the warm glow of a natural fire, and artifacts from the places I've traveled in the last two years. As soon as I could leave my family, I did. And I went as far as away as I could get.

Cigars are my favorite keepsake. There are several boxes, some antiques, holding cigars throughout my home. There are a plethora of maps as well. Mostly hand-drawn ones I've collected from the places I've traveled, mountains I've climbed, taverns I've explored. The other trinket I've collected a mass number of are weapons. A set of bow and arrows are showcased in the den. It's from ancient Greece, and one of my favorites. I never used it for fear of breaking it. Lilly's eyes widen when she catches sight of it. She blinks several times, as if doing so will make it disappear. My fingers itch to take the bow off the wall and let her hold it.

She noticeably swallows. I can practically hear her gulp. I know she's just now registering that she doesn't really *know* me. That she signed a contract handing her freedom over to me. And only now is she even beginning to learn who I really am. I don't like seeing her fear. Especially since she's only just gotten here.

"I think you'll feel better once we discuss things a little more in detail." I let my finger trail down her collarbone, down to her shoulder, pushing the fabric out of my way as I go. I only use my middle finger, my blunt nail scraping along her skin gently. Her eyes close, and her body relaxes under my touch. I've conditioned her to do that.

"For now, I'll allow you to be clothed." I talk softly, my words gentle and caressing. Calming her. "It'll be your first privilege that I'll take away. Do you understand?"

"Yes, Sir," she responds immediately. She's falling into character, so to speak. Remembering how we were inside of the dungeon of Club X. That's most likely what it was to her, *an act*, a character she was playing. But now it's real life. When she's done playing but realizes she can escape, that's when I'll see the real her. The piece that she's kept hidden from me while we played.

· · ·

"IF YOU DISOBEY ME AGAIN, THEN YOU'LL BE WHIPPED." HER HEAD falls back slightly at my words, her chest rising with a quickening breath. Again this turns her on; she's used to me giving her pleasure with the whippings. But there's no pleasure and punishment here. She has yet to go through a true punishment.

"Yes, Sir." I take her coat from the crook of her arm and set it on the foyer table behind me before returning back to her. She stands obediently, hands clasped in front of her, waiting for me to give her a command. This is the way she should have been from the start. Waiting and ready for me. That's how she'll always be in this house. I just need to train her. I step closer to her, standing in front of her but not touching. Her fingers twitch, but she stays still. "The third punishment is orgasm denial." I smirk at her as her eyes widen in surprise. "That's something you've yet to experience, isn't it?"

"Yes, Sir... May I ask a question?" She's hesitant and I can understand why, but I need her to know that she can always talk to me. There may be consequences if she speaks to me disrespectfully. But I always want to know what she has to say.

"While you're here you can speak freely. So long as you address me properly."

"How long?" I smile broadly at her question, holding back my laughter. My greedy little flower. My reaction makes her smile, her shoulders relaxing slightly.

"Are you already planning on getting into trouble?" I tease her, my middle finger now running up and down her throat.

"No, Sir." There's still the trace of a smile on her lips.

"Are you so certain that you're going to displease me?" I ask her, my finger pausing on her soft skin.

She takes a moment to swallow before answering again, "No, Sir."

"Your punishment will fit the crime. So the length of your denial depends on what you do."

I have to tell her about the cage. These punishments are for minimal offenses, if she does something out of character. But if she does something to intentionally upset me or disrespect me, then that's where she'll stay. I've seen the way she looks at the cages in the dungeon. The one I have for her is larger. There's curiosity behind her eyes, but it truly is a punishment. Both for her and for me. My hope is that I'll never have to use it, although I imagine with her curiosity she may ask me if she can go in, just to see what it's like. Just to tease me with her being unavailable.

"We have a lot to discuss." I splay my hand on her back, leading her away from the front door and farther into my house, her new home for the next month. "Come. Let me show you your room."

CHAPTER 15

Lilly

*L*uxury.

It's the only way I can describe my bedroom when I step inside with Joseph at my side, his eyes on my face, watching for my reaction.

I don't disappoint him. My jaw nearly drops to the floor as I survey the room, my breath catching in my throat.

An amused grin curls the corners of Joseph's lips up as he eyes my stunned look. He knows I'm floored by his impressive wealth, and he's enjoying every second of it. *Pure, unadulterated luxury.*

Seriously, I can hardly believe this will be my bedroom. The rest of the house is amazing and I can't wait to explore it all, but this... I shake my head. This is absolutely gorgeous.

I press a hand to my chest. This room is the stuff dreams are made of. It's large and spacious, contemporary, urban and chic, all in one. The walls are lined with an intricate high-gloss gray paisley wallpaper that literally takes my breath away, and soft lush white carpet that looks and feels like a mink fur coat. I kick my heels off as I let it all sink in.

As I move across the floor, my feet are enveloped by the soft carpet, and a soft sigh escapes my lips at the caress of it against my skin. It feels so good to walk on it. I've never felt anything like it. A large king-size bed with a canopy lies at the back wall, the soft white gossamer curtains billowing out from the gentle air circulating around the room. Above it is a tray ceiling painted a pale blue with a diamond chandelier in the very center.

Directly across from the bed lies an exquisitely shaped white hearth over a grey marble fireplace, with a large white recliner sitting in front of it, adorned with pale blue throw pillows.

I spin around, taking in everything from the crown molding, to the expensive finish of every piece of architecture in the room. With all the white, it really looks like a place of purity. Sweet innocence.

Like my virginity.

I try to push the unwanted thought away, not wanting to think about what the cost of the contract entails.

Then I see them. *The toys.* I shake my head. I must be imagining things.

I close my eyes, and then pop them open. *Nope.* Still there. I don't know how I didn't see them before, but now that I have, I can't *unsee* them.

They're all the color of the room, white and grey, so I guess they blended into the background. But not now. Now, they're all I see.

There are white whips hanging off the end of the bed frame, white riding crops on the wall along with large foreign objects that make me shudder at the thought of what they're used for. I start to walk to them, my hand at my throat, and as I do, I hear and feel Joseph walking behind me. I can hardly breathe. I stop in my tracks, lowering my head and just trying to breathe. This is why I'm here.

I lift my eyes and nearly laugh.

There's even a white cage in the corner of the room and a white bench with white leather straps.

I stare in disbelief, wondering how my eyes could have deceived me so. Here I am, enraptured in the upscale beauty of the room, when it's a goddamn torture chamber! A very nice, plush comfortable-looking one, but a torture chamber nonetheless.

Anxiety twists my stomach as I stare at these objects, knowing what they'll be used for. *How the hell did I get myself into this?*

I look over at Joseph and see his eyes on me. He hasn't said a word since we've walked into the room, content on watching my every move and expression as if trying to read my mind.

I part my lips to ask something, but then close them, my legs feeling weak. I don't trust myself to speak yet.

To hide my anxiety, I walk over to the closet and open it. It's pitch dark inside, and I have to search around for the light switch.

Once again, I have to keep my jaw off the floor.

Fuck. The closet is huge. It has its own island, and tons and tons of space. It's the kind of closet that every girl dreams about. With a ton of rack space to dump the latest trendy pumps on. But I'm surprised to see it mostly stuffed with feminine clothing; corsets, silk and lace lingerie. It looks like they're all my size, too.

After a moment, I turn off the light and leave the closet, walking back into the bedroom, feeling stunned.

Joseph is standing there where I left him, his eyes on me. My heart skips a beat at the hunger I see in them. A growing sense of dread rises from the pit of my stomach. I know what that look means. And I know what I haven't told him.

"THIS IS BEAUTIFUL," I SAY QUIETLY, TRYING TO KEEP MY VOICE steady, not wanting to betray the anxiety twisting my stomach.

An amused twinkle glints in his eyes. "I thought you might like it," he murmurs, his voice husky and confident.

"I don't think I've ever stayed in such a nice room before," I say, and then jokingly add, "Minus the whips, chains and cage of course."

Joseph huffs out an amused chuckle. "Those will have no effect on how well you sleep in that bed. You will find it quite soft, actually." For the first time, he takes his eyes off my face, casting a quick glance over to the corner of the room where the white cage is. "But if you disobey me…" his voice trails off, but I know what he means. It's almost like he's itching to see me in the cage.

I slightly shudder, my nipples pebbling. A part of me thinks I would like the cage. I'm turned on by it. But I think I would only enjoy it for a little while--an hour, maybe two, but definitely not for anything longer than that. The thought of being in it for more than several hours absolutely terrifies me. I clasp my hands in front of my dress, swinging my shoulders back and forth, trying to shake the nervousness that keeps running through my limbs.

Joseph steps forward, sensing my emotions, stopping a few feet from me. He reaches out and places a hand on my shoulder, halting my rocking. I almost groan at his touch, feeling small shocks where his skin touches mine.

Fuck, what this man does to me.

Up close, I'm enveloped by his masculine scent and it calms me, if only slightly. *Jesus*, I love how he smells.

"What's wrong, flower?" he asks me with concern.

I look into his eyes, and my heart flips. The hunger is still there, and it's enough to make my skin prick, my cheeks burning red. I know that it won't be long before that hunger will demand to be sated. I just need to... I swallow thickly. I need to tell him. I know it's going to happen soon.

"Can tonight be different?" I blurt out, my heart skipping a beat and then starting to race.

Joseph's eyes never leave my face. "Can what be different?" he asks, and his voice sounds so deep and low.

My forehead crinkles as I frown. Is he toying with me? He has to know what I mean with the way he's been looking at me since I've got here and that giant bulge in his pants that he's done little to hide.

My cheeks still burning, I gesture at the king-size luxurious bed. "Uh, you know."

A grin plays across his chiseled jawline. "No, in fact I don't."

Okay. Now I know he's toying with me.

I shake my head. "I just always thought... it's silly... but I've always been..." I search for a way to say what I want without giving myself away. "I'd like this to be outside our contract? I just... can we just pretend I'm not your Slave for the first time?"

Joseph shakes his head firmly, and my heart falls into my stomach. "I don't pretend, Lilly."

I search his face for some sign of softening, but his jaw is firm. I don't think I'll convince him. My heart races in my chest. All the ways I've imagined him fucking me have been ruthless. But right now, I don't want that.

"Can you be gentle at first?" I ask hopefully. "Just for tonight."

I see amusement flash in his eyes, but his expression remains flat. "That's not in my nature."

IT'S HARD TO KEEP MY FACE STEADY AND MY KNEES FROM SHAKING AS I look at him. I don't know what I should do.

I've never had sex before, but now I'm supposed to be able to endure a man his size, who's going to fuck me like a wild animal?

Holy fuck.

I'm just as scared as I am turned on.

More than that, I'm uncertain. I'm about to give away my virginity to a man I've hardly known for more than a few days. The realization nearly makes my head spin.

What the fuck is wrong with me?

My next words come out small and tiny sounding. "Is it going to hurt?"

God, I sound so fucking naive, but I can't help myself. I'm terrified.

Joseph reaches out, gently cupping my cheek. "The only pain I give you will be followed by pleasure."

Oh God. Yes.

I close my eyes, shuddering, hoping to find the strength to endure what's to come. I hear him as he takes a step closer, pushing me with him until the back of my knees hit the bed.

You could always end this, says that annoying voice. *You could just walk away right now.*

I don't get to answer it.

I feel Joseph move closer, invading my private space and pressing his hard body up against me. I want him. I've never known anything else to be as true as that single fact.

Fuck. I feel his hard cock pressing up against my hip.

And *damn*. It feels *SO* big. I take an unsteady breath. It's happening.

His hot lips suddenly press against mine, sending electricity shooting through every one of my nerve endings. I tilt my head back, my lips parting in a sigh, my nipples hardening and my pussy heating with need. The sensation is like nothing I've ever felt, and I feel like I'm being turned into pure liquid honey, ready to melt into him.

"You want me, Lilly?" Joseph stops kissing me to murmur, his hot breath scorching my neck.

I groan, wanting his lips back on me, not wanting the sensation to end. "Yes, Sir," I moan. "Please, Sir."

Even though his lips are at my neck, I can feel his grin, along with his throbbing cock pressing insistently against my pussy.

"Good girl," he whispers. I swallow thickly as he unzips the back of my dress slowly. I can hardly breathe as his hot breath sends chills down my body, his fingers brushing against my shoulders as he pushes my dress down my waist and over my ass. It falls into a pool at my feet.

His fingers tickle around my hips. I knew better than to wear undergarments. I only packed a few for the entire month, although I'm not sure he'll ever let me wear them.

He leaves an open-mouth kiss on the front of my throat, humming with satisfaction as his fingers move to my pussy. I stand still, waiting for any direction he's willing to give me. I can hear the words at the tip of my tongue, begging for me to say them. *Please be gentle with me. I've never done this before.* But instead I say nothing as he grabs my hips and lifts me onto the bed.

A startled gasp is ripped from my throat as my back hits the mattress. My heart races in my chest, beating uncontrollably. I glance up to see him unbuttoning his top button and pulling his dress shirt over his head. His muscles ripple in the soft light.

Holy fuck.

I can't take my eyes off of him as his deft fingers unbuckle his belt, and then the button of his pants. He slowly unzips the slacks, pushing them to the floor and stepping out of them along with his boxers. The only thing I can hear is my hammering heart. I lie as still as I can on top of the bedding. I need to tell him I'm a virgin. But I can't, the words refuse to come out.

He crawls onto the bed and hovers over me. His bulky shoulders make him look even more intimidating than usual. The look in his eyes freezes my body. Possession. Power radiates from his very being. He owns me. It's never been more clear to me that in this very moment. He. Owns. Me.

"Spread your legs for me." His voice is soft as he commands me, and then he gently kisses the edge of my jaw, trailing kisses toward my ear and down my neck. I do as he says, spreading my legs as far as I can. He moves between my thighs, his fingers cupping my pussy once again.

I'm soaking wet, shamelessly soaked for him.

He lays his body so close to mine. Only centimeters away. His forearm to the right of my head braces him as he strokes his cock, and gently pushes the head through my folds.

Tell him! I scream inside my head.

My body heats, and begs me to move. I don't. I lie perfectly still, waiting for him to take from me one thing I can never get back. I've committed to it. Fuck, I hope he can't tell.

"Are you ready for me, Lilly?" he asks with a different tone in his voice. Something I don't recognize. I nod my head quickly, swallowing the lump in my throat. "Are you ready to give me your virginity?" Shock paralyzes me for a moment. My mouth opens and closes, nothing coming out. He nuzzles his nose into the crook of my neck, giving me a moment to realize what he's said. I still can't respond when he kisses me sweetly on the lips. My eyes refuse to close.

"Tell me," he says, then kisses me again before moving away from me slightly to rest his thumb on my bottom lip. "You're ready for me?" he asks me, his eyes moving from my lips to mine. I can't deny the want reflected back at me. The pure desire. I nod my head once and with that simple response, the powerful man towering above me closes his eyes and groans as though I'm torturing him.

"Answer me," he says simply, his eyes still closed as his dick presses into my entrance.

"Yes, Sir." At my answer, he slams into me with a forceful thrust that makes my back bow and my neck arch, pushing my head into the mattress. I instinctively reach for him, my nails digging into his back. A silent scream falls from my lips. It feels like a pinch. A hard fucking pinch, followed by stinging pain.

He stays buried deep inside of me, my tight walls refusing to adjust to his thick girth. It hurts! The stinging pain refuses to dim as he stretches me. My eyes close tight, and my forehead pinches, willing the pain away.

He shushes me in the crook of my neck. His hand gently strokes the curve of my waist as he stays deep inside of me. I want to writhe under him and move away, but he holds me still, planting soft kisses down my neck to my collarbone and then back up my throat. Tears prick my eyes; I didn't think it would hurt like this. My heart isn't even moving. My body is so still, so paralyzed with the shocking pain. Joseph puts his hand between us and rubs my clit as he kisses me.

The sensation quickly morphs into something else. My body relaxes slowly and then tightens as my pussy heats, and tingling stirs in the pit of my stomach. I finally swallow, feeling my muscles ease and the pleasure increasing as the pressure builds.

"Does that feel good, my flower?" Joseph asks me in a low voice. I can only moan an answer at first. His hand moves from my clit as he pulls out of me slightly before pushing all the way back in. Fuck! My legs wrap around his waist, ankles crossing and digging into his ass. When he moves, oh God, when he moves, my sensitive nipples rub against his chest. I need more.

"Yes," I answer in a mere whisper as he pumps his hips again. And then again. Each time he brushes against my clit. The sensation becomes nearly overwhelming. Oh fuck yes. This is what I thought it'd be like. My body heats with a cold sweat breaking out along my skin. It's too much. I can't... I can't.

His fingers wrap around my hip, holding me down as his pace quickens. My nipples harden as goosebumps form over my entire body as a cold sweat breaks out, traveling along every inch of my skin. My nerve endings are on high alert. My forehead pinches as I realize I'm about to cum. My body slams into the bed, Joseph's hard thrusts pushing me higher and higher. I'm so close. I force the words from my lips, "May I-" He cuts me off before I'm able to finish.

"Cum freely," Sir says in a voice I've never heard, one laced with desperation, his speed increasing as he races for his own release.

The realization of what I do to him is my undoing. I make him lose control. I throw my head back, the intense sensation running through my body in waves. The first is slow, starting from my stomach and working its way out to each of my limbs, tingling the tips of my fingers.

Before the first is even finished, the next comes crashing through my body and as I feel him cum deep inside of me, the final wave forces me to call out his name, "Joseph!"

My body shakes and trembles. My heart is pounding so loudly I swear he can hear it.

As I try to catch my breath, Joseph slips out of me slowly, hushing me when I wince. I open my eyes to see his shining back at me.

He knew. My breathing comes in slower as he plants a kiss on my lips. I can't close my eyes though.

He knew.

CHAPTER 16

Joseph

*I*t's been a long time since I felt the warmth of a woman in my bed. It's been years. A soft sigh gently spills from Lilly's lips as she nestles into my arm. Her left leg is propped up on top of mine, and every little movement is making my dick even harder.

I own her. I could take her again right now if I wanted. But the sight of her sleeping so soundly is something I never thought I'd want to see as much as I do.

Her hair is a tangled, messy halo of golden locks. Her face is partially buried in the comforter that she has up around her neck. The warmth gives her skin a slight blush. I've seen her naked so many times. Last night I felt her raw, not only in the way I took her, but also in her emotions when she gave me something she can never have back. After I cleaned us up, I held her as a lover should, and I was happy to give her that. She fell asleep in my arms, and that's where she's stayed.

She's at peace and relaxed. It's an odd thing to me, the feelings washing over me as I look at her, something I didn't expect.

"Lilly," I say her name in an even cadence, and her breathing comes to a halt as she readjusts in her sleep, still not waking. I move my arm out from under her, the air feeling cool without her warmth.

Her head falls to the mattress without my support. She gasps, opening her sleepy eyes and bracing herself with both hands on the mattress. I give her a minute to wake and to recognize where she is. The moment she sees me, her pupils dilate with both recognition and desire.

I sit up on my knees, shoving my silk pajama pants down along with my boxers so my cock springs free. My little flower is such a naughty girl. She licks her lips staring at my cock, but she's as still as can be on the mattress as she waits obediently for my command. Such a good girl.

"What are you?" I ask her as I stroke myself from end to end, spreading the moisture over the head of my dick.

She breathes her answer, "Yours." Fuck, hearing her lust-filled voice admitting my claim to her with such pride makes me want her that much more. I reach down, grabbing her by the hair at her nape, fisting it and bringing her lips to my dick.

"Damn right you are," I tell her as her lips slide down my cock and my head brushes against the back of her throat. Fuck! She feels too good. It takes everything in me not to groan out loud and shove deeper down her throat. Although I have a firm grip on her, controlling her if I need to, I let her move at her own pace. She nearly gags on my cock, her wide eyes looking apologetic. I don't give a fuck. Her mouth feels like fucking heaven.

I buck my hips once, feeling her throat stretch around my cock. She takes it, her hands almost reaching up to grip me, but she quickly puts them back down, gripping her thighs. Her eyes water as I pump my hips, forcing her to take more, and holding myself at the back of her throat. Only for a moment, right before pulling out and giving her a moment to catch her breath.

She breathes in deep, keeping her mouth open and ready for more. Fuck, she's too good to be true.

She moans around my dick, loving how I'm using her. She gets on all fours, hollowing her cheeks as she sucks my length, eager to take more. Her tongue massages the underside of my dick and her throat closes around my head as she goes as far as she can, her nose almost reaching the coarse pubic hair. Again she moans and her lips push down, stroking my length as she blows me. She moves her lips all the way to the ridge of the head of my cock. It sends tingles down my spine, my toes curl and I nearly cum just from that sensation.

The tip of her tongue dips into the slit, licking up the small bit of precum that leaked out. She moves her hand up to stroke my dick, and that's what I've been waiting for.

Thank fuck she did it before I came. I'm quick to grab her wrists before she can touch me. I pull out of her mouth, pushing her backward and pinning her down on the mattress. Her eyes flash with fear as I hold her down, staring at her with narrowed eyes.

"Did I tell you that you could touch me?" I ask her, my head tilted. A spark of knowing darts across her blue eyes as she realizes what she's done.

"I'm sorry, Sir," she says as her hips tilt and her upper thighs clench. "I had no right." She gives in so easily, accepting what she's done. My fingers dig into her hip before loosening my hold on her and letting go of her wrist.

"Mistakes will be made," I tell her. "I'll allow you one warning for now." She stares at me, her breath barely coming in as she waits for her punishment.

I back away from her and her lips part to protest me leaving her, her eyes flashing with worry.

I've kept myself from her for so long, refusing to let her please me. And although it wasn't a punishment then, I'm sure she saw it as just that. But I have no intention of not taking from her every fucking day that she's here. She'll learn that soon enough.

"Get on your hands and knees," I tell her as I sit on my knees, ready to feel her tight cunt wrapped around me again.

She's quick to get into position, turning her body so her ass is the closest thing to me. I grip her hips nearly violently in a bruising hold and pull her quickly toward me, reveling in the sweet gasp that comes from her lips. She curves her back like a good girl. She's trying, I know she is. She's desperate to please me. I take her hair in both of my hands before wrapping it around my wrist, gripping and pulling her hair back slightly.

My fingers play at her wet pussy lips as I look over her body in complete submission to me. "You fucking love this, don't you?"

With her neck arched, her voice comes out in a higher pitch, "Yes, Sir." I nearly slammed myself into her tight cunt to the hilt without waiting for her response, but I stop before doing so after hearing those sweet words. But I already know that I can't.

She's swollen from last night. I spread her lips and see she's red. I'd love to ride her hard and fast, to give her the brutal fuck she truly desires. But instead I ease in slowly.

She feels so good, and I knew she'd feel just like this. Somehow I knew.

I slowly slip deep inside of her, letting her hair relax around my wrist and losing my grip on her. Taking her hips in both of my hands, I bend forward and kiss her neck. Her eyes are closed tight, and her mouth is pressed into a small frown. I know she hurts. My hand slips between her legs to rub her clit. I pull back on her clit slightly, exposing the raw sensitive side and press my middle finger down, rubbing merciless circles against her. Her eyes pop open as her mouth forms a perfect "O".

I stay buried to the hilt until her face softens to show more pleasure than pain. Her pussy strangles my cock as I move deep, sliding in and out of her. My fingers are wrapped around her hips and my stomach presses against her back as I bite down, nipping on her earlobe and making her gasp before I pull nearly all the way back and then slam into her. Her hands slip on the mattress, and she falls forward.

With her small body under mine, I buck my hips over and over. I brace my heavy body with one forearm, my other hand holding her hip and keeping her angled just how I want as she fights under me to control herself. I piston my hips, loving how her pussy spasms around my cock and the sounds of her wet cunt being so brutally fucked filling my ears.

Her cheek presses against the mattress with each blow I give her. Her eyes shut tight, and her teeth sink into her bottom lip. She's holding back her screams of pleasure, her hands fisting the sheet beneath us.

"Let me hear you," I tell her in a strong voice I don't recognize in this moment. I'm so lost in her touch. My heart beats fitfully, and my body heats then freezes with an intense pleasure that radiates outward. I'm so close to losing it. But I want her with me every step of the way.

Her mouth opens instantly, obeying me as I continue my ruthless pace. She screams out my name over and over, not addressing me as Sir but instead calling me Joseph. I wasn't expecting it, just like I wasn't last night, but my name on her lips sends me over the edge. I desperately rub at her clit as thick streams of cum fill her tight pussy.

Her small body shakes under me as her own release finds her. Thank fuck!

My mouth parts as I take in a sharp breath, loving the way her tight cunt strangles my dick.

I brace myself with my forearm, wiping the sweat off my forehead and gently stroking her side, until her body stops trembling and her breathing finally steadies.

My own breathing is coming in heavy as I sit up on my knees. Her small body is lying limp on the bed, her shoulders rising and falling with heavy breaths. Her eyes are wide open, darting from me, back to the bed as she stays still. Her body shivers uncontrollably, but I'm not sure if it's from a chill or from the intense pleasure of her orgasm. As I climb off the bed I grab the edge of the comforter and bring it up to her shoulders.

"Don't go back to sleep now, my flower." I kiss her forehead, loving how she closes her eyes and trembles beneath my comforting touch just as much as she did from the ruthless way I fucked her. I whisper against the shell of her ear, "We're just getting started."

CHAPTER 17

Lilly

I lie back against the mattress, my chest heaving, my pulse racing as I look up into his eyes. God, he's so handsome. I could look at his face all day. He leans in close, his hard body pressing up against my soft skin. Down below, I can feel his hardness pressing up against my stomach. I can feel it throbbing, pulsating along with my heartbeat as he brings his lips against my neck.

A soft sigh escapes my lips as I arch my back against the bed, pressing my body into him.

I want him.

I need him.

I'm just not sure if I'm ready.

He pulls back as if sensing my anxiety, his deep brown eyes searching my face.

"Do you trust me?" he asks softly, his breathing heavy.

I stare back into his concerned gaze, not sure what to say. Do I trust him? I've only known him for a few weeks, and while I am infatuated with him, I'm not sure if I trust him.

At the same time, he's treated me better than anyone else has ever treated me. He's shown more concern about my well-being than anyone ever has. Most of all, I'm sure he's willing to wait until I'm ready.

But I'm not going to make him wait.

Not today.

"Yes," I breathe, my heart in my voice. "I trust you."

His handsome face splits into a grin, his eyes sparkling with happiness. "Good."

As he comes in closer, bringing his lips close to mine, I relax my body and prepare to surrender myself wholly to him...

Smack!

The memory of being spanked jolts me out of the book I'm working on and I pull my fingers back from the keys of my laptop, my breathing ragged. I can still feel the sting of the paddle against my ass. Joseph disciplined me for talking back to him this morning.

At the time, I thought I was being myself and it was all just harmless banter. He even smiled as I was doing it. He played along. My heart warms at the memory.

But I was still *punished.*

Harshly.

My eyes fall down to my naked legs and I see the goosebumps covering them, the faint red marks my disobedience has earned me. I squeeze my thighs together, feeling my clit pulse, turned on by the sight.

I've lost my clothing privileges, all because I sat incorrectly at the table. Joseph wants me seated with my legs spread if I'm in a chair. His rules are simple and easy, but unnatural. I purse my lips. These punishments aren't really fair. But at the same time, I welcome them. Being bad has never felt so good.

They're erotic, sensual even, and they bring back memories of being whipped in the dungeon.

My nipples pebble, and my pussy clenches around cool air as I think about these *punishments.*

It's been a crazy last few days, and I still can't believe I gave myself to him. Or that he *knew* about my virginity. My fingers tap on the keyboard and I look over my shoulder and out to the hall, shifting on my bed with my laptop balanced on my thighs.

I was concerned I'd regret giving myself to him. But with everything I'm feeling, regret isn't even on the radar. Even when I unknowingly disobey him.

He's taught me so many things in such a short amount of time, gave me pleasure that I'd never dreamt possible. The way he makes me feel, taking my body, ravaging it, devouring it. *Owning it.*

I shake my head, at a loss for words.

I love it.

I love both sides of Joseph. The nice and caring side, and the dominant side. Although, he's been showing the dominant side more these past few days. It seems like he's controlling everything I do or say now. Just this morning he had clothes laid out for me that he wanted me to wear, along with the oils that he wants me to put in my hair. I love the smell of them actually.

And strangely enough, I want more of this. More of his control.

More of him.

Thinking about him makes me wonder what he's doing.

Crawling off the bed, I leave my laptop and go search through the house for him.

I look through several of the rooms, including his bedroom before I find him in his study. He's sitting at his desk, his head down as he writes in a notebook. It looks worn and I tilt my head, narrowing my eyes as I notice the binding is leather. His brow is furrowed; he's clearly focused on whatever he's writing.

I bite my lower lip as I look at him, my heart racing as my hand stills on the doorframe. He looks so gorgeous sitting there in slacks and a white dress shirt opened at the chest. I don't know if I should disturb him. He did tell me that I have permission to come to him at all times, but he looks busy and I don't even remember why I came to find him. I almost turn and leave, twisting on my back heel, but he looks up, freezing me in place.

I step fully into the doorway, clasping my hands out in front of me like he taught me to do, and then I wait patiently.

I don't have to wait long.

"Yes?" he asks in a low voice, slowly setting the pen down. My heart thump, thump, thumps.

Opening a drawer off to the side, he places the notebook into the drawer and then closes it, his eyes on me the entire time.

A feeling of suspicion washes over me at his actions. What was he writing?

Joseph clears his throat and says, "Lilly?"

I stare at him for a moment, noticing for the first time that he looks stressed; something's bothering him.

He's sitting in his chair, tense as can be, worry lines etched in his forehead. I've never seen him like this.

I lick my lips, hesitating to respond. I don't want to say anything now. I'm not here for anything important anyway. I was just coming to play around and do something to get punished, but it all seems so trivial now.

Joseph's going through something.

It's insensitive of me to expect him to stop what he's doing to indulge me. My fingers twist around one another. A strange sense of loneliness washes through me.

I think back to the hero that I'm writing about, with his dark hair and dark eyes, and how much he reminds me of Joseph.

"Flower," he growls warningly, his deep voice pricking my skin.

Shit. I have to say something now.

"I was hoping I could please you, Sir," I say softly. The moment the words leave my lips, I regret them. Looking at him, I know that he's not in the mood for playing.

His pause hurts almost as much as his next words. "Not right now."

I was expecting it, but it still hurts, a heavy weight settling on my chest. I try to turn away quickly before my face crumples into a frown, intent on running back to my room and closing the door behind me. I don't make it two steps before he calls me back to him.

"Come here," he commands me. "Now."

I bite my lower lip, holding back tears, and turn on my heel and make my way over to his desk to stand beside him. I don't know why I'm so emotional. But something about this moment is off.

He looks up at me, a sadness in his eyes that tugs at my heart-strings. "Kneel," he commands.

I obey his command immediately, sinking to my knees beside him. Swallowing, I look up at him, not sure if he's going to punish me, scold me, or both.

I startle when he reaches out and pets my hair softly. "You've been a good girl," he tells me. "You can put your clothes back on if you'd like."

My heart drops in my chest. I don't want to put my clothes back on. I want him to take me. *Punish me.* Anything.

"Okay," I say, rising to my feet, my throat closing. I try to hide my displeasure, but I can't keep the frown off of my face. I wish I could just disappear.

Anger sparks in Joseph's eyes. "I didn't tell you to get up," he growls, his deep voice low and dangerous.

My heart skips a beat and then starts racing, excitement coursing through my limbs. Maybe he will punish me after all.

I cross my arms over my breasts and try to think of something smart to say. But before I can say a word, he jumps up to his feet and grabs me by the wrist.

"I can see exactly what you're doing," he says in a calm, controlled voice. "I don't want you to deliberately disappoint me, do you understand?"

I stare into his eyes, my heart pounding. There's anger there, but a different kind. One that isn't attached to sexual emotion. I hate it. I hate that he's making me feel this way, like I've done something so horrible to turn him off.

"I wasn't trying to do anything-" I begin.

"Don't lie to me, Lilly," he growls, cutting me off. My heart clenches. I don't like this. I want to go back in time five minutes and never have stepped in here.

I square my shoulders, and rather than tell him how I'm feeling, how I'm craving his punishment in the pleasure that he gives me, and how I hate that he's in whatever mood he's in right now, I snap, "I don't know what you're talking about."

His grip tightens on my wrist, his eyes narrowing. I can tell he's pissed off that I won't tell him the truth. But fuck him. I don't have to give in to him when he doesn't give in to me.

His next words are cold and harsh. "Stop denying it."

Anger tightens my chest at his threat. All I wanted was to have a little playful fun, get each other off. It's not my fault that I'm begging for sex. He did this to me. He made me want it. He made me need it.

Need him.

Even now, I'm breathless with desire as he stares at me angrily, his lower jaw bulging out from being clenched tightly. But he doesn't want me right now. And that pisses me the fuck off.

Too angry to speak, I raise my chin in defiance, letting him know that I'm not going to do what he wants. He can fucking punish me.

That's when something inside of him seems to snap and he pulls me into him with great force, causing me to cry out in shock.

Next thing I know, his powerful fingers are wrapped around my chin, forcing me to look into his eyes. My blood turns to ice as I look into them, and for the first time that I've been with him, I feel very real fear.

There's darkness there. A cold emptiness that makes a chill shoot down my spine.

I don't know this man. Or what he's truly capable of.

And that terrifies me.

The next thing he says frightens me even more, his voice low and very dangerous sounding.

"Go to your cage."

CHAPTER 18

Joseph

She thinks she knows everything, and I've been pushing her to find her boundaries. To find that breaking point where she'll realize she isn't getting what she wants. So far, she's wanted to obey me. And every command she's met head-on. The perfect slave.

I knew at some point she'd break. I knew I'd ask too much of her. I imagined it would be something much more than simply not telling me that she's deliberately disobeying me. She's always had a problem expressing herself though, so I shouldn't be as shocked as I am.

I can read her so easily. I know she was disappointed. But this relationship isn't me being available to her. It's her being available to me. I'm restless in the leather armchair in the living room, her laptop on my knees as I read through the scene she's been writing. I've given her permission to write every day. When she feels the inspiration, she can do so. I huff a humorless laugh. I've given her permission to do whatever the fuck she'd like when my dick isn't in her. Maybe that was my first mistake. It's my fault she's in the cage.

I take a small sip of the whiskey before sitting the glass back down on the end table.

I scroll through her scene, reading about the collar the hero has given the heroine. She's romanticized everything. Her perception of what this lifestyle is, is missing an important aspect. The one where I have control.

This is why I didn't want a Submissive. My fingers tap on the short glass in my hand before bringing it to my lips again. I didn't anticipate that the boundary that would send her to the cage would be refusing to tell me the truth.

I thought better of her than that. Of everything I've asked her to do, that seems to be the least difficult. But maybe she doesn't want to believe it herself.

My eyes read over the next scene she's written, the hero of her book taking the virginity of the heroine. It's not difficult to see that it was inspired by how I took her. This hero kisses her sweetly, talks to her gently. He *makes love* to her.

This man is nothing like me. The stark contrast reminds me of where I came from.

I REMEMBER THE FIRST TIME I SAW MY FATHER KISS MY MOTHER. SHE was always quiet. Always in the background and never allowed to be around us. I didn't quite understand it. She wasn't allowed to interfere, that's what my father told us.

She approached him, her eyes wide with worry as she talked in quiet whispers, pleading with him for something. Her eyes kept darting toward us as we sat on the floor of the living room, cleaning the guns.

My father was rough with her. I watched as he grabbed the back of her hair so tightly he ripped some out. He kissed her hard on the lips, smearing her lipstick across her face before throwing her down on the ground. I remember how I jumped up, how my heart raced in my chest. I knew how hard my father hit, all too well. She landed hard, wincing with pain as she braced herself. But the look on her face changed when she saw me watching, slowly walking toward them. She shook her head, her eyes warning me to stay away.

That was what we had as an example. It sickened me. I loved my mother, and I couldn't watch as my father hit her. Day in and day out, she became an outlet for his anger. As my mother whimpered on the floor, I looked back to my brother. Wanting to make sure he was all right. We were only children. But the look in his eyes sickened me. It still does. The smile on his face showed what kind of a man he would be. If you can even call that a man.

That's the day I realized that my father was a sick fuck, and the cold dark look was echoed in my brother's eyes.

I DOWN THE WHISKEY AND CLOSE THE LAPTOP AT THE UNPLEASANT memory, setting it on the ottoman and rising from my seat. I ignore the fact that I feel like an asshole. I'm fully aware that she's under a different impression of what this is. She shouldn't be. It's my fault, and I need to fix this.

I look at the clock and see it's been an hour. The time has passed by slowly; tick-tock, tick-tock. I wanted to go to her every minute that she's been in there, but she needs to learn she can't top from the bottom. I'm the one with control, and she won't force my hand to get what she wants.

All the punishment she's received up to this moment has been for conditioning. The punishment was to help her learn how to please me. Although there's pain, it's always been accompanied by far more pleasure. She takes a simple punishment, and then she's rewarded for accepting it.

Not this time.

Hopefully this will be the last time. But I doubt it will be. There is a ferocity in her. A strength that she doesn't recognize. She may not know how courageous she is, but when most people see me, they cower. She was drawn to my power. That in and of itself shows courage.

My blood rushes in my ears, and my body heats as I move to her room. I open the door slowly, peeking in to see her curled in a ball on the floor of the cage. The cage itself is large enough for her to stand. I imagined her in the corner with her knees tucked under her chin, her arms wrapped around her legs.

And that's just how she is.

She peeks up over her knees as I close the door.

Her eyes are red-rimmed. She's been crying. Seeing her like this hurts me.

"Are you ready to behave?" I ask her, slowly walking toward the corner of the room. The cage door is slightly ajar; I didn't lock it, but I know she didn't leave it. It's not in her nature.

She can leave if she wants. At any time, she could go and break the contract. But she doesn't truly want to leave. She wants to fight me; she wants me to earn her submission.

And I fucking love the challenge.

This part of it though, I'm not sure I want to do again. I'd rather fuck her into submission.

I crouch in front of the cage, opening the door all the way. She watches me with wide eyes. When the door creaks open, her body stiffens as she says, "I didn't unlock it." I stare back at her as she continues, her voice soft. "I think you forgot to lock it, Sir."

"Did you leave?" I ask as I sit on the floor with my legs crossed. I already know she didn't. She shakes her head and whispers, "No."

"I didn't forget anything, my flower." I pat my lap, waiting for her to crawl out to me. "I'll never lock you in here. It's in our contract."

She seems hesitant for a moment, her movements stuttering.

"You did read what you signed, didn't you?" My voice comes out playful. I know she read every word more than once. I know she takes it seriously. Her lips show the trace of a smile, but it quickly disappears as she wipes away the tears under her eyes.

"Yes, Sir," she answers beneath her breath as she crawls out. She doesn't hesitate to come to me, nestling herself in my lap and resting her cheek against my chest. I comfort her, rubbing her back with firm strokes.

"You know I had to punish you, don't you?" I ask her.

She nods her head against my chest as her fingers intertwine nervously. "I do." She clears her throat and says, "I'm sorry, Sir, I shouldn't have lied to you. I shouldn't have tried to push you."

I kiss her hair, petting her as she apologizes. I hate this. It's something I knew that was going to happen, but I didn't expect my reaction. Or hers.

"I-" I clear my throat and shuffle her in my lap. I don't mind that she came to me. I'm dealing with my fuckface of a brother. He wants the money back. The money they planted on me to set me up. He's trying to get me back under the *familia's* thumb. It's not going to happen. "I will attend to you when I can. But sometimes you have to wait."

Lilly nods her head diligently.

I hook my finger under her chin, and look her in the eyes as I tell her, "Trust me, I would have much rather been spending time with you."

I kiss her, the taste of her tears touching the tip of my tongue as she gives into me, parting her lips. Her eyes are still glassed over with unshed tears. I brush my thumb along her cheek, and kiss her again. I say the only words I know that will make her smile again.

I brush my nose against hers and say, "I think you need to be punished, my flower."

I KNOT THE ROPE AT HER WRISTS, TYING THEM TIGHTER. HER LIPS PART, gifting me that beautiful sound.

Testing the give of the rope, I pull slightly, her small body falling forward. She's on her ass on the floor. Naked and waiting for me to command her.

I'm running out of these stupid rules. It's not about training her anymore, it's about pushing her limits and simply enjoying each other's touch.

I PULL HER CLOSER TO ME, HER ARMS BENDING AS MY LIPS BRUSH against hers. My heart seems to slow when I open my eyes and find her pale blue gaze shining back at me. There's a look there I should fear. Something that tells me I should end this. But I don't want to. I refuse to.

CHAPTER 19

Lilly

I let out a groan, rubbing soothing circles on my right ass cheek as I stop in the hallway outside of Joseph's room.

I'm sore all over. From being used. Deliciously used. But I need more of whatever it is he rubs on my ass after he's done spanking me.

Over the past several days, Joseph's given me nothing but sessions of rough, pleasurable sex. At this point, I can't tell if I'm aching from one of his spankings or his thick cock. I smile at the memory of this morning. No doubt the spanking when it comes to my ass.

It's a good problem to have. And I could definitely learn to love it. I just wish I didn't feel it right now. It's getting in the way of my snooping. A mischievous grin slips into place. I know I'm being a bit bad, but technically there's no rule against it.

For the past hour, I've been looking around the house, trying to figure out what Joseph's hiding. I *know* he's hiding something. A part of me is scared to find out. And the other part of me is hoping that I'm just being paranoid. I bite down on the inside of my cheek.

He won't tell me about his past. Or whatever the hell makes him hide away in his study. I'm sure as fuck not gonna sit around waiting.

The wooden floor creaks in the hallway under my weight the second I slip out of my room. Dammit. I'm not the best at being quiet. My heart stills and I stand frozen in the hallway, glaring at the wooden floorboards. After a moment, I straighten and continue on into his room. I practically tiptoe, my tongue stuck between my teeth as I sneak into his room. I love it in here. It's so... him.

Furtively I look around, wondering where I should start first, my heart pounding in my chest. I don't have much time. I don't know when Joseph will come out of his study, so I need to move quickly. I should hear him, I keep telling myself. I will definitely hear him when he comes up the stairs.

I purse my lips as I walk over to his dresser and start digging through it. I go through five drawers, but don't find anything but neatly folded clothes. Where else do people hide shit? I figured the dresser would be a gold mine. That's where I hide all my shit. I shut the last drawer gently, feeling a little let down. I look up and spot his bed, a smile curling on my lips. *The mattress.* I search underneath the bed and then push my hand below the mattress, between the box spring and the frame. I'm weak as shit, and holding it up actually makes me winded. *Nothing.*

"Come on," I mutter, looking around the room frantical-ly, "Everyone hides something under the mattress."

I get down on my hands and knees and look under the bed again. He's gotta have something somewhere.

I search the nightstands. Nothing again.

Frustrated, I stop and place my hands on my hips, biting my lower lip and thinking.

If I had a big house like this, would I hide anything in my bedroom? I mean, how stupid would that be? Maybe I'm in the wrong room. I sure as fuck can't search his study though. Not while he's in there at least.

I'm about to give up and leave the room when my eyes fall on the closet. The door is slightly ajar, and the light is on inside. My pulse picks up speed as I stare at it. I don't know how I didn't notice it already. I used to hide in the closets. The thought makes my heart hurt.

It's where I found my mother. I think she wanted me to find her before my father did.

He used to tell me how much I looked like her, until she killed herself. Then I would see that pained look in his eyes, and I knew it was what he was thinking, but he never said it again.

I know that's why he doesn't see me much; I remind him of her. I know it hurts him. I understand it. He still loves me, and I love him. Even if our family is scarred from what my mother did.

I bite my lower lip, shoving the sad memory back where it belongs, in the past, debating on whether I should go digging around more. I've already been looking for the past half hour, and Joseph doesn't spend very long on his own.

I should leave, I tell myself. *I'm not going to find anything in there anyway.*

I start to walk out of the room, but when I reach the doorway, I can't bring myself to leave without at least checking the closet. Though I know I probably won't find anything, who knows when I'll have another chance like this?

I spin around on my heel and walk quickly to the closet, swinging the door wide as I walk inside. It bangs against the wall, and I wince at the sound. I don't think he'll hear it though. Damn my eager ass.

Not wasting a second, I quickly go about inspecting the large closet, but I have to pause to suck in a sharp breath at the sight before me. *Jesus Christ.* He has *so* many suits. And they all look so fucking expensive. Who owns suits like these? I want to run my hands down all of the fine clothing, but I'm not here to look at his wardrobe. Focus, Lilly!

I go through several of the suits, checking in all the pockets, looking for something, anything that will tell me something about the past I feel Joseph is hiding. I come up empty. I look around, looking for a safe, some sort of bag, anything where something can be hidden. But I don't see a damn thing.

I'm about to leave the room when my eyes fall on a shoe box that's sitting inconspicuously next to a row of shoes. Looking at it, I know it's probably just shoes in there, but I can't help myself. I rush forward, nearly tripping to get to the box, and grab it. My heart stutters in my chest at the bit of racket I'm making. I only need one more minute.

Yes! Finally! There's a leather-bound book inside with a worn gold latch. I take it out, marveling at the high quality feel.

I open it, quickly glancing over my shoulder as I sit on the floor of his closet, to see pages filled with neat handwriting. One name keeps popping up off the page; *Passerotto*. I say it over and over again, whispering under my breath. I don't know what it means. I have no idea, but it definitely sounds Italian. I try to read some of the entries, and it's hard to keep up, but there's a lot mentioning of the *familia*. What the hell? Joseph is part of the Mafia? My heart beats faster, and my anxiety starts to grow.

I read a little bit further and find out that he's left *the family,* but it doesn't give me any relief. I scan an entry, my heart breaking in my chest. He watched his mother being beaten. He didn't do anything. I can tell by the way he's written it, he blames himself.

I get several more paragraphs in, so absorbed in the moment that I forget the time and where I am. I can feel my heart breaking as tears cloud my eyes. *Joseph.* I can't believe what he's been through.

A loud sound of footsteps coming up the stairs pulls my gaze from the pages of the book and a curse spills from my lips, "Oh shit!" I throw the book back into the shoe box and quickly set it back in its original place.

I'm about to run from the room when I knock over several suits on the clothing rack. My clumsy ass. Dammit. I'm the worst at this. Crap. I bend over to pick them up, but a metal glint catches my eye.

Holy fuck.

My heart jumps in my chest at the sight before me. A gun rack, hidden behind the fallen suits. It's filled with all sorts of guns.

"Tsk tsk," says a deep voice from the closet doorway.

I spin around, my heart pounding in my chest to see Joseph leaning against the doorjamb, gazing at me with amusement. I swear my heart wants to run away, and it chooses to try by climbing up my throat.

"Bad girl, my flower," he says playfully, a twinkle in his eye.

My heart is beating so fast it feels like it's about to burst out of my chest. I know I will be punished for this. And I know it will be the cage. I try desperately to come up with an excuse. Something. Anything. But I'm in his closet.

"Please sir," I plead, holding my hands out imploringly, "I was just looking around –" My throat is so dry as I speak. My body is tingling with fear.

"It's all right, flower," he says easily, surprising me. My heart doesn't believe him though, and it's still fighting to leave my body, ruled by fear. "There's nothing wrong with you having a little look. I want you to feel comfortable here."

"I'M SORRY SIR," I SAY SOFTLY, RELIEF SLOWLY COURSING THROUGH my blood.

Joseph motions at me. "Come here."

I look down at his suits that are on the floor, swallowing and bend to pick them up, but Joseph stops me with a terse, "Now."

That tone he uses makes me walk to him immediately, cringing as I step around his expensive suits left on the floor. He leads me back into the bedroom, pulling me by the hand and sitting me down on the bed. Gazing into my eyes, he gently strokes the side of my cheek, making my skin prickle all up and down my arms. I can still hardly breathe. I'm waiting for the other foot to drop, waiting for a punishment or admonishment. I knew what I was doing was bad. ...I also know I'm not really sorry. I'm only sorry I got caught. And I bet he knows that, too.

"There's nothing to be sorry about, flower," he tells me softly as if reading my mind. He pauses, and then gives me a playful nudge with his nose. "Unless you want to be sorry that you weren't waiting on my bed for me, naked with your legs spread wide."

A smile spreads across my face, and I let out a girlish giggle at his playful words. I really love these moments, when his playful side shines through. It's so different from the dark, dominating Master side. And I want more of it. I cup his face in my hand, looking deep into his eyes and rubbing my thumb across his stubble.

"I like you like this," I say softly, still not quite sure if he's really not mad at me. Maybe he knew I'd be looking. He always seems to know what I'm up to.

"Like what?" Joseph asks.

"I don't know, just when you're kind and playful."

He scoffs, shaking his head as he responds, "Those words aren't used to describe me very often."

"I REALLY LIKE THIS SIDE OF YOU," I SAY, PLACING MY HAND ON HIS. A moment of silence falls over us, and I feel compelled to ask, "*Passerotto?*" I'm not sure if I pronounced it correctly. Or if me prodding is going to tip him to the point of being pissed off. But I want to talk. It's in my nature.

Joseph hesitates for a moment, and I fear he might close himself off. But instead he grabs onto my waist and pulls me onto his lap. I gasp and hold onto him, not expecting it. He seems to pull me into his lap whenever we "talk." I like it. Yet another thing to add to my Things-I-Like-About-Joseph-Levi-list. I nestle into his lap and wait patiently.

"Yes. It means little sparrow."

"Who did that journal belong to?" I ask, although I'm certain it's his.

"My mother gave it to me when I was little…" Joseph's eyes are distant as his voice trails off. I place my cheek on his hot chest, listening to his heart and playing with the smattering of chest hair peeking through his unbuttoned shirt. I can sense that this is something he doesn't want to talk about, but I don't want to lose the opportunity to get him to open up.

"Go on… Please," I say very softly, stroking his hand and pulling away from him enough to look him in the eyes.

Joseph swallows audibly. But I'm pleased when he continues speaking. "I don't like talking about my past, but you seem to make me talk, my flower. I've had a fucked up life. There were a lot of times where I thought I wouldn't make it after the shit I had been through, after the shit I seen." He runs a hand down his face and looks past me.

The pain in his words pulls at my heartstrings.

"What did you see?" I ask, my voice barely above a whisper. I just want him to open up to me.

There's a long pause, and I can actually feel Joseph's heart pounding against my hand still at his chest. "A lot of death. A lot of murder."

I bring a hand to my lips in horror. "I'm sorry," I say in a choked voice, feeling tears well up in my eyes.

"It's okay," he replies thickly. But I know it's not. He's fucking hurting, and it tears me up. "I'd just rather not talk about it." My eyes flicker down to my lap, then back to his. I want him to talk. I want him to open up to me.

I know how he feels, not wanting to talk about things. But it helped me, so much that I know for sure I wouldn't be the person I am without having someone to confide in. Even if it was just a counselor at school. It's good to talk it out.

"Please?" I plead with him.

He shakes his head, and the look in his eyes tells me not to push him. I nod, trying not to feel like he's pushing me away. My eyes focus on the closet, where the journal is. Maybe that's his way.

I glance over at the closet. "Can I read it?"

"The journal?" he asks, and I immediately nod my head. "You can read it any time you wish."

We sit together in silence, and I swear I can hear Joseph's heart beating in tandem with mine. After a moment I turn in his lap, looking him in the eyes. I see the pain in his dark gaze, and I hate that I've partly caused it by bringing up the subject. I just want to help make it go away.

"I'm sorry," I tell him, rubbing his arm.

He doesn't respond. Instead, he leans down and kisses me on the lips very gently. Emotions swell up from my stomach and I find myself wrapping my arms around his neck and pulling him into me, smashing my lips into his with fiery passion.

I feel him hesitate for a moment, but it only lasts for an instant. He wraps his arms around my waist and pulls me back into the bed.

I've never felt more connected to anyone in my life. The more I learn about Joseph, the more I want him.

The more I fall for him.

And that could be a very dangerous thing.

Joseph

ALTHOUGH HER HIPS ARE STEADIED BY THE BENCH IN FRONT OF HER, THE rope tying her wrists behind her back and hanging from the ceiling is what's keeping her upright. Her ankles are bound to the bench and spread for me. Her hips are tied down as well. She's dangling naked, completely at my mercy. With the blindfold on, she doesn't know where I am. Each time my feet smack on the floor, her fingers twitch slightly. Her shoulders are going to be hurting her soon. This has to come to an end soon enough. I pull back on the blow as I smack the riding crop against her ass one last time. She yelps as her upper body is swaying, although her lower body is tied so tightly she doesn't move from the waist down.

Her ass is a beautiful shade of red. Some spots are a bit darker than the others. I trail the leather up the middle of her back; her body shivers, and her rose petal-colored nipples harden that much more. As I get to her arms and move forward, gently flicking the riding crop against her hard nipples, she moans.

It's only been thirty minutes, but she's so wet that her arousal is dripping down her thighs. I move the head of the riding crop up her neck and to her chin as I pull the blindfold off of her. The bright light startles her, and she sways away from me for just a moment as she closes her eyes. I allow it. Once she looks back at me, I bring my face closer to hers and plant a gentle kiss against her lips.

This is all because she got up from the table without asking for permission. Realistically, this isn't a punishment. I know she loved every minute of it. But that's what we're calling it.

"You do realize I own you," I tell her, my lips just an inch from hers. "You belong to me. Your freedom belongs to me." She holds my gaze as I speak to her. Her lips part in that beautiful way I've become addicted to.

She says her answer so sweetly, "Yes, Sir."

I walk around her, dropping the riding crop as I go and stroking my hard cock. I grip her hip in one hand although I don't need to, since she's not going anywhere.

I don't hold back when I fuck her.

And she takes it.

CHAPTER 20

Joseph

 *ou can't keep telling me no.*

I STARE AT THE TEXT MESSAGE, NEARLY BREAKING THE PHONE IN MY hand as I squeeze it, my anger rising and rising. I need to calm down. Every time this fuckface pisses me off, I fight with my flower. I'm not letting him come between us, and I don't give a damn what he wants.

I kept up my part of the bargain. I'm out.

They want the money back? They can come fucking get it.

I'm not dealing with their shit anymore. I pace the study, wanting to go back to the home I grew up in and beat the fucking piss out of him. But he never played fair. He'd pull a gun in a sword fight if he could. And he'd be damn proud of it. Going back there wouldn't be good.

The sound of Lilly turning off the water to the shower upstairs reminds me why I'm even letting him get to me. I finally have something worth giving a fuck about. This isn't the first or second or even the dozenth time I've had to put up with these assholes since I've left.

But lately I've been giving a fuck. I hear her pad across the bathroom upstairs. She's not a quiet little thing. Not in the least. The thought makes me smile until I hear the ping from my phone.

I scowl, looking down as my blood heats.

YOU DON'T HAVE A CHOICE.

PISSED. IF I HAD LESS RESTRAINT, I'D HURL THE FUCKING PHONE INTO the wall and scream out. Instead I calmly set it on the desk, staring at the phone and thinking of all the ways I'd love to kill him. I could have strangled him in his sleep. So many times I wanted to. I should have. Leaving that sick fuck alive was a mistake.

My desktop computer is still alive with light. With the sun setting and the thick curtains nearly closed shut, the study is dark. The faint glow of the computer draws me to it, back to the email Zander sent me.

IF YOU'D LIKE TO CHAT, YOU CAN REACH ME HERE.
-Z

IT'S THE THIRD TIME HE'S REACHED OUT TO ME.

He's yet to be straight with me, and I don't fucking trust him. I don't trust anyone.

My eyes dart to the ceiling as a thump followed by another thump tells me Lilly is up to something. I'm not sure what she's getting into, but I'm sure she'll be enjoying herself.

I have no one, I never have, but right now I need someone on my side. I need to protect Lilly. My fingers pick at my bottom lip. They itch for a glass of whiskey, to drown out the problems pestering me.

The men behind the scenes of crime each reach out to me, each wanting me for something. But not with her here. I can't do that to her.

My phone pings again, and I don't even have to get up or even touch the phone to see the message.

Answer me!

I feel the grin grow on my face. He never did enjoy being ignored. Fucking prick can go fuck himself.

We had a deal, I take the fall and I get the fuck out of the *familia*. What happened to loyalty? I clench my teeth and bite back my anger, finally doing the sane thing and silencing the cell phone.

I toss my cell phone back onto the desk, rising from my seat and ignoring my past.

Zander, my *familia*... I can deal with them later. I leave the study, slamming the door shut behind me.

"Lilly!" I call out for my flower. For my beautiful distraction.

As I make it up the stairway, I see her scrambling out of her room. I've never called for her like this before. When she catches sight of my anger, she falls to the floor and into a perfect bow. A beautiful display of submission.

Her wet hair is sticking to her face and lying on the wooden floor of the hallway.

I climb up the last few steps and walk slowly to her, watching as her chest rises and falls. She thinks she's in trouble. My lips kick up into a smirk as she trembles slightly on the ground.

"What were you doing?" I ask her with a bit of humor in my voice.

She answers clearly and quickly, "I was trying to rearrange something." My brow furrows as I lower myself to the floor and cup her chin in my hand.

As I bring her lips up to mine, her body stays still, just as she should.

I plant a small kiss on her lips before searching her eyes. "Re-arrange what?"

She swallows thickly. "I wanted to move the bed." I wait for more. At my silence, she adds, "So it would be across from the mirror." Her answer and the bright blush in her cheeks make me smile.

My flower. Ever the perfect distraction.

I rise, leaving her where she is and slowly taking off my worn leather belt. I let it slip through each loop on my pants slowly. "Did you ask permission?" I ask her. My voice is low and threatening. The punishment voice.

Her pupils dilate with lust as she shakes her head. "No, Sir."

I hold the belt in one hand, feeling my cock harden as I command her, "Get on all fours, now."

THE BELT CRACKS AGAINST HER SKIN AGAIN. "TEN!" LILLY CRIES OUT. Her hands are braced on the floor, her ass in the air. She's hanging over the edge of the bed, half on, half off. I run my hands down her trembling thighs and back up to her hot pussy. She's soaking wet for me.

"You asked for this," I tell her, dropping the belt on her bed.

Lilly moans before answering, "Yes, sir." I've learned she needs this; she doesn't have many punishments anymore. What used to be a method of conditioning, a tool for her training, has now become the reward. And I'm more than happy to give it to her. I need it, too.

I brush my fingers along her folds, ready to pleasure her. But I stop when I see how red and swollen she is. I've been using her often, and my touch is rough. It's not surprising that she's sore.

As I run my fingers from her entrance to her clit, I wait for her to tell me, but she doesn't. Her forehead pinches, and she bites into her bottom lip. I do it again and she closes her eyes tight, but still she doesn't tell me I'm hurting her. It makes me angry. All this time, and she still doesn't talk to me. She wants me to open up to her, but she can't even tell me when I'm hurting her? I close my eyes and let out a *frustrated sigh. She'll learn, I know she will. She's almost as stubborn as me, but I'll teach her.*

"Get on all fours," *I tell her as I unbutton my pants. I'm still waiting as I get behind her. Putting trust in the fact that she knows to tell me, and if nothing else she has a safe word. But she never utters it.*

"You asked for a safe word, Lilly," *I admonish her, placing my hand on her lower back.* "But you're not even using it." *She stills and looks back over her shoulder at me with frightened eyes. She realizes she's disappointed me. I leave her to grab the oil, and she gets up from her position, ready to protest, her soft voice apologizing.*

She's breathing frantically until she sees the ointment in my hand. This'll make her feel better.

"Did I tell you to move?" *I asked her.*

Lilly's quick to get back into position. "No, Sir," *she breathes. The oil is cool on my fingers, so I warm it for a moment, massaging it between my hands before pressing my hand against her pussy. She winces for a moment, sucking a breath between her teeth.*

I tell her as I massage her hot cunt, "I don't want to hurt you. If you desire pain, I'll give it to you in a way that's acceptable. But never like this." *Her eyes close as I speak. She should know better. I don't want to injure her. I can give her what she craves in other ways.*

"I'm sorry, Sir," *she whispers her apology.* "I just want to please you."

"You already do."

I move my fingers and spread the oil to her puckered hole, gently pressing my finger into her tight ring. My other hand is placed on her lower back as her mouth gapes from the sudden intrusion, and she nearly pushes away from me.

"Push back, my flower." *Her back curves as she obeys me, my finger sliding farther in.*

There's not an inch of her that I won't claim. But only when she's ready.

553

CHAPTER 21

Lilly

I lie in my plush bed, staring up at the ceiling, my breasts gently rising and then falling with each breath. I can't stop thinking about Joseph. All the things he's gone through. The terrible life he's had.

I feel for him.

I WISH I COULD BE THERE FOR HIM. BUT HE WON'T LET ME. I GRAB MY blue pillow I brought from home and hug it against my chest.

I know why. He wants to appear strong, doesn't want me to think he's weak.

He needn't bother. I know he's strong, surviving what he's been through. I close my eyes and shake my head. He just needs to let me in.

I know he drinks when I lie down at night, trying to suppress those unwanted memories, smother those dark feelings. I saw him last night, drinking while writing in his journal. My heart hurt for him, seeing him sitting there vulnerable, and in pain. I stare at the journal, now laying on my bed.

I hate to see him when he's like that. Alone with his thoughts. Consumed by his past. He becomes a different man and puts me aside. I *loathe* it.

He needs someone to help him get over his past. And I want to be that person.

Isn't that what I'm supposed to do? Be there for him, like he's trying to be here for me?

I just want to get to know him. I don't like how he shuts me out, or when he goes to his study late at night. I'm grateful he lets me read what he's written. In a lot of ways that's his way of talking it through. Talking to me.

He needs that. I know firsthand how powerful it can be to just talk things out. Even if it's just your school guidance counselor. Maybe if I open up to him, he might then finally open up to me.

Gathering my courage, I sit up in bed and roll over onto the edge, my feet dangling off the side. I'm about to slip into a pair of plush white slippers, when I hear an angry shout downstairs. My heart racing, I slip off the bed and rush from the room.

As I'm rushing up the hallway to Joseph's study, the voices get louder. He's arguing about something with another man. Their voices are muffled, so I can't understand exactly what they're saying, but it doesn't take a genius to know whatever it is, it's not good.

Stay out of it, the voice in the back of my head warns. I know I shouldn't go there. My blood is freezing, and my heart refuses to beat because yells are coming from both Joseph and someone else. It's more than a heated argument. But my feet are moving before I can stop them. I have to see. I have to make sure he's okay.

But I can't go unarmed. The thought chills my spine, paralyzing my movements before sending me quickly on a different path.

I make it down the hall into Joseph's room, the voices rumbling like thunder throughout the house, making my blood freeze. I hear Joseph yell something that sounds like an awful threat. I've never heard him sound so angry. Fuck, I'm scared.

I rush into Joseph's closet, shaking and trembling, my heart skipping every other beat. The room spins around me as I steady my clammy palms on my thighs. I can hardly breathe. What the fuck did I get myself into?

He was in the mafia.

He was a bad man.

I take in an unsteady breath, staring at the suits that block the gun rack. I didn't for one second think he had anything to hide other than his dark past.

My fingers are trembling as I push his suits aside and swallow thickly at the sight of the guns. I stand there for a moment, my heart thump thump thumping as the noises downstairs gets louder. Staring at all the cold hard steel, my heart bounces around like a fighter in a cage.

I've used a gun before, but only for target practice. I don't know which to choose.

But I don't have time to sit here debating with myself. Joseph might need me. My throat closes as I quickly grab one of the Glocks and check if it's loaded. It is. The click of the gun makes my heart pound faster, but I rush out of the closet and out of his bedroom, and down the hall to his study, holding the gun down carefully at my side and trying to be quiet for once in my life.

I stop to the side of the door of his study, my heart racing, and dare to peek inside. My heart pounds. Thump. Thump. Thump. The cold steel seems to heat as my palm sweats, making my grip on it weak.

Joseph's sitting at his desk, his face a mask of rage and there's a man in a black suit standing in the center of the room with his arms crossed across his chest.

They're arguing with each other, the man in black waving his hands sporadically before running his hand over his shiny bald head. Neither of them can see me from this angle, so I slip into the study, hiding behind the table, eavesdropping on their conversation. I can hardly keep my hands from trembling and the grip on the gun slips a little as I listen.

"The *familia* wants you back," the man is saying, his voice incredibly harsh. "Did you think they just forgot about you when you left?" He has a thick accent, but it sure as fuck isn't Italian. I'm trying to be quiet, but I feel like they're going to hear me just from my breathing.

"I don't give a fuck what they think," Joseph growls.

"Oh really? Do you really want to play this game?"

"I don't want to play anything. I'm done with that life. I'm a different man." The confidence in Joseph's voice makes me proud of him. I find myself nodding my head, although my heart is still begging me to get the fuck out of here.

The man in black lets out a harsh laugh. "You're not done until the *familia* says you're done." His quiet answer makes me want to peek around the table. My fingers grip the edge, but I can't do it. I'm frozen in place. "You can lie to yourself all you want, but it doesn't change the fact that you've killed in the name of the *familia*. That'll never go away, no matter how hard you try to forget, or no matter how many lies you try to tell yourself."

My heart stutters. *Joseph's killed people.* Goosebumps run over every inch of my skin.

There's a moment of silence, and I swear the only thing I can hear is the pounding of my heart. I'm afraid even Joseph and the man in black can hear it. Maybe that's why they're quiet; they know I'm in the room.

"You have ten seconds to get the fuck outta here," Joseph growls suddenly, his voice dark and deadly. My blood chills at the note in his voice. I don't think I've ever heard him so angry, so ruthless. It lets me know that whoever this man is, he's really gotten under Joseph's skin.

There's another pause, almost a hesitation, as if the man is wondering if he should press his luck and call Joseph's bluff. *Please don't.* My pointer finger steadies on the gun in my hand, although I'm too afraid to even open my eyes. I can barely hear the man respond, "The *familia* will be waiting for you."

He turns to leave, and when he does, I dare a peek from behind my hiding place. I catch a glimpse of dark hair, dark cold eyes and handsome features that remind me of Joseph's, except his are marred by the absolute ruthlessness stamped on his face.

For an instant, his cold eyes meet mine.

Fuck.

I sink down almost immediately, but I think he saw me. *I know he did.*

I can hear Joseph rise and follow the man out, the sounds of their shoes smacking against the ground so much softer than the sound of my wild heart. *He saw me. Fuck!!*

Before I can even move, Joseph returns and closes the door.

I sit there, clinging to the gun, my heart pounding, wondering what I should do. I'm fucking scared. I don't know what kind of shit Joseph is in, but I want no part in it. The man claimed Joseph killed before. He *killed* people.

AFTER A MOMENT, I DECIDE TO REMAIN HIDDEN UNTIL JOSEPH LEAVES the room, however long that takes.

But I don't get the chance.

"You can stop hiding now, flower," Joseph says, the sudden sound of his voice making my heart jump.

I close my eyes, swallowing thickly, and then slowly rise to my feet as a feeling of dread and two words run through my mind.

Oh fuck.

CHAPTER 22

Joseph

I can't stand the look in Lilly's eyes, accusing me. All this time she's been reading my journal, looking at me as though I'm a wounded animal. I don't want her sympathy. But her kindness and the sweet side she's given me have been addictive. I've grown to crave them.

Now she sees me for who I really am. What I represent, and where I came from. As if she didn't know. How did she think I got this fucked up?

You can't have one without the other.

"Hand me the gun," I command as I hold out my hand, and she's quick to look down at her hands as if only now realizing what she's holding. She rises slowly, her shoulders hunching in slightly and takes a step forward, handing it to me and quickly backs away. She looks around the room, still processing everything.

I gently set the gun on the table before turning back to her.

"What did you hear?" I ask her. More for her own safety than anything else. My brother isn't going to let up. I need to know what she heard.

She doesn't answer me. She stares at me wide-eyed with a mix of fear and something else.

I raise my voice and give her the command again, "What did you hear?" My heart hammers in my chest. I hate the look in her eyes. The way she's looking at me. I want my Lilly back. *My flower.*

"Nothing," she barely answers. Her voice is only just above a murmur. I narrow my eyes at her, hating that she's lying to me. I open my mouth to admonish her, but she cuts me off.

"I didn't sign up for this!" Lilly's voice wavers as she raises it. Her eyes are glazed with tears as her body trembles. Leaning forward, I can feel the anger radiating off of her in waves. As though I betrayed her.

"Who did you think I was Lilly?" I ask her, my head tilting and my voice low, filled with my own anger. She's a smart woman, she knew what she was signing up for. She had to know.

She stares at me with a look of contempt, but tears cloud her eyes. She shakes her head, unable to speak. She keeps looking at the door and then back at me. I can practically hear what she's thinking. She doesn't want me anymore. She doesn't want *this* anymore. I'm not the man in the books she reads. I'm not the poor boy whose memories of abuse are coming to front.

She thinks I'm *one of them*. One of the villains.

She swallows thickly and takes a step forward.

"Kneel," I give her the command, but she doesn't obey. She stares back at me, her eyes wide and disbelieving. My heart freezes. Don't deny me, Lilly. Don't do this. What we have is so good. It's so right.

"No," she says and shakes her head. "I want to leave!" she screams at me. My chest clenches with pain at the conviction in her voice. "The contract says that I can leave at any time." Her voice shakes as she speaks, mirroring the trembling of her body.

I can't let her go. I won't.

They've seen her. I saw the look in Ricky's eyes when he left.

They'd use her as a tool to get me. I take two steps closer to her, and she takes two away from me until her back hits the wall. She's staring back at me with her fists clenched, and her breathing is coming in sporadically. Her eyes flash with challenge, but they also contain fear. She's scared of me. It fucking kills me to see that look in her eyes.

I brace my palm on the wall beside her head, leaning forward and whispering into her ear, "You aren't going anywhere."

The only sound I can hear is her breathing. As though it contains her hate for me in this moment. She swallows thickly before answering, "You lied to me." The hurt in her voice is surprising. As if that's my biggest offense. Telling her she can go, and then taking it away.

I kiss her neck gently, but she's stiff and I wouldn't attempt to kiss on her lips at this moment. I pull away from her and rest my hand against her neck, my fingers wrapping around her throat in a possessive hold. "I've never lied to you Lilly," I speak softly, staring at her plump lips rather than the daggers in her eyes. "The game has changed though. You shouldn't have let him see you." I chance a look at her face, and her expression is one of sadness, her eyes staring at the hardwood floors.

Again she swallows, quiet and no longer fighting me. But that's only because she doesn't know how to fight back yet. She will, I know she will. She has too much fight in her to give up so easily.

"You directly disobeyed me," I say quietly; that draws her attention to me, and the sadness is once again replaced by anger. I prefer that. Because at least with anger, there's passion. I crave her passion.

"You need to go to your cage now." I deliver the blow.

Her lips part, and I can practically hear the words on her tongue, *"Yes, Sir."* But instead she snaps her lips shut, looking me straight in the eyes and refusing to obey yet again. It makes me want to smile. Her defiance, her new game move. I'll take it; I'll take anything she's willing to give me.

We're both quiet as I lead her to her room. I silently open the cage, and she gets in without a fight. That's not to say she doesn't have one. I can feel her disobedience rolling off of her in waves. I shut the door just as I did before, not locking it. I never have, and I never will.

She stares at me through the bars of the cage, with a look of pure hate shining back.

But she doesn't use her safe word, and I cling to that knowledge.

561

CHAPTER 23

Lilly

I lie in my bed, naked, the cool air from the ventilation system caressing my bare skin. I'm counting the days until this is all over. Just thinking that hurts my heart, my hand moving to it and tears pricking my eyes.

It hurts to think Joseph maybe isn't the man I thought he was. I knew he was hiding dark secrets, but this is just too dark for me. He won't let me leave. But as soon as he deals with this mess, as he says, then I'm gone. Money or no money, contract or not. I don't care.

It'll all be over. I roll over onto my side, clinging to the small blue pillow I brought with me from home and ignoring the pain in my chest.

At the same time, I don't want it to end. It's crazy. I both hate it and love it. Hate *him* and love *him*.

I blow out a frustrated breath as I think about my predicament, think about the position I'm in.

It makes me want to fight him, knowing he's keeping me here. And I'm getting addicted to it.

But even with the urge to be belligerent, I still obey him. Only to a degree. Pushing my limits, testing him. He knows it too, and that only makes me push harder. Because I want him to push me harder. The knowledge makes me lower my eyes to the beautiful white comforter.

And I still have feelings for him, even with my doubts. I can't deny how strong they are. How could I not?

A part of me hates myself for feeling that way. But I can't help it. I can't snap my fingers and erase what I feel just because Joseph may have done some horrible things. We have a connection, something that I've never had with anyone, though it feels very strained right now. Because of me. Because his past won't leave him alone.

I stretch out my leg, and lay it over the outfit he has laid out for me. My eyes are drawn to the beautiful short dress. Don't know why he laid it out. It's not like I'll be wearing it.

He wants to tempt me to wear it, that voice at the back of my head says. *So he can have a reason to punish me when I don't.*

As if he needs a reason. He can do whatever he wants to me.

He owns me.

I can't even lock my bedroom door.

I never have a moment of privacy.

That's the part my romance novels left out. The cold, harsh reality of never having a moment to yourself, never being able to do anything without approval. It was fun and games before, when I wasn't angry at him. When I wanted it as much as he did. But it changed.

I hate that I even have to ask to work on my novel. But it's not like he denies me that privilege. He always gives permission when I ask. Somehow, that makes it more infuriating.

I wish I could be more pleased with him. Instead, I feel like I'm a spoiled pet throwing a tantrum.

I'm so confused.

My thoughts are swept away as I hear the soft creak of the bedroom door.

I hear him walk into the room, but I only move my head just enough to peek at him. My breath catches at the sight. He looks handsome as usual, dressed in black dress pants and a white dress shirt opened at the chest. I don't get off the bed to kneel or greet him.

That's why I know I won't be wearing those clothes. I'm done play-ing. He can just throw me in the damn cage until he lets me go.

His eyes find my naked body and I blush fiercely, though I don't know why. It's nothing he hasn't seen before. Looking at him, I'm feeling so many emotions that I have to turn away, my chest heaving.

Anger. Hurt. Betrayal. Lust.

They're all there.

I startle slightly as I feel his arms encircle my waist. His hot lips find my neck and I find myself leaning back into him, my lips parting in a soft sigh, my nipples pebbling. I've missed his touch. My eyes close; he feels so good. My arm wraps around his, betraying me, but I don't care. I just want to feel him for a moment. Just a moment.

"I know you're still angry with me, Lilly," he says softly in my hair, his breath hot on my neck. I can feel his big, hard cock pressing against my ass, and I desperately want him inside of me. *Make love to me. Make me forget. Please, make me forget.*

I wish he couldn't read me so well. And I don't want to really respond. But I know he's expecting an answer.

"Yes, Sir," I say softly, my words sounding a bit stiff. I've come to hate them. But I love saying them at the same time. I'm just one big walking contradiction.

He runs his hand down my stomach, and circles it around my pubic hair. "When you shower, make sure you shave."

Anger swells up my throat, and I swallow. I'm glad he can't see me roll my eyes. He knows I'll shave; I just haven't gotten a chance to take a shower yet. I think he just knows that I'm pissed and wants to make me even angrier. He wants to rule over me. Fuck him!

"You're an asshole!" The words spew from my lips before I can stop them.

His arms leave my waist. I'm relieved and miss his touch all at the same time. I fucking hate how he makes me feel. "Why are you angry with me?" he asks, his voice even and low. Deadly.

I turn to face him, no longer able to hide the anger I feel. "You lied to me."

Joseph clenches his jaw. "I already told you that I didn't."

"And I'm supposed to believe that? That man said you killed people. How do you explain that?"

"Lilly, I'm going to ask you not to talk about that. It has nothing to do with us."

My jaw nearly drops as I stare at him with wide eyes. "Nothing to do?" I ask breathlessly, stabbing my finger into the mattress. "I'm a fucking Slave to a murderer! That's what I am! How do you think that makes me feel?"

Anger flashes in his eyes. I've really pissed him off by calling him a murderer.

He stares at me for a long moment, his chest heaving, the veins standing out on his neck. For a second, I think he'll even strike me. Maybe I just want him to, so I can have a real reason to hate him or at least a reason not to love him. But his next words make my blood run cold.

"Go to your cage."

I open my mouth to protest, but I snap it shut. It's useless. This is what I wanted anyway.

Tears well up in my eyes, but I fight them back. I don't know why I said anything. I should've known what would happen. All I needed to do was to shut the fuck up and keep counting the days until this was over.

I turn around, drop to my knees, and crawl inside my cage, hating him every second of the way.

He shuts the cage door before I'm even in the back of it. But he doesn't lock it. He never does. I wish he would. My heart breaks as I hold back the sob.

I glare at him balefully from in between the bars. He looks down at me with both pity and anger in his eyes. For some reason, it pisses me the fuck off, yet again.

"I'll spend every fucking day here in this cage if it means I can get away from you," I snarl with venom. I don't know why I say the words. I know I don't even mean it. But I can't help myself.

I regret it the moment I say it though.

I wait for him to say something nasty in response, but he doesn't. His face is an impassive mask, but his eyes are a storm of emotion. I've hurt him with my words, I can feel it. It hurts me to know that. I really shouldn't have done that. God, I'm such a bitch. Looking at the swirl of emotion in his dark eyes makes me hate myself.

He was opening up to me, and now he'll be closed off.

Fuck, I'm sorry. *I'm so fucking sorry.*

But I can't bring myself to say anything. My throat's closed off, and the tears roll down my cheeks.

I don't know why.

After a moment, his eyes heavy, Joseph turns and walks from the room, leaving me alone in my cage.

A feeling of guilt washes over me as soon as he's gone, along with a wave of loneliness and I can't stop the tears that are suddenly falling freely down my face.

I really should be careful what I wish for.

Joseph

HER NAILS DIG INTO MY FOREARMS, SCRATCHING DOWN MY ARMS AND leaving marks as I fuck her ruthlessly, claiming her once again. "Keep fighting me, my flower," I tell her as my hips buck into her and the bed shakes beneath us.

It's been three days since I've been able to feel the warmth of her cunt wrapped around my dick. Not that she hasn't wanted me, since her anger seems to only intensify her desire. I stare into her eyes, and she stares back at me with the same fierceness. In this moment I don't know who owns who.

She so close, I can see it on her face, but she's yet to ask permission.

"Are you trying to cum before I allow you to?" I pull away from her, pulling out of her warmth and leaving her on the edge of her release. I would have gladly given it to her, had only she asked. She breathes heavily, her blue eyes swirling with defiance.

The room fills with the sounds of our heavy breathing.

Hate fuck. Makeup sex. I'm not sure what this is, but I'm hopeful that once it's over, she'll forgive me. I want her to look at me the way she used to.

I crawl up her body, my hard dick wet with her arousal, pressing into her hip. Her expression softens as I gentle my hands at her hip. She doesn't know what to think as I kiss up between her breasts along her collarbone and up her neck.

"You only need to ask me," I say and stare at her lips, wishing I could kiss her like I used to. My eyes dart to hers, and I feel this familiarity of what used to be between us. I take a chance, pressing my lips to hers.

She kisses me back before breaking the kiss and asking, "Please, Sir." There's hesitation in her voice before she adds, "I miss you."

There's no trace of anger on her face. Only sadness. I'm not sure if this will last. But at least I have my flower for a moment.

CHAPTER 24

Joseph

The marks in the journal are smooth as the pen glides against the paper. The pages are worn and old at this point, and nearly come to the end. It's fitting, seeing as how I've come to the final scene between myself and my father.

THE ROMANOS WERE EASY TO GUN DOWN. THEY DIDN'T EVEN SEE IT coming. My father took the entire crew. Eighteen men. The first four littered the front of the restaurant with bullets. I remember how the glass broke, shattering onto the ground in splintered pieces. I stood in the background, my father to my right, my brother to my left. The screams and gunshots rang out clearly. Blood flooded the streets that night on both sides, although heavy in the Romanos. Their wives were with them. Their children were with them. Their deaths were quick. With a gun in each hand I walked up with my father, the glass crunching beneath my boots.

I shot a bullet in each of their heads from my guns. Evidence. I continued shooting until they were both empty. Part of me hoped that my father was going to put a bullet in the back of my head. Every bullet that went off, I expected it. I was meant to take the fall. And I didn't think that required me being alive at the end of this.

My father gave me a look with a hint of fear when he told me not to mention a single name. I already knew not to. What's more memorable than seeing fear for the first time in my father's eyes, was the cold look of my brother's face. I saw jealousy there. My father was willing to trust me with this task. A son who he knew never loved him. And my brother hated me for it.

Even if I was going to go away for life. He didn't like that I got any approval from our father, or any respect from the men of the familia. *But I didn't agree to do it for either of those reasons.*

I NEVER UTTERED A WORD. I WAS READY TO TAKE THE BLAME AND GET the death penalty or go to prison for life; I didn't care which. I deserved to be punished for my sins. All of them. But the cops let me go. They followed me, they waited. They were pissed I wouldn't talk, and they anticipated that letting me out would send up red flags to everyone on the streets.

They thought my *familia* would come for me. They thought the target they put on my back would have me running back to talk and give them the information they wanted in exchange for protection.

Their error was thinking that I gave a damn. I was ready to die. I didn't care how. It didn't matter to me who pulled the bullet.

My father didn't make a move. If anything, he knew I was honest, and he gave me the only thing I truly wanted. Freedom from his rule. But now that my brother is gearing up to take over, my past is coming back to haunt me.

I'm not going back. I don't care how many men my brother sends here. I'll kill them all before I go back. I just hope it doesn't come to that. I haven't pulled a trigger in a long fucking time. But I sure as fuck haven't forgotten how to do it.

The pen stills on the paper as I hear the faint padding of Lilly's bare feet against the floors behind me. Her anger has waned tremendously. She's not trying to fight me like she was before.

Maybe she's forgiven me. Maybe she's realized that she wasn't as angry as she thought she was. She was hurt because she thought she knew me.

In many ways she does though, more than anyone else ever has.

Or maybe it's because I stopped fighting her.

I've been going easy on her. I don't want to give her a reason to go back to that cage. I don't want to give her a reason to fight me any more than she already has. I don't see a way out of this, other than meeting with my brother. But to do that, I have to leave Lilly, and not something I can't risk. I *won't* risk her.

"Joseph?" she asks me.

Although she's used my real name, she still kneels beside the chair. I never know which side of her I'm going to get until she approaches me. It's a funny thing. I thought I didn't want a Submissive. I didn't want someone else to control what we do, and when and what our rules are. But Lilly's gotten under my skin. I'm bending for my flower. I'd rather do that than see her wilt.

"Yes?" I turn to her, petting her hair and waiting for her to look up at me.

She visibly swallows and clasps her hands in her lap. She seems nervous, which in turn makes me nervous, but of course I don't show her that. I'm her Master at all times, and I must be strong for her.

"What are you doing?" she asks, her eyes on the journal.

I pat my lap and say, "Come sit with me." She stands slowly and obeys me, but there's still hesitation in her actions. I've yet to earn her trust back. Even if she gives me these small moments, I know what we once had is broken.

I place my journal on her lap. My heart races in my chest, every bit of vulnerability I've ever had is documented within. I don't know why I write it all down. Maybe the dark scenes that haunt me late at night will leave me if only I write them down.

"I like to write things I remember." Her pale blue eyes focus on mine through her thick lashes. And then look back down to the journal. I can see those wheels turning in her head; she wants to ask more. I don't wait. I pull her closer to me, my fingers tickling the curve of her waist as I sit back in the chair. "I used to do very bad things, Lilly." My heart pounds in my chest as I confess to her, "I've written down some more for you." I swallow thickly. "These ones are just for you." My body chills at the thought of her hating me when she reads them. It's all the truth of what I've done. I can't forgive myself, but maybe she will. She's kinder than me. She met me when I'd tried to move on.

Her breathing comes in a little louder. She licks her lips slightly and then asks, "Why did you do them?" The hurt in her voice kills me.

"You didn't want me to turn out to be a bad man, did you?" She wants there to be good in all people. I can tell that about her. It's one of the qualities I find endearing about her. I think that's one of the reasons she's so angry with me. I disappointed her. But I swear I tried.

Her voice cracks as she answers, "You aren't a bad man." She can't even look me in the eyes as she says it. She knows she's lying, and it breaks my heart.

"I didn't have much of a choice." I know I had one, but it was kill or be killed. For the first time in a long time, she lays gently against my chest. Her small hand rubs circles over my heart. I miss her comforting touch.

"Would you like to read it?" The offer spills from my lips in an attempt to tell her what I had been through and explain without having to actually tell her. I don't want to recount it all over again. I put it into this journal so I can forget. But maybe if she knows everything, the explanation of how I left and why, she can forgive me.

She doesn't hesitate to nod, the word slipping between her lips, "Yes." The eagerness in her response makes me smile.

"This is different from what I thought it would be," she says softly. The way she speaks makes it seem as though what she's telling me is a secret.

"It is for me, too." I have to agree; this isn't at all what I had in mind when I first laid eyes on Lilly.

I wasn't lying when I said the game's changed.

"How is it different for you?" she asks, playing at the hem of her dress. I suppose I'll have to go first before she'll tell me what she was thinking.

"That the Master/slave relationship is only for short spurts. I'm not stupid, Lilly. I don't control you. But I don't want to, either." I want something different from her now. More than just acceptance as her Master. More than forgiveness. Although I'm not sure what, exactly.

She looks a little bit upset and hesitant. I wish she'd just forgive me. I want to put her at ease. That's all I've been trying to do for the past week.

"I'm sorry, I've been..." Lilly's voice trails off. "I knew you... I knew you had..." She looks away, unable to finish.

"It's in my past. I promise you." I just need her to believe it. I know she doesn't want to fight me anymore. "I'm not the man I once was." She must know it's true. She knows me better than anyone ever has.

Her nod is small, but accepting. I can see it in her eyes that she believes me.

"Where does that leave us? Both of us thinking this was something it's not... and you... figuring," she waves her hand in the air, shifting in my lap.

I cup her small chin in my hand, tilting those soft lips closer to mine as I say, "It just means that sometimes we'll play, and sometimes we'll just be us."

She looks up at me and asks, "And what is that?"

I don't know how to answer her, so I'm quiet.

"Even if we aren't playing, you still need to treat me as though I'm your Master." Although it's a statement, it feels as though I'm asking her a question. I feel wrong for telling her that since all this time we've nearly been playing scenes. But I know what she's about to read. And I don't want her to think any differently of me. I am her Master, and it should stay that way. Regardless of what she reads. Regardless of how well she gets to know me.

"Yes, Sir."

"HOLD STILL, MY FLOWER," I TELL LILLY AS HER BACK RESTS AGAINST the wall. "Hands at your side," I say as I push her palms against her thighs. She's naked before me, finally obeying me again. It feels as though we're playing house. Like this is all pretend. We're ignoring

what lies beyond these walls. My familia, *the fact that she can't leave. Pretending to be blind to what's meant to keep us apart.*

I get on my hands and knees, putting my face between her thighs and inhaling her sweet scent. Judging by her gasp, she didn't expect it. I smile against her heat before taking a languid lick and pulling back to look her in the eyes.

"Ride my face, Lilly," I tell her, noting how her eyes widen as she comprehends my words. "Take your pleasure from me. Cum freely."

I place my hands on the inside of her knees, allowing her legs to bend slightly. She rocks helplessly into my face, hesitant at first. But as I groan with approval, her hips grind harder and soft moans spill from her lips.

So long as she obeys me, I'll give her everything she wants. Every pleasure, every need. I just need her to obey me. I need her to stay with me.

CHAPTER 25

Lilly

J take a deep breath, my fingers trailing over the high quality leather of Joseph's journal. I'm partway through reading it. I don't know if I'm ready today for more of the bad things that I know I'll find out while reading it, but I'm going to go through with it anyway. I want to see what happened in his life. It makes me feel that much more connected to him.

A ray of sunshine hits the golden latch of the journal, reflecting a flash into my eyes.

I'm curled up in Joseph's sunroom, reclined in a white, plush fabric recliner, soaking in the warmth of the sun. The view from here is gorgeous. The sky is a clear azure blue, and the ground is covered with a thick layer of white snow that reflects the sunlight, filling the room with brightness.

It's lifting my mood. I'm already feeling better from these past few days with the new rules Joseph has set for us. I like the idea he had about playing scenes. And I love that he's opening up to me bit by bit. He's adding details and writing notes to benefit my understanding of what happened. He won't talk to me about it though; the journal is all I get. He won't even be in the same room when I read it. Even now, he's in the kitchen because he knows I'm reading it.

I open the journal to the last passage I stopped on and pick up where I left off. It doesn't take long before I'm deeply engrossed in his story. Now that I know how the story ends, everything he's written is so clear. But when I reach a passage that's so heartbreaking, about his mother, I can't keep the tears from falling from my eyes.

"This is hard," I say thickly, wiping the tears from my cheek with the back of my hand.

I have to close the book. I can't read any more right now. I just can't believe all the things that Joseph has gone through. I feel absolutely awful for him.

I haven't forgotten that he's keeping me here. That I'm a prisoner. But I wouldn't leave if he told me to. If he commanded me. I'd refuse.

As soon as I see him, I'm going to crawl in his lap and kiss him and try to give him all the comfort that I'm capable of giving. I know he doesn't like to be held and he doesn't like sympathy, but I need it as much as he does.

But for now, I'll keep playing our game and pretend like I don't know that he's avoiding me because I'm reading the journal. He'll pretend he doesn't know that it kills me to see what he's been through. I don't mind playing this game, because it only makes me closer to him.

I push the journal onto the ottoman and grab my laptop, wiping under my eyes and my nose as I move.

I need to relieve some serious stress. I sniffle again, opening up the laptop as I sag in the seat. Right fucking now. And there's nothing that helps me to relieve it more than writing. It's always been my therapy for when my emotions are heightened, or I'm feeling down. It's the perfect way to release my emotions. Joseph needs something like that. I told him that.

And he told me that's what I am to him. My heart hurts, remembering his words.

. . .

575

I OPEN ON MY LAPTOP SCREEN, MY MIND OVERFLOWING WITH IDEAS TO use for the story. It should be easy. I have so much material to work with. So many emotions to play off of.

I'm about to turn over to the Word document screen, when an email notification pops up on my screen.

FROM: AIDA WHITE
   To: Lilly Wade

SUBJECT: MY BABY IS GONE

LILLY

MY HANDS ARE SHAKING AS I TYPE THESE WORDS. I DON'T KNOW WHO to talk to, but I need to talk to someone. I haven't stopped crying since this morning. My baby is gone. I can't believe it. How I wish I would have turned my life around sooner. If only he would've waited just a little while longer and mommy would have been there for him. I feel like such a worthless piece of shit. I bet that's what you think of me. And you're not wrong.

THE POLICE CALLED ME THIS MORNING TO TELL ME THAT ZACH GOT into a fight. He was stabbed to death. He died this morning.

I KNOW YOU WERE SOMEONE THAT WAS IMPORTANT TO HIM, THEY GAVE me your email. You have to be someone special because he would talk about you when he called me. I just want to thank you for being there for my baby when I couldn't.

SINCERELY,

Zach's mom, Aida

I STARE AT THE SCREEN IN DISBELIEF, MY STOMACH TWISTING IN agony. I don't believe it. It can't be true. This has to be some sick cruel joke. I shake my head. This didn't happen. This woman is a liar. She's a liar!

I shake my head, pushing the laptop away, refusing to believe Zach is dead.

It might be one of his friends playing a joke on me. I can't accept this. It has to be! Tears roll down my cheeks as I rise out of the chair. Not Zach.

I refuse to believe it.

He was going to get his life together. Even the parole officer said it. Things were going to be better for him.

"It's not true," I say over and over in denial. "This is a bunch of bullshit!"

I have to believe it's not true, but a growing fear grips my heart. I have to find out.

I jump up from my seat and rush through the house in search of a landline phone. I find one in Joseph's study. My hands fumble over the ancient thing while I nearly rip the phone out of the wall in my haste to pick up the receiver.

I quickly dial the parole officer's number. I know it by heart. Pick up. Pick up! My fingers twist around the cord as I pace the small area.

It rings three times before someone answers.

"Hello?" a woman's husky voice answers.

My lips are suddenly dry, and my words stick in my throat.

It's okay, I tell myself. *You'll see. It was all a lie. He's okay*

I suck in a deep breath and then blurt, "It's Lilly Wade... I'm calling to... find out about... Zach White?" That's all I can manage.

I don't know if it's protocol to just say a name when calling to ask for information, but I can't say anything else. My throat feels so tight, I almost can't breathe.

The woman on the other end of the line gets it though, because I hear the tapping of keys.

Her next words nearly knock me off my feet.

"I'm sorry, Ms. Wade. He passed away this morning."

The phone slips from my fingertips and swings up against Joseph's desk with a bang. But I no longer care. The room is spinning around me. My heart is racing. I can't fucking think. Not him. I couldn't help him. But they were going to. They were going to save him. He told me they would. He told me he'd be fine!

Somewhere in the background, I hear the woman's voice coming out of the receiver, "Ma'am, are you there?"

I sink to my knees beside the desk, wrapping my arms around my chest, and begin rocking back and forth. Trying to calm myself. Trying to remember the moves I learned in yoga class to help me relax. But instead my rocking is fast. Too fast.

I'm not okay. It's not okay.

"No, no, no, no!" I repeat over and over, the tears rolling from my eyes, so hot my eyes are burning. I can't believe it. I failed him. I should have done more to help him. I should have snatched his ass and forced him in the car that day I saw him walk away from me.

It's all my fucking fault.

"Ma'am, are you all right?"

SHE TRIES AGAIN TO GET MY ATTENTION SEVERAL MORE TIMES BEFORE hanging up, the sound of the dial tone mixing in with my quiet cries.

I DON'T EVEN HEAR THE SOUND OF FOOTSTEPS, BUT I'M SUDDENLY pulled up into a hard chest by strong arms.

"What happened?" Joseph asks, pushing my hair out of my face as I try to calm down.

I can't answer him right away, the tears and sobs coming in even harder, seemingly brought on by his caring touch. But he waits patiently for me to get a hold of myself, his normally dark eyes filled with concern.

"Zach died," I sob when I can finally say the words. "He was murdered." Speaking haltingly, I tell him all about my relationship with the troubled kids in school and how I devoted a lot of myself to helping them and how special Zach was to me.

"I thought he was going to be okay." It's all I can say toward the end. His strong hand rubs my back in large, soothing circles.

Joseph frowns, squeezing me gently. "I'm so sorry. But this wasn't your fault, do you understand? You couldn't have changed what happened to Zach. No one could." I shake my head in denial before burying my face into his hard chest.

I want to scream at him, 'That doesn't make it right!', but when I pull away from him and look at the softness in his eyes, I know that he's only trying to make me see the truth. I couldn't save him, just like I couldn't save my mother. Just like my father couldn't save her. "Lilly, you can't save people from themselves. I know that. So much better than most people. But you try. And you never stop. You're a good person. Even if he's gone." I let out a small sob and try to pull away, but Joseph holds my chin firmly in his grasp and continues, "Even if he's gone, you can still help others. I'm sure you have. Even if you don't know it." He grips my chin and forces me to look into his eyes. The intensity that he gazes at me with actually stops my sobs and dries my tears. "I know you have."

I feel like shit. My heart is hurting. But I can't deny the power he has over me. I shake my head, not fully believing him.

His next words steal the air from my lungs. "You've helped me." He loosens his grip on me to brush the hair from my face as he says softly, "More than you'll ever know.

I stare up into his eyes, and I see something I've never seen before, something so powerful it makes me weak in the knees. Something I'm not sure that I'm seeing because it's truly there, or because I want it to be there.

That must be it. I'm only imagining the love I see reflected in his eyes.

CHAPTER 26

Joseph

J thought it was her that was playing a game when we started this. But it's more clear to me now that I was the one playing. The bottle of whiskey is empty. I keep bringing it to my lips, forgetting that it's gone, having nothing to take this pain away.

There's life beyond the hollow shell I've been living in. There's a reason to fight, there's a reason to *feel*. Lilly's shown me that. My heart hurts for her. I wish I could give her something to take the pain away. But nothing can soothe grief. I know that all too well.

Over the last few days, she hasn't been herself. I told her she's blaming herself for something she couldn't control. It's something no one could have controlled. But she doesn't want to believe that.

I'll show her with time. I'll help her however I can. I just want her to be happy again.

Knock. Knock. Two soft knocks from the front entry distract me from my thoughts.

I've ordered her a new laptop. I put the bottle down on the end table and quickly make my way to the door. I'm eager to get her something that will make her smile. She's been burying herself in her writing. I'm hoping this will make her happy. Even if it's only for a moment.

When I open the door without checking, my heart stops. I hate myself this very second. I should have known better. Fool! I'm a fucking fool for letting my guard down.

I stare down the barrel of two guns, held by men I don't recognize, but I know who sent them. I stand there numb on the surface, but internally I'm screaming. How could I be so fucking stupid? I don't have a gun. I have nothing! And Lilly's upstairs. Vulnerable. It's my fault.

"What do you want?" I ask without giving in to the fear and reflecting it in my voice. My hand grips the door keeping me upright, as though without it, I'd fall.

Lilly. She's all I can think about. I start to walk outside, my hand closing the door behind me, but they step forward, crowding my space. I need to get them away from here. As far away from Lilly as I can.

"We can discuss this somewhere else," I say easily, as they ignore me and continue walking forward, pushing me back into my foyer. One closes the front door and locks it. I start thinking about where every gun I have in this house is located. I have them stashed away in every room. My eyes dart to the corner of the foyer; the one here is behind these two assholes, so I won't be able to get to the gun in the closet. There are two in the living room though. I only need to get these assholes to follow me in there. But that's closer to Lilly. Fuck! I try not to clench my jaw and ball my hands into fists at the thought.

I'm not sure if these men know she's here. I can't risk them finding out. I wish I could tell her to run. To hide. I wish I could go back in time and never speak to her, never corrupt her with the sins of my past.

If only I could. I'd give it all up to keep her safe.

"You know how this ends, Joe," the one man says to my left. He's nearly bald and short, and his leather jacket is slightly too big for him. The man on his right is much taller, his military cut giving him an edge over the other fuckface. Both of them are holding their guns loosely. They're both arrogant. They think they've won. I take in a deep breath, quickly coming up with a plan. Something. Anything to keep her from them.

The bald man continues to point his gun at me as the other man asks, "We just need the code for your safe." I huff a grunt. Of course. Money. It's always about the money.

"And why would I tell you that?" I ask with a grin that doesn't reflect a single thing I'm feeling.

"Because if you do, we won't make you watch what we're gonna do to your girl." He smiles a crooked grin, showing his yellowed teeth. "We'll put you out of your misery first." The bald man's answer chills my blood. My heart pounds in my chest.

As I swallow thickly, registering what they're saying and trying not to give into the urge to beat the piss out of him, I see movement over the tall man's right shoulder.

Lilly.

I swear my heart stops. What the fuck is she doing?

"You need to go back where you came from," I tell the man standing in front of me, but I'm not speaking to him. I wish I could look at her as I talk, but I can't. I'm afraid they'll follow my line of sight, turn around and see her.

I'm fucking pissed as I say the same words louder. Both men seem thrown off by the command in my voice, but I don't care. I can't even think about them. She needs to listen. She needs to get out of here.

I dare to take a step forward when the floor creaks with Lilly's steps, it distracts them enough that they don't hear her; both men point their guns at my head. "You should go hide," I tell them, a sick grin on my face with false confidence in my voice. *Run, Lilly!*

Lilly must know that I'm speaking to her, but she doesn't listen. Of all the times I need her to just listen to me, now is the time. But she doesn't, she just continues forward, entering the foyer and holding a gun in her hands high, pointing at the tall man to my right.

"You have two minutes, Joe," the bald man says. "Or else Nicky here..." he sticks his thumb out pointing to the other man and turns his head slightly to look at him. My heart jumps up my throat when he does, because as he turns to look at his partner, he catches sight of Lilly. I see it all happen in slow motion.

Fuck!

He shouts and raises his gun at her, whipping around on his heels and I react instantaneously, pushing forward with all of my weight, shoving him down to the ground. All the sounds and screams turn to white noise, my lungs freezing, my heart beating frantically. A rush of heat takes over my body, nearly numbing me. I've never felt so much fear in my life.

"Run!" I yell at Lilly as several gunshots go off at once. Bang! Bang! Bang!

Lilly, not Lilly. My throat hurts from my screams as I fight for the gun. Trying to keep him from shooting it, but trying to look at Lilly. Run! Just run!

I hear her shrill scream as another bullet echoes off the wall. A stray piece of drywall falls into pieces and lands on the bald man's face. And then another gunshot, this one from the gun I'm fighting over. The jolt of the trigger being pulled loosens the grip this fucker has on it.

The bullet flies through the air and strikes me in my upper forearm. Fuck! I curse under my breath. In and out in the blink of an eye. I feel the urge to reach up and grab the wound, but I can't. I won't let it stop me from strengthening my hold on the gun. Nothing will stop me.

"Lilly!" I call for her. I can't hear her. "Lilly!"

My fingertips slip against the gun as the bastard kicks me in the gut. Both of us are wrestling on the ground, trying to rip the gun out from each other's grip. The pain from the shot in my arm shoots up and down my shoulder. I ignore it, merely clenching my teeth from the screaming pain as I continue to fight.

His head is close to the thick front leg of the foyer table. I could take a risk and stop fighting for the gun, going for his chin instead and try to slam his head into the hardwood. But that would mean letting go of the gun that I almost have a grip on. His fingertips fumble at the trigger again, a bullet whizzing through the air and landing into the plaster wall. He flinches from the sudden shot.

I take advantage of the moment, hurling my body upward. Using my forearm instead of my hand, I smash the back of his head against the leg of the table. It doesn't do any real damage, but it makes him close his eyes. I'm able to jump forward and sink my teeth into his forearm and grab the gun the second he loosens his grip on it. In a swift moment, the gun is in my hands and I don't hesitate to put a bullet through his skull. *Bang!*

My heart races as I quickly raise the gun in my hands and prepare to shoot the other bastard. But instead I find Lilly, staring at the man lying still on the floor. Three gunshot wounds are visible from the blood staining his shirt.

Lilly doesn't look at me when I call her name, still gripping the gun in both of her hands. She's shaking.

I stand slowly with my hands up, looking between the two men dead on the floor. There's blood spilling from their open wounds and pooling on the marble floor beside them. At least it happened out here, where I can easily clean up this mess.

I can hardly look at Lilly. I'm full of shame. It's because of me that she had to fight for her life. I couldn't protect her. I brought this pain to her. It's my fault.

She drops the gun to the ground, and it hits the marble hard with a loud thud as she collapses into my open arms. The moment I close my arms around her, she sobs into my chest, trembling uncontrollably. As if my touch broke the trance.

I've put up with my brother and father for years. But they brought Lilly into this, and that firms my resolve.

I kiss Lilly's hair softly, rubbing soothing circles on her back. But I stare straight ahead at the blank wall, knowing I need to kill them. Tonight.

CHAPTER 27

Lilly

J'm a ball of nerves as I sit in Madam Lynn's office, my mind on what just happened.

I killed a man.

I still can't believe it. It's nearly impossible for me to process. I keep thinking that I'm going to wake up and find out this was all some horrible nightmare. I pull my legs up into the chair, wrapping my arms tightly around my knees.

But it's too fucking real.

Never in a million years would I have thought I'd wind up in a situation like this. It's like a real life action movie. Hell, it's even like one of my romance novels. Except there might not be a happy ending for this one.

The thought chills my blood.

Even worse, I thought Joseph was going to die. I saw him die. I know I did. I couldn't pull the trigger as the man came after me. But I saw Joseph. I saw the bullet. My chest tightens as I remember the gun pointed at his head. God, I can hardly breathe remembering it. My heart felt like it was ripped from my chest. Even now I get cold sweats thinking about it. He was so close to death.

Had I not walked in right at that moment, he would've died. They were going to kill him.

I'm glad I shot that asshole. I'm glad he's dead. I'll never tell a soul. But I don't regret it. Not for a single moment.

And now I'm here. Stranded in an office in Club X. Joseph left me here, shoving cash into my purse and telling me that they'd protect me.

He pushed me away. He told me they would protect me, literally pushing me into the arms of people I don't even know.

And now I'm ready to leave. I rest my face on my knees. My eyes feel hot against my cool skin. I just want to get the fuck out.

I'm tired of being in this office. I either want to be with him, or I want to go home.

I'm tired of being a prisoner.

I know after what happened, he's pushing me away for my safety, trying to figure things out. And he wants me to be where he thinks I'm safe. I understand, I do. But I still don't want to be here. I feel helpless just sitting here and waiting around for I don't know how long.

I look around the office. It's so depressing. Just a medium-size room with a large oak desk littered with papers and not a single window.

Besides the lamplight, it's dark in here. Madam Lynn has been very nice to me and has done her best to make me feel comfortable with what she has to work with, but she hasn't come back in, I glance at the clock above the door, for almost two hours. I haven't seen *anyone* for hours. My heart flickers in my chest. I don't even know if Joseph is still here. I cover my face with my hand.

How could he just leave me here?

I shake my head and put my feet back on the ground. He has to know by now I can't live without him. Isn't it obvious that I love him? He must know.

Restless, I get up from my seat and pace the floor, wondering what the hell I should do. I want to leave, but I'm not sure if I'll be safe. And he told me to stay here. He practically pleaded with me to do as I was told.

The door opens, and I pause mid-stride as Joseph walks into the room. My lips part, and my breath halts.

My heart skips a beat at the sight of him. Dressed in dark slacks, a crisp, black dress shirt and coat, he looks pale and a little rough around the edges with a day's worth of coarse stubble around his jawline, but he's never looked so damn good to me. I'm so relieved to see him after being secluded in this room for hours.

"What's going on?" I ask him, immediately going to him.

He looks at me, holding me as I put my hands on his chest. But he doesn't answer me. My skin pricks with a chill. I know he's hiding a gunshot wound under his shirt. He has to be in pain. But I want to beat the shit out of him. Tell me what's going on!

I CROSS MY ARMS OVER MY CHEST, MOVING AWAY FROM HIM AND shoving the emotions down.

"You don't need to worry about it," he says finally, walking over to stand in front of Madam Lynn's desk. There's exhaustion in his voice, but he's doing his best to hide it. My eyes feel heavy and raw. I swallow thickly, not knowing what to do or say.

"YOU OWE ME MORE THAN THAT," I SAY WARILY. "YOU ALMOST DIED. I –" I swallow thickly.

And now I'll never be the same. The room is filled with nothing but the sound of my beating heart as he stares back at me, saying nothing. Offering me nothing.

I gesture sharply at him, pointing my finger at my chest. "I deserve to know."

Joseph shakes his head. "You don't need to know anything." His words are hard, but his eyes are soft. "I'm trying to keep you safe."

"Keeping me in the dark is not keeping me safe," I say with every ounce of sincerity I have.

When that doesn't get through to him, I add, "And I absolutely hate it here." I sound like a petulant child, and I hate it. But I really can't stand it here. I'd almost rather be in my fucking cage. And that's saying something.

His eyes study my face for a moment, and a twinge of hope goes through me. Maybe he'll change his mind. But when he speaks, his voice is firm. "It's the best place for you right now."

I START TO ARGUE WITH HIM WHEN THE DOOR SWINGS OPEN, AND IN walks a man I met when Joseph brought me in here. Zander.

I turn in his direction, taking in his appearance. With chiseled features and dark blond hair, he's a handsome man, dressed in a black suit with a white dress shirt. Tall and noble-looking, but with eyes like his, he looks like he holds just as many secrets as Joseph does. It makes me wonder if this club is filled with men like them.

I guess it would make sense. Men like these don't become rich and powerful without accumulating secrets.

Joseph turns away from me to meet Zander's gaze. "What did you find out?" he asks him.

Zander glances at me for a moment, as if debating if he should talk in front of me. But Joseph gives him a slight nod to go ahead. The pain in my chest eases slightly at his gesture. At least he trusts me with some things.

"I know for a fact it was your brother," Zander says. Like Joseph, his voice is deep and rich, and it has a kind of calming quality to it. He stares at Joseph as if waiting for a violent reaction. "He set you up."

Joseph's quiet for a moment, and I can only wonder what he's feeling right now. His own brother tried to have him killed? It's not hard for me to comprehend after reading his journal. I know it still hurts him though. It makes my heart ache for him. I couldn't begin to comprehend being in such a position.

There's a coldness in Joseph's eyes that scares me when he answers, "I already know that." It reminds me of death.

"Good, then you'll be taking care of that matter soon?" Zander asks, taking a seat in the corner of the room as if they're talking about a sale on dry cleaning.

My heart skips a beat as I realize what this is about.

I don't even have to hear him say it. I know he's going to kill his own brother. His own flesh and blood. Joseph's answer is short, "Yes."

"When you go," Zander says, crossing his left ankle over his right knee, "check your father's closet." Zander's words are firm as he stares at Joseph with a hard look.

I stand there numb, not believing the casual tone of this conversation.

GOD, I FEEL SICK. I WALK SLOWLY BEHIND JOSEPH TO THE FAR END OF the room, wishing I could disappear.

"I will," Joseph replies firmly.

Both men stare at each other for a moment, and then Zander gives Joseph a slight nod before leaving without another word.

As soon as the door clicks shut, I feel Joseph's eyes on me, waiting for my reaction.

"Please don't go," I plead, my voice nearly a croak, "you don't have to do this." My eyes are wide and begging for him to have mercy on me. I can't let him go. I don't know if he'll come back.

Joseph takes me in his arms, but he doesn't answer me. He holds onto me as I feel every last bit of hope slipping away. My nails dig into his shirt. "Please," I whisper. But there is no softening in his position. He's going whether I like it or not.

"I'll have tracking on my phone so you'll be able to see where I am," Joseph says, his voice soft, nearly sympathetic.

"I don't want to have to track you," I cry beneath my breath. "Just don't go! Please. Think about what you're about to do."

Joseph's voice remains firm. "I have. And that's why I have to do this." *Kill them.* The words seem to leap into my mind.

I sag against his firm body, tears burning my eyes. I don't want him to leave. I saw him shot, wounded and about to die. Now he's stepping in the line of danger again.

And it scares me like fuck that he might not come back. I cling onto him harder, feeling desperate and vulnerable and foolish, but I want him to stay. I want him to live. I can't save him if he leaves me.

"Please," I whisper against his hard chest as he tries hopelessly to soothe me. "I'm begging you."

Joseph's silent as he holds me.

"I have to go," Joseph tells me after a while, pulling back from me. Oh my God. It hurts like hell.

I try to cling to him, but he pries my fingers away from him, pushing me back against Madam Lynn's desk. I instantly feel cold. Abandoned.

"Let me go, Lilly," he says, his voice cold. God, he's breaking my heart. He's ripping it apart.

I shake my head, my throat throbbing from the aching pain. "No, you don't have to go."

"I'm leaving." His words are so cold now that I'm sure this time he means it. I take a step back, wrapping my arms around myself and trying to hold myself together.

He gives me a kiss on the cheek that makes me close my eyes, the hot tears rolling down my cheeks. "I gave myself to you," I speak just above a murmur. He pauses at the door, his hand on the doorknob, and turns to look at me. My skin pricks under his gaze as the tears roll down my face.

I try to say more. I try to explain what I'm feeling. But all I can think about is the first night he took me. I brush away the bastard tears.

Through my hazy vision, I see Joseph staring back at me. He looks like he wants to tell me something. For the first time since he's walked in the room, I see something in his eyes. That same look I saw when he comforted me over Zach's death.

Tell me, I urge him silently. *Tell me that you love me.*

I want him to say it. Because I know I love him.

Say it! my mind screams.

And it looks like he's about to do it.

I part my lips expectantly, ready to say it back.

But then he turns away and walks out, not saying a word as he shuts the door behind him.

It's not till he's gone that I realize I never told him either. I whisper in the empty room. "I love you, Joseph. You better come back to me."

CHAPTER 28

Joseph

I stalk through the dark hallways of the home I grew up in. If one could call it a home. The memories that haunt my dreams flash before my eyes as my quiet footsteps cause the hardwood floors to creak beneath my boots.

I expected to be nervous. I anticipated my heart beating turbulently with a cold sweat swarming over my body. Instead there's nothing. I hold the handgun in my gloved hand, the silencer pointing down to the floor. As I step closer and closer to the room my brother stays in, I feel resolute.

The Levi household is practically a mansion. A lonely one, full of empty rooms. The screams when I grew up used to fill the halls, I'll never forget that. I know every inch of this place

I also know the escape route and where it leads. I learned it when I was young, it was something that we all needed to know. My father taught me the layout for my own safety. It's probably the one good thing he ever did for me. And now I'm using it against him.

I used the escape route to come into the kitchen, completely undetected. There are no alarms from there up to here, there's nothing standing in my way of creeping into their bedrooms and killing them in their sleep.

A small part of me wishes I would only kill my brother. My father never came after me. It's all my brother.

At the thought of leaving my father alive, my heart finally races and adrenaline courses through my blood. That's not something I can do. He will come for me. He may not know it was me, but he would come for me anyway. He would come to force me to take over the business. He's getting old, and there needs to be a Levi to carry on the name. But when the night is through, there will be none left.

I'll make sure of that.

I adjust my grip as I approach my brother's door, my heart pounding in my ears. All I need to do is shoot him in his sleep. He's an easy target, a simple kill. He deserves a much worse death. I'd like to wake him; I'd like to beat him into a bloody pulp with my bare hands.

Killing him this way isn't justice, but I can't afford risks.

Not when I have Lilly waiting for me.

I imagined his door will be locked, and testing the doorknob proves that much true. It doesn't take me long to pick it though. He was in the habit of locking his door when we grew up. He was also in the habit of stealing from me and of hurting women in the middle of the night. The memories flash before my eyes as the lock clicks, and the doorknob turns.

The memories make me sick. Not just because of what I've witnessed, but because of what I allowed to happen. I didn't have to; I could have fought. I would have lost, but I could have at least tried.

I open the door so slowly that it barely makes a sound. But every tiny noise forces my heart to jump in my chest. I know for a fact he'll have a gun near him. We all did growing up. That was the only way to ensure our safety. I can't afford to wake him.

I can barely breathe as I stalk into his room, placing each step as silently as possible. My eyes had already adjusted to the darkness in the hallway, and the faint light from his windows only adds to my ease of seeing in the dark.

The covers are loose around his hips. His body is visible, an easy target. I get closer than I need to, just to get a better look at him as I steal the life from him.

There's no bang to my gun. No sound other than the harsh breeze of the bullet whipping through the air. His body jolts once as the first bullet enters his head, and then another. And then another. I waste three bullets on him, staring at his dead body without feeling as though it's not real. The last two were unnecessary, only a result of my anger. Each time I pulled the trigger, I thought of the look on her face as she stared down at the man who tried to kill her. The man she killed. I put the gun to his head and pull the trigger again.

Looking down at my brother, even dead he looks cruel. There was never any hope for him, no saving him.

My father's next. It's the only thought in my mind, and the only thing that keeps me from putting a fifth bullet into Ricky's skull as I leave my brother's room. My father's suite is at the other end of the hallway. I don't hesitate to go to him next. My brother's death doesn't faze me in the least. If anything, it gives me more strength to put my father into the ground next to him. That's where they belong.

My heart stops when I walk into the room. Not needing to pick the lock, it opened easily. My feet halt when the floor creaks beneath my weight. I'm unsteady as I count two bodies in the bed. One is my father, and the closest to me. His breathing is coming in heavy as he faintly snores in his sleep.

The other body is much smaller. A woman. And as the sound of my weight on the floorboards creaks through the night, she turns in her sleep. My heart beats erratically, my body heating and every tiny hair standing upright. I only planned on two deaths tonight. I don't want an innocent life caught in the crossfire. There's no way I can leave without seeing this through though. And I can't leave any witnesses.

I take one more step, pointing my gun at my father. I'm a few feet away, but all I need to do is put a bullet in his skull and I can leave, leaving the woman unharmed. *She doesn't have to die.*

My heart refuses to beat as the one last step I take is enough to wake the woman. She groans, stretching her arms and sitting up in the bed with a sleepy yawn, her eyes closed tight. Fuck! She rubs the sleep from her eyes as I take two steps forward.

The sound of my jeans scraping against one another fills the room and wakes her further. The silencer points directly at my father's head; I get one bullet off before the woman screams. It's all I need though. My father's head jolts as the bullet leaves a neat hole just to the right of the center of his forehead.

I can't think; I can't breathe. My body feels like it's heating to an unbearable degree. I don't know how I can save her. As I try to think, she does something she should know not to do. She turns her back to me, grabbing the gun off the nightstand. She grips it with both hands, turning toward me, ready to shoot me.

And for a split second I consider letting her.

What good have I done the world? Killing my father and brother were the last good things I could ever do. The best things I've done with my life. I've lived with no purpose for years.

The sound of her pulling the hammer back, the cold steel shaking in her trembling hands, loading the barrel of the gun with the bullet she intends to kill me with, triggers the memory of her, Lilly. Of my flower.

I need to live for her.

Without another thought, I pull the trigger. The bullet whizzes through the air, hitting her in her throat. She falls off the bed, the gun leaving her hand and falling with a thump onto the padded carpet.

I'm quick to go to her side, now that she's unarmed. I kick the gun to the side as both of her hands press against her throat, trying to stop the blood. My initial reaction is to save her. I kneel on the ground; she looks at me with wide eyes filled with fear. I press my palm to the wound in her neck even as she tries to helplessly push me away. The woman has fight, but there's too much blood. It pains my heart. I didn't want this.

"I'm sorry," I barely get the words out as her hot blood covers both of my gloved hands and soaks into the cream carpet.

I stare down at the dying woman. Her innocent blood is on my hands as I try to stop the wound from gushing blood. The pumps of hot liquid become weaker and weaker as her heart slows, and the life falls from her eyes. One deep breath leaves her, and she's gone. Another victim. I don't know who she is, but her death is on my hands.

. . .

THE SICK FUCK THAT MY FATHER IS, HE HAD TO TIE ME TO A CHAIR before he did it. I struggle against the binds at my wrists, but it's useless. My ankles are bound, and my thighs are strapped to the chair beneath me. So is my chest. I scream until my throat is raw and hoarse. For the first time in my life, my cheeks are wet with tears.

He's punishing me for not doing his will. For disobeying an order. I was trying to do what was right. I was trying to save the woman he wanted me to torture. And now I have no choice but to watch as he beats my mother in front of me. I look up at my brother, pleading with him to help.

"He's killing her!" I scream at him. Mother isn't even crying anymore. At first, she tried not to scream. She didn't want to see me upset. She told me it was okay. She told me she loved me. Even as my father slapped her across the face with the butt of the gun. But as he continued, his brutal hits coming with more force, she couldn't hold it back any longer. She begged him, just as I am now.

My brother looks back at me with the same look that my father's always had. Eyes filled with malice. The breath leaves my lungs, and my voice is lost as a shrill bang echoes in the small room. I hang my head low.

I was only twelve, and that was the last time anyone called me little sparrow. And the last time anyone told me they loved me.

I LOOK DOWN AT THE WOMAN ONE LAST TIME, WIPING HER BLOOD ON the sheets as I stand, towering over her and glancing back at my father. Her eyes are closed, and she's covered in blood. My father's eyes are open and cold and that's how they always were, staring at nothing. Beneath him blood pools into the mattress. The sheet soaks up the dark red liquid.

She may have died because I came tonight. To finish this.

I almost leave without heeding Zander's words, that I need to check the closet. My eyes dart to the double doors, and I take cautious steps to see what lies behind them. My body heats, knowing I'm trusting him. A man I don't know.

The door squeaks open slowly, the only sound in the room other than my own shallow breathing. The blood rushes in my ears, drowning out all other sounds as I stare at the monitors and video recordings of every inch of this house. Some areas I don't recognize. The screens flicker and move to rooms I've never seen before. It's surveillance, of this house and of somewhere else.

I watch them for a moment, each second passing, my body chills and my heart pounds. I remove the tapes, one by one. There are eight of them, and I stop the recordings before leaving. Had Zander not told me, there's no doubt in my mind I would've gone away for murder this time. The hard evidence is undeniable.

I walk to the door, stepping over the poor woman's dead body and turning my back to my father.

It's over now.

And not another body will be put in the ground because of that man. I close the door behind me and leave the way I came.

CHAPTER 29

Lilly

I've been tossing and turning all night. The back of my eyes is throbbing from a terrible headache, brought on by a lack of sleep. I think I've been up for over twenty-four hours, running on fumes.

I'm in a private room at Club X. The bed I'm lying on, a king-size plush pillow top mattress, is soft and comfortable. It practically begs me to go to sleep. But I can't. It's nice and all, but I prefer my room back at Joseph's house. Or his room, as long as he's next to me.

I can't stop thinking about him. I don't know if he's okay, or if he's even alive.

I swallow thickly as I see the dim light of morning peeking around the luxury curtains and then glance at the phone he left me.

The little dot that tracks his location is in the same spot. It makes me feel sick, like something's terribly wrong. The fucking dot won't move. I wish I could talk to someone--Joseph, or one of his associates, and be assured that he's okay. Anyone!

I called his phone at least a dozen times, but he hasn't answered. I knew he wouldn't in the beginning, but by now he should've.

My throat constricts and I roll over in bed, hating to think about it. Hating time for going so slowly.

Just come back to me.

A KNOCK ON THE DOOR BRINGS ME TO MY FEET FASTER THAN I WOULD have thought possible, my heart pounding in my chest.

I'm just at the door when Madam Lynn walks in.

She looks sharp as usual, dressed in a black dress that has ruffles at the bottom and black glossy heels, her hair pulled up into an elegant bun while wispy bangs frame her face. She looks perfectly fine. As though her friend isn't out killing his father and brother this very second.

Her face is solemn as she steps into the room and stops a few feet away from me.

"I'm here to tell you that you can go home now," Madam Lynn says softly. "Isaac set up a security system around your townhouse. You don't need it," she shakes her head gently, her eyes rolling as she adds, "He's peculiar about safety."

I part my lips to ask her about Joseph when there's a knock at the door.

Isaac sticks his head through the doorway, glances between the both of us, and then steps inside the room. Though I'm filled with anxiety, I can't help but notice the authority Isaac radiates. It reminds me of Joseph. Those chiseled features, the power and ruthlessness behind his eyes are familiar to me.

"IT'S DONE," ISAAC TELLS MADAM LYNN. "I'VE MADE SURE THAT NO one will gain access."

The look that passes across Madam Lynn's face as she glances at Isaac is one of extreme gratitude.

"But what about Joseph?" I ask. The hell with my safety, I want to know what's going on.

Madam Lynn exchanges a glance with Isaac and something seems to silently pass between them. My heart pounds harder in my chest.

I look back and forth between the both of them. "Where is he?" My body trembles with anxiety. Someone tell me something!

Madam Lynn is silent, and the look of sadness she throws my way makes my stomach churn.

"Please tell me what's going on!" I cry.

"You're better off without him," Isaac says finally, firmly. At the frown that crumples my face, he adds, "I'm sorry if it's not what you want to hear, but he's no good for you, Lilly."

"Isaac!" Madam Lynn snaps, and she looks pissed. And Isaac's shocked.

"IF HE REALLY WANTED YOU, HE'D BE HERE. NOT LEAVING YOU TO wonder where he's at," Isaac says.

"That's not true. You don't know him!" I cry out.

"Get out, Isaac," Madam Lynn says in a low voice. "I told you, you don't know him." Her voice is full of hurt. And from the look that flashes in his eyes, he seems genuinely sorry.

"OUT," MADAM LYNN SAYS IN A BIT OF A BRIGHTER TONE, SHOOING him away.

Isaac stands there for a moment waiting for her to look at him again, but she doesn't. He looks like he wants to tell me something. But again... nothing.

He presses his lips into a straight line and nods before leaving the room. At the door, he stops to tell me, "My team and I will be waiting to escort you home, Ms. Wade. Just come to us when you're ready."

I don't answer him. Fuck him for saying that. It hurts. I'm already hurting, and what he said was only salt in the wound. The only words I can get out are, "You don't know him."

The second the door closes, Madam Lynn says, "I was really pissed at Joseph." She clears her throat, taking the seat in the far corner of the room. The chair is a pale pink, and studded nails line the smooth leather. She runs her hands down the edge and it suits her. She looks like she belongs there.

"He's okay," she says and I stare at her with wide eyes. "Joseph is." My body sags with relief. "He called a few hours ago. It's over with."

A few hours ago? Her words hit me like a knife to my back.

"I'm sorry about Isaac. He doesn't know Joseph well." I can tell she's trying to change the subject, but I don't let her.

"Hours?" I ask her. Her expression tells me that she knows how I feel.

"He's safe. And he knows you're safe." I'm quiet as I sit on the edge of the bed, overwhelmed by so many emotions.

"He'll come for you. I'm sure he will." Her eyes are so full of sincerity, that I believe her. I believe that she truly thinks he will.

But her words don't give me the confidence I need. I want him here now. I want to watch that stupid dot on the phone coming closer and closer to me. Bringing him back to me.

But then I think back to the last look he gave me, and my doubts fall away.

I know what I saw in his eyes. And that wasn't a lie.

He loves me. And he's going to come for me.

And if he doesn't, then I'll go to him.

CHAPTER 30

Joseph

*T*he trunk closes at the foot of my bed with a loud clack. All the memories of my past have been placed inside, including my journal. I have no need for it anymore, no desire to write another word.

It's over.

There's not a single target on my back with both my father and my brother gone. Zander's assured me he'll keep his ear low to the ground. His finger's on the pulse of what's going on behind closed doors. I'm not sure what he wants from me, he's yet to ask. I don't like owing a debt to anyone if I can help it, but still I'm grateful.

Because of Lilly.

I want her back. I want her here, in my house and in my bed, just like I did that first night I saw her. She belongs to me now. So any protection I can take, I will. Even if that means making a deal with Zander.

As I grab my keys, they clink off the foyer table. The sound echoes with me as I realized the only reason I'll be coming home without her is if she doesn't want me. My hand hesitates on the door-knob, my mind replaying all the moments we've had in the past month.

We've grown together. I've been there for her, and she's been there for me. At least in my mind, that's what happened. I know these past two weeks she's been a prisoner, unable to go as she pleases. It was for her own safety, her own good. As I close the front door behind me, my body heats as I remember her in the cage staring at me with daggers in her eyes.

She could leave me now. She could walk away from me forever, and there's nothing I can do. I never locked the cage, and I never will.

The thought chills me along with the bitter cold February air. I forgot my coat. I don't give a fuck; I'm not going back. Not until I have her in my arms.

My strides quicken, and I hit the clicker to unlock my car. The faint *beep beep* rings out in the cold.

I'll be coming back with my flower. I know I will.

Just as I open my driver door, I see a car coming up the long winding drive. There's a dusting of snow over the clearing, and as the old red Honda takes the bend, the car drifts slightly.

My heart races in my chest, and I drop the keys onto the ground.

Lilly.

She regains control and takes it slower up the drive. I swear to God if she kills herself finding her way back to me, I'll never forgive her.

I leave the keys where they are as small specks of snow float down from the sky and Lilly parks her car in the driveway. She looks up through the windshield, hesitation clear on her face, that gorgeous vulnerability shining in her doe eyes.

My flower.

I try not to assume that she's come for me. That once again we desire the same thing. A harsh lump forms in my throat, the spikes threatening to suffocate me. My hands clench and unclench as the chill of the air starts to affect me.

I ignore all of it, walking to her driver door and opening it. She looks up at me warily as I offer her my hand. *Please don't deny me, my flower.* Be here for me. Please.

Her hand feels so small, so warm in mine. I've always known we were different, but I've grown to love how she complements me. She brings out a side to me that I don't want to lose.

We share a look, I'm not sure what mine reflects to her, but hers undeniably sends a chill through my body. She's looking at me as though she doesn't know what I'm thinking. I've seen it on her face a dozen times or more.

She should know what she means to me. And the fact that she doesn't makes me nervous. I'm not a man who likes to be nervous. It's not a comfortable feeling.

My hand splays on the small of her back, but I'm quick to pull her in close, wrapping my arm around her waist and holding her small body into mine as I lead her inside.

When I peek down at her, lowering myself to the ground to pick up my keys that are now freezing and coated with a thin layer of snow, I see a small smile on her lips. Nothing in my life has made me feel better. She makes me feel secure and wanted. I'll never let her go. Never. When you find someone who makes you feel like this, there's no reason to ever give her a reason to walk away.

She shivers in the doorway as I unlock the door, opening it and allowing the warmth of my home to spread through us both. Her heels click in the foyer as she continues walking without me. I close the door with my back to her, taking a deep breath. She came back to me. I can't let her leave. I close my eyes at that thought, realizing that's not what she needs. I need to give her a reason to stay of her own free will. I can't keep her here, but knowing that she's come here has to mean something.

I turn slowly to face her, her ankles cross slightly and she sways, standing there in the middle of the open doorway, her hands clasped and her coat hanging in the crook of her arm. She looks just as nervous as I feel. The sight of her reminds me of the first day I had her here. The same uncertainty, and just like before I know I'll soothe her worries. If only she lets me.

"I want you to stay for another month," I offer her, my voice echoes off the empty walls, walking to her and standing just inches in front of her. Technically our contract isn't over yet; Valentine's Day is tomorrow. But I want to bind her with the contract if I can. I don't want the days to pass and have no claim to her.

"Just a month?" she asks, a look flashing in her eyes. I like hearing the words "Yes, Sir" from her lips. But this may be even better.

"You want more, my flower?" I hope she says yes. Whatever she tells me she wants, I'll give her. I just need her to tell me.

I finally feel like I have a reason to live. And a future to look forward to with Lilly. I can give her whatever she needs. Whatever she asks for, I would happily provide her with. I'm sure she's realized that by now. Without her with me, I was clinging to the past just to feel. I don't want that anymore. I want her; all of her.

"I care for you Lilly," I stare into her eyes as I tell her, for the first time I think in my entire life making my feelings known for someone else. I feel vulnerable in this moment, and she looks back at me, not answering. She could reject me. It would crush me if she did.

My thumb rubs along her cheek as I cup her chin in my hand. Her hands gently wrap around my wrists as she leans into my touch. Her eyes close, and a look of pure happiness is on her face. It soothes the worry in me, but still I need her to tell me that she feels the same. I know the way we started wasn't what she wanted. It was a game of fools thinking we each knew what we wanted, when we knew nothing. But now I know. And I'm ready to fight for her.

"You can say you love me. I know you do," Lilly says teasingly.

Finally opening her pale blue eyes, it's as though she's looking straight into my soul. The look in her eyes doesn't match the tone of her voice. She needs me to tell her. I'm not sure if I'd recognize the emotion love. It's not something I grew up with, nothing I've ever felt before. But there's something different between the two of us. Something that drew me to her that first day. And something that fuels me to move mountains to be with her. To never let her go.

"I love you, Lilly." My lips brush against hers as I whisper the words. It must be love. "I love you."

"I love you, Sir."

HER WRISTS ARE BOUND BY THE THIN ROPE, THE END LOOPED OVER THE cast-iron loop above the headboard. She's bound to my bed where she belongs. Her movements are easy. The only reason the ropes are even there is to prevent her from spearing her fingers in my hair as I continue to lick between her legs. Her arousal is so sweet, so delicious. And all mine.

I crawl up her body, kissing my way as I go. Her thighs wrap around my shoulders and then down my sides to my waist. I've given her as much control as she can manage for this session. No holding still. No asking permission. All she has to do is feel and react. Although I did bind her wrists… she's greedy.

My fingers are wrapped around her throat as I settle my hips between her thighs, spreading her even more. My hard dick nestles between her sweet pussy. I kiss her lips with the intense passion I feel. I'm grateful for every moment with her. I'll never let her go. I need her too much.

"Who do you belong to?" I ask her.

"You, Sir, only you." I love how lust coats her voice.

"Only me for always," I tell her before slamming into her, all the way to the hilt, capturing her cries of pleasure with my lips. The headboard knocks against the wall with each hard thrust. It only fuels me to take her harder.

She is my one and only. And I'm hers.

EPILOGUE

Lilly

"Not this bullshit again!" I slam the book that I'm reading, *Don't Stop,* shut with a frustrated growl. How in the hell did I manage to find another book that pisses me off so much that I want to throw it across the room? And after I took every precaution to make sure I didn't?

This one was even worse than the last. The hero and heroine, Randy and Ada, made it through so many trials and tribulations that I was rooting for them like crazy toward the end.

I got really excited, turning the pages with bated breath. And it looked like their path was on its way to glory, only to find out that Ada was hiding a secret baby from Randy. A baby that was sure to cause major scandal between their families. The book cut off right there.

Ugh. It makes me so mad!

Like, who the fuck does that?

I can't say it enough.

I. Detest. Cliffhangers.

But even after all that, I'm dying to know what happened.

A thousand poxes on the author for doing this to me and making me wait! ...I know I'll end up buying the next one though. I blow a strand of hair out of my face as I toss the book onto the ottoman. I guess I'm a glutton for punishment.

I stretch out before grabbing my laptop and opening up my manuscript.

Last night I rewarded myself with writing a chapter of my new novel when I was finally finished my grueling lesson plans.

I'm excited about *both* the classes and my book.

The words for the novel are flowing easily. And I know with all the inspiration that I have, and the support of my awesome beta reader Jenna, I'll be able to do the book justice.

But it's my hobby. Not my job. I chew my bottom lip, holding back my smile. I got my old job back before the semester even started. Some anonymous donor came through and funded the *Children in Need Foundation.*

Anonymous. Joseph actually started to tell me it wasn't him when I pried. He didn't want me to feel like I owed him. He has no idea how much I owe him. But not in the way he thinks.

I can't believe how much he's helped me in the short time we've been together. How much we've helped each other. And lately, I've been able to have both sides to him, the Master and the gentleman.

A soft sigh escapes my lips at the thought.

Just thinking about it, I can't imagine my life getting any better.

The sound of heavy footsteps in the doorway causes me to look up, and my heart skips a beat at the dangerously sexy man who's standing there.

"Reading something?" his deep masculine voice asks.

Wearing dark grey dress pants and a white Henley open at the chest, his hair slicked to the side, Joseph looks like an absolute vision as he leans against the doorway with a grin on his face.

"Sir," I practically purr as he pulls away from the door and walks into the room.

I slip out of my chair and onto my knees, getting down on all floors and crawling forward like a vixen.

Joseph chuckles playfully at the sight. He's told me to do this when I want to play with him, and I take full advantage.

"Up," he orders me.

I rise to my feet and look him in the eye. Up close, I'm enveloped by that masculine scent that I love so much, and I inhale deeply, sucking in as much of him as I can.

Grinning, he wraps my arms around his waist and pulls me in close, delivering a soft kiss to my lips.

"I was," I reply to his earlier question when he pulls back, leaving me breathless.

He chuckles again. "I know. I could hear you yelling from across the house."

My cheeks turn red with embarrassment. I hadn't realized I'd been yelling like a maniac. But I guess that's what happens when you get smacked in the face with a cliffhanger.

"Sorry," I mutter.

Joseph quirks an amused eyebrow. "What happened in it that got you so worked up?"

"You don't want to know," I growl.

Joseph pouts. "That's not fair."

Neither was that ending. I still want to beat that author's ass like they're a Submissive from Club X. I don't bother saying it though.

"Life isn't fair," I say, giving him another kiss on the lips.

Joseph grins at me.

We stare at each other for a moment, and my heart feels full. I can't believe how lucky that I am to have this man.

"What?" I ask, breaking out of my thoughts to see Joseph gazing at me with a mischievous smile.

"I've got something for you."

My heart stalling in my chest, I watch as he produces a large, black velvet box. For a moment, I think it might be an engagement ring, but the box is far too big.

A faint smile spreads across my face and I shake my head at my eagerness. It's too soon to be expecting something like that. But I do want it. I want everyone to know that he's mine, and I'm his.

It will happen, I tell myself. *Eventually.*

I clear my throat, reaching out for it, and our fingers brush against one another and I feel that same spark I felt so long ago. Maybe not that long ago, but it feels like it with everything we've been through.

"Open it," he prods softly, pushing the box into my hands.

I keep the smile on my face although my throat closes, and I do as he says. My heart jumps when I see what's inside, my knees going weak.

"Joseph," I gasp, my eyes filling with tears, the air being pulled from my lungs. *Oh my God, oh my God,* I repeat in my mind over and over.

It's a collar, a beautiful one, black and silver, encrusted with sparkling diamonds. But it isn't the first thing that caught my eye.

There's a ring in there, too. I choke on my words for a moment, in shock but mostly just overwhelmed with so much happiness.

"What's this?" I somehow manage, my voice a breathless whisper, though I know exactly what it is. Staring at the ring, a platinum band with a large, sparkling diamond atop of it, it's suddenly very hard to breathe.

I imagined it moments before, but this doesn't seem real.

Joseph sinks to his knee in front of me, his heart in his eyes. My heart skips a beat and my skin pricks as reality sets in. The room spins around me as I stare down at him, and I feel like passing out.

"LILLY MARIE WADE, MY FLOWER," HE SAYS, HIS VOICE ACHING WITH emotion, "Will you marry me?"

I stare at him in disbelief, my throat so tight with emotion I'm barely able to fill my lungs. I can't find the words to answer. I'm stunned.

The silence stretches on for several long moments as I try to get over my shock. My chest heaves as I struggle to draw in breaths, my legs feeling like jello. Through it all, Joseph waits patiently, staying on one knee.

SAY YES, YOU IDIOT!

"Yes!" I'm finally able to croak when I find my voice, leaning down to wrap my arms around his neck and bury his face with tearful kisses, my heart pounding like a battering ram. "Yes, yes, yes! I'll marry you, Joseph!"

"Good." Joseph pulls me down into his arms, delivering a deep solid kiss to my lips. "Because I love you, Lilly. And I'm never letting you go."

I smile up at him through my tears, my heart aching from the unbelievable joy that fills my body and the happiness I see reflected in his eyes.

Delivering another kiss to his lips, I breathe out through aching lungs, "I love you too, Joseph."

Continue for book 4, Given.

GIVEN BOOK 4

PROLOGUE

ZANDER

*B*oth of my hands tremble and the adrenaline pumping in my blood makes my muscles coil, ready to fight. I grip the edge of the dresser to keep my body upright. I only need to breathe. A long and slow exhale leaves me, lowering my tense shoulders. I crack my neck before looking over my shoulder at her. *My sweetheart.*

I've never run from anything in my life. And I'm not about to start now.

But I should have run from *her*. I knew I should have walked away when I first laid eyes on her.

She's destroyed my control. Ruined my reputation. She'll be the end of me, I know it.

Her soft moans of pain from across the bedroom call to me. She's so beautifully broken. She *needs* me.

I took it too far, and I can't take it back.

They'll come for me; I'm certain the cops will be here soon. I'm guilty, and I have no one to blame. The evidence is all right here, and I can't deny a damn thing.

For the first time in my life, I don't see a way out.

There's no one I can turn to. No one who owes me who can make this right.

But I can't stop wanting her. She's gotten under my skin. And I won't stop fighting for her.

Never.

"Zander," she says and her small voice is choked. Her brow is pinched as her head thrashes from side to side and the doctor works on the deep lashes on her back. Agony rises through my chest; it stiffens my body. My eyes burn and my throat closes as I try to breathe.

She's stripped to the waist lying face down on the bed, her bottom half barely covered by a thin white sheet to keep the doctor's prying eyes from seeing even more of her.

I know what he thinks. What they all think since I took her.

I don't give a fuck. I pay him well to turn a blind eye, and that's exactly what he'll do. It's what they all do. They only want the money, and they'll do anything for it.

But not her.

My heavy footsteps are softened by the plush rug as I cross the master bedroom and walk to her. She lifts her head as I come closer, but the moment she does, she winces and sucks in a reluctant breath through clenched teeth.

I'm quick to gentle my hand on her shoulder, keeping my contact confined to the small area of soft skin without any wounds. "Don't move," I say and my voice is low, admonishing even. I hate myself. I'm so devoid of the ability to comfort that I can't even speak softly to her when she's... like this.

"I'm sorry," Arianna says quietly, her voice muffled from the mattress.

A chill runs over every inch of my skin. She has no reason to apologize to me. She never did anything wrong. Not since the first moment this started.

I swallow thickly, and the lump forming in my throat feels as though it scratches the tender skin on the way down. "It's alright." I try to soften my voice and put as much warmth into it as possible. I pet her hair with soothing strokes.

"I never should have left you," Arianna replies, her words coming out slow and full of genuine remorse.

She shouldn't have. This wouldn't have happened if she'd just listened. If she'd *trusted* me.

But it's my fault. Not hers.

"It's going to be alright," I say softly, crouching down so my eyes are level with hers. It's a lie. It's not going to be alright. I'm damn sure of that single truth. Everything is fucked.

But I'll tell her whatever she needs to hear.

I can't lose her.

I press my lips to hers, my hand cupping her jaw and my thumb rubbing comforting circles on her soft skin.

"Is it going to be okay?" she whispers against my lips. It's only when I open my eyes and see hers are still closed with tears running freely down her reddened cheeks that my heart shatters.

I wish I could tell her I'll take care of everything.

But it's not okay. And I can't fix this.

I know I shouldn't, but lying comes so easily to me. "Everything's going to be fine," I tell her. Her long lashes flutter and her gorgeous green eyes open to look back at me. So much raw vulnerability and something else are clearly evident in her gaze. Something that should push me away.

I didn't even want to take her when she was given to me at first. I should have refused.

Maybe even then I recognized what she would do to me. How she would change who I am, and destroy everything I've worked for. When they put me behind bars, they'll figure out everything. The corruption, the money, all the lies.

Even knowing that, I wouldn't hesitate to take her if I had the chance to do it all over again. My hand clenches into a fist, firming my resolve. Even if I couldn't change a damn thing, I'd still accept that sick fuck's offer.

She was given to me.

Now she's *mine*.

CHAPTER 1

ZANDER

I clasp my hands behind my back, staring out of the floor-to-ceiling window in my office. It's on the top floor of Penn Square, one of the three tallest skyscrapers in the city. My fingers run along the cold metal of my Tag Heuer watch as I let my gaze fall to the world beneath me. My shoulders are squared and the rush of the city flows easily through my blood.

This is where I thrive, where I make the deals that run this city.

"Are you listening to me?" my father's voice spills from the speaker on my desk, and the corners of my lips turn up into a smirk.

"I am." I answer easily with an air of confidence I learned from him.

"You never should have accepted." His words are sharp and firm. But he's right.

A heavy sigh leaves me as my eyes narrow at the park directly beneath the building. Although my blood chills at my father's words, I ignore him, cracking my knuckles and continuing to watch the specks of people moving about.

I'm the one that kept our family name from falling. We were going bankrupt because of *his* bad investments and trusting the wrong people. My teeth grind as I clench my jaw. Yes, I fucked up, but not nearly as much as he has. It's been almost ten fucking years of me rising to the top and carrying our legacy with me, creating not just a pristine reputation in the eyes of the community and business elites. I've also worked hard to create one of fear for those who run the underside of this city.

There are many men with power, but they all owe someone... and I happen to be that someone. My father's voice drones on as I move my gaze toward the streets. My father's still admonishing me for a single mistake.

A bad investment named Daniel Brooks.

That dumb fuck owes me a lot of money, more money than he should.

He knew how much debt he had, and he still gambled away my money. He thinks I don't know... I know *everything*. I was the first to know when the sum left his account and wasn't directly passed to mine.

This happens from time to time. *Everyone* owes me, and that's how I like it. It's only a matter of time before something gets between me and the money they owe me.

I don't care; I always come out on top, and that's what matters. Money isn't power, it's leverage. Being owed is power. True power. And that's what I want. It's what I have. But right now Brooks isn't an asset, and I have no way of knowing just how he's going to pay me close to the half a million I'm due. It's not the largest sum, but it's a deal that was public. A debt that many are aware of, and therefore, must be paid.

"Did you hear me?" My father's voice is low as I turn from the city to face my hard maple desk, my eyes focused and narrowed on the black corded phone that came with this office. It's at odds with the modern touches, but the line is traceable and I've been able to use that to my advantage more than a time or two.

"I did," I answer although I'd rather hang up the phone altogether. I don't wait for him to reply.

"Brooks owes me more than what's excusable. More than he's worth." I take my seat, leaning back and propping up my feet on the long, sleek desk.

"You can't allow him to get away with it." My father speaks with authority.

Brooks may be a high-up executive and think he's untouchable, but the alcoholic, gambling degenerate is going to give me my money one way or the other. And then I'm done with him. I have enough pull to bury him if I want. I tap my fingers on the hard wood top, debating. The *rap, rap, rap* echoes rhythmically and calms me slightly.

I could destroy him slowly. Cripple him financially and embarrass him in every way possible. But not many would know why, and he's too pathetic to waste that much time and effort on. No, I'll just take my money and be through with him. He'll hang himself on his own.

My eyes lift to the office door as a solid knock rebounds through the large space.

"Come in," I call out as my back settles against the leather desk chair, but my fingers never stop tapping on the desk as I wait for the door to open.

Charles walks in with a mask of indifference. I'm used to it. When I first met him all those years ago at boarding school, I thought there was something more behind his dark eyes. But now I know the truth; the only emotion I've ever seen reflected in his eyes is anger. It's that, or nothing. And I prefer nothing to his temper.

With short pitch-black hair and eyes to match, Charles is just as lethal as he looks. He didn't grow up with the lifestyle I'm accustomed to, but I made sure to make friends with him. It's been mutually beneficial.

I nod toward the phone before he has a chance to speak. Sharing a glance, he quietly shuts the door behind him, a soft click the only sound in my office.

"I'm going to have to call you back," I lean forward, speaking into the phone and preparing to hang up, knowing damn well that I won't return the phone call. There's nothing to discuss. He'll see me at the next social event and until then, the only thing he'll give me is shit over this debt.

Charles is silent as he takes a seat across from me. Placing an elbow on the arm of the chair, he stares back at me with his finger resting on his bottom lip.

Large black and white photos of the nighttime skyline decorate the wall behind him. The furnishings in my office are entirely black and white, with the walls painted a light grey. To an observer, my office may seem as if it's a minimalist and masculine design. And that's true, but more importantly, it suits me. Cold and simple. No room for bullshit.

I didn't even want the fucking blown-up photos, but I needed something to make the room seem... normal. Complete, even.

"We have a problem," Charles finally says after I've hung up the phone.

I may be deceptive. Born with a silver spoon in my mouth, I come off as playful and charming. They don't see me coming. And most of my clients never have a problem with me. The legal ones, anyway. It's a handshake and a smile, an exchange of money and profit. Those are ninety percent of my interactions. But the other ten percent, well that's where Charles comes in. I can't get my hands dirty. My reputation is everything.

He doesn't attend the social galas and business openings. He doesn't give a fuck about rubbing elbows and being seen with the right people. He meets his clients in back alleys. As far as anyone's concerned, he's an associate.

Everyone in my life is just an associate. And that's never going to change.

"And what's that?" I ask him as my lips kick up into a charming smile. It's always there. Even though it doesn't affect Charles, I can't help the false expression. I've learned to play this role. It pays me well.

"Brooks is a problem," he states and leans forward in his seat, grabbing a paperweight off my desk. It's a small slate cube, heavy with sharp edges. He runs his finger down one side.

Although he's not a threat to me, I can only imagine what he'd do with a weapon like that. I roll my eyes at what he just said and stretch my neck to look out of the large windows again as the sun sets behind us, darkening the room. I can't take another person telling me I've fucked up. I get it. I need someone to offer me a solution to fix it, not tell me the obvious.

"No shit," I say, waiting for his eyes to meet mine. It only takes a moment, and his movements stop.

"Are we offing him?" he asks me.

My blood turns cold, sending a biting wave through every inch of my body. It takes its time, slowly coursing through my veins. I don't take death lightly. Ending someone's life isn't as easy for me as it is for Charles. He grew up around it, made a career of it; killing is simply a way of life for him. They all have it coming and for good reason, but he's quick to take it that far.

I break the hold his dark eyes have on mine and stare at the large clock on the left-hand wall. It's simple and modern, so there aren't any marks on it. It's just a large white circle with contrasting black hands. The second hand sweeps by, rhythmically and perfectly. There's no sound, but I can only imagine the soft *tick, tick, tick* in sync with my own heartbeat.

I click my tongue, feeling the smile fade for a moment before turning my attention back to Charles.

"Who did he give it to?" I ask him. Brooks had the money in his account. I know for a fact what Danny Brooks was worth when I loaned him the investment. It should have been a good return, had he done what he was supposed to do.

"A bookie," Charles answers in a rough deep voice, setting the slate paperweight back down at my desk.

A huff of a humorless laugh rumbles up my chest.

"I'm guessing he thinks the bookie breaking his legs is worse than what you would have done to him," Charles adds and then cracks his neck and settles easily into his seat. He's probably right. Most of these men who work with contracts think I'd settle a dispute using the legal systems.

I'm sure Brooks thinks I'll sue him. But that takes so much time and sets a poor example. It would tarnish my spotless reputation as well. I don't set foot into courtrooms. I'm not interested in a lawsuit or having anything in the paper.

When someone doesn't pay me, I make sure I get more than my money's worth of retribution. I think back to the dozens of men who have tried to get away from me and their debts in the past. They can't run though. They can't hide behind the law, or in the shadows; *I own both.*

"So, what are you going to do?" Charles asks me, pulling me back to the present.

I sit up in my seat and lean closer to him, feeling that slick smile on my face. My blood heats and the resulting adrenaline fuels me. I speak slowly but firmly, staring hard into Charles' unforgiving stare as I say, "I want to know everything about Danny Brooks."

CHAPTER 2

ARIANNA

"They had rabbits, dildos and pulsators," Natalie shamelessly continues as she sets down her paintbrush in the cup of now-dirty water that sits between us. She's got an asymmetric grin on her face as she rises from her seat to step back and survey her handiwork. "It was *awesome*," she says and the smile doesn't fade as she stares at her canvas.

I stop my brush midstroke to look at her, arching a questioning eyebrow. Even dressed in pale blue overalls with old paint stains all over them, Natalie looks beautiful. She has the kind of natural beauty that comes equipped with confidence. Her dark brown hair cut in a short side bob sways as she crosses her arms and nods her head, and her large brown eyes widen as she steps forward and smudges a small spot on her canvas with her finger. The smile only fades for a moment until she's satisfied with the adjustment.

She lets out an easy sigh and her eyes sparkle as she meets my stare. I force a small smile back but avoid her gaze as I take in my own canvas. I've been in a cruddy mood all day. I was hoping painting would cheer me up. But so far, all I've done is paint a weeping willow that's truly crying because of how damn dark the picture is. A frown mars my face as I realize there's no fixing this.

I don't know what's wrong with me.

"Pulsators, huh?" I ask halfheartedly. "That's a new one." I shake my head as I set my brush down into the cup, dismayed with my lack of progress.

I pull my hair over my shoulder and twirl the ends as she continues, "Yeah. It's a little ball that goes into your cooch and vibrates." I stare at Natalie, slowly processing what she's saying. Thank fuck I have her as my roommate, sharing a two-bedroom apartment together in the middle of downtown. We split the rent to make costs bearable. But more than that, she's been my friend for years. Even through the darker times when I pushed her away. We picked up everything right where we left off when we reconnected.

Right now, I just don't give a shit about whatever sex toy party she went to last night.

I clear my throat trying to muster an ounce of her excitement as I say, "That sounds... fun."

Natalie pouts, her eyes dimming with concern. "What's wrong, Ari? Considering the stuff you're into," she says, eyeing me curiously, "I thought something like that would be right up your alley."

I feel like shit, but I just want to be alone. "I feel off. I'm just tired." I swirl the brush in the dirty cup to get some of the paint off the bristles. I speak without looking up, staring at the murky water, "I think I need some sun or something." I didn't expect her to come in here and join me, but I wasn't going to tell her no. Natalie's frown deepens and then she looks past me toward my bedroom door. "I'm sorry I'm being such a downer, Nat," I say, flashing her a weak smile. "I just feel like I woke up on the wrong side of the bed or something."

Nat stares at me for a long moment, chewing on the inside of her cheek before finally saying, "I'm a little worried about you, Ari." Her voice is delicate and cautious, but she doesn't need to be. I'm okay. I'm not where I was before.

I wave off her concern. "Don't be. I'm good." I nod at my canvas. "Just let me finish this up." I stare at the painting for a minute before pursing my lips. I should probably just trash it or paint the whole damn thing white and start over.

Nat gazes at me with suspicion. "You sure?"

I nod, picking my paintbrush back up and pressing the bristles against the side of the cup to get rid of most of the water. "Yeah. Tell me more about the party," I say, trying to change the subject back to her preference: sex. "It sounds like it was a lot of fun."

Nat nods, but her enthusiasm from earlier is dimmed, which makes me feel like shit. I hate spreading negativity.

I avoid her gaze entirely, shoving up my sleeves to add a bit of white paint to the background of the canvas. "It was. There's a bonus right now-" Nat pauses, and reaches out for my arm, her fingers wrapping just below my elbow. Her grip is so strong she nearly pulls me backward. "What the hell happened to your arm?" Although it's a question, there's an accusation underlying her words as she stares at my arm in horror.

Shit. I pull away from her grasp, clenching my teeth and feeling a bit irritated. A bit ashamed. My heart is still lodged in my throat and I can't respond for a moment. I'm feeling her judgment.

I part my lips to reply, to make up some lie, some defense, but then close them. Nat's seen the bruises before. This is nothing new. She knows where they come from, and she knows that they're there with my consent. That it's just a kink.

I try to swallow, but my throat is dry. I hate how she does this to me. She makes me feel guilty.

Nat places her hands on her hips and glowers at me when I offer no response. "Well? And don't tell me it was just how you and Danny like to play," she says but her voice cracks with pain. Her nostrils flare as she glares at my arm. "I don't believe it. Not this time." A part of me loves her for caring. Another part wants her to fuck off. We've gone around and around with this issue. It's how I've dealt with it all. It's the one thing that worked. Or used to work.

The very mention of his name sends a chill down my spine and causes my skin to prick with anxiety, although it never used to. If it weren't for Danny, I wouldn't be here. He helped me when I was at my lowest point in my life, saving me from darkness that was on the verge of swallowing me whole. There's no reason I should feel like this, but I do. I feel... afraid.

I pull my sleeve down, focusing on breathing and ignoring her. I need to talk to him. I'm not into this lifestyle like he is. It worked for a while, so he was right about giving it a shot. I'm just not sure I want to keep doing it.

But I owe him. And he's made it clear that he doesn't want to stop. Even if there's no sexual pleasure in it. He's not my boyfriend. Only my Master. He gives me the release I need to get rid of this sadness through an outlet of pain. But it's not working anymore. I don't know what changed.

"It's nothing," I say hastily, quick to cut her off the path she's heading down.

"Nothing?" Nat asks in disbelief. "That looked like a hell of a lot more than nothing."

I give her a big fake smile in an attempt to put her at ease, trying to hide the anxiety that's twisting my stomach. "It's not though, trust me. Really, it's nothing," I lie as my throat closes and my chest feels hollow, "I enjoyed it actually."

Natalie stares at me for a long time, her big brown eyes roving my face, searching for honesty.

Finally, she shakes her head and the moment she does, I feel a wave of relief. I can't lose her. I have no one else. *No one but Danny.* Even though I don't want him anymore. Not like that though. I never wanted him *like that*. "I know this is supposed to be," Nat takes in a breath as she looks to the door again and waves her hand in the air, "the thing you guys have, but I'll never be able to understand it. And quite frankly, it scares the shit out of me."

I don't blame her. Most people wouldn't understand. In fact, no one I know does. I don't even remember why I wanted this to begin with. He said it would heal me and in a way, it did. But it's grown to be something different, and it doesn't feel like healing anymore. It's turned into something else. "But if it makes you happy and you're getting laid, I guess that's all that matters," Natalie mutters, clearly upset, but at least she's leaving it alone. I'm not getting laid, although she doesn't have to know the specifics. I'll fix this. I just need to tell Danny that I don't want it anymore and that I'm fine without it. Although I really don't know if I am fine. I will talk to him though... soon. I feel guilty for even thinking about it. Danny's done so much for me; I owe him my life. I feel ungrateful for wanting to complain, but it's time for me to move on.

"Maybe you should try it sometime," I suggest playfully, trying to lighten the tone, but I immediately regret it.

Natalie shakes her head vigorously. "Hell no. I like my vanilla sex with pulsators just fine, thank you very much. I'll leave that freaky shit to you. "I huff out a dry chuckle, but I can't shake the feelings stirring in the pit of my stomach. I agreed to this M/s relationship, at at times I even wanted it. But now I don't know how to get out.

"Ari?" Nat asks, breaking me out of my thoughts. I refocus my eyes on her face. "You sure you're okay, Hun?" The words are on my lips. I could tell her everything about how I feel right now. Doing it would be like a weight lifted off my chest. I would finally have someone I could confide in about what's really going on in my life. But that's not what I do.

"Ari?" Nat presses when I don't respond. I flash her a smile and reply, "I'm fine," when deep down, I know I'm not.

CHAPTER 3

ZANDER

he Mercedes practically purrs as I park in the large, ten-story garage attached to the Parker business suite. This isn't the first time I've been in here. I don't own it, but I own plenty of men who sit behind the desks in this building.

And one of these fuckers is Danny Brooks.

The car door clicks shut and the alarm beeps as I walk across the concrete ground toward the entrance.

A smile creeps casually onto my lips as the greeter nods his head toward me, the automatic doors opening behind him. "Good evening, sir," he says in a raspy voice that's more comforting than anything else. His grey hair is barely noticeable under the tweed cap that matches his vest. As he smiles broadly at me, the wrinkles gather around his pale blue eyes.

"Good evening," I respond politely, heading straight into the building with a casual pep in my steps. The polished marble floors and stark white walls with gleaming steel framed ceilings make the interior seem so much brighter. Every bit of light is reflected off every surface. The sounds of heels clicking, people chattering and the large fountain in the center of the room spilling water over the edge immediately flood my senses.

It's almost five o'clock, close to quitting time and for a Friday, the main lobby is fairly empty already. But I know Brooks is still here. Charles knows his routine. He's useful for that, and damn good at what he does.

I head straight to the far wall, my hands in my pockets and the hint of happiness on my face. Always smile. *Make them wonder what you're up to.* I remember the words my mother told me once. Back when I thought it was playful... when I thought she was happy. I didn't learn the darkness behind her words until much later. Until it was too late.

The elevator doors open and a man in a crisp grey suit exits, all the while loosening the black tie around his neck and holding his briefcase in his other hand. Two women exit behind him, walking closely and speaking in hushed voices. As I enter the empty cart, I hear them laugh in unison, although it dims as the doors close, leaving me alone and in silence.

I push the button for the twenty-sixth floor, lighting up the ring around the number to bright green and instantly I'm ushered upward. My heart starts to race. It's not every day that I do this; in fact, it's a rarity. I hardly ever have to put pressure on my business associates. Let alone make them fully aware that they can't fuck with me and my money.

I don't enjoy this aspect, but it's a necessity. If you let one man push you around, the others will know they can push you, too. And that can't happen. *Ever.*

It only takes one time to fall. One chance for them to knock you down and tear you apart. Like what happened with my mother. She let them see behind the cracks, and she never recovered.

I shove my hands back into my pockets. I'm still wearing thin leather gloves. It's not so uncommon for them to be worn this early in March. But inside the building, it's warm. And I don't need to be seen wearing them and drawing any suspicion.

Ding.

The twenty-sixth floor comes faster than I anticipated. Showtime.

My dress shoes slap on the hard slate floor as I walk past the two office spaces on my right. My shoulders are straight as I walk with ease past the large glass fronts of the offices. They're all nearly identical in appearance, neatly lined up rows of glass boxes. Each one houses some sort of profession. I stop abruptly and turn on my heels as I spot 2614.

Although my blood's heating, my heart's hammering and I'm certain everyone can see the fire in my eyes, on the surface I'm the same man I always am. Nonthreatening, happy. Not a care in the world.

I keep my hands in my pockets and rock on my heels as I smile down at the receptionist. Forcing the charm to stay in place.

"Mr. Payne," the young woman at the front of the office behind a small white desk greets as she rises to her feet, finally feeling my eyes on her. "May I take your coat?" she asks politely, already holding out her hand. I've been in here several times before, but this is the first time she's remembered who I am.

"No, thank you," I say easily. "I don't have an appointment. I was just hoping to catch Mr. Brooks before he left." I think the woman's name is Delores. I'm almost certain of it. My eyes flicker to the name on her desk plate and I see it there, in thick bold letters. "I appreciate it though, Delores." She brightens at the use of her name. "Do you know if he's in?" I ask the question as I turn from her slightly, angling my body so she knows I'm headed that way.

"He is," she nods happily and takes a seat, scooting her chair back in.

"Have a wonderful weekend," I tell her, dipping my head and walking off as she calls out, "You too, Mr. Payne!"

My feet move of their own accord, everything seeming to narrow in my vision. The sound of my shoes against the thin, cheap carpet is being drowned out by the white noise ringing in my ears.

As soon as I stand in front of his door, every ounce of the facade is gone. I knock once, but I don't wait for a response. Instead I open the door and walk in, kicking it shut behind me as I put my hands back into my pockets.

I casually look over at Danny Brooks, who at first seems shocked but then annoyed.

"I'm not sure if you could hear me, Mr. Payne," Brooks starts to speak while his eyes are on me, but then he looks back at his screen and begins typing, the sound of tiny clicks accompanying his voice, "but I'm currently busy."

"I got your message," I tell him with my hands still hidden.

Brooks barely looks up to acknowledge me, his head still down as he types on the computer without pausing to answer me. "You'll have to make an appointment," he says and his voice is low as he blows me off. It's easy for associates to do when they first meet me and before they've finished doing business with me.

I walk slowly to the side of his desk and it's only then that he stops, his fingers hovering just above the keys. His lower back presses into the thin leather seat, making it creak as he sits straighter and finally acknowledges me. "Yes, it's going to take a little longer than I anticipated." He pinches the bridge of his nose as if I'm a bother to him. As if my mere presence has caused him undue distress or a headache.

The smile finally grows on my face as he continues to underestimate me.

"You aren't able to make the payment?" I ask him, although it's a question, not a statement. My feet move slowly, taking steady strides, rounding his desk but still staying a few feet away, seemingly nonthreatening as I lean back against the wall casually.

"I don't believe so." He types a word, maybe two and then gives me a look of irritation as he turns in his seat and lets out an exasperated sigh. "What can I do for you, Mr. Payne?" he asks in a voice laced with condescension.

I love it, the irony of it. But that's how men like him behave. They act as if *they* own you. When really they don't have a damn thing to their name, and *you* own them.

I shrug and look to my left. The blinds to his small window are closed, so the office is rather dark, and also quiet. It's nearly perfect. But the walls are thin. Luckily, it's past five on a Friday and Mr. Brooks is surrounded by empty office spaces.

I walk closer to him as I speak with an even cadence. "Why is the payment delayed?" I ask him, as if I'm curious. As if it's acceptable to go back on our deal. As if it's fine to piss away half a million that he can't afford to pay back.

The fucker scoffs at me and rolls his eyes.

I don't hesitate to rip my hand from my pocket, grab the back of his head and slam it on the desk. Once, then again. There's no blood; his nose didn't even hit the hard wood surface, only his forehead.

He's merely dizzy as I grab him by the collar and pull him up so his face is just beneath mine. "Was it a sure bet?" I ask him, my voice a sneer. My muscles are tight and coiled. I'm on edge and seeing nothing but red now.

"Zander-" he begins, and my name is a strained plea.

Brooks starts to speak, but I don't give him a moment to continue. I push him backward, his chair rolling across the floor as the backs of his knees smack against it. "There are no *sure bets*." I push the words through clenched teeth.

It wouldn't have come to this if he'd shown respect at least. It wasn't his money to piss away.

My grip tightens as I haul his back against the wall, slamming his spine against the drywall and denting it from the force. My teeth clench as my left hand forms a fist and I land a blow into his kidney. My muscles are taut and adrenaline is rushing through me. My head feels light; my breathing is heavy.

A loud grunt spills from his lips until I tighten my hand around his throat, feeling his blood rushing just beneath the surface and his throat giving in to the brute force of my weight. Both of his hands instantly reach for my hand on his neck, his blunt fingernails scratching against the glove on my hand. It's no use. I'm not letting go until he receives this message loud and clear.

I lean in close to his ear and hiss between clenched teeth, "You'll pay me all of it by the twenty-fifth of April. Or I'll destroy you." I pull away to look into his eyes. The milky whites have turned red around the edges, his face is a brighter shade of red, and his hands are still struggling at my grip. I hold his eyes, so full of sheer terror, only for a moment longer before releasing him.

I leave him there, heaving for air in a slump on the floor as I walk quickly to the door, shaking out my hand and ignoring the force inside of me begging to unleash itself. Begging for a fight.

"Wait. I have something you may want," Brooks calls out in a croak. His words stop me midstep, but I continue momentarily, ignoring him and turning the doorknob.

"I want my money, Brooks. I won't take anything else," I tell him firmly.

His eyes stare back at me with a darkness as I stand in the doorway.

"I know what you like most at the club," he says then noticeably swallows, the soft, sick sound filling my ears as he rights himself, still slumping against the wall.

"The club?" I ask flatly, my face devoid of emotion or interest.

"Club X," he says loudly and clearly. The name makes my blood run cold. I only go there to watch my investments, for appearances only. I'm not interested in anything beyond that, and I haven't taken part in any of the... activities for a reason.

"I know you like the Slaves." My eyes narrow, and I have to keep my feet planted before I crush this fucker's windpipe. Brooks continues, "But there aren't many. Take mine... for a month."

My heart beats loud in my chest and blood rushes in my ears as I finally move slightly backward onto my heels and open the door wider so I can leave this prick and get on with my life.

"You have until the twenty-fifth," I reiterate and turn my back to him.

"You don't want her then?" he asks with slight disbelief, and I quickly turn to face him when I hear him take a single step toward me. The moment my eyes lock with his, he freezes.

"No," I tell him with a chill in my voice. "You'll pay me what you owe me-"

"She'll go up for auction then." He nods sternly, not backing down from my cold gaze. "I'll get that money to you on time. I have three hundred thousand coming. She's good for the rest. I know she is."

His admission makes rage and adrenaline pump through my blood. "That's not *your* money," I answer him.

He shrugs slightly, seemingly more at ease now that he's figured out a way to pay me. "She's mine. She'll do what she's told."

"On the twenty-fifth, Brooks," I say one last time, turning and closing the door behind me as I go.

I'm on edge and uneasy as I slip the gloves off and shove them into my pockets. My strides are larger than normal, the outrage apparent no matter how much I'd like to hide it. As I pass the rows of desks, I know they can see me. The real me, but in this moment, I can't suppress it. I can only move faster and leave before I turn around and do something I'll truly regret.

CHAPTER 4

ARIANNA

*W*hack!

A strangled cry escapes my lips as my head falls backward, the stinging pain racing up my ass cheeks, spreading out to my lower back and traveling downward through my thighs. *Fuck.* It hurts.

My breath comes out in short gasps as I try to bear the wave of stinging aftershocks, my face twisted into a tight mask of pain. I try to remember to give my worries to Danny. To relax and trust him that the pain will give me pleasure in the end. It's all for a reason. Everything happens for a reason and I deserve this, but in the end, it'll be alright.

That's what I used to tell myself, and it did bring me relief in the past. At times, I even looked forward to it. I deserved this, and the end result made a weight lift from me. It was freeing. But not now. It's only mind-numbing agony now.

My heart skips a beat as I sense movement. And I brace for another one. But it doesn't come right away.

I can hear Danny behind me, his breathing deep and ragged, stalking me like I'm a wild animal that needs to be put down. But he doesn't have to do that. I'm chained to the wall, my hands cuffed above my head, my bare ass behind me, giving him complete access.

He just likes doing this. He likes building the anticipation of a hit, but never striking until I least expect it.

I hate it. As I wait for his next blow, I can't remember what I used to think about during these times. I don't remember them. *It wasn't like this.*

I wait in agony, my limbs taut and sweaty, knowing the next one is coming, even if I don't know when. I hear his footsteps move to my right side and then to my left. Then I sense him directly behind me. The sound of his breathing fills my ears and my heart pounds faster. It's coming. Everything goes silent.

A drop of sweat runs down my forehead, down my nose, all the way down my chin and drops to the plush carpet below. I swear my heart is about to race out of my chest as I wait, thumping so loud that I know he hears it. I feel dizzy as I grip the chains, bracing myself for what's to come.

"You're holding back," his voice calls out from behind me. My body relaxes at his words. *I am.* He knows me so well. "You need to give in," he tells me.

My head hangs in shame. This is my fault. I used to be ready for this, willing to give him my pain and it would make me feel better.

An animalistic grunt splits the air, followed by multiple lashes.

A tortured scream tears from my throat. Agony becomes my existence, my ass, thighs and lower back radiating a pain so strong my knees buckle. The hard cast iron cuffs scrape my skin as the full weight of my body pulls down toward the floor, my hands stretching out above my head as far as they'll go.

I try to silence my pain as the unforgiving metal digs into my skin. Danny's behind me, his breathing heavier and more shallow than before. I know he's getting off on this, his cock is hard as a fucking rock. It was the tradeoff. He'd take the pain of my past away in exchange for this.

The words are on my lips. I need to tell him, to let him know that I'm not okay and I can't give in like I used to. I don't want this anymore. *But what about everything he's done for you?* that annoying voice at the back of my head chimes in. *You wouldn't be here if not for him. And he knows what you need. You're only in this position because you won't listen.*

"Listen to me," Danny says softly, almost in a comforting voice as he cradles my chin in his hand. As if he knew exactly what I was thinking just now. "Give in to the pain, and it will set you free."

A feeling of guilt presses down upon my chest and I suck in a ragged breath. I hate it. I hate it even more because I know it's true. I wouldn't be here if Danny hadn't saved me. For a time, he made me forget the terrible loss I suffered. He made me feel like I'd repented in a way.

The sound of Danny moving again breaks me out of my preoccupation. I almost shake my head and tell him I can't. No. Not again. I don't think I can take anymore. I stay half-slouched. I don't have the energy to stand up straight. I just can't.

"Raise your ass," I hear Danny's deep voice command behind me. Goosebumps rise on my thighs as I tremble at the anger lacing his words. I want to tell him no. I want to tell him that I can't do this anymore. But the words stick in my throat when I try to speak them. He has my best intentions at heart. He did in the beginning, and this must be my fault. I'm the one holding back. I'm not well, and he knows it.

I try to rise and straighten my body, my legs wobbling like Jello. It's a chore to arch my back. I manage, but it's all I can do to keep myself in position. I weakly grip the chains that are holding me up, my limbs completely covered in sweat, my heart racing so fast that the room spins around me. *He saved me. He saved me. He saved me,* I chant over and over in my mind, mentally preparing myself for this. But the blow never comes. Suddenly I'm being released from the chains, Danny appearing at my side and jerking my cuffs loose. I gasp as he gently lowers me to the floor, hitting the plush carpet with a thud. My hands immediately go to my wrists. There are deep red indentations from when I strained against them, but they're not as bad as I thought. They still hurt like hell though. I look up, taking in my surroundings, my breathing ragged. We're in one of Club X's private rooms, one of Danny's favorites. It's absolute luxury, with a king-size bed in the middle of the room adorned with grey and white silk bedding, and ultra-plush pillows. A large canopy frames the sides with gossamer white curtains tied back against each post.

The walls match the colors of the bedding, grey and white, and have intricate designs, adding that much more luxury in the fine details. The floor is covered with thick, soft white carpet and the matching furniture is chic and contemporary, with a large loveseat at the foot of the bed and an oversized chair near the granite fireplace.

Then there are the toys.

A delicate glass china cabinet sits on the left side of the room, filled with whips, riding crops, and other devices. Nearby, there is a grey rack with white shackles.

And above me is the Saint Andrew's Cross that chained me to the wall. Plus, Danny.

His gaze holds nothing but disappointment. I look back at him, unable to control the anxiety I feel along with the pain. Although I'm naked, bared before him, he's dressed in grey dress pants and a white dress shirt that's unbuttoned at the chest, his dark blond hair adorned by his cold piercing hazel eyes. "What's wrong?" I dare ask, my voice sounding like a small, scared child's. And I truly am scared. I don't know what to think anymore.

"You," he says simply. "You're not behaving. You're making this harder than it has to be."

"Sir, I-"

"I only want to help you. I know you need this. You aren't well, Arianna."

"I- I-," I protest, trying to put some strength in my words, but failing. He's right. I'm not okay, but I just don't know if this is the answer.

"You don't trust me as a Master. I've done so much for you." I feel tears form in my eyes at his words. "Danny please, it's not like that. It's just…"

Danny leans forward, putting his face close to mine. The hurt in his expression is nothing compared to the anger in his blazing eyes. "It's just what?" he asks.

Tell him. He needs to know.

A lump forms in my throat, but I manage to mumble, "I feel like this isn't working anymore and it hurts, but there's no… there's nothing but pain. I didn't tell you because I don't want to upset you."

"It's only because you aren't trusting me." His voice is full of conviction. "Don't you remember how freeing it is? Why are you hurting yourself?"

After a moment, he takes a step back and stands up straight. "This has been coming for a long time now." His words are terrible. Not because they're angry, but because they're so quiet and fill me with overwhelming anxiety.

"What do you mean-"

Danny walks forward and unbuckles the thick leather collar from around my neck.

"Danny, what are you doing?" I cry in panic. I reach up to try to stop him, but he swats my hand away as easily as one would swat a fly, and pulls the collar free from my neck, leaving cold air to replace its warmth. He steps back with it clenched tightly in his hand, scowling at me with a coldness I've never seen from him before. Unconsciously my hands fly to my neck. It feels so strange, running my fingers along the bare skin there. It feels... empty. Like he's abandoning me.

"I told you so long as you didn't give up on yourself, I wouldn't give up on you." His words are carried with pain. He's given up on me.

My heart feels like it's been pierced by a jagged spear.

His next words turn my blood to ice. "You're going up for auction."

My jaw goes slack as what he says registers, my heart skipping several beats as I'm shocked into silence.

"You need to learn to trust me," Danny says. "And I think handing you over to another Master is the best thing for you right now."

I stare at him in disbelief, hardly believing what he's saying.

"I want you to know what it's like to miss me," he says. "To realize how good you had it."

But it's been so bad, I want to tell him, *so bad that I want to leave you.*

For weeks I've thought about ending this, but the fear of losing him and having no one that truly knows me kept me from doing it. To me, being with someone who doesn't know my history is terrifying.

"You can come back to me after you've learned your lesson," Danny says. "Maybe then you'll truly appreciate me."

"Danny-" I try to say.

He waves me silent. "I'm done. Prepare yourself for your auction."

With that said, he walks out, closing the door behind him.

I sit there on the floor, my skin prickling as a torrent of emotions goes through me. Anxiety. Anger. Sadness.

I don't know what to do. I'm so used to leaning on Danny for support to conquer my demons that I don't know if I can survive without him.

CHAPTER 5

ZANDER

The chill of the wind whips across my face, the hairs on the back of my neck standing to attention. The thick wool overcoat I have on shields everything but my neck and cheeks. I don't move to cover them though. The crisp morning air seems fitting as I stare down at my mother's gravesite. I was only ten when she died. I wonder what kind of man I'd be if she'd never left.

My heart beats slower as another gust of wind comes, harsher this time. Again, I don't move. I stand still, my hands shoved into my coat pockets.

I have her tombstone memorized, but my eyes still flicker over the engraved message.

Marie Payne
1958 - 1994
Loving wife, doting mother.
She will be missed.

I do miss her, as odd as it may be. I hardly knew her, but I miss what could have been. She's the one who taught me to smile behind the pain. She never stopped, until the last few weeks of her life. It all crumbled around her, the affair that tore them apart. People were always watching. Always judging. It was too much for her.

I clear my throat as I straighten my stance and take in a deep breath. When I come here, the smile that's perpetually on my face is nowhere to be found. I can't do it; I can't bring myself to smile when I'm around her.

Maybe that's why I come here so much.

I don't know much about her, if I'm honest with myself. There's plenty online, so I suppose I know as much about her as a stranger would who wanted to look her up. She had no family but us. She married into wealth and gave the Payne heir a baby boy. And then she had miscarriage after miscarriage.

Her name means misery. *Marie.* I remember she told me that once, and I didn't understand what she meant at the time. It's the Latin meaning. The sadness in her pale eyes is something that haunts me even till this day. How could my father not see it?

He'll never admit it, but I know she killed herself. He wouldn't let her leave. I remember the fights, the screams. That's what I remember most, even if I always had my eyes closed tight and my small hands over my ears. I'll never forget the way they'd raise their voices until I knew it must have hurt them.

I'd hide in the closet of my room whenever it happened. I stare at the small crack in the marble slab of her tombstone.

I never understood why they hated each other so much. Why they enjoyed hurting each other with their words. They must've; fighting was all they ever did.

My eyes settle onto the line, "doting mother."

I think children have to love their mother. It's something in them that's biological. It must be so, because I know I love her. Even without a single memory of her gentle touch or soothing words. I haven't a single one. The nannies were there for me when I was young. But they came and went like a merry-go-round. They got *too attached.*

The only constant was the fighting between my parents, and when that came to a halt with her death, there was only silence for a short time. And then my father started with me.

"*One mistake and you're ruined,*" he'd tell me all the time. I was to be perfect. Just like my mother was supposed to be.

I was good where my mother failed. I enjoyed charming people. I liked getting a reaction from them. I liked for them to see the boy I wanted to be, and not the hollow shell I became.

It's less amusing now, but it's vital to my survival.

Father taught me well.

My phone pings with a message at the thought and I'm slow to pull it out, even though my fingers are already wrapped around it.

When I finally take my eyes from the tombstone to look at it, a text from my father stares back at me.

Dinner on the 7th for the gala. You need to be there.

A grunt leaves me and I roll my eyes as I ignore it. I already know about the event. I'll be there just like I always am.

"He's still the same," I tell my mother as if she can hear me. I don't even remember why I came today. Some days just take me here. Usually when I'm not paying attention, or looking for a moment to think.

My father needs me now more than ever. As he grows old and his influence is waning, he's relying on me to a greater extent. I don't mind it. In my mind, I've always needed to step up. *If only I had back then.*

But this constant bitching and reminding me is unnecessary. I swipe away the text.

I nearly shove my phone back into my coat pocket, ready to shield my bare hands from the wind, but the picture of *her* is on my screen. *Arianna Owens.*

And with those gorgeous eyes staring back at me, I'm reminded of the last thing I care to remember. My mistake. Danny Brooks. I stare at my phone in my hand, the dim glow lighting the darkened sky. Isaac looked her up and gave me her information. *Arianna Owens.* I suppose in a way, she reminds me of my mother. There's a sadness there. Something that haunts her. She makes me feel like she needs to be saved.

I pinch the bridge of my nose, feeling ridiculous. "This is your fault," I say out loud, my voice drowned out by the harsh gusts of the wind.

She's beautiful, but her gorgeous eyes are haunted by something, darkened by what lies behind them.

I'm still enraged that Brooks offered me a month with her in exchange for a debt of hundreds of thousands that he owes me. The only claim he has to her is the collar around her neck.

My dick hardens at the thought of her on her knees, giving herself to me, pleasing me. I've been tempted before at the club, though I've never taken part. At least not in the open like that. These men are foolish to show their cards. My good friend Lucian paid the price years ago. Although now it's paid off for him, the burden of his past only goes to show that NDAs are nothing more than paperwork. They have no loyalty to them, merely sheets of paper; so easily shredded, so quickly forgotten.

Arianna's haunted eyes shine through the screen, staring back at me. I've seen her before. I've watched the way he drags her through the halls and leads her to the dungeon. She's submissive in her nature, but I don't trust her or his offer. I don't let anyone close for a reason.

And women make men fall.

I pull the jacket tighter around me and shove the phone back into my pocket.

I should stay away. I should take the money and let him fall on his own, carrying on with my life and ignoring the pathetic waste of life that is Danny Brooks.

But those eyes call to me. My contempt for him and what he represents make a side of me I try to keep suppressed rise to the surface.

And that's a very dangerous thing.

CHAPTER 6

ARIANNA

*Y*ou're going up for auction.

Danny's words run through my mind as I scrub at the spaghetti-stained plate vigorously, my eyes unfocused as I stare straight ahead into the wall, the rough Brillo pad digging into my soft skin. I've been at this for hours now, cleaning piles of dirty dishes after a day of hard work at the local shelter.

It was a packed house today, causing more chores to be done at closing. This job pays shit, but I don't mind. I couldn't care less about the money. It's about giving back and making my life have meaning. Coming here has always been my therapy, a way to escape my emotions. It's been cathartic for me to help people who are down on their luck, and it eases some of the guilt that plagues me.

But not today.

I scrub the plate harder, a mix of pain and anger running through my body. The whip marks are a mess of bruises along my back and thighs, and each small movement is accompanied with a hint of pain. It's a reminder that I'm alive, that I can *feel*.

I haven't been able to get my mind off Danny for more than a minute.

Even now, I can't believe what he said to me. That he's willing to put me up for auction like I'm just a commodity that can be bartered or sold at whim. And after everything we've been through. After everything he's done for me. All because I've been unhappy with our sessions. But I am broken. Something's changed, and I know I'm unhappy. What used to work isn't helping me anymore.

I suck in a painful breath as I look down at the plate that I'm scrubbing. The red stains are clinging stubbornly to the surface. No matter how hard I try, I can't seem to get them out. Just like how dark memories cling to me, sticking in my mind no matter how hard I try to rid myself of them.

If I could just forget. I drop the plate into the suds and let it fall to the bottom of the basin. My fingertips are pruned as I stare at them, remembering everything.

The thought summons a dark specter, one that always seems to pounce whenever I'm depressed.

I always had a drink in my hand. Even as I stumbled in my heels, a drink was sure to be there. Drugs? Yep. I was down for anything. I just wanted to fit in. I wanted others to accept me. I didn't go to college; I couldn't afford it, and it damn sure wasn't something my parents cared about. But I was at every party on campus.

That's where I met Natalie, although she just talked to me, bringing me into her group. It was different when she was there. It was better, but back then I didn't know. I just wanted to feel something. I needed something in my pathetic life.

I struggle against his powerful grip, my arms held back above my head against the bedpost, my eyes glazed and unfocused. I shouldn't be here alone in this darkened room with him, but I drank too much and let him talk me into it. Now I'm regretting it big time, but the words are lost in the haze of alcohol.

Chase lowers his handsome face down close to mine as the walls shake from the bass of the music blasting through the frat house. "God, I've wanted you all night," he says kissing my neck, his breath hot against my skin. "You asked for this."

I shake my head weakly, insecurity twisting my stomach. I didn't want this. I'm not like that. I don't want to be thought of like that. I didn't know when he led me up here. How did I not know? My head shakes and I feel so stupid, so foolish. So guilty.

I part my lips to tell him, the alcohol making my head feel so heavy. But he kisses me instead, and then pulls back to take his shirt off. No, I just need to tell him no. He'll listen. He's not trying to take advantage of me. It's my fault. "I thought you just wanted to mess around a little." My words come out muffled.

"What, baby?" he asks as he pushes my legs apart wider. I try to pull them closed, but his hips butt against mine. I was just looking to have a little fun.

His hands shove my skirt up and my arms are too heavy to push him away.

I didn't mean for it to go this far. I was reckless. It was my fault. I don't know if he heard me whispering no. It makes me feel a little better to think he didn't, and I don't know if that's more fucked up than the alternative.

My breathing is ragged as I shove the memory out of my mind and let go of the Brillo pad. There are red marks on my palm from where the pad has dug into my soft flesh, but I hardly notice it, a chill snaking down my spine. I stopped going to parties, but the reliance on drugs and alcohol didn't end. And one mistake led to another that I'll never forgive myself for. Even now, I still ache in my lower abdomen at the memory of waking up on a bloody mattress months later, my nightgown soaked with dark red blood. I didn't know I'd been pregnant until I had miscarried. More mistakes. More blame. More guilt.

That was enough to send me spiraling down into darkness; I just wanted to end it all. I had a bottle in my hand as my legs hung over the bridge. I'd drink the pain away and fall in. I was so done with making mistakes. But Danny saw me. *He saved me.*

And now... he's discarding me like none of that meant anything.

"Are you okay, dear?" a familiar voice asks, breaking me out of my dark trance. I whip my head around to see Clara, the head cook of the shelter, staring at me with concern. She's a large woman in her early fifties, with greying hair that's always arranged up high on her head in a loose bun. Her outfit, an oversized blue dress with a white apron, only makes her appear more matronly. She has a large oval-shaped face, lined with gentle wrinkles, and her hair contains striking streaks of grey that give her a distinguished look. I flash her a modest smile I hope she thinks is real. I try my best to keep my troubles hidden whenever I'm here, or anywhere really. I don't like to spread negativity. *Give your pain to me. Only me.* Danny's words from the night he first showed me the cane come back to me. I turn my back to her and grab the dish towel, drying my hands before turning back to face her. "I'm fine. Why, what's up?"

Clara nods at the dishes. "You seemed a bit distracted. You sure you're alright?"

I huff out a humorless chuckle. "Oh no, I just zoned out."

Clara places her hands on her wide hips, giving me a knowing look. "Are you sure you're okay?"

I flash her another smile, this one easier. "I'm positive."

For a moment, Clara looks uncertain as if she wants to press the issue, but then says, "Okay, I'm here for you if you ever need someone to talk to, okay honey?"

Warmth spreads through my chest and it's hard not to let the emotions I'm feeling play across my face. It touches me that Clara cares at all about what I might be going through. But then again, she wouldn't be working at a pantry that fed the homeless if she didn't possess so much empathy. There are so many people here who need help. And not because they were careless and reckless and hurting the people around them. They didn't choose it.

"Okay," I tell her with gratitude, "I'll keep that in mind."

"Make sure that you do." Clara gives me a heartfelt smile before going off back to her chores.

I spend the next half hour finishing cleaning up the last of the dishes and then head out behind the building with a bag of trash in my hand. It's full to the brim and heavy. I have to lift it with all my weight to make sure it doesn't drag on the asphalt and tear open.

I step out into the back alley, my skin pricking from the cool air sweeping through the area, goosebumps rising up on my flesh. A ray of moonlight shines down through the crack between the buildings, illuminating the walkway. I need to clean up back here; pieces of newspaper and some rotten food are strewn about, and the smell from the nearby dumpsters assaults my nose as I make my way down the small steps onto the cold concrete path. My car is parked around the side of the building, and it's just a short walk through the alley to reach it. But I need to dump the trash bag first.

I'm in the process of closing it when suddenly, rough and firm hands grab me from behind, clamping down on my mouth to stifle my cry.

My heart pounds as panic overtakes me, and I struggle against my captor, but whoever it is is too strong. Subduing my attempts to escape, I hear a grunt as I'm picked up off my feet and pressed up against the stone wall, feeling a rock hard body press into me from behind.

"Be a good girl," a familiar voice growls into my ear.

"Danny," I gasp with surprise, my heart hammering wildly as a hundred different dreadful thoughts run through my mind. I don't understand what's going on. "What are you doing here?" I cry.

Danny doesn't immediately respond, keeping me pressed up against the wall for several more moments, his breath hot on my neck. All the while, fear runs through me. He's never done anything like this before, and I can smell whiskey on his breath. He's taking joy out of keeping me guessing on his intentions while increasing the pressure on my back.

"Danny, please," I whimper as the pain grows, my eyes darting to the back entrance of the shelter. "Sir, please." I don't know what's going on. This isn't him.

Finally, he lets me go.

I gasp as I come free, turning around to face him, my chest heaving from my ragged breaths.

Danny's scowling at me, his hazel eyes blazing with anger. He looks out of place in this trashy alley with his expensive dress pants and shirt, his hair slicked to the side. I can even smell his vintage cologne over the filthy aroma of garbage.

"I've come to remind you how ungrateful you are," he growls. His words sting with a pain so raw, I can hardly stand up straight.

"Danny-" I pause and swallow the lump growing in my throat. I'm grateful. I am. I truly am.

"Don't you remember?" he asks me, gesturing around the grimy alley. "This is the same fucking alleyway I found you in. Before you went to the bridge. You were poor, broke, hungry and homeless. And I was the only one who was stupid enough to have pity for you."

I shake my head, unable to understand how differently Danny's treating me. He's never been this cruel and hateful with me before.

"Danny, please. It's not like that." My eyes dart from him to the door. There's a single light shining above it, and everything in me is pleading with me to run. But it's Danny. He saved me. He won't hurt me. "Why are you so angry with-"

"Did you once try to call me since taking your collar?" he demands, cutting me off. "Did you once try to beg me to take you back?"

"But you said I was going up for auction-" I try to reason with him. I don't know what to do. I'm so lost.

"I fed you, you ungrateful bitch!" Danny snarls, spittle flying from his mouth. "Helped you when no one else would. And look at you, ready to run from me the first chance you get."

I gape at him with shock.

"I saved you!" He continues his rant. "You were nothing but a drunk degenerate when I found you. And if it weren't for me, you'd be fucking dead!" His words cut through me, because they're true.

Tears burn my eyes as I gaze into his rage-filled face.

"Danny please," I beg, a huge lump choking my throat as I reach my hands out to him imploringly. "Please calm down and just listen to me…"

"No," Danny fumes. "I'm sick of listening to your pathetic whining."

"But-"

Danny rushes forward, grabbing me by the neck, and slams me back up against the wall. A gasp escapes my lips as pain radiates up my back and I struggle to pry his powerful hands free of my throat.

"Shut. The. Fuck. Up," he says nastily in my face, the smell of whiskey hitting me even harder now, his eyes blazing with a hatred that tears at my heart. "Your voice is *so* fucking annoying. I can't believe I listened to that shit for nearly two years. It's like nails on a fucking chalkboard."

Tears start streaming down my face as I choke against his grasp. His words are so biting and cruel.

"I just want to remind you that even though you're going up for auction, I still fucking own you," he barks. "I don't give a fuck whose collar you have around your neck. You're fucking mine. You got it?"

I'm unable to respond, his grip on my neck so strong that I can barely breathe.

He pulls me forward and then slams me back against the wall with enough force that it jars my teeth.

"I said you got it?" he repeats with fury. "The money is mine, and so are you. This is a fucking lesson and nothing else. I own you!"

"Yes," I croak, my eyes stinging and my lungs refusing to fill.

Danny holds me there for a moment, applying more and more pressure to my throat until I think I'm going to pass out. He lets me go at the last possible second, and I fall away from the wall, sinking to my knees onto the grungy ground, gasping, choking and crying.

"You'll do well to remember that," Danny tells me, uncaring that I'm bawling my eyes out at his feet, "because if you don't, you're going to wish I left you for dead."

"You're going up for auction, and then you're coming back to me."

I nod my head vigorously, needing him to know I'm obeying. I'm listening. "Yes, Sir." I croak out the words through the pain.

"There, there." His voice softens. "I don't know why you do this to yourself. All you have to do is listen." I hear his words, so gentle and comforting. Just listen. But everything in me is telling me to run. This isn't right.

"I'm sorry I'm so hard on you. I just know you aren't well." He crouches beside me and I flinch as he grips my chin in his hand. "You need me, you need this."

I nod my head as much as I can, staring into his eyes. But I see through him. In a split second, I see through it all. It's about the money. It hits me so hard, so brutally, I can't hide my expression.

His face morphs from the gentle attitude to one of cruelty. "You're going up there, Arianna." His voice is low. "I know where you live. I saved your life, it belongs to me now."

A feeling of despair washes over me as I choke on my tears, my neck throbbing.

"Just do what I say and everything will be alright."

CHAPTER 7

ZANDER

$\mathcal{M}$y hand has been forced in some ways. Well, not quite. I pick up the beer bottle and bring it to my lips as I sit at the table in the far right corner of the upper floor in Club X. *The auction room.*

I've never felt as if my hand's been forced. There's always a choice. However, it's undeniable that I'm backed in a corner with the knowledge that Arianna Owens will be on the stage soon. Sold to the highest bidder and if it's anyone else, that will be the money I'm paid.

"What are you going to do?" Charles asks. He's seated next to me at the small circular table. There are dozens of tables in the room that seat only two to three men at most. A mask covers his face just like most of the men here, including me. They all know who I am, but with his face completely covered by the smooth flat black mask that hides every inch of his features with the exception of his mouth, they have no idea who I'm seated with. He's lucky in that respect.

My fingers trail along my jaw, the hint of stubble rough beneath my fingertips. "I haven't decided," I answer him honestly.

He grunts a laugh and sits back in his seat, picking up the pamphlet to the auction and skimming the lines. I've done the same so many times when I didn't give a fuck about sitting here. Just doing my part to fit in and keeping my friends company while I take notes about the perversions of the other men in the room. *Always watching.*

I've never shown my cards. I've never given them an ounce of useful information to use against me if they so choose.

"I can't believe a place like this exists," Charles mutters under his breath. I turn to him, ignoring Madam Lynn, the owner of Club X, as she starts the show. I've seen these auctions a million times. I've never given a fuck about them. It's mostly a charade, no surprise at all who will end up with who.

My shoulders rise in a shrug. It's a fantasy really. Decorated and maintained to provide a false sense of a world that's temporary. Darkened rooms for men to spend their money and sate themselves, safety for women who want to give in to their dark desires. It's all an illusion, nothing more than that.

But as the first woman is sold as the hammer is dropped, I find my heart beating faster. The auction has never felt more real than in this moment.

The men are talking quietly to themselves. Arianna is next, according to the pamphlet. None of their eyes are on me. Instead they're focused on Brooks, who's seated on the far side of the room, at the table farthest away from me. His foot is tapping nervously on the floor as he leans back in his seat with a cigar, putting on a casual air. As if his very life doesn't depend on Arianna being sold to pay his debt.

I imagine most of the men here expect him to bid on her. Like it's a game between them. It wouldn't be the first time a Dominant or Master has sent his partner to the auction, some for play, others for punishment. But when he doesn't bid on her, the mood in the room will change. Each second that passes, taking me closer and closer to that moment, heightens my anxiety.

I can already feel the tense air growing as the men each decide for themselves if they're willing to take her.

She's the epitome of what a Submissive should be. Or Slave, rather. Since that's the preference she's taken at the club. She's only ever been with him, but he's put on quite a show with her before.

"How many have you come to?" Charles asks me, his voice low.

So low that the clinking of the ice in his short glass of bourbon nearly drowns out his words as he brings the glass to his lips.

Again I shrug, lifting my beer bottle to my lips and taking a sip. I answer him with a low voice, "Too many."

"How many have you won?" he asks.

"None," I answer him with clarity, setting my glass on the white tablecloth and looking straight ahead. The thick red curtains are pulled back and the lights focused on the stage, just how it always is.

Charles laughs a deep rough sound, and my eyes are pulled to his.

"How can you resist?" he asks with a warmth in his voice I've never heard before.

"Easy," I answer and take a quick look around the darkened room. "They're all watching."

"Let them see. Isn't that what this place is for?" He swirls the ice in his glass and drains the remainder of the bourbon as a waitress passes us. I eye him as he leans in her direction, ordering another. He seems more comfortable behind the mask than I've ever seen him before. As if it grants him a freedom he's never had. And I suppose it does. For him and many of the other men in here.

But I know all of the men in this room, and I'm not foolish enough to think that an NDA is enough to keep loose lips from using information within the walls of Club X as blackmail. As much as I'm fond of Madam Lynn, many things are beyond her control.

The first woman is sold to her own Dominant and the second is a new girl, unclaimed and looking a bit shy. She goes for a higher sum, having multiple bidders as the waitress comes back with another drink for Charles. No surprise there, and nothing out of place. Madam Lynn's expression reflects exactly what I'm feeling as Arianna walks out onto the stage.

The lights are focused on her, making her sun-kissed skin seem to glow. She takes in a shaky breath as she stands there, and her ankles cross and uncross as she clasps her hands in front of her. Everything slows down as her thin black dress swirls along her upper thighs. With the lights so bright, her vision is limited. It will take her a moment to adjust to the darkness in the crowd beyond the stage. But she's not trying. *She doesn't want to see.*

"We'll start the bidding at fifty thousand dollars," the auctioneer says.

Madam Lynn's gaze is focused on Brooks. She doesn't like surprises, and she's not used to them either. For a woman who's so submissive in nature, she controls every aspect of the club with an iron fist. But this is out of her control, and her resentment of that is reflected in her eyes.

The small room is quiet; a man clearing his throat and the skinny black heels shifting on the large stage ahead of us are the only sounds as the men wait to see what Brooks is up to. He takes a long and deep puff of his cigar, keeping his eyes on Arianna who's looking straight ahead at the barren wall in front of her.

After a moment he crosses his arms, ignoring the men and looking uninterested.

"Five hundred thousand," the auctioneer gestures to a man in the back. I take a quick look, not turning in my seat to see it's Nathan Blanchard. He's a simple man, vanilla in tastes, but has no knowledge of what it means to be faithful.

"Six," a man across the room says as he raises his paddle. I recognize his voice, as do most of the men here. That's the thing about masks. When the circles in the business world are so small, you can't hide behind a thin piece of plastic or leather.

A third man raises his paddle, and I take another drink. Listening to the auctioneer and glancing at Brooks who's merely smiling, confident his prized possession will buy him out of the debt he's in.

Each bid feels like a slap to my face.

Whoever wins her will use her for his own enjoyment. However he'd like. Of course there's a contract, set terms that Arianna will agree to. Her preferences are all laid out in the pamphlet sitting in front of me and in front of all the attendees. And she agreed to this. But I see the look in her eyes, and I know the way he treats her. *I know her past.* This isn't right.

I'm not interested in their money. My teeth grind against one another as the paddles continue to raise, the amount increasing with each bid.

The next two bids make my back straighten. My muscles are getting more and more tense.

Arianna's shoulders are rigid, but she stands tall, looking utterly gorgeous in the thin black chemise with a black rose held in front of her. Maybe it makes me a sick fuck, but the sadness only makes me want her more.

I raise my paddle, not uttering a word. It won't be the first time I've bid. But my normal cocky grin is absent. I'm not just fucking with someone as I usually am when I bid.

I've done that before, more than a few times although I always know the man I'm screwing with. It's always been in jest and light-hearted. But the winning bidder looks over his shoulder at me with disdain, and it's hard to keep the emotions off my face.

"Don't lose your cool," I hear Charles say as he lifts the glass to his lips.

I lean back in my seat and force a smirk on my lips.

None of these men know what's going on. They can think I've finally decided to indulge, but then they'll have ammunition. They'll use it against me.

From the corner of my eye, another paddle is raised.

"One point ten," the auctioneer's voice sounds out. "One twenty." I hear his voice over the loud ringing in my ears. My eyes focus on Arianna's. My heart beats slower, louder, drowning out everything else as I watch her close her eyes.

She's not meant for this. This isn't right. There's such an innocence about her, a vulnerability. I want to save her. I really shouldn't, since winning her will taint my reputation. I need to play this right.

It's just a deal I made with a man I shouldn't have. An error on my part. How many more mistakes can I afford?

"Going once," the auctioneer yells out. The sight of Arianna's large doe eyes opening and shining with fear is what breaks me from my thoughts. The quiet of the room comes back to me. The faint sounds of men drinking and hushed conversations fill the darkened room once again.

I can't let her pay for my sins.

I raise my paddle, and the auctioneer points in my direction.

"One point three million."

"One point four," I hear Brooks' voice, and it pisses me off. I lower my paddle and notice the way the other three men who were bidding look at him. As if they're not sure they want to press on. As if it was just a game to them. A rather expensive one.

"One point five," the auctioneer says as one of the other bidders raises his paddle.

I don't hesitate. "One point six million dollars."

"You look pissed," Charles tells me, not so quietly. It's an effort to smirk and look over at Brooks with a smile on my face, as if I'm merely playing. As if all the world is a game to me. Playing the part of a spoiled rich boy without a care in the world.

If only they knew.

Brooks plays with his paddle as if debating upping the amount. He can. And I can choose not to bid again. I can let him hang himself, but then his poor Arianna will go back to him.

Why is she even with him?

"Going once."

I hadn't questioned her motives before, but as the thought hits me, she could be in on this. The corner of my lips nearly drop as the auctioneer calls out, "Going twice."

They could be playing me for a fool. And I've just given them exactly what they wanted.

My blood chills as the realization washes over me. And I played into their hands because of her. Because of the thought of someone else having her.

"Sold!"

And I let them play me. I've never felt so fucking stupid before... but now that she's mine, I'll have to play this right. It's all about appearances. That's all it's ever been about.

My reputation, my family name, it's all on the line.

I'm simply a rich boy who fell for a woman and couldn't resist her.

This can't come back as a perversion. I crack my knuckles, one at a time. The only way to get around that is to be seen with her. Constantly. And not in fucking Club X.

CHAPTER 8

ARIANNA

The scribble of pen going across paper fills the room. *Scratch. Scratch. Scratch.* Anxiety twists my stomach as I watch Madam Lynn flip through the papers of my contract, signing where needed, her finely sculpted right brow arched in concentration. Her dark blonde hair is pulled into an elegant side ponytail and her makeup is dramatic yet flawless, her lips painted a bright shade of red. A diamond cocktail ring adorns her finger and a sparkling cuff that mimics a Submissive's adorns her right wrist, while her strong, yet simple fragrance tickles the tip of my nose.

The creak of a chair breaks me out of my reverie and I freeze, my skin pricking. I feel fucking sick.

He's watching me. It's all he's been doing since he stepped in the room. Watching me and saying nothing.

I try my best to avoid his gaze, my cheeks turning red and I readjust the hem of my dress to cover more of my legs. But his piercing blue eyes seem to draw mine to them. They're beyond gorgeous, but more than that, they're hiding secrets. *Dark secrets.*

Just like I am. Just listen to him. Do as he says. I'll figure a way out of this. I just don't know how.

The breath stills in my lungs as our eyes meet, heat flushing my throat. I've seen many handsome men here in passing, those that were bold enough to remove their masks while at play, but Zander takes the cake. His dark hair is perfectly groomed, his chiseled jawline immaculately shaved, his prominent cheekbones sharp enough to cut glass. He's dressed in a crisp dark suit, the white dress shirt underneath the jacket unbuttoned at the front. It goes without saying that he's a man of power and wealth, but he exudes much more than that. There's an aura of enigma around him, an atmosphere so strong that it causes my pulse to race and makes me weak in the knees. Zander stares back at me with an intensity that causes my palms to feel clammy, my body temperature rising. Even while looking intense, he looks so calm and composed, his legs spread out wide as if he owns the room. As if he *owns me*. And in a way, now he does. I let Danny use me. The thought makes my gaze fall for a moment. I'm going to find a way out of this. I just need time.

My eyes reach Zander's again and his gaze entraps me, as if he knows what I'm thinking. A small voice in the back of my head tells me he can save me. Another calls me a fool, reminding me how Danny *saved* me.

After a moment, I'm forced to look away, my breathing ragged. I can't take looking at him for more than a moment without my heart skipping a beat. It's almost as bad as when I was out there on the auction stage. Disgust twists my stomach as I think about what's happening. I shouldn't be here. This shouldn't be happening.

My skin pricks as I remember seeing Danny in the audience. It took a moment for his eyes to reach mine as I walked off the stage, sold and wanting to run. His eyes seemed to tell me that I was still his, and that no matter whose collar I put on, I only have one Master. My blood chills as I remember that murderous look. It was the same look he gave me in the alley. The look that said if I defy him, I'm a dead woman.

Anxiety threatens to overwhelm me, and I bite my lower lip.

Madam Lynn seems to sense my discomfort and she looks up from my contract, setting her pen aside on the polished cherry wood desk. "Are you alright, Arianna?" she asks gently. I glance at Zander and my heart wobbles again. He's still staring at me. I tear my eyes away and look over at Madam Lynn and shake my head.

"Yes, Madam," I say, lying. "Are you sure? she asks. "If you have

any concerns about the contract you're about to sign, please air them."
She pauses to gesture at Zander. "Don't be afraid, you can talk freely
in front of Mr. Payne. Anything at all that you want to say."

"I'm fine," I lie again.

Madam Lynn eyes me for a long moment. She senses something
that I'm not being forthwith, but doesn't press the issue. "Don't
worry," she tells me gently, offering me a forced smile. "Mr. Payne
will let me know if there's anything that needs to be said." She turns
to him, waiting for an answer and something passes between them,
although I'm not sure what.

"Mr. Payne, is there anything you would like to say before we
commence signing?"

"No," Zander says shortly, his eyes burning into my face.

It's just one word. But I'm nearly consumed by the sound of his
voice. It's so deep, rich and... sexy.

My cheeks burn as I'm filled with shame. I should not be having
these thoughts.

I look away from both of them, a feeling of worthlessness
descending upon me, a self-loathing that almost brings tears to my
eyes.

Madam Lynn looks between the both of us and then nods gently,
grabbing the stacks of papers.

"If you would just look over everything before signing," Madam
Lynn says. "As we discussed before the auction, you have the option
to terminate this contract whenever you wish during its term, but you
will forfeit the agreed-upon settlement if you choose to do so." She
slides the papers over to me along with her pen. The money. I just
need to get the money and give it to Danny. Then I'll be done. It
makes me a whore, but I'll survive. I'll live and start over.

I'm hardly able to concentrate as I flip through the pages and go
over the details of my contract. I feel so nauseated, I want to hurl as I
gaze at the dotted line, my heart pounding in my chest.

I don't have to do this, I try to convince myself. *I can go to the
cops.*

"Arianna?" Madam Lynn says softly. "Are you alright?"

The words are on my lips. I almost tell her, "I can't do this."
Instead I say, "I'm fine," as firmly as I can manage. I already know

Danny will get to me if I don't go through with this. He has wealth and power, and I have nothing.

Sucking in a deep breath, I close my eyes and quickly scribble my signature over the dotted line.

Madam Lynn gives me a tight smile when I'm done, taking the papers and pen and then sliding them over to Zander.

Zander slowly takes the papers and pen from Madam Lynn. I watch as if I'm not really here, as if it's not real, as he signs each dotted line that requires his name.

I shift in my seat, my skin pricking, my heart racing at the fire that burns in his eyes.

And as he signs the last line that requires his signature, I feel absolutely sick to my stomach.

Like I just signed my soul away to the devil.

CHAPTER 9

ZANDER

I stare at her from across the table, the door closing with a gentle click as Madam Lynn leaves the two of us alone in the conference room. It's rather small compared to the luxury of Club X. But I suppose it's only purpose is for signing contracts, so the plain white walls and simple necessities are all that's needed. In here there's no fantasy or illusion required. It's all business.

Arianna's head falls into a bow and she stays eerily still in her chair. Her eyes are focused on the floor. A darkness in me stirs with delight at her immediate submission to me. It's wrong to think that way and I ignore it, shoving it down and pretending it doesn't exist.

"Arianna," I say her name for the first time. It feels forbidden, too sweet to taste. The syllables linger in the air as she slowly raises her chin, her head still bowed slightly and her gorgeous eyes stare into mine. Deep into me, as if she can see through me.

"What are you doing?" I ask her, taking the attention off of me and back onto her lush lips. They're on the pale side, but a soft pink. Her makeup is soft and only there to emphasize her natural beauty.

"Whatever you wish, Sir." I nearly groan at her response. I'm not into power play in the bedroom. I have enough of it throughout the day to fulfill those needs. But she tempts me. It's the look in her eyes that tells me she needs what I can give her. She needs to be dominated, but not like this.

"May I call you Sir?" she asks me in a delicate voice that begs me to take her.

Her soft voice and perfect submission call to me. But I'm not interested in rules and games. The stakes in this game are much too high to play.

It hits me then, with her question, that she's mine. That I can do with her as I please. My dick hardens in my pants just thinking about the sweet sounds that would pour from her lips. I keep my back straight as I adjust my cock to keep it from pressing against the zipper.

I'd love to get lost in her lush curves and bury myself deep inside her. But this is business. And the desires I have aren't right. I tear my eyes away from her and look at the clock on the far wall. The second hand moves slowly, not a single tick audible as it moves seamlessly across the face. Counting time. That's what I'll be doing over the next month. That's all this is.

She's just another woman. My right hand sitting on the table balls into a fist at the thought, knowing it's not true. I rap my knuckles against the table. The steady tapping fills the room as I realize how fucked this situation is.

She's not just another woman. This would be too easy if she were. I wouldn't have come here if it were true.

"Do you know why I bid on you?" I ask her as my eyes lift to her heart-shaped face.

"Because you wanted me to obey your every wish," she answers in a gentle voice, the last word hanging in the air as I stare at her. *Yes,* a voice in the depths of my depravity calls out, begging me to take her as she offered. To give in and simply enjoy her.

"Do you know your Master offered you to me?" I ask her, although it's not really a question. I shouldn't have told her, but I want her to know, I want to see her reaction even more.

"Because my Master owes you?" she asks in a voice that doesn't show what she's feeling. It's all a cognitive process, with no emotion involved. She's hiding it from me.

"Yes, because your prick of a boyfriend owes me." I'm intentionally cold, wanting a response, and she gives it to me.

Her eyes whip to mine and her lips press into a hard line. For a moment anger rises inside of me at the thought of her defending him, but her words cut through it, silencing it.

"He's not my boyfriend." As soon as the words are spoken, her posture returns to what it was.

More than her submission, her anger and her determination that she doesn't belong to him make me want her that much more. Because she doesn't have any claim to him anymore. *Now she's mine.*

I haven't wanted anyone like this in a long damn time. Maybe not ever. It must be the forbidden aspect of it, the dark desires I've only ever observed from a distance. My eyes glance over her face, waiting for more from her, trying to determine what it is about her that's forcing my hand and only making me want her with more desperation as every minute passes.

She's a siren. Luring me to a depth that already has me making mistakes.

She's the reason I'm in this mess. I *felt* for her. This business isn't about emotions.

I rest my elbow on the table and lean forward, the legs of my chair scooting across the floor and making a screeching noise.

"Can I trust you?" I ask her, finally feeling a hint of a smile reaching my lips.

"Yes, Sir."

"Don't call me Sir," I immediately say and my command comes out sharp, but she doesn't flinch. My harsh manner doesn't affect her in the least.

"What would you like me to call you?" she asks in an even voice, perfectly still.

I let out a heavy sigh and sit back in my chair. My ankles cross as I look back at her.

"My name is Zander, and you can call me that."

Her lashes flutter as she nods her head and answers obediently, "Yes, Zander."

"I don't really like… the lifestyle," I tell her, that smile apparent as I start to spin a beautiful web, something to distract her maybe, something to hide behind. "As a kink, I understand it. But I'm not interested in having a Slave or a twenty-four seven power exchange."

Her posture relaxes slightly. "What do you like?" she says, and as she asks me the question, she licks her lips in a nervous manner and clears her throat, setting her clasped hands on the table. Her own mask is crumbling into pieces, and her true emotions are showing. Her voice is lowered and flat.

She's nervous, unhappy even. I'm taken aback for a moment. I hadn't expected this reaction.

"What do you think I like?" I ask her in return. My eyes travel over every one of her features, waiting for more information on her. Everyone has a tell, and I can spot a lie from even the most deceitful men.

"I'm not sure, to be honest." She swallows again and stares at her hands as she fidgets and pinches her fingertips. "I know I'm here to pay a debt. And that you'll use me," she adds and closes her eyes and takes in an uneven breath to steady herself. The smile falls from my face completely.

"I won't do a damn thing to you that you don't want. Let's make that clear right now." My firm voice makes her open her eyes. They're glassy with tears and something else, distrust.

"I promise you. If you don't want me in the least, you can walk through that door and this all ends."

"He'll-"

"He won't do a damn thing to you. Daniel Brooks owes me money; you don't owe anyone."

"I owe him," she breathes the words her face a reflection of nothing but pain. "I do," Arianna starts to say something, but she doesn't finish. I feel my forehead scrunch as I try to figure out what the hell she's getting at. And then it hits me.

"If you don't want me, you can simply leave." The words, *I'll forgive the debt and you'll be free* are on my lips, but a hiss of a whisper in the darkest part of my mind pleads with me to wait for her reply.

"I do want you," she says and her gorgeous eyes stare into mine again, piercing through me and threatening to learn every secret I hold.

I want to tell her to leave, to get rid of her. She already has too much power over me; she makes me weak. She makes me foolish. *But she wants me.* And I can't deny I crave the idea of her submitting to me.

"You're going to do everything I say." I don't think as I speak, another side of me taking over.

"Yes, Zander."

"We'll start tomorrow at six in the evening," I tell her, looking straight ahead and past her. My eyes focus on a small dimple on the white wall. An imperfection in the otherwise spotless facade of the conference room.

"What... what will you require?" she asks with slight hesitation.

"Whatever I want," I answer her simply. It's not the answer she wants, but she nods her head, her eyes focused on a dark knot in the center of the hard wood table.

"Until tomorrow," I say easily although not a damn thing in me is relaxed.

"Until tomorrow," she repeats in merely a whisper.

As she walks away, I find myself watching the sway of her hips and imagining taking her over and over. She turns to look over her shoulder one last time, her hand gripping the edge of the door. She licks her lower lip once, drawing my eyes to that beautiful mouth of hers. She starts to say something, but I can't hear her.

"Speak louder," I say and my voice reverberates off the walls. She startles slightly and lowers her head.

"I just said thank you." Her eyes don't meet mine as she says the words with an uneven cadence. The need to comfort her makes me grip the table harder, keeping me in place.

I nod my head once, watching her face as I dismiss her. "I'll see you tomorrow."

She leaves quietly this time, not looking back at me or meeting my gaze. It's only when she's left that I feel like I can breathe. It's also when I realize how fucked I am.

How Brooks paid his bills isn't any of my damn business. I never should have gone to that fucking auction.

I could have made an example of him and spared Arianna, such a sweetheart, so undeserving of this.

I made a mistake. And I know exactly why.

It's because of *her*. The temptation of having her, of owning her...
I caved to it.

I don't trust her. But I'll be damned if I don't want her.

CHAPTER 10

ARIANNA

Y es, because your prick of a boyfriend owes me.
Zander's biting words run through my mind as I turn over in my bed, a stream of early morning sunlight peeking through the blinds of my window. His words make me feel like a pawn. An object to be moved around on a chessboard and discarded when no longer useful.

I wrap my arms around my chest tightly, trying to ward away that worthless feeling that keeps threatening to suffocate me.

Madam Lynn's words come back to me. *You have the option to terminate this contract whenever you wish.*

Even Zander told me that I could leave if I didn't want him. But I didn't take the out he offered, and I'm ashamed. My skin pricks from the swell of emotion in my chest.

If I leave Zander, Danny will have me back. I'm a coward for hiding behind another man. Especially in this way. But knowing I'm temporarily his, gives me time and protection. My eyes stray over to my canvas. Painting almost always gives me solace when I'm stressed or feeling down. After stretching, I roll out of bed and ready my brushes and colors. I'm not even in the mood to go get coffee. I just want to paint and get lost in the art, forget about everything. I only get a few strokes done before the door opens behind me.

"Ari?" asks Natalie tentatively. It's odd, being in an apartment around someone normal when the reality of my life is nothing like hers. I don't fit in. I never have; I was always trying but never succeeding. I suppose it doesn't matter anymore. I turn around to see her standing in the doorway, still dressed in her pink polka dot pajamas, her hair tousled, peering at me with a grin on her face. "Yes, cavewoman?" I joke halfheartedly, mostly to try to hide my feelings, to pretend everything's alright. Natalie lets out a snort. "Cavewoman? Have you looked in the mirror lately? You're not exactly Cleopatra when you just roll out of bed either."

I huff out a mirthless chuckle. "Can't argue with that."

"Anyway, hater," Natalie says as she pulls her phone out of her pajama pocket, waving at me excitedly as she walks into the room, "you have *got* to see Sarah's ankle! She just got this tattoo done, and I love it!"

"Let me see." I wipe my hands on the cloth I use to clean up with, and take the phone from her hands to take a look. It's a picture of a black rose on her ankle. It's super realistic, but it only reminds me of the rose I held yesterday as I was sold.

Natalie grins at me as I stare at the photo. "Do you like it? I think it looks awesome." She taps her finger to her cheek, her expression turning thoughtful as I try to will the memory away and return to just pretending. "I'm thinking about getting the same one, but maybe on my wrist. And I was wondering if you wanted to be the one to do it?"

I don't immediately respond, my eyes still focused on the image of the rose.

"Ari?" Natalie presses, her voice filling with worry. "What's wrong?"

I tear my eyes away from the image to see the concern in Natalie's eyes. A part of me wants to tell her everything. About Danny. About the auction. Zander. But I ignore that part; I don't want to drag her into this, so instead I just say, "Danny and I aren't getting along right now." I'm unable to keep the frustration I feel with my situation from seeping into my voice. Natalie gazes at me with worry. "What's wrong? Did something get out of hand again?"

It sure fucking did.

It hurts me not to tell Natalie the truth. She's been my only friend for the longest time, and she's the only person I have left that I fully trust. But I know deep down telling her will do more harm than good.

I pass back her phone. "Not really. I just think we need a break from each other."

Natalie slips her phone back into her pocket and places her hands on her hips. "Come on, I know you're not telling me everything. Something got out of hand again and you just don't want to admit it."

Oh Nat, it's much, much worse than that, I think darkly.

"It's fine," I lie, hating myself for it. "I'm okay, don't worry."

Natalie's frown deepens. "You're lying to me."

I don't know how to respond. I can see that she cares so much about me. She knows about my troubled past and all of what I went through, and just doesn't want to see me hurt. But I don't know how to tell her without making things worse.

Right then, my cell buzzes on the nightstand.

I tell Natalie, "Hold on a sec," as I walk over to it, grateful for the interruption. It's a text message from Zander.

My driver will be at your apartment at 5:15 to pick you up.
The event is black tie. Wear a gown if you have one.
Be ready,
Z

"What was that?" Natalie asks, walking over, but I stick my phone back into my pocket before she can ask to see.

"Nothing," I reply, walking back over to my canvas while feeling like total shit for having to lie. "Just some dumb prick texting the wrong number."

CHAPTER 11

ZANDER

I admire punctuality. It says something about a lack of respect when a person is late. I half expected Arianna to be late for Marcus, my driver.

The cufflinks clink as I pick them up off the dresser and slip them into place, locking them and pulling down my sleeves slightly. I straighten my tie as I stare at myself in the mirror. I've always felt comfortable in a tux, but not today. Everything feels tight and suffocating.

I haven't given her a single reason to respect me, but she at least respects the contract.

It's obvious she doesn't want to do this, but I'll give her enough to desire at least a business relationship with me.

Tonight will be dinner, an interview in a way. That's all a dinner really is, just an interview.

I check my phone on the dresser, the dim light brightening the dark bedroom and see that the photographers will be there to catch a candid shot. I'll pretend I don't see them, just like I always do. I huff a humorless laugh at the ideal headlines PR is looking for.

Eligible Bachelor Falling Head Over Heels.

Love at First Sight for the Family Heir.

I can woo her. I'll get the photographs I need to create the image I want. I don't know how much I'd like to tell Arianna. My gut tells me to be truthful, to have her in on the charade. But the very thought of trusting her makes me panic.

I trust no one. But I can give her enough to go on.

The only loose end is Daniel Brooks.

My phone pings just as I set it back on the dresser. *Charles.*

I read the text silently and then pull back, running my fingers through my hair and slicking it back some before ruffling it in a way that looks careless. I take my time with it, making sure it looks just right.

Charles will take care of Brooks. I only need him to keep an eye on things for now. To make sure he stays in place until I figure out how to handle this.

Ideally, I can convince Arianna to keep the money for herself. The thought of Brooks' face when he finds out... how his expression will fall, that cocky glint in his eye will vanish.

But first, the interview. I need to know who she is and what she really wants. A background check can only tell you so much about a person, even one as in depth as what I received. *Don't disappoint me, Miss Owens.*

"She won't," the words slip past my lips as I shrug on my jacket. They hang in the air of my dark bedroom, holding a threat. I better be right about her.

My phone pings again, causing a spike of annoyance to run through me and this time it's Marcus, right on time with Arianna in tow.

I quickly make my way to the front doors, my strides so fast that I create a breeze as I climb down the stairs.

I breathe out a heavy exhale as I unlock the door, swinging it open and preparing for another evening of playing the role I was born into.

The moment I lay eyes on Arianna, the negative air that practically smothers me day in and day out, dissipates into the chill of early spring. Marcus is holding the door open for her, one of her small hands in his as her slender legs step out of the car one at a time, her heels clicking on the driveway. It's something about her expression that catches me off guard. Maybe it's the subtle way she brushes her gown and tucks a strand of her hair back as she stands tall as she takes in a deep breath.

She's as stunning as ever. I don't know what it is about her. She's not overly sexual, and there's not a single thing I can pinpoint that makes her exceptional. But every time I see her, my world pauses for only a moment. A single point in time where everything stands still, the air in my lungs halting and my heart slowing. There's a quality of innocence and sadness about her that makes me crave something I've never felt before.

I wish I could ignore it.

Her eyes widen when she sees me standing in the doorway staring back at her, and the smile I loathe creeps up and into place, but this time it feels different.

It's an odd thing that I've noticed. Everyone looks at me the same. Their eyes travel up and down my clothing, taking in the details. Businessmen before a board meeting, lower-level thugs at the corner of the street with information, even the vixens that wait late at night at the bars or casinos, hoping to sink their bright red nails into me for a piece of the money. They all look at me the same. Judging, assessing. I can practically see the wheels turning. Some are faster than others, but all of them have telltale signs of what they think.

Arianna is different. The expression on her face tells me she wants me, not my money. The lust turns her eyes glassy and makes her breathing come in short as her eyes linger down my body. But rather traveling back up to meet my gaze, she turns slightly away as the door closes and she thanks Marcus, her soft voice carried away by the gentle gust of the wind. It makes her hair blow, exposing more of her bare shoulder and her skirt clings to her right side.

When she looks back up, she doesn't meet my gaze.

"Miss Owens," I say loud enough for her to hear as I walk down the three steps to greet her. I make sure the charming smile is on my face as I wrap my arm around her small waist and plant a chaste kiss on her cheek. Surprise lights her eyes up and she doesn't respond for a moment. I don't know what she expected, but I'll surpass anything she's ever experienced. I'll make her want me. Want *this*. She'll play the part so well, because I'll make her believe it.

"Mr. Payne," her voice says my name in a sensual way that's seemingly unintentional.

"Just a moment, Marcus," I tell my driver as he stands by the car. Marcus nods once. He's an older man maybe in his sixties, but lean and cut from constantly working out. He takes pride in himself and what he does. He's always worked for me, ever since I was sixteen or so. I didn't trust him for years though. After all, it was my father who hired him. But on several occasions, he's proven his loyalty to me and that he can keep secrets.

Still, I'd rather him not hear what I have to tell Arianna. He may be trustworthy, but that doesn't mean I have to take an unnecessary risk. I haven't even confided in Charles. The less people who know, the better.

I lean in a bit closer to Arianna, whispering in her ear as I splay my hand along her lower back and lead her into the house. "We need to leave for dinner shortly, but I wanted a private word inside."

"Yes, Si- Zander," Arianna's posture stiffens at her mistake, and I almost regret my plan.., *almost*.

The moment we're inside, I shut the door and turn to her, slipping my hands into my pockets.

"I'd like you to be my girlfriend," I tell her simply.

She turns on her heels to face me, a look of not understanding on her face. "I'm sorry?" she asks.

I let out a charming chuckle, and walk the few steps to be closer to her. The house is so much warmer than outside, so much more welcoming.

"You heard me," I say and take her hand in both of mine. "I'd like you to be my girlfriend in place of what's written in the contract."

A knowing look flashes in her eyes and those beautiful lips part as understanding shows in her expression. Again, she doesn't respond like I thought she would. "A *fake* girlfriend?" she asks softly.

I pull away slightly and shrug as I reply, "I've never had one, so I'm not sure if it'd be all that fake." My words are casual, but calculated. I want her to believe in it. Of course it's fake. Yet another mask to hide behind.

Those dark green eyes pierce through me, not fooled by my tone in the least.

I ignore her prying gaze and the disappointment on her expression. "You'll be my girlfriend. Starting tonight, with a dinner date." I plaster a fake-ass smile on my face and wait for her reaction.

"Yes, Zander." Her posture stiffens now that she knows the rules of this game. It's an act and she's ready to play the part. But I don't want her to just play, I need it to feel real.

"Would you talk that way to your boyfriend?" I ask her. My jaw clenches at the thought of her speaking to Brooks like that. I ignore the jealousy creeping up my spine and sending a chill over every inch of my skin.

Arianna holds her clutch in both of her hands clasped in front of her and shakes her head slightly. "No," she answers honestly.

"Well then, it's just Zander, alright?" I tell her with a feigned casualness. "None of that..." I don't finish, not sure how to word her normal submission.

"I don't know how to..."

"How to what, sweetheart?" The little nickname parts from me without my conscious decision, but the way she reacts makes me want to say a million times over. The soft curves of her face brighten, and a beautiful pink hue rises to her cheeks. She lowers her head a little, closing her eyes and sinking her teeth into her bottom lip as she shakes her head slightly.

"How to," she starts to say with her eyes still closed and then opens them slowly, those gorgeous green eyes staring straight into me. The way only she can. "How to act tonight?" she asks in a voice so genuine, so sweet. Fuck, and all because I called her sweetheart? The shift in her is addicting. I love the smile. The light that I give her.

This is why I can't deny her.

CHAPTER 12

ARIANNA

*M*y heart feels like it's going to escape out my throat as I walk up the steps to Gargano's Italiano restaurant, my heels clicking against the stamped concrete. Wonder courses through my limbs as my eyes take in the gorgeous setting, the bright back-lighting illuminating the entire area with soft golden light.

I grip the railing as I walk beside Zander, his arm wrapped loosely around my waist. The stairway leads up to double doors that are surrounded by huge white Greek columns. There's a ten-foot male statue fountain halfway up the steps, the columns of water spraying high into the air. Surrounding the stairs is lush green landscaping, sprinkled with well-manicured walkways and white stone benches.

This is beautiful.

I'm so enthralled with the picturesque scenery that I only make it a couple of steps before I nearly trip over my dress. He told me to wear a gown, and this is the only one I had. The strapless chiffon fabric is forgiving and doesn't wrinkle which is a plus, but it's a bit long for my petite stature.

Shit.

Zander quickly tightens his powerful arm around my waist, saving me, pulling me against his hard body, and forcing me upright. The smell of his masculine cologne tickles my nose as I suck in a grateful breath, my skin pricking from the heat emanating from him. He smells like a fresh breeze and sandalwood. It's both calming and intoxicating.

"I'm sorry," I apologize softly from beneath lowered lashes, my face burning red with embarrassment. "I wasn't watching where I was going."

Zander told me to act like his girlfriend, but all I'm succeeding at is being awkward. I've never done this before, and my insecurity doesn't help. I feel like I'm not worth being on his arm, like it's obvious this isn't real. But I force a smile, trying to keep up appearances.

Zander smiles back at me, moving his hand to my hip, and despite my nervousness, I can't help but notice how handsome he is. He fucking *owns* the black tux and bow tie he's wearing. I've seen many men in expensive suits at Club X, but I've never seen anyone wear one like he does. He radiates, power, wealth and sex like the sun radiates light. I'm breathless, being this close to him. Like I'm drowning. And I don't want to come up for air.

He chuckles as he says, "I've got you. I won't let you fall." It's an odd thing, seeing how charming he is. I wasn't expecting him to be like this after the signing. I didn't expect any of this. And I don't know how to react.

"This place is beautiful," I say when I catch my breath. I'm trying so hard to be polite and act normal.

"If you think this is beautiful, wait until you see inside," Zander boasts. His teeth sparkle when he smiles. It's a beautiful look on him, that gorgeous smile, but it makes me feel uneasy.

Keeping a firm hand on my waist, he leads me up the stairwell. I raise my head, trying to look regal and confident on his arm.

As soon as we walk in, my breath catches in my throat as I take in the impressive architecture. Soft music plays over unseen speakers, setting the romantic ambience. We pass under impossibly high ceilings with massive archways that are decorated with silk sheers. I can see our reflections in the gleaming marble floors, and gorgeous intricate designs are inlaid across the surfaces.

The walls are painted a soft golden color and the sconces on the wall gives off a warm, fuzzy glow, infusing the room with an angelic-like radiance.

Tables are set with pure white cloth and the china and glasses are accented with gold. *Expensive.* This place looks fucking expensive.

And the people. Everyone here is dressed in their finest.

"You're right," I murmur, feeling extremely insecure. I lack the confidence of the other women around me. I have to look out of place on Zander's arm. "It is better."

Zander winks at me as we walk up to the reservation area, his arm resting possessively on the curve above my ass. "Told you." Seeing his playfulness eases my anxiety somewhat, though I clutch at him tightly to deal with my frazzled nerves.

Not a minute passes before a waiter dressed in uniform walks up to us.

"Do you have a reservation?" the waiter asks, his vest bunching slightly as he stands at the podium, flipping over a sheet of paper.

"Payne," Zander replies shortly although his voice doesn't hold an edge.

The waiter looks down at the booklet on the podium before nodding and motioning us out of the foyer. "Of course. Right this way, Mr. Payne."

As we follow the waiter and pass by rows of occupied tables, Zander tightens his grip on my waist and pulls me even closer, causing my skin to flush. It's like he wants to show me off to the world and wants everyone to know we're together. I even see a few women look our way, their eyes glued to Zander and traveling down his body, but then stopping at his hold on me.

I try to act confident, but I can't keep my eyes from nervously darting about. I feel like everyone knows I don't belong here. That I'm a worthless fraud.

"Remember to play your role," Zander says under his breath. "Act like you know me and not like you're a scared little doe lost in the woods." He whispers the words, but there's a playful smile still on his lips. His words have an immediate effect on me, and without even thinking, I gently place my hand on his stomach, feeling the hard ridges of his abs beneath his silk dress shirt.

"That's better," he says quietly.

I feel awkward as shit doing it, but I still like it.

We're led to a plush booth at the back of the restaurant. We pass what has to be a VIP section since the tables are more intimate, with lower lighting. I try not to look their way as Zander helps me into the booth before taking his seat.

"What will you have to drink?" the waiter asks while dropping menus in front of us and finishing up what felt like a speech about the fish of the day and something else. I can't concentrate on what he's saying with how fast my heart is beating.

"A white Zinfandel and I'll have a whiskey sour," Zander replies, not even bothering to ask me what I want.

"Of course, Mr. Payne." The waiter nods his head and walks off.

When he's gone, Zander focuses his eyes on me, the intensity of his gaze causing goosebumps to run down my arms. "You look beautiful."

My lips part with surprise as my cheeks flush. They're simple words, but they mean so much when they sound genuine.

"Thank you," I say softly when I can finally manage, lowering my lashes.

"You're welcome," Zander says, giving me that intense look that makes my skin prick.

For a moment, I get lost in his piercing blue eyes, wanting - no, wishing - that this was something more than what it really is.

"Why are we doing this again?" I blurt out suddenly. I bite my tongue after I say it. I wish I could take the words back, I only need to get the money and forget about all of this.

Zander arches an eyebrow. "Doing what?"

I gesture between us. "This... pretending..." I shift slightly in my seat, feeling so damn uncomfortable. "I just don't understand."

For the first time this night, Zander frowns and it makes me regret my outburst. "I already told you why," he says, keeping his voice low. "I don't want a Slave. It doesn't appeal to me."

And playing make-believe does? I want to ask. It's hard to believe a man like Zander not having *needs.* Sexual needs that revolve around power and domination. The thought brings a heat to my core, and I have to sit back in my seat, grabbing the napkin and delicately placing it over my lap.

"I'd rather get to know you first before having you crawl to me on your hands and knees," Zander says quietly.

His words have a clear effect on my body. I'd happily crawl to him. He must see the flicker of lust in my eyes, and the same is reflected in his. "You'd like that, wouldn't you?"

Right then the waiter returns with our drinks, saving me from responding. He sets a sparkling wine glass down in front of me and a mixed drink down in front of Zander.

"Are you ready to order, sir?" the waiter asks.

Zander nods. "A medium rare steak with crab cakes for me, and the stuffed lobster for my sweetheart." He says it again. Sweetheart. And a blush grows on my cheeks, heating my face and making me fiddle with the napkin to soothe my nerves.

"Wonderful selections, sir," the waiter says as he scribbles down the order and leaves us.

"What if I was allergic to seafood?" I have to inquire when he's gone.

Zander shakes his head. "I know you aren't. I want to appear that I know exactly what you want, like I've known you for some time. Remember, we're playing a role." He grins. "Besides, I know you'll love what I ordered for you. Promise."

"I'll take your word for it," I say softly, flashing a fake smile as I take in his admission that he knew I wasn't allergic.

"Smart girl." Zander grins as if pleased by my behavior. He takes a sip of his drink, his penetrating eyes glued to my face. He keeps them on me, literally making me squirm in my seat before asking, "Tell me, what do you do in your free time?"

I hesitate for a moment, glancing down into my glass, a slight flush coming to my cheeks. I wonder if he already knows.

"You can tell me," Zander says gently. "I don't judge." I look up at him, searching his eyes for the reason he's asking me, but I come up emptyhanded.

"I work at a soup kitchen, doing work for the homeless," I tell him. "When I'm not working, I like to paint."

"And you were ashamed to tell me that?" Zander asks.

I bite my lower lip. "It doesn't pay well." That's an understatement.

"But does it make you happy?"

I nod. "In some ways. I like helping people. It makes me feel… complete."

Zander eyes twinkle as he gazes at me. "I respect that, I really do. And I'd argue, loving what you do is more important than what a job pays."

"Do you really think so? My bills don't." It's a joke, but I sound absolutely serious.

Zander chuckles. "Can't say I can argue with that." Zander arches a curious eyebrow. "And what about your painting?"

I hesitate. I like my artwork, but I'm not sure if Zander will, or anyone else for that matter. I don't paint it for others; it's only for me.

"I think I have a picture here in my cell somewhere," I mumble.

"Can I see?" he asks, his tone filled with inquisitiveness that makes me want to show him.

I dig out my cell from my clutch and flip through the photos until I find a picture of one of my paintings. It's on the darker side with a woman lying down on a bed while looking out of a small window. It's not some picturesque painting. Not a classic, like a gorgeous land-scape of rolling green hills and an azure blue sky. She's haunted by something that keeps her in her room, although I don't know what.

My throat is dry as I pass him the phone, my palm feeling sweaty and my nerves making me nearly regret showing it to him. Zander takes more than a moment to look over it, his eyes moving slowly across the screen before passing my phone back. "That's beautiful, Arianna," he compli-ments me, a note of respect entering his voice. "You're very talented."

"It's a little…" I trail off as I try to think of the right word to defend it before he can question it, but he fills in the word for me.

"Haunting," he says and his voice is firm. "It's in her eyes."

I nod my head, not trusting myself to respond verbally. "It really speaks to how well you're able to paint emotions. Not everyone can do that."

I blush furiously at his praise, my self-confidence rising several notches. "Thank you," I say softly.

The waiter returns with both of our plates and I'm shocked to see how quickly time has gone by. The smell of sweet butter and herbs wafts toward me, and my mouth waters.

We're both quiet as the meals are set in front of us, although I notice Zander checking his phone.

"Is everything alright?" I ask him when we're alone again.

He gives me a smile, picking up his utensils and answers, "It's perfect."

CHAPTER 13

ZANDER

I'm rewarded with a small smile as I set my hand on Arianna's thigh as I readjust in my seat in the back of the Mercedes. I wonder if she's ever been treated this way before. It's not so difficult. A sweet gesture here and there, and alone time over a nice meal.

"I had a really nice time," she says so quietly I almost don't hear her. But then she clears her throat and looks up at me through thick lashes and speaks more clearly, "It was more than I expected, thank you."

But the way she's acting, it's as if she's never been fed. Like she's never been told that she's beautiful.

It's hard to believe it's true.

"Thank you for accompanying me," I tell her as the car slows down in front of her house.

I expected dinner to be filled with uncomfortable silence, but there wasn't a moment that conversation didn't happen easily and naturally. "We have a dinner this weekend as well."

"Another?" she says and her voice brightens and forces a small laugh from me.

"Yes, you may find it hard to believe, but I eat almost every day. Sometimes several times a day." The joke comes out easily and makes her smile. That sweet one that shows she's honestly happy. It warms my chest to know I put it there.

As Marcus stops the car, I'm quick to open my door and wait for his eyes to catch mine in the rearview mirror. I've got her from here. He stays in his seat as the car remains in park and I quickly shut my door and move to hers to help her out.

"I'm excited to do this again," she says with a sweet smile. She brushes a stray strand of hair from her face as the wind blows by and goosebumps grow along her arms. "Thank you... again," she says for at least the fifth time and this time rolls her eyes recognizing how absurd it is that she keeps thanking me. If nothing else, Arianna is full of gratitude and not afraid to show it.

"I am as well." I walk her up to her steps and stop, making sure that she knows I have no intention of going in. It's not about sex. I don't want her to feel pressured and judging by the soft look on her face, she's not in the least.

She turns on the first step, and rocks on her heels as she asks, "This weekend?"

I nod my head and answer, "Four days."

"Will I see you before then?" she asks me. There's a flash of hope in her eyes and I'm not sure if it's because she wants to see me, or if she thinks she won't have to be with me again until this weekend.

"I have a good bit of work to do," I tell her, although in the back of my mind I can't help but to think I'll have time in the evening. Late evening. She could always come and warm my bed. I brush off the thought but the hint of disappointment in her voice as she answers, "Oh, okay," makes me want to offer it to her.

Maybe not this week, but next.

"I'll be calling you. And you can do the same if you'd like. I'll message you if I think of anything," I tell her without thinking. I have no fucking reason to call her whatsoever, but just the offer brings that beautiful smile back to her face.

She tucks her hair behind her ear. "I'll call you then," she says and closes her eyes and shakes her head slightly. "Or you call me. I'll wait," she adds, then nods her head, looking so serious. "I'll wait for you to call me."

A rough chuckle rises up my chest as I lean forward and give her a chaste kiss goodbye. "Alright then, sweetheart."

Even in the darkened night, I can see that blush on her cheeks as she turns to go upstairs.

"Oh, Miss Owens," I call out her proper name, reaching forward and grabbing her hand in mine. "I had a package delivered for you," I say and pull her closer to me, and she doesn't resist my touch. I wrap my arms around her waist, letting them rest on the lower part of her back, dangerously close to her ass.

Although her eyes dart from my cheek up to my own, she doesn't push me away. I can see how her chest is rising and falling with quicker breaths now, and I fucking love it. I'm addicted to the way I so easily affect her.

"You did?" she asks with equal amounts of surprise and delight in her voice. The streetlights shine down on her in a way that casts shadows along the soft curves of her face. She looks up at me and all I can see in her green eyes is sincerity. I could get lost in the swirls of deep jade that shine back at me.

"I did," I say before I quickly kiss her lips. The kiss is soft and easy and I need to keep it that way.

It was only one night. An evening just to get to know her, just an interview, but I can feel it turning into something more. A desire for something I shouldn't want.

The reminder of why I'm holding her in my arms, why all of this is even happening is enough to break the spell of her hopeful gaze.

She's temporary. And a mistake I'm merely trying to fix. The knowledge makes my smile slip, but it's instantly replaced by the one I hate.

"I'll see you this weekend." I deliver another small kiss to the tip of her nose and step out of her embrace. She doesn't seem to notice my change in demeanor. "If you need anything in the meantime, you'll let me know."

"Of course," she replies and bats her eyes, moving the clutch from one hand to the other. "Really, and truly. Thank you for tonight, Zander." Her voice is so full of happiness, that I find my reasons for leaving so quickly disappearing into the dark night. But she turns from me before I can go back to her, her hips swaying and taunting me as she walks closer to the front door and grips the railing.

As I watch her walk up the steps, those gorgeous curves tempting me as the soft sounds of the night air swish by and make her dress cling to her, I finally answer her beneath my breath. "My pleasure, sweetheart."

CHAPTER 14

ARIANNA

My pleasure, sweetheart.

Zander's words linger in my mind as I step into my shared apartment and gently close the door behind me, feeling a heavy mix of emotions coursing through my chest. Zander has been such a gentleman. It was so unexpected; I don't know how to process it. It's hard not to feel butterflies, even knowing it's all fake.

I suck in a heavy breath, remembering how it felt to be held in his arms at the end of dinner. Zander made me feel special, like I was the only woman in the room. And even though I felt unworthy to be there with him, I wanted it to be real. I wanted desperately to think that he truly wanted me beside him.

It felt like that. It felt *real*.

I run my finger down the side of the package that was left for me. It's not hard to imagine that it's a dress for this weekend. The white box is large, yet light. My heart beats with anticipation to open it.

I spin around when I hear Natalie's shocked voice.

"Jesus Ari, what are you dressed up for?" She walks into the living room and adds, "You look beautiful!"

Natalie's in her favorite pair of pink polka dot pajamas, a half-finished cup of Greek yogurt in her hand, her jaw hanging slack. The television's on and running in the background, playing some rerun of one of the *Real Housewives* reality TV shows she likes to watch.

She sets her yogurt down on the end table next to the couch and walks over to inspect my dress.

My tongue is tied. I don't know how to tell her the truth. It all feels... dirty. "I was out with a friend," I lie.

Natalie studies me suspiciously. "What sort of friend? And since when do you go out dressed like that for *a friend*?" Although she's practically interrogating me as she crosses her arms, she has the hint of a smile playing on her lips.

I'm unable to answer her question. The butterflies fluttering in my stomach want to tell her about tonight. About dinner and how Zander treated me, but it's not real and it'll only complicate things to involve anyone else. Plus, I'm not sure what I'm allowed to reveal given the non-disclosure agreement I signed at Club X. I really wish she would stop prying. It puts me in such an uncomfortable position. She peers closely at me when I don't answer right away. "And what's this..." her voice trails off as if she realizes something. "Wait a minute... you weren't out there with Danny, were you? Is that why you don't want to tell me what's going on? 'Cause you told me you were taking a break with him, and you're really not?" Her voice raises, and the smile vanishes.

I roll my eyes at where her mind goes, holding the package a bit closer to me. I wish it were that simple.

Natalie persists, insisting, "I know you were with someone. I can smell cologne on you."

"It wasn't with Danny," I say.

Natalie presses. "Who then?"

I grit my teeth, wishing I didn't have to do this. "I can't say. Just a friend."

Natalie scrunches her face into a frustrated scowl. "You know what? Your sudden secretive ways are really starting to get to me."

I let out a sigh. "I'm sorry, Nat. I just don't want to say anything right now."

Natalie places her hands on her hips. "Well, when will you be able to say anything then? The suspense is killing me." She lightens the mood by exaggerating her last line and moving to snatch her cup of yogurt up again.

I remain tight-lipped. "I don't know. Soon."

Natalie stares at me for a long moment before letting out a resigned sigh and taking a spoonful of yogurt. "Okay. I'm going to let you off the hook for now. But can you promise me one thing?"

I'm on edge. "What?"

"Don't see that piece of shit Danny ever again, pretty please?"

"He's not a piece of shit," I say reflexively. I don't know why I say that. Everything Danny has done to me recently leading up to the auction says he is. And after what Zander told me, I should never want to see him again. But no matter how hard I try, I can't get over what he did for me.

He saved me. I really wanted to kill myself. I would have if he hadn't stopped me.

Natalie's jaw drops. "Are you kidding me? He beat the hell out of you for the past couple of months, and now you're defending him? What the hell is wrong with you?"

God, I don't want to fight. I toss the package down feeling like I'm in a no-win situation. But it's a tight spot that I put myself in. I seriously want to go into my room and curl up into a little ball. "Please, Nat," I plead, "I'm tired and don't want to talk about this right now."

Natalie stares at me long and hard, before finally shaking her head. "Fine. But I don't think I'll ever understand this relationship you have with him, and I don't think I ever want to." My throat feels tight as I take in her words. I didn't ask for her support and I understand that she doesn't like it, but it still hurts. "I'm going to bed. Don't forget to turn the lights off."

She disappears down the hall, leaving me alone.

I suck in a heavy breath as tears sting my eyes, my gaze going down to the package sitting on the sofa. I feel like crap having to lie to Natalie, but I don't know what else I can do.

Sighing, I slump down on the couch, running my fingers over the package.

I tear it open and stare in shock at what's inside. It's a beautiful gown, a white sparkly number, with glittering rhinestones that shimmer like diamonds. I run my fingers over the exquisite tailoring, thinking that it's the nicest gift anyone has even given me.

But just like tonight, just like the butterflies in my stomach, it's a lie.

I cover the dress up with the thin piece of white tissue paper and let my head fall back against the sofa.

None of this is real, and I need to protect myself and remember that.

CHAPTER 15

ZANDER

I turn down the radio as I pull off of the highway heading down to Arianna's place. It's nearly eight on a Friday, but it's the only night I can make time for her.

My turn signal clicks as I turn onto her street and remember the article in the paper this morning. It's nothing huge, and I doubt Arianna's read it. The picture of her is perfect, capturing the moment and sending the message that I'm no longer on the market. She may never even know about it unless she searches her name or someone points it out to her.

I want to be the one to show her. I can't wait to see her reaction when she sees. Although it does say, "mystery woman." The next one will have her name; I made sure of that.

I pass a row of condominiums. I hate this area in the city. The brick is old and worn, and graffiti covers half the buildings. She doesn't belong here. I grip the steering wheel tighter as I park out front of her building and look up to her apartment window. The lights are on.

It's a weird feeling, something like nervousness as I pull out my phone. It doesn't make sense, and I ignore it as I text her that I'm outside. I stare up to her window, waiting for a response. I let out a small laugh as I see her pull the curtains back to look outside.

The phone pings as I open my car door and I glance at it to see what she's said as I jog up the stairs. *Come on up.*

My heart flutters as I walk into the warmth of the building and see her standing in her open doorway.

"Hi," she says sweetly as she opens the door wider and bites her lower lip.

Her nightgown looks nothing like what I'd expect on her. It's a simple cotton thing, so thin that I can see the outline of her nipples. It's the colors that I don't expect. Patches of bright and neon colors.

"It's my roommate's," Arianna says, answering the unspoken question. She shrugs slightly before saying, "It's laundry day."

I turn to take her in, and something shifts. The flutters in my stomach turn to stone as she crosses her arms across her chest and avoids looking at me.

That smile I've been thinking about for the past few days, the one that's invaded my every waking moment, is nowhere to be seen.

"How are you?" I ask her out of curiosity as I walk into her apartment.

"Fine, how are you?" she answers with a politeness I've come to expect from her.

"Alright," my answer is a bit absent as I glance around her place. I've never seen the inside before. The walls are an off-white, typical in apartments, but there are so many photos on the wall that color the room. On the far wall of the living room there have to be at least thirty photos, all framed and hung in the shape of a heart above a lime green Ikea sofa littered with pillows in different colors. It takes me by surprise.

"Those are Natalie's," Arianna says and nods toward the living room.

"Ah," I walk in a few steps and lean against the banister.

"I didn't expect you," Arianna says in a way that makes it obvious she's uncomfortable with me dropping by unannounced like this. She tucks her hair behind her ear as she looks past me and back into the living room as she says quietly, "I would have cleaned up." Her entire demeanor has changed since I saw her last. My heart feels heavy in my chest, as if it's falling, it's an unnatural feeling, something I'm not used to.

"I thought I would surprise you," I tell her. "I wanted to make sure you got your dress."

I expect a smile, but instead she only nods and answers respectfully, "I did, and it's beautiful. Thank you so much."

My heart thuds once, then twice. Maybe this was a mistake. I run my hand through my hair, not knowing what the fuck to do. I don't have a significant other for a reason.

"I'm sorry," Arianna's voice comes out small. "I should have texted you to thank you."

My gaze travels over her entire body. She's uncomfortable, but presenting herself. Just like the auction. There's a small bit of paint on her elbow, and at first it looks like a bruise, but it's definitely paint.

"Have you done any more artwork?" I ask her, trying to change the subject. I can't leave her feeling like this. The gala is tomorrow and I don't trust whatever's going on in her head right now.

She nods her head, a bit of brightness lighting her dark green eyes. It makes my lips kick up into a smirk. "Let me see," I tell her.

"Oh," she takes a half a step back and bites her lip. "It's not really done."

My stomach drops at her confession, although she tries to back out of the excuse. "I can still show you," she says apologetically.

"No," I say and wave her concern away. "That's fine. If it's not done, I'll wait."

She nods her head and visibly swallows, awkwardness returning.

"I was just on my way to bed," Arianna says quietly. "I'm just tired, really."

"Alright then," I tell her, taking the cue to leave and feeling like a fucking jackass. "I'll head on out and go home."

She's a smart woman. She knows this isn't real, and whatever connection we had at dinner is long gone. My blood runs cold at the thought. A frown settles on my face and refuses to budge. *How did I fuck this up?* I shake the thought away. There was nothing to fuck up. It was stupid for me to visit her.

I open the door, seeing myself out, but she's quick to follow me. I stand in the open doorway. "I'll be with Marcus around six to pick you up tomorrow."

A small smile slowly grows on her lips and I'll be damned, but my heart flutters with hope.

"Come here," I say and cup my hand around the back of her head and bring her in for a kiss. My lips press against hers gently at first as she tilts her head and holds her body close against mine.

I'm just kissing my sweetheart goodnight.

A spark ignites between us as I deepen the kiss, letting my other hand roam down to her waist and pulling her even closer to me. The tip of my tongue slips between the seam of her lips and she parts them for me, moaning softly into my mouth and gripping my shirt in her hands. Electricity runs over every inch of my skin, a dark beast inside of me coming to life, wanting to hold onto her and not let go.

This is what we had before, and I don't want to lose it. I don't want to take another step away and never have this again.

"Hey," my voice is low as I pull back from the kiss and grip her chin in my hand. Her eyes are still closed, as if she's in a daze. I know I'm not the only one that feels this. "Are you alright?" I need to know. I don't want to lose her again. "Did Brooks message you?" I ask her even though I know Danny's not bothering her. Charles is still watching him and has his phone tapped. But something's not right with her.

"I'm just not feeling well," she tells me, although her eyes don't hold my gaze.

"Is there something I can get you?"

"No," she pulls away from me, holding the edge of the door, ready to close it. "I'll be alright."

I search her eyes and almost leave it be. I almost let her get away with brushing me off, but something comes over me. I push the door open wider and step back in. Arianna's eyes open wider and she walks backward, letting me invade her space and close the door behind me.

"You're mine, sweetheart," I tell her with a voice I don't recognize. "I need to take care of you." I let the flood of images that have kept me awake at night fuel my desire to keep moving. "Do you want that?" I ask her.

"When's the last time you got off?" I ask her, feeling my dick harden in my pants.

She turns to look behind her, swallowing and quickly answers. "My roommate is-"

"Get upstairs," I cut her off. I know exactly what Arianna needs, and I'm not going to hold back when I can give it to her.

I follow her up the steps, that lush ass swaying as I unbutton my shirt.

Arianna talks quietly as she walks in front of me, leading me to her bedroom. "It's just that I'm confused and I don't know how to react to it all." She opens her door and waits for me to walk in before closing it and locking the doorknob.

I don't hesitate to remove my shirt as she turns around. "And..." she starts to say, but then pauses mid-sentence as her eyes take me in. My sweetheart definitely knows how to boost my ego.

"I'm your Master, aren't I?" I ask her, taking the two strides to fill the space between us. "I do the worrying," I say as I cup her chin. My thumb brushes along her lower lip as her green eyes search mine.

"You are?" she asks me, her breath coming up short.

"I want to be," I say the words before I know how true they are. "Do you want me to be your Master, sweetheart?"

She nods her head once and whispers, "Yes."

CHAPTER 16

ARIANNA

"*Y*ou need to get off," Zander says, his voice low and husky, his thumb resting on my lips. I stare into his piercing blue eyes, desire heating my core.

"I-I-I don't think I can," I stammer. I'm starting to feel so very hot, the heat from his hard body causing my temperature to rise, my heart pounding in my chest.

"You can," Zander says firmly. "And you will."

He caresses the side of my face gently, his touch causing my skin to tingle all over. I close my eyes at the sensation, reveling in the feel of his gentle touch against my skin. I want to do as he says. I *want* to please him. But I don't know if it'll be easy. I've always used pain to get my release. And...

Danny's words play in my mind.

No matter whose collar you put on, I'm still your Master. And the only one to bring me pleasure is him. I can only have it through pain.

"Danny-" I begin to say. I need Zander to know.

"Isn't your Master anymore," Zander finishes for me. "I am. And I want you to get on that bed, spread your legs wide, and rub your pussy for me."

The intensity of his words causes my pussy to clench, my nipples pebbling against the flimsy nightgown.

Zander says, "You're wet for me already." It's not a question, but a statement of fact.

"Yes," I whisper, my pulse quickening, my breathing ragged. My body is still and tense.

Zander's fingers trail back down to my lips. He presses his thumb against them, demanding entry. I part my lips, letting him gently place his thumb on my tongue. "Suck," he commands me.

I do as he says, gently sucking on his thumb exactly how he wants me to. As if it's his cock. I don't close my eyes at first. I watch him and his reaction as I do what I'm told.

A soft groan escapes his lips and he closes his eyes briefly. When he opens them, he pulls his thumb from between my lips, leaving me wanting more, and asks softly, "Would you like to please me?"

Slowly, I nod my head, my clit throbbing. "Yes," I say, my voice barely above a whisper. Maybe I'm weak, but I desperately want to please him.

"I won't allow it," Zander says in his deep voice. My body freezes until he adds, "Not until you've made yourself cum."

I nod my head and take a step backward, the backs of my knees hitting the mattress. I haven't touched myself in… in over a year. I wasn't allowed.

Anxiety mixes with desire as I fall back on my bed and scoot myself back with my knees bent upward. Every move is deliberate and my eyes stay on Zander's, making sure that he's pleased with everything.

His breathing comes in heavier as he watches me. Zander grabs my desk chair, placing it in front of the bed. His eyes never leave me as he sits down, spreading his legs out wide. I can't help but notice the huge bulge pressing against his dark dress pants, straining to get out.

"Lift up your gown," Zander commands, his voice heavy. Husky. "Panties off."

I do as he says, pulling my gown all the way up to my upper stomach and push my underwear off. My fingers tremble as they push against my legs. Zander inhales sharply at the sight of me. I wait for him to touch himself, but he doesn't. His hands stay on his thighs.

"Touch yourself," he orders, his voice strained.

Slowly, I run my hand down my stomach and then between my

legs. Right before I touch myself, I freeze, anxiety washing over me. I'm not allowed to. I haven't been allowed in so long. *But Danny is not my Master anymore.* Still, it's hard to move forward.

I look at Zander for guidance, fear keeping me from obeying. "I haven't..." I look up at the ceiling before I continue. "I haven't in a long time," I admit.

Anger flashes in Zander's eyes. "You weren't allowed to touch yourself?"

I shake my head. "No. Or cum without... pain."

"You have my permission and that's all you need," Zander says, his voice tight. "Touch yourself."

Taking a deep breath, I place the tips of my fingers on my throbbing clit and rub a small circle against it with just a touch of pressure. Warmth flows from my belly outward, running a fire through my body all the way up to my neck. A soft moan escapes my lips as my head lolls to the side, my eyes still on Zander, my Master.

"Good girl," Zander groans.

I slowly move my hand up and down between my folds, and the touch is so foreign to me as my fingers spread the moisture back up to my clit.

"You're gorgeous like this," Zander says softly, the sexy tone of his deep voice causing my limbs to quiver. "You deserve this. Relax and just let go."

Another sigh escapes my lips as I arch my back, lifting myself up with the tips of my toes, and rubbing myself in a circular motion, faster and harder.

"Yes," Zander hisses.

His praise makes me want more. Keeping myself suspended and my back arched, the bed creaks as my ass sways, barely brushing against the bedding.

For a moment, I remember Natalie's home and I'm scared that I might be making too much noise. The last thing I want is for her to hear, but I'm too far gone now to stop. And I don't want to disobey him.

"Fuck," Zander groans. "I'm so fucking hard for you."

"Imagine my cock deep inside you," Zander says, his voice filled with lust, "filling you up."

I moan at his words, the fire raging hotter, rubbing myself faster, all the while staring into Zander's eyes.

"I want you to cum for me," Zander demands.

His command is my undoing. My back arches, the inferno inside of my stomach reaches a crescendo, sending shockwaves of pleasure all over my body. Wave after wave hits me and makes my neck arch, forcing me to look away from Zander. The room spins above me as waves of pleasure continue to radiate from my core and I lose all sense of time.

Zander's standing at the foot of the bed when I come back down from my high.

"On your knees," he commands me even as the dull ache between my legs continues to send shockwaves through me.

I instantly obey him, slipping out of the bed and onto the floor, falling to my knees at Zander's feet. My mouth parts as my pussy pulses and a wave of pleasure spikes through me.

He grips his belt at his waist, and pulls it out with one smooth movement, letting the hiss of the leather against the silk fabric fill the room along with the sounds of our heavy breathing. Zander tosses the belt to the floor beside him, but doesn't make a move, staring down at me expectantly.

My heart pounds as I realize he's waiting for me. I reach up and undo the button of his expensive dress pants and tug on the zipper, pulling his slacks and his underwear down around his thighs with one soft jerk.

I'm nearly slapped in the face as his thick dick springs free. My mouth waters as I look at it swinging back and forth before wrapping my fingers around his shaft. His cock pulsates in my hand, beating in tandem with my pounding heartbeat.

"Suck," he tells me, his voice strained as his fingers spear through my hair.

Slowly, I part my lips, allowing him entry to my mouth. I have to open as wide as I can to accommodate his size as his head gently pushes against my tongue, the sweet tang of his precum making me moan.

"Fuck," Zander murmurs, throwing his head back.

Gripping his shaft with my right hand, I swirl my tongue around his head, teasing it, before letting him go back further in my mouth.

I rock on my heels as I hollow my cheeks and take more of him into my mouth. He feels like smooth velvet over steel as I press my lips against him. Massaging, sucking, and pleasing him the best I can.

Zander moans again, placing his hands on either side of my head, taking control. He thrusts his cock all the way into my mouth, almost causing me to gag. He pulls out quickly, stroking himself once while I catch my breath. I open wide for him and wait. My hands are on my thighs, and I keep my eyes on his.

"Good girl," he says as he pushes himself back into my mouth. It's difficult, but I hold back my gag reflex as he thrusts deep inside of my mouth, his thick head hitting the back of my throat. Zander's breathing quickens as he picks up his pace, holding the back of my head firmly. My eyes sting with the need to breathe, but before it's too much he pulls out and then does it all again. It takes all my self-control to not pull away, his huge cock triggering my gag reflex with almost every thrust. But I love it. I want him to take all the pleasure he can from me.

"I'm gonna cum," I hear him groan above me, his breath coming in ragged pants.

His thrusts are short shallow pumps, but he remains deep in me as I feel his big dick grow impossibly hard in my mouth. *One. Two. Three.*

My fingernails dig into my thighs as he cums in the back of my throat. A strangled gasp escapes Zander's lips on his final thrust.

I swallow everything, taking it all and loving how I made him come undone. When he pulls away from me, I expect him to clean himself up, to leave me where I am and make me wait for him.

But he reaches down, gripping my chin in his hand and kisses me. I'm caught by surprise, his taste still in my mouth. It's only his lips, but still, I didn't expect it.

He pulls away, his breath still ragged as his eyes search my face.

"Did you enjoy it?" he asks me.

"Yes," I answer immediately.

He releases me and I instantly miss his warmth. I more than enjoyed it. *I need more.*

I HOPE ZANDER WILL BE PLEASED.

I glance over my appearance in the mirror, my heart skipping a beat at my reflection. It's the next day after our hot foreplay session and I'm getting ready for another date. Zander's taking me somewhere new tonight. Somewhere important. And I don't want to disappoint him.

I'm wearing the gorgeous white gown made up of sparkling rhinestones Zander gave me, my hair pulled up into an elegant French bun with wispy bangs framing my face. I had to watch a video on how to put my hair up like this, but it was worth it.

I hardly recognize myself.

With my dangling diamond earrings, dramatic makeup, and gorgeous gold bracelet I look like some wealthy debutante. Everything about my appearance says eloquence and beauty, even if the diamonds are fake. Still, I don't *feel* like I'll belong on Zander's arm. I feel like I'm just playing dress-up, hiding the flaws that lie just beneath the surface.

I don't think I can ever match up to the woman who's looking back at me in the mirror. That person I see, I don't recognize her. It's not the real me. I'm just a fraud.

I suck in a breath as I remember his warm lips pressed against mine. I got lost in the moment. Lost in him. I never wanted it to end. Just being around him makes me feel dizzy with euphoria. It's not supposed to be this way. It's just an act. It's all fake.

But why does it feel so fucking real?

Because he's my Master, a voice whispers in the back of my mind. The instant I think the words, my body relaxes.

My pulse races as warmth flows through my chest. I can't get over the way he looks at me. Like I'm *his*. It makes me feel wanted. Even if it is only for thirty days.

I shake off the feeling of anxiety rolling through me, the questions and fear. He'll take care of me. I close my eyes and try to believe it, but I know it's foolish. *This is temporary.*

He's going to be here soon to pick me up.

And I know the moment I see him, I'm going to go weak in the knees. It's what he does to me. He makes me powerless, but I want it. I want to give it all to him.

It scares me.

It makes me feel like I'm drowning.

And I don't want anyone to save me.

CHAPTER 17

ZANDER

The moment the limo pulls up, she's at the door to the townhouse, not making me wait. I should move and get my ass out of the limo to go to her, but I'm struck for a moment. She stands out against the dark red brick of the old building, her white dress brushing against her shapely legs as the wind blows, further emphasizing her tempting curves. She's striking, gorgeous even.

She's all I've thought about since I left her.

The trees and bushes along the sidewalk and in front of her building are barren. The buildings are old and worn; history has been unkind to them. Maybe her past is dark, but I know with everything in me, she doesn't belong here. Not anymore.

The wind is harsh, blowing her shawl and exposing her bare shoulders. She lets out a gasp that I imagine I can hear as she reaches for the edge of her shawl. It's blowing in the wind with the threat of losing it clearly on her face. Although the weather is more like spring than the end of winter, with the wind I know she must feel the chill.

She grips the iron railing, steadying herself on the landing of the stone steps as Marcus opens his driver's door to the limo. It brings me back to the moment, and I'm quick to get out so I can wave him back.

As my dress shoes slap against the paved sidewalk, my blood heats. She's sure to be noticed tonight, which will bring more attention than usual. That, combined with the news article, I'm sure will get people talking. My nerves prick at the thought. I usually enjoy blending in. The familiar is expected and also ignored.

She certainly isn't familiar, and I know damn well she won't be ignored.

I have to jog to meet her at the bottom of the steps. "You look beautiful," I compliment her as I hold out my hand. A beautiful blush rises to her cheeks as she sets her small hand in mine.

"Thank you," she says and her voice is small and full of genuine happiness. I don't know what she expects out of this, with me being her Master, but I can take care of her. And I intend to. I've almost messaged Lucian and Isaac a few times to ask what the fuck I'm supposed to do. I'm not going to let on to that fact though.

I hold her hand and open her door for her as a gentleman should. I wait for her to sit back in her seat before closing it and getting in on the other side.

It only hits me when we're alone in the back of the limo and Marcus pulls away that I'm really taking her to an event. I don't bring guests anywhere. I don't make appearances with any women, and I've never been seen with a significant other. Not that I've had them. A quick fuck to sate my appetite is all I've ever indulged in.

But tonight is different. It's a statement as well.

It's quiet for a moment, and I can see that it's getting to Arianna. Her fingers tangle with one another and more than once she parts her lips to say something, chancing a look up at me but then looks back to the floor of the cabin.

I finally break the tension. "I'd like you to do what I say tonight." She needs to be perfect. She needs to play the part well so that no one will question what we are, and my image will stay intact.

"Of course," she answers quickly, nodding her head. "I promise I'll do my best *and* it will be good enough."

I eye her and take in the conviction in her voice.

"Have you been to a gala?" I ask her, reaching across the cabin to the champagne that's sitting on ice. I uncork it with a flourish as she answers that she hasn't, but she's fully aware of how she's supposed to act and that she won't disappoint me.

The champagne pops, and the sound of it spilling easily into the first flute is accompanied by the sound of my heart beating in my chest. She continues talking nervously, but she sounds eloquent, even with the nerves evident. She's going to be perfect.

The glass flutes clink against each other as the limo goes over a small bump and I fill the second halfway.

"Champagne?" I offer as I set the bottle back down.

"Thank you," she says and accepts the glass with grace although she doesn't take a drink. I taste mine, the sweetness coating my tongue.

"You're a smart woman, so I'm sure you'll be fine," I tell her as I place my hand on her knee. "You'll be quiet for most of the night and simply stay on my arm."

"Yes," she answers quickly, both of her hands wrapped around the skinny stem of the glass sitting in her lap.

"As far as anyone knows, you're my girlfriend. It's a new relationship." I down the rest of the champagne and set the empty glass into its place, leaning forward and continuing to talk. "We met through a mutual friend if anyone asks, although I'll do my best to do most of the talking."

"Absolutely," she answers firmly.

I nod my head at her and let my eyes travel down her dress. "You really do look beautiful, sweetheart." I don't think about the words until they've left me. A pleasant sound comes from her lips. Not a gasp of surprise or a laugh, but something in-between. As if she's flattered, but that she doesn't believe me.

"I'm proud to have you by my side tonight. Do you know that?" I ask her.

She gazes at me for a moment, but doesn't answer quickly which isn't in her nature. She finally whispers, "Thank you." It makes me think she truly doesn't believe it. I need to change that.

I scoot closer to her and rest my hand on her thigh as I lean in and whisper against the shell of her ear. "A lot of the women in there are going to be jealous of you tonight."

She turns quickly in her seat to look me in the eyes. "Because they want you?" she asks softly. There's an expression in her eyes I don't recognize, maybe fear, but I'm not sure.

"No," I say and I can feel my forehead pinch as I continue, "Just because you're so beautiful." Her cheeks stain with that beautiful red and she looks away, pushing a stray strand of hair from her face.

Time passes as we both sway slightly in the limo, the comfortable silence stretching between us. My phone dings, and I'm quick to see who it is. With these functions, there's always someone who wants to ensure they'll be seen talking to me.

I've already missed half a dozen messages and two phone calls, several of which are from my father. I sigh and lean back in my seat, leaving the warmth of her small frame and focusing on work. She scoots closer to me, resting her hand on my thigh and leaning against me. I wait for her to say something, giving her the attention she needs, but she doesn't say a thing. I wrap my arm around her and continue to check my email as she lays her head against me and looks out of the window. She's simply happy to be held.

The limo comes to a stop, and it's only when Marcus opens his door that I realize we're here already.

"Wait here," I tell her as she reaches for the door. "I'll get out first, then open your door. You will not slide across the seat. Instead I want you to wait for me there," I say and nod toward her door.

"I can do that. I *will* do that." She holds my gaze as she answers me, and something flickers between us. She wants to please me. And I know she can. A small smile grows on my face and it's then that I realize I've been more of myself around her than I should have been. I've given her a glimpse behind the mask. Instead of feeling threatened, something else settles in my chest, leaning against my heart for a moment until I hear the rap of knuckles at my door. Marcus is waiting, asking for permission to open my door.

I pull the handle and step out, immediately struck by the bright lights at the front entrance and the sparkle of gowns adorned in jewels from the crowd out front. Many turn to look to see who's arrived. It's show time. I recognize four men instantly, sharing a knowing look between them as they nod my way.

I fasten the middle button of my jacket and turn my back to them as I walk around the limo to open Arianna's door. The conversations continue behind me and another limo pulls up behind us. Waiting.

As I open her door and reach my hand out for her, I know many of them are watching us. My heart hammers against my chest as I question if I've done the right thing.

If I'd kept her a secret, they'd have thought the worst of me. They would have come to the conclusion that I was just like Brooks. I need them to think otherwise. To believe in the character I've created. Most shouldn't know, but I'm not a fool. All men talk, and these circles are small but well connected.

It's reasonable for them to think that I've had a crush on her. And I'll be playing up that part tonight, starting with the kiss I plant on the back of her hand as she stands on the pavement.

A warm blush travels to her cheeks and she naturally smiles at me, batting her lashes and waiting for me. She's stunning and seems shy. She's acting brilliantly. Playing the perfect role, although the idea that it's an act makes me tense.

I whisper in her ear, "Be good for me." And then I plant a small kiss on her cheek. As I pull away to look into her eyes, something changes in her expression. She's stiff as she nods her head, and I question my decision to be so open.

To me, this is an act. But to her... maybe it is something else.

I plant a kiss on her lips, ignoring the spark igniting from the instant touch and wrap my arm around her waist.

She only breathes once we've made it to the foyer and, even then, she still looks struck with surprise. A good surprise.

If I can keep her like this all night, her presence will only make me look as though this is a genuine attraction.

I force the smile to stay on my face as my father walks toward me, a stern expression firmly in place as his eyes flicker to Arianna and then back to me.

I part with her for a moment, leaving her at the entrance of the foyer with the whispered words, "Stay here."

She doesn't have time to acknowledge me as I take large steps away from her to meet my father. My father is a loose cannon, and I don't like the way he looks at my sweetheart. And whatever he has to say, it won't be said in front of her. I won't allow it.

My defenses rise as he stops in front of me, talking beneath his breath.

"You brought her?" he asks with an air of disbelief. My expression is like stone, fixed in place. Even the jovial glint in my eyes stays in place.

"Why wouldn't I?" I ask him, feeling the smile on my face.

"From what I've heard, she should be in your bedroom... or someone else's." A huff of a laugh rises up my chest as I look away from my father and back to the crowd, turning to look over my shoulder and back to Arianna who's waiting for me patiently.

"Let me get her comfortable," I tell my father. "I'll talk to you later tonight," I say and pat his arm as if it was a pleasant conversation and he finally releases me. I have no intention of speaking to him again tonight. Or tomorrow.

Adrenaline races in my blood as I leave him behind me and walk toward Arianna. The entire crowd is stealing glances at her as I hold out my arm to her. Watching her. Watching *us*.

I do need to find out what he knows though, how the fuck he found out about her so quickly, and who else is aware of the situation.

And more importantly, I need to figure out where the information came from.

CHAPTER 18

ARIANNA

"I s it hot in here to you?" Dahlia asks, fanning herself with the fancy dinner menu that was given to all the guests in attendance. I tear my eyes away from the throng of people filling the dining room, turning them on Dahlia. I've been busy looking for Zander, who seems to have gotten lost in the crowd. Shortly after arriving, he led me to this table and told me to sit down after quickly introducing me to Dahlia and Lucian Stone.

It's been ten minutes so far, and he's still not back yet.

I pick nervously at my fingernails as I flash her a friendly smile, shaking my head, trying to hide my anxiety. This is yet another place that I feel out of place, a place where wealth and gaudy opulence is on proud display. It was easier with him here with me. All the guests are dressed in finery, and while I'm dressed similarly, I know it's all paid for by Zander. "No, it feels fine to me," I answer her.

Though we haven't spoken much since Zander ran off, I like Dahlia. She's gorgeous with a charismatic charm that makes me feel like I already know her. I've seen her in passing a few times at Club X, but never really talked to her before today. And I'm sure as shit not going to bring that up. I hope she doesn't recognize me. I keep stealing glances and she doesn't seem to make the connection. If she does, she's not judging me.

If she knew the circumstances, I'm sure she would be.

I think it's amazing that she's actually married to someone that is her Dom, although I guess it's more of a kink for them than a lifestyle. That's just an assumption though. I know he used to be her Dom. I nervously glance down to my fingers, tangling them as I remember seeing them in the club. I didn't know it was *him*, but I recognize her.

Lucian's been nothing but gracious to his wife. I glance over at him, noting how smooth he looks in his dapper tuxedo. He's a handsome man, and part of his personality reminds me of Zander's. Looking out into the crowd, he has an aura of power about him.

"Oh," Dahlia mutters, fanning herself fervently and wiping at her brow. I love the dress she's wearing, a white lace number that's provocative yet chaste. She practically glows in it. "I'm burning up."

As if summoned by her complaint, a male waiter in uniform shows up at her side with a tray of ice-cold drinks. They're made with a soda base, but that's all I can tell from the small bubbles on the glass and the ones still clinging to the crushed lemons and limes at the bottom of each.

"Would you care for a refreshment?" he asks us, offering the tray.

I expect Dahlia to down the cold beverage immediately, but she looks at the drink warily. "Is there alcohol in this?" she asks the waiter with her head tilted slightly.

The waiter, a young blond man with charming dimples, smiles and replies cheerfully, "It's the signature cocktail for this evening. Citrus vodka and Sprite."

Dahlia immediately shakes her head vigorously. "Oh no, thank you though. May I have a glass of water please?"

"Of course." The waiter nods his head before scurrying off.

Lucian places a hand on Dahlia's, rubbing it gently. "Relax, Treasure."

Despite my anxiety, a slight smile plays across my lips. I love the way Lucian calls Dahlia his Treasure. It makes me feel fuzzy inside, but also like I'm intruding on a moment when he looks at her like that.

"I'm trying," Dahlia replies, instantly at ease by her husband's touch.

Their breezy interaction stirs a longing in me.

"I'm sorry," Dahlia says, looking over at me and I realize I've been staring. Shit, I hope she doesn't think I'm being rude.

"No, no, you're fine," I speak quickly.

"I'm just not used to these things yet, and..." she pauses in her thought, glancing at Lucian as if looking for his consent.

He gives her a reassuring nod, lightly squeezing her hand. "You know I don't mind, Treasure."

A relieved smile spreads across Dahlia's face and she squeals to me, "We're four weeks!"

It takes me a moment to understand what she means. Four weeks... pregnant!

"Oh wow," I breathe. "Congratulations!" I can feel her excitement radiating off of her.

"Thank you," Dahlia murmurs, shaking her head. "I still can't believe it. I think I checked with the doctor at least five times before finally accepting it as reality."

"It must be an amazing feeling," I say.

"It is," Dahlia agrees. "And I have this guy over here," she stabs her thumb at Lucian, who chuckles, "to thank for it."

The two exchange a few looks and I smile, trying to let them have their moment by looking away and sipping the water in my hand while I turn back to the crowd and look for Zander.

I'm about to give up when I spot him near a huge column, talking to his father. A sinking feeling tugs at my stomach as I watch the two men speak to each other. Judging by his father's stiff body language and sharp gestures, I think they're arguing. Although with Zander's expression, maybe not. I feel caught in their exchange.

I wonder what they're fighting over. *Me*, a voice in the back of my head says as I take another nervous sip of my drink. I recognized Dahlia, so I wonder how many men recognize me. And I wouldn't have a clue. They all wear masks in the club. My suspicions are only increased when the man glances my way, a scowl on his face.

For a moment, I feel the urge to jump up and leave, but before I can move, Zander turns from the man, and strides toward us. I'm quiet as Lucian says something in Dahlia's ear. I peek up and he has a look of sympathy on his face. *He knows.* I feel sick. I feel Zander next to me before I see him.

"Is everything alright?" I ask Zander as he glides down into the seat next to mine.

Zander gives me a charming smile. "Of course."

He's so smooth with his response that I almost believe him. But I know what I saw.

"So how are things going?" Lucian asks Zander, still holding Dahlia's hand. I watch as his thumb rubs soothing circles on the back of Dahlia's hand.

Their conversation fades into the background as I sit there quietly, my eyes on Dahlia. I can't stop thinking about how happy she looks as she listens to the conversation, a hand on her belly. I bet she'll make a wonderful mother. My throat feels dry as I try to swallow, and I have to bring the glass to my lips and sip the cool water slowly.

"Arianna is an artist," Zander boasts, drawing me out of my thoughts. Lucian looks at me with respect. "Really? That's wonderful."

I blush furiously. "It's nothing really," I downplay. Zander's acting as if I'm an actual painter. I'm not. "It's just a hobby."

"Nonsense," Zander says. "I saw your work. It speaks for itself."

"It's not in any galleries or anything like that," I argue.

"Good enough for me," Zander says firmly.

My cheeks redden even more as Lucian and Dahlia observe our exchange.

"Well that's wonderful," Lucian says, grinning. "I've been thinking about getting a portrait of Dahlia done when she's further along." He glances at his wife, pride in his eyes before looking back at me to say, "Maybe you could do the honor?"

I don't have a moment to respond before Dahlia's eyes widen and she reaches across the small table to grab my hand. "I would love that," she says and her voice is so full of hope. She looks back at Lucian as though he's just given her a wonderful surprise. "Could you do something like that?" she asks me.

"I haven't done portraits before, but I could." I nod my head slightly although I feel anxious.

Zander reaches behind me and gently massages my back, causing sparks of electricity along wherever he touches. "I'm sure you can," he assures me, his tone encouraging.

I turn to look at him, to thank him, feeling a warmth and relaxation flowing through me, but the moment I do, I freeze.

I didn't know Danny was going to be here.

CHAPTER 19

ZANDER

I can practically feel him the moment he enters. That fucker, Danny Brooks. It's not because of his voice laughing behind me. Or the way Lucian narrows his eyes slightly and pulls Dahlia closer to his side. It's my sweetheart's reaction. Arianna tenses immediately, sucking in a breath between her teeth and straightening her back.

Her eyes lose the brightness that I've only just brought back.

I lean in close to her, ignoring the look from Lucian and rub the tip of my nose behind her ear. "Relax," I whisper into her ear and gently kiss the tender skin on her upper neck. Her soft hair tickles my nose as I do. I'm a hypocrite for telling her to relax. Nearly a dozen of the men in this room here know I've bought her. They know who she is, and they also know she used to be his.

She hasn't noticed the way they've been looking at her. But I have.

Not a single fucker in this room has a clue that this was designed by Brooks. That he gave her to me to pay his debt, and that this is all a facade. *Unless he's told them.*

I keep the smile plastered on my face as the thought hits me. Bringing the flute to my lips, I take a swig of the sweet champagne, the bubbles tickling the roof of my mouth.

If the men here know that he's given her to me, they're also well aware that I'm letting him pay his debts with her.

And that can't fucking happen.

I hear Brooks laugh again, although it's fainter this time and from across the room through a crowd of people. He should know better than to tell anyone about the arrangement. But he's not a smart man. I put the empty flute to my lips, the glass resting against my bottom lip.

A shiver travels down my arms as Dahlia gently touches Lucian's arm to grab his attention, completely oblivious to the entire situation. Arianna looks away, her head in the opposite direction as Brooks.

I'm struck by the sweet cadence of her voice as a waitress walking by asks for her drink. She politely tells her she's fine as I pass the empty glass to the young woman and she sets it on her silver tray.

"Would you like some fresh air?" Dahlia asks Arianna, and she obediently looks to me before answering.

Lucian speaks up before Arianna can answer, saying, "I could use a moment away from the crowds." His voice is low and only intended for his wife.

"Go ahead," I tell Arianna, nodding my head toward the French doors. She seems a bit more at ease and I think it'd be best if she got the hell out of this room.

"I need to go to the restroom; I'll meet you out there," I answer Arianna and expect her to simply obey. Her hand reaches out to grab my arm as I turn. She's quick to correct herself, shifting slightly with her expression falling and an apology on her lips.

"It's alright," I tell her softly before she can utter a single word, taking her hand in mind and rubbing soothing circles on the back of her knuckles. I stare deep into her dark green eyes and that's when her reality hits me.

I haven't even considered what she's been through. My stomach churns with a sickness. *What has he done to her?* In a room full of people, all the noises and lights dim to nothing, merely blurs in my periphery as I take in the sadness and fear behind her eyes.

"I've got her," Lucian says, snapping my gaze to his and breaking the small moment of clarity. As he reaches out to her in a casual manner, I nearly rip her away from him, from everyone. In the split second of a moment, I just want to take her away.

I clear my throat, remembering where we are. I straighten my suit and give her a small peck on the cheek. My hand splays across her lower back as I guide her toward Lucian. "I'll be right back, sweetheart."

With a tight smile, she nods her head obediently. Always obeying.

"Don't let her leave your sight," I tell Lucian low enough so only he can hear me. He nods and instinctively glances back toward the crowd, to Brooks.

The smile on my face is nowhere to be seen as I watch him take her away from me, his wife on his right and Arianna on his left.

THE SOUND OF RUNNING WATER FLOODS MY EARS AS I WASH MY hands, staring aimlessly at the lathered suds. The door to the bathroom opens at the same time as a stall door behind me, and it's a reminder that I'm not alone. That I should be performing, but I need to get the fuck out of here.

My eyes finally lift to the mirror, my demeanor not at all what it should be. I can't shake the feeling in the pit of my stomach when I realized she's not okay.

"Payne." The corners of my lips twitch as I hear that bastard's voice. They beg to force my expression into a scowl, but I fight it, concentrating on the fact that a third man is in the room. Stephen Ikabal. He's a clean-cut man with a penchant for younger women. He's been married for three decades, and I highly doubt he's been faithful for any of those years. But then again, she hasn't been either. They both prefer younger company, or so I've heard.

"Brooks," I say and finally tear my eyes away from Stephen in the mirror as he washes his hands in the basin two down from mine.

"How are you?" Brooks cocks an eyebrow, leaning against the granite counter and facing me. Stephen doesn't react, but he's a coy old man. I'm sure he's listening. Everyone's always listening. Always watching for a weakness. When you're on top, it's so easy to fall.

I force a charming smile onto my face as I dry my hands, my eyes on Brooks. He fooled me. I had no idea gambling was his vice. I thought it was sadism. The thought chills my blood and for a moment the charm, dimples and all, slips as I think about my sweetheart. It doesn't make sense how they fit. It just doesn't add up.

"Well, and you?" I answer him. Although I'm relaxed and engaging Brooks, I'm highly aware of Stephen's presence as he turns off the faucet and dries his own hands. I need him to get the fuck out of here. I want nothing more than to grab this asshole by the collar and shove him against the wall. I need to know what he's done to her to put that fear in her eyes.

Brooks nods his head, a smile on his face that looks cocky as his eyes flicker to Stephen as he passes us to get to the door. "Just missing my Arianna a bit." His voice is chipper as he shrugs his shoulders. Every hair stands on end as Stephen pauses by the trashcan before tossing in the balled-up paper towel.

A chill sweeps across every inch of my skin. I can only imagine what they think of her if he's been running his mouth. And I fucking hate it.

"I hope you're getting your money's worth," Brooks says beneath his breath, but loud enough for Stephen to hear on his way out. The creak of the door opening and then falling closed easily is the only noise in the room as my hand balls into a fist, the skin tightening around my knuckles to the point where I'm convinced it will split.

I don't wait for the door to close all the way; I don't even lock it like I know I should. I can't hold back the rage any longer.

I hit his jaw first, taking him by surprise. Maybe he expected me to act the part in this environment. After all, we're not all alone in his office. The soft classical music spills through the bottom of the door as I grip his collar and hit him again with my right fist, knocking his head backward.

This time he expects it at least and he hits me back square on the nose, the pain radiating outward up my cheeks and to the back of my head. It nearly makes me lose my grip on him, but I hold on. White noise rings in my ears as I quickly push him backward.

"She's not yours anymore," I sneer into his face as my hands clench, and I slam his back against the tiled wall. I hear a crack, but it does nothing to stop me. "You gave her to me, remember?"

My teeth slam against one another so hard that I swear they'll crack. He merely grins back at me, blood coating his teeth on the right side of his crooked smile.

As I talk, I can feel warm blood trickle from under my nose. My instant reaction is to slam him back against the wall, and I do it just to get the aggression out. "You owe me, and you'll pay me by the twenty-fifth." I decide then that even if I can't convince her not to give him the money, I won't accept it. I'll wait to pay her, I'll refuse to do it until after Brooks has paid me.

"Sure," he says with a glint in his eyes.

"I won't be paying Arianna, so you'll need to come up with that money some other way," I speak without thinking, holding his gaze and watching the arrogant expression morph into fear. It doesn't matter if or when I transfer the money to Arianna, I won't let him steal from her. I won't let him use her. Not anymore.

I let go of him when the fear is so strong that his body is stiff. I glance at myself in the mirror and see a black eye already forming, blood on my face and also my dress shirt. *Fuck!*

"And then what? What are you really going to do about it?" he asks as I grab a few paper towels and wipe the blood from under my nose. He doesn't move off the wall as he hisses, "I don't have the fucking money."

I don't answer him. I won't ever say it out loud. *I'll kill him.* Not for the debt, but for what he's done to her.

"We had a deal," he pushes the words through clenched teeth. "You have her and you can't go back on that!"

It hits me then what I've done. How I've lost control. I've provided evidence. Security cameras are littered in this building. Fuck!

"Payne?" Brooks calls out to me, but I ignore him. He means for it to come out strong as he stays behind me, standing tall and putting on a front, but his voice cracks with fear.

Tossing the paper towel into the trash, I open the door and almost make a quick right turn. I hesitate in the doorway. I need to get the fuck out of here; I can't be seen like this. But I need to get Arianna. The sound of another man coming down the small hallway makes me move. I have five minutes. If I don't have her in my grasp in five minutes, I'm coming back.

I keep my hand up, my fingers pinching the bridge of my nose and covering my face. To any onlookers, I hope it looks as if I have a headache. The cool air from the outside breezes by me as I get closer to the exit and a couple walks in.

I ignore them, I can't even see who they are and I don't give a fuck.

As soon as I get outside, I spot my limo and walk straight to it. I keep my strides wide and my pace fast. It's on the far left of the parking lot and the valet and a few guests are on my right, the sounds of them chatting and the brighter lights of the entrance dimming as I walk farther into the darkened lot.

I notice Marcus look up and see me, a surprised look on his face as I finally lower my hand and wipe under my nose. Dark red blood smears across the arm of my jacket.

That fucker. My steps are hard as I stalk toward the limo, my blood fueled with the desire to go back. I clench and unclench my hands before reaching for my phone. *My sweetheart.*

Thank fuck for Lucian.

As Marcus opens the door, not daring to look me in the eyes, I slip the phone from my pocket, only then realizing my knuckles are cracked and there's blood on them, too.

My blood runs cold as I settle into the seat. The door closes shut with a loud click and silences the cabin of the limo as I dial his number.

"Lucian," I say and press the phone close to my ear as I stare at the entrance, the light from the large glass doors and windows spilling out into the night.

"Zander?" he says and his voice is filled with surprise. Which is a good thing. It calms my racing heart.

"Arianna's still with you?" I ask as the driver's door opens and Marcus slips in. His eyes flash to mine for a moment in the rearview mirror.

"She is. Is everything-"

"Bring her to the front... please," I ask him quickly, grabbing a few tissues from the side compartment as I feel a bit of blood trickle from my nose. I resist the urge to slam my fist against the door.

Against anything. The anger is coming back. I shouldn't have left him like that. *He deserves so much worse.*

"Of course," Lucian is quick to agree, a serious note in his tone.

"Thank you," I barely get the words out, feeling in that moment that I've failed her.

Every muscle in me is wound tight, my heart beating chaotically. I've never done something so fucking stupid before in my life.

"To the entrance, Sir?" Marcus asks and I clench my jaw, nodding my head as his eyes meet mine again in the rearview mirror. My heart slows, and I reach for the whiskey as the limo pulls out slowly. I grab the glass and ice out of habit and pour two fingers into the glass. I sway slightly as we drive around to the front.

I'm able to down the glass before he stops the car and gets out, the cold ice clashing against my teeth. I don't even realize she's waiting for us until Marcus gets out and opens her door.

I run a hand down my face and put the cup back as she climbs in, her dress bunched in her hands.

My chest feels tight and my heart clenches as I watch her step carefully in and settle next to me. I've made a fool of myself. And her. All because of Brooks.

Next time, she doesn't leave my side. Not for a moment.

"I'm sorry," I choke the words out, reaching for her with my left hand, the one without the torn knuckles as Marcus closes the door. I'm so fucking ashamed. She deserves better than this.

She shakes her head easily, her brows pinched and her mouth parting as she takes in the sight of me. "Zander," she says and my name is barely a whisper on her lips.

She reaches up in an attempt to touch my face. From the look in her eyes, it must be bad. They're full of questions. But she doesn't ask them. She already knows the answers. I snatch her hand in mine before she can touch me.

"Don't," I tell her. At first, hurt flashes in her eyes, but I'm quick to add, "Just..." I trail off and take in a long inhale, not knowing what to say, or what to tell her. But I don't have to. She lays down, not waiting for me to finish as the limo pulls ahead. Her hair spills over my leg as she rests her head in my lap. Laying her cheek against the designer pants.

I slowly pet her hair, moving it from her face and smoothing it out. She lets out a comfortable sigh. As she nestles her head into my lap, looking aimlessly into the cabin of the limo, her small hand wraps around my knee. Her thumb rubs small circles. "Was it Danny?" she asks me.

"Yes," I answer her easily.

"Are you okay?" she asks me in a cautious breath.

"Fine," I reply and I'm short with her, my voice hard as I continue. "You'll never go back to him." Her finger halts in its rhythmic path as I say the words with authority, as if I can command her. For now, she may be in a contract, but I'm not a fool, I can't force her after the thirty days are done. She doesn't owe me a damn thing, and what's more is that I don't want to force her.

She doesn't answer me, and her body is stiff, but I continue to pet her hair and then run my fingers down her shoulder to the dip of her waist and back up.

"I don't want you to."

Her cheek rubs against my leg as she nods her head, but she still doesn't answer me.

She has no idea what I feel for her. She may think she's still just a pawn and a bargaining chip.

But I'll be damned if she ever sees that asshole again.

I'm never letting her go.

CHAPTER 20

ARIANNA

"Y ou should really let me take a look at your eye," I say to Zander once we step inside his estate and make our way to his bedroom. I'm following behind him, not even taking in his house as he leads me up the stairs.

My heart is still reeling, twisting in my chest with a mix of emotions, my mind running with a million questions.

I don't know what Danny did to him, but I feel caught in the middle. I feel like I'm the one to blame. He was there because of me. Had to be. Now Zander is paying for it.

Zander doesn't answer me as he pushes open his bedroom door and walks over to the mirror to peer at his face. Even roughed up, he looks sexy as fuck, his bloodstained dress shirt torn open at the front, his hard, tanned flesh on display.

"I'm fine," he mutters. But it's not reflected in his voice.

"Well let me-," I start to say, coming up behind him.

"I'm good," Zander cuts in. My forehead's pinched and I'm silent for a moment as he takes off his suit jacket, tossing it to the side, and then removes his ruined dress shirt, tugging it over his head. He takes it off and lets it drop to the floor, seemingly ignoring my presence.

I can't help my frown and need to back away from him, feeling slightly dejected. He's blowing me off when I want to know what happened. I let out a heavy but silent breath of frustration as my gaze drops to the floor and I chew on my bottom lip. I wish he'd just talk to me. I need to know what's going on. I feel guilty, like Zander's bruised face is all my fault. And this is only making me feel worse.

"Hey," Zander says, getting my attention before he lifts my chin up so my eyes meet his. "It's okay." He says the words with conviction, and I almost believe it. "I promise you."

I nod my head slightly and my voice cracks as I answer him, "Okay."

"I'm still pissed. At Danny, and at myself." He drops his hand as he adds, "But I promise you that everything is alright." His eyes search mine and I finally let his words sink in. I believe him. I trust him.

"I'm just glad you're okay," I say quietly.

"I'll always be okay," Zander replies with confidence, his hand cupping my cheek again. "It's you I'm worried about."

"Me?" I ask.

Zander nods, gently stroking the side of my face. My skin warms with his gentle strokes, my pulse quickening.

"I'm fine," I answer him. "Really, I'm fine." His eyes search mine for a long moment.

"You've been denied so much. I want to give you... more."

His words leave me with a pain in my heart that I don't quite understand and I feel as if I'm in a trance staring into his eyes. I wish I had words, but I don't. I step closer to him, just wanting to feel him. All I know is that I need his touch.

"You looked so beautiful tonight," he says softly.

A flush comes to my cheeks as I breathe, "Thank you."

"And I've been waiting all night for this." He kisses me, pressing his lips softly against mine. It's sweet and short, but it leaves me wanting more when he pulls away.

"I need you," he says, his voice low and heavy.

I don't even think about the words as they leave me. "Take me," I moan, my heart pounding in my chest, hungry for more.

Zander spears his fingers through my hair, cradling the back of my head, and gives me a deeper kiss, this one filled with swirling tongue and unbridled passion. I melt into his hard body, feeling weak in the knees, but he holds me up with his powerful arms.

I moan into his mouth, fire heating my core, my skin blazing from the heat of his hard body. He sucks on my tongue in response, pulling me closer to him. Down below, I can feel his hardening cock against my stomach.

He breaks away from our kiss, his lips finding my neck, his hands sliding down my back to cup my ass. I moan, throwing my head back, his lips burning into my flesh.

"Fuck," he groans, his lips near my ears as he smothers my neck with passionate kisses. "I want that sweet tight pussy on my cock." I go limp in his arms, weak from his passion, and he picks me up, carrying me to the bed.

He lays me down gently, his breathing ragged, his eyes on my face and shining with lust as he climbs into the bed, making it creak as he places his hands to either side of my head.

"You're so fucking beautiful," he tells me, his voice low and hoarse, his breath hot on my face.

"I want you, too," I answer him quickly. I do. I've never wanted something so much.

Zander's lips find my neck again, pecking, kissing, licking, causing me to throw my head back, my nipples pebbling and my body burning up in flames.

He makes way down my neck, pausing briefly to pull my gown above my shoulders, and then tossing it carelessly onto the bedroom floor. Next off comes my bra, Zander practically tearing it off and slinging it across the room. His eyes immediately feast on my hard nipples, his chest heaving as he moves in and takes a nipple into his mouth. He swirls his tongue around it at first, teasing, tweaking it, before sucking on it with great force as my back arches in response.

I buck slightly at the sensation, biting down on my lip as I grab onto the bedding. He gives both nipples equal attention, alternating from one to another before moving down my stomach, his lips kissing every inch of my sensitive skin along the way.

When he reaches my hips, he grabs my panties and pulls them off, baring my glistening sex to him. Below, I hear him inhale deeply and bury his face between my legs before taking a languid lick of my pussy.

"Oh," I moan as his tongue flicks against my clit back and forth.

I try to keep still as he tastes me and sucks my clit, pleasure stirring in my belly. But before I reach my peak, he moves in closer, causing the bed to creak as he hoists both of my legs around his shoulders, burying his face into my pussy, clamping his mouth down on my clit as hard as he can.

"Oh God!" I yell as he has his way with me, savagely tasting me and sucking on my clit until the pleasure is too much.

A fire builds in my core as he goes to town on me, and I grip the bedding with both hands, digging my nails into the plush comforter. His keen blue eyes look up at me but it's so hard to look back, my neck wanting to arch away, my body begging me for both an escape but also for more.

Keeping his eyes locked with mine, Zander plunges two thick fingers into my pussy while keeping his mouth clamped down on my clit with great force.

His forceful touch, his relentless sucking, and intense gaze are all I can handle, the fiery storm exploding with fury from my core, ripping through my body like a level six tornado.

"Fuck!" I scream as my body is rocked by explosions of insane pleasure. All the while, Zander keeps me in place, his eyes locked on my face, his mouth clamped on my pussy as my limbs convulse violently from orgasm after orgasm. "Zander!"

I don't know when he lets me go, I'm so overwhelmed with ecstasy, but suddenly he's stripping in front of me, pulling off his pants and underwear, letting his cock spring free as he tosses his clothes onto the floor.

"Now it's my turn," he growls hungrily, lining his thick cock up between my legs and thrusting inside of me without hesitation.

I gasp as he enters me, feeling him fill me, stretching my walls, while he groans with utter rapture.

"Fuck," he says, his deep voice low and heavy, "You're so fucking tight."

He places his hands to either side of me to balance himself, getting into position to pound harder into me, while my hands drift instinctively down to his chiseled ass, my fingernails digging into his flesh.

His breathing is ragged as he steadies himself, all the while keeping up his ruthless pace. When he gets his balance, he fucks me harder and deeper, rocking the bed back and forth, the headboard starting to bang against the wall.

The smack of flesh hitting flesh fills the room, mixing in along with the sounds of the banging headboard. *Smack. Smack. Smack. Bang. Bang. Bang.* I can't scream. I want to scream out my pleasure, but my body feels paralyzed from the intensity of it all. I feel another storm brewing as I moan out his name in what feels like a whispered plea, barely able to take his entire length, his cock going so deep I almost think it's almost too much.

Zander picks up his pace, his chiseled hips thrusting violently inward, faster, harder, his moaning becoming louder as I feel his cock grow impossibly hard inside of me. It's coming. I know it. And I want it. *All of it.*

His powerful thrusts slow down to deep, rhythmic ones, the bed indenting each time his body smashes into me with such force that I fear the box spring might break.

"Fuck, I'm gonna cum," I hear Zander moan while the fire inside of my core ignites again.

One. Two. Three. Four. Each thrust is deeper and harder than before, and on the fourth, Zander throws back his head as he goes balls deep inside of me, and cums violently.

My thighs are quivering and shaking like an earthquake as a tidal wave of pleasure hits me and I moan his name over and over.

"Zander!" I cry, feeling his dick still contracting inside of me while my walls squeeze every last drop out of him.

Finally, he pulls out of me and falls onto the bed on my right side, his chest heaving from exertion, his body covered in sweat. Both of us need to catch our breath.

As he walks away from me, I'm struck by the realization that my body is shaking with an intensity I've never felt before. Every emotion feels as if it's overwhelming me.

I've had sex before. I've had other partners and came before.

But this is different.

It's so strong, so powerful, it's... too intense. I place a hand over my racing heart as he flicks on the light to the bathroom.

The shockwaves pulse through me as I try to calm down and try to ignore what my heart is telling me.

CHAPTER 21

ZANDER

*M*y light blue gaze stares back at me in the mirror of the dresser. A dark ring is around my left eye. This isn't a good look. My eyes travel to Arianna's form on the bed behind me as I slip the Rolex around my wrist and tighten the band. I don't even need to look as I do it, it's been the same every morning. But there's never been a woman behind me.

In my room, on my bed.

Her gorgeous body is nothing but a small lump on the bed, hidden beneath the thick grey comforter. She's getting to me. I'm breaking rules for her. A deep inhale makes my back crack slightly as I close my eyes, wincing slightly from the bruise on my face. Last night... things are changing. Fast. And it's hard to admit it.

I got into a fucking bathroom brawl over her. *It was worth it.*

Work is calling me. I'm already late. I button the top of my dress shirt, not knowing what to do about my sweetheart.

Right now... and later. Once all of this is done. I'm sure as fuck not kicking her out, but I don't like that she'll be in here. Alone.

With cold blood running through my veins I quietly walk to the end of the bed, my jacket and shoes waiting for me.

The clock on the nightstand reads 6:40. Late for me, but Arianna's still asleep. A genuine smile curves my lips up when I hear her soft snoring. It's adorable. *She's* adorable.

With her mouth parted slightly, the soft sound is accompanied by her shoulders rising slightly, her dark hair a messy halo around her angelic face.

She's so beautiful. So innocent.

I rip my gaze away, slipping the first shoe on and tying the laces tight.

My daily routine. Nothing has changed. I almost roll my eyes at the thought, pulling the lace even tighter.

Everything's changed.

It's not because of Arianna. I refuse to think that she's the reason I'm slipping, making one mistake after the other. It's Danny Brooks. I keep making errors in my judgment when it comes to him.

The thin laces dig into my fingers as I tie the second shoe and rise from the bench at the end of the bed, picking up my coat and walking quietly to the nightstand where I tossed my keys last night.

I have to close my eyes when I catch her sweet scent. It's like citrus with a hint of honeysuckle. I wonder if she knows how alluring she is. Lying there so beautifully, her body so soft and warm with curves that only tempt me that much more.

A dark voice in the back of my head whispers, in nearly a hiss, *you can take her. She's yours. You own her.*

But the stolen moments we've had are because she wanted me. Because she needed me.

I don't want her to think I'm the kind of partner Brooks was. The thought disgusts me. My nose wrinkles and I turn sharply away from her, hating the vile image of that prick. If that's what last night was for her, I'll never forgive myself. She's not a whore for me to use. Not to me. My heart beats faster, slamming against my chest.

The keys jingle against one another as I snatch them quickly off the dresser. I can be a Master worthy of her. Not a sick fuck who uses pain as a threat. I don't ever want to cause her pain, and I know she doesn't need it. Even if she thinks she does. Holding the car keys in my hand I walk away from her, intent on leaving both her and my thoughts behind me.

I'm halfway across the room when her soft voice calls out. "Zander?" My name is soft, but also scratchy, the morning evident in her tone.

I stop in my tracks, the floorboards beneath the thick carpet creaking slightly. My body tenses, realizing I have to address her now. She knows I heard her.

I turn slightly, relaxing my body and treating her the same way I treat everyone else. With a facade of ease. It comes naturally.

"Good morning," I greet her and feel the fake smile on my face without consenting to it.

She props her small body up on her elbow and shoves the hair away from her face. Blinking several times, each time seeming more and more awake, she stifles a yawn and rises slowly into a sitting position gripping the comforter in her hands and bringing it up over her naked body. I'm not sure if it's because she's self-conscious or if she doesn't want me seeing her.

In the soft yellow morning light spilling in between the thick curtains, she looks radiant. I *want* to see her, every last inch of her, just like I did last night. *But it's only fair that she hides herself behind a blanket, while I hide behind this smile.*

Her dark green eyes dart to the bedroom door and then back to me as she asks, "Do you want me to get ready?" Another yawn creeps up on her, and from the look in her eyes she's obviously embarrassed by her exhaustion.

"You don't have to," I say and my voice is strong, slightly harsh perhaps.

"Are you sure?" she asks me sweetly. "I don't mind... I know you probably don't want me in here..." Her voice trails off as she picks at the comforter and then laughs a little, this sweet little sound that's so pure.

My smile softens and I'm moving toward her before I even realize it, my strides easy and comfortable. I have the urge to sit on the bed, she even scoots slightly, making room and straightening a little, although the comforter sags slightly in front of her. Just a glimpse of her cleavage is showing, modest, but tempting. Just like my sweetheart.

I almost sit with her, but then I remember. *Her gift.*

It was meant to be a thank you for attending last night.

"I got you something," I tell her without thinking. Instantly, her expression softens. Those sweet lips slowly turn up and her eyes sparkle. I run my hand through my hair, wondering if it's stupid. All the while I'm going to the closet and gathering the small bag to give to my sweetheart. Her eyes flicker to the empty side of the bed, a warm red hue filling her cheeks. My spot that she made for me.

Utterly gorgeous. A huff of air leaves me as I look at her. She really doesn't get how tempting she is. How a woman like her could ruin a man like me. Losing control, coming undone all because of her. It's already happening. And she doesn't even know it. My feet remain planted where they are, even though my body wills me to sit next to her. I have to hold back.

I clear my throat as I hold the bag out to her. At the faint sound, Arianna finally looks at me. I watch her face as her slender fingers pull the paper away.

The thick wrapping paper crinkles as she pulls the package out of the bag and tears it open from the seams.

The moment she realizes what they are, her eyes brighten and a wide smile makes my chest fill with confidence. She's so true to her feelings, her reactions so natural.

And she loves the gift.

"Brushes?" she asks me with that smile still on her face. Her eyes aren't on me though; she's peeling the last bit of tape from the package of paintbrushes. I had no idea such a thing could cost so much.

"I thought you'd like them," I answer her simply.

She tilts her head, focusing all of her attention on me as she puts it all to the side and rises to her knees, pulling the comforter with her and planting a small, chaste kiss on my lips.

My eyes stay open the entire time and although her lips are pursed, I swear she doesn't stop smiling. She pulls back quickly, that beautiful red flush all over her skin and says softly, "Thank you. I love them."

I stare at her a long moment, realizing how genuinely happy she is with such a small gift. But the clock from the nightstand calls my attention with the faint click of the hand.

Late. I'm late.

Reality sets in, and I give her a nod. "I'm happy you like them. I've got to be going now."

An awkward tension settles between us.

"Do you want me to go?" she asks, the warm color fading and a wall of armor slowly rising around her. The small moment is over, enjoyable though it was.

"No," I say, but even I can hear the hesitation in my voice. I strengthen it as I add, "You can stay for as long as you like."

I lean forward, my legs pushing against the bed making it groan and a hand bracing myself on the bed. I cup her jaw with my other hand to kiss her quickly, pulling back slightly and staring at her lips for just a moment. She doesn't open her eyes until I let her go.

CHAPTER 22

ARIANNA

J run my fingers over the paintbrushes, my gift from Zander. They're the most beautiful brushes I've ever seen, with high quality mahogany handles, exquisite markings and fine, durable bristles. I press them to my chest, a fuzzy feeling swirling in the pit of my stomach. I feel like a stupid little girl, but I don't care. It's nice to be given something that means so much. Even if it didn't mean much to him.

These are even better than the gown Zander gifted me. And I can see myself putting them to good use, already thinking about the masterpieces I'll paint. I'll cherish them long after this contract is over.

When this is *over*.

The thought makes me sick to my stomach. I'm getting used to Zander and his charming personality, and I feel like I'm just starting to get to know him.

But do you really know him? says that annoying voice in the back of my head. *This is all supposed to be fake, a make-believe courtship. You can't really know a man who is hiding behind a facade.*

I chew my lower lip, dropping the brushes into my lap.

I don't want to believe that everything Zander says or does is inauthentic. When he looks at me, fire burning in his eyes, it looks real.

Each time I'm with him, I can *feel* the emotion emanating from him. I *feel* the connection we have between each other. It can't be fake, can it? Why would he ask me to stay as long as I like, if it was make-believe?

Because he wants you to believe it's real.

I don't know what to believe at this point. I feel so many conflicting emotions. I want Zander. And I want him to truly want me, too. But I know less about him than I do about Danny. And that doesn't sit well with me.

The voice resurfaces with, *Well, you have the whole house to yourself, why don't you find out?*

For once, I agree with the voice. I set the brushes aside and roll out of bed, my feet causing the floor to creak as I slip on one of his shirts and walk out of the bedroom and into the hall.

I take a tour of the house, going room from room looking around for anything untoward, taken in by the opulence. I'm really impressed with the house, every room filled with expensive furniture and superbly decorated. It's large, luxurious and beautiful. But after a while, it starts to feel empty. There are too many rooms for just one man. Zander has to be lonely living here.

But he has me now.

I huff out a chuckle at my wishful thinking as I run my hand over a painted glass vase in one of the extra bedrooms. I bet it costs more than what I make in a month. For how long will he have me? A month? Two? I shake my head. It might be not much longer than that.

I make my way back into the hallway, my bare feet padding along the gleaming hardwood floors. I try to get rid of the overwhelming feeling that I don't belong here, but with each step the gnawing feeling in the pit of my stomach grows and grows. I'm about to turn around and go back to the room to grab the gown and my purse to get out of here, when I see a picture frame on a small dark stand near the entryway to one of the common areas of the house.

I pick it up out of instinct. It doesn't belong here either. I already know it. While everything else in Zander's house is expensive and each item holds an air of luxury, this picture frame is common. And the photo inside it, just a snapshot.

It's an old family picture with Zander, maybe ten years old, with his father and a lady who I presume to be his mother. She's a beautiful woman, with long, flowing blonde hair and a shapely figure. I can definitely see where Zander got some of his looks from.

But what attracts me most to her is the way she looks at Zander. It's the way all mothers look at their children. A heavy feeling settles on my chest as I stare at his mother's face.

It takes me a moment to realize that I've met Zander's father, but not his mother. I find it odd that he's never mentioned her before at all. The idea hits me that I should Google Zander's family. I bet there's at least some dirt on his father... maybe some on Zander, too.

I'm so dumb. I should've done this the moment I found out about Zander.

I'm quick to go back to the bedroom and take out my cell. I bring up the web browser, tapping in Zander Payne. The first few results yield nothing. I go several pages without seeing anything actually related to Zander or his family. It's all business news. I let out a sigh of relief when I don't really find anything. At least Zander doesn't have a sinister past.

I'm about to search for something more specific when one headline grabs my attention

Rich Socialite takes her own life after husband's affair.

Marie Payne, forty-eight-year-old wife of wealthy hedge fund investor Thomas Payne jumped to her death after learning of her husband's years-long affair with his mistress. Sources say in the week leading up to her death, Marie was so distraught she locked herself away in her room for days at a time, refusing to come out for food or drink.

Marie leaves behind a young son, Zander Payne...

"Oh," I breathe, tearing my eyes away from the article, tears filling my eyes. My body seems to go cold all at once, the large bed feeling like an abyss as I bring the comforter up and around me. I check the date on the article and think back to how old Zander was.

He was just a boy. I wipe under my eyes as the sting of the tears hits me out of nowhere.

· · ·

735

No wonder why he keeps secrets, I say to myself, shaking my head and holding my tears at bay. *No wonder why Zander doesn't trust people.*

I thought I had a painful life, but at least I'm still alive. A lot of my issues, I caused myself. Being a problem child, being wild and partying. But his mother's death? Zander had no control over that. No control over the betrayal that led to such an earth-shattering loss.

Letting out a deep, trembling sigh, I turn my phone off and settle into the comforter, imagining how hard that had to be on him. I'm no longer in the mood to go snooping around. After finding that out, a part of me is content in letting Zander keep whatever secrets he has close to his chest. It probably gives him comfort, more control over his life. And who am I to say that he owes me complete access?

I look toward the door to his bedroom, feeling a swell of emotion. I need a release. I need to do something that'll make me feel better.

There's only one thing that I know will do that.

I throw the covers off of me and go back through his house looking for his office. After finding pen and paper, I make my way to the piano room, sprawling out on the floor.

And I begin to draw.

CHAPTER 23

ZANDER

*M*y hand tightens on the leather shifter as I park my Mercedes in the garage. I lean back in my seat after turning the keys and pulling them out. My forehead is pinched as I stare at the garage door to my home.

She's still inside.

I didn't expect it. There are monitors and cameras set up throughout my home. I'd be a fucking idiot not to have them with the sheer number of people who come in and out. From the housekeeping service, to caterers and business associates.

I wasn't surprised when she started looking through my things. I rest my head back against the leather, staring at the door and remembering how I watched her on the computer screen rather than actually working today. I'd already decided phone conferences would have to substitute for my normal meetings, considering the faint darkness under my left eye. I canceled three of them though so I could focus on watching her. During the fourth and fifth she stayed on my screen, lying on the floor, sprawled out and tempting me to come back to her. To pull her tempting body into mine, but also to see her drawing.

My sweetheart is a beautiful distraction.

And she's still here.

Or at least she was when I left the office nearly fifteen minutes ago. The realization that she could be done with her art makes me exit the car in haste. Shoving the keys into my pocket, I open the door and kick it shut behind me. The garage is at the side of the house, and I'm well aware that my pace is much faster than it usually is. I'm curious to see if she's still sprawled there on the floor of the piano room, waiting for me.

My dick hardens in my pants as the mental images of me lying on the ground next to her and slowly teasing her shoulder with my finger-tips until she shivers plays in my mind. But when I get to the foyer and see her spot empty, my steps slow and my heart pauses in my chest. She's been here for hours. Taunting me to come home.

I stare at the gleaming hardwood floor. How the fuck have I missed her? How cruel would it be for her to leave just as I've come home when I've been wanting her all day? The seconds split and time moves slower as anger seeps in. *She's mine.* She should be here. Waiting for me.

I know it's unreasonable. Even as my jaw clenches, I know I shouldn't think that way. This is *pretend.* It's fake and merely a result of my poor judgment, but nonetheless, *I want her.* And she was fucking here all this time.

"Oh!" the small sound of her gasp from behind me grips my atten-tion. I school my expression, turning slowly to see her standing in the kitchen. I haven't missed her. The adrenaline stops pumping in my blood. My heartbeat settles, and my body instantly relaxes at the sight of her in the middle of the kitchen. My sweetheart didn't slip through my fingers. She's right where she belongs.

Her dark green eyes are wide and she shuffles her feet as she stares back at me. She pulls her hair around her shoulder, her fingers nervously twirling the ends. "I wasn't sure-" she starts to say some-thing, but stops as I walk toward her in the open kitchen, my strides slow and deliberate.

"I'm surprised you're still here," I say and the lie comes out with an unnatural tone in my voice that I don't recognize.

Arianna doesn't notice as she clasps her hands and shakes her head. "I'm sorry. I didn't have work today, and I got caught up." Her hands fly outward as she blurts out an excuse, and the paper she's been working on waves in the air as she moves her hands.

"What's that?" I ask her, nodding to the sketch. I resist the urge to take the few remaining steps forward and snatch it from her. I want her to *want* to show me.

"Oh," she says and looks at the paper as if it's the first time she's seen it. As if it didn't encompass the last few hours of her time.

"May I see?" I ask, but the words come out as a hard command instead of a question and I wish I could stop them. I wish I could soften for her. But that's not who I am. "Please," I add and clear my throat.

She doesn't react to the harsh tone, instead she obediently hands me the paper and the thrill of her listening to me makes my blood heat with desire. Such a small thing. So insignificant really. But she makes me feel powerful in a way I haven't felt before. She makes me want to command her; it's a dangerous thing for her to play with me like this. To tempt me, but she doesn't realize she's doing it.

She bites down on her bottom lip as I take the paper from her. I'm gentle with the edges, and I make sure not to touch any of the marks. Her eyes watch where I touch the paper, and her fingertips are covered in ink of some sort. I shake the paper slightly, finally getting to see what she's been working on all this time.

And it's beautiful. I knew she wouldn't disappoint me.

It's just a sketch of the room. Of the piano, really. But the way it's done romanticizes the barren room. Something about the subtlety of the lines, the delicate details and shading. There's a softness to it that I've never felt in that room myself. But it's what she sees. What she *feels* being there. It makes me see it in a different light.

"You have such talent, sweetheart." I lift my eyes from the sketch to her eyes and love how much light shines back at me.

"Thank you," she says in a whisper, a blush coloring her chest and moving up to her cheeks.

"You should do this... for a living." Her long lashes whip up as she stares back at me. "It's a crime that you do anything other than this."

I expect a smile in return, but instead she answers kindly, but firmly, "I can't. I have work, and... I just can't."

"I'll get you a studio tomorrow," I say out loud without thinking.

It was a fleeting thought in my office, but hearing her now, I know I need to get her one.

"A studio?" she asks me with disbelief.

I nod my head, my brow furrowing as I second-guess what it's called. "For your art," I state and gesture to the paper in her hand.

There's still a look of confusion on her face. Her soft lips part, but no words come out. She clears her throat, looking away from me.

"What's wrong?" I ask her, taking another step closer but standing an arm's length away. The warmth from this morning is gone. The girl I held in my arms last night isn't the same one standing in front of me.

"It just seems... a bit much?" she responds after a moment.

I can tell she's trying to distance herself. She's already waiting for this contract to be over maybe, so she can stop playing the part. So she can just go back to being herself. *To being Brooks' possession to barter off when he sees fit.* The second the thought comes to my mind; jealousy ravages my thoughts.

And for the first time in years, I show it, my expression, my stance, everything shows what I'm feeling and thinking. I can't stop it. Arianna takes a small step back, fear clearly evident as she reacts to my anger.

I shake my head slightly, letting out a heavy exhale and pinch the bridge of my nose, hating that I've scared her. I don't want to hide anymore, but my anger isn't for her. None of it. But this is why I hide it.

"You're playing the part of my girlfriend." I start speaking without thinking. Convincing both of us that a studio is necessary for this... game. "They'll expect me to pamper you," I finally open my eyes and chance a look at her. "I would do anything for someone I want to impress." *For you,* that dark voice in my head whispers. *For someone I want to love me.*

I ignore the thought, a chill traveling down my spine as Arianna slowly nods her head. She visibly swallows, still a bit unsure of herself.

But she answers with the words I want to hear. "Okay," she says and her voice is soft, meant to appease me. "Thank you."

My eyes search hers, but she isn't looking at me. I chance a step toward her and cup her jaw like I did this morning. Her posture softens and she pushes her cheek against my palm, her small hand cupping the back of mine and her eyes shining back at me with vulnerability. "Let me spoil you, sweetheart," I speak slowly. "Just for the rest of the contract."

I've told many lies in my life. So many deceitful things have left my lips. And I know full well the words that just slipped past my lips are nothing but a deception.

I said them only to get her to cave to me. I want her to submit to me. I can feel that darkness in me rising. A possessive side is controlling me. And I don't stop it. I don't even want to suppress it.

She's making me weak. And for the first time in my life, I don't give a fuck.

CHAPTER 24

ARIANNA

et me spoil you, sweetheart.

Zander's words run through my mind, causing warmth to flow through my chest. I told him yes, only for the contract. *But that was a lie.* I want to get lost in his world and become his plaything. I want to fulfill his every desire; all while being spoiled by him. It's a fantasy and it's dangerous to get lost in it, but I am. I'm becoming consumed with the thought of being *his* and losing sight on what the reality of this situation is.

Each day that passes I feel more at ease, wanting more and more of what he has to offer.

I suck in a deep breath as I gaze out the floor-to-ceiling windows, remembering the way he looked at me the other day. There was something in his eyes. Something that told me what we have feels real. I want to believe it. But it's too good to be true. And like most things that are too good to be true, it's easy to be fooled. I don't want to be that girl, hoping and wishing for something that can never be, all while ignoring the truth. Everyone knows that in real life there are no Prince Charmings and no knights in shining armor. Still, I'm drawn to him like a moth to a flame.

"There you are," says Zander's deep voice behind me.

I turn around with my eyes closed, wanting to believe in the fantasy. And when I open them, I'm lost in the world I want. In the make-believe. He's leaning against the doorjamb in the doorway, wearing dress pants and a matching dress shirt, looking classically handsome and sexy as fuck. My breath halts in my lungs, refusing to leave the moment. This is real. If only I could hold onto it.

"Here I am," I say, flashing a light smile, ignoring my racing heart, the fear and every other thing that's going to rip us apart and leave me shredded into nothingness. I can pretend. For him.

Zander grins at me, walking over to deliver a warm kiss on my lips. I like this smile. There's something different about it than the way he smiles at everyone else. This one is just for me. I think it's the way his eyes brighten and the skin around them wrinkles. I nearly melt into his hard body, my knees going weak from *that* look.

When he pulls away, I'm breathless and feeling drunk on lust. If he wanted to take me right here, right now, I wouldn't dare object.

"Are you ready to go see the studio?" he asks me, gently rubbing my arm and causing sparks to flow through my body.

I gaze up into his eyes, seeing the caring warmth reflected there.

All the questions are right there, on the tip of my tongue. Is he going to keep me afterward? Does this feel the same to him? I'm falling into a dark abyss and I'm terrified; I just want to know that he'll catch me. But closing my eyes and imagining he will makes the fall that much easier, that much more enjoyable. Even if there's nothing but the hard, cold unforgiving ground there to meet me when this is all over.

His eyes stare back at me as the questions makes my stomach flutter, but my lips stay closed tight. My heart is clenching in agony because I already know the answers, I already know the truth.

And I refuse to appear ungrateful. He's gone through the trouble to rent a studio for me. I won't ruin the moment.

Besides, I want to live in the fantasy.

Before I can reply, my cell goes off in my pocket.

"Sorry," I tell Zander, fishing it out, my fingers fumbling with the tight jeans.

Zander's low, rough chuckle makes my cheeks heat. How does he do this to me? All that warmth leaves me in a sharp wave as I check the screen, my blood running cold.

Seeing the look on my face, Zander asks, "Who is it?" I hear his words, but I don't want to answer. He moves closer to me, invading my space. I feel caught between the two of them. Caught between my past and what could be. It's falling away from me, slipping past my fingertips as the phone rings again in my hand and Zander leans forward.

"Danny," I whisper even though me responding at this point isn't necessary, Zander can see for himself.

"Answer it," Zander says firmly.

"But-" I protest, not wanting this to happen. I don't want to be a part of this anymore.

"Answer it." His words are like stone, hardened by his resolve.

Dread pressing down on my chest, I tap the answer button and put it on speaker.

"Hello?" I ask weakly, although I'm staring at Zander. His eyes aren't on me; his focus is on Danny. I'm lost in the battle between the two of them, back to being nothing but a pawn.

"Where are you?" Danny asks coldly.

I swallow back a nervous lump in my throat. "I'm at home," I answer without thinking, my voice devoid of life.

"Don't lie to me."

I clear my throat and straighten my back. I can't hide from him, or my past. "I'm out." He doesn't own me. He's not my Master. *No one is.*

"You're with him," Danny says matter-of-factly. "And you must really think I'm a fucking idiot if you think I think otherwise."

I don't bother arguing.

"I need you to leave him now," Danny tells me firmly, in a voice I recognize all too well. One that makes me want to obey. A voice that *made* me obey once upon a time. "Right now. You're no longer his property."

My mouth is dry as I reply, "Danny, I-" Deep down inside of me, I feel the need to tell him no, but as the word climbs up my throat, it's as if I'm being strangled. The word refuses to leave my lips, to be heard by the man who saved me, by the man who beat me. I'm at war with myself and stuck in the middle of a battle between two men.

"I said leave!" Danny screams on the other end of the line, the dark side of him he showed me in the alley coming to the surface. "Or you're as good as fucking dead!"

His jaw clenched tightly, Zander snatches the phone out of my hand, leaving my body trembling on its own.

"Brooks," Zander growls, his voice dropping so low that my skin pricks with more fear than I thought possible at the sound. "You ever threaten Arianna again; it'll be the last thing you'll ever do. She's not going anywhere. She's mine. And you're going to pay me the money you owe me. Every. Fucking. Penny. Or you're going to wish I would've killed you back at your office."

Zander hangs up the phone, his eyes blazing with murderous rage. "You'll never speak to him again. He isn't going to touch you."

I don't say a word as a dozen different emotions course through my body. The threat is very real. My body sways as the shock of what's transpired hits me. *You're as good as fucking dead.* Over and over his words repeat in my head.

"You're never going back to him," Zander tells me firmly. "Ever."

"What's going to happen?" I ask, my voice barely above a whisper.

"I'm going to make sure he pays," Zander practically growls, tossing the phone onto the end table. It takes him a moment for him to look at me, and when he does his demeanor changes. "You're safe."

He reaches out to me, gripping both of my shoulders and lowering his eyes to mine. "Look at me, sweetheart." I instantly obey him, but I question my instincts. "You're alright, and everything is going to be alright." His words are like a soothing balm, but the wound too deep.

The only thing I'm truly aware of is that nothing is alright.

CHAPTER 25

ZANDER

*T*here's a gentle breeze outside; it blows the light dusting of snow as it falls, twirling before coating the hard ground. It's April and the cold should be moving along, winter done and over, but the chill has lasted longer than it should. I rest my hand against the window, it's cold as ice against my heated body.

He's done.

They're the words I texted Charles. It's long past due for Brooks to be put in his place. Come Monday, there will be nothing left of him.

I turn, looking over my shoulder at Arianna as she wraps her arms around her knees. She's staring into the fire, listening to the crackling as the billows of soft grey smoke spill from between the split logs.

She hasn't been the same. I hate how much control he has over her. How weak he's made her. She keeps saying he saved her, but she has no idea how wrong she is.

"Sweetheart," I call out to her and she lifts her head from resting on her knees and stares back at me with the desire to be commanded in her eyes. She's lost and scared, just like she was before Brooks got his hands on her. He kept her that way, molded her to believe something else. To believe she was better when he only made her suffer that much more.

I'm going to fix her. It's the only thing I give a damn about anymore.

"I want you to come here," I tell her as I walk to the edge of the rug. She's still on her ass, curled beneath the heat of the fire, but she makes a move to come to me. She nearly crawls. For the split second that she's on all fours, I want her to. The idea of her crawling the few feet and waiting on her knees to please me makes my dick twitch with need. *Soon.* I'm ready to give in, but only once she fully submits. And that starts tonight.

She slowly rises and I can see in her eyes that she questions if she should have crawled to me. If she wanted to, she should have. It's as simple as that. She'll learn. I'll learn with her. And together we'll enjoy that depraved darkness we both desire.

"Do you want me?" I ask her. Her eyes spark with fear, the green flecks mixing with a light gold and shining back with panic.

"I… Yes… I-" she doesn't answer with confidence. Her eyes look down at the plush rug beneath her bare feet.

"You need to know what you want, sweetheart. If you can tell me, I'll give it to you."

"But for how long?" she finally asks the question that's been holding her back. My lips turn up into that smile, the one I love. The one that reflects the happiness she gives me. I brush the stray hairs from her face with the back of my knuckles and lean forward, my hand cupping her chin.

I whisper, my lips nearly touching hers. "However long you'll let me have you."

"I don't want to leave," she tells me with her eyes open, but there's a pain in her voice caused by her confession. Our hot breath mingles as she says, "You make me weak."

The words are like a knife to my heart. If only she knew. I'm the weak one. Only for her.

I press my lips to hers and let my hands roam her body. My fingers trail down to the dip in her waist before I pull back, leaving her to stand on her own, although she almost stumbles.

"Undress for me," I tell her as I grip the ends of my shirt, forcing myself to hold anything other than her. She doesn't hesitate, although her eyes spark with a hint of anger for leaving her in the heat of the moment. The fire crackles and sparks behind her, lighting her with shadows dancing over her slender body as she slowly strips, dropping her clothes to the floor in a puddle at her feet. I do the same, mimicking her movements until we're both naked before each other, bathed in the glow of the fire and nothing else.

"I want you," she whispers, and her simple words contain so much power. They're so raw and full of a truth that's undeniable.

I step forward, closing the space between us as my toes dig into the plush rug and confess, "I want you, too."

Her lips crash with mine and her fingers spear through my hair as she moans into my mouth. Yes! This, this is exactly what I want.

My blunt nails dig into the flesh of her ass as I lift her up, parting her thighs and nestling my dick between her legs as I lower her to the floor beneath us, sinking into the rug in front of the fire.

The soft fur of the rug is nothing like the feel of her skin. So delicate, so easily bruised and broken. But I want her like this. Every part of her moving with me, wanting me just as much as I want her.

I leave open-mouth kisses along her body, over every inch. My hot breath trails along her skin. Her hips buck and those moans of desperate need fill the air as I toy with her, teasing her just as she's teased me.

"Please," she moans my name. "Zander, please."

She'll never know how much power she gives me when she calls for me like that. When she shows me how much she needs me. How much she craves my touch.

"On all fours," I breathe the command and she's quick to obey, turning over her body, her hair swishing over her shoulder. I let my teeth scrape along her neck before sucking gently at the tender skin in the crook of her neck.

Her plush ass grinds against my cock, begging me to take her and claim her as mine. But this is for her. For her to claim me.

"Take from me, sweetheart." I place my hand on the small of her back as I line my dick up between her hot folds. She's already slick, already wanting me. "Take what you want."

The way she looks at me from over her shoulder teases me to slam into her. To take everything from her and overpower this beautiful creature who's submitted to me.

But there's so much more power in having her take from me.

Her back arches beautifully, her ass rising slightly as she reaches between her legs and grabs a hold of me. A rough groan vibrates up my chest and soothes me as she slowly eases herself backward, her hot cunt taking all of me achingly slowly.

Her hips push back until she's pressed against my groin, her hot cunt filled with my cock. Her forearms brace herself and she leans forward, her head thrashing from side to side as she moves on and off my dick.

My head falls back and my fingers dig into the flesh of her hips. They itch for me to hold her still and fuck her like I want to. But I hold back. Waiting for her.

She rocks herself on and off my dick, her tight cunt sucking me in and making me regret the decision to give her control. My fingers dig deeper, wanting more. Her soft moans turn to ragged breaths as she picks up her pace.

I have to let go of her, warring with the need to take over and pin her down. I fall forward, my hands gripping the rug as her pussy clamps down on my dick. I kiss along her spine, traveling upward and letting her hair tickle my nose as she cums violently, urging me to spill myself deep inside of her as her body trembles with the shock of her orgasm.

A cold sweat breaks out over my body, and I finally feel like I can breathe. Her body sags on the floor, limp and sated, but I'm not done with her.

"Good girl," I tell her before nipping her earlobe and propping her back up and onto all fours. She turns to look at me over her shoulder, her breathing frantic.

My hands are gentle as I trail them down her back, catching my breath and positioning my knees so I can take her hard and fast. I only give her a moment, only waiting to see her lower her front to the floor to steady herself and then look back at me with her mouth parted.

I slam into her, buried to the hilt without any mercy as she screams out. I piston my hips, taking her over and over with a relentless pace.

I'm already close to cumming. The sight of her taking pleasure from me was enough to be my undoing. Her fingers dig into the carpet and her pussy spasms on my cock. "Zander!" she screams out my name as I pound into her over and over. My toes curl and the very bottom of my spine tingles as I thrust my hips once, twice, and one last time before cumming deep inside of her.

My body falls forward as she shakes beneath me, the waves of her own release racing through her. My hand grips hers as my body covers hers, and I kiss her shoulder tenderly.

"Never question if I want you," I tell her softly. "Never question if you're mine."

She breathes out heavily, strands of hair falling in her face. Her gorgeous eyes stare back at me and she answers, "Yes, Zander," as I kiss her shoulder one last time.

CHAPTER 26

ARIANNA

*T*he crackle of spent logs and the scent of wood smoke fill the room as Zander slips on his dark blazer over his white dress shirt and adjusts his cufflinks in one smooth flourish. I bite my lower lip as I watch him check out his freshly shaven appearance in the bedroom mirror. He has to know that he looks good. This is just habit.

After adjusting his black tie, he turns around, his piercing blue eyes focusing on me.

My skin pricks as the intensity of his stare summons a dull ache between my thighs, a reminder of the passionate night before.

"You'll be fine while I'm gone?" Zander asks me, giving me his boyish grin that makes my heart skip a beat.

I grip the grey silk bathrobe in my hands, pulling it tighter around my chest. "I think so," I say. I pause, not knowing if I should pry, but hesitantly ask, "Where are you going?"

Zander's grin quietly fades. "I have some business to take care of."

I want to ask him what kind, but I stop myself. There's a reason he keeps his secrets, and maybe he doesn't trust me with them yet. But he can't keep them from me forever.

He can too, says an annoying voice at the back of my head, *this is all pretend.*

Fuck you, I want to tell the voice. I don't need any negativity shitting on my rainbow right now. I just want to be happy for once.

I shove down my anxiety and ask, "Do you know when you'll be back?"

Zander raises his right hand to glance down at his platinum Rolex. "I think around six. I'll bring back dinner."

Damn, that's a long time. What the hell will I do until then?

I try to keep my disappointment from showing, but I barely manage. "Okay."

Zander crosses the space between us, hooking his hand beneath my chin and tilting my head back to force me to look into his eyes. "Don't be sad, sweetheart," he says softly. "I have something for you to do while I'm gone."

"What?" I ask, my mind racing with what it could be.

His boyish grin grows wider. "I bought an easel and painting supplies for you so you could work here when you're not in the studio. I set it all up in the piano room."

A feeling of warmth goes through my chest and I stand on my tiptoes to give him a kiss on the lips. "Thank you," I breathe with gratitude when I pull away. My cheeks hurt from the wide smile on my face, but I don't even try to hide it.

Zander winks at me. "I thought you might like it." He gives me several more kisses that leave me wanting more before pulling away. There's a look of regret on his face as he gazes at me, as if he wishes he could stay. "Don't go anywhere while I'm gone, and do not answer your phone if you don't know who it is. I don't want you in contact with *him.*"

I nod my head slowly, my anxiety slightly rising at his serious tone. "I won't." I promise. It's not like Danny's threat feels real, it doesn't. But I feel safer here with Zander. I don't want to see Danny at all. Just the thought makes a chill run through my body. I don't want to talk to him. I don't want anything to do with him, and I trust Zander when he says he's taking care of it.

Zander gives me one more quick kiss on the lips. "Later then, sweetheart."

He walks over to the door but before he can leave, I call out, "Wait."

Zander turns, arching an eyebrow in question.

"What am I supposed to paint while you're gone?"

His brow furrows in thought for a moment and then he gives me that boyish grin. "I don't know. Surprise me."

With a wink he's gone, leaving me alone in the room. I listen to the sound of his footsteps receding down the hallway until they fade into the distance. After a minute, I hear the roar of the engine of one of his cars start up outside as he drives away.

I chew on my lip, wondering what I could paint for Zander. Looking around the room, I feel like he has expensive taste. Hmm... An item of wealth, maybe? Power? I shake my head. No, I don't think he'd like that.

I got it! Remembering his reaction to my painting of the woman, suddenly I have an idea and my face breaks out into an excited grin. My fingers itching with excitement, I rush out into the hall toward the piano room. I stop just outside of it, grabbing the picture frame off the stand just outside the door.

When I walk into the room, the breath catches in my throat.

"Ohhh," I say softly, butterflies in my stomach.

Zander's set up a chair and easel on the dais with the piano, pointing it toward the floor-to-ceiling windows so I could paint with the breathtaking backdrop in front of me. He even went to the trouble to have the painting supplies set out and ready. All I have to do is sit down and start painting.

This is so sweet of him. So unexpected.

Tears pricking my eyes, I walk up the dais and set the frame upright on the piano. I take a seat at the easel and look at the brushes. When I choose the right one, I dip it into a deep earth tone shade of brown and begin painting.

Over the next several hours, I lose all sense of time as I work on the painting, frequently casting glances at the picture frame, trying to get every detail and nuance right. I don't take any breaks and I get so lost in my art, not even getting up to go to the bathroom. And by the time I'm close to done, my back is aching and my right hand feels nearly numb.

"Almost there," I whisper, setting a brush down into a small cup of water on the stand next to me. There's a bit of paint on Zander's shirt I'm wearing, but I'm sure he won't mind. I fucking hope not. "It's missing something," I murmur, staring hard at the painting, a replica of Zander's mother, Marie.

I stare at it long and hard, trying to figure out what it is. Finally, I snap my fingers.

Her smile. A feeling of joy sweeps through me, a rush of euphoria I always get when I'm close to finishing a work of art. It's not quite right. There's life to the smile I see in the photo. A tenderness that shows her love for Zander. And it's missing from this canvas.

"Once I get that done," I say happily, loving how it all looks, "it'll be perfect."

And I hope Zander will love it.

I'm about to pick up a paintbrush and apply the finishing touches, when I hear a faint ringing sound. I pause, frowning, straining my ears. I can't tell exactly where the sound is coming from, but it sounds like it's in the other room.

I pick the paintbrush back up, but now that I've heard the sound, I can't unhear it. I've got to know what it is. Sighing, I place the paintbrush down and walk into the adjoining room, one of Zander's studies.

Ding. Ding. Ding.

It's my cell, laying on his desk.

When I see the messages on the screen, my heart leaps up my throat.

It's Natalie. Fuck!

I've been so worried about Danny that I forgot to call her.

That's not true, says the annoying voice at the back of my head. *You were too wrapped up with your lover Zander to care.*

I'm really starting to hate that fucking voice right now, especially because it reminds me how much of a shitty friend I've been.

Sucking in a deep breath, I pick up the phone, reading through some of the messages.

Nattybatty95: Hey Ari! I got some crazy shit to tell you! I can't wait to get home to talk to you about it :P

Nattybatty95: Where you at, chica?

Nattybatty95: Is something wrong? :(

Nattybatty95: Why aren't you home yet?

Nattybatty95: WTF

Nattybatty95: I'm filing a missing persons report if I don't hear from you within the next day

The last message sends me into a panic and my fingers are flying across the keys before I even have time to process.

Artistchick96: Hey nat! Don't go filing a police report!!! I'm totally fine! Don't worry. I just took a mini vacation that's all

My cell chimes with an immediate *ding.*

Nattybatty95: Ari! Thank God you're alright! I was just about to file that report on you

Thank fuck she didn't. Jesus.

Artistchick96: No need! I'm okay.

Nattybatty95: Holy shit, you scared me to death! I thought you'd been kidnapped or something

My fingers fly across the touch screen.

Artistchick96: Nope. You're still stuck with me.

Nattybatty95: Wait, where are you? And where the hell have you been!?

I pause before responding, biting my lower lip while I think. I feel awful about the worry and panic I've caused Natalie. And I can't believe I haven't thought to send her a message while I've been staying over here with Zander. But deep down, I know a part of me didn't want to contact Natalie because... I knew she'd be trouble.

If I told her I was staying somewhere, she would've pestered me with endless questions.

God, I feel awful.

Sucking in a deep breath, I type out a quick message, ignoring her last message.

Artistchick96: hey... are you home?

Nattybatty95: No, but I will be in about a half hour.

Nattybatty95: Why what's up?

I hesitate, my heart pounding in my chest. As bad as I feel about keeping Nat in the dark, I'm not sure if I want to do this. *But if I don't give her at least something, she might grow suspicious.*

. . .

ARTISTCHICK96: I WANT TO MEET UP. TO TALK ABOUT SOMETHING.

I'm barely done pressing send when the screen lights up with another *ding.*

Nattybatty95: I'd definitely be down for that. Burning rubber to get home.

Artistchick96: See u there

Another *ding.*

Nattybatty95: What's this all about? Is it Danny?

I turn off the phone instead of answering. It'll take too much to type to tell my story, and I'd rather think about what I'm going to tell her on the way over. I still haven't decided if I'm going to tell her the truth yet, or make up some story.

But whatever I'm gonna do, I need to go there quick so I can get back before Zander's home. Glancing at the clock on the wall it's almost one, so I don't have too long, but it's still plenty of time.

Don't leave here without telling me. His words echo in my mind before I can take a single step.

For a moment, I'm frozen with indecision, not sure what to do. Zander was explicit about not going anywhere without asking for his permission.

But Natalie's my friend. And she needs to see me to feel secure. I can't leave her worrying about me like that.

Deciding that Zander will have to get over it if he finds out, I quickly get dressed and take off without looking back. He'll get over it. I glance at my purse a few times, wondering if I should text him. But I don't. Instead, I turn up the radio and try to relax, but it's impossible.

A heavy weight settles on my chest just thinking about opening up to Natalie. I don't know what I should do. Tell the truth. Or lie.

There are no pros to either one. I tell the truth and Natalie goes nuts, wanting to call the police. I tell a lie, and I feel like a shit face asshole.

I lose either way.

Whatever I do, I'm still going to apologize for being an absentee friend these past few months. It's really not fair how I've treated her after all she's done for me.

When I pull into my usual parking space at the apartments, I don't see Natalie's car anywhere, but I figure she'll show up any minute as I step out of the car and head up inside. The familiar scent of Natalie's perfume hits me as I step through the doorway and I feel a sense of nostalgia.

I've been so wrapped up with Zander, I forgot how much I've missed my friends these past few days.

I walk down the hallway and go into my room. I toss the keys on my dresser and head over to the closet to grab some more canvas, but before I can open the doors, my eyes are drawn to a note on my bed.

My stomach drops in my chest when I pick it up and read it:

Ari

I know I haven't been the best friend to you lately, always bugging you about the problems you're having with Danny, but I'd just like to tell you I'm just concerned about your well-being. I don't mean to be intrusive when I'm trying to figure out what's going on. I just care about you and want what's best for you. I really do hope that you'll tell me about your problems one day.

Until then,

Love always,

Crazy Nat

Tears sting the back of my eyes as I read the message.

"Oh Nat," I say softly, swallowing back a large lump in my throat, "Why do you have to make this *so* damn hard?" Now I'm *really* dreading our conversation. A part of me wants to leave now before she comes back, so I don't have to deal with the situation. But I'm not going to take the easy way out. I'm going to wait until she's here to decide which action I take.

I reread the message several more times before placing it on my nightstand and walking back into the living room to wait for Nat.

I flip through channels on the TV, thinking Nat is going to walk through the door any minute. But almost thirty minutes later, she's still not here. I glance at the time, my anxiety growing. Zander said he'd be back at six, and it's almost two.

I turn back on my phone to text Nat to see what's going on. Before

I can type a letter, the last message she sent before I turned my cell off pops up.

Nattybatty95: Hey I'm going to stop by A.C. Moore to get some supplies so we can chat while we paint. I have a feeling this is gonna be a juicy talk. ;)

Artistchick96: Okay. I'm here at the apt already... but can you hurry? I need to leave here by 5:30.

No sooner than I'm done texting, there's a knock at the door.

My heart jumps in my chest, my hand gripping at my shirt. *It's Natalie.* It has to be. She's probably back with her hands full of painting supplies. I let out a breath and try to shake off the dread.

Knock. Knock. Knock.

"Coming," I call, slowly getting up, and moving as fast as I can.

I take a deep breath when I place my hand on the door handle. Muttering a quick prayer, I swing the door open and put on a cheery smile, "Hey Nat-"

My heart freezes as I see Danny standing only a foot away with a demented grin on his face. He's dressed in his usual dress pants and dress shirt, except his eyes are bloodshot, his hair isn't finely coiffed as usual and his clothes look rumpled.

"Expecting someone else?" he sneers. A whiff of alcohol hits me and I immediately know he's been drinking.

"Danny?" I gasp. "What are you doing here?" It's hard not to tremble and keep my voice even. I wasn't expecting this at all. Zander's words come to me unbidden.

Don't leave the house without telling me.

"I've come to collect my debt," he growls, his eyes boring into me with a hatred that causes my skin to prick.

"What? What are you talking about?" I try to move, to slam the door in his face, but my body feels frozen, paralyzed with fear. He takes enough of a step in that I can't slam the door. *I can run though.*

"I followed you here," he says, his voice low and dangerous. "You know what?" I ask after swallowing the lump growing in my throat and being as firm as I can manage. "You're making me feel uncom-fortable. I think you should leave." It's hard, standing up for myself. But I don't have to take this kind of abuse from Danny. Not anymore. My hand feels hot as I push slightly on the door.

"You're really asking me to leave?" Danny demands in disbelief, his nostrils flaring as he splays his hand on the door, keeping it from shutting.

"You've been drinking," I say, "and don't look well. It's for the best." My heart beats chaotically. If I just act like everything's fine, it'll be okay. I'm in control. "Please leave." I hold his gaze, straightening my back and willing him to go and leave me alone.

For a moment, I think Danny is going to comply with my wishes, his head bowing. But when he looks back up at me, my blood runs cold.

"I don't think so," he says, his voice dark and deadly. Without warning, he rushes forward.

Crying out in alarm, I try to slam the door, but it smacks against his foot and he forces it open with a feral grunt. The door hits me straight on and I stumble, falling onto the floor. Heart pounding like a hammer, I scramble forward on my hands and knees while simultaneously reaching for my cell in my pocket.

I open my mouth, preparing to scream as loud as I can. But cold, powerful hands clamp down on my mouth from behind, muffling my cries. His hard body falls on top of me, knocking the phone out of my hand, but I grab it, forcing it into my blouse to hold onto it.

Kicking and bucking, I struggle violently, but I'm no match for Danny's strength. He presses down hard on my neck, cutting off my air supply. I strain against his grasp, my heart pounding so hard I think it will burst. Danny increases the pressure, growling in my ear like the monster he is.

I grow weak, my vision dimming black around the edges.

It only takes about five seconds for me to go limp.

"I gave you to him," I hear Danny's voice growl from somewhere far away as I fade off into darkness. "But now I'm taking you back."

CHAPTER 27

ZANDER

"*Y*ou look like shit."

I look up at Charles and see him smile. Grunting a humorless laugh, I lean forward and toss the papers back to him.

"I guess that's what happens when you get your hands dirty," he says with a glint in his eyes.

"You couldn't be happier, could you?" I ask him.

"Just surprised you risked your pretty boy face," he says with a smirk.

"You're not the only one," I mutter beneath my breath. My father hasn't let it go. *Everyone knows.* I'm a disgrace. Or so my father tells me. I haven't responded to him, and I won't. He'll never understand. She's worth more than anything. She's worth far more than my reputation. If my father could understand that, my mother may still be breathing.

"What's going on with her?" Charles asks me, catching my attention with his tone.

"What do you mean?" My heart races a little faster with him questioning me about her. I don't want anyone to question it.

"The money-" he starts to ask, and I cut him off. I'm so fucking sick of talking about money. So much fucking money runs through my hands. I don't need it. I'm tired of chasing it. I just want to live a full life. One with her.

"I'll give her the money, but it's not going to him. It's just for her." My voice is flat, but firm.

"So it's just the month?" Charles asks.

My stomach drops at his question. She said she doesn't want to leave me and I believe her, but only time will tell if she's actually happy. If I can give her enough. "I'd rather it not be."

His brow raises as he leans back in his seat, the leather groaning. "It seems... expensive."

I shrug, not knowing what to say.

"How do the contracts work?" Charles asks.

"It's just a month," I explain, and my voice is flat. "After that, I'm keeping her."

"Paying?" he asks, resting his ankle on his knee and tapping his foot.

"No." I'm harsh with my answer, narrowing my eyes. He raises his hands defensively. "She's not a whore," I say and I practically spit the words. Is it too much to think she'd want me without my money? I don't entertain the thought. I refuse to think she'd leave me. She's not in it for the money. She'll stay when the contract is over. I'll make sure of it. Whatever she desires, I'll give it to her. I'll spend every cent of my wealth on her to keep her happy.

"I'm just asking out of curiosity."

I'm about to tell him to mind his own business when he adds, "They're an interesting thing, the auctions."

I glance at the screen on the computer as he talks. The living room is empty, the house quiet and cold without her in it.

"I imagine a woman would put herself up for auction... if she knew about it."

I check the cameras to the house again, but Arianna's not home yet. She knows to be home when I get back. My only request is that she greet me when I get home. If I had it my way, she'd never leave, but I'm not so selfish to think that's possible.

"Your sweetheart isn't home yet?" Charles asks me, and there's a slight mocking tone in his voice. I just give him a sharp look and don't say anything.

"It's different, seeing you like this," he says.

"Like what?" Weak. I've never felt as though Charles was an enemy, but his tone makes me question.

His answer surprises me. "Like you give a fuck."

I stare at him, searching his face for his intentions, but I don't have to guess.

"I'm jealous," Charles admits and then looks away, staring past me and out to the window behind me. The dark night of the city sky playing shadows across his face.

"Jealous?" I ask him, a smile creeping onto my lips.

"Not jealous of your face," Charles answers with a smirk. I huff a laugh and lean back in my seat.

"It's good to see you happy," Charles says with a lowered voice. I meet his eyes and I know with everything in me he's being genuine.

I prefer not to let the emotions dictate my response. I shake them off, leaning back in my seat and resting my chin in my hand. "I'll be happy when Brooks is out of the picture."

"Changing the subject," Charles says, the grin fading from his lips. It's quiet a moment until he answers, "Soon."

"When is it happening?" I ask him as I pick up the slate block, and the edges seem sharper to me than they ever have before.

Charles shrugs, "It all depends on what you'd like." He takes out his phone, tapping the screen and bringing up Brooks' information. "He's predictable. If you'd like it to look natural, that can be arranged. I suppose it just depends on when and where."

I nod my head once, debating on what to respond, but Charles interrupts me, "We have a problem."

There's an urgency in his voice that makes me sit up straighter. I wait for him to continue as he watches the phone, his body stiff.

"Where's Arianna?" he asks me.

"She should be at my place s-"

"He was at her place. He changed his routine. He went to her house."

My hands grip the edge of the desk. "He's on Fourth Street?" There's only one reason that Brooks would go there. I take out my own phone and message Arianna to text me back and stare at the screen. Willing her to text me, but nothing comes.

I can't wait. "When was he there?" I ask Charles, my voice fighting to hold back the panic I feel. She's been gone for hours. My thumb taps across my phone and I call her. The phone rings and rings, but there's no answer. Everything in me stills, he's gotten to her.

Charles nods his head as he taps on the screen of his phone. "Three hours ago." I hang up the phone and realize that's right when she left. *He was watching her.* I call her again. Ring. Ring. Ring.

"Where is he now?" I ask him as my ice-cold blood slowly pumps through my veins.

"His place."

"On Andrews?" I confirm, already grabbing my keys off the desk and leaving for the door.

"Yeah," Charles says as he grabs his coat and comes up behind me.

"He has her. I know it."

Charles nods his head, throwing on his coat as I open the door.

"You're coming?" I ask him.

He nods his head once, the mask of indifference on his face morphing as he smiles at me. "I can't let you have all the fun." His humor does nothing to ease me. Right now nothing will make me feel as though I haven't already lost her.

"We'll get her back, Zander," he tells me as he places a hand on my shoulder.

I don't answer him. The door closes behind us as I stalk to the elevator with purposeful strides. I'm not letting him take her. I'll kill him first.

CHAPTER 28

ARIANNA

hoosh!
The sound of the whip sings through the air before lashing against my bare back. *Crack!*

A strangled scream rips from my throat, echoing in the hollow basement as blazing pain shoots up and down my flesh. I weakly struggle against my binds, sweat beading my brow. I'm suspended, naked, held up by chains hanging from the ceiling.

It's useless to fight. My head lolls to the side as my aching body screams at me to do something, yet I'm too weak. I never had a chance. I woke up in this position, and every ounce of my body is sore from fighting.

Despair consumes me.

The only thing I feel is pain.

I scream and scream again until my voice is raw and cracking, shaking against my binds, my back on fire. After several agonizing moments, my head drops forward and I hang limp against my bindings, my limbs trembling as a cold sweat breaks out all over my body. I don't know if he's going to hit me again, but I don't even know if I'll even feel it, my vision blackening around the edges.

"I gave you everything," Danny says behind me, his boots thudding against the cement floor as he paces behind me, his voice filled with utter contempt.

My eyelids open at the sound of his voice. He hasn't spoken since I woke up. My voice is sore from screaming, from begging and pleading. I can feel the cool air blowing over the open lashes and it stings with a pain that's indescribable, but even that isn't enough to scream over. The only movements, the only sounds I have the energy for are those that are instinctual. And even then, it's dulled by exhaustion.

I lick my dry, cracked lips. "Danny... please," my voice croaks as I cry weakly, tears streaming down my hot face. "You don't have to do this." I think I say the words, but my eyes are so heavy, my body so weak and the pain so unbearable, I'm not certain of anything.

"He wants to keep you?" Danny asks angrily.

I swallow back the lump of fear in my throat as I try to think of a response. I clench my sweaty hands, my fingers brushing against the rough metal and the raw cuts at the sharp cuffs shoot a pain down my arms that makes me wince.

"And you want him too, don't you?" Danny's words are just a whisper. His voice is eerily calm. I try to pick my head up, my throat too dry to answer.

I hear him drop the whip. My heart slams in my chest, and my body stiffens. I think that's what I heard. Please God, please. I can't take any more.

"Well he can have you back," Danny whispers next to my ear. His breath feels so cold. Everything feels so cold. "As soon as I'm done with you," Danny says as he wraps my hair around his wrist and pulls my head back too sharply, a scream tears through me as my neck is ripped to the side.

The moment he lets go, I hear him pick the whip back up and somehow, I'm able to cry again. Not that it will do me any good. I can't save myself. I'm powerless and pathetic.

Dread presses down on my chest as his whip sings through the air and I cringe. *Whoosh! Crack!*

Whoosh!
Crack!
Whoosh!
Crack!

My mouth opens wide in agony, saliva dripping from my lips, but I have no voice left to scream with. I buck, shudder, and strain against my bindings, my back feeling like it's being flayed to the bone.

With each painful lash, the room spins around me, my breathing becoming shallow, ragged.

My heart is becoming sluggishly slow.

When the darkness finally claims me, I'm incredibly grateful. I only pray it will swallow me whole.

CHAPTER 29

ZANDER

*I*f the cops had seen-" He won't fucking let it go. I spend the whole way here. He's had her for nearly four hours. Four fucking hours.

"Enough," I snap at Charles. He won't shut the fuck up. I get out of my car which I've parked a block down from Brooks' house and slam the door.

"You need to be quiet," Charles says and grabs me, gripping my shoulder and slamming me against the car.

All I can see is red.

I push against him, but he pushes me back.

"He has her!" I scream at him, but he doesn't relent, slamming my head into the car and pushing his face against mine.

"Calm the fuck down," he says through clenched teeth. I wish he hadn't come with me.

I use all of my weight and push him off of me. He stumbles backward and nearly falls on his ass.

"He's going to see you coming."

"Let him!" I scream, my voice hoarse and my skin so fucking hot I can barely stand it. I just need her back. I turn from him and take quick strides, my eyes focused on the house at the end of the barren street.

"He could kill her," Charles calls out to me, and it's only then that I pause. My heart freezes in my chest. No. I clench my teeth and move my hand to the gun at my waistband. I hear Charles' footsteps walk up behind me slowly, with determined steps. "If you barge in, he could kill her."

I'm silent as I stand there, feeling a wave of nausea threatening to come up.

"We both know he didn't take her for a chat."

"Stop it," I tell him with my eyes closed. All I can see is her face, her smile. I can practically hear her laugh.

"You need to listen to me. You need to restrain yourself."

My hands ball into fists and my blunt nails dig into the fleshy part of my palm. "Just go then. Lead the way, but no more waiting. I need her."

Charles slaps a hand on my back, and it's hard and firm. He moves ahead of me and I lift my eyes to watch his back as he moves off the sidewalk and hides in the shadows of the trees along the large estates.

He looks over his shoulder and I'm quick to move, my heart pounding so hard it's the only thing I can hear.

Thud. Thud. Thud. Each beat is another second she's in there with him.

I can't hear a damn thing, a loud ringing in my ears is the only thing I can focus on as Charles leads me through the scattered trees to the side of Brooks' house.

I don't even realize he's picking the lock until I try to shove him away. I just need to get to her.

I can feel it in the pit of my stomach. He's hurting her. He has for years, but now it's personal. I stand there watching Charles shoving the pick into the lock and twist it slightly before I hear a muffled scream.

The blood drains from my face, and ice replaces my blood as Charles' eyes meet mine.

"Open it," I mouth the words to him. My hand slowly travels to the cold steel of my gun. My reddened vision becomes focused. Adrenaline is bringing life to the hatred burning inside of me.

The door clicks and slowly opens, and I move in front of Charles. He doesn't stop me as I move through the house. The floorboards are creaking loudly under my weight. I don't stop, all I can hear is that scream, her pain. It compels me to go to her, a pull so strong, so violent that nothing can stop me. Nothing will keep me from her or save him from death.

She screams again as I come to a stop in the narrow hallway to a heavy door with an old steel knob. I test it and the knob turns easily, her scream louder as I creak it open.

My heart pounds in my chest as I hear the swish of a whip and the crack of it against her skin. The lights are dim as I move down the stairs, my gun held out in front of me.

Time slows as I see her, hanging there from the chains with him behind her. Pure hatred shines in his eyes as he pulls the heavy whip back over her shoulder, ready to strike her again.

It only takes two shots. *Bang! Bang!*

He wavers on his feet, staring down at his chest where the small holes in his chest seem to vanish, but quickly blood seeps through the fabric and spreads along the woven threads.

I keep my arm up, the kick of the gun still traveling up my arm as he falls to his knees first, his head tilting back up to me, his forehead pinching and his hands moving to his chest. It's not long before he falls forward, his face slamming against the ground, his body lifeless.

My feet move down the steps, going closer to him. I don't take my eyes off of him as I empty the gun into his skull. *Bang! Bang! Bang!*

I keep pulling the trigger even after it's empty. His dead eyes are open and staring back at me as blood pools around his disfigured face.

It's only the sound of her whimper that tears me away from him.

"Don't touch her!" I scream at Charles, making him flinch as he puts both his hands up.

There's so much blood. Lashes mar her back, her shoulders, her thighs. Everywhere. He tore her flesh open. I don't hesitate to pick her small body up, relieving the weight that's pulling her wrists against the metal cuffs.

"Zander," she says and her voice is so weak as her head droops to the side.

"It's alright," I tell her quickly as Charles works on the locks at her wrist. He must've found the key somewhere, because they're off in an instant. Her arms are falling like dead weight and making her face twist in pain.

She cries out as I turn her body, cradling it and feeling the warmth of her blood soaking into my shirt and against my arms.

"Here," Charles says and passes me a white sheet. I question using it for only a moment before wrapping it around her body, not tightly. Every small movement makes her wince with pain.

"Talk to me, Arianna," I tell her. Her eyes look as if she's staring far off into the distance. "Arianna," my voice cracks as I say her name.

I'm too late.

"We need to get out of here," Charles says as he looks around the cellar. My shoes have traveled through the blood, tracking footprints wherever I've been. "I need to call for clean up."

My heart races as I realize what's happened. What I've done.

"Hopefully there's time," Charles says so softly I'm not sure if I was meant to hear him.

My body shakes as I hold her closer to me, carrying her weak body up the steps and letting Charles lead the way. "I've got you," I whisper, kissing her hair. "It's alright," I tell her even though I'm not sure it is. My body is so cold, so numb.

Sirens scream in the background as we walk away from the house.

"We should have gotten the silencer," Charles mutters beneath his breath, opening the car door for me.

We would have time to clean up. Time to hide the evidence if we had stopped to get his equipment like he'd told me to.

Arianna groans with pain in my arms, the blood seeping through the thin white sheet.

But then my sweetheart might not have survived.

CHAPTER 30

ARIANNA

I groan softly with the twinge of pain as the doctor works on mending my back. My hands fist the comforter and my head thrashes from side to side. I'm on pain meds, but the prodding and stitches bring sharp pains that won't go away. I'm alive though. "Zander," I croak, barely able to force the words from my lips. I try to be still, feeling the cool air sting my open wounds, but it's hard. It just *hurts*. I've never felt so much pain in my life.

In the background, I hear heavy footsteps softened by plush carpet, coming toward the bed. As the footsteps get closer, I lift my head to see Zander, his face a tortured mask. But my movement proves to be a mistake as horrible pain runs up and down my back. I suck in a sharp breath through clenched teeth, trying my best not to cry out. I don't want him to see me like this, but I need him here. I just want him to hold me.

A large but gentle hand touches my shoulder where there aren't any wounds.

"Don't move," Zander says, his voice low and sounding like a soft rebuke.

It hurts me to hear that tone in his voice. "I'm sorry," I tell Zander quietly, my face pressed against the mattress, my lips mashed together. I'm sorry I ever left. I'm sorry I couldn't fight harder. I'm ashamed. I brought all this on Zander. And now Danny's blood is on Zander's hands. Guilt mixes with anxiety in my stomach, making me feel sick.

"It's alright," I hear Zander reply, his voice softer now. Even through my pain, a warmth flows through my chest.

"I should've listened to you," I say remorsefully. *And none of this would've happened.*

"It's going to be alright," Zander repeats. He crouches down so his eyes are level with mine.

My heart skips a beat at his handsome face so close to mine, his masculine scent calming me. His gaze pierces through me, his heavenly blue eyes clouded with emotion.

I attempt a smile as Zander leans in, pressing his lips against mine, his hand cupping my jaw while his thumb rubs soothing circles on my cheek, causing my skin to warm from just his touch alone. But he murdered someone. I heard what Charles said. There wasn't time to hide anything. They're going to know. They're going to come for him. I'll tell them everything. They can't blame Zander. They can't... I can hardly breathe, and the reality makes me dizzy with agony. "Is it going to be okay?" I whisper against Zander's lips, my heart in my throat, my eyes shut from the pain. *Please tell me that it is. Please tell me that everything is going to be okay.*

"Everything's going to be fine," he says softly.

My eyes flutter open and I see his piercing blue eyes gazing at me. His jaw is clenched, his expression conflicted.

I look back at him, my heart still in my throat. I have the sudden urge to tell him that I love him. That I want to be with him forever. He really saved me. I truly owe him my life.

But I can't find the strength to speak the words as I watch the look in his eyes change.

Deep down, I know that he's lying to me.

Everything isn't going to be okay. And it's all because of me.

CHAPTER 31

ZANDER

I wish I could just pause time. If only it were possible. The soft sounds of Arianna sleeping peacefully are the only sounds I concentrate on. If I don't, all I can hear is the bang of my gun. The thud of his body hitting the floor. The sound of her scream.

I close my eyes, wishing the image would go away. It's not the blood from the bullet holes spilling onto the floor that makes my stomach turn with sickness, it's Ariana's blood stained on the cement under her and caked on her back.

I grit my teeth, my hands fisting the sheets as I try to contain the anger.

A soft moan makes me open my eyes as Arianna twists on the bed, nestling closer to me and giving me a warmth I'm in desperate need of.

Her small hand meets my chest, and instantly her body relaxes and she moves closer in her sleep as I put my arms over her waist.

Her simple touch calms the anger inside of me. I feel raw and powerless with her next to me. I'd do anything for her. She turns me away from everything I've ever known. It means nothing compared to her touch.

I've sacrificed it all; I already know I'm going down for this.

Charles messaged me this morning, there's too much evidence. Video surveillance from the gala, her blood, his blood.

We both knew it as I stood over Brooks' dead body. There was no going back. No hiding it. I'm only biding my time until they come for me.

If only I could pause this moment and stay with her forever.

"Mmm," Arianna's soft voice brings my eyes to hers. They flutter open and she yawns, covering her mouth with her hand. As she moves her arm, she winces, a reminder of the pain from the wounds on her back.

I wish I could do more for her. I feel like I failed her. *In so many ways I have.*

"How do you feel?" I ask but my voice croaks and I have to clear my throat. I haven't slept, and that's evident in my voice. My eyes feel heavy and my body is begging for me to let go, but I can't. I know I only have a few moments left with her. I won't waste them sleeping.

"Okay," Arianna answers me, her hand moving to the stubble on my jaw. I take her hand in mine and kiss her palm, making that sweet smile form on her face. I love that smile. It should always be there. She deserves that happiness.

"Do you need any more meds?" I ask her, my eyes automatically flashing to the clock. It's nearly eight, she can't have another dose for two more hours.

"I'm fine," she says with the soft smile still there. "Really," she leans forward and hides the pain that's clearly there to kiss me on the lips.

I don't waste the moment, I pull her closer to me, holding on to her small body carefully and gently and deepening the kiss. I part her lips with my tongue, slipping it along the seam and then stroking her tongue with mine. Our tongues mingle in a dark dance of desperate need. Her moans fill my hot mouth as she pushes herself against me. Her breasts press against my chest, and her leg brushes over my knee.

I nip her bottom lip and look down at her. Her dark eyes look up through her thick lashes and her lips part. Our hot breath fills the air between us.

A moment passes with a spark igniting between us. Not lust, something stronger. *So much stronger.* Her lips part and she almost has a chance to say the words, but I don't let her. I push my lips against hers, muffling anything she could say and putting every ounce of passion and need into my touch.

I can't bear to say it, knowing how this ends, but I hope she can feel it. That's all I need. As long as she can feel it, it'll stay with her forever.

As I break the kiss, I hear the banging on the front door. My heart freezes, but it's not from knowing that I'm done. That I'll be in jail soon and on the stand for murder. It's not the threat of life behind bars, or the death penalty that makes my heart stop. It's the look in Arianna's eyes and the way her nails dig into my arm as I pull away from her.

"No," Arianna whispers, her head shaking as I move off the bed, ignoring her attempt to keep me with her in the safety and warmth of the comforter.

"I have to," I tell her with my back to her. I'm not going to run. I know that's not an option. I take in a breath as the bed groans and Arianna grabs her sweater off the floor, throwing it on and ignoring the pain she must be feeling and running through the hall to catch up to me. Her bare feet pad on the floor as a voice says through the door, "Zander Payne, open up! We have a warrant!"

"Go back to bed, Arianna," I command her, but she doesn't listen.

I clench my teeth as the banging of a fist on the other side of the door echoes in the foyer.

"Zander," Arianna pulls on my arm, begging me to look at her. She swallows thickly, looking at the door as the banging continues.

"Sweetheart," I tell her with the semblance of a smile on my face. "It's okay," I lie to her. It hurts to do it. "Just go back to bed," I say and my voice cracks. I brush the hair away from her face and cup her chin.

Bang! The knock at the door sounds so much louder.

"Coming!" I call out and at my voice, Arianna hunches forward, tears falling down her cheeks.

I lean down and kiss her lips, tasting the salt before resting the tip of my nose against hers. "You'll be alright," I tell her in a soft voice. It's meant to comfort her, but it only forces a sob from her throat.

She cries quietly behind me in the middle of the foyer as I unlock the door and open it, stepping aside. Each beat of my heart seems slower.

Four cops stand at my doorstep, the first pushing the door open wider as he steps through.

"Zander Payne?" the man asks. He has dark skin and dark eyes to match. Tall and broad shouldered, his voice doesn't match the intimidation of his presence. The man is deadly, that much is obvious, but his voice is calm and level. Professional even. "I'm Officer Richter, and this is Officer Lawson."

I nod my head, meeting his eyes and waiting for the arrest.

The man behind him, Officer Lawson, comes in with cuffs already out. "Turn around sir, we have a warrant for your arrest." The second officer speaks this time, a much shorter man, with tanned skin but lacking the same forceful presence as the first man. His voice still echoes authority though. And I listen, turning around and putting my hands behind my back.

I don't ask what I'm being arrested for, maybe I should. I should have prepared this better. But the truth is, she was never a part of my plans. None of this was supposed to happen.

"Zander," Ariana's voice is full of pain as the metal brushes against my skin. It's cold and the clinking of the cuffs is loud as the metal closes around my wrists. A strong hand rests on my shoulders as I'm pushed against the wall. My cheek is flat against the drywall as the man pats me down.

"You have the right to remain silent. If you do say anything, it can be used against you in a court of law. You have the right to have a lawyer present during any-"

"I did it!" Arianna calls out. I can't see her with my face still pressed against the wall. My eyes pop open, and my heart races as her words hit me. I try pushing back against the man holding me, but his hold is unforgiving.

"I killed Daniel Brooks. I did it!" Ariana shrieks and runs forward, toward the cops. I can hear the commotion behind me. I push against the man holding me, and this time I'm forceful. "I shot him. I can tell you everything. Please don't take him."

"Keep quiet!" I yell at Arianna, whipping my body around. I'm so off-balance I fall over, tripping over the cop's boot as Arianna's being turned around by Officer Richter.

"Don't say anything!" I wrench my head around, craning my neck as I lie awkward on the floor with the cuffs tight on my wrists, the cold metal digging into my flesh and shooting sparks of pain up my shoulder, begging her to look at me as I scream out. "Arianna!"

"Take 'em both," Officer Richter tells the other cops.

I stare at Arianna's back, watching as they cuff her.

"Don't touch her!" I scream out so loud my throat hurts. "She didn't do it!" I shout at them.

"If I were you, I'd wait for your lawyer," Officer Richter tells me as one of the cops ushers her away. My heart is beating so loud; the sound is deafening.

"Arianna!" I scream for her as I'm heaved off the floor and shoved against the wall as I try to run to her. "Stop!" I scream out. My face is shoved against the wall, and the harsh crack bruises my cheekbone.

"She didn't do it," I breathe out the words. "Leave her alone!" The sounds of them walking her out of the house mixes with the blood rushing in my ears. "Arianna!" I scream again, but she doesn't answer me, instead I'm left with silence. Only the two officers and myself remain, alone in my foyer.

"She confessed to a murder, we have to take her in," Officer Lawson says close to my ear. His breathing is ragged from dragging me up and keeping me still against the wall.

"I'll repeat what I said, Mr. Payne." Officer Richter comes into view. His tall frame hovers over me as he tells me, "You should wait for your lawyer."

"She didn't do it." I look him in the eyes, letting him feel my conviction and the truth in my words. She never should have said anything. What was she thinking? My heart twists with a pain that's indescribable.

"She's hurt," I tell them as the man behind me spreads my legs. "She's-"

"She'll be alright, Mr. Payne."

"She didn't do it," I tell him again. I plead with him to let her go, she can't take the fall for this. I won't let her. "She's not feeling well, and she-"

"It doesn't matter. You need to let the law handle this."

The fight that's been absent since I brought my sweetheart home comes back. I won't fight for myself. I'll take the punishment I deserve. But I won't let them touch her. She's innocent. She's always been innocent.

I look him square in the eyes as I tell him, "I need to call my lawyer."

CHAPTER 32

ARIANNA

I rest my head on the interrogation table, letting out a heavy exhale. *I won't tell them anything.* I don't care what they say. Or what they do. I refuse to talk. The table is so cold. It makes me want to sleep. I'm so tired. So exhausted. Anxiety twists my stomach as my heart pounds. I assumed they would lock me up right away, toss me in a cell, and throw away the key. But instead I've been left in a room. I don't know how much time has passed. There isn't a clock in here. Nothing. I'm just alone.

I resist the urge to look behind me. I know they're on the other side of that one-way mirror, looking in. Watching me. I told them I shot him. I don't know how many times. When they asked me why, the answer was easy. But then they asked questions I couldn't answer. Where I got the gun. Why a man's shoe prints were found at the scene. I went silent. I won't say anything that can implicate him in murder. I'm trapped and alone. I turn my head to the other side, letting the chill calm my heated skin.

All for Zander.

I lift my head, sitting back in the metal chair as I remember the look in his eyes when he laid me on the bed. It touched me in ways I couldn't imagine. Made me feel like I was the most precious thing. Like I was *his*.

A tear threatens to fall down my cheek, but I fight it back. I can't break down. Not here. Not *now*.

There's no way I can let Zander take the fall for me. Danny is dead because of me. He killed him to save me. I'm not going to let Zander pay for my mistake. Just the thought of him going to prison for the rest of his life fills me with so much guilt and shame.

No matter what they do or say, I can't let them break me. I pick at my nails, wishing for some miracle. Hoping that telling them what he did to me is enough. *It should be.* Shouldn't it?

I keep my neck stiff, staring straight ahead when the door to the interrogation room opens and booted feet smack across this floor. I even keep my head down as the two hardened detectives sit down at the table across from me.

"Are you ready to speak with us, Miss Owens?" Detective Richter asks harshly, a thirty-something tall man with a chiseled jawline and a receding hairline, his deep voice filling the small hollow room like a bass. Out of the side of my eye, I can see him staring at me with an irritated scowl, his muscular arms folded across his chest. Dressed in a plain white dress shirt and blue jeans, he's not wearing a badge, his gun holstered at his waist.

"I already told you I did it."

The two men share a glance before Detective Richter replies, "You need to give us more than that."

I don't say a word.

"You don't have to be afraid to speak," his partner, Detective Lawson, says more gently, resting his elbows on the table and leaning forward with his hands clasped. He seems the more levelheaded of the two, with short dark hair, broad shoulders and a large nose. Unlike Detective Richter, he has a badge, a large golden ornament, proudly on display on his right breast. He doesn't have a gun. "You're away from prying ears now and can speak freely." He waits for a moment to see if I'll respond before saying, "We promise you, we're just trying to do our best to help you."

I nearly snort out a laugh at the bullshit. Though I'm not well-versed in law or cop tactics, I at least know that they are not my friends and they are not trying to help. I would be a fool to trust them.

I keep my head down, clenching my jaw. If they're expecting

they'll get me to talk, they'll be waiting a damn long time. I'm not saying shit other than what I've already told them.

The sound of the clock ticking on the wall fills the silence. *Tick tock, tick tock.*

"Look up when Detective Lawson is speaking to you," Detective Richter says irritably, suddenly.

Go fuck yourself, I want to growl, but don't.

I know Detective Richter is only doing his job, but he has no idea what I've been through. And if he thinks being firm with me will get him what he wants then he's sadly mistaken.

"Don't make this hard on yourself. We all know you're lying."

I freeze, wondering if they really do. I almost part my lips to say, "How?" but then remember the tactics the cops use. No matter what they say to me, I need to stay quiet. It's better that way. I'll be quiet, I'll get a lawyer. They can blame me for killing him when they see what he did to me. I'll claim self-defense, or maybe insanity. I pick at my nails, the fear and anxiety weighing heavily against my heart.

"Do you honestly expect us to believe a woman like you killed Danny Brooks when he had so many enemies?" Detective Richter demands.

I remain silent.

Detective Richter snorts when he sees I don't react. "Or let me put it better for you; do you honestly expect us to believe that a woman in your condition, a woman who'd just been beaten within the inch of her life, was in any position to kill her lover?"

Again, I don't respond, keeping my face stoic and pointed downward against the table, even though the word lover throws me off.

Just a little while longer, I tell myself.

"You're making this hard for yourself," Detective Lawson says in a way more calming tone. "We don't want to see you locked up for a crime you didn't do. All you have to do is tell us why your new boyfriend killed him."

I stay still, clenching my jaw, my eyes closed tightly.

Silence descends upon the room.

Detective Richter starts to say something, but he's interrupted by a knock at the door.

A young man sticks his head in, opening the door just enough and says, "Someone here to see you, Detective Richter."

Detective Richter glances at me, his jaw clenching. "Can it wait?"

The man glances outside the door and then shakes his head.

Detective Richter sighs and gets up from his seat and nods to Detective Lawson before leaving the room.

It's quiet when he's gone and I stay in the same position, feeling sharp pricks along my back. I shudder at the thought of having to sleep on a hard bed with my aching wounds.

"Don't be unnerved by Richter," Detective Lawson says, breaking the silence. "He tries to get a rise out of all our interviewees, to put them off guard."

I ignore him. He can try to be nice all he wants, but he's not getting anything out of me.

"You can talk to me," Detective Lawson presses. "I'm on your side here."

I continue to sit there, not saying a word. I just want this all to end.

Detective Lawson inhales as if to say more when the door opens, and in walks Detective Richter with an impeccably dressed woman in a business suit, her shiny blonde hair finely coiffed.

"Up, Miss Owens," Richter practically barks.

For the first time since coming into the interrogation room, I lift my head up, wondering what the hell is going on.

"Why?" I demand, my voice sounding hoarse and raw from screaming the other night. "Is it time for me to go to jail?"

Before he can answer, the woman next to him says, "Hello Miss Owens, I'm Dana Mills, the lawyer that's been hired to represent you."

"What?" I ask, my face twisting in confusion. "I didn't hire-"

"Mr. Payne hired me as your counsel," Dana says.

I try to keep my hands from trembling. "I'm guilty. I've already admitted that I'm the one who killed Danny Brooks. I'm going to jail."

Dana has a sad expression on her face as she gazes at me, but it quickly turns professional once again. "Please come with me. We've got to get you prepared for your pretrial hearing."

CHAPTER 33

ZANDER

*M*y hands are white-knuckled as I grip onto the back of the wooden row of seats in front of me. This isn't real. It can't be. This isn't how it's supposed to go down.

"Just stay quiet," my father says from my right and it's a damn good thing my grasp is on the bench. The need to beat the shit out of him is riding me hard. He got me out. He pulled his strings and got me out. *But she's still in custody.*

"She didn't do it," I tell him again. My voice is raw, my eyes stinging and bloodshot. I haven't slept, eaten. I look and feel the same.

"Get yourself together," my father says through clenched teeth as if anyone in here could hear him.

There's hardly a soul in the courtroom. The judge isn't here yet, but the defense, Miss Mills, and prosecution are at their benches as is the court reporter and a few people occupying several seats of the benches where my father and I are. Although we're alone in the row.

"She didn't do it," I tell him again, this time turning my head to face him. He's clean-shaven and his suit is crisp. If anything, he looks better today than he has in years. I'm slumped forward and next to him I imagine I look the opposite. Unkempt, although my suit is at least clean and pressed.

I let out a shaky breath as the back door opens in front of me, just to the left of the witness stand and a cop ushers my sweetheart in.

My heart crumples in my chest as I lean forward. She doesn't look at me. Her eyes are on her hands as she walks in.

I hate my father. I hate trusting him. He promised me she'd be alright. But this is too much.

Please don't say anything, Arianna.

They couldn't charge me with her confession. My father's spinning stories in the press and coming up with plans and deals. But all of them leave her here in the courtroom to face the charges. I only need to hear the bail amount so I can pay it and take her away.

We can run. I'll run forever with her. I have enough money. I'll take her wherever we can hide.

"All rise," the bailiff says in a commanding voice and I lift my heavy body, but I don't move my eyes away from my sweetheart.

Her hair sways as she stands, and I get a glimpse of her profile as she turns her head to watch the judge come through the heavy double doors on the right. Her cheeks are reddened and tearstained. The sight of her in an orange jumpsuit shreds me.

My father's hand rests on my shoulder and I slowly pull my eyes away from her to look into his gaze. The same eyes as mine.

"She'll be fine," he tells me beneath his breath. The bail hearing continues as I search his face for something to give me confidence in him, trying to settle the disdain rising to the surface.

"And what are the allegations against the defendant?" I hear the judge's heavy voice call out.

"Murder in the second degree," the prosecution answers the judge.

"I need her out of here," I tell my father, my body trembling with the need to go to her. The skin over my knuckles feels as though it will split if I grip the bench any harder.

"She shouldn't be there-" I tell him, but he cuts me off.

"Quiet," my father hisses, the admonishment clear in his voice. I've never needed him. Not for one goddamned thing in my life. But right now I do.

"She's not a flight risk," I hear my attorney say. Dana's the best there is. She'll get her out. But I need it to happen now. Today.

"On the contrary, it's evident that she has access to financial means. Enough to flee the country."

"What access?" Miss Mills asks with disbelief. The room spins around me as I take in the words, white noise drowning out parts of the conversation as I turn back to Arianna. She's staring ahead just as she was on the stage at the auction. *Accepting her fate.*

"She's involved with an individual with enough money and means, and reason might I add, to carry her out of the country." My heart sinks in my chest. No. No. They can't keep her.

"The charges against my client, make it clear that no one else is in danger of-" my attorney rebuts.

"She confessed to murder," the prosecution cuts off my attorney.

"What was said is inadmissible, she was under duress at the time and the prosecution is well aware of the circumstances."

"I did it!" The words are ripped from my throat as I stand there, staring at the judge. I can feel her eyes on me as I step out into the aisle, finally letting go of the bench.

My father reaches for me, grabbing my arm and shoving his hand over my mouth. I turn in his grasp and land my fist against his jaw, the stinging pain ringing through my numb body.

"Zander," my father looks back at me with his hand over his jaw. There's a bit of blood covering his teeth and spilling out onto his hand. His face isn't one of anger, there's no hate. His expression is simply one of denial.

"I shot Daniel Brooks twice." I turn and face the judge, only then aware of the sounds of the people around me and the flash of a camera.

"Zander, no!" Arianna's soft voice travels to me, her words full of pain. I close my eyes, ignoring her plea. She never should have tried to pull this shit. I won't let her. I swallow thickly and continue.

"I came to his home and saw the defendant there. I knew she was there." My father tries to cut me off, but I continue. "I came with my gun and I shot him." The words leave my hollow chest, each one ripping and clawing at my throat on the way out, begging to take the memories with them. "I killed him, and I'd do it again."

"This is a stunt, your Honor," the prosecution calls out, his voice high and carrying an air of disbelief.

I catch sight of my attorney but she's looking at my father, her lips pressed together.

Through all the banging of the gavel, the chatter of the people behind me, the attorneys arguing and judge speaking over everyone, all I can hear is Arianna. "Zander, no," and her small cry breaks my heart.

I hear the footsteps of the cop's shoes against the thin carpet of the courtroom before his hands are on me.

CHAPTER 34

ARIANNA

"You're a free woman, Miss Owens," Dana tells me as we pull up to my shared apartment with Natalie, the smooth hum of the Mercedes engine running.

Her words bring me no joy. I don't want to be free. I shouldn't be here.

I suck in a sharp breath as Zander's words ring in my mind. *I did it! I shot Daniel Brooks twice.*

I shake my head at the memory, filled with despair. He should've kept quiet. He should've let me take the fall.

Seeing him dragged from the courtroom nearly brought me to my knees.

Noting the anguish on my face, Dana gently pats me on the knee. "That's a brave thing you did, trying to take the fall for Mr. Payne."

I make a face. "Brave? Or stupid?" The question is rhetorical. What I did wasn't smart, but smart doesn't matter in this case.

A wistful, empathetic expression comes over Dana. "I think we've all done something not so wise in the name of love, Miss Owens."

I inhale deeply at the word *love*. It's true. And something I've known for a while now. I love Zander. And I don't want to see him rot in a jail cell on my behalf no matter what he did.

"Don't worry," Dana assures me at my distant, pained expression. "Everything is going to work out fine."

"Do you think so?" I ask, feeling a small glimmer of hope.

Dana gives me a confident nod. "Mr. Payne is a resourceful man. And so is his father. If anyone can figure a way out of this mess, they can."

I know she's trying to comfort me, but she can't know that for sure. Zander committed murder. Even confessed to it. I want to believe that things are going to be okay, but right now, I'm not seeing a way out.

"Thank you," I say to Dana, giving a nod and flashing a weak smile. "I really appreciate all your help."

"You're very welcome, Miss Owens," Dana replies. "Take care."

I open the door and step out of the vehicle and watch as she drives off in her gleaming chrome Mercedes-Benz. After a moment I turn around and take in the apartment building, noting the cream-colored stucco walls and the units that are almost too close together.

It feels strange coming back here after everything I've gone through. And I dread having to go inside, knowing the questions that await me there. But I have to do it. I need someone to confide in.

My heart races as I make my way up the stairs and to my apartment with Natalie. By the time I reach the door, my breathing is heavy and ragged, a little from climbing the stairs and some from the crushing anxiety that I feel.

"What the hell is going on, Ari?" Natalie demands as soon as I step through the door.

My chest fills with warmth slightly at the sight of her. I haven't seen her in days and I'm grateful to finally lay eyes on her face. She looks beside herself, her hair's a mess, and it looks like she's lost a few pounds in the little time since I last saw her.

"Your mug has been plastered all over the news!" Natalie hisses when I don't answer right away. "It's crazy!" She shakes her head in anger. "I tried getting into the courthouse to see you, but I couldn't get inside." She pauses, peering at me with concern. "Is it really true?"

"Is what true?" I ask.

"Did that Zander... Zander Payne... Did he really murder Danny to save you?" Natalie asks with intensity.

I stare at her for a long time, setting my keys down on the counter and recounting the last few weeks. It hurts to take in a breath as I look back at her wide, pleading eyes. Slowly, I nod my head. "He did... if he hadn't..." my voice trails off as pain pulses my back. My wounds have been healing, but they still hurt like hell. I don't know when the pain will stop. If it will *ever* stop. I'll have scars for the rest of my life, but none of that matters compared to what Zander's facing.

"Jesus," Natalie mutters, shaking her head. "I can't believe it." She looks up at me, her eyes shining with relief. "Thank God you're still alive." She comes forward to give me a hug.

I hold her at arm's length. "Please don't touch me."

She covers her mouth quickly, pain reflected in her eyes. "I'm sorry," she breathes the words. She visibly swallows as I lower my arms. "He hit you? Right?" Danny did?" Her words are slow, said with a lowered voice.

I turn around and lift my shirt slightly up my back for a brief moment. Natalie recoils as I turn back around, her face twisting in disgusted disbelief.

Silence falls over the room for a moment.

"I need you to tell me everything," Natalie says, finally breaking the silence. She looks shaken to the core, visibly trembling.

"I don't want to talk, Nat." My voice is soft. I don't want to do anything except wait for Zander to be released. Tears leak from the corners of my eyes. He can't go to jail for me for the rest of my life. I don't think I could live with the guilt.

"Please, Ari?" she asks as I brush the tears away. "I've been worried sick about you since this all started. I don't think I can go another minute without knowing what happened." She shakes her head, tears filling her eyes. "Not after..." she pauses and swallows thickly, "seeing that."

I suck in a trembling breath, more tears threatening to spill from my eyes. The pain in Natalie's voice causes my knees to go weak and I feel like crumpling to the floor. I stumble over to the couch and sink down into the cushions, wanting to curl up into a tiny ball. Crossing my arms across my chest, I bite my lower lip and lower my head. The shame, guilt and anxiety are almost too much for me to take.

I've been a shitty friend, keeping secrets and leaving Natalie in the dark.

A moment later I feel the space beside me dip as Natalie takes a seat and a warm hand gently touches my shoulder.

"Please don't do this," Natalie begs, her heart in her voice. "Please don't push me away right now."

The pain in her words lances my chest.

"Ari?" she presses. "Please. My heart is aching."

When I can manage over the lump in my throat, I tell her, "I'm so, so sorry for keeping things from you. I never meant to hurt you."

"Oh honey," Natalie says, her voice filled with unshed tears, aching with sympathy. "You don't have to be sorry for me. I'll be fine. I'm just happy that you're okay."

I try to respond, but I can't get any words out.

Natalie keeps rubbing my shoulders until I'm all cried out, softly whispering soothing comfort in my ears. "Can you forgive me?" I ask hoarsely when I finally recover, looking at her with red-rimmed eyes. Natalie grabs a tissue from the end table and dabs at the tears on my face. "Oh, Ari... there's nothing to forgive. I love you, and am here for you no matter what."

Her words are almost enough to send me into another bout of tears, but I swallow them back.

"I just need to know what happened," Natalie says softly.

I stare at her long and hard. Her eyes are puffy and swollen. I didn't notice it when I came through the door.

Sucking in a deep, trembling breath, I tell her everything. About Danny and his abusive, manipulative ways, his debts, him owing Zander, using me as collateral for the auction, Zander's confession. *Everything.*

"Shit, Ari," Natalie whispers when I'm done, her eyes filled with tears and horror as she shakes her head. "I never knew."

"It's awful," I say weakly.

There's pain in Natalie's face. And it's hard for me not to avert my gaze. "Why didn't you tell me?"

I pick nervously at my blouse. "I don't know. I felt like... I was trapped. The club, it has NDAs. I'm not supposed to talk to other people about it unless I've been permitted."

"You could've still told me," Natalie said, looking hurt. "I would've never told anyone."

I let out a distressed sigh. "I know, Nat. I just didn't know what to do and I didn't want to disappoint you. I'm sorry. "Nat grabs my hand and squeezes it. "Don't be." She gives my hand another gentle squeeze. "I'm just glad you're alive."

I close my eyes, remembering the brutal lashes Danny gave me and whisper, "Me, too."

"And I'm glad that bastard Danny is dead," Natalie says with venom as though my thoughts summoned him to her mind.

I part my lips out of habit to defend him, but then close them. For the first time I can remember, I have no urge to come to Danny's defense. It used to come so easily to me, like a reflex, but now I owe him nothing.

"I'm glad he's gone too," I agree, and mean it.

There's a moment of silence and I can only hear the sound of my heartbeat.

"So what happens now?" Natalie asks. "What's going to happen to Zander?"

It's the question that's been on my mind the moment I saw him dragged out of the courtroom. I like to believe with all his money and power, Zander could somehow find a way out of this. He's too smart, charming and cunning to let himself be locked away for the rest of his life.

But deep down, I know his chances are slim. He confessed. They have all the evidence they need to put him away. And no amount of money he has is going to save him.

A heavy sigh escapes my lips and I grip Natalie's hand tightly as I reply, "I really hope so, Nat. I really do."

CHAPTER 35

ZANDER

One slip, and your world crumbles around you. My elbows rest on my knees in the large cell. The holding area is quiet, the only sounds coming from a vent above my head and occasionally a door opening or closing. I lift my head to stare at the steel bars.

I'm fucked. I take in a deep breath, exhaustion weighing me down. There's nothing I can do or say to protect me. Judgment day has come. I let out a shaky laugh that echoes off the empty walls.

How ironic. All the shitty things I've done, the laws I've broken and corrupt deals I've made, and yet I'm going to be sentenced for the one good thing I ever did.

The smile fades as I see the look in Arianna's eyes. The fear. The realization of what was happening.

I run my hands through my hair, my eyes glassing with tears. The hardest thing is walking away from her. *My sweetheart.*

It's only been hours since the hearing. Hours since they cuffed me and took me here.

I was silent in the interrogation room. I'm smart enough to shut up when I'm alone.

A long sigh leaves me as I slump against the cold brick wall, staring aimlessly ahead. It's odd how much relief I feel that it's all over. No more deals and corruption, no more hiding in the shadows and watching, but smiling when the lights are on me. No more pretending and playing their game.

Even if I somehow get out of here, I'm done. I'm through with all this shit.

I want more from life. I want a real life. One with Arianna.

Women make men fall to their knees

I wouldn't change a thing. But now I'm not there for her.

I close my eyes slowly, picturing her sweet smile. Genuine happiness. She gave that to me and I'll be damned, but I want more.

My eyes open and the vision of her disappears. If only I could go back and somehow hide it. No. I'd need to go back to before. To when he gave her to me. I'd go back then if I could and hire Charles to end him.

I should have. I made so many mistakes, tripping and stumbling all the while my eyes were only on Arianna.

She made me fall, and now I only want to get up for her.

The sound of the large door at the end of the hall opening, snaps me back to the moment.

Several sets of shoes slap against the hard floor as they make their way closer to me.

I stay still, my heart beating slowly and my blood chilling. I know how this all ends, but I can't help to wish for an out. Someone who owes me, someone I've helped in the past who can pull strings. But there's not a single name I can think of. None connected to Judge Pierce. And I've confessed in a room of eyes and ears.

I should have played this smarter, but I couldn't think. Not with her taking the fall for me.

The warden doesn't look at me as he slips a key into the lock, opening the large cell door by pulling on the first bar. Behind him are two men.

The first I recognize as my father's lawyer. Not my own. Nathanael Goldman.

My father's behind him. Immediately I stand up, rising to meet them. The warden closes the door behind them as anxiety races in my blood. I can hardly look my father in the eyes, but somehow I do. I may have killed Brooks, but he deserved to die.

"I know you didn't do it." My father's voice is full of pride and confidence.

"I did," I look him in the eyes as I answer. My father's jaw clenches and he looks to his right, to the lawyer he's brought with him.

"I didn't hear anything," Goldman answers, leaning against the bricked cell wall, with his eyes focused through the bars and on the door at the end of the hall.

I look back to my father, staring into his eyes that reflect disbelief and something else. Disappointment. Never in my life have I seen him look at me like that. I have to tear my eyes away from him. Shame seeping into my blood. My father's done a lot of wrongs in his life.

But I murdered a man.

"He hit her," I say the words and my bastard emotions come through, making my voice crack. "He beat her so hard, so violently, she couldn't even move. There was so much blood."

"Zander..." my father's voice is nearly a whisper.

"I'm sorry, but I don't take it back." My eyes close tight as I sit back on the bench, the image of her on the floor refusing to leave me.

I jump back at the feel of a strong hand on my shoulder. My eyes fly up to meet my father's. His eyes are glazed as he nods my head. "I can understand that."

He starts to sit next to me, but stands tall instead, running a hand down his face. "I just," he takes in a deep breath, looking at the wall and lowering his head. "I don't want to believe it," he says in a low voice.

"I couldn't help myself," I tell him as I stare at my hands, feeling the anger pouring out of me as I killed him. Stealing the life from him and making sure he'd never strike her again.

"You'll never speak of this." My father turns to face me again, his voice coming in stronger. "Ever. To anyone."

I stare at him, not understanding. "I can't lie on the stand," I tell him.

His brow furrows for a moment and then he shakes his head before he says, "There won't be a trial."

I'm dumbfounded, still not understanding. "You aren't the only one who didn't like Daniel Brooks. And your Arianna wasn't the first woman he struck." My father shares a look with Goldman before continuing. "If you'd just been quiet, she would have gotten off." Anger flashes in his eyes for a moment as he continues, "If you'd just listened to me and kept quiet-"

I rise from my seat, meeting my father eye to eye. "I couldn't risk her," my voice comes out firm and barely hiding a threat. I'll never risk her. I won't ever let her pay for my sins.

It's quiet for a long moment. My chest rises and falls with sporadic breaths, remembering how she took the fall for me. I wish she hadn't. I wish she'd never said a word.

"It doesn't matter. You're still my son. I'm not letting you sit behind bars."

"It'll be out in the papers."

My father scoffs. "It's already out!"

I lower my head, my blood heating. My reputation is ruined.

"Payments have been sent," Goldman says softly from the far side of the cell.

"Right, right," my father says, pacing the room. "We can romanticize it?" my father asks Goldman.

The lawyer nods once, his eyes flickering to my father's before turning back to outside the cell.

"So what's going to happen?" I ask, for the first time feeling as though there's hope.

"You'll be free from charges based on inconsistent evidence. And the papers will paint it as if it's a tragedy and Daniel Brooks was a monster-"

"It's the truth," my voice is hard as I cut him off. "What he did to her," I say and my hands shake as they clench into fists.

"What's important is the fact that you'll be fine," my father says with a hard edge as he walks to the far wall, the wheels turning in his head. A bit of a breath leaves me, and I nearly fall forward.

"It's done then?" I ask with disbelief.

My father turns sharply toward me and says, "So long as you fucking listen." I stare into his eyes, but I don't see a hint of anger, only fear. I nod my head once, swallowing the lump in my throat. I'm stunned; I've only ever felt a sense of competition between the two of us. But all I have for him in this moment is gratitude. He's sending me back to her. The thought makes me close my eyes, and her beautiful smile comes back to me.

"You love her?" my father asks, taking me by surprise. I don't answer him. I know with everything in me that I do. But a man like him wouldn't understand.

"I loved your mother," he says as if reading my mind.

My father motions toward Goldman.

"Just make sure she loves you back, Zander." My father's voice wavers as he starts to leave the cell.

"She does," I answer him quickly, making him halt in his steps. I may be a fool in many ways. But there's no doubt in my mind that she loves me as much as I love her.

My father turns to look at me, a genuine concern in his eyes.

"I know she does," I tell him before he can say whatever's on his mind. "I know she does," I repeat and my voice is low, but the conviction is there. I don't need to prove anything to anyone, but for whatever fucked up reason, I need my father to know that she does.

He nods his head once, his eyes on the floor of the cell. His lips part again, but no words come out. He pats his hand against the bars and Goldman gestures to whoever's waiting. The sound of heavy boots coming closer down the cement hall echoes off the walls.

"I hope you're right, son," my father says in a low voice. A small bit of doubt creeps into the back of my mind. She's never said the words. And neither have I. She has no idea. She's never known.

"You'll be out within the hour. Just don't say anything," Goldman tells me as the warden opens the cell and the two of them leave me alone. My thoughts are consumed with what will happen to Arianna now that Brooks is dead.

I have a contract to keep her, but she doesn't have to stay.

I'll do anything I can to keep her.

CHAPTER 36

ARIANNA

They look so happy. Standing in the hallway of Zander's estate, I grip the picture frame in my hands, a solo tear rolling down my right cheek. They look like the perfect family. Zander, with his gorgeous smile. And his two parents looking on as if they're so proud of their son.

My heart aches as I stare at the portrait, my eyes on Zander's mother. She's gone now. And if she knew what was going to happen to her son, she'd probably be devastated. Guilt presses down on my chest as another tear rolls down my cheek.

This is all my fault.

I wish I could tell him that I'm sorry. That I didn't mean for any of this to happen. That I wish I could take it all back. I wish I could go back to the very beginning. When all of this started. I wish I'd killed Danny myself.

A huge lump forms in my throat as try to hold back the tide of tears that threaten to fall from my eyes.

The guilt is almost enough to choke on.

It wasn't supposed to end up this way.

I squeeze the picture frame against my chest, despair and anger coursing through me.

"You okay, sweetheart?" asks a deep, sexy voice.

I look up and cover my mouth with my hand, nearly collapsing on the floor.

"Zander!" I cry, setting down the picture frame on the oak wood stand with shaky hands. It falls over, but I don't care. I have to run to him. To feel him. I bury my face into his chest and hold him with everything I have in me. *I'll never let him go.*

"How did you..." my voice trails off as I'm at a loss for words when I lean back to look at him.

He smiles weakly down at me, his eyes focusing on a stray strand of hair in my face as he brushes it away and leans forward to kiss me. The simple touch melts me. My body relaxing into him, finally feeling the warmth of his body. "I'm not going to be charged."

His words hit me slowly, taking their time before I fully comprehend what he's saying. I pull away from him out of shock, but he holds my lower waist close to him as I stare into his eyes.

I can't speak. My voice is robbed from me from the shock. I shake my head slightly and ask, "No charges?"

"Nothing."

"How?" I finally manage softly.

Zander's eyes go dark momentarily, his body tensing. "My father has his connections," he replies, his voice low. "He's still owed a lot of favors."

"Is everything...," I breathe when I get over my shock. "Is everything okay? It's over?"

I can barely breathe as he pulls me into his chest. His hand is gentle on my back, but still it stings to the touch. "Sorry," he breathes into my hair as I settle against his chest. I don't give a fuck about my back. Not right now. I bury my face into his shirt, just breathing him in. "It's all over."

I don't want to let go.

I'm afraid if I do, I'll lose him forever. And I'll never have a chance to hold him again.

"I've got you," Zander whispers as he kisses my hair. "And I'm not letting you go."

I close my eyes, and nestle deeper into him. *Don't, please don't ever let me go.* "There's something I've been wanting to let you know for a while now. Something that I've wanted to say but haven't had the courage." I talk with my eyes closed, but he pulls back to look into my face and I have to stare into his eyes to tell him.

Zander arches an eyebrow with curiosity. "What's that?"

A large lump forms in my throat.

"I love you, Zander Payne," I tell him, my voice aching with emotion.

Zander doesn't respond immediately, causing my heart to skip as I wait for his response. It's beating so fast and hard I'm sure he can feel it pumping against his chest. But when he breaks out into a handsome grin, I know I have nothing to worry about.

"And I love you too, Arianna Owens," Zander says softly, coming in for a deep, passionate kiss. "And I always will."

EPILOGUE

ZANDER

"hey'll be expecting you," my father's voice comes out clear on the phone.

"I understand that," I answer him simply, walking out of the kitchen, with the phone to my ear. It's the *Gala of the Year*, the third one with that title so far.

Veronica Marsett is hosting it for her charity, and over four hundred attendees will be there. Most of whom I know firsthand, and half of them will be expecting me to address them. To notice them publicly and pose for photo ops. To rub elbows, as my father used to say when I was younger.

These are the scenes that matter most. It's all about who you're seen with.

But with my Arianna, my sweetheart hardly sleeping, I doubt she's going to want to go. And if she's not with me, I'm not going.

I don't want to be anywhere without her by my side. Because my father's right. It's all about who you're seen with. That's who matters. And right now, she's the only one who matters to me.

Even if he saved me. He can wait. Business will always wait from now on.

"You're really going to snub them?" Oddly enough, my father's voice holds only a trace of admonishment.

"It's not a snub, she's not feeling well."

My father's silent on the phone for a moment. The glow from the fire in the back of the library lights the dim room. The floor-to-ceiling curtains are closed tight on the far end, but the ones closest to me are open, just enough for someone to peek through.

I keep the phone to my ear as I peek out and see the snow settling on the ground. Early February has brought enough snow to lock us in for weeks, but I'm fine with that.

I turn around to face the large leather sofa as my father starts talking. It groans as Arianna shifts her weight on it to get comfortable. Her hand rests on her swollen belly, but she's sleeping soundly.

I hate that she can't fall asleep in bed with me; I guess I'll have to start sleeping out here.

"There are deals to finalize and if you're seen with the right investors, that will make their bids rise." He tells me things I already know, but I simply don't care anymore. There's so much more than money. More than power. There's love.

Arianna's belly rises with a deep breath as she slowly rolls onto her side, dragging a cream chenille throw with her as she goes.

There's a feeling of being complete. Of not wanting anything more than what you already have.

A soft sigh of satisfaction falls from her sweet lips.

"I'm sure they'll understand," I speak softly into the phone, but Arianna's eyes flutter open. A small smile spreads on her face when she sees me.

It's a genuine smile, one that makes me reciprocate.

My feet move of their own accord, drawn to her. I crouch down to the floor beside her and plant a kiss on the tip of her nose.

"I have to go," I tell my father, cutting off whatever reason he's trying to convince me of to go.

"Wait!" I'm surprised from my father's sharp voice, it takes me aback and I flinch, pulling the phone away slightly.

Arianna rises on her elbow, wiping the sleep from her eyes and staring at the phone. She's not used to my father's temper and to be honest, it's been a long time since I've had to deal with it. I won't let her witness this. I rise to my feet, straightening my shoulders and preparing to tell my father off.

He's been agitated lately with me leaving more and more work in his hands, or simply to let go. There are plenty of investors, and I'm not interested in certain deals anymore. Not when I have so much to protect now.

My lips part as I suck in a breath, prepared for the worst, but I wasn't anticipating the words that come from the other end of the phone.

"The baby shower, that's next month?" my father asks me, clearing his throat and waiting for a response.

A deep crease settles in my forehead as I turn back to look at Arianna over my shoulder.

"It's next month, yes." I wait for a moment, still feeling tense and on edge as Arianna stands up, holding her stomach as though it will fall if she lets go. She's so beautiful, carrying my child. There's been a glow about her since she found out.

"I'd like to go," my father says with firm conviction.

"It's not for men," I say and the words spill out of my mouth with disbelief.

"Sure it is, we'll go at the end... Your mother loved that." I'm taken back by his confession. "You go at the end with a gift for her and help load all the things. It's what you do," he says matter-of-factly. "It's probably the last thing I did right with your mother. But I know it's a good thing to do... and I want to help you."

My body's frozen in place as Arianna walks toward me, one hand rubbing soothing circles over her swollen bump and the other bracing a hand on her back.

"Sure," I answer my father. The vision of what he must've looked like back then plays in my mind. Maybe they were happy then, all those years ago.

"It's settled then. I'm sure I'll see you before then?" The words come out as a question.

"Sure," I say again, wrapping an arm around Arianna's waist as she leans into me, her eyes wide with questions, but her body relaxed.

"Very well then, I'll talk to you soon." There's a silence between us for a moment, and for the first time in years, I feel the urge to tell him I love him. As though it's real, but I don't. Maybe another time.

The line goes dead, and I pull the phone away from my ear to stare at it in my hand.

"Are you alright?" she asks and her voice is soft, tinged with concern.

I toss the phone down onto the sofa a few feet away and turn her in my arms. Her belly rubs against mine as I pull her in close. "Of course."

She eyes me warily, her one eyebrow lifting with skepticism.

"Everything is wonderful."

That sweet smile plays at her lips again and she nods as she says, "It is, isn't it?"

I kiss her lips softly, but she deepens it. My greedy sweetheart. I'm more than happy to give her more. I'd hand her over the world in exchange for what she's given me.

When she breaks the kiss, I whisper between us, "I love you."

"I love you too, Zander."

ABOUT THE AUTHORS

Thank you so much for reading our our cowritten novel. We hope you loved reading it as much as we loved writing it! Stay connected at our socials below!

Willow Winters
Facebook
Instagram
Willow's Website

Lauren Landish
Facebook
Instagram
Lauren's Website

Standalones
Inked: A Bad Boy Next Door Romance
Tempted: A Bad Boy Next Door Romance
Mr. CEO